Joshin' Around

Joshin' Around

A surprise Navy SEAL dad, friend's sister, instalove, alpha male, scared woman, cowboy romance book.

Heart's Destiny Book 6

Leah Mae Wright

Contents

Dedication

To my grandmother, Beulah Mae Wolf.

*Thank you for inspiring most of my passions and
hobbies in life. Because of you I went to my first
professional wrestling match, cheated the system to go
to my first gym before I was old enough to be allowed
to use their pool, and read my first romance novel. If it
wasn't for you, I wouldn't have turned all three
passions into careers.*

I love you mostest, Granny Grunt!

Introduction

Lt. Josh Burleson was known as the jokester of his family due to his penchant for finding the humor in life to help him deal with the darker aspects he saw in his job. Raised on the family ranch, he'd been taught to work hard and play harder. And his playtime wasn't limited to just joshin' around with his family and friends.

As a Navy SEAL, he wasn't lacking when it came to available women to spend his nights with when he wasn't off on a mission. With him also being one of the Burleson bachelors, it wasn't just the frog hogs who chased after him. As a single guy, he'd had more than his fair share of one-night stands, starting with the buckle bunnies who offered themselves up back when he was a teenager, competing in the team roping competitions of the rodeo with his twin, and ending when he met the woman that he fell in instalove with at Christmas.

As soon as Josh saw Cait walk into his childhood home for a late Christmas celebration, he fell head over heels for her. But after seeing the toll of military life paid by the relationships of his fellow SEALs, Josh knew he couldn't pursue anything with her until after his minimum service requirement was over. So Josh did the only thing he could do — he started a long-distance and leave-time friendship with Cait while making plans to get out of the Navy to move home and marry her.

While home during one of his leave times, Josh sent in a DNA sample to an online family tree site like the rest of his family. When the results came in, he saw an extra person listed as sharing fifty percent of his DNA in the Parent-Child section of his DNA match list on the site. Floored by the realization that he was a father, Josh had to put his plans to build a relationship with Cait on hold. He needed to settle the situation with his child, and his child's mother, before he could commit to moving home to pursue the lovely Cait.

Cait Campbell wasn't sure she'd ever feel comfortable going out and dating again after the trauma her family had endured over the past few years. Not only had her brother lost his first wife, but both he and Cait had been injured in the drive-by shooting that ended Mari's life. While her physical scars had long since healed, Cait wasn't so sure the internal ones that kept her trapped in her brother's house ever would.

When her brother had the idea of moving their family from San Diego to Texas, she developed high hopes of moving on with her life. Getting away from the cartel hub of the city and learning about life in a rural area seemed like just what she needed to move past her agoraphobia and start feeling social again. She even felt an instant attraction to one of the men she met during her first week in Heart's Destiny, Texas.

Then she found out their move was her brother's way of hunting down the head of the cartel, who had targeted them back in San Diego, and her fear of leaving the house came back tenfold. And even though the one man she'd been attracted to in the last two-and-a-half years was the same man who ultimately killed the leader of the cartel to set her free of her fear of another attack on her family, she still didn't think she could have more than a little light flirtation with Josh because of his dangerous career as a Navy SEAL.

When Josh's son showed up at the wedding reception for his sister and Cait's brother, they faced even more barriers to the relationship they both secretly craved. Could they come together to form an unconventional family? Or would all that joshin' around just lead to trouble and more heartbreak for Cait?

DISCLAIMER: This surprise Navy SEAL dad, friend's sister, instalove, alpha male, scared woman, cowboy romance book contains references to past gun violence, profanity, and graphic sex scenes, as well as multiple scenes with the hero rescuing kidnapping and rape

Leah Mae Wright

victims alongside his fellow SEALs and family members. It is
intended for adult readers (18+) who are not easily offended.

Chapter One

Cait Campbell was excited to go meet a few of the locals at a late Christmas celebration on one of the nearby ranches in the quaint little town of Heart's Destiny, Texas, where her brother had relocated their family. But she was also nervous about whether or not she could attend the large gathering without having a panic attack.

I can do this, she mentally told herself, trying to get over her fear of going out in public by giving herself an internal pep talk. *I'm not in San Diego anymore. The cartel who did the drive-by at Brody's birthday party isn't here in Texas. Mikey moved us across the country to keep us safe. I'm safe here. Mikey's safe here. Brody's safe here. This is a party, not another chance for them to try to kill us.*

Crap, I have to remember to call Mikey by his middle name — Ian — so nobody will know he's the same person who tried to take down the cartel. My brother's name is Ian now. And I'm Cait, not Caitir.

Cait had always liked her full name. She'd never met another Caitir and had loved the stories her brother told her about how her grandparents had picked the Scottish name for her to honor their heritage. She was only three years old when they died, so she didn't have any memories of them, other than memories of the stories Ian told her about living with them on a farm until they passed away. After Keith and Carol Campbell died, their daughter, Lorna, moved her children, Caitir and Mikey, off the farm to San Diego.

I bet that's why Mikey, ur, Ian thinks moving us to a rural area is such a good idea. He wants to recreate some of those happy memories of living on the farm with our grandparents to help me get over my fear of leaving the house and getting caught in another drive-by in the city.

Leah Mae Wright

I'm sure he's thinking the possibility of getting a job on a ranch will push me to leave the house once we move in next week. And with a ranch being a really big farm, he's hoping it will be similar enough to our grandparents' farm that I won't need him to go with me to feel safe while I'm there.

After being shot in her right shoulder and arm and suffering from a concussion after hitting her head while diving for cover during the drive-by shooting that killed her sister-in-law a little over two years ago, Cait had developed an intense fear of leaving the house. Her brother had also been shot twice as he protected his son by covering the then two-year-old with his body. When they were all released from the hospital, the DEA faked Mikey's death, moved them to a safe house on the other side of the city, and helped her brother change his name to keep the cartel he'd been undercover trying to infiltrate from finding him.

Even though her name hadn't been released as one of the victims of the shooting, Cait had been afraid one of the cartel members who were there might recognize her from the modeling and acting jobs she'd done using the stage name Caitir Skye, her first and middle name. So, in addition to leaving her career and going to work as Ian's live-in nanny for Brody, she started going by Cait in the hopes that anyone who saw her name would assume it was short for Caitlyn, like most women who spelled it that same way, and wouldn't realize she'd been there to be able to identify the shooters.

Unfortunately, her plan to lay low until the cartel members were all captured, and the danger passed, ended up taking so long that she developed a full-blown case of agoraphobia. Before that horrible day when her family was targeted by the cartel, Caitir had always been a strong, independent woman. But two years later, after hiding in her brother's house, cowering in fear of what might happen if she went out in public, she was surprised she'd even been brave enough to get on the private plane for their move to the small town just outside of San Antonio, Texas.

When she looked in the mirror now, she missed seeing the vibrant woman she'd been before. She'd been so outgoing, socializing regularly with her friends and classmates while getting her bachelor's degree in performing arts and the one semester she'd completed toward her master's degree in screenwriting. She'd paid her way through school with the local commercials, print ads, and plays she'd started padding her résumé with, hoping to use them to get noticed for her eventual move up to Los Angeles. But being shot derailed all her Hollywood starlet dreams.

Not that she truly believed she had the looks or self-discipline to maintain the diet required to retain a thin enough figure to actually become a movie star. That was why she'd decided on the screenwriting degree, so she could work behind the scenes in the industry she loved.

Now that they were in another state, and over a thousand miles away from San Diego, Cait hoped to start getting over her fear, venturing outside the house, and getting back to her old self. She might not ever feel safe enough to want to see herself on the big screen, or even a billboard ad, again. But at this point, she'd be happy to feel safe enough to want to participate in any kind of entertainment production, even if it was only communicating virtually as a screenwriter, who never actually had to go on set.

Her major goal now was to get over her fear of being in public and interacting with others enough that she could one day go back to school to finish her master's degree. She already felt like she was well on her way to achieving her first step toward that goal by broadening her circle of acquaintances, after spending some time outside her room at the bed and breakfast and socializing with the Hunters.

But who could resist when Mandi and Meemaw Hunter insisted we sit down for girl talk? With not having a strong motherly or grandmotherly influence in her life before, Cait had no experience in evading their, slightly manipulative, charms. Especially when they were pulling her out of hiding and helping her reconnect with the vibrant young woman she'd once been, who loved meeting new people and exploring the world around her.

While she hadn't ever dreamed of being a housekeeper, she knew she had plenty of experience doing the job, since that was what she spent her time doing whenever Brody didn't need her undivided attention. That had been his nap time when he was younger, but now that he was at the stage where he wanted to do more for himself and didn't nap as often, she gave him things to do in the same room with her whenever she spent time cleaning up at home while her brother was at work. If Mandi Hunter was right about her being able to bring her nephew with her to work, cleaning the houses on the ranch they were going to for this late Christmas party, then she hoped this job could be her next step to getting back to her old, outgoing self in the near future.

And that's going to start now with me being brave enough to go meet a few of the people who live in Heart's Destiny, Texas. Cait had to hope that this first step back out into the world would be the hardest. And once she got over that hurdle, she'd breeze through driving again and going to more public functions on her own. In the meantime, she knew she could rely on her brother to help her feel safe on these short outings.

She looked over at her brother, who was clearly wearing a fake smile as he drove them from the bed and breakfast where they were staying to the ranch where the party was being held. *He's just nervous because this is the first time we've gone out as a family to any kind of celebration since that day. But he's alert and watching for threats to be able to protect us, just like he was at both of the small airports we had to go through to take the plane Trent arranged for us to move here a couple of days ago. So, we're perfectly safe.*

Cait had always looked up to her brother and gone to him for guidance with most aspects of life. After their childhood move to San Diego, their mother had gone through a downward spiral of drugs and bad decisions in her choice of boyfriends. Ian had stepped up then to start protecting his little sister. He was only seven years older than Cait, but she always saw him as more of a father figure. Even in her earliest memories of life when he was a preteen, she'd seen him acting as the adult in their family.

When he graduated high school and started taking college classes, he continued living at home, even though he was eighteen and able to move out. At eleven years old, Cait knew he'd only stayed in their hellhole of an apartment to keep her safe. When their mom and her loser of the month were arrested a couple of years later, her brother stepped up to take custody of her.

Because she couldn't remember a day of her life when her brother hadn't been the one acting as her protector and guardian, Cait had more respect for him than any other man she'd ever met. So much so, that prior to the shooting, she'd compared every guy she even thought about dating to her brother to determine if the guy was worthy of spending time with.

Needless to say, she wasn't nearly as experienced with men as her friends had been back before they were all cut out of her life after the shooting. But at twenty-six years old, she knew she needed to get over her fear, so she could be the independent woman her brother raised and set him free to have a life of his own again.

Cait smiled at her brother, hoping to reassure him that she was okay with going to this party, before turning to watch out the window to see a little bit of the town on the drive. She enjoyed the park-like setting of the grounds of the bed and breakfast before they turned left on Walker Road. They passed a couple of businesses, including one that smelled heavenly, called the Burger Barn. Brody made a comment about being hungry, which made her laugh because he wanted to stop for burgers instead of going to the party.

Since her brother seemed too preoccupied with watching their surroundings and ensuring their safety to respond to his son, Cait promised her nephew that there would be food at the party, smiling into the back seat at him as they passed a residential area and then a large white church. They turned left off of Walker Road and onto Rogers Road, passing a wooded area on the left and fenced-in pastures on the right. They then made a right turn into a driveway, leading to a wrought-iron gate with a stylized B in the middle. Above the gate was a wooden sign that read, "Burleson Ranch".

I wonder if they're related to the people who own the Burleson gas stations? Cait didn't pay much attention to the big businesses that were often in the news, or know anything about any major companies, other than the talent agency she'd worked with and a few of the clothing companies she'd modeled for a few years ago. But before she quit driving to stay at Ian's house all the time, she'd often stopped for gas at one of the Burleson stations because it was usually a few cents cheaper than the other chains.

Ian followed the Hunters through the gate and around some grassy pastures and a couple of barns to a large, white, plantation-style house, where he parked along with the rest of the guests coming from the bed and breakfast. Cait looked around at the other houses that surrounded this one, hoping they would give her a sense of safety with this area of the ranch being like a mini-neighborhood instead of a public space.

"Maybe this wasn't such a good idea," Cait mumbled, just as Ian got out of the car. Seeing several cars in the driveway, as well as several more parked at the cluster of family houses around them, she suddenly feared she'd attempted too big an outing for her first time outside the bed and breakfast, where they'd been staying for the past couple of days. Even though she was nervous, she somehow managed to follow her brother's lead to unbuckle her seat belt and get out of the rental car, sucking up her fear to try to get past this first hurdle to feeling whole again.

"It'll be fine, Cait," Ian reassured her, as he lifted Brody from his car seat to carry him into the gathering. "If there isn't a job you're comfortable with here, then at least we'll have made some new friends by the end of the day."

"Maybe." Cait bit the inside of her lip as she tried to gather all her former bravado to be able to go into the party. *They're friends of the Hunters, so surely these new people will be just as friendly and welcoming as they've been. This is a celebration and nothing to be afraid of, Cait. You can do this!*

Ian smiled at her reassuringly as they walked onto the porch of the mansion-sized home behind the Hunters. Cait was in awe of the three-story plantation-style house with huge white pillars that reminded her of Ashley Wilkes' house in **Gone with the Wind**. The interior was just as beautiful, though Cait didn't notice much of the décor once they were inside and surrounded by people.

Breathe, Cait, breathe. In. Out. In. Out. Do not panic before you've even been introduced to the hosts of the party. Cait continued her internal pep talk as she looked at her brother to try to center herself and calm down.

As the Hunters started making introductions, Ian looked around at the crowd of people around them. Knowing her brother was scoping out the people around them to keep her and Brody safe, Cait relaxed a little, though she was still quiet and only nodded at Jon and Bob Burleson, instead of shaking hands with them like her brother.

As David and Mandi Hunter were telling Jon and Bob Burleson about Ian's new job in town, Cait took a moment to look around the room. Unconsciously, she picked out places she could hide if someone pulled a gun in the middle of the party.

It was a beautiful dining room with three extremely large tables situated in a U shape around the room to provide seating for so many guests. She wasn't sure what would replace the Christmas decorations that adorned the walls and various side tables and cabinets, but she assumed it would be priceless artwork and antiques to match the style of the home.

I hope I don't get too nervous and accidentally break something, if I get the job cleaning this place.

She recognized a couple of the wrestlers, who were also staying at the B and B, and apparently, worked with the Hunters' sons, which she'd learned from Mandi and Meemaw Hunter as they talked to her at breakfast on her first morning in town. The wrestlers had apparently been here before, since they immediately started to mingle like they were old friends with the other attendees.

It was as she was letting her eyes wander over the crowd to make sure she knew where to find the nearest exit in case she started to panic that she saw the most attractive man she'd ever seen. *Holy! Wow! Who is he?*

He looked to be about the same size as her brother, so she guessed about six-foot-four and two-hundred-something pounds like Ian. His royal blue Henley and jeans were more form-fitting than the button-downs and slacks her brother usually wore, so Cait could tell he was ripped with muscles. Not that she would have noticed if her brother was as muscular as the local hottie, even if he wore more revealing clothing. But his appearance would just be the first way she compared a man she was interested in possibly dating to Ian if she reverted to her pre-shooting habits.

Oh, wow, and he's wearing cowboy boots! I didn't get the appeal of the cowboy romance novels my friends were all into a few years ago, but seeing that hot cowboy in person has suddenly made it clear.

The stranger's hair was darker than Ian's dark blond, more of a mousy brown like hers since she quit adding blonde highlights for modeling. His hair was stylishly cut, not too long, but also not as short as her brother wore his. This man also had a much less serious look on his face than either of the Campbells had worn for the last couple of years.

He was smiling at something that was said by the group of people around him, which made the laugh lines around his mouth show from across the room. She guessed he was somewhere between her age and her brother's, so that put him in his late twenties or early thirties. Even with the laugh lines keeping her from describing him as having a boyish appearance, she'd be surprised if he was younger than her twenty-six. And since he didn't have any other signs of aging marring his otherwise youthful face, she also didn't believe he was older than Ian's almost thirty-three.

Cait couldn't tell what color his eyes were from so far away. But when he looked up and their eyes locked on one another for the first time, she felt the strangest sense of butterflies swarming in her belly.

Oh, no, I don't need to get an upset stomach before I'm supposed to eat as part of this party! Hopefully, it's just attraction causing these internal flutters, and they'll go away when I'm not looking directly at him. If it's nerves from being in a crowd and causes me to lose my lunch in front of that cowboy hottie, I'll be mortified.

It wasn't just his good looks that drew her attention. The other men around him were just as attractive, though maybe not as buff. But there was something about this one man that made her feel like she was supposed to know him, like she could run into his arms, and he'd protect her from everything she'd ever feared in life.

She barely caught herself before she involuntarily took a step toward him, feeling drawn to him in a way that she'd never been attracted to anyone previously. Not any of the male models she'd worked with over the years. Not even the boyfriend she'd finally lost her virginity to in her sophomore year of college. Nope, only this smokin' hot cowboy elicited these strange feelings.

Get it together, Caitir! You can't go chasing after a guy when you're not even sure you're going to be able to make it through this party without having a panic attack or tossing your cookies.

"I'm gonna take them out to the kitchen to introduce them to Hazel and Susan," Mandi announced, drawing Cait back into the conversation around her as she motioned for Cait, Ian, and Brody to follow her. "And also, to find out where we should have them sit for dinner."

Cait followed right behind Mandi as she walked through the dining room and down a hall to the kitchen. Once there, they found a group of women working to put the finishing touches on the lunchtime meal they'd have for the party.

"Ian and Cait Campbell, this is Hazel, Bob's wife, Susan, Jon's wife, and Rosa, whose husband, Carlos, manages the ranch. But I haven't seen him yet today to introduce you to him." Mandi pointed to each of the women as she said their names. "Ladies, I'd like to introduce you to Cait, Ian, and Brody Campbell. Hazel, Cait is the woman I told you about, who might be able to take the housekeeping position you have open."

"Oh, yes," Hazel smiled at them as she wiped her hands off on a hand towel. "The one who would need to bring her nephew while her brother teaches at the middle school."

"Yes, ma'am," Cait timidly confirmed.

"Please, call me Hazel. I know ma'am is supposed to be polite and all, but it just makes me feel old before my time."

"It's nice to meet you, Hazel." Cait returned Hazel's welcoming smile, relaxing a little at how hospitable the women seemed to be. *Thank goodness! Those flutters were just from looking at the cowboy hottie. I can do this without getting nauseous. I just have to make sure to avoid looking at him for the rest of the day.*

"You too, Cait. And as much as I'd love to talk to you about the job, it'll have to be one day next week, when I'm not rushing around like a chicken with my head cut off tryin' to get everyone fed."

"Of course," Cait agreed, inwardly cringing at Hazel's morbidly strange expression.

"I wasn't sure if you have a seating chart for today or not, but I wanted to check before I just directed them to take a seat anywhere," Mandi explained why she'd brought them to the kitchen.

"Oh, no, we don't have a seating chart," Susan informed them as she gave Hazel a strange look. "But I'll still take ya'll out and introduce you to our kids, so you can mingle with people closer to your age, instead of hangin' out with us old ladies."

"Hey, speak for yourself," Rosa chastised with a grin. "I for one, don't see any old ladies in this kitchen."

"Me either," Hazel chuckled while waving them all out of the way, so she could open the oven to take out the rolls that smelled divine. *Oh, they're going to be a fun group to work with if I'm able to take the job.*

Cait followed Susan as she led them back to the dining room. Ian followed along behind her, still carrying Brody. He'd been awfully quiet the whole time they were in the kitchen, making Cait wonder what he was thinking about to be so distracted, since he was normally the more outgoing of the two of them. Well, at least for the past two years.

Knowing he was too distracted to have comprehended the conversation in the kitchen, Cait wasn't surprised when Ian tapped her on the shoulder and asked, "Which Mrs. Burleson are we following?"

"Susan," Cait whispered in response. "Jon's wife."

Cait couldn't elaborate further about Susan planning to introduce her and her brother to the adult children of the Burlesons. She was suddenly struck mute by the realization that Susan was directing her to sit at the table across and one seat over from the man who made her insides flutter earlier.

No, no, no! Cait silently freaked out as she took one of the two empty seats not too far from the end of the inside of the U of tables. *I can't deal with flutters and wanting to date again until after I know I'm able to keep from freaking out every time I leave the house, so I need to avoid the hot cowboy, not sit with him for lunch!*

"Family, this is Ian Campbell, his sister Cait, and his son, Brody. Beside you, Ian, is my niece, Charlotte, and across the table is my son, Justin. Beside Justin is Amy Lawton. She's starting work with Justin in the lab next week. On his other side is my other son, JJ. Then we have my nephew, Josh, and across the table from Josh, and seated next to Cait is Josh's twin brother, Jake."

His name is Josh. And I'm sitting next to his twin brother. Oh, dear Lord, please don't let me have a panic attack or toss my cookies with him or his brother watching me.

~~~

Josh Burleson was standing in his family dining room, talking to his siblings and cousins when he first felt like he'd been struck by lightning. He looked up, saw the most beautiful woman in the world, and knew she was *The One*. All his life, he'd heard the stories of having that feeling the first time one of his elders had seen their soulmate. Hell, not just his elders. Two of his brothers, the oldest and youngest of his five siblings, had just recently felt the same
~~~

phenomenon. So, he knew what it meant the instant he felt that jolt through his whole body.

His youngest brother, Anthony, had married Kay and adopted her two daughters within two months of meeting her. And they were already expecting another child. Then, at Anthony and Kay's wedding reception, his oldest brother, Bobby, had seen Brie and felt the same jolt of awareness. It took a little of their mom's matchmaking to move Brie in with Bobby less than two weeks later. But from what Josh had seen in the time he'd been home from where he was stationed in the Navy for a Christmas visit, Bobby and Brie (Whom they'd recently found out was actually Brooklyn Barns, the heiress who went missing on Thanksgiving, and was using her pen name to keep anyone from tracking her down.) were well on their way to more than roommates.

Josh couldn't believe he was the next of the Burlesons to fall in love at first sight. But as he watched the gorgeous woman with blondish brown hair walk through the dining room behind the Hunters, he knew it had happened, whether he was ready for it or not.

Considering he had nine more months before his five-year minimum service commitment to the Navy after leaving the Naval Academy would be up, Josh knew he shouldn't pursue the lovely lady just yet. During his time in the Navy, including his time as a midshipman while in college, the year and a half he spent in BUD/S, parachute, SQT, and SEAL-specific medic training, and in his years as a SEAL after his training, he'd seen too many of his buddies' relationships fail because of not being home with their women.

Oh, he knew he wouldn't cheat on the curvy woman in an emerald-green dress, whom he couldn't stop staring at, the same way some of the guys had on their wives or girlfriends over the years. But he also couldn't expect a woman that spectacular to wait at home and worry about him, while he was off on missions around the world instead of being home to take care of her.

He'd known long before now that he couldn't put the woman that he was meant to spend his life with through the stress of being a SEAL wife. So, as soon as he'd graduated from the Naval Academy and gone to BUD/S training to become a SEAL, Josh had vowed to not get serious about a woman until after his time as an active SEAL was over. Not that he'd really gotten serious about anyone he'd dated during the four years he was at the Naval Academy. To be totally honest, Josh's dating life had always consisted of one-night stands and weekend flings because he knew none of those women was his soulmate, since he hadn't ever felt that jolt of lightning with any of them.

Fuck, I'm gonna hafta play it cool and just be friendly for now. At least, until after I break the news to my CO that I'm not staying in past September. Josh started putting together his plan for coming home more often during the next nine months as he watched the tall, curvy woman of his dreams walk up to be introduced to his dad and uncle. *Damn, she's taller than pretty much all the other women here. Hell, she's at least a couple of inches taller than Char and Julie, and they're the tallest women in our family.*

It was as those introductions were being made that he finally realized there was a man and child there with the woman he wanted to claim as his. *Fuck, no! She can't be married already! Fate is not that cruel!*

As the men around her conversed, the object of his attention turned her head to look around. When their eyes met across the room, Josh couldn't contain his smile. Her expression conveyed her feelings of attraction to him, even though she was too far away for him to see them in her eyes.

No, she's definitely not married. Or if she is, it's not happily. So maybe she'll be free by the same time I'm outta the Navy.

"Dude, why are you grinnin' like a loon?" JJ, Josh's cousin, gave him a curious look, bringing him back into the conversation going on around him.

"No reason," Josh shrugged, reluctantly turning his gaze away from the bombshell across the room. "Just happy to be home for the holidays, instead of stuck in the sandbox like some of my buddies."

"We're happy you're home too," his twin cousins, Jen and Julie, chimed in unison.

Josh was also a twin, but he was still dumbfounded by how his cousins often thought the same things at the same time to be able to complete each other's sentences or talk in unison without missing a beat. He'd always felt closer to Jake than his other siblings, but they'd never felt like they were so close that they were sharing the same mental wavelength to know what the other one was thinking.

He continued talking with his cousins and the GWA wrestlers, who'd joined them while he was ogling his brown-haired beauty, for a few minutes about the likelihood of his team being spun up and him having to leave town before the first as he currently had planned. When they started moving to sit down, he looked back over where he'd last seen the woman that he wanted to make sure he met before the party was over, only to be disappointed by not being able to find her in the room.

She couldn't have gone far, he thought as he took a seat between JJ and Jen. *She just got here and most likely didn't leave before the party has even gotten started. So, surely, I'll have the chance to meet her before the party's over.*

Josh's prayer of meeting his dream woman was answered a few minutes later, when his Aunt Susan walked up and directed the newcomers to fill the empty seats across the table between Jake and Charlotte.

"Oh, let me introduce you." Aunt Susan spoke loud enough to be heard over the conversations going on around them. "Family, this is Ian Campbell, his sister Cait, and his son, Brody."

Fuck yeah! He's her brother. And she's not wearing a ring, so she's not already married. Which means she can marry me and become Cait Burleson just as soon as I get outta the Navy. Cait Burleson. Yeah, I like the sound of that. Josh mentally tried out the name he hoped she'd one day have as he locked eyes with his soulmate once more. Her blue-green eyes, which reminded him of the ocean in Southern California where he'd been stationed for BUD/S, widened with recognition as she took the seat beside Josh's twin brother. *Fuck! Why didn't I sit there and have Jake sit here?*

"Beside you, Ian, is my niece, Charlotte, and across the table is my son, Justin. Beside Justin is Amy Lawton. She's starting work with Justin in the lab next week. On his other side is my other son, JJ. Then we have my nephew, Josh, and across the table from Josh, and seated next to Cait is Josh's twin brother, Jake."

Josh was surprised Aunt Susan didn't introduce her daughters, who were sitting beside him and Jake. But when he glanced over, he could see that Jen and Julie were focused on their conversations with the wrestlers on their other sides. *Yeah, she's not gonna interrupt what looks like two of her and Ma's matchmaking success stories in the making.*

"Nice to meet you all." Ian looked around the group to acknowledge each of them as he took his seat with his son on his lap.

The conversations around them started back up, but Josh only heard a low murmur, as if he was sitting in the middle of a ***Peanuts*** cartoon. He was too keyed in on observing Cait to comprehend anything he was hearing from his cousins, siblings, and the GWA wrestlers they were talking to at the time.

Josh catalogued everything he could about Cait, from her oval-shaped face to her button nose, to her wide mouth that he couldn't wait to see wrapped around his cock. *Fuck! I have to stop picturing that or I won't be able to stand up to get my plate in a few minutes without everyone around noticing I'm sporting wood.*

Cait looked shyly down at her lap, giving Josh the impression that she was too innocent to understand the meaning behind the sparks flying between them. *Shit! Or maybe she's embarrassed because she can tell by my expression that I'm getting hard from just looking at her.*

She only looked up briefly when Justin raised his voice, getting everyone's attention as he spoke to the newcomers.

"What brings ya'll to Heart's Destiny?"

Cait's attention was quickly diverted back down as her nephew, Brody, demanded his aunt's attention by crawling from Ian's lap to hers.

"I'll be starting a new job in town in a little over a week," Ian replied to Justin's inquiry.

Awesome! They're not just here for vacation, so I can take my time getting to know her every time I'm home on leave until I'm done in the Navy.

"Oh, what do you do?" Amy asked enthusiastically.

"I'm a middle school English teacher," Ian replied curtly.

Josh saw his sister Charlotte's lips move, but he assumed she was talking to herself, since she didn't speak loud enough for him to hear her from across the table and three seats down.

"What about you, Cait?" Justin turned the questions to the woman Josh wanted to know more about.

Thank fuck, I know he's into Amy, so I can thank him later for being friendly to Cait without wanting to kick his ass for hitting on my woman.

"Are you just visiting your brother for the holidays? Or are you moving to town as well?"

"I'm, uh, moving here, too." Cait didn't lift her eyes off of her nephew as she replied to Justin.

Fuck, she's so sweet, shy, and absolutely adorable.

"Cait helps me out by taking care of Brody while I'm working." Ian reached over to pat his sister's shoulder reassuringly.

Ah, a good big brother, who takes care of her when he knows she's uncomfortable. Hopefully, he won't object too much when I ask his sister out.

"Looks like you've definitely got your hands full with that little cutie." Amy leaned over the table for Josh to be able to see her from the other side of JJ and Justin and waved at Brody, who shyly looked up at her from Cait's lap. "How old are you, Brody?"

Brody held up four fingers before burying his face in his aunt's shoulder, but he never said a word. Seeing the boy in Cait's arms, Josh easily pictured her holding their children, and hoped the image in his head would be their reality sometime in the not-too-distant future.

"Sorry, he's shy around new people." Ian tousled his son's hair as he smiled across the table at Amy. "He's four, but it'll be an hour or two before he'll tell you that himself."

"Oh, I understand that," Amy laughed, wiggling her fingers at Brody, who was twisting on his aunt's lap and peeking out shyly. "I was the same way when I was a kid."

"Susan said you're starting a new job next week," Ian stated, monopolizing the conversation with Amy, when Josh wished Cait would share a little more. "What do you do?"

"I'm a chemical engineer. When I was here last month for Anthony and Kay's wedding, Justin told me about all the R and D projects he has going on to try and make Burleson Incorporated into a more environmentally friendly company, and I couldn't turn down the opportunity to help make that happen."

Justin took over then, elaborating on what Amy had just disclosed. "Don't let Amy fool you. It took me a whole week after she schooled me on how I could do more than I already had planned in the lab before I convinced her to move here and implement her ideas to improve our projects."

"No, you were only vaguely hinting that I should come work at Burleson. Once there was an actual offer on the table, I accepted immediately."

Just as Josh was about to ignore Justin and Amy's conversation with Ian to ask Cait more about herself, Charlotte redirected the conversation. "Ya'll need to stop with the lovey-dovey eyes and fussing at each other like an old married couple. Or our mothers will let their matchmaking success go to their heads and keep trying to set the rest of us up."

"Oh, no, we're not," Amy sputtered, motioning between Justin and herself as she denied that they were flirting. "There's no lovey-dovey anything with us. We're just friends. And, um, coworkers starting next week. Or I guess, technically, Justin's my boss starting next week. So, we can't ever be anything more than friends."

Josh could tell by Justin's expression that his cousin didn't agree with Amy's assessment of their relationship. *I wish you luck, Cuz. Hopefully, neither one of us will have too hard a time lassoing our fillies in the new year.*

"Is that why we were seated here instead of with the Hunters, who actually invited us to this dinner? So your mothers could play matchmaker?" Ian looked pointedly at Charlotte before turning to glare at Jake, who was seated beside his sister.

Damn, maybe it's a good thing I'm not in Jake's seat. I'd hate to get off on the wrong foot with my future brother-in-law by kickin' his ass for that dirty look.

"Technically, it was our aunt who seated you between my sister and I," Jake pointed out, smirking at Ian. *Damn, maybe Jake and I have more of that twin thing to have similar thoughts after all. Hopefully, he's not getting any ideas about my girl. I'd hate to have to kick my brother's ass to stake my claim.* "But, yeah, I'm sure Ma enlisted the help of her best friend, Mandi Hunter, and our Aunt Susan, to try to pair us up."

"They've been doing it for years," JJ chuckled from beside Josh. "They've just stepped it up a notch with any new people in town since Anthony found his new bride outside of Heart's Destiny."

"Most of the time, we just laugh it off and appreciate making a new friend, like Justin and Amy." Josh motioned to his cousin and Amy with his thumb before pointing across the room at Bobby and Brooklyn. He was pretty sure he was about to stir the pot and really aggravate Ian, but he wanted to see how Cait responded to his explanation of the lightning strike they'd obviously both felt a few minutes earlier. "But since Ma's matchmaking seems to have worked with Bobby and Brie, she and Aunt Susan are hoping that success snowballs into marrying us all off. But unless lightning strikes the instant you meet someone in our family, you don't have to worry about a trip down the aisle. It's either love at first sight or not at all for the Burlesons."

Cait's head popped up and her bright blue-green eyes lit with recognition as their eyes locked on one another once more. *Yeah, baby girl, I'm talkin' 'bout that jolt of lightning we feel every time we look at each other.*

"You all really believe in love at first sight?" Josh didn't take his eyes off of Cait, as her brother questioned the Burlesons around him, so he didn't notice if Ian realized what was going on between him and Cait or not.

Yeah, sunshine, you and me are the real deal, love at first sight, and destined to be together forever.

"I've never felt the tingles myself, but it's common knowledge that our family tends to know immediately when they've met their mate," Jake replied when nobody else responded to Ian's question.

Josh almost called bullshit on his brother's claim to have never felt the tingles of love at first sight. He knew Jake still felt those tingles every time he saw Kara Thompson, just like he had when they were little kids and Jake picked on Kara for misspelling "cakes" when she drew the logo for her mom's bakery, which she now owned and ran since her mom passed away. But he also knew his brother was in denial about what those tingles meant, thinking they couldn't be the same things all their elders described for meeting *The One* because he was too young to remember when they first started.

He also knew if he called Jake out on his feelings for Kara, then Jake would start to dig into Josh's sudden understanding of the love-at-first-sight feeling and figure out he'd just met *His One*. Since he knew he needed to bide his time with making a move on Cait, Josh kept his brother's secret. For now, anyway.

"For as long as there have been Burlesons on this land, they've fallen in love at first sight." JJ took over for Jake in explaining the history of how Heart's Destiny got its name. "Our third-great-grandfather, Jonah Burleson, saw Emma Rogers on the train out of San Antonio going to Laredo, declared her his heart's destiny, and followed her off the train to settle here. Twenty-some years later, when there were finally enough people here to form a town, he named the town Heart's Destiny to honor her and their love."

"Their son, Joshua, who I'm named after, fell in love with our second-great-grandma, Sarah, the first time he met her at a cattle auction in Dallas." Josh continued the family history lesson without taking his eyes off Cait. He smiled brightly when he saw her eyes dilate as he spoke.

"Joshua and Sarah's son, Robert, who our dad and brother are named after, met our great-grandma, Sylvia, while on a business trip to the east coast. He stayed a little longer than planned on that business trip and had her moved home and married to him within six months." Jake grinned before continuing. "I know he fell in love at first sight, but since it took him a little while to seal the deal, I have to wonder if she took a little convincing before she fell for him."

"Our Pappaw Jerry told us stories about how he had to keep making several trips to Oklahoma to court Memmaw Judy." JJ nodded his head at Jake. "While he knew the moment he met her, it took him almost a year before he won her heart."

"And of course, there's our parents." Josh motioned between himself and Jake.

"And our parents." JJ motioned between himself and Justin. "They all fell in love at first sight, too."

"Not to mention Anthony and now Bobby in this generation," Jake added.

"Gracious, did the Burlesons only have boys until the current generation?" Amy questioned the predominance of males born in the Burleson family lineage.

"No, there were a couple of girls before us," Charlotte replied, expanding on the family history without continuing the love-at-first-sight discussion. "Our great-grandpa, Robert, had a sister, Elizabeth, who died during a flu outbreak when she was fourteen. And Jonah and Emma had a daughter, Mary, whom my house was originally built for, but we don't have a clue what happened to her after she left the ranch to serve as a nurse during World War I."

"She went off to serve and never came back?" Cait finally broke eye contact with Josh and turned to give Charlotte a wide-eyed look. Josh instantly missed having her undivided attention, but he was glad to see her opening up and actively participating in the conversation, instead of continuing to look so shy and scared of them. "Do you think she died in the war?"

"No." Charlotte shook her head as she replied to Cait. "I found boxes of her stuff that were sent home at the end of the war, including a stack of love letters. I think she fell in love with someone she met while serving in France, and either stayed there to marry him or went back to his home after the war."

"So, ya'll could have some distant cousins out in the world and not even know it." Amy succinctly stated the possibility that the Burleson family had been trying to figure out for a hundred years. *I wonder if anyone will tell her about the multi-billion-dollar trust those possible cousins are set to inherit if we can find Mary Burleson's descendants.*

"Yeah, I think so." Charlotte nodded her head. "When Tia was staying with me a couple of weeks ago, she suggested we all do one of those online DNA tests to see if we can find our long-lost family. I've been thinking about it, but I don't want to be the only one doing it, ya know?"

"I'll do it with you, Char." Justin quickly volunteered.

"Yeah?" Charlotte looked at Justin quizzically, like she couldn't believe he would volunteer to submit his DNA for testing.

"Of course." Justin grinned at her before turning to look in Josh, JJ, and Jake's direction. "We should all do it, don't you think?"

"Sure, why not?" JJ chuckled.

"Absolutely," Josh exclaimed, happily stepping up to support his sister in her quest to solve the family mystery. But then he realized those tests didn't just link people to long-lost relatives. They also showed how much DNA you shared with your immediate family members. He deliberately pointed at Jake, setting up for a joke about one of them being switched at birth and not actually related to the rest of the family. "Maybe it'll explain how we're twins, but nothing alike."

"We'll probably find out you were switched at birth," Jake interjected before Josh could get it out.

Damn, maybe we do have that twin thing after all.

"What about ya'll? Any of you wanna spit in a tube with the rest of us to see if you can find any long-lost family?" Jake turned his question to the Campbells and Amy, not bothering to interrupt the conversations Jen and Julie were having with the wrestlers sitting on the other side of them from Josh and Jake.

Cait looked over at Ian with an almost scared expression. Ian shook his head at his sister before looking back up at Jake and saying, "I know all I need to know about our family, but thanks anyway."

What the fuck? Why does my Katydid look so freaked out about finding out about her family? Josh recognized the instant he thought of the pet name for Cait that he should probably skip any reference to the grasshoppers when he actually started using one of the terms of endearment that he'd been trying out for her in his head.

"What do you say, Amy?" Justin directed his question specifically to the woman beside him. So, Josh kept his focus on Cait as the conversation went on around him. "If I order a bulk lot of DNA tests, will you take one with me?"

"I, uh, I don't know," Amy stuttered. "I mean it would be kind of cool to find out about my dad's side of the family that I don't know anything about, but it's kind of scary to think of what I might possibly find that I don't really want to see."

"Like what?"

Yeah, like what? Josh wondered the same as his cousin, not sure what could be bad about finding more family. *Unless maybe we find out our ancestors are notorious criminals or have some kind of medical issues that we hope none of us inherit. Is that what Cait's afraid of finding?*

"I mean, those things don't just tell you who you're related to." Amy's voice sounded tentative, drawing Josh's attention when Cait turned to look at Amy. "They also give you a detailed racial breakdown. And while I know I'm mixed with both my dad and grandpa being white, I'm not sure I want to know if the mixing started back when one of my Black ancestors was raped as a slave. Things don't always go well for Black people on ***Finding Your Roots***, ya know."

Fuck! I didn't even think about the atrocities we could all find in our family trees with ancestors who weren't as color-blind as our folks raised us to be. Damn. I need to make sure I'm more sensitive to those things in the future with our family expanding. I don't want to accidentally stick my foot in my mouth and hurt anyone's feelings, especially the people who could be my new in-laws in the near future.

"Yeah, I've worried about what we'll find in our family history before Jonah and Emma started this branch of the family, too." Charlotte reached across the table and placed her hand on Amy's. "Since Jonah was born in eighteen-sixty, we could find that he was the product of one of those rapes and given the last name of the man who tortured his mother, which would taint the Burleson name as being on the wrong side of our American history. Or his parents could have been plantation owners, which would still put them on the wrong side, even if his father wasn't a rapist. But even as hard as all that will be to learn, I still want to know how much of Memmaw Judy's Native American ancestry flows through my blood, and if I have a Black fourth-great-grandma that I would be proud to claim in my family tree for the strength she showed to live through that horrible time in history and raise a man as good as our third-great-grandpa, Jonah. Not to mention all the possibilities on the Rogers' side of the family that we know nothing about."

Damn, Sis, if teaching doesn't work out for you, you should go into promoting DNA tests, Josh thought, just as his mother called everyone to line up to fix their plates. *Now I'm really curious about what all we'll find when we submit our DNA samples.*

"Okay, I'll think about it." Amy acquiesced as they all started standing to go fill their plates.

As he went through the line with the rest of his family and their friends, both new and old, he couldn't keep his eyes off Cait. He desperately wanted to switch seats with his twin when they got back to the table, but he knew if he suggested it, his whole family would soon start teasing him about being the next to fall for the schemes of their matchmaking mommas.

No, I need to bide my time and take things super slow. She's too skittish for me to start laying the groundwork for us to be more than friends when I can't be home full-time to work on the relationship.

Josh ended up spending the majority of his time that afternoon trying to draw Cait into the conversations going on around them as they ate, opened presents, and played a few games. All the while, he was planning the timeline he'd have to follow to transition out of the Navy and start to pursue his soulmate.

Chapter Two

Cait was still freaked out two days after the conversation she had with her brother, when Ian told her that their move to Heart's Destiny was so he could help find the head of the cartel, who had ordered the drive-by shooting a little over two years ago. Ian had diligently tried to convince her that Rojo was the only one left who hadn't been captured in a raid in the local area back in November. But Cait had enough knowledge about the cartel, from spending several years hanging around her brother and his former partner in the DEA, to know that Rojo would have immediately started recruiting to rebuild his organization as soon as he knew he'd evaded the raid. So, even though her brother assured her that she was safe, with nobody who might recognize her from the day they were shot in the vicinity of where they now lived, she didn't feel as safe as she had the week before when she thought they'd left the cartel back in San Diego.

Ian doesn't know who might have talked after the shooting or what they might have told their boss. Rojo might not know I'm Mikey's sister, but he could have heard one of those men describe me. And if he's heard my description, then he could tell his new followers to look for me, even if he doesn't have a clue that we moved here.

She'd been looking forward to going sightseeing on Saturday after successfully venturing out of the bed and breakfast and their new home multiple times over the previous week. She'd not only made it through the party on the Burleson Ranch, but she'd also managed to drive herself for a couple of outings. One to the hardware store while Ian was busy setting up their furniture in their new home, and another time going back to the ranch for her interview to get her new job. But after talking to Ian and finding out they weren't as far from the cartel as she'd thought, Cait rapidly regressed back into the agoraphobic person she'd become after the shooting.

Now she had to have her brother drive her to her first day on the job, and she wanted to sink down in the seat so there was no chance one of the new cartel members would see her as they drove through town. She hated feeling so scared and wanted to go back to the time when she wasn't so constantly afraid. But after this setback in what she thought was progress to achieve some semblance of her previously normal life, Cait wasn't sure that even being told that everyone in the cartel was behind bars would be enough to reassure her that she was safe again.

"Remember what I told you," Ian tried to reassure her as he drove along the gravel drive between pastures and barns to get to the house they'd visited a little over a week before for the late Christmas party. "The ranch is like Fort Knox. You're safe here. If you weren't, I wouldn't feel comfortable leaving either you or Brody here while I'm at work. So, try to relax a little bit. If you keep looking so nervous, you're going to blow my cover. And while I don't think it will put us in danger if the Burlesons find out why we really moved here, I'm sure Jake doesn't want his family to worry about him being a part of this operation as part of his job."

She'd learned at the Christmas party that Jake and Josh were both still in the Navy and didn't live on the ranch full-time, which she'd found both disappointing and a small relief. She was disappointed that she wouldn't get to see Josh all the time, but she was also relieved that she'd be able to work on her issues from being shot without being tempted to pursue a relationship with him before she'd healed some of the traumatic, invisible scars. Ultimately, she'd decided it was better that she had the time to take care of her mental health without having to fight her attraction to Josh the whole time.

She hadn't cared as much about Jake not being on the ranch full-time. He seemed friendly enough, but he didn't make her tingle like his brother did, so it wasn't a big deal if he was around or not.

But then, over the weekend, her brother had filled her in on Jake's job with Naval Intelligence, and how he worked with various other law enforcement agencies to coordinate their cases when they overlapped. Apparently, that was how Ian had met Jake a few years ago, and also why Jake had helped Ian set up his new teaching job as a cover for why he really moved them to Heart's Destiny. Now she wished Jake was stationed here in town, so he could be her brother's backup to help keep them all safe.

"Okay, I know," Cait groaned, tired of hearing the broken record her older brother had become in the past two days. "We're safe as long as we're on the ranch, so Brody and I will both stay here until you come to pick us up this evening."

Cait wasn't sure what a few cowboys armed with hunting rifles, to protect the cattle from any coyotes or cougars who might wander onto the ranch, were going to do to protect the women and children, who weren't anywhere near the grazing land of the cattle, if a cartel gang armed with AK-47's showed up and started shooting near the houses. But she'd given up arguing with her brother about issues that he knew a lot more about than she did.

She was just going to trust that his years of experience working undercover with the cartel, and all the training he had to go through with his various law enforcement jobs before he spent almost a decade working with the DEA, would be enough to know what needed to be done to keep her safe. If Ian was assured that Jake had all the proper safeguards in place to keep his family safe, then she would trust him. And she'd even try not to jump at every loud noise she heard while working on the ranch.

"Thank you," Ian sighed the words more than said them, making it obvious he was just as tired of the argument as she was. "Now, you guys have a good day. Brody, you stay where Aunt Cait can see you and have fun with the workbooks I put in your book bag."

"I will Dad," Brody grinned, reaching for his backpack before Ian could even get him unbuckled from his car seat.

"I love you." Ian hugged his son before setting him on his feet beside the car. He then pointedly looked at Cait as she walked around the vehicle to take Brody's hand and walk him into the house, where she was supposed to report for her first day of work. "Both of you."

"I love you, too," Cait smiled at her brother and gave him a one-armed hug before walking away, so he could get to his new job at the middle school on time.

"Aunt Cait, aren't we supposed to knock?" Brody looked up at her suspiciously, as Cait opened the door and walked into the unlocked house.

"Most places, yes," Cait acknowledged her nephew's wisdom. "But when I talked to her for the interview, Hazel told me to just come on in and look for her in the kitchen."

Brody still looked at her like he wasn't sure about that, but he followed along as they made their way through the house to the kitchen, where they found not only Hazel, but also Bob and their two granddaughters sitting down for breakfast. Tia and Maria had quickly befriended Brody at the Christmas party a week before, convincing him to join their team for the game portion of the day as soon as lunch was over.

"Aunt Cait, why didn't you tell me I'd get to play with my new friends today?" Brody didn't give her a chance to reply, tearing his hand from hers to run over to the table to sit down beside Maria.

Cait would have been surprised by her nephew being so outspoken in front of the adults in the room, considering how he was normally shy in front of people he wasn't around all the time. But she'd witnessed firsthand how Hazel and Bob had treated him like another one of their grandkids at the Christmas party, right down to having a stack of presents for him and insisting Brody call them Memmaw and Pappaw. He might have only known them for a short time, but they'd quickly cemented their places in his heart from day one.

"We can't play for long," Maria informed them. "Mom and Dad have to go back to work, so we've gotta fly out as soon as they finish packing our stuff."

"Sorry, I didn't realize we'd be interrupting breakfast," Cait apologized for her nephew's rude interruption, not feeling anywhere near as comfortable as Brody in her new employers' home.

"Nonsense," Hazel waved her apology off. "Grab each of ya'll a plate and visit until the kids leave for the week."

"Oh, we already ate," Cait started to object before her nephew cut her off.

"But we had yucky eggs." Brody made a face that caused the girls to giggle. "And they're having toast with syrup, so I wanna eat again to try it."

"It's good to know eating at home and then wanting to eat again five minutes later at Memmaw's house isn't a phenomenon limited to my kids," Hazel chuckled, bringing a slight smile to Bob's lips.

"It's French toast," Tia corrected Brody between bites.

"You realize that French toast has eggs on it, right?" Cait arched an eyebrow at Brody as she grabbed him a plate.

"No, it's just toast, isn't it?" Brody leaned over to look closer at the stack of French toast on a platter in the center of the table before turning to look at Hazel. "Memmaw wouldn't mess up toast by putting yucky eggs on it. Would you, Memmaw?"

"Oh, boy, Memmaw," Bob chuckled. "I'm not sure how you're gonna get your shenanigans to work when you're already disappointin' Brody by putting yucky eggs on his French toast."

What shenanigans? Cait wondered, slightly confused by Bob's statement.

"It's not French toast without the eggs, Pappaw." Tia gave Bob a strange look, almost like she was also confused by Bob's words.

"But it's okay, Brody," Maria interjected, reaching over to pat Brody's hand. "You can't taste the eggs. Memmaw makes them yummy by putting them on the bread and frying most of the yucky out." She leaned in like she was going to whisper to just Brody, but apparently hadn't learned to lower her voice yet. "And we cover the rest up with syrup."

"Maybe I should try a bite of yours to see if I like it first," Brody suggested, looking over at Maria's mostly empty plate.

"Okay, you can have that piece." Maria pushed the smallest bite to the edge of her plate closest to Brody. "But get a clean fork to eat it with."

"That's very sweet of you, Maria." Cait praised the girl as she handed her nephew the fork she'd gotten for him from the stack on the island.

"She's already practicing, so she'll be a good big sister when our little brother is born," Tia explained.

"And she's obviously learned from your good example of how to be a fabulous big sister," Hazel praised her other granddaughter.

"Oh, it is good!" Brody shouted as he chewed.

"Swallow before you speak, Brody." Cait corrected Brody's bad manners. "And use your inside voice."

Brody quickly swallowed the bite in his mouth before reaching for one of the pieces of French toast on the platter to put it on the plate Cait had placed in front of him. "Sorry, Aunt Cait."

"Yeah, that's gonna hafta be one of the first lessons we teach our baby brother," Maria pointed out. "Or maybe Mommy and Daddy should give us a little sister instead."

"I hate to break it to you, Maria. But they don't get to choose if the baby is a boy or a girl," Tia informed her sister. "So, we'll just have to teach him or her about manners, no matter if the baby is a brother or a sister."

"What about you, Brody?" Hazel pulled Brody into the girls' conversation. "Would you like to have a little brother or sister like Tia and Maria?"

Oh, now I see the shenanigans Bob was referring to, Cait mused, remembering the conversation about the matchmaking efforts of the Burleson matriarchs a week earlier. *She's thinking she'll get Ian to date one of her daughters by being Brody's honorary grandma and inviting the whole Campbell family to every social event she hosts.*

Too bad her efforts probably won't work on him any better than they'll work on me with Josh already back on base and not around to tempt me.

~~~

Saturday, January 12, 2019

Josh couldn't believe his twin was running a covert op in their hometown and hadn't told him about it when they were there for Christmas. Or that Jake was running the op to find a cartel kingpin with Ian Campbell and not their older brother, Bobby, who was the police chief in Heart's Destiny. *Fuck all that! The really unbelievable part is that he read me in, so Ian can use our cabin as a tactical operations center without Bobby or anyone else in the family finding out about it.*

Most of the land comprising the Burleson Ranch was flat and great for grazing cattle. They had streams and ponds throughout the property with oaks and other native trees to provide natural breaks between the various pastures, though they also fenced them, so the cattle didn't wander into the woods or over into a pasture they weren't supposed to be in, or out to the oil fields.
~~~

But there was a small area in the far southwest corner of the property that was hilly and densely covered with thorny mesquite bushes and trees. Since that ten-acre section of land wasn't safe for cattle to graze, the Burlesons had always left it as nature intended, fencing it off from the rest of the ranch so they didn't end up with a cow trapped in the thorny bushes that they'd have to go in to rescue.

But boys being boys, Jake and Josh had to go explore the area as young teenagers, thinking it was a good place to escape from the constant chaos of their large family. When they were fourteen, they stumbled across an old cabin that they assumed was either someone's hunting cabin, or an attempt at a homestead back before their ancestors bought the land. It took several summers and weekends, when they told their family they were "camping" by one of the creeks not near where the cattle were grazing, for them to fix the place up to make it livable. But by the time they graduated high school, they had a comfortable place they could go to not risk having one of their family members walk in on them when they were alone with a girl.

Josh hadn't ever trusted one of the buckle bunnies he'd hooked up with back in his teenaged, rodeo days to take them there, preferring to take his conquests to the trails on the north side of the Walkers' land or back to whatever hotel they were staying at while they were in the area. But he knew his brother had used it for that purpose a couple of times.

Since college, when Jake had expanded his computer knowledge to include security systems and video surveillance, they'd made a few upgrades to the cabin. A couple of those had required letting their best friends, Aiden and Leo Walker, in on the secret location and swearing them to secrecy. But until Jake called him earlier in the day, they'd both vowed to not let anyone else in on the secret lair. They'd promised not to even bring a girl there unless she allowed them to blindfold her, so she couldn't tell anyone else where to find their secret hideaway. Now, Jake wanted Josh to not only show Ian where the cabin was located, but also to help him move his tactical gear there and give him full access to the place.

Guess we really are growing up, if we're givin' up the Wonder Twins' Secret Lair. Since they would be turning twenty-eight years old in two-and-a-half months, Josh realized it was probably time for them to start acting more like adults instead of childishly keeping their hideaway a secret. *I just thought we'd hold off on adulting until we hit thirty.*

In thinking about all the ways he wanted to adult, Josh's mind instantly drifted to the things he wanted to do with Cait. It probably wasn't the smartest move to start thinking about all the ways he wanted to get naked and dirty with her while he was flying his Cessna 172 to the small airport on the south side of San Antonio closest to the Burleson Incorporated headquarters to meet her brother. But Josh had never claimed to be the smartest of the Burlesons. He gladly gave that honor to his brother, Jake, before they even made it to kindergarten. Though since his little brother, Anthony, had adopted Tia, Josh kinda wondered if she was smarter than all the rest of the Burlesons combined.

Since the flight from Virginia Beach to San Antonio had become second nature to him over the last few years, Josh was able to picture Cait being there to greet him at the airport while still keeping an eye on his instruments to safely make the flight. He longed for the day he pulled his plane into the private hangar he kept there for when he was home on leave, and she really could be waiting there for him because it would be his plane's new permanent home. He hoped their relationship would be far enough along by then that they could lock up the hangar and strip off their clothes right then and there, too eager to be together to wait until they got home.

While he had every intention of taking his time and savoring every moment of the first time he made love to Cait, Josh also knew there would be many more times in their lives when one or both of them would be too impatient to endure a slow, sensual screw. So, since meeting Cait and having to take care of his sexual needs with his own hand in the shower, his most frequent fantasy for the last two weeks was a fast, fervorous fuck.

Josh imagined the day he'd fly home from Virginia for the final time. He'd pull his plane into the hangar and rush through his post-flight tasks to get to Cait as soon as possible. Then, just as he closed the roll-down door to block the view of anyone else using the runway, Cait would come out of the office completely nude.

"Hey, Cowboy, it's about time you got home," Cait greeted him. Josh wasn't sure why his imaginary version of Cait called him by the call sign he used as a SEAL, but he was going with it.

"Hey, Darlin'," Josh grinned at Cait as he stalked toward her, already stripping off his clothes.

"No, not Darlin'. That's too stereotypical for half the guys in Texas to call every woman they meet. I think I'll stick with Sunshine, 'cause she's from Southern California, and seein' her smile is like havin' a ray of sunshine brightening my day."

"Hey, Sunshine," Josh grinned at Cait as he stalked toward her, already stripping off his clothes. "Sorry it took so long, but I got here as soon as the Navy let me leave."

As soon as all of Josh's clothes were strewn across the floor of the hangar, Cait leaped up into his arms, wrapping her arms around his neck and her long, sexy legs around his waist. Their lips met in a passionate kiss as the head of his cock nudged past the soaking-wet outer lips of her pussy.

With one hand cupping her ass and the other in her hair, Josh carried Cait over to the plane, so he could press her back against it while he slid the rest of the way home in the tight sheath of her cunt. No further words were needed as she writhed in pleasure while he set a brutal pace with his thrusts.

Josh used the hand on her ass to control the way she slid up and down on his cock, but moved the hand from her hair down to cup her perky tit, lightly pinching the turgid, pink nipple between his thumb and forefinger. The whole time he fucked her, he claimed her with his kiss.

Cait returned his ardent passion, their tongues tangling in a sensual dance as her nails dug into his back. Josh reveled in the slight sting of pain from her clinging to him, trying to hold on for the wild ride as her cunt started to clench around his cock.

"Fuck, yeah, come on me, Cait," Josh commanded, only breaking their lip lock long enough to grunt out the words as he continued to fuck her through the orgasm.

Josh quickly came out of the fantasy when the nose of his plane dipped, realizing instantly that he'd gotten so caught up in imagining fucking Cait that he'd dropped his hand from the yoke to grip his dick through his jeans. He leveled off and forced himself to banish his fantasies of Cait until he was safely on the ground in San Antonio.

Fuck, I can't zone out like that when I'm getting close to the more populated areas where I have to check in with Air Traffic Control.

Luckily for him, he only had another half hour or so before he landed. So, he was easily able to focus on all the self-announcements he had to make as he passed through the airspace of the various airports in San Antonio. By ten p.m., he'd landed, refueled, and taxied over to the hangar where he was meeting Ian.

That gave them four hours to pack everything up, drive the hour to Heart's Destiny, unload, and drive the hour back to the airport for Josh to be able to fly back to Virginia Beach and be on time for a team meeting at noon the next day. *Hopefully, Ian doesn't have too much gear to pack up. And won't mind if I nap while he's driving, since I won't get another chance to sleep until at least eighteen-hundred hours tomorrow.*

"Hey, Josh, thanks for meeting me here," Ian greeted him with a nod of his head as he carried a crate out of the hangar.

"No problem." Josh dipped his chin toward the crate of computer components Ian was carrying. "You got everything already packed up?"

"Yeah, when Jake told me you were flying in for just a few hours, I figured you wouldn't have time to stick around for packing and unpacking. So, I came back here a couple of hours early to take down the surveillance cameras I'd put up and pack everything. This is the last of the stuff to load in my Range Rover." Ian lifted the crate a couple of inches.

"Cool." Josh pointed toward the side door that Ian had just come out of from the hangar. "You need me to lock up before we head to the ranch?"

"Yeah, I guess you can." Ian sat the crate down and fished a couple sets of keys from his pocket. "You'll need to go back in and lock both doors after you pull Jake's truck out."

"Damn, Jake didn't tell me we're moving his truck, too," Josh groaned as he took the keys from Ian. "Guess that means I get to drive it instead of napping on this first leg of the move."

"Sorry, man," Ian shrugged as he picked up the crate once more. "But since you don't have to wait around while I pack and unpack, you should have an extra hour to nap before you have to take off."

"Naw, it's fine," Josh shook his head, knowing he wouldn't be able to sleep that long, even if he laid down on his bed in the cabin because of worrying about being late for PT the next morning. "It won't be the first time I've gone for thirty-six hours without sleep. And I can guarantee it won't be the last, either."

They both chuckled lightly as they walked away from each other. Ian went to his Range Rover in the parking lot, where he loaded up the crate and got in the driver's seat. Josh went in the side door of the hangar, opened up the roll-up door closest to the truck, drove the truck out of the hangar, and then went back in the hangar to lock everything up. He then led the way to the cabin hidden in the southwest corner of the Burleson Ranch, with Ian following him in his Range Rover.

"Damn, Jake wasn't joking about this being a secret lair," Ian chuckled as they each got out of their vehicles once they parked at the cabin. "I was seriously worried about scratching the paint on the trucks to make some of those sharp turns through the overgrowth to get back here."

"Yeah, we put those in to make it look like the trail dead ends to keep people from snooping too far off the main road," Josh grinned, remembering back to when he and Jake were sixteen and they'd measured their trucks to figure out how far back to cut the bushes to be able to drive to the cabin without scratching the paint jobs. "We went through way too much touch-up paint when we first started driving and hadn't figured out we needed to measure how far back to cut the underbrush for this trail. It's a wonder our folks didn't figure out where we were gettin' all those scratches on our trucks."

"Damn, you guys have had this place that long?" Ian gave him a surprised look as they started unloading the vehicles of the crates and boxes that Ian used to pack up his gear.

"Oh, yeah, we actually found it when we were fourteen," Josh informed him as he unlocked the door to the cabin for them to enter and walked over to key in the security code to keep the alarm from signaling to Jake that someone was in the cabin. "It was just a shell then, with the log walls being the only thing still left from whenever it was originally built. But hanging out with the Walkers all the time helped us learn what we needed about construction to be able to fix it up a little at a time. Not that we could do much when we camped out here before we were old enough to drive and get part-time jobs to be able to get the supplies we needed to fix it up. For the first couple of years, we patched the holes in the roof with tarps 'cause we couldn't sneak real building supplies out here in our backpacks or on the back of our four-wheelers."

"Wow," Ian looked surprised as he looked around the now fully furnished three-bedroom, two-and-a-half-bathroom cabin. His eyes seemed to catch on the kitchen in the open-floorplan living space. "Wait! How do you have electricity and running water in a cabin nobody else knows about?"

"We did have to let a couple of the Walkers in on the secret when we needed help upgrading the existing well and septic system," Josh admitted with a shrug as he directed Ian to the third bedroom, where he and Jake planned to store their tactical gear when they got out of the Navy. "I was fine wiring up the solar panels for electricity, but I draw the line at working with electricity near water and anything to do with sewage, so we let the experts handle those tasks."

"This is the room we planned to use to store our tactical gear after getting out of the Navy." Josh pointed to the two gun safes they had in the otherwise empty room as he sat down the box he'd carried in. "I don't know what all you have for this op, but there should be plenty of room for you to be able to store your weapons and whatever else you have in here. If you need more space, or access to the security feeds, you're welcome to take over Jake's room, since that's where he has the primary monitors for all the cameras on the ranch."

"This should be plenty of room for what I need." Ian sat down the crate he'd carried into the cabin. "Though if he's already got surveillance cameras set up here, I'll have him send the feed to my phone, so I don't have to put up more."

As they carried in the rest of the boxes and crates, Ian filled Josh in on more of the details of the op, including his personal interest in capturing the man who'd ordered the hit on him that took his wife's life at their son's second birthday party being held in a park in San Diego. Josh had to fight not to show the overwhelming emotion he felt when he heard that Cait had been caught in the crossfire on that fateful day.

Fuck! I bet that's why Cait's so shy now and kept looking to Ian for reassurance at the Christmas party. She must be terrified if she knows they moved here to try to catch the cartel ringleader.

"So, does your sister know why you moved here?" It was all he could do to keep his voice even as he questioned Ian. "Or is she as in the dark as the rest of our family is about Jake's involvement?"

"I thought I could keep her in the dark," Ian confided with a rueful chuckle. "But then within days of leaving San Diego, she seemed practically cured of her fear of leaving the house. So, I had to tell her about Rojo being in the area to keep her from wanting to go with me to explore San Antonio."

Oh fuck! I can't imagine that went over well. I hope that hasn't caused her to be afraid to leave the house again.

"How did she take the news?" Josh finally voiced the question when Ian didn't elaborate further.

"Not as well as I'd hoped," Ian sighed. "I thought it would just deter her from wanting to go into San Antonio. But she's quit going anywhere alone again. And only feels safe enough for me to leave her side at home and on the ranch. And the only reason she feels safe enough to work for your mom is because I assured her that the ranch is as well protected as Fort Knox."

Josh wasn't sure he agreed with that assessment of the security on the ranch, but he allowed his lips to turn up in the slightest smile to reassure Ian that his sister and son were both safe while they were there. Yeah, they had gates that required an access code to get onto the main part of the ranch where the family all lived, but nobody ever locked their doors in the main cluster of homes. So, if someone with nefarious intentions ever snuck past the gate, they wouldn't have much of a problem breaking in at any of their houses.

Fuck! It doesn't even matter that we were all taught to shoot as kids, when the only guns that aren't locked up are Bobby's service weapon when he's on duty and the guns the hands carry in case a snake or other predator gets into one of the cow pastures. Hell, I don't even think Dad carries a gun when he takes Tia and Maria on a trail ride, though he probably should in case of snakes.

Josh spent the rest of the time he was helping Ian carry in his gear with his mind volleying back and forth between how to make the ranch safer and how to help Cait get over her fear of going anywhere without her brother. Other than reminding his dad that the snakes' brumation period would end in the next month or so, Josh wasn't sure what else he could do to increase the number of people carrying a gun while walking around the ranch. And he felt completely useless when it came to helping Cait, knowing it would take the capture of everyone in the cartel before she'd ever have a chance to feel safe again.

If Ian and Jake haven't accomplished that by the time I'm finished with my minimum service requirement and able to get out of the Navy, then I'll make it my mission to hunt every fucking one of those bastards down. And then I'll start trying to coax her out on dates to help her feel safe everywhere again.

Chapter Three

Sunday, February 3, 2019

Cait felt like she was really starting to settle into this new phase of her life since her family moved to Texas. With her brother focusing his search for the head of the cartel in San Antonio, which was at least fifty miles away from Heart's Destiny, she had less fear that she'd be recognized and targeted again while in town. She still limited the places she was comfortable going without her brother there to protect her to their house, the Burleson Ranch, and the Hunters' Bed and Breakfast. But she'd managed to brave going to church with Ian there, and had started to socialize some with the Burleson women and the friends they introduced her to at church. That socialization was limited to when they were on the ranch, like at Brooklyn's birthday party earlier that week, or at church, but at least she was making friends. So, she no longer felt as isolated as she'd become the past couple of years.

She'd been surprised to learn that the woman she knew as Brie Brooks was actually Brooklyn Barnes, an heiress from Georgia who'd fled from her father's estate in the middle of the night to escape an arranged marriage to a man more than twice her age. But in the month she'd spent getting to know the younger woman, she'd really come to like the author, who was living with and dating Josh's oldest brother, Bobby.

Brooklyn and Bobby had to leave town the day after her birthday to go deal with her father and some legal issues in Georgia, which Cait hoped were going well for the couple, so her new friend could come back to continue living on the ranch permanently. Though Cait doubted Brooklyn would continue working with her as a housekeeper for very long, if she was able to gain control of her inheritance, she hoped they could continue to build their friendship, the way she was with the other women on the ranch.

Jen, Julie, and Becky Burleson were all only a few months older than Cait and shared one of the homes on the ranch that Cait cleaned each week, so she felt closest to them. Charlotte was not quite three years older than Cait, but she seemed so much more mature than her and the other Burleson women, probably from living alone instead of sharing a space with her sister and cousins.

After spending the last month getting to know the family, Cait could clearly see why Hazel was trying so hard to push Charlotte and Ian together. Not only did their maturity levels seem to match up, but they also had the common interest of both being middle school English teachers.

Cait had been skeptical of Hazel's matchmaking on her first day working for the Burlesons, especially pertaining to her and her brother. While she thought she'd one day be open to Hazel playing matchmaker for her and Josh, she knew she needed some time to get over her agoraphobia before she'd be ready to dip her toes in the dating pool again.

She hadn't fully opened up to Hazel to explain why, but after working with her for the last few weeks, Cait had made it clear that she was working on getting over her fears, so she'd be ready when Josh finally got out of the Navy. Thankfully, just knowing that she was amenable to being fixed up with Josh in a year or two was enough to satisfy Hazel for now.

When it came to her brother, however, Hazel was a little pushier than Cait thought was appropriate for having just met them. As far as she'd known when they first moved to Heart's Destiny, Ian hadn't even looked at another woman since the day Mari died, so she hadn't thought he was over the loss of his wife enough to consider dating yet. She'd tried explaining that to Hazel, but the older woman hadn't seemed to agree.

Cait had tried to stay out of Hazel's matchmaking plans as much as she could, even running interference for her brother when she thought he needed it. But then she'd noticed the way Ian kept looking over at Charlotte when they were in church the week before, and started to wonder if maybe he just needed to find the right woman before he'd be ready to start healing a little from the tragic loss of his wife. It was because she'd seen her brother's interest in Charlotte that she'd finally relented and allowed Hazel to send Brody to the stables to spend some time with Charlotte.

That had almost ended up with Ian realizing she was in on the matchmaking plot because of Charlotte wanting to take Brody on a trail ride. But thankfully, Cait had quickly covered her part by calling Ian and not letting on that Brody had gone to the stables where she couldn't see him for a few minutes. As far as he knew, Charlotte had her horse in the paddock between her house and the stables and that's where Brody had seen her while Cait watched him playing outside through the window as she cleaned.

Since then, Brody had talked non-stop every night over dinner about Charlotte and the horses. And Ian hadn't done a very good job of disguising his interest in Charlotte every time his son mentioned her name. Oh, he'd tried to act nonchalant and as if he was only curious about Brody's enjoyment of horseback riding. But after seeing her brother when he first started dating Mari, Cait knew his tells and recognized his attraction every time Charlotte came up in conversation.

Ian giving a repeat performance of watching Charlotte at church this morning only reinforced Cait's belief that he might be ready to date again. Or at least, he wanted to spend some time with Charlotte, even if he was only ready for friendship just yet.

So, when her friends invited her to come to the ranch and go riding with them, Cait made sure to sneak a moment with Hazel, under the guise of asking for the recipe for the casserole she'd brought to the potluck lunch, to make sure Hazel knew to extend the invitation to Ian and Brody.

It might be sneaky and somewhat manipulative, but Cait knew Ian wouldn't accept the invitation if Brody wasn't there to hear it. But her kindhearted brother was too great a father to ever say no to something his son would enjoy so much. So, now they were pulling up the driveway on the ranch for all of them to go horseback riding together.

"Park at Charlotte's house," Caitir instructed her brother as he drove into the cluster of houses she cleaned for her job with the Burleson family. She had to stifle her smile at seeing that little twitch of Ian's eyes when she said Charlotte's name. She pointed to the small brick house on the opposite side of the gravel drive from the large, white, plantation-style home, where he normally parked when he came to the ranch to drop her and Brody off each weekday morning and pick them up each weekday evening. "It's a shorter walk to and from the stables, and I have a feeling we might need that after horseback riding."

Cait had only spent a few minutes on Thursday and Friday when she was finished with work, learning a little from her friends about how to mount a horse and hold the reins to walk the horse around the paddock. But even that few minutes sitting in a saddle was enough for her to know their inner thighs would be sore after a longer ride. Based on the look her brother gave her as he parked, she didn't think he had any clue about how much of a workout he was in for by going on this ride.

"This is gonna be so much fun," Brody beamed as soon as they got out of the vehicle and started walking in the same direction Charlotte was toward the stables.

"So much fun," Cait agreed, stifling a giggle at the way Ian was blatantly staring at Charlotte's backside. *Oh, yeah, Hazel is definitely right about him being ready to date Charlotte.*

"Hey, ya'll ready to break out of the paddock and go for a real ride?" Charlotte turned to greet them as they walked into the stables.

"Yes!" Brody shouted his agreement. "But I need my helmet first, Miss Char."

"Of course," Charlotte agreed, smiling at Brody. "Let me grab that for you first thing. Then we'll get you started brushing one of the horses while we tack them up for the ride."

Charlotte turned and walked over to the room on the left side of the stables that Cait's friends had informed her was called the tack room. She barely stepped inside before she returned with the child-sized motorcycle helmet that Brody had worn the other two days Charlotte had been teaching him how to ride.

As Brody put on the helmet, Charlotte walked back to the tack room and loaded up with all kinds of other equipment that she carried to the stalls where the horses were waiting. Several of the other Burlesons were also grabbing the bridles and saddles and stuff they needed to prepare the horses for riding, so Cait just stood there waiting for Charlotte or one of the others to direct her where to go and what to do.

After her nervousness was noticed while outside with the horses earlier in the week, she was pretty sure they were all giving her a moment to go through the positive affirmations her therapist had taught her to be comfortable with being in an outdoor space after the shooting. She hadn't thought they'd done much when she was back in San Diego, but she hoped they'd be helpful here in Heart's Destiny.

I'm safe here. This isn't the park. The cartel can't do a drive-by here. Breathe in the fresh air and blow out the fear. As she inhaled the smell of hay and horses, Cait wasn't so sure her former therapist was correct about the fresh air part of that mantra, but she blew out the fear anyway.

"What do we need to do first?" Ian nodded at Justin and JJ as they walked out of the tack room and toward the horse stalls.

"Grab a brush and follow me," Justin answered with a smile as he carried a couple of harnesses toward a horse's stall.

Ian stepped over to the tack room, but he was only in it for a moment before he came right back out, holding two brushes. He handed one to Cait and one to Brody before going back for a third for himself. They all followed Justin into the stall, where he was working with a horse that Cait hadn't seen the Burleson women work with earlier that week.

"We have to groom the horses before we put the saddles on, so we make sure there's nothing in their hair that might cause saddle sores while we're riding," Justin explained, showing them how to brush the brown and white horse he'd just put one of the harnesses on and attached to a strap on the wall of the stall.

"Miss Char already taught me how to do this with Westley." Brody grinned at Justin, obviously not as shy as usual when there were horses present. "What's this horse's name?"

"This is Michelangelo." Justin smiled down at Brody as he continued to brush the horse. "He's a little younger than Westley and the horse I rode the most growing up."

"Nice to meet you, Michelangelo." Brody presented his hand to the horse for it to smell him before he started brushing his hand over the side of the horse's neck. He turned to look up at Justin. "Which horse do I need to start tacking up to ride?"

"We can get you set up to ride Michelangelo if you want," Justin stated, grinning down at Brody. "Or we can see which of the other horses are available to let you pick your favorite."

"We're tacking up Pocahontas for Cait." Jen poked her head into the stall and motioned for Cait to follow her.

Cait carried the brush with her as she followed Jen out of the stall and over to another stall across the aisleway in the center of the stable, where there was a chestnut brown horse with a black mane and tail.

"Which horses are still available for Brody and Ian to pick from?" Justin hollered down the aisle as he followed the girls out of the stall.

"Tornado and Raphael," Charlotte shouted back from a stall farther down on the opposite side of the stable.

"You guys named your horses after the *Teenage Mutant Ninja Turtles*? Where are Leonardo and Donatello?" Cait heard the laughter in her brother's voice as he questioned the naming pattern of the Burlesons' horses while he stood in the aisle between the stalls.

"I'm riding Leonardo," Tia yelled from a couple of stalls down. "And Daddy is riding Donatello."

"Well, then we have to ride Raphael, so all four of the *Turtles* can stick together," Ian chuckled.

Cait followed Jen's instructions for how to brush down Pocahontas, losing track of the other conversations in the stable once they stopped shouting between stalls. Once they were finished with their horses, Julie and Becky joined Jen and Cait in the stall with Pocahontas, showing her all the steps for tacking up the horse.

"I can't believe you're goin' along with Aunt Hazel's matchmaking plans for Charlotte and Ian," Julie whispered, obviously not wanting anyone outside the stall they were in to hear their conversation.

"She's not just goin' along with 'em," Becky chortled. "She actively helped set this one up."

Cait gave Becky a wide-eyed look over the top of the horse between them, hoping she'd lower her voice, so her brother wouldn't overhear the conversation.

"What?" Becky whisper-shouted. "We all know you don't need her recipe for cheesy chicken and rice casserole."

"Come on, Cait, give it up," Jen whispered, shaking her head. "We thought you were on our side with stopping all the setups. Why are you helping the Matchmaking Mommas?"

"I was right there with you about stopping them at first," Cait shrugged, keeping her voice low as she explained her change of opinion. "But then I saw how interested Ian is in Charlotte. I love my brother and want him to go back to being the happy man he used to be before he lost Mari. So, if the Matchmaking Mommas can help bring him back to life by setting him up with the only woman he's even remotely looked twice at in the last couple of years, then I have to help them."

"Okay, I can see your point," Jen and Julie whispered in unison.

"Besides," Cait added with a smirk. "If Hazel keeps the Mommas focused on Ian and Charlotte, they aren't trying to play matchmaker for any of us."

"Okay, I guess I'm willing to sacrifice my sister to the Matchmaking Mommas," Becky sighed. "If it keeps them from trying to set me up with Surfer Josh again. Yeah, he's hot and all, but on top of traveling all the time so I couldn't really see him, his having the same name as one of my brothers makes it impossible for me to seriously consider dating him."

"For real," Jen agreed. "It's bad enough we all have to refer to him as 'Surfer Josh' when he's in town to keep from getting the Joshes mixed up. I can't imagine having to scream 'Surfer Josh' in the middle of an orgasm to keep from being creeped out by calling out our cousin's name."

Cait had to giggle with the rest of the girls, though she really didn't have a problem calling out "Josh" in the middle of an orgasm. At least, not during the self-induced ones she'd had while fantasizing in bed at night since meeting Josh and the rest of the Burlesons.

Although, now that the girls have pointed out that there are two men named Josh who come to town on occasion, maybe I'll start calling him Cowboy Hottie in my fantasies, so I don't accidentally start picturing the wrestler while using my vibrator.

"I'll help Cait with finishing up and leading Pocahontas out, if ya'll want to go ahead and get your horses lined up for the ride," Becky suggested, pointing at Jen and Julie.

"Sounds good," the twins chimed in unison before walking out of the stall.

Cait followed Becky's instructions to swap out the harness and lead currently being used to anchor Pocahontas to the wall for the bridle that attached to the reins for her to be able to direct the horse once she was ready to ride. Once everything was in place, and Becky was assured it was all properly cinched down to stay attached to the horse, they walked Pocahontas out of the stall to go line up behind Jen and Julie.

Julie introduced Cait to the other horses, Hurricane, who was lined up in front for JJ to lead the ride, Jen's horse, Belle, and Julie's horse, Jasmine, while Becky went back into the stable to get her horse, Ariel. Becky put Ariel in line right behind Pocahontas, so Cait realized she'd be riding between Julie on Jasmine and Becky on Ariel.

Charlotte followed her sister in lining up with her horse, Westley. Brody was with her, though they didn't stay standing near Westley for long because Brody wanted to go meet all the other horses.

JJ soon led Ian and the horse she assumed was Raphael, since that was the name of the horse she'd heard her brother pick to ride earlier, out of the stable to line up behind Charlotte. Brody quickly ran over to his dad to take him through the line of horses and introduce him to all of them as the rest of the Burlesons started lining up their horses behind the one Ian and Brody would ride together.

Oh, JJ must be in on the matchmaking scheme too, Cait mused when she noticed he'd worked the lineup, so Ian would be right behind Charlotte all afternoon. She couldn't help but smile at him as he walked by to mount his horse.

Once everyone was lined up, they all started getting on their horses for the trail ride. Cait followed the instructions to mount Pocahontas that she'd been given a couple of days before when Charlotte had let her practice on Westley, since she didn't have enough time between when she finished work and Ian was due to pick her up for her friends to tack up another horse.

She heard Charlotte trying to instruct Ian how to mount his horse, but was surprised when she turned to watch him and saw him ignore her directions. *Oh, Mikey, that's not the way to convince her to return your romantic interest.*

When she saw Ian asking Anthony for help in getting on the horse, Cait turned back around to face the front. She knew better than to point out Ian's rudeness right then. Unfortunately, she wasn't sure she could point it out to him later either, not if she didn't want him to figure out that she was trying to help with the matchmaking plot to push him and Charlotte together.

Yeah, I should probably back off on how much I help Hazel for now, she decided as they started on the trail ride. *Let nature run its course for a while. And maybe look into the benefits of equine therapy for my PTSD and agoraphobia. If nothing else, learning about the horses will give me something to talk to Josh about the next time he's home on leave.*

Cait smiled then, happy to have the start of a plan for helping herself heal, and hoping to be able to build a foundation of friendship with Josh that could one day lead to more.

As they rode, Cait tried to keep up with the conversations going on around her. But thinking about Josh while experiencing the bouncing movement of riding a horse led her thoughts to wander toward following the advice of that old country song about saving a horse and riding a cowboy. *Yeah, I really wouldn't mind riding that Cowboy Hottie!*

Cait tried to picture Josh naked from her memories of him in the tight jeans and Henley he'd worn at Christmas. But when she pictured him laid out on her bed back at her brother's house, she knew the image was wrong for where she'd feel comfortable possibly having sex with him in real life. *Eew! No! Not where Mikey or Brody are sleeping down the hall. Stick to the cowboy theme, Caitir! Maybe in a hayloft out near the cows where it's unlikely anyone would walk in on us. Or maybe the hay barn where the girls said the horses' feed is stored, but after everyone else has gone in for dinner, so again, nobody would walk in on us. Yeah, that works.*

Once she had the setting in mind, Cait easily pictured Josh laid out on one of the horse blankets like they put under the saddles when tacking up the horses. Only instead of the blanket being draped over a horse, it was spread out over several bales of hay to provide them with a soft bed for their wild ride.

"Mount up and ride, Darlin'," Cait imagined Josh commanding in that sexy southern drawl that made her panties wet whenever he spoke.

"I will, Cowboy," Cait replied in her head, picturing herself naked, kneeling between his spread legs and stroking his long, thick dick. *"But first I've gotta make sure you're ready for me."*

She was only guessing about his size based on the size of the bulge she remembered seeing in his jeans a little over a month before. Having only seen a couple of small dicks in real life, she had to guess what something that made that big of a lump down the leg of his jeans would look like erect and unconfined by his clothing. She just hoped what her girlfriends had said about bigger being better really were true, since that's how she was imagining being with Josh.

"Oh, I'm ready, Sugar," Josh assured her as his cock twitched under her ministrations. "But if you wanna take a little time stroking and sucking my cock, then you need to sit on my face, so I can make sure your pussy's wet enough."

"Oh, I like the way you think, Cowboy," Cait agreed, moving into position for a little 69 before they fucked.

Though she'd never actually enjoyed oral sex in the past, Cait imagined she'd love sucking Josh's dick, even if she couldn't take all of it because he was bigger than her previous partners. Especially if he reciprocated by being the first man to go down on her.

Cait used her hand to stroke the base of Josh's cock while using her mouth to bob up and down on the tip and first few inches of his shaft. At the same time, Josh licked, sucked, and slurped at her sex, like a starving man devouring a feast. His expert oral skills took her to the brink in what seemed like only seconds, sending her flying to the point that she lost her rhythm and his cock popped out of her mouth. "Oh, yes, Cowboy!"

"Fuck, yeah, Darlin', you gotta ride my cock now," Josh groaned, gripping her hips, and lifting her up to spin her around and slide her down. "I need to be inside you when I come."

Somehow, they were lined up perfectly for her to sheath his length, feeling only pleasure even though he was bigger than she'd ever taken before. Cait pushed up on her knees, running her hands over the muscular planes of his chest and abs while bouncing up and down on Josh's decadent dick.

"You enjoying the ride, Cait?" Becky's words brought Cait out of the fantasy and back to the moment.

"Yes, very much," Cait nodded, knowing she was blushing at being called out for not paying attention to her friends.

"Oh, yeah, I bet you are," Julie smirked as she turned to look back at Cait.

Thank goodness, they can only see me blushing, and not how hard my nipples are, or how wet my panties are from that hot fantasy. So, they probably just think I'm distracted and don't know what I was actually thinking about just now.

Unless, oh shit, did I make a noise or an O-face when I had that little orgasm? Cait realized that the way the saddle was rubbing against her clit had helped her have a minor release when her alter ego came on Josh's tongue. *I didn't call out his name, did I? No, I was just thinking Cowboy, not Cowboy Josh or even Cowboy Hottie.*

Hum? I guess Cowboy works a lot better than Cowboy Hottie for my fantasy lover. Now if only I can get over the rest of my agoraphobia and get close enough to Josh to possibly call him that in real life with his dick buried deep inside me.

~ ~ ~

Monday, February 18, 2019

There were some days when Josh loved his job as a Navy SEAL. He loved the feelings of camaraderie with his platoon and pride in his work for helping keep his fellow Americans and America's allies safe. But then there were other days when he had to question his sanity for risking his life around the world, when he was needed at home on the ranch to keep his loved ones safe. Days like the one he was currently having, when his job was to go rescue a politician's spoiled daughter from pirates off the coast of Somalia, were the ones when he most questioned his sanity.

Knowing the cartel responsible for shooting Cait in the past was now in South Texas where they could come after her again, Josh wished he could leave these missions in the capable hands of the other guys on his SEAL team, so he could be back at home protecting her. If anything happened to her while he was unable to be there for her, Josh knew he'd feel guilty for his prior commitment to the Navy keeping him from taking care of the woman he knew he would love for the rest of his life.

Unfortunately, he had no choice in the matter. He'd made the commitment to be a Navy SEAL, so when Americans needed rescuing, he had to step up and focus exclusively on his job. *Fuck! I have to trust that Ian and the rest of my family will be there to protect her while I'm over here protecting someone else's loved ones.*

United States Senator Kurt Lexington was on a vacation with his family to the small island nation of Kala in the Indian Ocean, when his twenty-one-year-old daughter, Keri, went on a sailboat tour that didn't return to port. The next day, the badly beaten sailboat captain had limped his boat back to the dock without any of the other crew or passengers. Before he allowed the paramedics to take him to the hospital, he insisted on speaking with Senator Lexington. The captain's wife was among the hostages, and he knew he'd only be able to get her back if the senator called for assistance from back in Washington D.C. because Kala didn't have the resources to mount a rescue mission that was likely to be successful.

Kala was a small island about halfway between the eastern coast of Africa and the Seychelles. At one point in time, it was a British colony, but the island became an independent nation in the 1960s. They now elected a President and representatives of the National Assembly every five years. Because the people who lived there were not indigenous to the island, but rather transplants from the United Kingdom, and other former British colonies, the national language was English, and ninety-five percent of the people believed in some form of Christianity as their religion.

With the recent rise of terrorist activity in their nearest neighboring countries of Kenya and Somalia, Kala was actively trying to convince the United States government to help safeguard their nation, so they wouldn't lose their largest source of income — tourism — to the pirates and other terrorist groups that were starting to encroach on the territorial sea surrounding the island. Josh assumed that was why Senator Lexington and several other prominent politicians had recently been invited to visit Kala. He just wished the politicians who traveled there had thought to bring a security detail with them to protect their families.

Josh's SEAL platoon had been gearing up for a different mission in response to the recent upsurge in terrorist activity in Kenya by al-Shabaab, when they were rerouted to Kala to rescue Keri Lexington. Well, half the platoon had been rerouted to Kala. Josh was leading the eight-man squad on the rescue mission while the other lieutenant in the platoon, Tucker Holt, was the officer in charge of the other half of the platoon, which was going on the original mission in Kenya along with another SEAL team. They were scheduled to help safeguard a school being built by an American aid organization after the recent attacks on teachers in the area until the organization could arrange private security. If everything went as planned, Josh and his squad would be joining the rest of their team in Kenya by Wednesday.

Once the intelligence officer working with their platoon at the Naval Support Facility in Diego Garcia confirmed the location of the boat, which they believed Keri and the rest of the hostages from the sailboat were being held on, Josh's squad was sent from a government port on the island of Kala on a Mark V Special Operations Craft to get within striking distance. Josh then split his squad into two four-man fire teams, so they could take two Zodiac boats to raid the pirate vessel and have enough room to bring back all the hostages.

Chief Petty Officer Asher "Smasher" Brantley, who was the second-in-command in their squad, led Petty Officer First Class Jayden "King" Presley, Petty Officer Second Class Regan "Mr. President" Johnson, and Petty Officer Third Class Ty "Beef" Wellington in one Zodiac, while Lieutenant Josh "Cowboy" Burleson led Petty Officer First Class Kalua "Mudslide" Kai, Petty Officer Second Class Oakley "Shades" Slade, and Seaman Lane "Pie" Shepherd in the other.

As they were gearing up to board the two Combat Rubber Raiding Crafts, known as Zodiacs, to sneak up on the pirate's ship, Josh got to thinking about the men there with him and his time working with them. Since Josh had informed his commanding officer that he would be leaving the Navy at the end of his minimum service requirement, Asher Brantley was tapped to go to Officer Candidate School in order to maintain the ratio of two officers and fourteen enlisted sailors in the platoon.

Asher was one of the members of their team that Josh had worked with since his first day as a SEAL. Asher had earned his call sign of Smasher long before Josh joined the team, but he'd heard the story about how a group of girls had been playing a game of *Smash or Pass* in the bar all the guys went to during BUD/S, and Asher was the only guy there that all the women voted to smash. So, the rest of the guys started calling him Smasher in tribute to how easy it was for him to get laid. The fact that his name was part of the call sign was just a bonus.

Jayden Presley and Kalua Kai were the other two members of the squad that had been on the team longer than Josh. Jayden was an African-American from Mississippi, who got the call sign of King because he shared the same last name as the king of rock-n-roll and did a damn good imitation of him. Since his family had all started talking about sending in their DNA to be tested by an ancestry site, Josh had been bugging Jayden to send in a sample to see if he was actually related to Elvis.

Kalua was Hawaiian and the most laid-back of all the guys on the squad. When the frog hogs got to be too talkative about inane bullshit like reality television, Kalua was the only one of them that had the patience to listen to it. From what Josh understood, that ability to listen to the most mundane of stories was what earned him the call sign of Mudslide.

Apparently, a cocktail waitress had heard someone call his name and thought they were asking about drinks made from Kahlua Coffee Liqueur, so she went into a long dramatic monologue about the various cocktails made from the liqueur, and ended the impromptu bartending lesson by saying that her favorite was a Mudslide. The guys thought it was hilarious that Kalua had sat there smiling at her the whole time and the nickname stuck.

Regan Johnson was one of the guys who went through SEAL training with Josh. In fact, Josh had been one of the guys to come up with Regan's call sign back in BUD/S. Regan had been the first to call Josh "Cowboy" after seeing him in his cowboy boots when they first arrived on base for training, so Josh felt it was only fair that he had a say in coming up with Regan's call sign. While his first name wasn't spelled the same as the former president's last name, having the names of two former presidents made calling him Mr. President a no-brainer. Though with it being so much of a mouthful, whenever they went on a mission, they all shortened it to Prez.

Oakley Slade was also in the same SEAL training group as Josh. The guys had all started calling him Shades because Oakley is such a popular brand of sunglasses. Oakley had hated the call sign at first, but when *Fifty Shades of Grey* premiered in theaters while they were in SQT, he suddenly changed his tune. Oakley quickly studied up on

BDSM and told all the ladies that he got his call sign because he was a Dom. He'd been using the nickname to help him get laid for the last four years.

Ty Wellington joined the team a year after Josh and had been trying to get Josh to change his call sign ever since. Apparently, Beef was a nickname he'd been plagued with since high school, and his fellow SEALs had just continued using it. Evidently, Burleson Beef was well known all over Texas and not just in Josh's hometown. So, when Ty found out that Josh had been raised on the ranch where Burleson Beef originated, he thought Josh should take the call sign and give him a new one. Josh had just joked that he couldn't think of a better person to represent the family brand and claimed to adopt Ty as an honorary Burleson. When they weren't in the middle of an op, Josh often called him Burleson Beef instead of just Beef.

Lane Shepherd was the newest member of their platoon and was only halfway through his first deployment cycle. During his first week with the team, they'd given him the call sign of Pie as an ode to the Shepherd's Pie that had been served in the mess hall. He hadn't liked it at first, but then when they took him out to the sports bar they frequented and he heard the stories about Shades and Smasher's call signs, he changed his mind. Lane promptly started using the nickname to get the ladies' attention by saying he'd been given the nickname because he liked to eat poontang pie.

Fuck, I hope I wasn't that crass and obnoxious when I went out looking to hook up back when I was his age. Aw, fuck! That woulda been the end of high school and the first semester of college. So, yeah, I probably was just as much of a jackass looking to hook up. Josh quickly shut down any thoughts about the parties and wild nights he and Jake had back in their first year at the Naval Academy, wanting to keep his focus on the mission and his squad as much as possible.

Lane was still in the single digits when counting the number of times the platoon had been spun up for a short-term op since he'd joined them a year ago. But Josh could already tell he was going to make an excellent SEAL.

Hell, with me leaving when my minimum service requirement is up in September, I won't get to see how the kid does on a full deployment.

Damn, when did I turn into the old guy who calls all the younger guys "kids"? Josh shook his head at his mental reference to his old age as he took his place in the Zodiac.

Looking at the men around him, Josh suddenly felt every one of his almost twenty-eight years. He was the second oldest among them, with only Asher having a few months on him. The other six guys ranged from as young as Lane's nineteen to Jayden and Kalua's twenty-three.

Fuck, now I understand why most of the guys take the enlistment track, instead of going through the academy to earn a commission as an officer before becoming a SEAL. They're all gonna get to do more as SEALs than I have before they're ready to settle down with a wife and kids.

As the second Zodiac launched, Josh looked over at Asher and had to wonder if his friend had chosen to switch to the officer track to be able to move over to a command position in preparation for when he was ready to leave the SEALs to have a family as well. Technically, that had been Josh's initial plan instead of getting out of the Navy altogether. He'd thought he'd spend at least twenty years in the service, with the first ten being school and the SEALs and the last ten being mostly desk duty, commanding a SEAL team instead of actively going on missions.

Of course, he'd also assumed he'd meet the woman of his dreams in Virginia Beach, and she'd want him to stay there for work after they got together. But when he'd met Cait in his hometown, his future plans changed in an instant. Seeing her in his family home made it clear that it was time for him to move back to Heart's Destiny to pursue her.

Fuck, after learning about the reason her brother moved her to my hometown, though, I really wish I could move her to Virginia Beach to keep her safe.

Josh knew that wouldn't be possible. She wouldn't ever want to leave her brother and nephew. After what Ian had told him last month when he was there to move his temporary tactical operations center, Josh was pretty sure the Campbells were so close that Cait might never want to move farther away from her brother than living in the house next door to him.

Good thing I like the guy, since I'll probably end up being next-door neighbors with my future brother-in-law. Josh chuckled at his mental quip.

"What's so funny, Cowboy?" Mudslide lifted his chin at Josh to acknowledge his inappropriate timing. "You're normally much more serious going on an op like this."

Not wanting to jinx the possibility of the future he saw for himself and Cait by mentioning it as they were going into a dangerous situation, Josh mentally switched to mission mode and pointed out the irony that Kala could also be an acronym. "Just thought it was funny that we've come to Kala to *Kick A Little Ass*."

"Damn straight, we're gonna kick a little ass," Pie agreed as Mudslide and Shades laughed along with him.

They all quietened down as the pirate's ship came into sight. Both Zodiacs slowed their speed to decrease their engine noise as they approached the mostly dark ship, cutting the engines completely to paddle in once they were close enough they might be heard from the ship.

The plan was to assail the vessel in the middle of the night when most of the pirates would be asleep, so they would only have to deal with a couple of them guarding the hostages. They wanted to secure the pirates to be prosecuted for their crimes with as little loss of life as possible.

Everything seemed to be going as planned as they climbed aboard the cargo ship. With suppressors on their weapons, they silently took out the two men patrolling the deck before they could alert the rest of the pirates by firing the AK-47's in their hands. Smasher led his fire team to the bridge to take command of the boat, while Josh led his fire team below deck to locate the hostages. But as the SEALs made their way below deck, they soon realized they hadn't waited quite late enough to start the rescue.

According to their intel, there were between six and ten pirates who'd raided the sailboat and ordered the ten passengers and four crew members onto their cargo ship. The sailboat captain claimed to have only seen the six men with machine guns, with two of them separating him from the rest of the hostages to deliver the beating before sending him back with their ransom demands. The intelligence officers, who'd flown drones with infrared cameras over the area to locate the cargo ship, had reported that they counted ten crew members on the pirates' boat, with the thirteen hostages being held in the cargo hold.

Fuck! I wish Jake coulda been the one flying that drone. Then I'd know the count was right from the heat signatures on the ship.

As they approached the mess hall, Josh heard what sounded like a raucous celebration. He held up his fist to signal his men to hold while he assessed how many of the people in the mess hall were hostiles and how many were the female hostages the pirates had separated from the men to torment for the night. From the sounds he heard, Josh quickly surmised that they should have added the two estimates of how many pirates were there together to get closer to a more accurate number.

"Bridge secured," Smasher announced over the comms just as Josh realized his squad was outnumbered by a lot more than they'd originally thought. "Two hostiles down. We're headed your way, Cowboy."

Four down total, Josh realized. *And I've counted at least ten male voices in the mess hall. And there's probably at least two guarding the other hostages in the cargo hold.*

Josh used the hand signals they'd all learned early on in their training to indicate the count and approximate locations of the combatants, as well as the presence of at least half a dozen of the hostages. The four men separated into pairs to breach both doors into the mess hall at once. With Pie on his six, Josh led the charge to take out the pirates, knowing Smasher's fire team would be right behind them.

It wasn't as clean as it would have been if they'd caught them while they were sleeping and been able to detain them for questioning and prosecution by the authorities in Kala. But catching half the men with their pants down at least evened the fight considerably. With the women either on their knees or being held down on the tables, picking off the bastards who were raping them was like shooting fish in a barrel.

As he scanned the room, Josh momentarily saw Cait in place of the women he was there to rescue, knowing that could be her fate if she ran across the cartel and became a target for their human trafficking operation. But Josh couldn't let himself be distracted by imagining the woman he loved in the middle of the horrific scene they'd interrupted, because the men waiting to take their turns weren't unarmed or as easily caught off guard as the men with their pants down in the middle of committing their heinous crimes.

"Stay down," Josh commanded the hostages as he felt a round whiz by his shoulder.

Josh and the rest of his squad returned fire until all the pirates in the mess hall were eliminated. He then tried to calm the hysterical women, who were wailing from the trauma they'd just endured. "You're safe now, ladies. We're American SEALs here to take you back to Kala."

Most of the women quieted as the men started speaking softly and pulling out the extra t-shirts and emergency blankets that they carried in their combat kits. They whispered words of reassurance as they handed over the items for the women to be able to cover up, since their clothing had been ruined, taking special care to look them in the eyes, so they wouldn't be as self-conscious about their nudity.

Josh fought to keep his expression from showing his anger at how these women had been mistreated, as he asked if any of them needed immediate medical care. They all shook their heads in the negative, even as they continued to look at him and the other men warily.

Yeah, after what they just went through, they probably don't want any of us to treat their injuries at the moment. But since I don't see any obvious broken bones or open wounds, I think it'll be okay to wait until we can get them to a hospital with female doctors and nurses to take care of them.

"Damn, Cowboy, did you leave us any targets to take out?" King quipped as the other half of their squad entered the mess hall.

"Yeah, I'm guessing there are at least two still down in the cargo hold," Josh replied as he looked over the women to determine if any of them had calmed down enough to be able to give them more information. "Along with the rest of the people we're here to rescue."

"This is only half of them." Keri Lexington tentatively gestured to the dead men laid out around the room with one hand, while hugging her midsection with the other arm.

"There were twenty pirates?" Josh wanted to ensure they had an accurate count to keep from being surprised as they moved through the rest of the ship to clear all the cabins, the cargo hold, and the mechanical rooms.

"Yes," the woman Josh recognized as the sailboat captain's wife confirmed. "They only had five or six board our sailboat, but as they've rotated out watching us and moving us around the boat, I counted twenty total."

"Then we still have six to find," Prez announced, nodding at King.

"Mudslide and Shades, stay here and protect the women while we go find the others," Josh ordered, turning to exit the mess hall until a delicate hand on his forearm stopped him.

"Do you know if my husband made it back to Kala?" The sailboat captain's wife looked up at him imploringly, obviously afraid to hear her husband hadn't survived the beating he'd received before being sent back with the ransom message.

"Yes, ma'am," Josh assured her with a cautious smile. "He's recovering in the hospital, and anxiously waiting for us to bring you back to him."

"Thank you," she sobbed, releasing his arm as her tears started to slip from her eyes.

Mudslide stepped in and took over assessing her and the rest of the women, so Josh could go with the rest of his squad to finish clearing the ship. Josh was grateful for his teammates at that moment, needing a second to separate himself from his empathetic feelings to be able to stop himself from continuing to picture Cait in place of the victims they were rescuing. If he let his mind go down that road, he wouldn't be able to do his job. And not just because he'd get sloppy with anger at the thought of her being violated the way these hostages were and risk collateral damage to the innocents he was trying to rescue.

Whenever he thought about home and Cait, he started to feel guilty for how many people he'd had to kill in the line of duty, wondering if his loved ones could still care about him if they knew about the dark place in his head that he had to go each time he pulled the trigger with a person in his sights. Though after the scene they'd walked in on in the mess hall, Josh almost felt glad that they'd had to kill the majority of the pirates, instead of capturing them for a future trial. While he thought the bastards got off easy with only taking a few bullets for their monstrous crimes, it eased his conscience to know they couldn't rape another woman ever again. Those were definitely kills he knew his family would agree were justifiable.

The six SEALs moved through the ship in pairs, calling out "clear" over the comms each time they verified a space was empty. They managed to detain four militants, who were asleep in their cabins, and took out both of the men that had been left guarding the male hostages.

Once they verified the rest of the ship was completely empty, they called in for the law enforcement vessel from Kala to pick up the prisoners and secure the ship. Once the Kala officials took over the crime scene, the SEALs took the freed hostages back to the island for medical treatment.

Witnessing the couples being reunited and clinging to one another as they boarded the Zodiacs brought Cait back to the forefront of Josh's mind. It made him realize just how close Cait was to her brother, knowing he was the only person she'd had to lean on when she was caught in the cartel drive-by. Wanting to be the one she turned to in the future, if she ever had to deal with another traumatic situation, only fueled Josh's desire to leave the Navy and move home to Heart's Destiny.

Fuck! Ian better catch every fucking member of that cartel before I move home in September. Otherwise, I might just hafta recruit a few friends and hunt them down myself.

"Do I know you from somewhere?" Keri Lexington's words brought Josh back out of his head.

"No, we've never met before." Josh shook his head, but smiled to keep from scaring the traumatized young woman.

"I swear I know you, or I've at least seen your picture before," Keri claimed, looking up at him with more than a little hero worship in her eyes. "What's your name? And don't give me the nickname you guys give out to maintain your anonymity. I know the other SEALs call you Cowboy, but that's not a name I might recognize. And I'm sure my dad has a high enough clearance level to find out your real name, so you might as well just tell me and save your bosses and his staff the hassle of playing phone tag for me to find out."

Josh was surprised at how quickly she'd reverted from the scared victim she'd been when the SEALs first rescued her, back to the entitled socialite attitude he'd seen on the social media posts included in her profile while they planned for the mission. It was almost like she had repressed any memories she had of being sexually assaulted by her captors only an hour before.

Her sudden attitude shift almost elicited a sarcastic response from Josh about her father's clearance level not meaning shit for what she was allowed to know. But he somehow managed to bite it back, unable to completely see her as she had been before being kidnapped because he hadn't forgotten the horrific scene he and his men had witnessed when they were on the pirates' ship. Instead, he took a deep breath, shrugged, and retained his stoic expression as he quietly kept watch of the water around them for the rest of the trip back to Kala.

Not that it mattered much that he didn't tell Keri Lexington his name. As soon as they disembarked back in Kala, Senator Lexington insisted on meeting each man on the team that rescued his "little girl" and giving them his contact information in case they ever needed a letter of recommendation. And of course, Keri was right by his side as he shook each of their hands and went through all the introductions, acting like nothing bad had happened to her at all.

"Burleson? As in Burleson Incorporated?" Senator Lexington arched an eyebrow at Josh.

"Yes, sir," Josh nodded as he shook the older man's hand, not elaborating about his position on the board.

"I knew I recognized you!" Keri hollered, bouncing in her borrowed t-shirt at her father's side. "You're part of the family that rescued that runaway bride from Georgia, whose father was holding her hostage and planning to marry her off to one of his friends to steal her inheritance. You weren't in the pictures I saw online, probably because of being a SEAL and all. But you look enough like the rest of your family that I should have realized who you are immediately."

"Guess it's a good thing you're getting out, Cowboy." Smasher slapped Josh on the shoulder. "Being part of a famous family isn't exactly ideal for staying incognito on covert ops."

"OMG! Was the article I read correct when it said the SEAL in the family was the one to rescue the heiress? Are you getting out of the Navy to marry her?"

"No," Josh refuted the insane claims of some of the less reputable articles his brother had been having to deal with for the last three weeks. "Brooklyn rescued herself back on Thanksgiving, and I didn't even find out her real identity until Christmas. And she's marrying my older brother. Definitely not me."

"No, Cowboy's gettin' out to try lassoin' a different filly," Beef chimed in, exaggerating his Texas twang, as if he'd been raised in the country instead of being a city boy from Dallas.

"How do you know that?" Josh looked at Beef in surprise that he'd figured out Josh had his sights set on Cait when he hadn't talked to anyone about her specifically yet.

"Because you haven't even noticed another woman for the last two months," Beef shrugged as the other guys around them nodded in agreement.

Damn, he's right. Who'd have thought that would be how I'd screw up my just-acting-normal routine to tip off the guys?

"Well, regardless of why you're leaving the Navy," Senator Lexington interjected, obviously ready to go back to his hotel with his family instead of listening to more SEAL team drama. "I owe you a debt of gratitude I can never fully repay for rescuing my daughter. So, please don't hesitate to call if I can ever do anything for you or your family."

"Thank you, sir. But that's really not necessary." Josh felt awkward anytime he was praised for doing his job, especially when his job included killing others, regardless of whether he thought they deserved to die for their transgressions or not. "I'd rather you focus on seeing to your daughter's well-being. In fact, she really needs to go straight to the hospital to be evaluated after everything she's been through the past couple of days."

Josh really didn't want to be the man responsible for telling the senator that his daughter had been raped. But since she hadn't gone straight to the paramedics on site like the other women who'd been held hostage, he was afraid he might have to disclose the information more publicly than in his after-action report.

"Oh, yes," Senator Lexington sputtered a moment, looking at his daughter like he was just then realizing she was only wearing an oversized t-shirt and still had blood spatter on her exposed skin from being in close proximity to the pirates when they were killed. "I just wanted to thank you all before riding with her in the ambulance. But we're going to the hospital now."

Once the senator and his daughter walked away, the SEALs started packing up their gear to head back to their temporary base for the rest of the night.

Leah Mae Wright

"Man, rich people are weird," Pie shook his head as they carried their stuff to the vehicles they were assigned to use while on Kala. "If that'd been my sister, my parents would have been checking her out more thoroughly than the paramedics, and wouldn't have looked twice at us until after they knew she had a clean bill of health."

"I think it's because he's a politician," King chuckled. "Not all rich people are more focused on their public image than their family's well-being. Cowboy's family is loaded, but he'd never be caught glad-handing like a politician when someone he cares about was hurt."

"Hell, I seem to recall Cowboy telling a few politicos to 'back the fuck off' when they wanted our AARs as soon as we got back to base from that Afghan mission a couple years ago," Prez interjected. "And he didn't even know the kids we rescued and were trying to check on."

"I always forget Cowboy's loaded 'cause he doesn't act like the rich-bitch snobs I grew up being tormented by," Pie shrugged. "But I guess you guys are right that the senator was acting weird because he's a politician, and not just because his suit cost more than my car."

"I don't know if I should be flattered by all ya'll's bullshit just now or not," Josh chuckled, shaking his head. "But I have a feeling that ya'll are just bringin' up my family money to get me to cover the bar tab when we get back home."

"Of course we are," Smasher slugged Josh in the shoulder. "That's what we're all gonna miss the most when you leave us in a few months."

Yeah, I'm gonna miss ya'll, too, Josh thought, knowing that's what they all meant when they teased him. *But even once I get home and have a family, I'm still gonna call and check in on everyone on the team regularly, so we won't lose touch completely.*

Chapter Four

Cait was really getting frustrated with her brother not being able to find Roberto Rodriguez. Rojo being on the loose in the area wasn't just exacerbating her fear of going out in public. Having to go home early every evening, so her brother could go searching bars and seedy neighborhoods in San Antonio for him once Brody was in bed, was also limiting her time socializing with the Burlesons when they had birthday parties and other get-togethers during the week, when she could easily stay on the ranch after work. It also meant she'd had to decline invitations to other events, like the Sweetheart's Ball and the Burleson women's Galentine's celebration on Valentine's Day, Aiden Walker's birthday party on Wednesday of this week, and multiple book club meetings with her friends, like the one she would miss that night. And she was really irritated by not being able to start working toward getting over her fear and embracing life again.

When her new friends started talking about the books they were reading, she'd started bringing her Kindle to the ranch, so she could at least download a few of the same books to discuss them during her breaks. But since most of her breaks during the day were spent with Hazel, Susan, Rosa, Mary, and Brody, Cait only felt comfortable critiquing the sweet romances. And the time she spent with the women her age, when she could talk about the naughtier romances they recommended, was usually spent in the stables or paddocks with Brody too close by working with Charlotte and the horses for them to have any kind of adult discussion.

She missed the days when she could have girl talks with Mari and her other friends in San Diego, and wished she could figure out a regular time when she could hang out with her new girlfriends to have that bonding experience with friends in her life again. Not that Becky, Jen, or Julie would want to hear about how Josh had started playing a part in her sexy dreams for the last three months, but the other women they'd introduced her to in town might be open to giving her some advice about how to handle her attraction to him.

But maybe I shouldn't talk to any of them about him, so I don't hear about which of them he dated in high school or how many of them have slept with him. Oh, hell no, I definitely don't want to risk hearing stories about any of them having sex with him.

Cait refocused on folding the bedding she'd just gotten out of the dryer at Becky, Jen, and Julie's house, trying to block out all thoughts of Josh with other women. *Why am I worrying about this? It's not like we're together or anything.*

Hell, he's probably just like all the sailors in San Diego. With a woman in every port, why would he ever even look twice at me? And even if he did look, he'd only be interested in a hookup for a night or two. Considering the way he goes all over the world as a SEAL, I'm sure he'd never be happy settling down with a woman who only feels safe being alone at home and on his family's ranch. And if my brother doesn't arrest the rest of the cartel soon, I might never be able to get over this fear to be a woman he could actually take on a date.

As she carried the sheets upstairs to put them away, her cell phone rang in her back pocket, bringing her back to the moment. She quickly stacked the bedding in the linen closet before pulling the phone out to answer.

Weird. Why is Mikey, ur, Ian calling me at this time of day?

"Hello?" Cait cringed, knowing her brother could clearly hear the angst in her voice, since the word came out sounding like a question. She ran to the closest window to check on Brody, assuming her brother would want to verify they were both safe, since he was calling when he should still be in the middle of teaching a class.

Brody was playing with the barn cat, whom he, Tia, and Maria had named Speckles, in the yard between the house Cait was in and Charlotte's house. He was clearly waiting for Char to finish her workday at the middle school to take him over to the stable to work with the horses.

"Hey, Cait," Ian sighed, sounding weary over the phone. "I don't want to alarm you, but I do need to make sure you and Brody are both safely inside."

"I'm inside, just finishing up putting away the bedding I washed and changed today," Cait assured her brother, trying to ignore his comment about wanting them both indoors. "And watching Brody out the window, where he's playing with Speckles while waiting on Charlotte to get home to ride the horses."

"I'd feel better if you brought him inside with you for the afternoon. And maybe go work with Hazel for the rest of the day."

"Why? What happened? Did he show up at school or something and now you're afraid he's coming here for us?" Cait was proud of herself for not saying Roberto Rodriguez's name out loud as she questioned her brother. She was being careful not to mention him whenever she was on the ranch, in case one of the Burlesons overheard her conversation with Ian. While she knew some of them knew about Ian's past with the DEA and the reason they'd moved to town, she didn't want to alarm any of the women she'd become friends with who didn't know what was really going on.

Before her brother could answer her questions, Cait quickly ran back down the stairs and out the side door to get to Brody, suddenly afraid the relative safety she felt on the ranch was about to be shattered.

"No, he hasn't shown up at the school," Ian claimed. "And I don't think he's likely to go to the ranch. But he has apparently seen me and had someone follow me home to know where we live."

"Oh, gawd," Cait sobbed, clutching a hand to her chest, and stepping back inside the house, so Brody wouldn't hear her break down at realizing she'd just lost one of her safe spaces.

"It's okay, Caitir," Ian went on in a soft, soothing tone. "I caught the guy who broke into our house on video and am working with Bobby, so the local cops can arrest him. He now knows about my mission here and has set it up for us to stay with his parents on the ranch until the whole cartel situation is over. I promise, you're still safe there on the ranch. All this does is prove that I'm on the right track with my leads for where to find Rojo, so I can turn over the rest of the investigation to the local police."

"So, you're out of it now? You're not going to go hunting for him every night anymore?" Cait needed that reassurance that her brother would be safe, so she could at least quit worrying about him being shot again while trying to find Rojo. *But is he really safe since someone from the cartel broke into our house? What if they go after him while he's at school or coaching the baseball team?*

"Yeah, I'm out of it," Ian assured her. "Well, other than continuing to keep you and Brody safe. And keeping Charlotte safe when we're at school, since I think he's seen me talking to her."

"You think he might come after you at the middle school? Or while you're coaching?"

"No, outsiders stand out too much in this little town, so I don't think Rojo will risk trying anything so public here," Ian reassured her.

"Okay," Cait sighed, praying her brother was right and finally releasing a breath she hadn't realized she'd been holding. "So, what do I need to do now?"

"Like I said, I'd feel better if you and Brody were both inside with Hazel until I get there," Ian restated in the normal take-charge tone of voice she expected from her brother. "She knows what's going on and might need your help in getting guest rooms ready for us. Bob also knows the real story, but as far as anyone else knows, we're staying there for a little while because we had a pipe burst and flood our place. As soon as I'm done here at the station, I'm going to go home and pack each of us a week's worth of clothes and stuff. So, text me if there's anything specific you want me to get for you."

"Okay, I can do that," Cait agreed, wiping the tears from her eyes as she did a walk-through of the house to make sure she hadn't left anything out of place before going back outside to get Brody.

They said their goodbyes and Cait informed her nephew it was time to go back to Hazel's house for a little while. Once there, Hazel set Brody up with an afternoon snack and sent him up to the top-floor game room to play video games while they freshened up the second-floor bedrooms where she, Ian, and Brody would be sleeping for the foreseeable future.

"I'd put ya'll on the third floor so you could have a little more privacy, but Jake and Josh will be home next week," Hazel informed her as they made up one of the beds. "And they'll both expect to sleep in their old bedrooms up there. But since Anthony and the girls won't be using their old bedrooms, they're our guest rooms for now."

Cait's ears perked up at hearing Josh would be home for a visit soon, but she didn't want to appear too eager to see him in front of Hazel. "Oh, I didn't think they'd get leave time again so soon. I thought that was only a once-a-year thing."

"It wasn't even that often when they first graduated from the academy," Hazel divulged. "With Josh going through SEAL training for the first couple of years, he didn't have the opportunity to use his leave time, so it rolled over. Now he's gotta take at least sixty days this year or he'll lose it. So, he's planning on taking two weeks at the end of every quarter to be home for the Burleson board meetings, plus Thanksgiving week to make sure he doesn't lose any time."

"Of course, Jake doesn't have as much leave built up as Josh, since he used some during his time working on his master's degree," Hazel continued. Thankfully, she didn't seem to notice that Cait was only interested in hearing about Josh's time off. "But anytime they're working in the same area, they schedule their leave time together if they can, so we're hopeful that he'll be able to make all the board meetings and major holidays this year, too."

As Hazel continued talking about her sons and how much she missed them when they were off in the Navy, Cait's mind drifted to how she was going to handle staying in the same house as Josh for a couple of weeks. On the one hand, she was thrilled to see him again and loved the thought of him being there during the day to make her feel safe while her brother was at work. But on the other hand, she was worried about him coming home and possibly being pulled into the investigation because of how small the Heart's Destiny Police Department was and Josh being military trained to hunt down terrorists.

Yes, she knew it was irrational to be afraid of him being shot by someone in the cartel while he was home on leave, when he was more likely to be shot at while on missions as a SEAL. But having only seen Josh on the ranch and not geared up for a military mission, Cait had blocked out how risky his job was and pictured him sitting at a desk planning missions for the other SEALs instead. Having been shot by the cartel while wearing leggings and a sweater at her nephew's second birthday party in the park, it was much easier for her to comprehend the risk of Josh being caught in another cartel drive-by while home and not suited up for a SEAL mission.

She found her mind wandering back and forth for the rest of the afternoon, jumping between wanting him there to be her protector and wanting him to stay in Virginia, where Hazel had informed her he was currently stationed, to keep him safe from what she feared would happen. Ian might not have wanted to alarm her with his call that afternoon, but he'd still sent her into a spiral of anxiety she was struggling to conceal.

By the time he got to the ranch at almost seven that night, Cait had gone mostly numb. She didn't pay much attention to the conversation going on around her as she sat down to dinner with Ian, Brody, Bob, Hazel, Bobby, and Brooklyn. When Ian finally excused himself to take Brody upstairs to put him down for bed, Cait decided to go soak in a nice hot bath.

The bedrooms on the second and third floors of Hazel and Bob's home all had Jack and Jill bathrooms. Ian and Brody would be sharing a bathroom, but the room Cait was staying in shared the bathroom with what had been a playroom for the Burlesons when they were kids, so she had it all to herself.

Maybe listening to an audiobook while I soak will take my mind off of all the ways the cartel might come after us, she thought as she stripped off her clothes and put on her waterproof, bone-conduction headphones before turning on the audiobook app on her tablet. *If nothing else, I might be able to relax a little bit by picturing me and Josh during the sex scenes while I masturbate in the tub.*

~~~

Wednesday, March 27, 2019

A lot had happened since the last time Josh had been home to Heart's Destiny to see his family. His oldest brother, Bobby, had settled his fiancée's legal situation with her father with the help of Josh's twin. When they came home from Georgia the first time, they brought back the couple Brooklyn thought of as her foster parents. Joe and Mary Turner were now living in the south bunkhouse, helping out on the
~~~

ranch and supervising the renovations for the bunkhouse to become the second Madeline Ashbury House as part of the charitable organization Brooklyn and Bobby had started. They'd also started the merger of Ashbury Industries into Burleson Incorporated on that first trip. Josh only knew that because he'd had to give his dad his power of attorney to place his board vote for him on the expenditure to buy out Brooklyn's family business.

That wasn't the only thing his dad had used that power of attorney for the previous month. Josh hadn't known it at the time because of being spun up on the missions in Kala and Kenya, but Bob Burleson had also signed for Josh when they added all their Avington cousins to the Burleson board of directors and released the trust that had been held for them for almost a century.

While he and Jake hadn't been able to be there to send off their DNA samples yet, the rest of his family had gotten their results and already solved the hundred-year-old family mystery about what happened to their second-great-grandaunt, Mary Burleson. They'd discovered that she'd married at the end of World War I and moved to Georgia with her husband.

His family had figured it all out because his brother, Bobby, recognized the name of one of his friends from his time in the Navy on their DNA match lists. And now they were welcoming their Avington cousins to their first board meeting since they'd found out they inherited a fortune that had been held in trust for them, along with shares in Burleson Incorporated.

Josh vaguely remembered meeting Blake Avington when Bobby brought him home with him on leave during his first year in the Navy, but walking into the board meeting was his first time meeting the rest of his new cousins. He knew Bobby had met all of Blake's family when he visited them in Georgia during another of their leave times back then, and most of the rest of the family had met them when they discovered the link on the DNA website, so he felt a little left out by not recognizing any of them before they started making introductions. Even though Jake had also been on base and hadn't submitted his DNA yet either, he'd gotten to meet the cousins when he went to Georgia to testify in the trial of Bobby's fiancée's father.

Needless to say, Josh was extremely grateful for his Uncle Jon starting the meeting by making introductions. "Wow, ya'll are as bad with the B names as we are with the J names." Josh chuckled after being introduced to Byron, Barrett, Blaine, Brady, and Blake Avington.

"Hey, we don't all have J names," his sister Becky objected.

"No, but six out of ten for our generation definitely makes it the most popular first initial in our family," Josh replied, shaking his head. "I just thought it was funny that it was a similarity among our family to pick a letter like that and stick to it."

"Yet another reason for me to veto the name Jimi Hendrix Burleson for this little one." His sister-in-law Kay rubbed her hand over her baby bump as she looked lovingly at his brother Anthony.

Josh wasn't sure why his sisters-in-law and nieces were present, since these meetings were normally limited to current board members only. But he was sure his sisters and female cousins welcomed the additional ladies present to keep them from being so outnumbered by the men in the family.

"Then I'll have to veto Braden," Anthony shrugged in reply to his wife. "So we don't steal a name one of our cousins might want for their kids to keep up the B name tradition."

"As much as I'd love to know what ya'll are gonna name my first nephew, I don't think we have time for ya'll to figure it out right now," Jake smirked across the table at their brother and sister-in-law.

"Yes, we do need to get this meeting started," Uncle Jon agreed before requesting reports from the various division heads.

After Julie told them all about how things were transitioning with a couple of companies they'd acquired since the last board meeting in December, JJ reported on the increased energy production that quarter from the various wind and solar farms they'd brought online following the environmental cleanup of former oil well sites. Josh didn't really pay much attention to the numbers, but he was interested in what he had to say about the methanol production facility they were putting in between the ranch and refinery, which would basically recycle the cow manure produced by the cattle they raised for beef production. He'd decided he wanted to talk to his dad about being more involved in caring for the herd when he moved back home after his time in the Navy was up, so he figured he'd need to know the new procedures they'd put in place for collection since he'd last worked full-time on the ranch, almost ten years ago.

"I actually need to pass along an idea for a brand name for our manure-based methanol." His cousin Justin smiled from his seat on the other side of Jake. "Moothanol."

Josh stifled a chuckle at the tongue-in-cheek reference to the cow shit their methanol was derived from. *And they all used to pick on me for joshin' around with ideas.*

"Moothanol?" Uncle Jon raised an eyebrow as he questioned the suggestion. "Where on earth did you come up with that idea?"

"Amy actually gave me the idea when I was showing her the quality control lab at the new facility." Justin's grin widened as he said Amy's name.

Damn, I wonder if he's that happy because he's finally getting somewhere with her. Or is he still just pining for her the way I'm longing for Cait?

"She also suggested sponsoring a monster truck made up to look like one of the cows on the ranch to promote it," Justin added.

"That's actually a pretty clever idea." Justin's sister Jen grinned at him.

"Who's Amy?" Barrett Avington looked around the room before his eyes landed on Justin.

"Our lab manager," Justin replied curtly, though the look in his eyes made it clear he was warning their new cousin away from his girl.

Oh yeah, he's definitely still in the friend zone and worried about one of our new cousins poachin' his girl.

"And the girl Justin's pining over, so don't even think about asking her out," Bobby added, giving their new cousins the warning Justin hadn't verbalized.

"Wouldn't dream of it." Barrett held both of his hands up in surrender. "I was just wondering who she was to try to figure out why she couldn't give her suggestions straight to the marketing department."

"Amy's had a lot going on the past couple of months," Jen informed them. "Now that life's calming down some, I'm sure she'll be able to send them an email with her suggestions."

Damn. Guess that's why Justin hasn't made his move yet.

"Speaking of the issues Amy's had to deal with since starting to work here," Uncle Jon interjected, turning to look at Justin and Jake where they were seated side by side. "What's the latest on the lab tech we had to let go?"

"She's still sitting in jail awaiting trial," Jake answered, surprising Josh that his twin had been in the know and hadn't shared the info with him.

"And luckily, she hadn't contaminated any of the other supplies in the lab," Justin continued. "So, everyone else in the lab was able to get back to work within a week of her arrest."

"And the other issues you found on the security footage have been resolved?" Byron Avington, the oldest member of that branch of their family, and the other four Avingtons' father, questioned.

What issues with the security footage? Josh felt extremely out of the loop. He knew it was hard to keep him informed about everything with him going radio silent every time he was spun up for a short-term op. But since that had only happened a couple of times so far this year, he thought he should be better informed than he was about the things going on in his family business. *Damn! Guess I haven't been getting all the updates about the company from Dad like I thought. But I'll be back in the loop once I finish up with the Navy and move home. Though maybe I should take over some of the security tasks here, so Jake and Bobby don't have to try to squeeze it in with their other jobs.*

"Yes," Justin replied, nodding his head.

"I actually spent the week, when they weren't able to run experiments in the lab, assisting Amy in retraining everyone in the lab on the rules and regulations of their jobs." His cousin Jen was the vice president of human resources, so Josh assumed that training was part of the stuff she would have gone over with any of the employees who worked in the lab when they first started with the company. "Though, it probably wouldn't hurt to keep up some spot checks on those cameras to make sure they all listened."

"Yeah, I'm still remotely checking those each day," Jake admitted.

"And I made sure they all know that if I catch anyone horsing around in the lab or playing phone games when they're supposed to be working, they'll be next in line to lose their job just like Tara," Justin added.

"Maybe not just like Tara," Jen giggled. "I mean, we can't exactly have them arrested for playing phone games."

"You know what I mean." Justin shook his head at his sister. It was as close to an eye roll as he thought Justin would get. "They've been warned, and the written reprimands are in each offender's HR file, so if they're caught not paying attention to active experiments while playing on their phones, they all know they won't have a job anymore."

"Very well," Uncle Jon put an end to the lab discussion. "Now, what have we got going on in the entertainment division?"

"Actually, that's why Kay and Brook are here today." Becky pointed to their sisters-in-law. "They came to me with a suggestion about content for the streaming service we want to develop. And the more I look at the costs for acquiring outside content and the vast number of other streaming services that already carry the same content we'd only be able to purchase limited rights to carry, the more I agree with them that we need to produce our own original movies to set us apart from the competition."

"So, you want to produce movies as well as the theatre productions you've been focused on?" Their dad looked surprised at the suggestion, which confused Josh.

Damn, Becky used to be such a Daddy's Girl that she would have told him about her ideas first to have him help her develop a plan to bring them to fruition.

"Yes," Becky answered, smiling at their dad, Bob. "Starting with adapting Brook and Kay's books into movies we'll release in theaters all across the country, until we have enough content to fill a streaming service."

"This seems like a rather expensive endeavor that won't have any return on investment for at least a few years with trying to make enough content to fill a streaming service." Byron's blank expression matched his flat tone, making it clear to Josh that he wasn't supportive of the idea.

"Yes, that's why we want to release the movies to theaters at first." Becky's smile and positive attitude never faltered as she explained her thought process. "We'll make back our production costs with box office sales, and the streaming service will be almost a hundred percent profit when we finally roll it out. I have a PowerPoint breaking down all the numbers to show this option is, in fact, much more profitable than purchasing the rights to share other people's content and competing with a dozen other streaming services, some of which are free to the consumer."

Wow! Look at you, little sis. All confident and assertive. Josh couldn't help but smile at his sister, happy to see her coming out of the shy shell that had kept her behind the scenes in most of the school plays and theater productions that she'd always seemed to want to act in instead. While she'd always been more outgoing than Charlotte when hanging out with a small group of friends and family, she always seemed to get a serious case of stage fright anytime she was asked to speak or act in front of a room full of people, even when the room was only full of their family. So, Becky being able to present anything in the meeting seemed like a positive step for her to possibly be getting over that issue. *Maybe if we do this movie division, Becky will get the chance to fulfill her dream of acting.*

"Please, set that up to show us." Uncle Jon motioned for Becky to hook her laptop up to the SmartScreen on the back wall of the conference room.

"Just how many books do you have ready to be made into movies?" Blaine Avington inquired, looking at Brooklyn and Kay, while Becky started setting up the presentation.

"I have five out so far," Brooklyn replied.

"I only have one published," Kay admitted, her lips turning up in a half-smile. "But I already have a dozen more plotted out that I just need to finish writing."

"Same here." Brooklyn backed up Kay's statement about future book plans, also smiling. "And we both know other indie authors who would love to have their books made into movies as well."

"But we'll have to buy the production rights for books by other authors." Byron scowled, obviously not liking the idea of adding the expenditures necessary to expand the entertainment division of the company. "Which brings us back to the same problem with spending a fortune on the rights to content that could be sold to other streaming services as well as ours."

"Technically, we have to buy the production rights to Kay and Brook's books, too." Charlotte stood up for their sisters-in-law to be paid what they'd earned by writing the original content for the movies.

"And production rights are different than distribution rights." Becky pointed to the slideshow she had started. She skipped forward a few pages in her PowerPoint to one outlining the differences. "When we buy the production rights to a book, the author can't sell those same production rights to another movie producer for the specified term of the contract with us. And as the production company for the movie, we have full distribution rights for that movie. But if we buy distribution rights to movies made by other production companies, they don't have to be exclusive in who they allow to stream their movies."

"So, the authors won't have the right to distribute the movies we make from their books elsewhere?" Byron looked pensive as he asked the question.

"No, because the movie is actually our product that we've made," Becky answered. "The production rights contracts I've looked over do have a provision for the authors to earn residuals from the sales of the movies made from their work, but they have no say in how we distribute our work product."

Becky closed out of the slideshow option for displaying the PowerPoint to be able to go back to the beginning of the presentation and started reviewing all the details. Josh once again let his mind wander when she started in with a bunch of numbers. He could clearly see the bottom line that she expected to increase the company revenue by, so he didn't feel like he needed to know all the mundane aspects of the plan to cast his vote in favor of adding movie production and streaming to the entertainment division of Burleson Incorporated.

Once Becky was finished, they ordered in lunch and voted to allow her to move forward with setting things up to start making their first movies. Then they moved on to a proposal from Byron to take some of the daily accounting and human resources tasks off his plate as the head of the company he'd started.

Josh was really interested in hearing about Avington Security, especially when he learned that most of the men the Avingtons employed were former SEALs and other military special forces operators. He didn't think he'd want to work with them full-time after he moved home, but he'd consider helping them out on occasion if they were shorthanded and he wasn't too busy on the ranch.

When he mentioned being able to help them out whenever he was home on leave or once he left the Navy, Josh also suggested making Avington Security a full-fledged division of Burleson Incorporated, instead of just contracting with them to handle the accounting and human resources paperwork. Surprisingly, Jake backed his suggestion, though Byron wasn't completely sold on the idea just yet.

After they finished voting on everything they had to vote on, they were released from the conference room, so the newest board members and anyone who wanted to go with them could tour the main office. Their sister Char pulled him and Jake aside as everyone stood up to leave the room.

"I wanted to make sure ya'll know I still have DNA test kits for you at my house," she informed them.

"Oh, yeah, okay," Josh nodded, unsure if taking the tests was really necessary since their family mysteries had already been solved by everyone else's results.

"Cool," Jake smirked, slugging Josh in the arm. "We might be late to the game, but we can still find out which one of us was switched at birth and isn't really a Burleson."

"Whatever, Bro." Josh slugged Jake back, unable to resist horsing around with his twin, even though they knew better than to get into a full-blown wrestling match in the middle of the company conference room.

"And ya'll better get all that roughhousing out of your system before you get to the house," Charlotte advised. "The Campbells are already dealing with enough right now. They don't need the two of you acting like fools and teaching Brody to misbehave while they're staying at Mom and Dad's."

"The Campbells are staying at Mom and Dad's?" Josh blurted the question at the same time his twin apologized and agreed with their sister.

"Sorry, Char. I promise not to negatively influence your protégé."

"Protégé? What the fuck?" Josh was really confused now, wondering which of the Campbells Jake was referring to as Charlotte's protégé.

"Oh, you haven't heard?" Jake slung his arm around Charlotte's shoulders and grinned at Josh. "Ma's been using Brody in one of her matchmaking schemes to get Charlotte and Ian together."

"No, she hasn't," Char protested, shaking her head as she shoved Jake's arm off her shoulders. "She only gave him permission to play with the barn cats. Brody wandered out to the stables all on his own."

"Uh-huh, sure he did," Jake chuckled. "And Ma hasn't invited Ian to join you on trail rides since you started teaching Brody to ride?"

Charlotte rolled her eyes at Jake, but she didn't refute his assertion that their mom had pushed the little boy to go hang out with Charlotte to get her to spend more time with Brody's dad.

Damn. I wonder how Ian feels about being matched up with Charlotte? Josh was so caught up in the possibility of Ian not being able to insist his sister was off limits if he started dating Josh's sister that he missed the rest of his siblings' discussion as they walked out of the conference room and caught up with the rest of their family.

Fuck! Char's probably gonna think I'm a bad brother for hoping Ma's matchmaking works out for her and Ian. But damn, I hope they end up together, so he can't have any objections to me dating Cait.

Not that I can start dating Cait while I'm home for the next couple of weeks. But if she's staying on the ranch, then maybe I can use this time to start building our friendship.

Fuck! What am I thinking? If they're staying on the ranch, then something must have happened with Ian's investigation into the cartel to make them not feel safe at home.

Considering what Ian said back in January about Cait not feeling safe being alone anywhere but at home, having to stay on the ranch is probably driving her crazy. I don't wanna make that overwhelmed feeling worse by coming on too strong, but maybe having a friend to talk to might help.

Josh didn't relish the thought of his family finding out that he'd been shot in the line of duty and hadn't told anyone but Jake. But if sharing his experience with Cait would help her realize he understood her fear of another shooting and wanted to help her heal from the trauma, then it would be worth the risk of her possibly mentioning it to his mother.

Hell, if it helps her to have someone else who understands what she's been through to be able to lighten her load by talking about her experience with someone other than Ian, then it'll be worth the lecture I'll get when Ma finds out.

Besides, it's not like I could really hide it from the rest of the family for very much longer. If I spend any kind of time working on the ranch this summer while on leave, there's no way I can keep a shirt on in the scorching South Texas heat to keep the scars hidden.

Leah Mae Wright

Josh was brought out of his head when the family finished the tour and started heading off, either to their offices in the headquarters building or to their vehicles to head home for the evening. Since Jake had loaned his truck to Ian to use while searching for Rojo, he'd ridden with Josh from the airport to the meeting after Josh flew them in that morning. Now Josh was glad his brother needed the ride to pick up his truck at their cabin, so he could spend the trip to Heart's Destiny questioning his brother about what was going on with Ian's op to cause the Campbells to temporarily move to the ranch.

Jake's probably gonna figure out how I feel about Cait when I insist on being brought in to help hunt the bastards down while we're home. Especially since I probably won't be able to be as covert with my feelings as I was at Christmas because of wanting to watch her like a hawk to make sure she's as relaxed and comfortable as she can be while the cartel is still on the loose.

~~~

Cait felt even more anxious sitting down to dinner with all the Burlesons and Avingtons gathering at Hazel and Bob's home than she had the day her house was broken into. It had been better the first few days that her family was staying on the ranch, when it was a much smaller group of people gathered around the table. Then she could sit with her brother and nephew and felt comfortable getting to know the Burlesons they were eating with at each of the different meals. But with the Burlesons' newfound cousins coming in the night before, and Ian focusing his attention more on Charlotte the past few days, Cait had felt herself going into a shell of shyness that she'd apparently developed in the last couple of years. She'd tried to bring herself out of it by sitting with Jen, Julie, and Becky to have her friends to talk to during the meal. But somehow, she'd ended up sitting between Becky and Josh, and having Josh that close to her brought out her anxiety in a whole different way.

It wasn't just the flutters he caused in her belly every time they were in the same room that were getting to her. She also felt tingles every time he accidentally brushed against her because of them sitting so close. Every light brush of his leg against hers, as he shifted in his
~~~

seat, lit up erogenous zones she hadn't even realized she had before. *There must be something wrong with me to cause my pussy to get wet every time our knees or feet bump against each other.*

Being so close to him also allowed her to discern his intoxicating aroma. Unlike a lot of guys who seemed to overdo it with body sprays, Josh smelled like a potent earthy mix of the outdoors on a rainy spring day and whatever soap he'd recently used. It was such a light, fresh scent that it let the powerful pheromones in his natural musk draw her in like no man ever had before.

The way he joked around with his sister and cousins didn't help her situation any, either. Normally she was turned off by guys who showed their affection by teasing the way he was with Becky, Jen, and Julie about how they were all going to be hitting on the actors they'd be working with when they started making movies at Burleson Incorporated. But with Josh, the lighthearted banter almost seemed endearing.

No, it's not the way he's picking on them that's turning me on. It's the way it feels like he's putting his arm around me every time he reaches around me to torment Becky that's making my nipples hard.

"Dang it, Josh," Becky hissed, slapping Josh's arm as he pulled it back. "If you don't stop pulling my hair and snapping my bra, I'm gonna freeze all your underwear again."

"Good luck with that, Sis," Josh chuckled. "I quit wearing them the first time you did that."

OMG! He goes commando? Cait barely stopped herself from looking down at his crotch. *And now I've completely lost it. It's not like I can actually verify that by looking through his slacks. Maybe I should quit reading so much sci-fi and fantasy romance, so I quit having delusions that I have x-ray vision.*

"You did not," Becky argued. "You were only fourteen at the time, so Mom would've noticed if she suddenly didn't have to wash your boxers."

"Naw, Jake made up for mine not bein' in the laundry by changing every time he…" Josh's voice trailed off as Jake elbowed him from his other side.

Josh's shoulder brushed Cait's as he tried to get away from his brother, causing more tingles that temporarily distracted Cait from the conversation. She completely missed whatever Jake hissed at Josh.

"Sorry, Bro," Josh croaked, leaning into her even more as he held his hands up in surrender to Jake. "I promise I wasn't gonna break the vow. I was gonna say every time you showered after gym class."

"Cait, you wanna move to this side of the table?" Jen offered.

Since Jen was in the corner seat on the inside of the U of tables and there were fewer seats on that side than the outside of the U where she was currently sitting, Cait wasn't sure where Jen expected her to sit on the other side of the table.

"So our neanderthal cousin doesn't squish you," Julie finished her sister's thought.

"Oh, sorry, Cait," Josh apologized, sitting back up in his chair and turning to look directly at her. "I didn't mean to invade your personal space while joshin' around."

"Seriously, Josh? I thought you'd outgrown your narcissistic phase." Jen rolled her eyes at Josh.

"Why would you think that when he still acts like a kid every time he comes home?" Becky shook her head at Jen.

"It's not just when he comes home," Jake interjected. "Josh pretty much acts like a kid anytime he changes out of his NWUs."

"What are NWUs?" Cait hadn't ever heard the term and was curious.

"NWU stands for Navy Working Uniform," Josh explained, smiling at her in a way that made her heart flutter. "It's the Navy's version of camo." He then turned his head to look at his twin. "But if you're classifying any kind of joking around as acting like a kid, then you're wrong, Bro. I only get super serious and quit being witty when I'm in the middle of an op. And even then, I might pop off a one-liner to relax the guys as we're gearing up or before we go silent on Infil."

"What the hell are you jokin' about on Infil?" Blaine Avington turned in his seat at the next table behind Jen to glare at Josh.

"Usually, somethin' to get the guys pumped up," Josh shrugged. "Like when we inserted on the island of Kala to deal with some pirates on the Indian Ocean, I pointed out the irony of goin' to Kala to *Kick A Little Ass*. Finding a little humor like that is how I keep the darker aspects of the job from getting to be too much. It seems to work pretty well both for me and for the men I lead."

"Okay, yeah, I guess that is acceptable," Blaine smiled as his brother across the table chuckled.

Becky reached around Cait and slapped Josh on the shoulder. "Wait, were you on the team that just rescued that senator's daughter who was kidnapped by pirates? Weren't they vacationing on Kala?"

"Sorry, Sis," Josh shrugged then winked and grinned, making Cait wonder if Becky had guessed correctly. "Missions are classified, so I can neither confirm nor deny when I was there or what I was doing."

Cait was glad he wouldn't talk about his missions. Hearing about them would make the danger he was in on a regular basis seem more real to her, which she needed to avoid to keep from spending her every waking moment worried about him once he left to go back when his leave was over.

"Oh, yeah, they probably send in SEAL team six for those special missions, right? And that's not the team you're on, is it?" There was a teasing tone to Becky's voice that almost sounded like she was playfully insulting her brother for not being on a specific team.

Why does it matter what team he's on? All the SEALs are badasses, no matter what team they're on.

"What you're calling team six is actually DEVGRU," Josh explained, shaking his head at his sister. "And no, I'm not on DEVGRU. I'm on team two."

Josh didn't elaborate on the differences between the teams, stopping the conversation instantly by stuffing his last bite in his mouth and standing from the table to carry his dishes to the kitchen.

"Dang it," Becky huffed. "I didn't mean to piss him off."

"Don't worry about it, Sis," Jake consoled Becky. "He's not pissed. He just can't talk about the different teams and their missions, so he walked away to get us to change the topic before he comes back. Though you might want to go lock up your underwear drawer before he sneaks over to freeze all your bras."

"Crap!" Becky jumped up from her seat and started gathering her dishes. "I'll probably have better luck hiding Mom's satellite dish bowl, so they don't end up in a giant block of ice." She then took off toward the kitchen.

"We'll go stand guard at the house!" Jen and Julie jumped up and ran after her, barely pausing long enough to grab their dishes.

"He wouldn't really go steal her bras to freeze them in that giant bowl filled with water, would he?" Cait couldn't imagine Josh being that mean to his sister. Yeah, she'd seen how much he loved to pick on her, but it was playful, not malicious. She couldn't imagine he'd do something that might damage her expensive delicates.

"Naw," Jake shook his head and grinned. "At least not right now while they're awake and could catch him in the act. But after the girls froze all our boxers at that slumber party when we were teenagers, we've both kinda wanted to get back at them."

Cait was surprised to hear the vengeful sentiment from Jake. He always seemed so laid back, much like Josh.

"What?" Jake shrugged. "It seemed like it took forever to get all the ice around them to melt. And it was at least a month before we found all the bowls they hid in every freezer on the ranch. So, they kinda deserve a little retribution."

"What's up with the girls runnin' through the kitchen to toss their dishes in the sink and hightail it out the back door?" Josh nodded in the direction of the kitchen as he sat back down with a plate full of pie.

Cait had helped make three different kinds of pie that morning. They made four each of the three different kinds of pie — strawberry pie, coconut cream pie, and lemon-lime pie, which Hazel called Mistake Pie because she'd accidentally used frozen limeade in a lemon pie recipe years ago and her family loved her mistake more than the original pie recipe. And Josh had a piece of each on his plate. His pieces were so big that if there had been a fourth flavor of pie, he'd have reconstructed a whole pie from the four pieces.

How on earth can he eat all that and still have abs that show through his t-shirt?

"Becky thought you might be pissed at her for picking on you about not being in DEVGRU," Jake explained with a smirk.

"Why would I be pissed at her for that?" Josh shook his head as he loaded his fork with a large bite of strawberry pie. "I'm not even eligible to train for DEVGRU since I've only been on team two for a little over three years."

"Yeah, I told her you're not pissed," Jake chuckled. "But I also warned her that she might want to lock up her underwear drawer, so you don't freeze her bras."

"Ya'll can pick on me all ya want about still acting like a kid for how much I like joshin' around, but I've outgrown childish pranks like that." Josh dug in, finishing off the strawberry pie before moving on to the coconut cream pie.

"No, you haven't," Jake argued with Josh. "You just won't go to that extreme for the same reason I won't. We're too grossed out by just the thought of touching our sister's underwear."

"No, I've matured past mean pranks like that, I swear," Josh promised. "I prefer verbal humor now."

"He did snap her bra tonight," Cait interjected, unsure if that proved he wasn't afraid to touch Becky's undergarments or that Josh was still childish enough to enjoy physical humor.

"That was actually an accident," Josh admitted. "I was trying to lightly run my finger down her back to give her the sensation of a spider crawling on her, and accidentally hooked my finger on her bra strap. It only snapped because I jerked my hand back when I realized what I was touching."

Cait couldn't help but laugh at the ornery little boy look on Josh's face.

"Hey, what can I say? It's a brother's job to bug his sisters. So, I'm always gonna do my job to be the favorite brother." Josh made a goofy face that kept Cait chuckling. "I'm sure Ian does the same with you."

"Not for the last couple of years," Cait admitted without thinking as she looked back on life with her brother. Mikey had been just as mischievous as Josh was this evening when they were living on their own after he got custody of her. Prior to that, his jovial pranks were limited to when they were off by themselves because he had to be serious whenever their mom or one of her boyfriends was around. After meeting Mari, he often included her in their lighthearted joking around, but he always made Cait feel included. Since Mari was killed, however, Ian had been stoic and serious almost all the time, only slightly smiling on occasion, but never really laughing with anyone except Brody.

"That's when his wife was killed, right?" Josh's whispered words brought her out of her mental trip down memory lane to realize he'd finished off the coconut cream pie and was about to start on the lemon-lime pie, while she hadn't even finished the last couple of bites of her dinner.

"He told you about that?" Cait's eyes popped up and locked on Josh's hazel orbs. She was shocked to realize Josh knew a little about their history, wondering when he'd had time alone with Ian to get her brother to open up.

"Uh, yeah." Josh looked around before turning back to her and softly suggesting, "How 'bout we go sit on the porch to talk a little more privately?"

When Cait froze in place, nervous about being alone with the man she was seriously crushing on, Josh wiggled his eyebrows and sweetened his offer. "I'll split this last piece of pie with you."

"You're not afraid of getting cooties from my fork touching your pie?" Cait joked, referring back to the way his siblings had suggested he still acted like a kid earlier.

"Naw, I can fix that," Josh grinned. "Hand me your butter knife."

Cait arched a skeptical eyebrow at Josh, unsure why he wanted her knife instead of using his own.

"I put mine in the dishwasher when I went to the kitchen," Josh informed her as he motioned toward the table for her to look for herself.

She handed over the utensil before picking up her fork to finish off her dinner. He quickly wiped the knife off with his napkin before using it to cut the pie in half.

"Now we can use your knife and fork to move your half onto your plate, so we don't accidentally swap spit."

No, apparently there won't be any swapping of spit between us. No matter how much I keep dreaming of more intimate ways I'd love to swap bodily fluids with you than sharing a piece of pie.

They worked together to transfer the pie to her now empty plate before picking up their dishes and stepping out on the porch. Once they were alone and sitting in the swing, Josh filled her in on how he'd found out about Ian's mission in Heart's Destiny. He told her about flying in to help Ian move his tactical operations center in the middle of the night before revealing that Ian had told him a lot more about the day Mari was killed than Cait was comfortable with him knowing.

Cait dropped her fork to her plate on her lap, losing her appetite as Josh offered to listen if she ever wanted to talk about being shot.

"You don't have to talk about it if you don't want to," Josh cajoled. "But I thought it might help to have a sounding board, other than your brother, who's been through something similar and understands how you're feeling."

"You've been shot?" Cait's heart rate sped up as her anxiety level skyrocketed at the realization of just how dangerous his missions were and would continue to be as long as he was in the Navy.

"Yeah," Josh nodded before setting his empty plate on the table beside the swing. He looked around, like he was double-checking that nobody else was around to see him, before lifting the right side of his t-shirt to reveal a circular bullet wound right below his ribs. "It's why I don't take my shirt off while I'm anywhere Ma could see the scars and freak out about my job."

Cait was too fascinated by the perfection of his abs and the line of his obliques — which she knew would form a V if she could see his other side at the same time — to pay attention to what Josh was saying about his injuries as he twisted to show her the exit wound on his back.

Holy shit! He's so ripped, he has an eight-pack. And even his low back muscles have lines of definition that point to his ass. Cait really didn't even notice the scars because of how drool-worthy his body was otherwise. It wasn't until he lowered his t-shirt that she came back to her senses.

"I was scared shitless the next time I went out on a mission," Josh confessed with a sympathetic smile. "So, I totally understand why you might be afraid to go anywhere in public where another mass shooting could happen. And I wanna do anything I can to help you feel safe again."

Cait wasn't sure there was anything Josh or anyone else could do to ever make her feel truly safe again. But now that she was no longer distracted by the perfection under his shirt, her anxiety amped back up, causing her to feel like she was already too close to having a panic attack to be able to talk it out with him right then.

"Oh, uh, okay. Thanks." Cait shyly smiled up at him.

"No problem, Sunshine. That's what friends are for, and I'm sure our families are gonna be lifelong friends."

Friends. Great. The man I'm all hot and bothered for only sees me as the damaged girl his family has befriended. Cait was so caught up in the melodrama in her head that she didn't even register that Josh had started calling her by a pet name that indicated he wanted to be more than friends.

Cait plastered on a smile that she hoped he couldn't tell was fake and promptly changed the subject. "Well, Friend, how about you tell me all about the ranch? I've been learning to ride the horses some from your sisters and cousins, but I've yet to see a cow on this cattle ranch."

"Yeah, the girls all avoid the cows, claiming they don't wanna meet their future dinners while they're still mooing," Josh chuckled. "But while I'm home the next couple of weeks, I'll be helping out in the birthing barn. So, I'll gladly take you over there to see a couple of the calves if you want."

Josh continued to talk her through the different parts of the ranch and how the cows were moved around the various pastures, depending on their stage in the life cycle, what pastures needed a season to regrow, and whether the cows were being kept for breeding stock or raised for beef production. Cait was fascinated by learning how the beef came to be on her plate, but she could also see why the other women on the ranch didn't want to meet the cows that lived there.

She eventually finished eating her slice of pie as she sat there talking to Josh. They ended up talking most of the night, getting to know one another's likes and dislikes, and swapping stories about their childhoods with their siblings.

It wasn't the grand romantic connection she wished she could have with Josh, but she felt like she'd made a new friend by the time they finally went inside to go to their separate beds.

Now I just have to figure out how to keep him in the friend zone in my dreams, too. Yeah, I doubt that'll happen anytime soon. Getting over my crush on Josh is going to be a lot easier said than done. But maybe if I stop mentally chanting his name when I'm masturbating and start fantasizing about some random Cowboy who just happens to look a lot like him, then I'll eventually get over my broken heart to be able to find my real Mr. Right someday.

Chapter Five

Josh felt like he'd taken the right steps in befriending Cait the night before. He'd thoroughly enjoyed their time sitting on the porch, lightly moving the swing back and forth while talking about anything and everything they could think of at the time. Well, maybe not everything he could think of, since they had kept the topics strictly platonic.

He'd had to leave his t-shirt untucked all night to try to cover up the way his dick kept getting hard every time he thought about all the ways he wanted to make love with Cait. Since he was constantly thinking about wanting to lean over and kiss her, or carry her up to his bedroom to do more than kiss her, he'd battled with his boner all night. It got so bad that he had to jerk off as soon as he got to his room, so he didn't have to ask his brother to take him to the hospital for having an erection that lasted too long.

They'd found out they had a few things in common besides having both been shot in the past. Though he knew he was stretching it to say her former job as a model and his enjoyment of looking at models was really something they had in common, he thought their love of movies counted. They also both liked to read in their downtime, though again, the genres they chose differed.

So what, if we prefer different genres in books, movies, and TV shows? Or that she would rather act in the sappy love stories that I would only watch to see her acting?

No, scratch that. I couldn't handle seeing her kissing her co-star unless I acted as her love interest.

But I will be doing an online search for any Caitir Skye modeling photos I can find from her time modeling in San Diego.

During their talk, Cait had filled him in on the particulars about using her first and middle name for her stage name, but she didn't elaborate on why she preferred the shortened version of her first name most of the time now. Josh just assumed it was because it was such an unusual name that she didn't want to have to explain it to everyone she met. He thought it was a cool name and a great way to remember the grandparents she'd lived with on a farm until she was three, when they passed away and she moved with her mom and brother to San Diego.

He still couldn't believe how close they'd lived to one another when he was in Coronado, California for BUD/S and they somehow hadn't met back then. Being fresh out of the Naval Academy, he'd frequented some of the same bars that Cait had mentioned going to when she was in college. They'd figured out that she was in her junior year at San Diego State University when he was there. He knew that technically the base was over fifteen miles from the university, but he still thought they could have been in the same clubs on the same nights during his six months there.

It just wasn't our time to meet, I guess, Josh thought as he hopped in Jake's truck to ride over to the police station. *Neither one of us was in a place in our lives to be able to settle down and get serious about a relationship. And I wouldn't have been able to walk away from her if we'd hooked up back then.*

"Dude, you alright?" Jake gave him a curious look, stopping Josh from going down the mental rabbit hole of how his life would have changed if he'd met Cait four-and-a-half years before the first time he saw her.

"Yeah, I'm fine," Josh assured his twin. "But when I was talkin' with Cait last night, we realized we coulda run into each other while I was in BUD/S. Now I can't help but wonder if I'd have been able to do anything to help prevent the need for this op now, if I'd have met the Campbells almost five years ago when I first got to Coronado."

"Naw, you couldn't have changed anything." Josh shook his head as he drove them to the meeting they were having with their new cousins, the HDPD, the DEA, and Ian to figure out the best course of action for taking down Roberto Rodriguez. "I met Ian three-and-a-half years ago when I caught some chatter on the dark web about drugs being smuggled into the US with sailors coming home from deployment. Even working on another case with him, I wasn't given any info on the cartel case to be able to help. So, there's no way he woulda shared that info with some random guy who wanted to date his sister back when you were in BUD/S."

No, but maybe he woulda shared it with his brother-in-law, Josh thought as they parked, knowing if they'd met back then, he would have married Cait as soon as she'd agreed to it. Not only because he couldn't wait to make her his wife, but also to keep the male models she worked with back then from hitting on her. *And Cait wouldn't have gotten shot if she'd have moved with me when I left BUD/S.*

Josh pushed those thoughts from his head as he walked with his brother into the police station. As they made their way over to where Ian was talking with the receptionist, Mabel, Josh caught the tail end of their conversation.

"No, not another break-in," Ian reassured Mabel. "But I am here for a meeting with Bobby, so I probably won't be able to get away with sitting out here flirting with the beautiful women of the HDPD today."

"Hey, are you flirting with my girlfriend?" Jake walked around Ian and threw his arm around Mabel's shoulders. "You'd better knock that off, or I'm gonna tell my sister on you."

Ian lifted his hand to his chin, doing a standing imitation of *The Thinker* sculpture similar to what Josh had seen in a movie or two. "Hum, maybe making Charlotte jealous will bring out her feisty side. This could be a good plan."

"Sorry to burst your bubble, man, but Char doesn't have a feisty side." Josh slapped a hand on Ian's back, remembering how his older sister had always been more serious than his younger sister. While Becky had problems with public speaking when they were younger, she was definitely the one most likely to show her bratty side to the people she cared about. "You picked the wrong sister for that."

"Oh, you boys, quit picking on Ian," Mabel interjected. "He's a good man and perfect to bring Char's feistiness back out."

"Oh, I think he already has," Bobby chuckled as he walked up from his office in the back of the building. He nodded at the group standing there as he stopped beside Mabel's desk. "Or at least her sadistic side. You still walkin' bowlegged after she made you spend the first two days of spring break on the back of a horse?"

Ian groaned and moved his hands down to cover his junk. "Seriously, guys, you've got to tell me the secret to lessening the impact on the boys while riding."

"There is no secret," Jake shrugged. "Ya just gotta toughen up."

Damn, I should probably tell him to wear a jock strap next time, but you'd think that would be obvious, since I'm sure he was taught to wear one for baseball. Josh might not wear traditional underwear except when he was required to under his Navy dress whites, but he always wore a jock for any athletic activities he'd participated in since he was a kid, including horseback riding, and still donned one for PT and missions in the Navy.

"And this is why we're not going to be spending our time here on the back of a horse," their cousin Barrett laughed as he and his brothers and father joined them.

"Oh, boy, Paisley is gonna be so disappointed that she's working the night shift this week and missed out on all the handsome men ya'll brought with you for this meeting." Mabel fanned herself before extending her hand in Byron Avington's direction. "Hi there, handsome. I'm Mabel. Welcome to Heart's Destiny."

"Byron Avington. Nice to meet you, Mabel." Byron lightly shook her hand, but the cousin, who was technically in Josh's father's generation, looked slightly uncomfortable being the target of the HDPD receptionist's coquetry.

Josh had to grin at how blatantly the woman, who was at least a couple of years older than Byron, flirted with him.

"Back off, Mabel. He's married," Bobby warned.

"So's your daddy, but I can still enjoy the view whenever he comes around without poachin'." Mabel waggled her eyebrows suggestively, causing Josh to chuckle. "Now, ya'll head on up to the briefing room before you get me in trouble. Dusty's already taken the donuts up there and corralled Dougie and Jagger before they left for patrol."

Josh followed his brothers and cousins up the stairs and into the briefing room, taking a seat beside Jake, who was already pulling up his computer.

"You know I already have him scheduled to Skype in, right?" Jake nodded his head at Ian's phone in his hand.

Ian looked surprised at Jake's statement as he took the seat on the other side of Jake.

"Dude, you've either been out of the game too long, or my sister really has you distracted," Jake laughed as he hit a few keys on the computer in front of him and the DEA team appeared on a large screen at the front of the room.

"Maybe a little of both," Ian sighed, sounding weary after everything he'd endured in the course of trying to take down the cartel.

"Don't worry man, we've got ya covered," Jake assured Ian as he slapped a hand on his shoulder. Then he turned to the rest of the room and took over, starting the meeting by introducing everyone in the room.

DEA Agent Trent Jones then took over the introductions for everyone on his team in San Diego, whom they were meeting with over Skype.

Once all the introductions were concluded, Byron Avington kicked off the meeting by informing everyone that he'd already read over all the files Jake and Bobby had provided him with to be up to speed and ready for Avington Security to step in and take over the search for Roberto "Rojo" Rodriguez. Byron also detailed the experience Avington Security had with working investigations with the FBI and ATF in Atlanta, along with several local and state police forces and various branches of the military, to make it clear that they were better prepared than Ian had been in trying to hunt the man down on his own.

"Damn, I should probably get the director in here to negotiate a contract with you before we actually start coming up with a plan for our next steps in tracking Rojo," Agent Jones declared, shaking his head. "But since Jake said he was bringing in his cousins to brainstorm, not hiring an investigative team, I didn't think to ask Director Jameson to come in early today."

"Can you authorize us to go in without your director signing off beforehand?" Byron asked Trent.

"Yeah, but I can't authorize an expenditure over five-thousand dollars, which an investigation of this magnitude would obviously be." Trent shook his head as he explained the need for a contract through the director of the DEA for outside investigators due to budgetary reasons.

"If your only concern is the money, then you don't have to worry about a contract. I just need to know my men won't be treated as vigilantes or charged for whatever happens when we go in and capture this guy. If you can give us the authorization to work on behalf of the DEA to bring in your fugitive, then we're good."

"Yeah, I can authorize that," Agent Jones nodded.

"And even if he couldn't, I could just deputize all ya'll before we get started," Bobby quipped, causing a few chuckles around the room.

Byron smiled, looking around the room at his sons, then the Burlesons, before turning back to look at the screen at the front of the room to see the DEA agent's reaction to his next statement. "Since my family likes to keep financial matters private, I'm sure you haven't heard all the specifics of how we recently found out my great-grandmother was the long-lost Burleson heiress. But because of finding that out about six weeks ago, there's been quite a few changes to our family business. One of which is that we're now able to take on cases with law enforcement agencies on a pro bono basis."

Yeah, his last name may be Avington, but Byron just showed his Burleson side, Josh thought, knowing his family funded a good portion of the public services in Heart's Destiny.

"That's not even the best change in the company," his cousin Blaine chuckled.

"No? What's the best change in the company?" Josh arched an eyebrow at his cousin, curious about what Blaine thought trumped their newfound billionaire status.

"Turning all the accounting, human resources, and other paperwork we hate doing over to the pretty ladies at the Burleson headquarters," Blaine smirked.

Josh had to chuckle as he remembered seeing all of his new cousins interacting with the women in those departments on the tour of the Burleson Incorporated headquarters the day before. *Damn, I bet he's hoping to get to turn in some of that paperwork in person. Maybe I shoulda pointed out the benefits of having an office in our corporate headquarters when I suggested bringing Avington Security in as a division of Burleson Incorporated yesterday?*

Barrett reached over and smacked his brother on the back of the head. "I thought when you turned thirty, you'd mature enough to quit being a sexual harassment lawsuit in the making."

Byron gave his sons a look that made them all straighten in their seats, even the ones not horsing around, before bringing the meeting back on topic. "Well, now that we know there's no need for a contract, let me tell you my plan for finding Roberto Rodriguez and bringing him in."

Byron explained how he planned to send a couple of his employees from Georgia undercover in San Antonio to see just how much of the operation Rojo had recovered since the bust in November. Since Ian had obviously been recognized at the Community Mission Shelter and had possibly put Charlotte on Rojo's radar, Byron wanted him to stay in Heart's Destiny, working as close cover for Charlotte while his team took over the search for Rodriguez in the San Antonio area.

Oh, boy, Char's gonna love that! I wonder if Byron made that decision after Ma told his wife Blair about her matchmaking plans?

When Byron finished detailing his plan without mentioning anything about having someone working as close cover for Cait, Josh decided to take on that duty for himself. At least for the next couple of weeks while he was home, anyway. He could stick close while he was on the ranch and use their new friendship to keep his family from realizing he planned to move home and pursue her romantically. He just wasn't sure what he would do to keep her safe if the cartel wasn't caught before his leave was over.

Fuck! Cousin Byron and his team better find that bastard Rojo before I have to head back to Virginia. 'Cause there's no way in hell I'm gonna be okay with having to ask one of them to watch over my girl for me.

~~~

Sunday, March 31, 2019

Cait had thoroughly enjoyed the last couple of days on the ranch, even though Josh being home wasn't helping her get over her crush on him. Though she didn't spend any time actually talking to Josh on Friday while she was working, she had several times throughout the day that she could have sworn she felt him nearby, often right before catching a glimpse of him out the window while she cleaned. It was the strangest feeling, almost like her body was perfectly attuned to recognize his presence and tingled to alert her to look for him. *Yeah, I don't think my girl parts got the message that he just wants to be friends.*
~~~

Friday afternoon, once she was finished working, he joined the group at the stables working with the horses just long enough to get her attention before taking her to the birthing barn to show her the two newest calves born on the ranch. She had to insist that Josh didn't tell her the fate of the cute baby cows she met, suddenly wishing she was a vegetarian when he teased her by claiming he'd named them Steak and Brisket.

Needless to say, on Saturday morning when Josh offered to take Brody to see the cows while Ian and Charlotte were out of town fulfilling their coaching duties, Cait had declined. Instead, she made plans with Becky, Jen, and Julie to spend some more time learning how to ride and care for the horses, so Brody could have more practice time in a saddle, even though Charlotte wasn't there. She was pleasantly surprised when Josh joined them and started teaching Brody about roping, instead of heading back out to tend to the cows.

Seeing that hot cowboy sitting on a fence and teaching her nephew how to make a lasso had given Cait all kinds of ideas, which were completely inappropriate to have while she was supposed to be babysitting Brody. Apparently, her thoughts about all the other ways she could imagine him using rope while they were naked and off somewhere private showed so clearly in her expression that her friends could read them with no problem.

Jen and Julie had joked about Cait needing to talk to Brooklyn and Kay about her shibari fantasies because they didn't want to ruin theirs with any mention of their cousin that she was obviously crushing on. And Becky had teased her about it being weird to watch Cait ovulate while drooling over her brother demonstrating what a good dad he'd be one day.

Cait couldn't deny her attraction to Josh any longer, but she did swear her friends to secrecy. She'd convinced them that she was only enjoying the view, telling them that she knew it couldn't ever be more than friendship as long as he was in the Navy. She couldn't quite bring herself to tell them that she didn't think Josh was interested in more than friendship with her, though.

As she walked down the stairs to join the group of people gathered at the Burlesons' home for Josh and Jake's birthday party, Cait really wished she could convince her heart that she didn't want more than friendship with Josh. Although, she thought her heart might have gotten the message when she saw him surrounded by a bevy of beautiful women. The heartbreaking sight made her want to retreat to her room for the night. Not that she could with such a large audience watching her descend the stairs.

The dining room was packed with people to the point that they spilled out into the foyer. There were way more people there than had attended Brooklyn's birthday party back in January or JJ's party at the beginning of the month. Because of the massive number of people there, they'd moved a couple of the tables out of the dining room and opted not to serve a sit-down meal. So, everyone was standing around mingling and making it difficult for Cait to even get across the room to the table, which she'd helped set up with drinks and snacks before going up to shower and change for the party.

She felt stupid for having changed into the nicest dress her brother had brought to the ranch for her to have to wear to church. While she hadn't worn it either of the Sunday mornings they'd gone to church, she put it on specifically for this party because she wanted Josh to see her in it.

It was a sapphire blue, sleeveless, ruffled hem, bodycon dress that flared out just above the knees with the hem hitting her mid-calf. The form-fitting dress, with a strappy shoulder accent in front and a deep V in the back, which prevented her from being able to wear a bra with it, was the sexiest dress she owned.

The bonus was the royal blue color and how it brought out the bluer aspect of her blue-green eyes. Her mother always told her that she got the green in her eyes from her father, so Cait constantly tried to downplay it, wishing her eyes were more of a pure blue like her brother's.

Looking around to see that everyone else was dressed casually, or business casual with slacks and a button-down sans tie being as dressy as any of the guys were dressed, made her feel completely out of place. Even Charlotte, who normally dressed up more than the rest of the Burlesons, was in a more casual dress than Cait. Char was wearing the same tea-length flower print dress she'd worn to church that morning. *Maybe I should go back upstairs and change?*

"Wow! You look hot, Cait." Becky greeted her, waving her over to where she was standing with Jen and Julie.

"I feel like an idiot for being more dressed up than everyone else," Cait admitted to her friends. "But it was either this or one of the t-shirt dresses I wore to church the last couple of weeks. And I didn't realize when you guys said you'd be wearing dresses that you meant you'd be wearing the dresses you wore to church this morning, or I would have done the same."

"Oh, gosh, I didn't even think about you not having your full wardrobe while you're staying here," Jen gasped. "I would have told you to come borrow something from one of our closets if I'd realized your brother only packed you three dresses."

"Really?" Cait arched an eyebrow at Jen, wondering how her friend, who was four inches shorter and at least twenty pounds lighter than Cait, hadn't realized that Cait couldn't fit in any of her tiny clothes. "Do you own a dress that goes below your knees? Because every dress I've ever seen you wear would be a mini-skirt on me. That is, if I could squeeze my big ol' butt in any of them."

"I think she was offering you free rein in my closet," Julie pointed out. "Since I'm a couple inches closer to your height."

Yeah, that might have worked back when I was model thin, Cait thought, rolling her eyes at her friends. *But not with the twenty-five pounds I've gained in the last two years.*

"It's no big deal," Cait shrugged, not wanting to get into how she felt like an Amazon when compared to all the women on the ranch. "If Ian doesn't go get more of our clothes this week, then I'll get online and order a few things." She didn't mention that she'd become an expert online shopper in the last couple of years, so she didn't have to leave the house, even when she outgrew her old clothes.

"Well, you look great, so don't worry about feeling overdressed," Jen advised.

"And it appears our cousin noticed," Julie added with a grin. "Considering he keeps looking over here."

"I doubt that," Cait disagreed, but she had her back to Josh, so she couldn't be certain. "When I saw him earlier, he was too busy appraising his harem to even notice that I walked by him."

"Oh, no, that's not his harem," Julie chuckled. "That's the Thirsty Threesome. Jackie Adkisson, Melody Martinez, and BJ Willis."

"They were a year ahead of us when we were in high school," Jen added, shaking her head. "And in the same class as Justin, Josh, and Jake."

"They were two years ahead of me and Anthony in school, but we still heard all the stories about them." Becky made a gagging face. "They were always after whichever one of our brothers or cousins they could get their claws into."

"Not just our brothers and cousins," Jen whispered. "Rumor has it, they offered to gang bang the whole football team. But I don't know if they ever actually did it."

"No, I don't think they did," Julie agreed with her sister.

"But they did offer to all three do Anthony at one time," Becky informed them. "Thankfully, he was dating Nancy at the time, and adamantly turned them down loud enough for everyone in our gym class to hear him."

"Seriously?" Cait couldn't believe the stories they were sharing about sexual acts the three women had tried to instigate in high school. Things she still wouldn't consider doing seven years after she graduated.

"Oh, yeah," Jen nodded. "We weren't in the class to witness it, but we still heard about how they'd gone to cheerleading practice early to catch Anthony in the gym."

"And he roasted them by announcing to everyone that his brothers had warned him to stay away from the three of them to keep from getting an STI," Julie continued for her sister.

"I'm surprised they're here considering how bad my brothers embarrassed them back then," Becky added. "But I guess at least BJ's sister isn't here."

"That's probably because Tammi Jo thinks Bobby still has a restraining order against her," Jen chuckled.

"From the look on Josh's face, I think he might want to get a restraining order against Barbara Jean," Julie giggled.

"I guess badass SEALs aren't trained to evade the advances of the Thirsty Threesome," Becky laughed.

Cait couldn't resist any longer. She had to turn and look at Josh, even though she was afraid he'd see her jealousy written plainly on her face.

Leah Mae Wright

Josh and Jake were surrounded by a blonde, a brunette, and a redhead. All three of the women seemed to have boundary issues, touching both of the twins suggestively without caring that there were children present at the party. They both kept fidgeting to get away from the girls, but none of them seemed to notice.

"Maybe we should go rescue Josh and Jake," Cait wondered aloud, just as Josh's face transformed from an uncomfortable expression to a wide smile. *Or maybe not, since he seems to be enjoying their interest.*

Before any of her friends could reply, there was a loud bark of laughter from the other side of the room, drawing everyone's attention. Cait took advantage of the distraction to slip away from her friends, going out the back entrance to the dining room and sneaking up the back staircase to her room.

If anyone asks why I left, I'll tell them I was overwhelmed by the number of people there, she decided as she stripped off her dress and jumped in the shower to wash off the makeup she'd put over her scars to be able to wear it. *Hopefully, only the girls will realize it was jealousy and not the crowd that sent me back into hiding. At least I know I can trust them not to tell anyone why I really bolted.*

~~~

Josh wasn't sure how he'd lost track of Cait in the crowd at his birthday party. He'd just seen her looking at him from across the room and smiled at her. Then he was momentarily distracted by the loud laughter of some of the girls he'd grown up with, and when he turned back to look at where Cait had been standing with his sister and cousins, she'd disappeared. He scanned the crowd, thinking she'd be easy to spot because of being the tallest woman in the room. But no matter where he looked, he couldn't find her.

Damn it! I bet she's overwhelmed by there being too many people here. I swear I'm gonna strangle whichever one of the Walkers it was who started spreading the news about this party at church this morning. I don't know why they thought it was a good idea to invite everyone in town, but it's clearly a disaster.
~~~

"Are you even listening to me, Joshy?" BJ Willis whined the question as she dug her nails into his bicep.

"Nope," Josh replied to the woman, who still went by the nickname she'd earned in high school for having a goal to give every guy in school a blow job. Oh, she claimed it was because her name was Barbara Jean, but Josh knew the truth from being in the room when some of his classmates came up with it after they found out she'd sucked off half of them. "Sorry, I wasn't interested in any of ya'll in high school, and I'm still not interested in any of ya'll now. So, I'm gonna go hang out with the people I'm actually in town to see."

Josh pushed his way through the three women his high school classmates had dubbed the Thirsty Threesome to make his way over to where Ian was standing with Charlotte and JJ. He'd tried to be as polite as he'd been raised to be, but he was done. He couldn't believe he'd wasted the whole time Cait was at his birthday party in that smokin' hot dress, trying to be a gracious host to the mean girls from high school.

"Where's Brody and Cait?" Josh hoped asking about Ian's son first would cover for his interest in finding out what happened to Cait.

"Since Maria and Tia aren't here, Isabella Diaz offered to play video games with Brody, so he's not bored waiting for cake," Ian chuckled and looked around. "As for Cait, I'm not sure. I saw her earlier, though, so I'm sure she's around here somewhere."

"Izzy's like ten years older than Brody, isn't she?" JJ gave Ian a curious look.

"Yeah, eleven, actually," Ian sighed. "My boy apparently has a thing for older women, and I just couldn't bring myself to burst his bubble by pointing out that I'm paying her to babysit."

"He does not," Charlotte rolled her eyes and slapped Ian's arm. "She's joined us working with the horses during Spring Break, so he sees her as another horse expert that he can learn from, just like everyone else here on the ranch."

"No, I think Ian's right," JJ disagreed with Charlotte. "I've seen the way Brody follows Maria and Tia around when they're home."

"He's too little to start crushing on girls," Char argued, making it clear to Josh that she was already more invested in a relationship with Ian and his son than she wanted anyone to know. "He just prefers hanging out with them because they're the closest to his age on the ranch."

"I hate to tell you this, Sis," Josh smirked at his sister. "But there's no such thing as being too young to have a crush. And from what Brody told me yesterday when I was teaching him about ropin', I think his biggest crush is on you."

"Ah, so it was you who thought it was a good idea to give rope to a four-year-old," Ian glared at Josh.

"Yeah, I already told Ma I'll replace the lamp he broke and made him promise to only practice tying the lasso while he's inside," Josh assured Ian, raising his hands in a placating gesture as he relayed the conversation he'd had as he walked down the back stairs after changing clothes when he got home from church earlier in the day.

"I told you it had to be one of my brothers being a bad influence on him," Charlotte pointed at Ian before turning to Josh. "And I told you and Jake both not to do anything stupid in front of Brody."

"I didn't do anything stupid," Josh defended himself from his sister's allegations. "I started teaching him about calf ropin' when he asked about the different events kids can do in the rodeo. I figured it'd be a lot safer than teaching him about mutton busting."

"And what did you tell him to practice on?" Char's eyes flared with irritation.

"Fence posts, the same way Pappaw taught me," Josh informed his sister.

"Apparently, you weren't clear in your instructions," Ian chuckled, waving a hand between himself and Charlotte. "While you were off with the cows this afternoon, he tried to lasso us."

"Damn, sorry," Josh apologized, feeling bad for getting the kid in trouble. "I'll talk to him again and make it clear he can only lasso fence posts until I get him a ropin' dummy made, if you think it'll help."

"No, it's fine," Ian waved him off. "I think he learned his lesson after the way Charlotte squealed when the rope hit her back."

"Shit, Char, are you okay?" Josh really felt bad then, imagining a welt from the rope on his sister's back. "It wasn't bad enough to break the skin, was it?"

"I'm fine," Char shook her head. "It didn't hit my back. It hit my butt, which was well protected by my jeans. It just startled me and wasn't really hard enough to hurt."

"Shit, sorry," Leo shouted from across the room and drew everyone's eyes in his direction. "No harm, no foul. Just a friendly gesture."

Josh took advantage of whatever Leo was yelling about being a distraction for his sister and cousin to pull Ian aside for a private conversation.

"I still haven't seen Cait come back in the room," Josh whispered to Ian. "Do you think her anxiety was triggered by this place being packed with people she doesn't know?"

"Fuck," Ian hissed out the expletive. "Maybe. I thought since she can handle the crowd at church that she could handle the additional people at the party. But she's normally glued to my side to feel safe when we're out in public, so it's possible this was too many people for her to handle without me being close to her."

"Do I need to kick everyone out to help her feel more comfortable?" Josh figured ending the party early might piss off a few people, but he didn't care about that. He just wanted to make sure Cait wasn't suffering because of a party for him.

"No," Ian shook his head. "I'm sure she just went up to her room for a bit. I'll go check on her and make sure I stick close to her if I can convince her to come back down."

Ian excused himself to go upstairs just as Josh's mom called for him and Jake to come blow out the candles on their cakes. Josh made his way over to the table where she was lighting the candles on side-by-side cakes, keeping up appearances as best he could while watching the doorway for Ian and Cait to return.

Thankfully, everyone had listened when he and Jake had insisted that they donate to the Madeline Ashbury Foundation instead of buying them birthday presents, so he only had to plaster on a fake smile long enough for the crowd to sing *Happy Birthday*. Then he could cover his worried expression by stuffing his face with cake.

When he saw Ian come back into the room without Cait, he decided to ditch his birthday party to carry a piece of cake up to her. He had to wait until his mom had finished doling out cake to half the town while he and Jake graciously accepted all their well wishes before he was able to escape with two plates and forks in his hands.

He sat the plates down long enough to stuff a soda bottle in each of the front pockets of his slacks before picking them back up and ducking out the back of the dining room to sneak up the back stairs. With his hands full, he couldn't knock on the bedroom door, so he lightly tapped it with the toe of his boot.

"I told you I'm fine, Ian," Cait huffed through the door without opening it.

"It's not Ian. It's me, Josh. I brought you some cake."

"Oh shit," Cait cursed so softly that Josh barely heard her. "I'll be there in a minute."

He wasn't sure what she was doing, but he could clearly hear her scurrying around in the room. *Fuck! Did I catch her in the middle of changing clothes? You don't have to put anything back on, Sunshine. In fact, I'll gladly take my clothes off, too, just as soon as you let me in the room.*

Unfortunately, she wasn't naked when she finally opened the door. *But she is awfully cute in those PJ's,* Josh thought as he looked her over from her bare feet, up her long legs, to the turquoise blue sleep shorts and t-shirt with whimsical beach scenes printed in a random pattern that covered all the parts of her he really wanted to see. He liked seeing her without makeup and wearing a towel on her head, where she'd obviously just gotten out of the shower. *If only I could strip all that off of her and take her back to the shower.*

"Sorry, I, uh…" Cait's voice trailed off as she stood there, obviously struggling to come up with an excuse for why she left the party when it had barely gotten started.

"Had a panic attack from being stuffed in a room with so many strangers," Josh finished her sentence for her.

"Yeah, something like that," Cait blushed, lowering her eyes like she was too embarrassed to face him.

"Don't worry about it, Sunshine." Josh walked past her into the room to set the plates on the dresser, so he could pull the sodas out of his pockets before they got too hot to be drinkable. "I know every single one of those people, and they were still too overwhelming for me to want to hang out down there any longer."

"Really?" Cait looked up at him in surprise.

"Yeah," Josh nodded to the door she was still holding open. "You might wanna shut that door before our voices carry downstairs, and Ma realizes we're eating in the bedroom."

Cait quickly closed the door without making a sound before walking over to see the treats he'd brought her.

"I probably should have gone out and grabbed us a couple of burgers from the grill to go with the cake," Josh half-shrugged as he pushed a plate and soda toward Cait. "But I didn't want to get caught trying to sneak out of the party, or risk bringing you a cold burger, if I couldn't escape the party animals fast enough."

"Party animals?" Cait giggled, picking up the fork and cutting into the pineapple cream cake that had always been Josh's favorite. "You make it sound like there's a rowdy frat party going on downstairs."

"Well, the Walkers did invite the girls from our graduating class in high school, who were voted most likely to spend more time at frat parties than in college classes," Josh quipped, grinning at her before taking a bite of his cake.

Cait rolled her eyes at him before opening her soda to take a drink. When he expected her to return the banter, Cait continued eating her cake.

Damn it! I know better than to mention other women when I'm talking to a woman I'm interested in, so why the hell did I just stick my foot in my mouth? Josh contemplated how he could change the subject as he continued to eat his cake.

While the silence between them wasn't exactly awkward, Josh still wanted to make sure she wasn't suffering in silence and trying to fight off a panic attack until after he left the room. "So, are you really okay? Or are you gonna have a full-blown panic attack just as soon as you can shove me out the door?"

"I'm really okay," Cait assured him with a smile. "I may have had a panic attack in the shower as soon as I got upstairs earlier, but I'm fine now."

"Okay," Josh nodded, though he wasn't sure he totally believed she was completely over the episode. "But I know from experience that sharing our feelings with others helps to lessen the mental load from traumatic events, or even mild panic attacks, so I'm here to listen whenever you're ready to talk it out."

"I did telehealth appointments with a therapist for about a year after the shooting," Cait admitted while looking down at her plate and scraping the last of the crumbs of her cake into a pile before smashing them between the tines of the fork to be able to eat them.

"Did they help?" Josh didn't think they had since she'd seemed to develop a fear of going out in public during the same time period, but he wanted to know what she thought about the therapy sessions.

"Yes and no," Cait sighed, picking up her soda and walking over to sit on the end of the bed. "I had a lot of nightmares at first and it seemed to help with those. But no matter what the therapist tried, she couldn't convince me it was safe to leave the house when we still lived in San Diego. That's when it got to be more irritating than effective because I got sick and tired of telling her, 'No, I haven't left the house this week,' every session."

"So, how did you go from never leaving the house in San Diego to moving here and going to work and church and stuff?" Josh wanted to know what had helped her gain that little bit of progress, so maybe he could help her feel comfortable increasing the number of places and situations where she felt safe around others.

"Ian pushed me out of my comfort zone for the move," Cait huffed, but her lips turned up in the slightest smile. "And then once we got here, we had to stay at the bed and breakfast until our furniture was delivered, so I was kind of forced to come out of my room for meals. And the Hunters pretty much made it impossible to hide in my room the rest of the time. Since I thought we'd moved a thousand miles away from the cartel, I pushed myself to try to do more, too. I was doing really well that first week and a half, even driving by myself to go to the store and for my interview with your mom. But then I found out why Ian moved us here…"

Josh wanted to go sit beside her and pull her into his arms to comfort her while she gathered her thoughts to continue, but he wasn't sure she'd appreciate the gesture. So, he sat down on the floor and leaned back against the dresser instead, making it easier for them to maintain eye contact.

"Once he explained that the cartel had moved their operation to get away from the heat his investigation had brought down on them in Cali, all my fears about being recognized by the guys who shot up the park that day came back, only now they feel ten times worse."

"So that's the big issue," Josh nodded, finally understanding why she fled the party and struggled with going anywhere but the ranch and church. "You saw the shooters that day and are afraid they'll come after you again if they see you because you can identify them to the cops."

Cait nodded in agreement, but her tentative smile didn't reach her eyes.

"So that's why the extra people here tonight caused you to panic," Josh continued working through his thought process aloud. "They haven't all been vetted as safe by Ian like everyone who's normally on the ranch. But why is it you seem to be okay at church?"

"I figured cartel criminals wouldn't be there," Cait shrugged. "Even if they wanted to try to use religion as a cover for their illegal activities, I doubt they'd attend the same church as the police chief. Besides, I'm usually sitting next to Ian when we're there, and I know he's always carrying at least one weapon to defend us."

"Yeah, I guess those are pretty good reasons to feel safe there," Josh chuckled. "Though maybe you might feel safer in other places if we worked on ways you can defend yourself when Ian's not around." *At least until I move home to be able to step in and protect you twenty-four-seven.*

"Ian's always been good about making sure I know where his guns are and how to use them," Cait informed him. "But it's been so long since I went for target practice that I'm not sure my aim is good enough to risk using one of them to stop an intruder when I'm home alone with Brody."

"Well, that's one thing we can fix this week," Josh grinned. "It won't be some fancy gun range like I'm sure Ian took you to in San Diego, but we've got lots of secluded places on the ranch where we can line up empty pop bottles to use as targets. That's how Dad and Pappaw taught all of us. I don't know if the girls have kept up with it, but I'm sure they can all show you where to find a gun or two while you're working. Not that I think you'll need it here on the ranch."

Josh cringed, thinking he'd screwed up by not acknowledging her legitimate fear of how many people she didn't know had made it past their security. "Well, except maybe on nights like tonight when some of our buddies think it's funny to bring people, who we wouldn't normally let through the gate, to a birthday party." Josh half-shrugged, as he grinned at the mental image of Cait chasing the Thirsty Threesome off the property with his old Daisy rifle. "But if you wanna run off the mean girls who keep trying to corner me down there, I'll run upstairs and grab my BB gun for you. We can sneak out the back for me to teach you how to use it first if you want. And maybe grab a burger or two, so you have a more nutritious dinner than pineapple cream cake."

"No, thanks," Cait laughed, and he finally saw the mirth in her eyes. "I think I'll skip the opportunity to find out if BB's are strong enough to pop implants to keep from giving your brother a reason to arrest me."

"Probably not from a pump-up air gun," Josh shook his head, remembering back to how many times he had to pump the rifle to pop the balloons Pappaw had tied to the fence for Josh to shoot at when he was a kid. "But now I'm curious if implants could work as an extra layer of body armor for women in the military or law enforcement."

Cait looked at him like he was crazy, but she was also smiling slightly at his random, weird way of thinking.

"What?" Josh smirked. "I mean, I know silicone and saline can't stop a bullet, but what if they could encase them in Kevlar? And if Kevlar is safe to implant in the body, then would it be possible for a plastic surgeon to put a layer just under the skin for those of us who don't want boobs but wouldn't mind protecting a few more areas than our body armor covers?"

"You're insane," Cait laughed, rolling her eyes at him.

"Yeah, maybe," Josh shrugged and grinned, happy to be the one making her laugh. "But since that's what everyone said about Thomas Edison when he was working on inventing the light bulb, I consider it a compliment. Besides, I know you secretly wish you had some implanted Kevlar on the day you were shot, just like I do."

"No, I don't," Cait disagreed, her smile only slightly dimming. "I'd rather have been wearing some Kevlar football pads, so I wouldn't have the scars. But if I had implanted Kevlar, I'd have even more scars from the surgeries to implant it than I got when they removed the bullets. Like you, I got lucky that both wounds were through and throughs. Well, the shoulder was a through and through. The arm was more of a graze."

Cait lifted the sleeve of her t-shirt to show him the little line on the inside of her right bicep, turning her arm so he could see it without having to move closer to the bed.

"Wow, that looks a little like the scar I got on my inner thigh from climbing over a barb-wire fence when I was a kid," Josh chuckled self-deprecatingly at the memory.

Cait lowered her sleeve and pushed the neckline of her shirt over for him to see the circular scar just above her clavicle. "I got lucky that I was ducking when the second one hit, so it only went through my trapezius and didn't hit any bones or major blood vessels. The doctor was able to go in through the entrance and exit wounds to stitch the muscle back together, so the scars are small enough I can cover them with makeup if I wear something where they show."

Remembering the strappy shoulders he'd seen on her sleeveless dress earlier in the evening, Josh wondered if she'd covered them with makeup to go down to the party. *Fuck! I bet looking at the reminders of that day to cover them with makeup really amped up her anxiety right before walking into a crowd of strangers. No wonder she had to leave almost immediately after she walked into the party.*

"Does it help you to forget they're there if you cover them with makeup?"

"I don't know," Cait shrugged. "Tonight's the first time I've tried it. Most of my clothes cover them, and I pretty much forget about them unless I see them in the bathroom mirror when I'm getting into or out of the shower."

"Yeah, that's pretty much the only time I remember mine, too," Josh agreed with a smile. "And yours are smaller than mine, so most people probably wouldn't even notice them, even if you didn't cover them with makeup."

Josh didn't mention that he would have noticed them no matter how small they were because of how closely he wanted to inspect and memorize every inch of her body.

"My therapist tried telling me that we see our imperfections as bigger than they are, but I don't know how true that is."

"Oh, I'm sure that's probably true for a lot of things, not just the size of our scars," Josh nodded. "Though I think my scars are bigger than yours because I was shot with a bigger caliber bullet than you were."

"Are you really pulling out the *mine's-bigger-than-yours* line?" Cait put a hand on her hip and glared at him. "Is that your way to get me to quit whining about being shot?"

"No, absolutely not," Josh shook his head and held his hands up in surrender. "Being shot hurts, even if it's with a paintball gun that doesn't break the skin. And you took two bullets where I only took one, so you absolutely have the right to whine about it all you want. I'm just pointing out that the scars are so small that they do absolutely nothing to detract from your beauty."

Cait twisted on the bed to grab a pillow, which she promptly threw at Josh. "Using your charm and giving me compliments are not going to get you out of the dog house, mister."

Josh easily caught the pillow before it smacked him in the face. He fluffed it up and put it behind his head. "Thanks, Sunshine. That's a lot more comfortable than leaning my head against that drawer handle."

Cait rolled her eyes and shook her head at him once more, but she didn't stop smiling. Josh took that smile as a win, thrilled to be the one making her smile.

"Why do you call me Sunshine?"

Cait's question threw him for a loop. He knew it was too soon to tell her how he felt about her and that the term of endearment was meant to subtly show his feelings for her. And he also knew telling her that her smile made him feel like he was basking in a ray of sunshine sounded too sappy for just friends. So, he made up a quick reply and hoped she'd drop the subject.

"You're from California, which I think of as always sunny," Josh shrugged. "And you wear a lot of yellow, which again makes me think of sunshine. So, I figured if I call you Sunshine, I won't accidentally call you Caitir in front of someone you don't want to know your full name."

"Makes sense," Cait bobbed her head from side to side, causing the towel to drop from her head onto the bed. She finger-combed her wet hair as she continued. "And yellow is my favorite color, so that's why I wear it so often."

"My favorite color is blue, like the dress you were wearing earlier," Josh confided to change the subject.

"Yeah, that's probably my second favorite color," Cait agreed, smiling and nodding.

They ended up sitting there talking about absolutely nothing important for the rest of the evening. Even though they talked about mostly inane topics, Josh didn't want to walk away from their conversation to go to his room for the night. But when Cait couldn't stop yawning, he knew he had to let her get some sleep.

"Alright, Sunshine, I'm gonna call it a night and go get my beauty sleep." Josh stood, as Cait tried to cover another yawn.

"Yeah, I don't think that's going to do much good," Cait teased with an ornery grin.

"Yeah, I know I can't really get any more beautiful," Josh smirked as he handed her pillow back to her. "But as you well know, once we've reached the maximum beauty level, we have to stay on schedule for the maintenance plan."

Cait rolled her eyes at him and smacked him in the abs with the pillow.

"Sorry, I deserved that," Josh held his hands up in surrender. "But it's my birthday, so I get to be a little narcissistic today. I'll go back to normal tomorrow, I promise. Now please make my birthday wish come true."

Josh opened his arms to show her he wanted a hug, but she just looked at him skeptically.

"What exactly was your birthday wish?"

"A hug goodnight from the most beautiful girl at my birthday party." Josh hoped Cait could see the sincerity in his eyes as he gave her the compliment that he shouldn't have been so subtle in giving her a minute earlier.

"Well, I guess I can't deny your birthday wish," Cait giggled as she stood and wrapped her arms around his waist. "Happy birthday, Josh."

Best birthday ever, Josh thought as he held the woman of his dreams in his arms for the first time.

Chapter Six

Cait was having a hard time getting through the evening at Bobby and Brooklyn's wedding reception, and her panic was only partially brought on by being in the ballroom at the Hunters' Bed and Breakfast in a large crowd of people. The majority of it was her jealousy at having to watch Josh perform his duties as a groomsman with another woman glued to his side.

After their talk on his birthday, Cait had started to think her attraction to Josh was mutual. He'd called her beautiful, and she thought she felt his arousal when they hugged. Oh, he didn't blatantly say, "You're beautiful, Cait," like she longed to hear. Josh's compliments were subtle and hidden in his snark, but Cait recognized them for what they were. Or at least, she thought she did.

She'd also thought a lot of his banter as he followed through on his promise to take her out for target practice was his subtle way of flirting with her. While she still didn't think it could go past the flirting stage for the time being, she'd hoped they might be laying the foundation for a relationship at some point in the future. She'd even pictured them settling down together on the ranch one day. It would have to be after she felt more like her old self, and Josh finished up his stint in the Navy, but she'd seriously believed it could happen.

It was only because she knew both her brother and Josh would be there to keep her safe that she'd felt strong enough to go to the rehearsal dinner the night before and now the wedding and reception. But after seeing how Brooklyn's friend Ashley had monopolized Josh's attention at the rehearsal dinner last night and was continuing to do so throughout the reception, she no longer felt like Josh even noticed she was there.

While Cait had danced with her nephew at the dinner the night before, Josh had danced with Ashley. Every time she thought she'd felt Josh's eyes on her, she'd turned to look only to see him looking at the other woman exclusively. By the time the rehearsal dinner was over, Cait's heart had been thoroughly cracked, if not completely broken, by the way Josh had ignored her.

During the wedding, when she couldn't take her eyes off of Josh standing at the front of the church, he'd kept his gaze on the preacher, the happy couple, or the woman standing opposite him as a bridesmaid. She'd been dreaming of him standing there waiting for her at the end of the aisle to become her husband, while he hadn't looked in her direction once. And seeing him smiling down at Ashley as he offered her his arm and walked her back up the aisle had made it clear that he wasn't as opposed to the younger woman's attention as he'd been to the women he went to high school with throwing themselves at him during his birthday party.

Now, sitting at the reception, it seemed as if they were living through a repeat performance of the night before. Only this time, Josh was in a tuxedo, instead of slacks and a button-down.

Why does he have to look so damn hot all the time? Slacks and a button-down — hot! Cowboy boots and jeans — smokin' hot! But in that tux, he epitomizes all my royal book boyfriend fantasies! And it totally sucks that having Josh as my love interest will obviously only ever be a fantasy!

Cait knew she was being extremely rude by sitting there focusing on watching Josh across the room instead of paying attention to the conversation going on around her. But she couldn't really care less about the car show Hayden and Hudson Walker were talking about, so they had no chance of distracting her from watching Josh.

Hopefully, Kara and Summer will take them up on the dates they're working their way up to asking about for next weekend, so I won't have to publicly turn either of them down.

They almost piqued her interest when they mentioned the rodeo, thinking back to what Josh had told her about competing in the team roping competitions with his brother when he was home on the ranch. She briefly wondered if Josh would be competing, and if she could be brave enough to go and watch him. But then Hayden mentioned it wasn't for another couple of weeks, and she knew Josh would be back in Virginia by then.

Thankfully, Summer, whom she'd learned was the nurse at the Heart's Destiny Clinic who'd given Brody his shots during their first week in town when she sat down and introduced herself, changed the subject by telling Ian that she'd heard all about him from her brother, Ryder, the middle school physical education teacher. Unfortunately, the way Summer was batting her eyelashes and giving all her attention to Ian made it clear that she wasn't interested in either Hudson or Hayden any more than Cait was. While she knew her brother didn't return Summer's interest because of clearly being taken by Charlotte, Cait worried that Summer's actions would cause the Walkers to redirect their flirtations back at her.

She was saved from whatever Hayden had turned to her to say when the speeches started as they finished their dinner. Not that turning in her seat to watch as each member of the wedding party, including Josh and Ashley, gave a speech about Bobby and Brooklyn was much higher on Cait's list of things she wanted to do right then.

Once the speeches were concluded, the emcee called all the single ladies to the dance floor. Cait wasn't sure she really wanted to be in the crowd trying to catch the bouquet. But since she hadn't really had the chance to hang out with the women she felt like she was actually friends with at the wedding events so far, she took the opportunity to walk toward Jen, Julie, and Becky, hoping to at least hang out with them for a few minutes.

"Hey girl, come hide in back with us." Becky grabbed Cait's hand and pulled her away from the main crowd of women and off to the opposite side of the room from where she'd been sitting. "We're trying to make sure none of us accidentally catch the bouquet."

"You don't want to catch the bouquet?" While Cait didn't really want to catch it either, she thought at least one of the other members of the Burleson family would want to be the one to catch it.

"No, definitely not," Jen and Julie stated in unison, shaking their heads.

"And since the Matchmaking Mommas seem to have included you in their scheming today, we know you don't want to either," Becky added with a smirk. "'Cause we all know they've rigged it so the garter will go to whoever they have picked to pair up with whichever woman catches the bouquet."

"Seriously?" Cait arched an eyebrow at her friends, barely seeing in her peripheral vision when Charlotte caught the bouquet.

"Oh yeah," Jen, Julie, and Becky all replied, nodding their heads.

"Watch," Becky continued, pointing to where Ian was standing holding Brody as the women started to disperse. "I guarantee Ian will catch the garter."

Cait continued standing off to the side with her friends, so she could see her brother and nephew clearly, as the guys all took to the floor, and Brooklyn sat down in a chair for Bobby to remove her garter. Bobby made a big production of hiding under the poufy skirt of Brooklyn's wedding dress, which was hilarious considering he was almost six-and-a-half feet tall and had to practically sit on the floor to get low enough to get under it.

Bobby finally crawled out from under Brooklyn's wedding dress, whispered something to his new bride that made her blush, and gave her a peck of a kiss before standing up and turning toward the men on the dance floor. He clearly scoped out the room to decide who to toss the garter toward.

Sure enough, the girls were right. Bobby shot the garter like a slingshot straight at Ian, but Brody actually caught it first, dropping it into Ian's hand.

"Told you," Becky smirked as the girls started walking back toward their seats while Ian and Charlotte posed for pictures.

"Oh, no, Daddy!" The flamboyant photographer, who'd introduced himself as Philippe at the rehearsal dinner the night before, wagged his finger at Ian. "You bring that boy with you. Half the people in here got baby fever from seeing him assist you in catching the garter, so we have to include him in the pictures."

Cait had to giggle at her brother's reaction to loudly being called "Daddy" by another man. He was clearly uncomfortable with being the center of attention, but he was trying valiantly to keep it from showing so he wouldn't hurt the other man's feelings. Ian wasn't homophobic in any way, but he'd always had issues with stage fright whenever he felt like everyone in the room was watching him. That was why he'd had trouble even helping her run lines to prepare for an audition whenever they had other people at their house. Even when it was just the two of them and Mari.

She wished she was close enough to hear the conversation as Brody wrinkled his nose and furrowed his brow, so she could help her brother keep from making the situation more awkward. But then she saw Brody tug on his father's jacket sleeve and whisper something that made Ian chuckle, and she realized he was no longer uncomfortable.

"Oh, I hope that new baby doctor is prepared for all the immaculate conceptions that just took place from seeing this," Hayden shouted, just as Cait took her seat.

"Dude, the girls might have all just ovulated, but I don't think they can actually get pregnant without…" Hudson loudly argued before he was cut off by a feminine shout of "Enough!" from somewhere behind them and a roar of laughter from the rest of the crowd.

Cait sunk down in her seat, embarrassed to be seated at the same table as the Walkers at that moment.

"Oh, come on, Char," Philippe scolded loud enough for everyone in the room to hear him. "Don't ruin my shot by rolling your eyes at that, when we both know you were among the ovulators."

"Philippe!" Charlotte screeched in shock.

"What?" Philippe shrugged. "You know Nico and I would have both joined you if we had that equipment. As it is, I'm going to have to hope showing our surrogate these pictures will speed up our baby-making process."

"What are they talkin' about, Dad?"

Oh boy! Brody would pick now to be brave enough to speak loud enough that everyone in the room could hear him.

"Something you don't need to know about until you're older," Ian chortled as Philippe instructed them all to smile once more.

As the conversation continued to carry across the ballroom, Cait realized that Brody might not have been speaking any louder than normal. *Who'd have thought this big a crowd could be so nosy that they're capable of being so quiet we could hear a pin drop in the hallway outside the ballroom?*

"We should have just left Ian out of these pictures," Charlotte grumbled as Philippe directed them to change poses to make it look like she was trying to decide between Ian and Brody. "Since Brody's the one who actually caught the garter to be my future groom."

"But Dad said I'm not old enough to marry you yet, so he's gonna marry you first, so you can get married next."

"Actually, Kay's sister, Randi, is going to be the next woman I know to get married," Charlotte disagreed, shaking her head. "So, I guess I'll get a do-over on finding my future groom at her wedding."

"You don't need a do-over," Ian growled, showing his interest in Charlotte more than Cait thought he wanted to at that moment.

"You're right, I don't," Charlotte smirked as she pulled her hand from Ian's. "I'll just wait for Brody to grow up and marry me."

Philippe continued to snap picture after picture as Charlotte turned her back on Ian and leaned down to kiss Brody on the cheek, making it look like she'd chosen his son over him.

Oh, Char's going to make my brother work for it, Cait thought as Ian played up the jilted lover role for the camera. *Maybe I should ask her for tips on how to get Josh's attention. But not now. I need to wait until after everyone in the cartel has been arrested, and I can start feeling safe going to events like this without having to sit with my brother.*

Until then, I'll just keep being friendly when he is, and pretend it doesn't bother me to see him flirting with other women the rest of the time. I was an actress after all. So it shouldn't be too hard to act like I enjoy my role as Josh's platonic friend.

~~~

Monday, April 8, 2019

Josh was ready to kick his own ass for whatever he'd done over the weekend to cause Cait to stop responding to his flirty banter. He thought he'd been playing it so smoothly with her since his birthday, sneaking in compliments and longing looks whenever they could get some alone time, but not actually making a play for more than the hug he'd asked for on his birthday. But then he hadn't had the chance to talk to her even briefly at any of the wedding events he'd had to participate in as a groomsman over the weekend. Since then, she seemed to have reverted back to the shy woman she'd been at Christmas, who barely said a dozen words in his presence, and refused
~~~

his offer to take her for more target practice when he could have been alone with her the day before.

Hell, I wanna be proud of her for successfully attending the wedding on Saturday and Justin's birthday party last night. But I'm afraid she only suffered through them to avoid having me bring her cake to her room again.

As he stroked his dick in the shower after working with the cattle most of the day, Josh tried to think of what he could do to get them back to the flirtatiously friendly stage of their relationship before he had to leave town again on Wednesday. Unfortunately, he couldn't think of anything that might help because he kept drifting off into fantasies about fucking Cait instead.

Knowing he had to hurry if he was going to make it on time to the four o'clock meeting with his brothers and Avington cousins to get an update on the status of their search for the head of the Rodriguez cartel and all of his associates, Josh quit splitting his focus and concentrated on how tight he imagined Cait's pussy would feel on his cock. Picturing her naked and wrapped around him as he pounded her into the shower wall, Josh quickly shot his load, making sure to rinse his semen down the drain before he finished cleaning up.

He heard his phone beep with an incoming text as he was getting dressed, but didn't rush to check it because he knew he hadn't exchanged numbers with Cait. *I really need to do that before I head back to base, so I can keep working on building our friendship, even when I can't physically be near her.*

As he was putting on his boots, Jake banged on his door. "Grab your guns. Rojo kidnapped Char."

"Fuck!" Josh cursed, rushing to his closet for the tactical kit he'd felt paranoid about bringing home with him while he was on leave. He couldn't bring his Navy issued firearms, since they were locked up on base, but he had his personal weapons that he hadn't wanted to leave locked up in his apartment in Virginia Beach. *Guess I wasn't all that paranoid after all.*

He met Jake, who was carrying his own gear bag, in the hall and they rushed down the stairs and out to Josh's truck. Byron Avington jumped in the back, surprising Josh with how agile he was for a man his father's age.

"Bobby said you'll know where the softball field is, so the boys are following you," Byron informed them as they all buckled up.

Josh started the extended cab Ram that he'd had since high school and left in his hanger at the airport in San Antonio when he wasn't home in Heart's Destiny. As Josh started driving, Jake pulled his computer out of his bag.

"What are you pulling up?" Byron leaned forward to look over the seat at Jake's screen.

"Traffic cams from around town," Jake replied without taking his eyes off the computer.

"My brother's a cyber stalker," Josh quipped, trying to keep from being freaked out by their sister being kidnapped. He had to put himself in mission mode to keep from worrying about how that bastard could be hurting Charlotte. He also had to push Cait from his mind, otherwise, he'd worry about the possibility of the cartel going after her at the ranch. "But at least his hacking habit should give us an idea of where to find Char."

"If I can figure out which vehicle he might have her in," Jake added. "Looks like Ian is already pulled over on the side of Rogers Road, so pull up behind him. That way we won't get caught up in the extra traffic from the parents coming to pick up their kids from softball practice in the parking lot on Brahman."

Josh followed Jake's parking advice and pulled off on the side of the road behind Ian's Range Rover once they reached the ball fields. Byron's sons pulled up right behind him and they all got out of their vehicles to run over to where Ian was sitting in his SUV. They crowded in around his driver's door to get the latest update and Josh noticed that Ian was also on his computer.

"What are you doing on the computer when my sister was just kidnapped?" Josh growled the question angrily, irritated that he and Jake were duplicating each other's work, when one of them could be coming up with a tactical plan to rescue Charlotte.

"Pulling up her location from the tracker in her necklace," Ian admitted without taking his eyes off his computer screen.

Josh then looked at the screen to see a green dot moving away from Heart's Destiny on the map. *Holy fuck! How'd he convince Char to wear a necklace with a tracker in it?*

"Damn, and ya'll called me a cyber stalker for accessing the traffic cams on the way over here," Jake quipped as he leaned in front of Josh to look at Ian's screen. "I'm guessing, since the pink dot and blue dot are both on the ranch, Char's the green dot moving away from town on one-thirty-two."

Damn, he has a tracker on Cait and Brody, too. Wonder what it'll take to get him to give me access to Cait's tracker?

"Yeah," Ian grunted in response to Jake's statement as the dot indicating Charlotte's location turned off the two-lane state highway into an area not marked as a road on the map used by the program.

The Avingtons were talking about gearing up and making a plan to free Charlotte from her captors, while Josh, Jake, and Ian watched the tracker's movement slow down on the screen.

"That's all farmland out that way, isn't it?" Josh pointed to the area on the screen where Charlotte and her abductor appeared to be stopping, trying to remember who lived out that way, since most of his friends from school lived closer to town.

"Yeah, let me grab my laptop and see if I can find the land records to get an idea of what we're going into out there." Jake turned and walked back to Josh's truck, where he'd left his laptop, just as their brother Bobby walked up.

"I've got Dougie and Chase taking statements and processing Char's car, and Dusty, Jagger, and Gabe are on their way here to assist in going to rescue Char, if you have a location pinpointed." Bobby nodded toward Ian's computer.

"I've got an idea of a location." Ian handed his computer over to Bobby, so he could see the location on the map.

"Fuck! I should have thought to check there back in November," Bobby snapped before explaining. "That's the old Gruber farm. Mac Gruber died a few years back, and the place has been abandoned ever since. His kids moved out of state like twenty years ago and haven't ever come back to deal with selling the place."

"Any idea how many structures are on the premises that we'll have to search to find Char?" Josh lifted his chin at Bobby, hoping he could give them an idea of how best to set up the mission.

"Only two that I can find in the land records," Jake answered as he walked back over with his laptop in hand. "The house and a barn. But who knows what might have been added without a building permit."

"Too bad we can't get permission to fly a drone over the place." Josh looked at Jake, wishing they had access to the equipment his twin had controlled back when Josh first got through training and Jake was the intelligence officer assigned to his SEAL team.

"Bro, you know the drones I have on the ranch don't have near the capabilities of the ones I use for recon when sending in a SEAL team." Jake shook his head as he reminded Josh of the small drones they'd bought to play around with on weekends and while they were home on leave.

"They have cameras," Josh shrugged, figuring they were as good as they'd get in their small hometown. "All we need is a visual of the structures we need to breach to make a plan."

"Don't we need a warrant to fly a drone over a private residence?" Ian looked back and forth between Jake and Bobby.

"I'll add that to the request I'm taking to the judge while everyone else is gearing up," Bobby stated matter-of-factly before pointing at Jake. "And I'm assuming that your license for flying Navy drones is valid in Texas."

"Of course," Jake smiled. "Hell, that FAA license is probably a lot more valid here than it is in the Middle East."

"Then let's all head over to the PD to finish up the paperwork and gear up while Jake goes back to the ranch to get his drones," Bobby directed.

Josh drove Jake back to the ranch to get one of the drones from their rooms while everyone else headed over to the police station to start gearing up.

"Did anyone tell Ma what's going on?" Josh couldn't stop thinking about the possibility of Rojo sending some of the other members of the cartel to target the women on the ranch while the men were all off searching for Char.

"Yeah," Jake assured him. "And Dad's bringing a couple of hands back up to the house to stand guard with him and keep everyone else safe while we go rescue Char."

"We should probably have everyone gather there, so they're not walking around outside in case someone from the cartel does try to get onto the ranch," Josh suggested. *Fuck, this is gonna freak Cait completely the fuck out. And there's not a damn thing I can do to make it easier on her 'cause I've gotta go help rescue Charlotte.*

"Already taken care of, Bro," Jake reassured him. "Everyone's on lockdown either at the house or one of the Burleson buildings until Bobby gives them the all-clear."

Even knowing that precautions had been taken to make sure Cait and everyone else on the ranch were safe, Josh had to go inside when they got to the ranch to make sure Cait was with the rest of his family, where he knew she'd be well guarded by his father and the ranch hands. Sure enough, he found her sitting in the family room with his mom, Aunt Susan, Brooklyn, Rosa, Mary, and Blair.

The women were all huddled together in what he could only describe as a prayer circle. His dad, the ranch manager, and Brooklyn's honorary father figure were talking quietly as they watched over them.

Josh lifted his chin at his dad, who nodded in acknowledgment of Josh's unspoken request to keep Cait safe. Then he slipped back outside to see the hands patrolling the perimeter, getting back in his truck just as Jake came back out of the house with his drone in hand.

Bobby already had their Uncle Doug sign the warrants by the time Josh and Jake made it back to the station. Since Avington Security had brought more than enough Kevlar and black tactical clothing for all of them and it wasn't an official SEAL mission, Josh opted to use as much of the Avington Security equipment as he could instead of donning his NWU. But since Byron hadn't thought about bringing night vision goggles, Josh pulled those out of his kit along with his favorite personal weapons.

Since he was the officer in charge of his SEAL squad, it felt weird for Josh to sit back and let Bobby and Byron take the lead in planning their mission. But considering this was technically a police raid and not a military op, he knew his place was to back them up and make sure they all came home without any extra holes in their bodies after capturing the cartel.

His brother and cousin were clearly on top of things with the planning, causing Josh to have to rush to change clothes to catch up with them. They had everything together so fast that the Avington team in San Antonio didn't have time to get to Heart's Destiny to go with them, leaving them with only twelve men going in to rescue Charlotte. Bobby was leading three additional HDPD officers, their five Avington cousins, Ian, Jake, and Josh.

Josh could tell Ian was worried they needed to wait for the other Avington Security guys or his friend with the DEA to send in additional manpower. But after getting to know his cousins and learning they'd all either been SEALs or had gone through the same Navy law enforcement training as Bobby, Josh was pretty sure they could pare the squad down to just his biological family and still be able to complete the mission successfully.

As they caravanned out to an overgrown field a half-mile away from the entrance to the old Gruber farm, Josh said one final prayer for all of their safety and a successful mission. When he parked, he took a moment to close his eyes and picture Cait. He couldn't think about her while doing the job they were there to do, but he wanted one last moment of seeing her face before he completely shut down all his emotions to be able to focus on the task at hand. He didn't think this would be any more dangerous than the other missions he'd been on as a SEAL, but he wanted that moment of thinking of her in case it was his last.

By the time he caught up with everyone else, who were all gathered around Ian's Range Rover where Jake was sitting in the passenger seat, his brother had already launched the drone. Josh looked at the footage on Jake's computer screen over his cousin Barrett's shoulder.

As the drone made the first pass over the farm, they made note of three structures on the premises. The farmhouse and barn that Jake had already told them should be there, and a newer metal building set off by itself toward the back of the property.

"Fuck," Ian cursed under his breath, garnering the attention of all the men, who were trying to figure out which building was most likely where Charlotte was being held.

"What pissed you off about that third building?" Byron Avington prompted Ian from the back seat of the Range Rover.

"That's most likely where they've set up a brothel," Ian explained, pointing to the screen where Jake had the drone focusing on the metal building. "Or where they're trying to set up a brothel if it's new since the raid in November."

"So that's where they've got Char?" Josh pushed around his cousin, so Ian could see him from where he was still sitting behind the wheel, and raised an eyebrow in question.

"Not likely." Ian shook his head. "Not this soon after kidnapping her. Even if they were hosting a party tonight, they'd only bring the women they already have trained to the brothel. If I had to guess, she's being held in the farmhouse, and they're using the barn to hide their vehicles."

Jake maneuvered the drone to get a closer look at the area surrounding the buildings to see if they could figure out how many people were milling around on guard duty. They only found one person walking around outside the brothel. Ian told them that was standard procedure for when the girls were there, but the johns hadn't arrived for the night yet.

"Barrett, you take the brothel with one of Bobby's officers," Byron instructed, pointing to his oldest son.

"Gabe, you go with Barrett," Bobby directed Gabe Garcia, one of the patrol officers. "Arrest the guard if you can, but your most important job is to communicate with any women who've been trafficked from Mexico that don't understand English, so we can help them get home safely."

As they were giving out those instructions, Jake flew the drone around the barn to see that it appeared unguarded. *Guess they aren't too worried about the women escaping and trying to get to their vehicles to get away.*

"I'll head over to the barn to disable the generator," Byron announced. "Cutting their power will cause just enough confusion to put them at a disadvantage when ya'll go into the house. But I'd like an officer with me just in case there's a guard in the barn."

"Jagger, you go with Byron." Bobby pointed to Jagger Youngblood, the other patrol officer with them. "Secure the barn before he goes to cut the power at the generator."

"You got it, Chief," Jagger saluted Bobby.

"There's at least two guards walking around outside the house," Jake alerted them. "I don't want to take the drone down low enough to see on the porch in case they figure out we're coming from seeing it. And the visuals aren't close enough for me to determine if the two I saw on the last pass are the same two I saw on the first pass."

"What can you tell us about their typical numbers from when you were undercover?" Byron looked at Ian as he asked the question.

"If that's a training house for the brothel, then there can be up to a dozen guys there to guard it and keep it running. The master bedroom would be used to house the women, with the secondary bedrooms set up for the guards to train them before they go to the brothel. If there's an office in the house, they'll set it up for whoever's in charge of the local operation. And if there's not an office in the house, they'll set one up in the dining room or another room in the common area of the house. But I'm not sure how that might change if Rojo is using the house as his headquarters." Ian ran a hand through his hair, obviously irritated by not knowing exactly what they'd be walking into.

"Okay, we'll treat it as a training house and deal with whatever adjustments we have to make on the fly," Byron stated, patting a hand on Ian's shoulder. "The rest of you divide up, half going in the front and half going in the back. I'm guessing the bedrooms are upstairs, so Ian should focus on heading there to look for Charlotte. Bobby, you and Dusty need to look for the office. That way, you can arrest Roberto."

"We're with Ian to look for Charlotte," Jake insisted, waving a finger between himself and Josh.

"Perfect. That leaves Blaine, Blake, and Brady to cover you if there are more guards inside than what we've seen out on the grounds."

They made sure they all had everything they needed, from handcuffs and zip ties, in case they had to secure more than a dozen prisoners, to their protective gear and weapons with plenty of ammo. Josh was glad he'd grabbed his night-vision goggles as he attached them to his helmet, knowing he'd need them when they cut the lights, if any of the rooms they needed to clear were windowless or had the windows blacked out to keep the trafficking victims from using them to escape. They left their vehicles in the field, hiking through the overgrown fields between them and their target buildings with weapons drawn.

They coordinated their movements via earbud two-way radios, so they all knew when Jagger secured the barn. He had one guard in cuffs and reported the barn clear, allowing Byron to cut the power and give the rest of them the upper hand as they made entry into the other two buildings. Josh went with Bobby, Jake, and Ian to the back of the house while Detective Dusty Deere, Blaine, Blake, and Brady Avington prepared to make entry from the front.

As they approached the back of the farmhouse, Josh snuck up behind the guard patrolling, and choked him out without making a sound. He cuffed him and added a gag, just in case the man woke up before Byron and Jagger made it over to finish securing him with the other prisoner.

Dusty and Bobby took turns on the comms, alerting the others that the guards patrolling outside in front and back of the farmhouse were secured and ready to be taken to transport back to the jail.

Bobby led the way through the back door as soon as the power was cut, announcing, "HDPD, we're here with a warrant," at the same time Dusty made the same announcement as their half of the team made entry from the front. Barrett reported that the guard at the brothel was in custody, just as Josh followed his brother through the back door into the kitchen of the farmhouse. They all four opened fire on the man sitting at the table, who had shot at them instead of lowering his weapon and cooperating.

"One down, kitchen clear," Bobby barked, his voice echoing through the earpiece in Josh's ear.

"Two guards eliminated in the living room," Blaine announced over the comms as Josh, his brothers, and Ian made their way out of the kitchen and into the dining room.

Just as the next cartel asshole raised his weapon in their direction, Josh put a bullet between his eyes. "Dining room clear, one more target eliminated."

The two squads met in the downstairs hallway, where they quickly cleared a bathroom, family room, and what was probably at one time a bedroom that was now being used for drug storage. As they continued moving through the farmhouse, they eliminated at least half a dozen more men inside, communicating with the rest of the team each time they cleared a room.

Barrett and Gabe also continued to report in his ear as they dealt with the men they found in the brothel. Josh wasn't sure if they were more cartel members than expected, or if they were customers who were already there to partake of the services. But either way, it didn't sound like they were going down without a fight.

Damn. You'd think some of these assholes would be smart enough to hold their hands up to show they're surrendering, instead of trying to win in a shootout.

Once the main floor was completely cleared, Bobby and Dusty split off to search for the office while the rest of them started pairing off to clear all the bedrooms on the second and third floors.

"This looks like all smaller bedrooms set up as barracks," Brady commented as they started searching the second floor.

"Then we should probably head up to the third floor to find Charlotte in the master," Ian decided.

"Let's split into three-man teams," Josh suggested. "We'll go find Char, while ya'll make sure none of the guards are sneaking in a nap."

Just as Josh went to follow Ian and Jake up to the third floor, Bobby called over the comms, "Josh, bring those night vision goggles to the center hallway on two. I think we've found the office and it doesn't appear to have any windows."

The layout of the second floor was strange in that there were three hallways leading off from the front stairs. The ones on the right and left side of the house ran the full length of the house to meet up with the hallway off the back stairs, with doors on both sides of those hallways all the way to the end. The center hallway was only about three feet long and only had one door at the end. Josh would have thought the room had windows out the back of the house, except as he'd come up the back stairs, he'd seen the solid wall where he expected to see the center hallway. He'd also seen Blaine and Brady step into a room at the end of one of the other halls that appeared to go behind the room in the center of the house. It was a weird layout, but Josh agreed that it would be the most likely place for the cartel to put their office because of looking like a closet more than a room from the outside.

"What's the plan?" Josh looked to his oldest brother as he lifted his hand to his night-vision goggles, preparing to flip them down into place over his eyes.

"You kick the door in and tell us where the target is, if the light from the windows behind the stairs isn't enough for us to see in the room," Bobby directed Josh.

Josh knew it sounded a lot simpler than the execution would probably play out. He just hoped that Rojo wouldn't have a flashlight in that room with him to make his goggles ineffectual. *And hopefully, it's cloudy enough outside that I won't be an easy target for him standing in the doorway once I get it open.*

Josh flipped the goggles down just before he kicked in the door. He quickly scanned the room to determine how many people were in the office, only seeing one man, whom he assumed was Rojo. "Eleven o'clock," he announced as he stepped to the side for Bobby and Dusty to enter the room behind him.

"Roberto Rodriguez, you're under arrest. Lower your weapon," Bobby's voice boomed as he walked in holding his flashlight on the head of the cartel.

"Go to hell," Roberto shouted, trying to shade his eyes from Bobby's flashlight to be able to take aim at them.

As Rodriguez started calling for his guards to assist him, Josh holstered his weapon and started inching closer to the target to be in place to make the arrest as soon as the weapon was lowered. He stuck to the shadows outside the beam of light Bobby was shining at their target, sneaking up close enough to be able to disarm him if he didn't give up willingly.

"The rest of your men have already been arrested or eliminated," Bobby informed the cartel head. "So, nobody's coming to save you."

"I don't believe you," Roberto hissed as Josh inched closer. "You might have taken out the men guarding the exits, but I have many more patrolling the grounds who will have heard the gunfire and come running to take care of you pigs."

"No, we took them all out," Bobby stated confidently. "And the only way you're gonna get out of this alive is if you lower that weapon and turn yourself in."

As Roberto started in on a rant, yelling for his men once more, Josh activated his comm unit and whispered, "Go dark, Bro."

Thankfully, Bobby must have heard him over the racket Rojo was making because he shut off his flashlight. That's when Josh stepped in and grabbed for the gun in Roberto's hand. He knew his brother wanted them to take the cartel leader in alive. Otherwise, Josh would have preferred to just shoot the son of a bitch, the way they had with everyone else who'd aimed a weapon at them as they made their way through the house. Knowing this was the bastard responsible for Cait's injuries because he ordered the drive-by shooting, Josh wished he could spend a little time torturing him before taking him out. He wanted Roberto Rodriguez to actually suffer for his crimes and have no chance of ever coming back into their lives, so Cait could have the peace of mind to know she was safe.

As they struggled for the gun, Roberto raged in rapid-fire Spanish. Josh had studied Spanish in school, but he was only able to catch about every fourth word, most of them expletives. He gripped the barrel of the weapon in his left hand as he tried to twist the gun out of the other man's right hand while fending off blows from Roberto's left hand with his right. Just as Josh thought he had the gun almost free, Roberto pulled the trigger, not realizing that Josh had twisted the barrel back in his direction.

Josh was grateful for the fire-resistant combat gloves he wore, as he felt the heat of the barrel when the gun discharged. *Damn! And I didn't even get to pull the trigger,* Josh thought just as he heard a woman scream from the other side of the room. He couldn't turn to look in her direction at the moment, though, because he had to finish taking the weapon from Roberto Rodriguez's hand before assessing any injuries.

Josh caught the sudden look of shock on Rojo's face just as he wrested the gun from his hand. When he stepped back to make sure Roberto couldn't try to get control of the weapon again, the cartel leader fell to the floor.

Bobby turned his flashlight back on while barking into his comm, "Get the lights back on now!" Josh assumed he was talking to Byron, since their oldest cousin was the one who had cut the power from the generator.

Josh secured Rojo's weapon before crouching down to see if the cartel ringleader was still alive. His eyes were open, but stared up lifelessly. Josh could clearly see that the bullet had entered Roberto's abdomen just below the ribs, with an upward and left-angled trajectory that pretty much guaranteed it was a heart shot.

"Have you been hit?"

Josh wasn't sure whom Bobby was talking to until he heard his sister stutter, "Nah-no. Just scared."

Fuck! Char was in this room with Rojo! Why didn't I see her when I first looked around?

"Stay there," Bobby ordered just as Josh announced, "Target eliminated."

"Or don't, since it's safe to come out now."

Josh stood and turned to see Bobby helping Charlotte up from where she'd apparently been hiding under a table near the door.

Ah, so that's why I didn't see her. She was smart enough to hide as soon as the lights went out, I bet.

"The rest of the room is clear, Chief," Dusty Deere reported as Josh noticed his Avington cousins double-checking that Char wasn't the only one hiding under a table.

Bobby pulled a key from his pocket and removed the handcuffs from Charlotte's wrists. Charlotte rubbed her sore wrists as soon as they were free of the shackles and looked around the room with wide eyes.

"Where are Ian and Jake?"

"I'm here, Princess," Ian announced, running into the room and scooping Char up into his arms. "And Jake's upstairs with Antonio."

Damn, I guess he's done pussy-footing around and he's finally gonna make his move on Char, Josh grinned as Ian and Charlotte kissed like they were the only two people in the room. *Thank fuck! Now I know he can't say a word about me going after his sister as soon as I'm able to move home for good.*

"I hate to interrupt ya'll's romantic moment, but we need to check Char over for injuries and start taking statements," Bobby announced, totally interrupting the way Ian and Charlotte were making out like teenagers.

Josh followed the group as they made their way back downstairs to meet the paramedics and other law enforcement agencies that he hadn't even realized Bobby had already called in. That was when he got his first glimpse of the women and children who'd been held up on the third floor in the master bedroom, where Jake and Ian had gone looking for Charlotte.

Seeing the scared expressions on the faces of the victims made Josh eternally grateful that Cait wasn't among them. He felt guilty as fuck for being glad it was Charlotte that had been kidnapped and not Cait. But Char seemed to be handling the ordeal a lot better than he thought Cait would have, considering the trauma she'd already endured at the hands of the cartel.

At least, now I can tell her the bastard she's most afraid of is dead and won't ever be able to hurt her again.

After turning over Rojo's weapon to his oldest brother, Josh stepped up to help assess injuries while Bobby worked with the Medina County Sheriff's Department and Texas Rangers to start sorting out all the legal issues for arrests outside the Heart's Destiny city limits. Thankfully, the women and children who had been held in the farmhouse weren't in as much need of medical assistance as the women who'd been out at the building that was set up as a brothel. When he saw they were having to be helped or carried up to where the paramedics set up a triage tent, Josh knew they'd also have to get the proper state and county departments involved with taking care of the trafficking victims, so they could go back to some semblance of their normal lives.

I wonder how many of these women and children are gonna end up living in the Madeline Ashbury House on the ranch because of not having any place to go home to? Josh wondered as he treated a few minor injuries from the men in the large metal building trying to use the women as human shields. *I hope Brook's prepared to bring in a counselor to help them deal with the mental aspects of their time in captivity.*

If she does, maybe I can get some advice from the therapist she brings in to figure out how I can help Cait feel safe in public now that this cartel mess is over.

Fuck! Is it all over? I know that DEA guy said Rojo was the last of them that needed to be rounded up after they did that raid back in November. But clearly, he's been recruiting since then. Are they a hundred percent sure that everyone he's recruited since then was here this evening? Or is Cait always gonna feel like she has to watch her back to make sure one of these cartel bastards doesn't come after her again?

Josh knew that wasn't a question that could be answered right then, so he made a mental note to check in with Bobby in a couple of weeks to verify they'd gotten them all. *And if any of the assholes are still out there, I'll work with him to catch every last fucking one of them, until I know my Cait is safe.*

Chapter Seven

Cait struggled to get back to normal after spending the afternoon and evening before praying for Charlotte's safe return to her family after she'd been kidnapped by the cartel and that none of the men were hurt while going to rescue her. After getting a phone call from one of his sons, Bob had assured them that everyone was safe, and the situation was over just before dinner the night before. But none of them had come back to the ranch until early in the morning for Cait to see that for herself.

She was especially upset with her brother for not calling to tell her what was going on or that he was safe and uninjured after the rescue. She'd only known he was actively involved in going to save Charlotte because she'd been working with Hazel, cleaning the house she'd been staying in for the last couple of weeks, when they got the call that Char had been taken and Ian was the first on the scene.

She'd seen the way Josh and Jake had rushed out of the house carrying backpacks that were no doubt loaded down with guns and whatever other tactical gear Josh wore on his SEAL missions. She'd been terrified at the realization that Charlotte had been abducted by the same cartel that had orchestrated the shooting she'd been caught in a couple of years before. And even more petrified to realize that her brother and the man she was crushing on were both about to go in guns blazing, risking their lives to rescue her.

She hadn't felt like she'd held herself together nearly as well as the other women around her. Hazel had quickly called all the women on the ranch to shelter together while her husband and the men working on the ranch stood guard over them. Cait felt extremely guilty for needing Hazel to comfort her during her breakdown, when it was Hazel's daughter who'd been abducted.

Once she'd finally calmed down, they started praying for all of the men who'd gone to rescue Charlotte to be unharmed as they performed a successful mission and brought her home. As they were praying, she'd felt Josh's presence momentarily. She looked up, wanting to ask him what had happened that he'd come back home so soon, but he'd only peeked in on them for a second.

She'd later found out from Bob that Josh and Jake had only come home to pick up a piece of surveillance equipment that they needed before going back to the police station to set up for the mission. And she only learned that because of being in the kitchen helping to start dinner when he was talking to Hazel about the status of their children.

Hazel had been worried about Becky being stuck at the theater where her office was located, since everyone else in the family had been instructed to shelter in place until they got an all-clear notification from Bobby. Luckily, Becky had been able to get one of the police officers not working the kidnapping case, and who also happened to be her cousin, to drive her back to the ranch, so she was home when they finally got the call that the men had successfully rescued Charlotte.

That was all the news they'd received until everyone finally started returning to the ranch in the wee hours of the morning. Ian had finally come waltzing in at five in the morning, looking like he hadn't slept a wink. He then insisted on going to work as if nothing had happened the day before. His only words to Cait had been to tell her to relax, that it was all over, and he'd give her details that evening when he was finished with work and baseball practice.

The Burleson and Avington men who'd been on the team to find and rescue Charlotte had all gone to bed, sleeping away the morning. When Cait hoped to get a moment to ask Josh what had happened after he woke up that afternoon, he told her that he'd have to tell her later because he had to go debrief with the DEA and Homeland Security.

Her only solace from the stress of the previous day's events came from Josh's parting statement as he left for his debrief. *"I promise you're safe, Sunshine. The head of the cartel is dead, along with the majority of his closest friends. And everyone else is in jail, so there's nobody left to want to take out witnesses to their previous crimes."*

She would have said that taking care of Brody had been another source of comfort for her during the harrowing events of the past two days, but with her grandchildren out of town, Hazel had taken over the tasks Cait normally performed for her nephew. Since the boy had no living grandparents that were actively involved in his life, Cait appreciated how Hazel had taken him under her wing and treated him as if he was one of her grandchildren.

She also knew Hazel had needed the distraction of taking care of Brody to keep her mind off of what her daughter might have been going through while in the custody of the cartel, so she hadn't objected to stepping back and letting Hazel and Brody bond a little more. Considering how close she felt to having a breakdown, she was appreciative of the time to work on her own, so she wasn't at risk of her nephew seeing her in such a state.

As dinner time came and went with no sign of Josh or her brother returning for the second day in a row, Cait really started to worry about how much trouble they were in for whatever happened the day before. She wasn't as knowledgeable as her brother when it came to the specifics of law enforcement, but she didn't think a small-town police chief like Bobby could deputize his brothers, cousins, and a family friend like Ian to go raid a cartel compound to rescue a woman most of them were related to.

At the very least, she suspected there was some conflict of interest in the family of a victim going on a manhunt. But at the worst, she feared they would all be charged with some form of vigilantism and possibly murder, since Josh had made it sound like they'd intentionally killed Rojo and some of his henchmen.

It was all she could do to keep the tears at bay as she helped clean up after dinner while Brody was upstairs getting his bath before bed. She wasn't sure what she'd do if her brother went to jail for taking the opportunity to get revenge on the man who'd ordered the hit that killed his wife. She knew she'd be given custody of Brody if anything happened that prevented Mikey from being able to raise his son. But even the generous salary she earned from working for the Burlesons wouldn't be enough to cover all their household expenses and pay Ian's legal fees.

And I doubt the Burlesons will want us as permanent house guests, or even want me to keep working for them, if Ian's quest to hunt down the head of the cartel caused half their family to be arrested for murder.

Hazel had just suggested that Cait go up and try to relax in a nice hot bath, obviously seeing how stressed out she was, when the back door opened and Josh, Jake, and Ian walked in. Cait sighed out a relieved breath at seeing the three of them, hopeful that their presence meant they weren't being arrested anytime soon.

"Oh, you boys must be starving after spending so long at the police station." Hazel tried to usher them over to the table while she started pulling the leftovers from the fridge to feed them.

"No, Ma, we ate with the Homeland agents," Josh assured her, kissing the top of his mom's head as he hugged her to stop her progress at the refrigerator. "Jane delivered a feast from the diner, so we didn't miss a meal."

"But she didn't bring dessert," Jake grumbled, rubbing a hand over his abs. "So, I'll gladly take whatever sweet treat ya'll made today."

"Cait, let's go upstairs and talk while we pack to move back home," Ian suggested, taking her arm to usher her out of the room, as Jake and Josh indulged their mother's need to take care of them by sitting down for dessert.

They were stopped at the bottom of the back stairs as a fresh from the bath Brody ran down them announcing, "I'm done in the bath and ready for another piece of cake, Memmaw!" He stopped in his tracks as soon as he saw his dad. "Dad! You're home! Did you catch all the bad guys?"

"Yeah, Brody, we got all of them," Ian replied, ruffling Brody's wet hair while arching an eyebrow at Cait. Clearly, her brother was confused about what Brody had been told about why he wasn't around for the last two days.

"Good. Now that they're all in jail, you can go back to work at the school, so you can be home in time for dinner." With that, Brody hugged his dad's legs and then ran off to the kitchen for his second dessert of the evening.

"We kept him distracted as much as possible yesterday, but when you weren't here for dinner, he started asking questions," Cait explained as she walked up the steps with her brother by her side. "I went with the same story Mari used to tell him when you were working undercover. Though I'm not sure how much longer he'll be satisfied hearing you're off catching the bad guys to keep everyone else safe because his questions are a lot more detailed now than they were when he was one."

"Well, thankfully, now that the Rodriguez Cartel has been officially disbanded, I won't be going to catch the bad guys anymore," Ian chuckled as they walked into the bedroom she'd been using during their stay on the ranch.

"Is it really over? None of them are going to come after us again?" Cait wasn't sure she could believe that there wasn't someone in the cartel that might want to finish the job they'd attempted with the drive-by. Or that they'd really be safe if they went back to the same house where the cartel knew they lived.

"Yeah, it's over," Ian assured her as he leaned against the dresser.

Suddenly feeling weak in the knees, Cait sat down on the end of the bed and looked up at her brother. "Please tell me everything you can, so maybe I can start to believe they won't come after us again."

"Okay, but we need to start packing everything up, so we can move back home tonight while I tell you," Ian agreed.

Reluctantly, Cait started gathering her clothing and toiletries to put them in her suitcases, while Ian went into detail about what he'd done to search for Rojo since they'd moved to town. He explained how he ran into Charlotte a couple of months back while tailing a vehicle he believed was driven by Roberto Rodriguez, which was when he thought they were seen together to put Charlotte on the cartel's radar. He expounded with how Rojo had been hiding out at the shelter where Charlotte volunteered in San Antonio, and had suddenly left when Ian started accompanying her there.

They finished packing her things and moved to Ian's room to pack his stuff as he detailed how the cartel had followed him to scope out his routine and had pinpointed when Charlotte would be most vulnerable for them to kidnap her and use her to torment the undercover agent they hadn't been successful in killing after all. Then he started telling her about the raid the day before, only stopping when Brody came in after finishing his extra serving of cake.

They finished packing and moved everything back to their rental on the other side of town just in time for Brody to go to bed. Cait wasn't sure she'd be able to relax enough to go to sleep in the house she knew the cartel had broken into only two-and-a-half weeks before. At least, not without additional reassurance from her brother that the cartel was no longer a threat to their family.

After unpacking the bare essentials and changing into a pair of pajamas, she met her brother in the living room for a nightcap and to finish their earlier conversation. After growing up with their mom's constant use of alcohol and drugs to block out their life, neither of them were big drinkers. But after the stress they'd been under recently, neither of them was opposed to a single glass each to calm their nerves. "So, you're sure you got everyone this time?"

"I didn't personally get them." Ian shook his head. "In fact, I only shot one of them. And no, that one wasn't Rojo. It was the first one we ran across in the farmhouse, who shot at us instead of surrendering. I was too busy looking for Charlotte and the rest of the hostages, while the rest of the guys dealt with making arrests and clearing the way for me and Jake to make it to the third floor, where the women and children were being held."

"But Rojo is dead, right?" Cait picked up her wine, needing something in her hand as she told her brother about what Josh had mentioned earlier in the day. "That's what Josh said as he was leaving to go back to the police station this afternoon. That the head of the cartel and the majority of his closest friends were all dead, so we're safe now."

"Well, Josh would know," Ian chuckled ruefully, shaking his head. "Since he's the one who took Rojo and half the rest of them out."

"Josh killed Rojo?" Cait gasped, setting her glass down without taking a drink, afraid she'd drop it as she started shaking.

She struggled with mixed emotions at hearing that Josh was the one who permanently ended Roberto Rodriguez's reign of terror over her family. She was relieved to know that his death meant she and her brother were most likely safe from being targeted by the cartel in the future. She also felt more than a little bit of hero worship toward Josh for being the one to set her free. But she was also terrified that Josh might end up in prison for his actions. "He's not going to be arrested for murder, is he?"

"Josh?" Ian looked at her in confusion. "No. Why would you think he'd be arrested for murder?"

"Because he's not law enforcement," Cait elaborated with a half-shrug. "And this wasn't exactly a sanctioned SEAL mission for him to have a reason to be able to go in and kill people. So I've been freaking out all day, worrying that you, the Avingtons, and the Burlesons, other than Bobby, will be arrested for acting as vigilantes, instead of waiting on the DEA and Homeland Security to come in and rescue Charlotte."

She barely stopped herself from blubbering out a long rant about her fear for the future if she had to try to cover Ian's legal fees while supporting herself and his son had he been arrested.

"Well, you don't have to worry about that," Ian smiled as he picked up his tumbler of scotch. "We were acting on behalf of the DEA and under Bobby's authority as the chief of police. And I'm pretty sure we were all sworn in as officers of the Heart's Destiny Police Department at some point yesterday. Besides, we only shot at the assholes who raised their weapons toward us instead of surrendering. Hell, I don't think Josh even intended to shoot Rodriguez. I wasn't in the room to see what happened, but everyone who was in there at the time reported that Josh had holstered his weapon while attempting to disarm Rojo and the gun went off in the struggle, killing him. So even if Homeland wanted to throw a fit about not waiting for them to go in, it was a clear case of self-defense. Or at the very least, defense of his sister, since Charlotte was handcuffed on the other side of the room at the time."

Cait's stomach felt like it was trying out for the Olympic gymnastics team when she heard that Charlotte was in the room with Roberto Rodriguez and could have been caught in the crossfire during the raid. Ian might not be ready to admit to having feelings for Char just yet, but Cait knew it would have devastated him to have lost another woman he cared about to that monster's violence.

She quickly picked up her wine glass once more and promptly chugged it, needing the alcohol to help her block out the realization that both her brother and Josh were in just as much danger as Charlotte had been the day before.

"Whoa, Caitir, slow down," Ian admonished, taking her glass from her hand, and placing it on the coffee table. "I'm safe. Charlotte's safe. None of us are going to be in any kind of trouble for taking down the last of the Rodriguez Cartel, so you have no reason to worry anymore."

"You're absolutely positive they don't have another compound somewhere? And everyone who might have a grudge against you for being undercover and taking them down is either dead or behind bars, where they can't try to retaliate?"

"Yes," Ian assured her, taking her hands in his to stop her from wringing them incessantly. "And everyone who actively participated in the drive-by has been eliminated, either in the raid yesterday or one of the raids Trent's team has led in the last two years. I personally verified that with him today after he identified the bodies in the county coroner's office. So you don't have to worry about anyone coming after you to keep you from identifying them as one of the shooters in San Diego, either. It's all over. Now we get to enjoy living peaceful lives."

Cait wasn't sure she knew how to live a peaceful life. Even hearing the cartel threat to her family was over wasn't enough to make her feel like all danger was eliminated from the lives of the people she cared about. Josh was going back to where he was stationed in the Navy the next day, and she knew she'd still be worried about him being in danger. So was his brother Jake, and while her feelings weren't nearly the same for him as they were for Josh, she'd still worry about him because of his close relationship with Josh and her own brother's friendship with him that she'd clearly seen the past couple of weeks.

Thinking about the friendships her brother had developed since they moved and also about the possibility of him starting to fall in love with Charlotte, Cait had to wonder where he'd want to live now that his location wasn't dictated by the job he was assigned by the DEA. "Are we going to stay here? Or move back to San Diego?"

"I want to stay here," Ian admitted, releasing her hands, and leaning back on the sofa to relax. "I've enjoyed the last few months of feeling like Brody is getting a little taste of what life was like on the farm when we were kids. But I don't want to hold you back if you want to go back to San Diego to restart your modeling and acting career."

"No, I don't want to go back to San Diego," Cait blurted, hating the thought of living so far away from her brother. She wasn't going to allow herself to think about her biggest reason for not wanting to move out of Heart's Destiny — being able to get updates on Josh from her friends, who just happened to be his relatives. "I'm going to need a little time to really believe it's safe for me to do more than I've been doing since we moved. And if I ever get to where I want to try acting again, I'll talk to Becky about trying out for a role in a play at the theater or in the movies they're about to start making."

"That sounds like a good plan," Ian nodded, smiling at her.

Cait returned the slight smile, but she could tell he was still holding something back. She didn't think it was about the cartel or the danger having passed. He kept looking at his phone, sneaking glances with just his eyes shifting to look at the device laying on the coffee table.

I wonder if he's hoping Charlotte will call or text him? Cait watched as Ian sipped his scotch and glanced at his phone once more. *Thank goodness, big brother is out of the undercover business. He's not very good at hiding his tells. But if he doesn't want to talk about his feelings, I'm not going to make him. Instead, I'll be a good sister and give him some alone time, so he can call the woman he so obviously wants to be with.*

"Well, it's been a long day." Cait stretched her arms over her head and faked a yawn. "I'm going up to bed. Goodnight, Mikey."

"Goodnight, Caitir." Ian smiled as she stood and walked upstairs to her bedroom.

Hopefully, reading a hot romance novel before going to sleep will help me dream about sex with Josh, instead of having nightmares again, like I did last night.

<div align="center">~~~</div>

Wednesday, April 10, 2019

Josh hated that he hadn't had the opportunity to clear the air with Cait before he had to leave town again. Everything just got so crazy the last couple of days that he hadn't been able to sneak any time alone with her to talk about why she seemed to be putting up a wall between them. Part of that was because he couldn't physically be in the same space with her while dealing with Charlotte's kidnappers and giving his statement about the events surrounding the rescue to a half dozen different divisions of law enforcement. But he knew the biggest problem was that he'd needed time to process everything that had happened and keep it compartmentalized in his brain, so Cait never

136

had to see the cold, calculated side of him that he only ever let out when he was on a mission.

He never wanted to dim the light inside her by sharing the darkness he had to live in to be able to do his job without regrets. Hell, he hated that some of his family members had witnessed how he was able to turn into a cold-blooded killer when he went into mission mode. Yeah, they'd all fired back whenever they were being shot at, but Josh knew he was the only one who'd intentionally aimed to kill with headshots.

Other than the HDPD, every agency he'd spoken with about his participation in this op had asked him why he didn't aim for center mass like the rest of the guys, the way they were all taught. He'd pointed out that he wasn't a law enforcement officer and explained that with his SEAL missions, he'd come across too many terrorists wearing either body armor or suicide bomb vests. Center mass shots weren't effective when fighting the war on terror, so the SEALs had to change their strategy for the use of lethal force.

After years as a SEAL, headshots were now ingrained in Josh to the point that he no longer played paintball wars with his friends and family because he found it hard to aim for anything else. The only reason he'd been able to go target shooting with Cait was because they were shooting at empty plastic bottles and cans, instead of shooting at human-shaped targets.

He just hoped that once he was out of the Navy and no longer needed to go into mission mode on a regular basis, he'd be able to retrain his brain to more recreational forms of shooting. *Fuck! Pop will think I've lost my mind if I go for headshots to run coyotes off the ranch before they can attack the herd.*

As he was packing the last of his things, Josh started coming up with a plan for how to banish that dark place he found inside his head when he went into mission mode. Unfortunately, he was afraid it would include some time with a therapist and not just setting up a target course for him to practice going back to center mass shots, so he'd one day be able to go play paintball with his brothers, cousins, and friends again.

But fuck, I'll happily go through hours and hours of therapy if it'll help me be the man Cait needs me to be. Maybe I should start it now, so I'll be completely ready to move us out of the friend zone in four-and-a-half months when my terminal leave starts.

Josh felt a little bad about not telling his family that he was getting out yet. He'd made all the arrangements with his commanding officer and was literally just biding his time until his squad left for deployment without him in August. But he knew anything could happen between now and then, so he didn't want them to get their hopes up about when he'd be coming home for good, only to dash them if things went sideways when his team was spun up for a short-term op before he was completely out.

Yeah, it'll be much better to surprise them when I come home for Labor Day and tell them I only have to go back to sign my discharge paperwork once my terminal leave is over.

With everything more settled in his head, he started carrying his bags down to his truck for the drive to the airport. Just as he stepped out the front door, he noticed Ian pulling out of the driveway after dropping off Cait and Brody. *Thank fuck! I didn't miss her completely.*

"Josh!" Brody hollered as he ran up to Josh, just as he stepped off the porch. "Where are you goin'?"

"Gotta go back to base, Bud," Josh smiled as he ruffled the kid's dark hair that he must have gotten from his mother, since it was so much darker than his dad's or even his Aunt Cait's. "But I'll be back in about two-and-a-half months for another visit."

"Can you stay long enough to see how good I am at ropin' fence posts?" Brody looked up at him hopefully as he pulled off his backpack and started digging around for the length of rope Josh had given him.

"I don't know," Josh grinned as Cait walked up to where he was standing with Brody. "Does your aunt have time to walk over to the paddocks with us before she has to start work?"

"For a few minutes," Cait agreed with a shy smile.

"Then let me put my bags in the truck, so we can go rope a few fence posts before I leave." Josh walked the short distance to his truck and placed his bags in the back before turning to look at Brody, who was trying to pass his backpack off to Cait. "Ya'll wanna leave your bags here too, so ya don't hafta carry 'em?"

"Yes, thank you." Cait walked over and set her purse down next to Josh's duffel, pulling her phone out of a side pocket and sticking it in the back pocket of her jeans, as Brody put his backpack beside Cait's purse.

Awesome! Now we can exchange numbers while watching Brody, so maybe I can get us back to a little flirting over text while I'm not here.

As Brody took off running ahead of them toward the paddocks, Cait placed her hand on Josh's forearm, which he took to mean she wanted him to walk with her so they could have a private moment to talk. "I wanted to thank you for what you did on Monday."

Yeah, that's not really what I wanna talk about with her. Josh wasn't sure how to respond to her thanks for doing the job he never wanted her to think about him doing. "Nobody needs to thank me for going to rescue my sister."

"While I'm elated that you got your sister out of that situation, that wasn't what I was thanking you for," Cait smiled up at him as they continued walking. "I was thanking you for killing Rojo, so I don't have to worry about him sending anyone from the cartel after me or my family anymore."

"What makes you think I'm the one who took him out and not one of the others?" Josh hoped Ian hadn't told his sister about how he'd let his dark side out during the raid of the cartel's compound.

"Because Ian told me last night that you were the lucky one who got to pull that trigger," Cait shrugged like it was no big deal.

"Yeah, I didn't pull that trigger," Josh laughed ruefully, unable to take the credit for the one kill he would have proudly claimed on Monday's mission if his brother hadn't insisted on trying to take the asshole alive. Though he probably wouldn't have ever told Cait about it, so she wouldn't see even a sliver of his dark side. "I was trying to disarm him, and he pulled the trigger himself, not realizing that I'd twisted the barrel of the gun back toward him in my attempt to take it out of his hand."

Cait shuddered as she came to a stop, just as they got to the backside of Charlotte and JJ's houses, and looked up at him with an expression of pure fear on her face. "Mikey didn't tell me how close it came to Rojo killing you instead of…" Her voice trailed off as she covered her mouth with her hand and started to sob.

Mikey? That must have been Ian's name before he changed it after his cover was blown.

"Hey, it's okay, Sunshine," Josh tried to console her, stepping up behind her and rubbing his hands over her shoulders, when she turned her back toward Brody so he wouldn't see her breaking down. "I was wearing body armor, so I'd have been fine even if I hadn't twisted the barrel away from me."

Fuck! Why did I think it would be better to tell her how close I came to being shot than to let her see how bad I wanted to shoot him in the head as soon as I breached that door?

Cait spun around and buried her face in his chest, wrapping her arms around his waist. "Next time you go on a mission like that, promise me you'll snipe the bastards instead of getting close enough they can shoot you."

The words were so unexpected coming from sweet, innocent Cait that Josh couldn't stop the bark of laughter that escaped him as he wrapped her in his arms. *Maybe she can handle that dark part of me that's okay with killing criminals and terrorists, after all.* "I'll be sure to tell my CO that I have new orders from home for how I'm allowed to participate in combat ops."

Before Josh could really enjoy his time holding Cait, Brody disrupted their moment by yelling, "Hey, are ya'll comin' to watch me ropin' or not?"

Cait pulled out of his arms and wiped the tears from her face as Josh hollered back, "Yeah, Bud, we're comin'."

Though not the way I'd really like to be comin' with Cait.

"I'm sorry, I got your shirt wet," Cait apologized unnecessarily, as they started walking toward the paddock once more.

"Aw, it's fine," Josh shrugged, running a hand over the small wet spot. "I doubt anyone will even notice, since a black t-shirt can't really get any darker when it's wet."

They stopped outside the fence and watched as Brody entered the paddock to start roping the fence posts on the opposite side from where they were standing. Josh was impressed with how well Brody was doing with only having about a week and a half of practice. They praised him profusely, wanting to encourage his continued safe practice of only roping fence posts in a space where he wasn't likely to hit anyone with the rope.

Josh felt like he'd reverted to his awkward pre-teen phase as he stood there trying to figure out how to ask Cait for her phone number, so he could text her while he was back on base. As he stood there thinking, he realized that he normally didn't have to ask for a woman's phone number. They usually gave them to him without him ever asking. And he normally trashed their numbers as soon as the hookup was over.

Even when he was in middle school and just starting to be interested in girls, they'd often passed him notes in school with their numbers. So, he couldn't remember ever having to ask for a number since he was twelve or thirteen and asked for one of his sisters' friend's number, when she visited the ranch for some kind of party they were having.

Damn! Has it really been fifteen years since I had to ask a girl for her number? It figures that when I finally want a woman's number, she's not aggressive enough to offer it up.

But Dad always said the right woman would be worth all the hard work a man had to do to win her heart. So, I'm sure asking for her number will be the easiest of the things I'll need to man up and do for us to have a future together.

While Josh was thinking about what to say as a segue to exchanging numbers with her, Cait pulled her phone out of her pocket and started taking pictures of Brody as he continued to rope fence posts.

Perfect! Josh thought as he sidestepped a little closer to Cait and nodded down at her phone. "Can I see that for a second?"

"Sure," Cait agreed and handed him her phone. "You going to brave getting closer to that wild cowpoke and get me some better pictures?"

"Naw, I'm not that brave," Josh chuckled as he adjusted the settings on her screen to take a selfie. He put his left arm around her shoulders as he extended his right arm with her phone to take a picture of the two of them together. "I'm gonna take a selfie of us and text it to myself to use as your contact photo in my phone."

Josh clicked the photo just as her jaw dropped in surprise at what he was doing.

"No, don't use that one," Cait protested as Josh pulled his arm back in to start sending the text. "Let me at least smile first before you take a picture of me."

"Well, then smile, Sunshine," Josh directed, extending his arm once more and waiting until they were both smiling up at the phone to take the next picture.

He then quickly sent both photos in a text message to his phone before saving his number in her contact list with the smiling photo. Josh grinned as he handed Cait her phone back. Then he turned and hopped the fence to go give Brody a few more roping tips before he had to leave to fly himself and Jake back to Virginia.

He knew he probably should have said something more to her to set up his plan for texting her over the next couple of months. But if he'd stood there beside her a moment longer, he'd have leaned over and kissed her. And he knew it was way too soon for that step in their relationship.

Fuck, maybe it's a good thing I've gotta go back to base today. Hopefully, I can keep resisting the urge to claim her as mine anytime I see her when I'm home on leave before I'm able to come home for good. Lord knows, hanging around her so much this time around has made waiting to get our timing right difficult.

But I guess I know it's the right course for us because my cock isn't the only thing hard.

Chapter Eight

Wednesday, April 24, 2019

Cait was still having a difficult time letting go of some of her irrational fears a little over two weeks after the cartel had been dealt with and Josh had killed the man responsible for the drive-by she'd been caught up in back in San Diego. Oh, Josh still refused to take the credit for shooting Roberto Rodriguez. But in Cait's opinion, Josh had heroically ended the cartel kingpin's reign of terror. Of course, Cait's opinion was based on having lived the first thirteen years of her life with a mom whose drug problem was fed by the cartel and being shot by the cartel while at her nephew's second birthday party in the park. Even if he didn't pull the trigger, knowing Josh had a hand on the gun when it discharged in the scuffle clearly caused her little crush on him to develop into a full-blown case of hero worship.

She had to wonder if he could tell how she was falling for him from the way their texts had gotten flirtier over the last week than they'd been the first week they started texting. She might still be scared to go out in public without her brother there to keep her safe, but knowing Josh could also protect her had clearly helped her get over any trepidation she had about possibly dating him.

Since he was just as flirtatious in his texts as she was, Cait had started to realize that maybe the attraction between them was mutual after all. She'd decided that his behavior during the time he was part of his brother's wedding party was an anomaly. He hadn't really been ignoring her, just doing his duty as a groomsman.

Once the distractions of the wedding and Charlotte's kidnapping had passed, he'd been right back to goofing around with her the same way he had the rest of the time he was home on leave. *Joshin' around,* Cait mentally corrected herself, loving how he claimed ownership of his playful personality. His playfulness and easy friendship had gone a long way to making her feel comfortable starting to come out of her shell while he was there with her. And his consistent praise via text had given her the confidence to feel more like her old self than she had in years.

Wow! Talk about taking baby steps, Cait mentally scoffed at herself. *Witty repartee in text is about the littlest baby step I can take to being back to my old self. And I'm not even sure I can count going off alone with him for target practice as a step, since we never left the ranch, where I already feel safe by myself.*

But if things keep going well over text, maybe next time he's in town, we can try going on a date. Even if we just go to dinner at the Burger Barn or Pistol Pete's Pizza, going out in public with someone other than my brother will be a major step for me.

And if I take that big a step in the right direction, maybe I'll get rewarded with a goodnight kiss from that cowboy hottie.

If Cait was truly being honest with herself, she'd admit that she wanted a lot more than a goodnight kiss from Josh. But even though he starred in all her dirtiest fantasies, she wasn't sure they could ever have anything more than a short-term fling during one of the times he was home on leave. But if she ever had a chance of trusting a man to take her out again, she was pretty sure Josh would be the first man she'd feel safe with to try it.

She was almost certain that she was more than half in love with him already. And more than a little afraid that giving in to her attraction for a short-term fling would cause her to fall so hopelessly in love with him that she'd never want to be with another man. It was situations like she currently found herself in that really made her miss her sister-in-law, whom she'd previously confided in, even when she didn't feel comfortable talking to her college friends.

Cait was starting to get some of the girl time she missed back, though, having grown more comfortable talking about sex and other women's issues with her new friends since moving to Heart's Destiny. It was kind of unavoidable when they all started talking about how hot the sex scenes were in the latest book they read. They'd also given her some great recommendations for the various vibrators she should look at on the It's My Pleasure website. She knew she could talk to any one of them about her feelings and get some excellent advice on how to deal with them.

Not that she would share how she felt about Josh with his sisters and cousins as they all gathered with their other girlfriends from town for a book club meeting at Becky, Jen, and Julie's place on the ranch. But she could have if her crush was on one of the Walkers or some other guy in town that wasn't one of their relatives.

As she walked in and took a seat on one of the sofas in the room she thought of as a family room, Cait realized that maybe she couldn't have talked about her feelings for any of the other guys in town because she didn't know the familial connections of any of the Burlesons' friends. *Yeah, I might have to stay quiet this time and take notes in my phone to keep track of which local men each of these ladies mention tonight,* she thought as she took a sip from her water bottle.

While this would be her first time attending a book club meeting, Cait had heard from her friends how they always seemed to compare the men they knew to the men in the books they were reading during their impromptu book discussions whenever they got to hang out together for any length of time. But since she couldn't see how Josh would have anything in common with the main characters in the books they were currently discussing, she hoped to avoid any mention of him during this get-together with her friends.

She assumed the rest of the ladies there would be respectful of Charlotte, Becky, Jen, and Julie by not mentioning any of the Burlesons during their discussion, which she hoped meant she wouldn't have to fight her jealousy at hearing one of the other ladies there talking about having a crush on Josh.

Her phone beeped, signaling an incoming text, so Cait pulled it out of her pocket to switch it to vibrate to keep from interrupting the meeting. When she saw Josh's name on the preview of the text at the top of her screen, she couldn't stop herself from opening it. *I'll just send him a quick reply to let him know that I'm not free to text yet tonight. Since everyone else is still getting drinks, I doubt they'll notice how I'm being rude by using my phone instead of socializing.*

Josh: Hey, Sunshine. How's it going?

Cait: Good, but I can't talk right now. I'm at a book club
meeting.

Josh: Book club? That group my sisters were talking
about? What book are you reading?

Cait: Yeah, that book club. And the current book is *"Lost
and Found"* by Lexi Blake. But I think we're going to
talk about how it ties into the rest of the series, too, &
not just that one book.

Josh: Are you talking about the dirty parts of the book?
{Kiss emoji} {Eggplant emoji} {Peach emoji}

Cait: {Blushing Face with Hand Over Mouth emoji}
Maybe? Or maybe we'll talk about how much hotter it
is to listen to the audiobook since the male lead has a
sexy Scottish accent.

Josh: Is it just foreign accents you're into, Sunshine? Or
does my Texas twang work on you, too?

Cait: Why do you want to know? Are you planning to
learn a sexy accent to get me all hot & bothered?

Josh: Only if I have to. {Smirking Face emoji} But I think
my normal accent might already work for you.

*Oh, you have no idea how much your Texas twang already makes
me want to drop my panties for you, Cowboy,* Cait thought, not
realizing her friends had noticed the faraway look on her face as she
texted. She quickly figured it out when Jen and Julie flanked her as
they sat down on the sofa with her.

"Who are you texting to get that dreamy look on your face?" Jen
leaned in from her right side, trying to look at her phone screen.

"That's got to be our cousin Josh, since Surfer Josh hasn't been in town recently for ya'll to exchange phone numbers," Julie pointed out from her left side.

Cait shot off a quick text to explain why she wasn't continuing the flirtatious conversation.

Cait: Gotta go. Book club is starting.

"Sorry," Cait apologized as she switched her phone to vibrate, stuffing it in her bag as she got out her Kindle in case she needed to reference one of the books during the meeting. "He's been texting to check on me every few days since the whole cartel thing. And when I went to turn my ringer off for the meeting, I figured I'd better let him know why I wouldn't be replying for a bit, so he wouldn't get worried."

She'd already told her friends about being shot in the cartel drive-by and how Charlotte's kidnapping and subsequent rescue had brought back some unpleasant flashbacks and nightmares, so she thought they'd buy her concerned-friend excuse for why she was texting Josh.

"Yeah? If he was just checking to make sure you're not still having nightmares, then why were ya'll talking about sexy accents and whether his gets you hot and bothered?" Cait looked over at Julie in shock, surprised that her friend had been able to read that much of the text conversation before she'd been able to switch screens.

"Your cousin Josh's accent gets me hot and bothered," Ashley Myers giggled from her chair to Julie's left, fanning herself as if just thinking about Josh was heating her up.

"Yeah, but you know we don't stand a chance with any of the Burleson boys," Heather Deere commented as she took her seat and rolled her eyes at her friend before turning to look directly at Cait. "But Cait might have a chance with him. Did ya'll have that love-at-first-sight feeling the first time you met him?"

Cait had only briefly been introduced to Brooklyn's friends back at Brook and Bobby's wedding, so she didn't know them well enough to feel comfortable talking to them about her instant attraction to Josh from the first moment she saw him. Luckily, with so many women in attendance, one of the others quickly filled the silence, so she didn't have to reply to Heather's question.

"Josh doesn't need to fall in love to get in a girl's panties," Kayla Scott chuckled as she plopped into a chair on the other side of the room. "At least, he didn't on prom night. But that was nine years ago. I suppose he could've outgrown his man-whore years since then."

Did she just admit to sleeping with Josh on prom night? Cait felt like she might need to leave to keep her jealousy in check if they kept up this topic of conversation.

"Gross," Becky exclaimed, acting like she was gagging as she squeezed onto the opposite sofa between Brooklyn and Amy Lawton, Justin Burleson's girlfriend. "Can we, please, not talk about my brother getting in anyone's panties? I'd rather not lose my appetite before the pizza gets here."

"We were just trying to find out if Cait and Josh are the next to fall victim to the plotting of the Matchmaking Mommas," Jen informed everyone in the room. "But we definitely don't want any of the dirty details about our brothers or cousins."

"But that pretty much puts all the hot guys in town on the do-not-discuss list," Lexi Wilder pouted, crossing her arms over her chest and elbowing Cassidy Reilly beside her in the process. "Since they're all related to at least one person in this room."

"Oh, crap, we can't even discuss how Ian Campbell compares to Ian Taggart now that his sister has joined us," Sierra Sadler interjected, slumping in her seat. "And I was looking forward to grilling Charlotte about how accurate the size description was when Big Tag was at the nudist resort in *Lost Hearts*."

Cait remembered the scene in question and how she'd wondered how Josh would compare to all the dicks that were described. But when she realized that every woman there thought her brother looked like Ian Taggart and several were wondering if his dick was as big as the book character's dick was described, she felt more than a little nauseous. *Thankfully, I didn't realize the similarities between my brother and Ian Taggart before I read* **Love and Let Die**, *or I might not have been able to get through it. And I will definitely be calling my brother Mikey again from now on.*

"I don't think I want any pizza now," Cait choked out, covering her mouth, and pretending she might puke.

"Don't worry, Cait," Cassidy consoled her with a placid smile from across the room. "I don't think Char's gonna give us any more details about Ian's magic peen."

"Ya'll got all the details you're gonna get on Valentine's Day," Charlotte glared in Sierra and Cassidy's direction before turning her stare at Kayla. "And I don't want to know how my brothers or cousins compare to the dicks described at the nudist resort in Bliss, either. Well, not unless it's the one that went into hiding."

Char gave them details about Mikey's "magic peen" on Valentine's Day? First of all, gross! I don't even want to think about Mikey having that body part, much less know how and when Charlotte's seen it. Second of all, I guess they've gotten closer than I thought. I mean, I knew they were friendlier than Char wants her mom to know, but I didn't realize they'd gone past friendship way before I even realized they were friends.

Yeah, I don't think I'll ask Char for tips on getting Josh's attention after all. Not only would it be as weird for her to discuss my attraction to her brother as it would be for me to discuss her carnal knowledge of my brother's junk, but I also know I'm not ready to move as fast as they seem to be. So, I wouldn't want to act on any of her tips that might push us past the flirtation we've been doing this week.

"Oh, that scene was so funny," Becky chuckled, pulling Cait back into the conversation. "I seriously hope we can work a deal with Lexi Blake to make her books into movies, just so I can figure out how to put that scene in the film and not go over an R rating."

Cait wasn't sure how she planned on not going over an R rating while making films about BDSM romance novels, but she was intrigued by the prospect. *But I suppose, if the production company that made* **Fifty Shades of Grey** *could do it, then so can Becky and her team.*

Maybe if I can get to the point where I feel safe going back to school, I can find a college nearby that has a master's in screenwriting similar to what I was doing in San Diego? Or maybe a school that has the program online, so I can finish my degree, even if I can't ever completely get over my fear of leaving my safe spaces alone?

If I can get back into something like that, I'm sure I'd enjoy the challenge of helping Becky convert our favorite books to movies. And

Leah Mae Wright

I might even be able to work up to going to her office without being scared out of my mind.

Cait let her mind wander to the possibilities of movie scenes as the ladies around her placed their pizza order and discussed the storylines that carried over from Lexi Blake's other series into the ***Masters and Mercenaries: The Forgotten*** series they were currently reading. Since she hadn't read the ***Nights in Bliss*** series or the fantasy series the ladies mentioned yet, she couldn't comment on the characters from those series that the other ladies were talking about.

It wasn't until they mentioned Josh again that what they were saying even registered in her head. "I'm sorry, Becky. I was still picturing how you're going to make all these scenes work on the big screen and missed that. Can you please repeat it?"

"I said I don't buy Tucker as an evil doctor any more than I would believe it if someone told me they'd wiped Josh's memory and turned him evil," Becky repeated. "I think once their memory was wiped, they'd revert to type. So, if Dr. McDonald tried wiping Josh's memory, he'd still be the easygoing, jokester of our family. So, Tucker was probably just as kindhearted before she wiped him as he is once he was rescued."

"Oh, yeah, I completely agree with you," Cait nodded, focusing her reply on the book character instead of how Becky used her brother as an example. "And with the way they can't find any record of him other than Rebecca's memories of Dr. Reasor, I think he might have been an undercover agent of some type, trying to bring down Dr. McDonald."

"That's gotta be it," Jen agreed. "I just hope Lexi doesn't leave us hanging through all the other Lost Boys books to tell Tucker's story."

"I think I'd be more devastated if she makes him the traitor who fooled us all with his nice guy act," Amy interjected. "Than if I have to wait a couple of years for her to write the other four Lost Boys books and she leaves his story for last."

The ladies all agreed that there was no way Tucker could be the traitor before moving on to how badass the women were portrayed in all of Lexi's books. As Brooklyn discussed how hard it was to write strong female characters when she didn't feel as tough and independent as she wanted her characters to be, Cait thought about the lessons she could learn from the female leads in her favorite books.

Oh, she had no desire to be a badass female operative or heroic doctor out to save the world like a lot of Lexi Blake's characters. But maybe she could take some of the lessons they learned in the course of their stories and apply them to her life.

"Does anyone else see something of themselves in some of these book characters?" Cait held up her Kindle as if it held all the answers to her problems, while the ladies around her looked at her in confusion. "Rebecca Walsh went on a two-year sexual sabbatical and hid in her lab to avoid living her life. I pretty much did the same thing after being shot, only I hid in my brother's house and then here on the ranch when he moved us here. But by the end of the book, she's embracing her sexuality and facing the challenges of living her life. I want to figure out the mental process she had to go through, so I can quit hiding and start living my life again. Though I'd rather not almost die again to get to the next chapter of my life."

"But you're open to meeting your soulmate, so he can push you outside your comfort zone?" Kenzie Martin arched an eyebrow at Cait.

"I mean, if he comes along and is as hunky as a book boyfriend, I wouldn't be opposed to meeting the right man," Cait shrugged, trying to cover her thoughts about Josh possibly being that man already. "But I don't think a man is required for me to push myself to make a few changes. In fact, I should probably deal with a few issues on my own now, so I can be ready for him when Mr. Right does come along."

"Oh, absolutely, you can't wait for him to come along and fix whatever issues you're dealing with…" Charlotte agreed before she was interrupted.

"Wait, you were shot? When was this? And why haven't I heard about it?" Sierra questioned, looking at Cait with a shocked expression.

"Yeah, at Brody's second birthday party," Cait admitted, surprised that her friends hadn't already shared her story, considering how gossipy their small town was. "In the same drive-by when my sister-in-law was killed."

"With the amount of drive-bys they have in California, it's no wonder you didn't feel safe leaving the house after that," Kayla commiserated. "But you don't have to worry about that here. Even San Antonio isn't big enough to have that kind of random violence."

"Oh, it wasn't random," Cait corrected Kayla's mistaken impression. "Mikey, ur, Ian was the primary target of the cartel because his cover was blown. And we moved here for him to track down the leader of the same cartel because they moved here after the DEA raided their compound between San Diego and Tijuana."

"And I'm sure that same cartel kidnapping me a couple of weeks ago has brought up your bad memories as much as it did Ian's." Charlotte gave Cait a sympathetic smile before everyone who wasn't in the know started inundating her with questions about the kidnapping.

"Why don't we go replace that bottle of water with a glass of wine?" Julie whispered her suggestion to Cait as Char recapped the events of the kidnapping and rescue for their friends.

"That's the best idea I've heard all night," Cait agreed, getting up to go to the kitchen with Julie and Jen for a little liquid courage to get through the rest of the meeting.

As soon as the three of them were alone, Julie grabbed another wine glass and motioned back and forth between the open bottles on the counter for Cait to pick which she wanted while her twin started the interrogation. "Now that it's just us, spill. What's really going on between you and Josh?"

Knowing she couldn't get out of confiding in her friends, Cait pointed at the white wine she knew was the sweetest and confessed, "I've been attracted to Josh since the first time I saw him. But when he killed the evil overlord that ordered the hit on my brother that resulted in me being shot, too, my little crush exploded into a full-blown case of hero worship. But a couple of friendly hugs and a few flirty texts are all that's really happened between us."

"We were kinda preoccupied at Christmas and didn't see the sparks flying when ya'll saw each other the first time," Julie admitted hesitantly as she handed Cait her glass of wine.

"You were preoccupied with Dion at Christmas," Jen corrected her sister, shaking her head and smiling mischievously. "But I was sitting right next to Josh, and I couldn't get his attention to ask him a question as soon as Cait sat down. With his head turned away from me, I couldn't see his eyes to know for sure, but I'm betting he felt the lightning bolt our parents told us about feeling when meeting *The One*."

"No," Cait disagreed, downing more than half the wine in her glass as she remembered the strange feeling she had every time her eyes met Josh's during that first encounter with him. *Surely, he wasn't trying to tell me he felt that lightning bolt for me when he mentioned it while everyone was talking about how the Burlesons fall in love at first sight. Was he?*

"Yes," Jen argued with a wide smile.

"Even if he didn't feel it at Christmas, I saw it on Josh's face whenever he looked at you while he was home a couple of weeks ago," Julie claimed, also smiling as brightly as her sister. "Ya'll are destined to be soulmates."

"Oh, yeah, definite soulmates," Jen agreed with her twin.

"Maybe there was some mutual attraction, but there weren't any lightning bolts," she lied, not wanting to get her hopes up that the twins were right about her and Josh being soulmates. *And I really don't want to examine the way he looked at me while talking about lightning striking when Burlesons met their soulmates. I'm sure I'm just looking back through rose-colored glasses and imagining his look meant more than it actually did because the twins just put that idea in my head.* "Besides, it can't really be more than a long-distance flirtation or maybe a brief fling when he's home on leave."

"Oh, you might have the same bad timing I'm having with Dion," Julie nodded as she refilled all their wine glasses. "But Josh won't be in the Navy forever. So, do like I'm doing with Dion and enjoy the long-distance-friends-with-bennies phase of the relationship for now."

"I still can't believe you're willing to settle for only seeing him a few times a year," Jen sighed, shaking her head at Julie. "I'd be too worried about what kind of diseases he could get from all the women throwing themselves at the wrestlers while they're on the road all the time."

"That's because you didn't feel the same connection with Liam that I did with Dion," Julie shrugged. "When it's the real deal, you trust your partner not to cheat." She paused long enough to take a sip of her wine before adding, "And Skyping with him every night when we can't get our schedules to match up to be in the same city makes it really easy to trust him."

"I'm sure surprising him in his hotel room whenever the GWA is in a city we have a subsidiary where you can go work for a day keeps him on his best behavior, too," Jen giggled, pointing at Julie.

"Only if you consider kinky his best behavior," Julie grinned, wagging her eyebrows suggestively. "He is the best I've ever had in bed if that counts."

"Now you're just bragging because you got laid this week," Jen pouted, rolling her eyes at Julie.

"You should've come with me to Austin on Monday," Julie shrugged, just as the doorbell rang. "I'm sure one of the guys woulda helped you out."

Luckily, they were called back to the family room as the pizza arrived, so Cait was able to escape the awkward conversation about Julie trying to help her sister hook up with one of the GWA wrestlers. Since Julie had only told Jen, Becky, and Cait about her booty calls with Dion, the subject was dropped completely by the time they were back in the middle of the meeting with the rest of the women.

Cait was also glad that everyone seemed to have dropped any curiosity they had about her and Josh as the meeting went on. She knew she'd have to talk to Becky at some point about the things she'd discussed with Jen and Julie, but that could wait until it was just the four of them.

And maybe, since he's her brother, she'll have a better idea of how Josh feels about me than the twins. Until I hear it from him or someone closer to him than his cousins, I'm not going to believe he wants to be more than my flirty friend. There's no point in getting my hopes up, just to have them dashed if he's not really interested in me.

~~~

Sunday, April 28, 2019

Josh stared at his computer screen, feeling completely dumbfounded by the results of the DNA test he'd sent in the month before while he was at home in Heart's Destiny. He'd only been joking with his brother about one of them being switched at birth and not related in any way, so he didn't think he'd come across any surprises when he
~~~

looked at his DNA match list. And when he looked at how much DNA he shared with Jake, he wasn't surprised to see they shared forty-nine percent of their DNA. In fact, all of his siblings were in the immediate family category and shared between forty-seven and forty-nine percent of his DNA. Below that, he saw the close family category where his Uncle Jon, Aunt Maggie, and all his first cousins appeared, just as he'd expected. No, what he found confusing about his DNA match list was the extra person listed in the parent-child category that shared fifty percent of his DNA, just like his mom and dad.

"Holy fuck! This has to be some kind of mistake. Like maybe I'm a triplet, not a twin, and there was some kind of mix-up in the hospital when we were born. And I just share a little more DNA with the other triplet than I do with Jake." Josh tried to talk himself into believing the convoluted story he was crafting in his mind, not wanting to acknowledge the possibility of one of his random hookups resulting in a child he didn't know anything about.

He picked up his phone, thinking he'd call Jake and have him hack into the website to find out more about this mystery match. But then he decided he'd better check with Charlotte first to see what she'd learned in all the research she'd been doing on the family tree and with the DNA match lists of the rest of the family since her birthday back in January.

"Surely, she checked out a match this close to us when she was going through the match lists to find our fourth cousins. Triple J has to be showing up a lot higher than the Avingtons on her match list, too." He swiped through the screens to pull her up in his contact list before hitting the green button to connect the call.

"Hey, Josh," Char answered, sounding cheerful. Josh hoped that was because she had no residual effects from being kidnapped just a few weeks ago. "What's up?"

"Hey, Char," Josh sighed, unsure how to ask his sister about his unknown DNA match in a tactful way. "So, I, uh, got my DNA results."

"Yeah?" Charlotte sounded curious about why he was calling to tell her that he'd gotten the results.

"Yeah, and I'm confused about some things," he admitted, wishing he'd called Jake first.

"Okay," Char drawled the word out, clearly trying to prompt him to tell her more.

"I, uh, have an extra match in the parent-child category that I don't recognize."

"Seriously?" Charlotte screeched, blasting his eardrum to the point that he pulled the phone from his ear and put her on speaker.

"Yeah, I'm serious," Josh confirmed, placing his phone on the desk beside his laptop. "And I was hoping you might have looked at the same person on your match list to be able to tell me how we're related to them."

"Yeah, give me a minute to get my computer and I'll look at it on my account."

"Here, use mine." Josh wasn't a hundred percent certain, but he thought that was Ian's voice he heard in the background.

Guess they aren't trying to hide their attraction to one another from Ma any longer.

"Thanks." Charlotte was back to sounding happy, making Josh wonder just how far along his sister was in her relationship with Cait's brother.

Damn. I guess things are moving a lot faster for them than anyone back home has mentioned when I've talked to them since coming back to base.

"You have to authorize me to look at your DNA matches, so I can see the one you're talking about." Charlotte's statement kept Josh from thinking about how his sister's relationship with Ian would affect his potential future with Cait.

"How do I do that?" Josh had decent computer skills, but he'd left all the mundane details of computer tasks to his brother, who practically lived with one glued to his hands. He could probably figure out how to give his sister access to his account on the DNA website if he wanted to dig around on there, but it was a lot faster to just let her walk him through the steps, so he could do it while they were on the phone.

Josh dutifully followed Charlotte's directions to give her authorization to look at his DNA test results. Once he was done with that, he clicked back to his DNA match list and listened to the clicking of keys as Charlotte apparently did the same on her end.

"Um, Josh, this looks like you have a kid out there you don't know about," Charlotte sputtered, sounding as shocked as he'd been when he first saw the extra fifty-percent match.

"You sure it isn't another brother? Like maybe Jake and I aren't twins, but triplets with one of us being stolen at birth? I thought maybe that could be the case since we were born in the hospital in San Antonio and Jake comes the closest to fifty percent of his DNA matching mine." Josh hated how frantic he sounded as he laid out his theory.

"I mean, I suppose that could be possible," Charlotte hesitantly agreed. "Let me look for this Triple J on my match list and see how much DNA I share with him to see if we have enough shared DNA to be siblings."

Josh fidgeted impatiently as he heard Charlotte clicking on her computer once more. *Fuck! Please let her share almost as much DNA with Triple J as I do.*

"I only share twenty-eight percent of my DNA with Triple J," Charlotte informed him. "And this says there's a hundred percent chance that he is either my grandparent, grandchild, half-sibling, aunt or uncle, or niece or nephew. So, it looks to me like someone has put her child's DNA up on here and you're coming up as the baby's daddy."

"Fuck," Josh groaned, wishing he'd met Cait back when he was in BUD/S, so he would have quit sleeping around years ago instead of just a few months ago.

How the hell am I supposed to tell her I have a kid I don't even know? Will she even want to be a stepmom to my kid?

Hell, for that matter, how am I supposed to find out about the woman who put up the child's profile, so I can step up and be its dad? Josh looked back at the profile to see the blue icon in place of a picture. *To be his dad. Fuck, I have a son. And now that I know about him, I'm damn sure gonna be the man my boy deserves for a dad. The best, just like my dad's always been.*

"How am I supposed to find the kid to step up, when all she's listed on his profile is a username, which doesn't identify either of them in any way, and that they joined the site and last signed in on it last month?"

"I guess you have to hope you have enough information on your profile that she can identify you and reach out," Charlotte advised. "Maybe send them a message on the site to let them know you want to step up and give them your phone number to contact you, so they know how whenever they sign in on the site again."

"Yeah, okay, I can do that," Josh sighed, wishing his baby momma had at least listed a phone number on the profile. "Any idea how I should word this message?"

"Be nice. Don't go into too much detail about how you want to step up, so she doesn't think you're going to try to take her baby away from her or take over her life," Char suggested. "Maybe say that you're surprised to find out you might be a dad and give her your number to call you, so ya'll can talk about getting to know one another."

"Do you think I should tell her about me?" Josh wondered aloud, thinking maybe a few details about him might help his son's mother recognize him from when they met and conceived a child. "Like maybe to break the ice and get her to tell me a little about herself, so I can try to remember when we might have hooked up?"

"Maybe a little?" Charlotte sounded skeptical about how much he should share. "But maybe ask more about the baby instead, so she doesn't get her hopes up about being more than co-parents with you."

"Oh, yeah, good point," Josh agreed, clicking on the message button on the site to start drafting a message. "How about this? 'Hi, I just saw my DNA match list for the first time and was surprised to see that I might be Triple J's dad. I'd love to get to know more about him and talk to you about how I can be a part of his life. Please give me a call at 830-555-5674.' Is that too short? Or enough info for now?"

"That's probably enough information for now," Charlotte agreed. "Ya'll can exchange more when she calls you."

"Thanks, Char. And, um, maybe don't mention this to anyone else in the family until I find out more about the baby." While Josh planned on calling Jake as soon as he got off the phone with Charlotte, he didn't want to be inundated with calls from everyone else in his family when he didn't have anything to share with them yet. He also didn't want a lecture from his dad about how he'd screwed up by having a kid he hadn't planned on ahead of time.

Josh was meticulous about always wearing a condom, so he knew there was nothing more he could have done to prevent an unplanned pregnancy other than never having sex. And while he had no desire to be with anyone but Cait now that he'd met her, his younger self had been too much of a horndog to have followed the abstinence plan for the last thirteen years. *Hell, until I met Cait, I don't think I went thirteen days without hookin' up with someone except when I was deployed. And once I went off to college, I know it was at least once a week that I swapped out fuck buddies, except when my duties with the Navy made it impossible to go out that often.*

"Don't worry," Char reassured him. "I won't say a word to anyone."

As soon as they said their goodbyes and disconnected the call, Josh swiped his phone screen to dial his twin. Before he sent the message he'd drafted while on the phone with Charlotte, he wanted to see if Jake could find out anything from the profile on the DNA site. *Like maybe an email address or phone number that can lead to a physical address. This is something that really needs to be done in person, not in an impersonal message on this website.*

"Hey, Bro, what's up?" Jake answered after only one ring.

"I'm in need of your superior cyber-sleuthing skills," Josh blurted instead of a greeting. "Is there any way you can hack the DNA website to get me info on one of my DNA matches that's not listed on his profile?"

"Maybe?" Jake didn't sound as confident as he usually did when it came to the things he could do with a computer.

Josh assumed Jake's caution with hacking in the last couple of years was because he was under more scrutiny since moving from the Little Creek base, where he'd previously been stationed while working with the SEAL teams, up to Alexandria, Virginia, where he commuted into Washington, D.C. to work in the National Maritime Intelligence Center.

"I know you don't like hacking if it's not part of your job, but this site shows I have a son out there that I don't know how to find," Josh explained with a desperate, pleading quality to his voice that he'd never heard before.

"Holy shit! Yeah, give me a second to see what I can find for you." Jake's reaction was pretty much exactly what Josh expected from his twin. Momentary shock, followed immediately by buckling down to take care of business. "What's the username on the profile?"

"Triple J," Josh told Jake as the phone line filled with the sounds of Jake clicking away on his computer.

After several minutes of silence other than the noises Jake was making with his keyboard, he finally sighed, "All I can find is an anonymous email address from a free service. With a little time, I can possibly determine the city where the email address was set up. I wouldn't trust anything I could find that might be closer than that, though. If they did put a name and physical address on the email account when they set it up, I doubt it's legit, since they didn't put anything identifiable on their DNA profiles. Since those services don't require a physical address or even proof of identity, we might lose the trail if they used an IP address at say a public library instead of their home to set up the email."

"So, even you might not be able to find my son?" Josh hated the thought of not being able to track down his child.

"I'm gonna do everything I can," Jake sighed. "But it's not that hard to remain anonymous online by using burner phones and public Wi-Fi. And if the mom wants to track you down and check you out first, you know to make sure she didn't sleep with some jackass who might abuse her or the baby, then she could easily take those precautions to keep you from being able to find her before she's ready to make contact."

"So, I should go ahead and send this message on the DNA site to give her my contact information?" Josh wondered if he should give her more information about him to make it easier for her, if she was trying to check him out before telling him about his son. "Char suggested I keep my first message to a bare minimum, but I can't help but wonder if I should tell her a little more about me, so she'll know she can trust me with our child."

"Yeah, I agree with you, just make sure you don't give her so much information that you scare her off," Jake advised.

"Yeah, Char was trying to keep me from making it seem like I wanna take over her life or something," Josh chuckled. "But I'm worried that if I make it clear that I only want to co-parent with her too early on, then she won't return my message at all. I'm ashamed to admit it now, but the women I was with the last few years have all been frog hogs. And I'm sure more than one of them would use having my child as a means to land a husband simply because I'm a SEAL."

"And you aren't interested in marrying anyone but Cait," Jake continued his train of thought.

"Exactly," Josh agreed. "But I don't want to miss out on my son's life just because I don't want to marry his mom."

"So, don't mention exactly what you do in the Navy," Jake suggested, sounding completely nonchalant about the whole thing. "Maybe talk more about growing up on the ranch and having a big family that will welcome both of them with open arms. Just don't mention how Ma might start trying to play matchmaker as soon as she meets your baby's momma."

"Definitely not," Josh chuckled.

"How is this gonna affect your plans for getting closer to Cait every time we're home on leave?"

"I don't know," Josh admitted. "We've been flirting a little via text the past couple of weeks, but maybe I should back off on that and keep us firmly in the friend zone until I get everything settled with my son and his mother."

"Damn, sorry, Bro," Jake uttered apologetically. "I know how much you want to have more with her. But maybe it's better if you slow things down, so she has time to really heal from the trauma she's been through the past few years before you try to push her out of her comfort zone. Besides, you don't want to overwhelm her by asking her to help you transition into being a dad when she's not the kid's mom."

Since Josh hadn't told his brother about his plans to leave the Navy in a few months, he couldn't really explain that he wasn't planning on pushing Cait to move in with him on base once they started dating. But even if he had informed his brother about his plan to slowly help Cait get over her fear of going out in public by taking her on dates once he moved back home to the ranch, Josh couldn't argue with Jake about not wanting to overwhelm her with the changes coming in his life.

They talked for a few more minutes before Josh hung up the phone and rewrote the message he'd started drafting to the mother of his child.

To: Triple J

From: Josh Burleson

Hi, I just saw my DNA match list for the first time and was surprised to see that I share 50% of my DNA with Triple J. I'd love to get to know more about him and talk to you about how I can be a part of his life.

I don't know how much we might have talked the night we were together, or how much you might remember about me. But to refresh your memory and hopefully make you feel more comfortable talking to me about our child, I thought I'd tell you a little about me.

I'm 6'4", between 225 and 230 pounds, depending on whether I've been doing more cardio or more weight training the week before I step on a scale. I have medium brown hair and hazel eyes.

I'm currently in the Navy, but looking forward to moving back to the ranch where I grew up in Heart's Destiny, Texas, when my time is up in September. I haven't told my family about that yet, so please don't mention it to them if you meet them before then. ;)

I come from a big family, who are all going to be thrilled to meet you and our son. I'm a twin, and my brother and I are the middle two of six kids. I'm older than Jake by 3 minutes, so I have an older brother, an older sister, two younger brothers, and a younger sister. Of the six of us, they'll all tell you that I'm the jokester. But I promise my joshin' around is never malicious. I

just like to make the people I care about smile as
much as possible.

Hopefully, I'll get to add you and our son to that list
of people in the near future.

Please give me a call at 830-555-5674. I look
forward to hearing from you.

Josh

Josh read over the message a couple of times to make sure he was happy with it before clicking his mouse over the send icon. As he sat there watching his screen and hoping for an instant reply to his message, Josh's phone beeped with an incoming text message. He looked down and saw Cait's name beside their selfie as the preview of the message flashed momentarily on his screen. He was torn about whether or not he should read it and reply.

On the one hand, he knew it would be rude to ignore the message completely. That would set them a lot farther back in their friendship than he wanted. But on the other hand, he knew he couldn't keep up the flirty texts they'd been sharing for the last week without moving them out of the friend zone.

"Maybe it won't be a flirty text, so I can reply but keep it friendly instead of lacing the reply with innuendo," Josh hoped as he swiped across his phone screen to open the text message.

The first thing he saw when he opened the message was a sexy selfie of Cait in a low-cut top. He was so focused on the swell of her breasts that he didn't even notice the background of where she'd taken the pic. His cock instantly responded to the sight of her creamy flesh on display, engorging to the point that it almost escaped the top of his sweatpants.

"Fuck," Josh groaned, wishing he could reply to the message, but knowing nothing he'd say would be appropriate for them just being friends. "I hope she pulled her top down just to take this picture and covered those glorious tits back up before anyone else saw her."

He had to tear his eyes away from the image to read her message, hoping he could come up with a friendly reply to the text portion of the message without mentioning the photo.

**Cait: Just heard a funny story about you, your brothers, &
cousins naming certain body parts while swimming in
this creek. So I had to sneak down here for a moment
to send you a pic as inspiration for helping me name a
couple of mine.**

"Fuck," Josh moaned, drawing the word out to multiple syllables.
"I definitely can't reply to that message and keep us in the friend
zone."

He closed the message without replying. "Hopefully, she'll send
me a joke or something in the next couple of days and it won't be a big
deal that I didn't reply this time."

Chapter Nine

Cait's mood had progressively plummeted lower and lower each day that went by without a return text from Josh. She'd thought their flirty banter and innuendo-laced comments meant he returned her attraction and wanted to add a few benefits to their friendship. But since he ghosted her as soon as she tried to lead them into the shallow end of the sexting pool, she realized that she'd greatly misunderstood the meaning behind his side of their conversations.

Why on earth did I think it was a good idea to send him a picture of my cleavage and ask him to help me name my boobs?

She'd known taking a moment to herself by the creek and pulling her v-neck t-shirt down in front to reveal more of her assets than she normally showed off to take the selfie to send to Josh was a mistake within a millisecond of hitting send on her phone. Seeing the pic on her screen as it was sent, she noticed the scar just above her collarbone was just as noticeable as the valley between her breasts.

Seeing that scar again obviously killed any attraction he might have had to me.

Yes, she knew Josh had seen the scar before and didn't act like it was a big deal. But she wasn't sure how close of a look he got at it since he primarily looked her in the eyes whenever they were talking.

Come to think of it, he always seems to look at my face and not at my body. I thought it was a Burleson trait to show their respect for women, since none of them look anywhere but at a woman's face, unless the Burleson man in question is looking at his wife or girlfriend.

Since Josh never let his eyes stray from my face, except for the brief glances when I showed him my scars, he obviously has no plans for us to be more than friends. So, I really stepped over the line by sending him that picture and trying to be flirty.

"Cait, are you in here?" Becky's voice calling out through Charlotte's house where Cait was currently working brought her out of the downward spiral in her head.

"Kitchen," Cait called back as she continued to put away the dishes from the load she'd run in the dishwasher earlier that day.

"Hey, are you almost done here for today?" Becky bounded into the room. She was a ball of energy and looked to be too excited to be able to sit still for more than a second.

"Yeah, this is my last task here before I'm supposed to go help Susan set up for Jen and Julie's party tonight." Cait wasn't really in the mood for a birthday party, but she plastered on a fake smile for her friend, not wanting to bring down anyone else's mood.

"Excellent, then you can help me wrap Antonio's presents," Becky beamed, her smile so bright it was almost blinding. "We're combining Jen and Julie's birthday party with Antonio's Gotcha Day party."

Antonio was a little boy that Charlotte had been working with at the shelter where she volunteered in San Antonio. He was among the hostages that were rescued from the cartel the day Charlotte was kidnapped. Charlotte wanted to foster and possibly adopt him after the ordeal, but the Department of Family and Children's Services had blocked her every effort to check on him.

Apparently, when they were moving the previous weekend, Kay mentioned something about her and Anthony's plans to adopt a little boy as soon as they found an orphan named Antonio because that was the name of the little boy Anthony saw in his dreams about his future family. When Charlotte heard the little boy's name that her brother and sister-in-law planned to adopt, she told them about the little boy, whom she knew needed a home.

Thanks to the foundation that they'd started, Brooklyn and Bobby were able to help Kay and Anthony with all the red tape they had to go through to be able to go see Antonio and start the process of fostering and possibly adopting him. They had a hearing scheduled earlier in the day to see if it would be possible for them to move forward, but Cait hadn't heard how the hearing had gone, since none of the Burlesons who had gone to the courthouse had returned home just yet.

"So, the hearing went in their favor, I assume?" Cait shut the dishwasher after putting away the last of the dishes.

"Yes, they have temporary custody for now and should be able to finalize the adoption in six months," Becky proclaimed, bouncing with excitement. "So now we're scrambling to make sure he has plenty of clothes and toys and everything he needs for his first night in his new home. Kay gave us his clothing sizes, so I picked up a few clothing items here in town. Mom and Dad are picking up some of the stuff we can't get here while they're in Hondo. Same with the cousins who are still in San Antonio. And Char is meeting up with Ian to get age-appropriate toys. Since Antonio is just a few months older than Brody, we all figured he'd be the one to know the latest and greatest toys that boys their age will like."

"If Antonio's into the same things as Brody, then you might want to get him some of the same rope that Josh gave Brody last month," Cait pointed out as she watched through the window as her nephew continuously practiced roping fence posts. "That's kept him interested longer than any of the toys he got for his birthday and Christmas."

Becky looked out the window at Brody and chuckled. "Yeah, Mom's already pointed out that Brody and Antonio are both at the age my brothers were when they were more interested in building forts out of the boxes than playing with the toys that came in them."

"Yeah, that sounds about right," Cait agreed with a more real smile, remembering how Brody had done something similar with the boxes for his action figures to destroy at Christmas. "Where are we meeting to wrap all this stuff?"

"Mom and Dad's, since that's where the party's gonna be," Becky informed her.

Cait double-checked that everything was in its proper place and grabbed her purse to head out of Charlotte's house. "Give me a minute to round up our little cowpoke, and I'll meet you over there."

"I'll be in the family room, up to my eyeballs in wrapping paper," Becky grinned as she headed for the front door while Cait went to the back to get Brody.

Once she got Brody washed up from his time outside and set up at the kitchen table with a snack, Cait joined Becky in the Burlesons' family room to wrap presents. She quickly shot off a text to her brother to pick up something for Antonio from her before grabbing a roll of wrapping paper and getting started on the stack of boxes Becky had prepared.

"Texting Josh?" Becky teasingly arched an eyebrow at Cait as she took a seat after putting her phone in her purse.

"No," Cait sighed as her momentary reprieve from thinking about how she'd screwed things up with him ended. "I think I bungled any chance I had at more than friendship with him last weekend."

"How?" Becky looked over at her with a shocked expression. "Last I heard ya'll were all flirty and well on your way to long-distance lover status. Not that I want to hear any of the details about that with my brother, but it seemed like ya'll were both happy with one another."

"After that conversation with Brook, Kay, and Amy when we heard about how your brothers and cousins named their junk while swimming in the creek by Kay and Anthony's house," Cait confessed, feeling herself flush with embarrassment as she confided in her friend. "I took a little walk down there while everyone else was leaving. I then sent Josh a selfie with the creek in the background and my shirt pulled down to reveal my cleavage and asked him for ideas on names for the girls."

"Oh, gawd," Becky cackled with laughter. "I can't even imagine the crazy names Josh would come up with. So, what did he reply?"

"That's just it," Cait shrugged as she pulled off a piece of tape to adhere the wrapping paper to the box she was wrapping. "He didn't reply. I haven't heard back from him all week, not even when I texted to apologize for the inappropriate text."

"That doesn't sound like Josh." Becky's face screwed up in a confused expression. "He's normally really good about replying to texts. Maybe he's off on a mission and hasn't had a chance to even see your message?"

"Yeah, I'm sure he immediately replies to your messages with no problem, but you're not sending him stuff like that." Cait didn't mention how Josh had promised to tell her if he was spun up for a short-term mission and would be unreachable, so she wouldn't worry about him if he didn't reply to a message.

"True," Becky chuckled, then cringed as if thinking about sexting her brother. She shook her whole body as if shaking off the icky thoughts. "But with how Josh was acting with you the last time he was home, I doubt he's intentionally ghosting you. When Dad gets home, I'll ask him if either of the twins have told him about being incommunicado for a bit. He's usually the one they keep updated with their whereabouts, even when it's classified, and they're not supposed to tell anyone."

"How was Josh acting with me the last time he was home?" Cait couldn't think of anything he'd done or said during his time on leave that made her feel like he treated her any differently than any of his other friends or family members.

"He was constantly maneuvering to sit next to you at every meal," Becky chortled and rolled her eyes at Cait when she opened her mouth to object. "And he stared at your butt anytime you had your back turned to him."

"He did not," Cait protested, picking up a stack of precut ribbons and tossing them at Becky.

"He did too," Becky giggled as she batted away the ribbons raining down on her. Once they all landed, she quickly gathered them up and tossed them back at Cait. "I thought it was gross at first because he's my brother and shouldn't be perving on anyone like that. But I decided not to pick on him about it because I didn't want to screw up my chances of having you as a sister-in-law one of these days."

"Whatever," Cait reciprocated the eye roll as she pulled one of the ribbons from her hair and stacked them back up neatly. "I think the closest we'll get to that is if my brother marries your sister."

"Oh yeah, those two are awfully cozy lately," Becky nodded in agreement. "But I'm still hoping for an even trade. When Char becomes a Campbell, you need to become a Burleson."

"Sorry, Becky, I don't think that's going to work out the way you want it to." *No matter how much I might want it even more than you do.* "Now let's change the subject, so I can get in a party mood, instead of being bummed about messing up my chance of having that delicious piece of man candy."

"Yes, definitely time to change the subject," Becky agreed while making a gagging motion with her mouth. "If only to keep you from referring to my brother like that again."

Cait couldn't help but giggle at Becky's mortified expression. The laughter helped her put Josh and his recent lack of communication out of her mind, so she could enjoy the rest of the evening celebrating with her friends. Her nephew running into the room wanting to help them wrap presents also distracted her from her otherwise constant thoughts of Josh.

"Who are we wrapping these for?" Brody held up a pair of jeans from the stack of clothes that Becky was boxing up that looked pretty close to his size. "They won't fit Aunt Jen or Aunt Julie."

With Tia and Maria being on the ranch for the past couple of weeks since their parents were off work in preparation for when Kay would have their baby brother, Brody had picked up their habit of calling all the adults on the ranch by the same aunt or uncle monikers that the girls used. Well, except for Char. Cait had to wonder if Brody recognized what was going on between his father and Charlotte, and secretly hoped to call her Mom one day.

"No, these are for Tia and Maria's new brother, Antonio," Becky explained as she handed Brody the bottom half of the box she'd just filled with an outfit for him to put the lid on and hand it over to Cait.

"Their new brother's name is Sam," Brody corrected, shaking his head at Becky.

"The baby in Kay's belly is Sam," Cait clarified for her nephew. "But the little boy they're adopting is Antonio."

Brody still looked confused as he put the lid on the next box and stacked it up for Cait to wrap.

"And since they get to bring him home with them from court today," Becky added. "We're combining Jen and Julie's birthday party with his Gotcha Day party."

"What's a *got-choo* party?" Brody's little brow furrowed in even more confusion.

"Gotcha Day," Cait corrected as Becky giggled at the way Brody made the word sound like a sneeze. "It's like an extra birthday party for kids who are adopted to welcome them into their new family."

"What's 'dopted?"

Cait really wished her brother was there to answer his son's questions. But since he wasn't, she knew she had to push through and try to give the boy an explanation that he would understand, without having to know all the atrocities that Antonio had probably faced to get to the point of being adopted by the Burlesons.

"It's when kids who don't have parents anymore get new ones." Cait looked at Becky, hoping her friend might have an idea for how to explain it better.

"So, I can 'dopt a new mom since mine's in heaven?"

"Adopt," Cait corrected. "And technically, if your dad gets married again, his new wife could adopt you to become your mom."

"Just like Anthony adopted Tia and Maria to become their dad," Becky added. "And now Anthony and Kay are adopting Antonio because he needed both a mom and a dad."

"How big is Antonio?" Brody carefully pronounced the other little boy's name for the first time, looking at Cait to make sure he said it correctly.

"He's a few months older than you," Cait informed her nephew with a smile. "So, I'm sure you guys will have a lot of fun together."

"But don't be upset if it takes a little while before Antonio wants to play with you," Becky warned, placing a comforting hand on Brody's arm after handing him the last box. "He's really shy and doesn't talk very much when he first meets new people. And he's probably gonna be scared meeting so many new people all at once at the party."

After living for who knows how long with the cartel, Cait assumed Antonio being shy and unsure around new people was to be expected. And probably the least of the issues he might have developed in response to the trauma he'd been through in his young life.

"It's okay, Aunt Becky." Brody returned Becky's comforting gesture by patting the hand she still had on his arm and showed how he was wise beyond his years. "I remember how scary it was to meet everyone at Christmas. I'll be nice to my new cousin like Maria and Tia were with me when ya'll welcomed me into your family."

Cait had to wonder if Brody's four-year-old way of thinking led him to believe the Christmas party they'd attended when they first moved to Texas was also his Gotcha Day party, after the way she'd just described what they were doing for Antonio. She didn't get the opportunity to clarify his understanding, however, because Hazel and Bob returned home with several more bags of things they needed to wrap to prepare for the party.

Yeah, I should probably let Mikey handle the rest of Brody's questions about adoption anyway. Cait grinned, thinking about how her brother might react to her trying to explain the discussion she'd just had with Brody. *Yeah, I won't tell him my suspicions about how Brody might have misunderstood this conversation, and let him figure it out on his own when Brody finally gets to the point where he starts calling Charlotte his mom.*

~~~

Friday, May 10, 2019

Josh couldn't believe it had been almost two weeks since he first sent a message to the mother of his child, and he hadn't heard anything back from her. He also couldn't believe he'd held out on texting Cait just as long. But with the whole baby revelation shaking up his life, Josh didn't feel like he could devote his attention to Cait the way she deserved. So, he felt stuck in limbo, unsure how to move forward with her, while waiting to find out how he was going to have to rearrange his future plans to include his son in his life.

As he sat in the local sports bar with most of his platoon, Josh wished Asher was back from officer candidate school, so he could ask for his advice on how else to search for his son and his son's mother. He would have talked to the other lieutenant in his platoon, since he was about their age and had started talking about wanting to settle down, but Tucker Holt wasn't at the bar that night for some reason.

Not that he really thought either of them would be able to help him any more than his brother already had in finding out where his son lived. Jake had traced the location, where the email address associated with the Triple J profile on the DNA site had been created, to an IP address in a public library in Alexandria, Virginia. Unfortunately, that didn't narrow down the search as much as Josh had hoped, since the person opening that email account could be any one of the approximately seven-hundred-thousand people who visited the Alexandria library each year.

Josh had tried to remember all the women he'd hooked up with during the time period between nine and eleven months before the Triple J profile was created, thinking that might help Jake in searching online to see if any of them were now in the Alexandria area. But Jake had pointed out that the baby might not have been born within the
~~~

same month that the mother submitted his DNA to the site to make him realize that there was no way to narrow down the time frame when he slept with the boy's mom the way he'd hoped.

Josh then tried to remember every hookup he'd had while visiting Jake in Alexandria since he moved there in 2017. Again, he assumed the mother had to live in the Alexandria area, so it seemed reasonable to think he'd met her while he was visiting his brother there. Of course, Jake had to shoot down that theory as well, reminding Josh that she could have met him anywhere since he first started having sex and only moved to Alexandria recently. Or that she could live in one of the other suburbs of Washington, D.C., and intentionally went to Alexandria to set up the accounts to throw him off the trail because she feared her child's father wasn't as upstanding as the Burlesons were raised to be.

Now he was at a loss as to what else he could do to find his son. And he was starting to feel desperate to find the boy because he couldn't, in good conscience, continue with his plan to pursue Cait until he had a handle on the situation with his child and his child's mother.

Fuck! It would be a disaster if I start a relationship with Cait and then this woman blindsides her with my child. And even if I tell her what I've found on the DNA site to give her some forewarning about the possibility of me finding my son, I'm sure she'll feel displaced in my life while I'm trying to work out custody and visitation with his mother.

I know she wouldn't have any reason to be jealous of the time I'll have to spend with my child's mom to be able to see him, but I also know how hard it can be for a woman to believe that in a brand-new relationship. And if the worst-case scenario happens and the woman ends up being the type to try to bag a SEAL or after the Burleson fortune, then I'm sure she'll do something to intentionally put a wedge between me and Cait. And there's no fuckin' way I wanna risk Cait being hurt like that.

"Yo, Cowboy, why you growlin' at your beer?" King nodded at the mostly full beer sitting in front of Josh. "Did it have the audacity to get hot while you were sittin' there starin' at it instead of drinkin' it?"

"Naw, the beer didn't do anything wrong," Josh chuckled before taking a big swig of the warm brew.

"Then what's got you in a mood tonight?" Prez lifted his chin in Josh's direction. "Normally by now, you'd be three beers in and coming up with the best ways to prank the new guy."

"You know the new guy joining the team when I leave and Smasher moves up is just transferring from another team, right? 'Cause they can't send someone straight out of training on deployment with ya'll."

"Yeah, but we still need to make him feel welcomed properly to our team," Regan grinned. "And we can't do that if our fearless leader is too grumpy to give us some good ideas before bailing on us. So, tell us what the problem is, so we can either fix it or kick its ass. And then you can help us come up with a brilliant idea for how to welcome the new guy to our team."

Josh wasn't sure the guys sitting with him were mature enough to give him any advice on handling fatherhood, and he doubted they'd have any better ideas for tracking down his child than Jake had already tried. But he figured if he could trust them to have his back during an op, then he could trust them with the news of his surprise son.

"Ya'll know my whole family did the DNA thing to track down our relatives," Josh started after choking down the last of his warm beer and motioning for the waitress to bring him another.

"Yeah, you said they found some cousins and solved a long-time family mystery with that," Kalua nodded, leaning in to hear the story over the noise of the bar from the other end of the table.

"Yeah," Josh confirmed. "Last time I was home, I sent in my sample, not thinking there'd be any big surprises, since most of the family had already got their results by then."

"Oh shit!" Regan's eyes went wide as he stared at Josh. "You found something bad in your DNA, didn't you?"

"Oh, I found something," Josh chuckled self-deprecatingly. "But I don't think it's necessarily a bad thing." He took a deep breath and slowly let it out before confiding in his friends. "I found out I have a son, which I actually think is pretty great news. But since I can't find anything but a bare-bones profile on the DNA site that doesn't give me his name, age, or any other identifying information, I have no idea how to find him to step up and be his dad. And his mom isn't responding to the message I sent her on the site, so I'm kinda stuck in limbo with no idea what I'm gonna hafta do to be a part of his life. And now I'm kinda worried that I won't be able to move home to go after my girl because I'm gonna hafta stay in Virginia to try to find my son first."

"You sure he's in Virginia?" Jayden tilted his head in thought as he examined Josh, like he was trying to figure out how to give him bad news or something.

"Whoever set up the email address and profile on the DNA site was in Alexandria, Virginia, back in March," Josh informed them. "Jake was at least able to figure that out by tracing the IP address where they were set up. But they used a computer at the public library, so he hasn't been able to get any more information than that. And yes, before you ask, he did go to the library and try to get the computer sign-up sheets for that day, but apparently, they don't keep them."

"Seriously, they don't record computer usage in their main computer?" Regan looked surprised.

"Nope, it's a paper sign-up sheet," Josh confirmed. "And apparently, they log how many people used the computers at the end of each day and then shred the sign-up sheet."

Josh had also been surprised when Jake told him how old-school the system was for using library computers. While the users had to have a library card to be allowed to sign-up to use them, the library didn't even keep track of computer usage on the patron's account because computers weren't checked out like library books.

"So, whatcha gonna do if she doesn't reply?" Mudslide interjected, appearing concerned. "Alexandria's too big a city for us to go on a weekend recon mission and have any chance at finding your kid or his mom."

"Hell, if she hasn't changed that much from the time we slept together, then that might be more effective than Jake's suggestion of putting together a list of all the women I've ever hooked up with, so he can try to track 'em down online," Josh chuckled to keep from groaning about the impossible task his brother had suggested. He was really starting to regret how much casual sex he'd had over the years. "At least I might recognize anyone I've previously fucked, even though I don't remember most of their names."

"Could be worse," King smirked, imitating the Elvis lip curl.

Josh wasn't sure how the situation could be worse, but he looked at Jayden as he waited for him to finish his gibe.

"You could be more like Smasher and not even ask their names. Or more like Shades and blindfold 'em, so you won't recognize the woman if you do eventually find her."

"Hey, I'll still recognize the women I've topped," Oakley scoffed, flipping off King from his seat at the opposite end of the table from Jayden. "I might hafta have some of them open their mouth real wide and picture my cock between her lips to be sure, but I'd recognize every one of them."

"Damn, our squad should really be renamed the Navy Sluts," Beef quipped as he picked up his soda.

Josh momentarily thought about admonishing Ty for using the derogatory term. But when he looked around the table at the men his sisters would most likely label as man-whores, he had to admit that they'd all been promiscuous enough over the years for the term to be considered an accurate description.

Damn, I really wish I'd met Cait years ago, so I wouldn't have to lump myself in with the rest of the Navy Sluts.

"So, are we Slut Team Two or SEAL Team Slut?" Pie queried, sparking a debate among the rest of the men.

"I highly doubt any of us would be able to get laid if we started calling ourselves either of those," Prez pointed out, making Josh laugh at the ridiculousness of his teammates.

"Now that you've got Cowboy laughing again, how about we get back to what we can do to find his son?" Kalua interrupted the team-name conversation to get them back on topic.

"I say we get Cowboy's mom to send us a bunch of his baby pictures and go check out the parks in Alexandria tomorrow morning to see if we can find a kid that looks like him," Lane suggested, showing how naïve he still was at nineteen.

Hopefully, turning twenty next month will help him grow out of some of that, so he's not too ill prepared when he hits the sandbox on deployment in August.

"Damn, Pie, you trying to get us all arrested for acting like pedophiles?" King reached over and slapped Pie on the back of the head.

"I'm not saying we should act creepy toward the kids." Lane rubbed a hand over the back of his head. "But if we find a kid that looks like it could be his, then we can narrow down the women Cowboy has to check out to see if he recognizes his baby momma."

"No," Josh barked, his voice taking on the commanding tone he normally reserved for when he was out in the field with his squad. "We're not doing recon at parks or anyplace else where kids and families might hang out to try to find my son. Being arrested for stalking kids is a surefire way to guarantee I'd never get to see him. I'll just keep trying to come up with a list of names for my brother to research."

"How are you supposed to remember that many names?" Ty skeptically arched an eyebrow at Josh.

"For real," Pie nodded in agreement with Beef. "That's gotta be a huge number of women to remember."

"At least fifty or sixty a year," Shades smirked. "And as old as you are, you've probably been bagging the babes for at least ten years."

"Damn, I'd hate to try to remember all the names of the women I've hooked up with just since high school, and I'm pretty sure I'm still in the double digits." Beef shook his head. "I can't imagine having to remember five or six hundred over a decade."

Josh wasn't about to correct their count by admitting that he'd been hooking up at least once a week with a different woman from the time he turned fifteen until he met Cait just after Christmas, with his only dry spells coming when he was deployed or spun up for a short-term op. The count of women he'd been with during that additional almost three years would probably be double what Beef estimated his total count to be. *Fuck! I'm probably close to eight or nine hundred hookups over the course of my life. I really was a slut before I met Cait.*

"Yeah, well, if we don't have any luck with that by the time I go home at the end of next month, I'll tell my dad what's going on and ask his advice."

"You haven't told your dad about having a kid?" Oakley might have been the one to pose the question, but it was clear to Josh from their expressions that everyone else at the table wanted the answer just as much.

"No, I figured my folks need to hear that kind of news in person," Josh admitted. "Other than ya'll, I've only told Jake and Char. And the only reasons I called to tell them were because I thought they might be able to help me find him and know what I should say to get my son's mom to let me be a part of his life. And they've both been sworn to secrecy until I figure out what's going on with my son and his mother."

Josh tried not to worry about what Ian might have overheard when he called Charlotte while still in shock after seeing his DNA match list the first time. *Fuck! I hope he understood not to say anything to anyone. Cait's gonna need to hear the news from me, not her brother.*

As the guys brainstormed a bunch of bad ideas for how Josh could find his son and his son's mother, he continued to brood. Between his worry about Ian having said something to Cait about his son and his inability to figure out what to text her since the day he found out he was a father, Josh feared his chance of having a meaningful relationship with Cait was FUBAR — fucked up beyond all recognition.

And there's not a damn thing I can do about it with fifteen-hundred miles between us. I can try apologizing next time I see her in person. But I don't know that it'll do much good if I can't find my son and settle things with his mother before then. But maybe, if I come up with a good enough excuse for not texting her, then I might be able to salvage the friendship. And maybe that will be enough to one day earn me another chance with her.

Chapter Ten

Josh felt like he was barely trudging through life after two months without any progress in finding his son or having any kind of communication with Cait. He knew he must have looked like a zombie as he sat through the second quarter board meeting, only paying attention to how his dad voted to place his vote on the various acquisitions his cousins had suggested. He was too worked up about how he was going to handle seeing Cait again to pay enough attention in the meeting to even know what had been discussed. Josh was so caught up in his inner turmoil that he only realized the meeting was over when everyone else started getting up from the table.

"Hey, Josh, gimmie a ride back to the ranch," his father insisted, slapping Josh on the back as they walked out of the conference room. "I rode in with Jon this morning and I don't wanna wait around for an hour while he deals with paperwork in his office before headin' home."

Bob and Jon Burleson might be the co-CEOs of Burleson Incorporated, but it was no secret that Bob preferred the manual labor of running the ranch and let Jon handle as much of the "boring business stuff" in the office as possible. Oh, he still had plenty of paperwork to do to keep track of all the details of maintaining two thousand head of cattle on their family ranch and overseeing the beef production on a dozen other ranches around the state that they worked with to provide Burleson Beef to the masses. But Bob didn't mind so much when the paperwork included veterinary records, breeding, calving, and weaning schedules, and pasture rotations. Especially if he got to spend a good portion of his time actually working the land and interacting with the animals.

"Sure, Pop," Josh agreed, knowing his dad probably wanted the time alone with him because of seeing how unlike his normal self he was acting during the meeting.

Guess it's a good thing I planned on asking for his help while I'm home for the next couple of weeks. I just thought I'd be talking to him tomorrow while we're deworming and moving the calves ready to be weaned into their new pasture, not in my truck on the way home today.

They were both quiet on the ride down in the elevator with Anthony and his family. Josh was surprised that Kay and the kids had come to the board meeting with his youngest brother. Though he supposed he probably shouldn't be considering Kay looked like she'd swallowed a beach ball and could go into labor any second. Josh smiled, knowing his little brother probably wouldn't let her out of his sight now that they were within the last two weeks before her due date.

It was also nice to get to see how his new nephew, whom they'd adopted since Josh's last visit home, was settling into the family. Antonio wasn't nearly as reserved as his family had warned him to expect, talking a mile a minute with his sisters about their plans for when they got home. But then again, when Josh had met Antonio on the day the cartel was dealt with, the little boy was only shy and reserved with the first responders that Charlotte hadn't told him about previously. He was perfectly fine acting like a normal kid with Charlotte, Ian, Bobby, Jake, and Josh.

"I have to stop in the ladies' room again before we leave," Kay whispered to Anthony, barely loud enough for Josh to hear.

"Sam playing soccer with your bladder again?" Anthony smiled down at his petite wife, leaning over to rub a hand over her very pregnant belly.

"Bladder, kidneys, pretty much any organ he can reach to punch or kick," Kay giggled and grinned, covering Anthony's hand with hers to move it over to a different part of her protruding abdomen.

Fuck, I hope I get to share the whole pregnancy experience with Cait one of these days, Josh thought, smiling at his brother and sister-in-law as the elevator doors opened and the kids led the way out into the lobby.

Even though he regretted missing out on his son's birth, Josh was almost glad he hadn't been involved in his child's mother's life while she was pregnant. It might be selfish of him, but he wanted his only experiences with obstetrician visits and feeling his child moving while in utero to be with Cait.

And just like that, Josh was back to thinking about how he could smooth things over with Cait after not replying to her texts for the last two months. *Fuck! I don't want to lie to her and say I had to go dark on a mission and then wanted to apologize in person because of how long I was gone.*

But I don't want to tell her about finding out I'm a father yet, either. 'Cause if I do that, then I'll have to tell her how I'd planned to work us up to dating by the time I'm outta the Navy. And I don't think she's ready to hear all my plans for our future together. At least, not yet.

Not that I can really plan anything while I'm still in the dark about my son. Hell, I can't even guarantee I'll be able to move home in a few months like I originally planned. And she's not gonna wanna come with me if I have to move to wherever my kid lives to be able to see him regularly.

So, I'm just gonna hafta lie to her and tell her I forgot to warn her when I got spun up and then felt like I needed to apologize in person.

"Why don't you tell me what's runnin' through your head?" Bob brought his son back to the moment just as they got into Josh's truck for the drive to Heart's Destiny from the corporate headquarters in San Antonio. "So I can help you come up with a plan to deal with whatever's got you in such a grumpy mood."

"I'm trying to come up with a good excuse for why I quit texting Cait," Josh sighed, trying to figure out how to tell his dad about the son he couldn't find as he put on his seatbelt and started his truck. "And I can't tell her the real reason 'cause I haven't been able to resolve the situation yet."

"Yeah, you're gonna hafta quit talkin' in riddles and start makin' more sense for me to be able to help you, Son." Bob's tone was jovial, but his use of the word "Son" felt like a knife to Josh's heart.

He turned the truck back off and turned in his seat to face his dad as he talked to him. "So, after seeing me flirting with her the last time I was home, you probably figured out that I felt that bolt of lightning you always told me about the first time I saw Cait."

Bob nodded and smiled at his son, not needing to say a word to show he was following along as Josh spoke.

"Last time I was home, just before I headed back to base, we exchanged numbers and started texting. Things were moving along wonderfully, making me think we could really start dating when my minimum service commitment is up and I'm able to leave the Navy in September."

"You're planning to come home in September?" Bob's eyes widened in surprise as he blurted the question, which was a major departure from the stoic man Josh knew his dad to be.

"Yeah, Pop," Josh nodded, making his dad smile. "I talked to my CO back in January to start the process. I'll be on desk duty for a couple of weeks when the rest of my team deploys in August, and then be on terminal leave starting the first of September until all my leave time is used up. I'll have to go back at the end of September to sign all the final paperwork and pick up the last of my stuff before turning in my apartment keys, but I was plannin' on spendin' as much of that leave time as possible here in Texas to start pursuing Cait."

"Was plannin'?" Bob arched a curious eyebrow as he repeated the two most pertinent words in Josh's last sentence back to him. "You're not plannin' that now?"

"I don't know what I'm plannin' now," Josh confessed, shaking his head. He turned back to face forward before slamming his head into the headrest in frustration.

Bob didn't say a word as Josh took a moment to just breathe. He felt his heart racing as he opened his mouth to admit what he'd found in his DNA results two months ago, turning to face his dad once more so he could see his father's reaction. "I looked at my DNA results as soon as I got the email that they were ready and found out I have a son I didn't know about," Josh blurted, the words coming out so fast he wasn't sure he enunciated every syllable.

"I've been doing everything I can for the last two months to find him, but only know the email address and profile for him on the DNA site were set up at a library in Alexandria, Virginia. I've sent messages on the site, but haven't heard anything back. And to be honest, I'm not even sure they've been read, even though the profile shows it's been accessed since I sent the first one. I was planning on pulling Jake aside tonight to have him check again for me while we're both home and not busy at work to see if he can tell if my messages have been read or not."

"Okay," his dad drawled, his face blank, as if he didn't know how to respond to the bomb Josh had just dropped on him. "And now you think you're gonna hafta move to Alexandria to find your son and be a part of his life?"

"Yeah," Josh nodded. "That's the other thing I was gonna talk to Jake about tonight. You're the only one I've told about getting out of the Navy, so I was planning to break that news to him and ask if I can crash at his place while I'm there trying to find my son and settle things with his mom. I'm hoping I can work it out where I can bring the boy to Texas for our time together, so I can eventually move home. But without knowing if I'm gonna hafta buy a house there to be able to see my son, I can't keep flirting with Cait. That's why I couldn't reply to the sexy text she sent me the day I found out about him. And I don't know how to backtrack to just being friends with her after starting to steer us toward more."

"And you know she's at the house, so you're delaying driving us home until I tell you how to get out of the mess you've made for yourself?" Bob arched an eyebrow at his son as he pulled a handkerchief from his pocket and wiped the sweat off his forehead. "You know we can go in one of the other gates and have this talk on the tailgate while looking over the cows, right? She won't know you're there and we can at least have a little bit of a breeze while we figure things out."

"Sorry, Pop," Josh chuckled and turned back to the steering wheel to start his truck once more.

As soon as the engine came to life, Bob adjusted the air conditioning to cool off the cab while Josh backed out of the parking space and started the drive to the ranch.

"Before we try to figure out what you're gonna say to Cait, let's try to narrow things down on finding your son," Bob started as Josh drove. "How many times have you gone without protection?"

"Never," Josh replied, hoping to stave off a lecture from his dad. "And before you ask, no, I've never had a condom break either."

Even when it was just a quick hookup, I've always slowed down long enough to be careful putting them on. Josh barely stopped himself from voicing the thought, not wanting to discuss the casual relations he'd had in the past with his dad.

"Okay, so that means we need to narrow it down to women you've dated in Alexandria," his dad suggested, making Josh cringe at the word "dating" because he didn't think one-night stands really counted as dating. "Surely, there's not that many of them, right?"

"I've made a couple dozen trips up to see Jake since he moved there," Josh admitted. "And I've already given the names from those trips to Jake for him to try to track them down online." *Well, all the names I can remember, anyway. I probably shouldn't tell Pop that I only remember first names for most of them.* "None of them have panned out so far. But as he likes to point out to me, just because she opened the email and profile in Alexandria, it doesn't necessarily mean she lives there or that she lived there when we hooked up."

"So ya'll haven't been able to narrow down the list of potential mothers at all?"

Josh didn't have to take his eyes off the road to see his dad's face to know he was disappointed in him. The feeling was so strong in his father's voice that he almost felt suffocated by it.

"I can say she's not one of the girls I went to high school with," Josh offered, knowing that only decreased the list of possible baby mommas by about ten percent.

"No, with the way everyone gossips in Heart's Destiny, we'd have known about it a long time ago," Bob chuckled. "Even if she moved away to have the baby, your momma would've heard about it at one of the hen parties in town."

"True," Josh chuckled along with his dad, glad that he'd moved on from his disappointment to try to find some humor in the situation. "And I've spent the last two months trying to remember every other woman I've ever been with and sending their names to Jake. So, hopefully, he'll find her soon and then I can start getting to know my son."

"I don't wanna know how many names are on that list, do I?"

"Probably not," Josh admitted sheepishly. *And he really doesn't wanna know that I can't even remember half of them.*

"This is exactly why I tried to tell all you boys to wait until you met the right woman," Bob sighed. "But I suppose I shoulda expected something like this to happen. Hell, with four boys who didn't listen to my advice, I probably shoulda expected more than one grandbaby being found when we all sent in our DNA to that site."

"For real," Josh snorted. "Since Jake, Anthony, and I all learned our player behavior from Bobby, I'm kinda surprised he wasn't the one who found a kid he didn't know about."

"Naw, he always stuck with buckle bunnies before he met Brook," Bob disagreed, shaking his head. "With the rodeo coming through town so often, we'd have heard about any of his babies before they were born. Even though your ma quit going to the rodeo when ya'll quit competing, she's still friends with the other rodeo mommas in town. So, she woulda heard the gossip within a month of when the woman in question started showing."

Considering he didn't think his mom knew that Justin and Amy were expecting before they announced it almost two weeks ago, Josh wasn't so sure she would have heard about some random buckle bunny turning up pregnant and immediately gotten suspicious that one of her sons was the father. But he wasn't about to contradict his dad.

"Okay, well, it sounds like you and Jake are already doing all you can to find the boy," Bob stated, bringing the conversation back around to Josh's issues. "But if that's a very long list, maybe we should give it to Byron. We can pay one of the people on his cyber team to spend all their time working on it. And maybe they can find results faster than Jake can with him having to only work on it in his spare time."

"I wasn't planning on telling the rest of the family until I know more about my son," Josh sighed. "But you're probably right about the Avingtons being able to put someone on it full-time being faster than what Jake's been able to find in his limited free time."

"I'll talk to Byron about keeping it discreet until we know more," his dad assured him. "And I won't even tell your mother. Nobody would be able to find the boy if she knew and could spend all her time bugging them about their progress."

"I don't know," Josh grinned, teasing his dad. "Ma would probably be the most diligent about searching for her grandson. She might be the perfect person to tell to find him faster."

"Only if you want her to fix you up with your son's mother instead of Cait," Bob quipped, smiling mischievously.

"No!" Josh barked out his objection, not wanting to even think about the possibility of his mom trying to fix Cait up with anyone but him. "Cait's the only woman for me. And I'm the only guy for her."

"Then I guess we'd better figure out how to get the two of you together before your ma starts thinkin' you might have other options," Bob chuckled. "What's your plan for apologizing for not texting her?"

"I don't have one," Josh confessed. "I thought about telling her I was on a mission and didn't see her messages until I got back to base. And then I didn't want to apologize over text because it was so many weeks later that it really needed to be done in person. But since the only time I got spun up since I was home last was like three weeks after I stopped texting her, it would be a pretty blatant lie. And I don't want to lie to her either."

"You could just tell her that you had some things come up that you can't tell her about and couldn't give her the attention she deserves at the time," his dad suggested. "It's the truth, just without the details you're not ready to share with her yet. And also, something that you had to explain in person because of feeling guilty for not replying to her texts promptly."

"That's…" Josh trailed off, trying to think of the right word to use. "Perfect. Ya know, Pop, if you ever get to where you wanna retire from ridin' herd, you could probably make another fortune by writing a book with all the great advice you've given out over the years."

"I think I'll leave the writing to my daughters-in-law," Bob laughed. "Though I think they might be pulling your ma and sisters into their latest endeavor."

"Oh?" Josh was curious about what Kay and Brooklyn would write that they'd need to collaborate with the other women in the family about.

"Yeah," his dad scoffed. "They pulled out the photo albums, family journals, and a few boxes of old letters from the various attics on the ranch to use as reference material for a historical romance based on our ancestors. And I caught your ma talkin' to some of her friends about sharing their family stories, so they can make it into a whole series about the people who founded Heart's Destiny."

"I can't imagine Becky or Char wanting to read a book about Grandpa Jonah and Grandma Emma having sex." Josh cringed at the thought of any of his ancestors appearing in any of the books his Pappaw Jerry had called "bodice rippers" back in the day. "So, I doubt they're really helping Kay and Brook write their story."

"They've supposedly changed the names and only loosely based the first story on how Jonah and Emma met." Bob shook his head as Josh exited the highway in Heart's Destiny. "They even changed the name of the town to try to keep people from figuring out it's based on our area. But I'm sure as soon as they start describing the ranch, all the women in town will know exactly where it's set and who it's about. Especially if Becky turns the book they're planning to publish next month into a movie."

"Well, look on the bright side, Pop," Josh chuckled, planning to rile up his dad just a little. "Now you know our production company will be putting out a new series of westerns for you to enjoy. And you might even get to watch Becky make 'em on the ranch."

"Damn," Bob groaned, dropping his head back on the headrest. "We might have to have a talk with her about scouting out locations on the other side of the state. And we might need to go back and veto putting a movie screen in at the theater."

Josh couldn't stop laughing at the realization that they'd just voted that morning to add a movie screen at the Destiny Playhouse, so they had a local theater to release their movies in, instead of expecting their family, friends, and neighbors to drive to the next town over to watch them.

But I like the idea of being able to take Cait on a date in our local movie theater. He was so caught up thinking about making out with Cait in the back of the theater that he forgot to go in the back way on the ranch to avoid seeing her before he had his plan finalized for what to say about ghosting her for the last two months.

<p style="text-align:center">~~~</p>

Just as Cait finished up the last of her tasks for the day at Justin and Amy's house and started walking over to check in with Hazel to make sure she didn't need to do anything else before leaving, she saw a familiar blue truck pull into the driveway. *No, no, no! Why'd he have to show up just as I'm about to leave? Couldn't he have waited thirty more minutes to get here? Then I'd be off the ranch and able to safely avoid having to see him until Monday.*

She'd known he was coming home for the Burleson Incorporated board meeting that day and staying through the Independence Day holiday and the week after when his nephew was due to be born. That was why she'd parked the car that Mikey insisted she start driving to and from work at her girlfriends' house instead of at Hazel's where she knew Josh would be staying. She hadn't wanted to take a chance on him blocking her in and her not being able to avoid talking to him.

Even though he hadn't replied to her sexy selfie text or the text later that week apologizing for overstepping the boundaries of their friendship by sending the pic, she had a feeling he wasn't going to let her gracefully pretend it hadn't happened when they saw each other again. She was afraid he'd humiliate her by teasing her about acting like one of the Thirsty Threesome, the same way he'd teased his sister and cousins about chasing after the actors in the films the company had decided to start producing the last time he was home.

So, to avoid running into him as he parked and got out of his truck, Cait darted across the gravel road to walk behind Susan's house and the empty house that Kay and Anthony had moved out of a couple of months ago to go in the back door at Hazel's to check in. Since he'd parked in front, she assumed Josh would go in the front door and carry his things up to his room before going to the kitchen to let his mom know he was home. So, she thought she had plenty of time to check in with Hazel in the kitchen and sneak back out and over to her car without having to talk to him.

Unfortunately, when she finally made it the long way around the other houses on the ranch and stepped into the kitchen at Hazel's house, she realized she was wrong about what Josh would do first when he got home. He was standing in the kitchen, hugging his mother. And appeared completely oblivious to the havoc he was inflicting on Cait's senses of peace and contentment.

When it became obvious that he wasn't going to text her again after her shameful selfie, she'd tried to evict him from both her heart and her head. She'd forced herself to stop asking her friends if they'd heard from him and had successfully banished him from her fantasies while using the toys she'd ordered from It's My Pleasure. She hadn't managed to kick him out of her dreams when she was asleep, but while she was awake, she had full control of who she imagined pleasuring her.

Granted, her orgasms weren't nearly as good when she pictured being with one of the Hollywood Chrises that all her friends gushed over as they'd been when she fantasized about Josh. But none of her self-induced orgasms were worth the tears she'd shed after realizing that making love with Josh would only ever be a fantasy for her.

Just pretend he's not here, she told herself as Hazel finally released Josh from her embrace to notice Cait had entered the room. *Pretend he's Anthony or Bobby and be polite, like you would with one of them, instead of acting embarrassed for how badly you bungled being friends with him.*

"I just wanted to check and make sure you didn't need me for anything else before I head home," Cait finally muttered, looking directly at Hazel, and not acknowledging Josh in any way.

"Oh, no, I'm all good," Hazel assured her with a smile. "But are you sure you can't stay for dinner?"

"Sorry, I already have plans for the evening," Cait lied, hoping nobody would ask for specifics. *A hot bath and a good book count as plans, right? Maybe not as exciting as whatever I'm going to hear over dinner from Brody that he and Mikey did in San Antonio today, but I don't really need excitement in my life. A relaxing evening is just what I need right now.*

"Oh," Hazel gasped, looking surprised as she stepped over to give Cait a quick hug. "Well, don't let us keep you, then."

Cait returned the older woman's brief embrace, realizing how quickly she'd adjusted to how huggy all the women in the Burleson family were. *Not just the Burleson family,* she mentally corrected. *Every woman in Heart's Destiny seems to be huggy.*

"And I'll look forward to hearing all about your date on Monday," Hazel announced as they released their grasp on one another, her eyes gleaming with mischief as she smiled at Cait.

Oh! She's conniving to make Josh jealous. Cait grinned at the thought. *She might think it'll get him to make a move on me, but I'll gladly use her scheming as cover for how hurt I was by him ghosting me.*

"Now, Hazel, you know I don't kiss and tell," Cait teased, wiggling her eyebrows as she backed toward the door. "See you Monday."

Cait waved as she slipped outside, eager to escape the room where Josh was standing slack-jawed. As soon as the door shut behind her, she speed-walked to her car.

"Cait, wait," Josh called out, following her out of the house and not letting her get away without talking to him.

"Damn it," she hissed under her breath, wishing their eight-inch height difference didn't give him such an advantage in a foot race. She opened her car door and tossed her purse over to the passenger seat to give her time to school her features before turning to face him. "Sorry, I'm kind of in a hurry right now. But I'm sure we'll see each other sometime next week to be able to catch up or whatever."

"I won't take too much of your time tonight, I promise," Josh smiled as he leaned against her car. "I just wanted to apologize for not replying to your texts the last couple of months. I had some things come up that have taken all my focus. I wish I could have given you the attention you deserve to see where things could go between us, but it's just not possible right now. And I didn't know how to tell you that over text, especially when I wasn't in a good mental place at the time."

Josh smiled wryly before breaking eye contact and sheepishly looking down at the ground. "Besides, apologies really need to be done in person. So, I'm sorry I was an ass. I hope you can forgive me, and we can go back to being friends."

He wishes he could give me the attention I deserve? What the hell is that supposed to mean? That I'm some kind of attention whore who's too needy to fit into his busy schedule?

And what kind of mental place does he have to be in to send a text that says, "Sorry, I can't talk right now," or "Going on a mission. I'll text when I can," instead of just ignoring me altogether?

I understand that he can't tell me about classified information to be able to explain his mental state when something goes wrong. But that doesn't mean he can't show me the common courtesy of checking in once in a while, so I know he hasn't been killed on one of his missions. Cait fumed internally while trying to maintain a blank expression on her face, so Josh couldn't see the mix of hurt and anger she was currently feeling.

The way you've checked in with your friends in San Diego? The snarky voice Cait heard in her head sounded an awful lot like her college roommate, Tiana Karimova. They'd quickly become best friends when they had all the same classes during their first semester of college. So, when Mikey had started dating Mari, Caitir had moved to give the couple more privacy. Since Caitir had needed a roommate to cut her living expenses, Tiana had moved out of the dorms to split the apartment with her BFF.

Crap! I really can't be mad at him for doing the same thing to me that I've done to Tiana, and the rest of the girls we used to hang out with, since being shot. And since he seems to be pretending not to notice the inappropriateness of my sexting, I should probably let him off the hook for rejecting me, too.

"No apology necessary," Cait smiled at Josh as she planned to reach out to Tiana when she got home that night. *Since I don't have any of my contacts from my old phone, maybe I can find her on social media?* "I completely understand that you can't keep in touch while you're off defending our freedom. As far as I'm concerned, our friendship hasn't changed."

"Good, I hated thinking I'd screwed things up between us," Josh smiled at her, making the butterflies in her stomach start flapping their wings double-time. "So, you've got a date tonight? Does that mean you're more comfortable going out in public now?"

"Oh, no," Cait shook her head, starting to panic about not being able to keep up the ruse with Josh scrutinizing her. "It's just dinner and a DVD at the house."

That's not really a lie. I am cooking dinner when I get home and I'm sure Brody will want to watch **Toy Story** *for the billionth time before going to bed. Josh doesn't need to know that my "date" is with my brother and nephew.*

"But you are driving yourself now," Josh prodded, nodding down at her cute little Kia Rio. "That's a pretty big step that you didn't seem to want to take a couple of months ago."

"Yeah, but just to and from work," Cait admitted with a self-deprecating shrug. "And only because Mikey insisted, so he can do more with Brody over the summer."

"Mikey?" Josh arched an eyebrow. "You mean Ian?"

"Yeah," Cait chuckled, feeling silly for why she insisted on going back to using the nickname derived from her brother's first name. "He started using his middle name after his cover was blown with the cartel. But after you guys dealt with them, I figured it's safe to go back to what I've always called him. And after the girls pointed out his resemblance to one of my favorite book characters named Ian, I can't call him that anymore."

"Yeah, considering the kind of books ya'll read, I bet that was an uncomfortable comparison for you," Josh chuckled.

"To say the least," Cait agreed, giggling as she realized she could share the creepiness with Josh. "The really funny part is that in the book series, Ian's married to a woman named Charlotte. And before you ask, no, your sisters-in-law didn't write that book series."

"Yeah, I'm afraid to read the books my sisters-in-law have written," Josh admitted, shaking his head. "Though it was fun to pick on Pop about the movies my sister is planning to make from them, especially the one he mentioned earlier today about our ancestors."

"Are you talking about the **Heart's Desire** series?" Cait grinned, seeing her chance to needle Josh a little more. "I read an advanced reader copy of the first book they're publishing in a couple of weeks. I loved Jeremiah and Ella's story and can't wait to start helping them convert it into a screenplay."

"Jeremiah and Ella?" Josh arched an eyebrow.

"Yeah, they said they had to change the names for some reason," Cait shrugged, acting like she didn't understand why the Burlesons wouldn't want their third-great-grandparents' names used in a book inspired by how they met and named the town. "I think Kay did the same with her contemporary **Devine** series. Katrina and Anton from her first book, **Kissing Kat**, remind me an awful lot of her and Anthony. And the couple in the second book in that series, **Winning Rhonda**, reminds me of her sister Randi and her husband James, but in the book she calls them Rhonda and Jack."

"Yeah, now I really don't want to read my sisters-in-law's books," Josh cringed.

"Oh, but I didn't even tell you about all the secondary characters," Cait teased, unable to hide her grin as she revealed the name of the most interesting of the characters in Kay's contemporary romance series. "I think Jeff Brown, Anton's brother, might be based on you."

"Please tell me Kay hasn't written a book about Jeff Brown falling in love," Josh groaned, shaking his head.

"Not yet," Cait admitted with a grin. "She told us the other day that her next book is going to be about the oldest Brown brother, Ronnie. But I'm sure she'll get to Jeff's love story eventually."

"And you're going to help her convert all of them to screenplays, so my sister can make them into movies?" She couldn't tell if Josh was nauseous at the thought of his likeness being portrayed in a movie, or if he was happy for her to start using what she'd learned in the semester she'd completed toward her master's in screenwriting.

"That's the plan," Cait shrugged, not wanting to appear too excited about changing jobs sometime in the next month. "We haven't worked out all the details yet, so it's just something I'm doing in my spare time for now."

Cait didn't want to admit that she was dragging her feet on committing to a full-time screenwriter job until Becky agreed that she could work exclusively from home or on the Burleson ranch. She knew Becky was trying to help her get over her fear of going out in public by pushing for her to work from her office at the Destiny Playhouse, but she just didn't feel ready for that big of a step yet. Besides, her brother still needed her to watch Brody during the day until he was old enough to start school, so she couldn't commit to a typical work environment where she wouldn't be allowed to bring him with her for another couple of years. Not to mention the fact that Hazel would need some time to find her replacement for her current job.

"Well, please don't be upset if I'm only willing to watch the movies you work on that aren't based on my sisters-in-law's books," Josh smiled. "But know that I'm proud of you for taking that step to follow your dreams, even if I can't watch all your movies."

"Thanks," Cait nodded, wishing she didn't still feel a little awkward talking to him. "I've, uh, got to get going."

"Yeah, sorry for keeping you longer than I promised." Josh looked a little bummed as he pushed off of her car, so she could leave. "I guess I'll see you later. Have a good night."

"Yeah, you too," Cait returned the sentiment as she got in her car, wondering if their friendship would always feel as strained as it did right then.

~~~

Josh wasn't really in the mood to go to a bachelor party for his youngest brother's boss, Rick Robertson. But since he'd known the bride-to-be, Fiona Harrison, for as long as he could remember, he kinda felt obligated to at least make an appearance at their joint bachelor and bachelorette party, along with the rest of his generation of his family. Even his Avington cousins were at the party, since they were providing security for one of the women wrestlers who'd picked up a stalker. Josh had offered to back them up at the various wedding and holiday events if they needed it while he was in town, which was yet another reason he had to go to the party. He just hoped he'd be able to smile and be friendly if Cait showed up with her new boyfriend.

He hadn't been able to get any more information from his mom about Cait's date the night before. And his sisters and cousins had all been tight-lipped about who the poacher could be when he'd asked if they'd heard who the Matchmaking Mommas had started pushing together since he was home last.

He scanned the room as soon as he walked into Tully's Roadhouse, but didn't see Cait in the crowd of women filling up the front room. He stopped at the bar and ordered a beer from Leo Walker, thinking it was a good excuse to dawdle until it appeared everyone had arrived, so he could see if Cait brought a date to the party.

"You lookin' for someone in particular?" Leo prodded as he handed Josh a long neck. "Or just tryin' to decide which one of these lovely ladies you might wanna hook up with tonight?"

"Naw," Josh lied, not wanting to reveal his feelings for Cait to his childhood friend until he was actually free to act on them. "Just scoping out the place to be prepared in case my cousins need backup while working security for the GWA."

"Yeah, I heard we're supposed to be on the lookout for any strangers who might show up in town this week," Leo nodded toward the Avington Security guys at the end of the bar, letting Josh know that
~~~

the whole town was on alert for the stalker without mentioning any details.

"Well, since it looks like they've got the front room covered, I'll head on back to play a little pool with the guys." Josh paid for his beer and dropped his change in the tip jar before giving up on waiting to see Cait arrive and going to the back room. He knew he couldn't keep hanging around at the bar any longer without his friend figuring out his real reason for stopping there instead of going to the back and ordering his beer from the waitress like he normally did.

He made the rounds, saying hi to a few of his friends, whom he hadn't seen since the weekend of Bobby's wedding and a few he hadn't seen since Christmas or Thanksgiving when they'd all been in town for Anthony's wedding. He eventually ended up at a table with Ian, watching Jake and Aiden Walker playing a game of pool.

"I didn't realize you were here since I didn't see your sister in the front room when I got here." Josh tried to act nonchalant as he tried to coax Cait's whereabouts from her brother.

"No, she stayed home with Brody," Ian offered before taking a drink of his beer.

"Really? I thought the kids were all going to a lock-in at the church tonight." At least that's what he'd heard from his oldest niece earlier in the day. Tia was excited to get to spend some time with her GWA friends while they were in town for the week, since she was still home for a couple more months while Anthony and Kay were on paternity and maternity leave.

"I think that's mostly just the kids from out of town," Ian shrugged. "And since Antonio isn't going to be there, Brody didn't want to go."

"Yeah, Ma said those two are almost as inseparable as Jake and I were when we were kids," Josh chuckled. "I'm surprised she isn't babysitting both of them tonight."

"Oh, she offered. But I think Cait needed the excuse to be able to stay home tonight." Ian sighed, his expression turning troubled. "I don't know what I'm going to have to do to convince her it's safe for her to go out of her comfort zone again."

"I saw yesterday that you've at least got her driving to and from work," Josh pointed out, hoping Ian could see what a major accomplishment that was for her. "That's a pretty big step in the right direction."

"Yeah, but she only drives between our house and the ranch, and won't even take her car to the gas station without me with her," Ian huffed. "And I still have to be with her to get her to go to church or the B and B, though I don't have to stay right by her side the whole time we're at one of those two places anymore."

"What about other places?" Josh was curious about how often Ian was able to get her to go shopping like she'd mentioned in their last text conversation. "I know she said something about you taking her shopping a couple of months ago."

"Yeah, but I still have to be right by her side the whole time if we're anywhere but the ranch, church, or the B and B. And she won't go to anything outdoors unless it's on the ranch. I don't know how I'm going to convince her to go to the fireworks next week."

Josh hated what he was about to suggest, knowing it would kill him to see Cait with her new boyfriend. "Maybe she'll feel more comfortable if she has both you and her new boyfriend with her."

"What new boyfriend?" Ian looked confused at Josh's suggestion.

"She and Ma were talking about her date last night, so I assumed she had a new boyfriend." Josh held his hands up in surrender at the angry expression on Ian's face. "I guess the date didn't go well if you don't think they're serious enough for him to help her want to go to the fireworks."

"Cait didn't have a date last night," Ian denied the claim, shaking his head. "She watched Brody, so I could take Charlotte out."

"Really? She didn't have her date come over for dinner and a DVD while you were out?" *Holy fuck! Did she lie to me about her plans? Why would she do that?*

"Oh, she had dinner and watched a DVD last night, but the movie was **Toy Story**, and her only dinner companion was Brody," Ian assured him with a smirk.

"Huh, I guess I misunderstood," Josh shrugged, hoping Ian couldn't see how jealous he'd felt at the thought of Cait dating anyone but him. *Was that the plan? Trying to make me jealous by lying about a date?*

Or maybe she was trying to make me regret not texting her back after she sent me that sexy selfie? Fuck, it about killed me to think I was too late to make my move on her yesterday.

Or possibly she did it to cover up how much it hurt her when I didn't comment on how hot she looked in that pic.

Fuck! I bet that's it. She doesn't want me to know how she really feels about me because she thinks I was rejecting her. And I can't do anything more than be her friend, for now, to reassure her that the feelings between us are mutual.

"Maybe it'll help if I get my brothers and cousins to stick close too, so she knows we're all there with you to keep her safe?" *Even if she still feels like she needs an army of protectors to prevent another mass shooting like before, being able to go to the town square for fireworks will be a major step in helping her heal some of her mental wounds.*

"Maybe?" Ian bobbed his head from side to side like he was contemplating how having the whole Burleson family there to support Cait would help.

Cool. If he's able to convince her to come to the fireworks, I'll bring her a set of earplugs to keep the popping noises from bringing back bad memories.

"But I have to wonder why you're so interested in helping my sister start getting back out in the world." Ian examined Josh like he was looking for any slight sign that Josh had nefarious motives for getting close to Cait. "Because I would think you might have other things you need to deal with before you can show any kind of interest in my sister."

Fuck! I knew he heard my conversation with Char when I first asked her about my son's profile on the DNA site. But I'm sure as fuck not gonna talk about that with him while we're standing here in the middle of a bunch of the gossipiest guys I know.

"I like Cait," Josh shrugged, trying to act like it wasn't a big deal. "She's a nice girl who doesn't deserve to feel trapped by her fear because of what happened with the cartel."

Ian nodded and gave Josh a knowing smile.

Damn, he sees right through my cover of friendship and knows I'm attracted to his sister.

"And yeah, I've got a lot goin' on and can't consider a romantic relationship with anyone right now. But that doesn't mean I can't be a good friend and support her in healing from her past trauma. If you were having trouble going to outdoor events after being shot in a park, I'd offer to hang out with you to help you through that first time, too."

"Fine, I'll talk to Cait about sitting with you and your family at the fireworks," Ian conceded, his smile going flat as he closely examined

Josh. "But only because I think it'll be good for my sister to start going out again, and I know she feels safe with you after what happened with Rojo."

Josh nodded as Ian paused to take a drink of his beer, not wanting to push his luck by saying anything more.

"But you'd better not hurt my sister in any way," Ian pointed at Josh with his bottle as he gave him that protective brother glare that Josh and his brothers had all used on the guys they grew up with to keep them from dating their sisters. "While I think you might be good for her in the long run, if you don't deal with your baggage before you try for more than friendship with her, you could set her back big time."

"Yeah, I know," Josh sighed as his shoulders slumped in defeat. "That's why I have no intention of stepping out of the friend zone until everything's settled and I'm out of the Navy."

"Why do ya'll look like you're at a funeral instead of a bachelor party?" Jake interrupted their conversation after wiping the table with Aiden. "Ya'll pissed 'cause ya know you won't be able to beat me either?"

"Naw," Josh chuckled, already having a plan for how to bring his brother down a peg or two. "I was recruiting Ian to help me set up the pool table I'm buying our nieces and nephews while I'm home this week. And all I had to promise him to convince him to help me carry the heavy ass table up to the game room in Anthony's house is a front-row seat when Tia takes your crown as the family pool shark."

"You think Tia can beat him when none of us can?" Aiden arched an eyebrow at Josh like he thought he was delusional.

"Oh, yeah," Josh chuckled. "She's way smarter and faster at mental geometry and physics than Jake, so I'd bet she'll beat him within an hour of her first time picking up a pool cue."

"Seriously? You think she's smarter than Jake?" Aiden didn't look like he believed Josh. "She's barely a teenager."

"Dude, she's thirteen and just finished her first semester of college." Josh would have rolled his eyes at Aiden, but he wasn't a teenage girl like his niece. "Yeah, she's smarter than Jake. Hell, she's smarter than everyone in this room combined. Don't believe me? Ask Anthony. He'll tell you how she amazes him with how she figures out problems before he's even finished reading them."

"Yo, Anthony," Aiden shouted across the bar, obviously planning on doing just that.

"Dude, you don't have to pull Anthony away from his protective dad position, watching for Kay to have a contraction," Jake interjected, shaking his head. "I'll gladly concede my title as the smartest Burleson to Tia. Hell, Maria doesn't demonstrate it as much as Tia, but I think I've even lost second place to her. And I have a feeling I'll only be holding on to third for a few more months because those girls are teaching Antonio all their genius ways."

"Give it up, Bro," Josh teased, slapping a hand on Jake's shoulder. "With Kay, Brook, and Amy all having babies this year, you won't even stay in the top five past Christmas. And it won't be long before the rest of us start procreating, and then you'll be lucky to stay in the top ten."

As the evening progressed with the guys debating which of them would have the smartest kids, Josh couldn't help but wonder how his son would fare in comparison to his nieces, nephews, and cousins' kids. *Damn, I really need to come up with some more ideas for how to find him.*

I know the guys were way off base with some of the places they suggested I scope out in Alexandria on our days off. But maybe I could go to the library where the email and DNA profile were set up and run into my son's mother the next time she goes back to check on the results?

Chapter Eleven

Cait was a nervous wreck, having the strangest feeling of her insides vibrating with her anxiety, as she sat among the Burlesons for a cookout on the town square to celebrate Independence Day. She'd been adamant that she wasn't ready for an outdoor event anywhere but on the ranch where she knew she'd be safe. But over the last few days, her brother had gradually worn her down and pushed her way outside her comfort zone to get her to come to the town festivities.

First, Mikey had pointed out that most of the Burlesons would be there, so she'd be just as safe in the middle of town as she would with them protecting her on the ranch. He'd even recruited her friends to try to talk her into coming along and bringing her version of an American Flag cake. Cait had tried to get by with just making the white cake topped with whipped cream, strawberries, and blueberries and giving it to the girls to take to the cookout. They'd taken the cake to a family dinner the night Sam was born to use as his birthday cake instead, apparently not caring that Sam, Kay, and Anthony weren't there to enjoy it. Not that Sam could enjoy a birthday cake as a newborn, but Cait imagined Hazel would have taken his picture with it the way she'd taken his picture with everyone who'd gone to see the baby in the last two days. And each of the gifts that they'd brought with them.

Josh had also stepped up to try to get her to go to the fireworks, making sure she knew he'd stay right by her side to keep her safe the whole time. As they'd fallen back into their easy friendship, like the past two months of him ghosting her hadn't ever happened, his pleas had been the hardest for Cait to reject. She knew she'd be safe from anyone attacking the crowd with Josh there to protect her. But she also knew how devastating it could be to her heart if she didn't maintain a friendly distance between her and Josh. So, she'd somehow found the fortitude within herself to be able to tell him she'd have to think about it without actually committing to going.

Ultimately, it was her brother and Brody that broke her down and made it obvious she couldn't say no to going. Mostly Brody. Mikey was planning to propose to Charlotte after the fireworks, and he wanted Cait there to celebrate with them afterward. Had it just been Mikey proposing, she'd have suggested she stay home to set up a surprise engagement party for afterward. But when Brody told her that he was going to ask Char to adopt him at the same time his dad proposed, Cait knew she had to be there to support her nephew as he asked for his greatest wish — to have a mom again.

It wasn't until after she'd already agreed, and they were walking out the door to go to the town square that Mikey informed her that Charlotte wouldn't want him to propose in front of a crowd. So, after they ate, he planned to take Charlotte and Brody to the other side of the City Hall building to watch the fireworks and make their proposals.

Needless to say, she felt extremely uncomfortable as she watched Mikey, Brody, and Charlotte walk away while she sat at a picnic table with her girlfriends and a few of their brothers. Josh following through on his promise to stay right by her side might have helped decrease her fear of being shot in another drive-by, but she still struggled with her body's response to his nearness being way more than friendly.

God bless Victoria's Secret for putting enough padding in their bras to hide how my nipples get hard anytime he's close enough I can smell his earthy mix of the outdoors and soap that must contain the strongest pheromones on the planet.

"What's up with Ian taking off and leaving you here?" Josh looked concerned as he lifted his chin in the direction her brother was walking as he motioned with his hand for Jake to take the seat on her other side that Mikey had just vacated.

Cait smiled politely at Josh's twin as he sat down on her other side, grateful that the Burlesons were such good friends that they'd step up like that to try to help her feel safe. Though she had to admit, if only to herself, that she'd probably feel just as safe with just Josh there with her as she did with Jake and JJ also at their table and Justin and Bobby at the tables on either side of them with their significant others and their families and friends.

"Mikey and Brody have a surprise for Char at the end of the fireworks," Cait replied, not wanting to spoil Mikey and Charlotte's moment when they shared the news with her family. As she looked around, she wondered if they'd share their engagement news that evening or not.

Considering Char's family wasn't all there, she assumed not, knowing Charlotte would probably want to tell her parents about the engagement first before spilling the beans to the rest of her family. Hazel and Bob were off taking care of their grandkids, while Kay recovered from giving birth only two days earlier. And that meant they were watching the fireworks from the ranch, since Antonio could only handle short bursts of time in large crowds of strangers.

Cait had noticed how the grandmothers of the town had taken turns keeping the kids occupied in separate rooms at the various wedding events she'd attended the last couple of months, and she assumed that was their way of taking care of Antonio's anxiety after his ordeal with the cartel. At that moment, she kind of wished she was still a kid to be able to hide away with Antonio and the town grandmas whenever she felt anxious, too.

Without her parents here, I bet Char won't want to announce their engagement tonight. So, I really didn't have to be here for a celebration that's probably not going to happen. I could have watched the fireworks from the safety of the ranch, or out my bedroom window, and be there for them when they actually announce they're getting married instead.

"And this surprise is more important than making sure you feel safe out in the open like this?" Josh shook his head, obviously irritated at Mikey for not considering her in his plans.

Cait shrugged, not wanting to make the situation more uncomfortable by verbalizing her own mixed feelings about the events of the evening. She felt guilty for feeling abandoned by her brother, when she should be nothing but happy for him being able to move on after losing Mari. But while she was thrilled for Mikey and Charlotte finding each other and falling in love, she had to wonder how she'd fit into her family after her brother remarried.

Yeah, she knew she'd still be needed to watch Brody, while Mikey and Char were at work during the school year. But she didn't want to be the third wheel, living with the newlyweds because she didn't feel safe living on her own.

She couldn't admit it to anyone but herself, but she kind of resented Mikey for pushing her to heal faster than she was ready to, so he could move on with his life. After everything her brother had done for her, practically raising her since she was born, she really felt guilty for her bitterness at him for pressuring her to be more independent.

Yeah, she wanted to be independent again, to feel safe doing normal daily activities like going to town events and the grocery store on her own without having a panic attack. But she felt like she needed to do those things at her own pace. Being pushed into doing more than she was ready for felt like it was more traumatizing because of the pressure she felt to heal on someone else's timeline.

At the same time that she hated feeling rushed to get better on her brother's timeline, she also wished she could move on as quickly as he was, so she could live the life she truly wanted. She was thrilled for her brother to have found love for a second time and ecstatic to see him start to go on with life with a healed heart after the trauma they'd both endured.

Mikey deserved to live a happy life without the burden of taking care of his baby sister. She truly believed that deep in her heart. But she also had no clue how to push past her issues to quit leaning on him so much and give him his freedom.

Maybe if Mikey moves onto the ranch for him and Brody to live with Charlotte, I can ask the girls if they have room for another roommate? Or maybe one of them will be willing to move in with me, so I won't be all alone in our house?

No, even if switching jobs increases my salary enough for me to be able to afford the rent on that house, I won't feel any safer with one of the girls living there with me than I would have living with Tiana in San Diego after the shooting.

If only Josh lived here instead of on base. I'd feel safe with him as my roommate. But do I really want to lean on another person to make me feel safe? Why can't I be on my own now that the cartel is no longer a threat? I know how to use a gun to defend myself. I even remember quite a few of the self-defense moves Mikey insisted I learn when I was a teenager. So why do I feel like the only way I'll ever feel comfortable living on my own is if I convince Mikey to put one of those HGTV tiny houses in his backyard for me to live in?

She was so lost in her own thoughts, she missed whatever her friends were saying in response to Josh's irritation. Not that she could truly comprehend what was being said around her when Josh put his arm around her shoulders, either, but at least she forgot her worries about her future living situation.

"Come on, Sunshine," Josh smiled, urging her off the bench with a gentle pull of his arm. "We're moving to lay down, so we have a better view of the fireworks."

"Oh, um, okay," Cait stuttered, following along in a Josh-induced daze as he walked her over to a grouping of blankets that were laid out on the lawn of the town square.

If we're only going to be friends, he really needs to stop acting like a protective boyfriend and calling me Sunshine.

Josh settled her on the center blanket with him while his siblings and cousins surrounded them. "Relax. With all the extra security my cousins brought into town to watch for Allissa's stalker, nobody's gonna be able to pull anything to hurt you here. They're securing the whole square, not just the area over there where the GWA crew is setting up."

"Besides," Becky added from her blanket on the other side of Josh. "If I'm right and Ian is proposing to Char, then you'll be part of our family soon. And we were all raised to protect our family, so you're just as safe as if you had a half-dozen clones of Ian surrounding you."

While Cait knew Becky meant the statement to be comforting, and she did feel safer with several of the Burleson men surrounding her, she kind of wanted to cringe at the thought of Josh as a clone of her brother. *No, no, no! Mikey will have the Burlesons as in-laws after he marries Charlotte. Josh won't actually be my brother-in-law.*

"Oh, here, before I forget." Josh reached into the pocket of his cargo shorts and handed her whatever he pulled out, amping up the tingles she always felt when they accidentally touched, as his work-roughened fingers touched her palm.

Cait looked down at her hand to see a set of earplugs in a tiny, sealed plastic bag, taking a moment for the tingles to pass before registering what she was holding. "What are these for?"

"To block the sound of the fireworks, so they don't cause flashbacks," Josh informed her as he opened a second set to put them in his ears.

Cait was confused as to why Josh was putting in earplugs to prevent flashbacks of gunfire. Oh, they'd both worn ear protection when they went target shooting a few months ago, but she didn't think he could wear that while on his SEAL missions. *So, if he doesn't use earplugs when he's most likely to get in a shootout, why is he using them now? Just to make me feel like I'm not alone in needing the precaution?*

"Thank you," Cait choked out, trying not to tear up at his thoughtful gesture. She quickly opened the bag and followed Josh's lead in squeezing the earplugs down to make them small enough to go into her ears before inserting them and allowing them to expand to fit snugly. "How do you do your job if you have to put in earplugs to prevent flashbacks at fireworks shows?"

Josh held his hand up to his ear, indicating he couldn't hear her question. So, she raised her voice and repeated herself.

"Oh, I don't have flashbacks," Josh smiled, shaking his head. "I just figured I'd need them to know how loud to talk so you can hear me."

Yeah, he's using them to keep me from being the only freak wearing earplugs at an outdoor concert and fireworks show. Cait wasn't sure what she was going to do to stop herself from falling even more in love with Josh, when he kept doing sweet things like this that made her feel like he was taking care of her because he thought of her as more than a friend.

"Ya'll can both quit yelling!" Jen turned on her blanket to grin at them.

"Unless you're passing out earplugs for all of us!" Julie added, also grinning.

Josh reached into his pocket and pulled out another set, tossing it at Julie. "Sorry, I only have one extra pair with me. Ya'll will have to share."

"Weirdo!" Julie tossed the earplugs back at Josh, just as the band stopped playing and the sound system switched over to playing prerecorded patriotic music, which she could barely hear through the earplugs.

Leah Mae Wright

Even though the earplugs had already muffled most of the crowd noise to the point that she mostly felt the music instead of hearing it, Cait could sense that the crowd had hushed at the first fiery explosion in the sky. She laid back on the blanket beside Josh, wishing it was acceptable for friends to scoot a little closer and cuddle. She kind of felt like she needed the extra assurance she was safe while watching her first fireworks show in years. But even if it was acceptable, she knew she couldn't take that comfort from Josh. Not without risking even more of her heart than she'd already lost to him.

Maybe one of these days, it won't hurt so much to just be his friend.

And maybe I should reach out to my therapist in San Diego to get a referral for a telehealth therapist that takes my new insurance. Maybe they can help me deal with the heartbreak of unrequited love at the same time they give me some tips on how to push myself outside my comfort zone, so my brother doesn't have to do it for me.

~~~

Sunday, July 7, 2019

Josh felt like he'd won the lottery as he sat through the speeches at Fiona and Rick's wedding reception with Cait by his side. One of the benefits of not being part of the bridal party at this wedding was that he got to pick where he sat, instead of being paired up with a bridesmaid, as he'd been at Bobby and Brook's wedding. Though considering his sister Charlotte was the maid-of-honor and she was sitting at the same table he was, instead of being at the head table, Josh assumed the seating chart was less rigid because the Harrisons and Robertsons were bucking tradition. Either that or the only reason he and Jake weren't seated with their mother's pick of eligible women was because she was too busy basking in the afterglow of getting another grandchild earlier in the week to interfere with the seating arrangements.

Regardless of why he'd gotten lucky with the seating, Josh was glad that Cait was the only single woman at their table. And she was sitting between him and her nephew (well, until Brody bolted to go sit with the other kids), so none of the other guys in town could hit on her.
~~~

Oh, yeah, technically, Charlotte was still single, but the rock Ian had put on her finger made it clear she wouldn't be for long. Besides, she was his sister, so she didn't count. And neither did the only other woman at their table — his sister-in-law Brooklyn.

Unfortunately, even though he was in the perfect spot, Josh couldn't take advantage of the seating situation to make a move on Caitir yet either. So, he had to continue the just-friends act that he'd suffered through for the last week.

Yeah, I'm definitely gonna go to the library in Alexandria on my next day off once I'm back on base. I have to be more proactive in finding my son, 'cause waiting on Jake or the cyber team at Avington to find his mom online is taking too damn long. And I need to have things settled there before I finish my time in the Navy, so I can come home and take things to the next level with Cait.

Josh felt a pang of jealousy as his sister returned to their table after giving her maid-of-honor speech. He wanted so badly to be able to lean over and kiss Cait on the cheek the way Ian kissed Charlotte as she took her seat.

"Oh, geez," Char gasped in response to whatever Ian whispered in her ear. "I didn't even think of that being the reason they chose to have their families up there instead. Yeah, we probably should, but I think I'd rather it just be you, me, and Brody at the head table, instead of having my parents up there with us."

"We can do that," Ian agreed, grinning at Char, and triggering another wave of jealousy in Josh. He wanted to be able to make wedding plans with Cait the way his sister was with Ian. "But it'll most likely just be the two of us, since Brody will probably ditch us to go sit with his cousins like he did tonight."

Josh smiled as he watched his sister look around for Brody, who was sitting at the table to their left with Bob, Hazel, Anthony, Kay, and their four kids.

Damn, I hope the kid realizes he can't grow up to marry one of his cousins, Josh thought, remembering back to Bobby and Brooklyn's wedding, when Brody had said something about waiting for Maria to catch the bouquet for him to catch the garter to be able to marry her.

"I can't believe Kay feels up to being out and about like this so soon after having a C-section," Brooklyn sighed, also looking over at the table where Kay was sitting. "I'm exhausted just carrying Maddie around, and she's not even born yet."

"Don't worry, Brie-Baby, you'll bounce back just as quick. That's one of the benefits of being a Burleson," Bobby chuckled as he leaned over and kissed his wife's temple, leaving his arm around her shoulders as he pulled back. "Once the baby's born, you can focus on recovering 'cause there's always a half dozen of us around to carry the baby while you get your energy back."

Josh was just as jealous of Bobby and Brooklyn's relationship as he was of Charlotte and Ian's. *Fuck! I can't wait much longer to start a relationship with Cait, or I'll go crazy from wanting to kiss and touch her the way my siblings do with their significant others.*

"And even when some of us have to head back out of town for work, Mom will always be there to babysit whenever you need a break," Jake added, nodding his head at their mom holding baby Sam, so Anthony and Kay could have time to eat their dinner. "And if ya'll can get in there with Anthony and Kay to keep her distracted with grandkids at events like this, maybe she'll be too busy to pull any matchmaking mischief on the rest of us."

"Is that how ya'll got to sit here with us, instead of being paired up with a couple of the single ladies in town?" Bobby arched an inquisitive eyebrow as his eyes darted back and forth between Josh and Jake.

Josh shook his head, not wanting his older brother to call their mom over to correct the situation.

"Yep," Jake replied at the same time.

"Cait's one of the single ladies in town," Josh pointed out, tilting his head in Cait's direction, where she was seated beside him. *Fuck! I hope Bobby and Char don't realize how happy I am to be sittin' by her.*

"Yeah, but Cait's on the ranch all the time now, so she's like another sister," Jake disagreed with Josh.

Thanks, Bro. I knew I could count on you to help me deflect them from figuring out I'm attracted to Cait.

"You realize having Brie on the ranch all the time was the ploy Ma used to match us up, right?" Bobby looked at Jake like he thought Jake might be the one attracted to Cait, since he seemed to be protesting too much. "And if she could get one of ya'll to move home and stay in the same house with Cait, she'd do it in a heartbeat."

"Maybe I should move into the spare room with Jen, Julie, and Becky, instead of moving into your house, Char," Cait piped up, looking nervously at Josh. He knew she was worried about living alone for the first time more than having one of them move in with her.

Hell, she's probably just as nervous about her safety living with the girls, since she won't have her brother there to protect her if something happens. Fuck! Maybe I should tell her I'm getting out of the Navy and will gladly move in with her in September. No, fuck, I can't do that yet. Not when I'm still not sure I'll be able to move home immediately.

"If that's where you'd feel most comfortable, then I'm sure the girls would be glad to have you." Char smiled reassuringly at Cait.

"I'm surprised Ma hasn't already tried to talk you into moving into my old room at her house, so these two'll be right across the hall whenever they're home on leave." Bobby nodded his head at the twins while grinning at Cait.

"Oh, she's mentioned the abundance of empty bedrooms at her house," Cait giggled, seeming to relax a little at the change of subject, instead of being put on the spot about her choice of living arrangements after Ian and Char move in together. "But I pointed out how she needs to keep those bedrooms available for out-of-town guests whenever the GWA rents out the whole B and B."

"Smart thinking." Josh grinned, hoping to keep her more at ease by holding his hand up for a fist bump with Cait. "Way to keep Ma from matchmaking."

Cait giggled as she bumped her fist with Josh.

Damn, I love being the one to make her laugh.

Their conversation was cut short when the emcee called out over the microphone, "If we could please get the gentlemen to clear the dance floor, it's time for the single ladies to gather for the bouquet toss."

"Hey, where are you going?" Ian grabbed Charlotte's hand, when she stood to go with Cait to try to catch the bouquet. "You're not single anymore. You're engaged, so you don't need to try to catch the bouquet this time."

"Exactly, I'm engaged," Charlotte retorted, pulling her hand free while grinning mischievously at her fiancé. "Not married yet, so I still have time for another do-over before getting hitched."

Ian made a face as Charlotte smiled at him and sauntered off to join the group of ladies gathering on the dance floor.

"Damn, I guess Mabel was right in sayin' you'd bring out Char's feisty side," Josh chuckled as he turned in his seat to watch Cait. *Fuck, if she catches the bouquet, then I'm gonna hafta fight for the garter.*

She looked beautiful in her sunny yellow dress, even though she seemed to try to fade off into the background instead of getting in the middle of the fray where the women of the GWA were talking smack. Josh was so focused on looking at Cait that he missed seeing Fiona toss the bouquet. All he knew was that Cait wasn't the one who caught it, as he watched her walking back toward their table as the dance floor cleared once more.

"And now let's get the single gentlemen on the floor for the garter toss," the emcee announced.

Josh got up and took a spot on the floor beside his brother, though he had no intention of trying to catch the garter. As he watched Rick look around before taking aim and shooting the pink garter at Dean Hunter, Josh had to smile at how the Matchmaking Mommas had clearly influenced Fiona to tell her husband whom to target.

He was shaking his head at the obvious setup as he walked back toward his table, catching the tail end of some rather unexpected PDA between Char and Ian as he took his seat.

"Dude, I know ya'll are in love and all," Bobby groaned, tossing a balled-up napkin at them to break their kiss. "But I don't need to see you playing tonsil hockey with my sister."

Josh agreed with Bobby, fighting the urge to gag as a way to pick on his sister a little.

"You guys have some weird sayings in Texas," Cait laughed, shaking her head at Bobby.

Char and Ian just looked at each other and shrugged, smiling at one another before Charlotte finally got off Ian's lap and moved back to her own seat.

"Hey, Darlin', you need to come back up for pictures," Dean hollered across the room, twirling the pink garter on his finger, and grinning at his coworker who'd apparently caught the bouquet while Josh was staring at Cait.

Allissa seemed to be reluctant to go back out on the dance floor for pictures, but she eventually took the seat Philippe directed her toward. There were numerous catcalls from around the room, as Dean got down on one knee in front of Allissa at the direction of the photographer.

Josh mostly ignored the rude remarks from their friends, trying to think of something to say to get the conversation at the table started again. But just as he saw Dean putting the garter on Allissa's leg, he heard Liam shout, "Guess this means you're next to get married!"

Dean obviously couldn't let the taunts of their friends pass without commenting, turning to look at the crowd instead of up at Allissa as he hollered back, "Yeah, well, if this means we're the next to get married, then ya'll can all plan to come back here for our wedding on our Labor Day break in September."

"Sorry, Dean. That week is already spoken for, so Fiona can be here as my matron of honor!" Charlotte shouted, surprising Josh with how boldly his normally reserved sister had just announced her engagement to the whole town.

"Guess that means we'll have to plan a Thanksgiving wedding, Darlin'," Dean corrected as he wagged his eyebrows suggestively at Allissa.

"I still don't understand why ya'll are in such a rush to get married that you can't schedule it for when we've already put in for leave time this year," Jake grumbled, drawing Josh's attention back to their table, instead of continuing to watch the couple getting their pictures taken. "It's gonna be hard to get the extra time off with only two months' notice to our commanding officers, especially since we're both already planning to be off the last week of September to be here for the board meeting."

Shit! I guess I shoulda told him about my plans to leave the Navy before now. Josh realized then that he'd gotten distracted by talking to Cait and then thinking she was on a date, so he hadn't had the conversation with his brother that he'd planned to have the day of the Burleson board meeting.

"Can't you just swap the last week of September for the first week?" Charlotte looked back and forth between Jake and Josh with a worried expression on her face. "You can always Skype in for the board meeting, but you can't Skype in for my wedding."

"Yeah, possibly," Josh smiled at Char, hoping his little fib would help calm her nerves about him and Jake not being at her wedding. "As long as I'm not spun up for a short mission that week."

She doesn't have to know that I'll already be on terminal leave the first week of September, and there's no chance of me being spun up. After the way Jake covered for my attraction to Cait earlier, I can't tell them all now and throw him under the bus about swapping his leave.

"Sorry, Sis, but we don't really have a choice about when we have to run an op," Jake apologized with a half-shrug. "But if you move the wedding to the end of September or the end of December, you know we'll both most likely be here since we put in for those leaves last year."

"But Justin and Amy are already planning their wedding for the end of December," Josh pointed out, shaking his head at Jake. *Dude, quit getting her worked up by pressuring her to push back her wedding. It's not that hard to swap leave weeks in your cushy desk job.*

"What's the matter, Princess?" Ian reached over and brushed a tear from Char's cheek.

Josh turned to glare at Jake when he saw Char tearing up, wishing they had some sort of twin telepathy, so he could make sure his brother got the message.

"We can't wait any longer than the first week of September to have the wedding," Charlotte sobbed, leaning over into her fiancé's chest. "Or I might not fit in my wedding gown."

Why wouldn't she fit in her wedding gown? Josh wondered, confused by how dramatic Char was acting because it was so out of character for her.

"Oh, sweet Charlotte, don't worry about that." Ian pulled her into his arms as she cried on his shoulder. "I'm sure the gown can be tailored to fit, even if you gain a few pounds between now and then."

"Not with the corset-style bodice on my dream wedding dress," Char wailed, lifting her head to look up at Ian as she cried uncontrollably. "I can't squeeze a baby bump into a corset, so we have to get married before I start showing."

Holy fuck! Char's pregnant?

"Okay, well, then we won't move the wedding date," Ian reassured her. "And if Jake and Josh can't be here, then I'll pick some different groomsmen."

"Did you say something about a baby bump?" Hazel appeared out of nowhere, hovering over Charlotte and Ian's chairs and still cradling baby Sam in her arms. "Are you gonna give me another grandbaby soon?"

"So much for not telling anyone until after the first trimester," Char choked out as her tears started to subside.

"I'm just glad it was you who spilled the beans and not me," Ian chuckled, grinning at Charlotte.

"It's still your fault for choosing my brothers as your groomsmen," Char quipped as she pulled back slightly to wipe her tears.

"I'll make it up to you later, Princess," Ian promised as he released Charlotte, so she could turn and confirm what everyone in the room suspected after her inadvertent announcement.

"Yes, Mom, we're adding to the family in February."

"Oh my goodness!" Hazel squealed, drawing the attention of everyone in the room. "Did you hear that, Sammy? You're gonna have another cousin in February!"

"Geez, Ma, chill," Anthony chuckled, taking his son from Hazel's arms. "You're gonna bust Sam's eardrums, tryin' to announce your next grandbaby to the whole state of Texas."

Josh joined in with the rest of his family as everyone congratulated Charlotte and Ian. He was happy for them, even though he was also extremely jealous that they were already getting to start their family together, while he was stuck in limbo and couldn't do the same with Cait.

~~~

Saturday, July 13, 2019

After a week of pondering her future living situation, and getting a couple of emergency telehealth appointments with a therapist to help her deal with the massive changes happening in her life, Cait still wasn't sure where she'd be living at the end of the day, as she started
~~~

packing the things in her bedroom for the move to the Burleson Ranch. She'd been given three options — Charlotte's former home, moving in with Jen, Julie, and Becky, or staying with Hazel and Bob in the same room she'd used after the Campbells' rental house had been broken into earlier in the year. And so far, she'd only been able to rule out staying with Hazel and Bob because she knew she'd need that space between her and Josh every time he came home on leave to try to fall out of love with him.

The other two options both had pros and cons to them that she had to take into consideration while making her decision. The pros of living with her friends included having them there if she ever got scared and getting more girl-talk time when they were all home for the evening. But the cons were what worried her, including being farther away from her brother and the other men on the ranch, whom she'd feel more comfortable having close by to defend her if she needed it, and not really taking a step forward in exerting her independence.

The pros of moving into Charlotte's former home included being closer to her brother in the house catty-corner across the gravel drive from where he was moving, having JJ right next door to her, and taking the major step of living on her own while surrounded by friends and family, who would all make her feel safe to start spreading her wings a little. She'd also still have her girlfriends right next door on the other side, the closest access to the stables if she felt the need for a little equine therapy, which her therapist had pointed out would be a big benefit to moving to the ranch, and the most space where she felt like she could escape to be alone when she needed it.

The cons of moving into Charlotte's former home were that she'd feel guilty for living there with the Burlesons refusing to let her pay for her rent and utilities. And that she was afraid the nightmares might come back from knowing she was alone in the house. Not to mention the fact that if Josh or Jake got out of the Navy, or one of their Avington cousins decided to move to town, Hazel would try to move them in to be her new roommate for one of her matchmaking schemes.

But she does know about my attraction to Josh, so she'd probably only try it with him. And there's no way he's getting out of the Navy anytime soon, so I probably don't have to worry about him moving in as my roommate being a con to living on my own in the only vacant house on the ranch.

Besides, with Justin and Amy building a house down on the south side of the ranch, their house will be vacant by the end of the year. And JJ has way more empty bedrooms than I will. So, even if they have a family member who wants to move to the ranch, they'll have a house or a room with JJ for them. So, they won't need to double up with me.

And I really do need to prove to myself that I can live alone. Yeah, it's with the safety net of being on the ranch. But if I can't do it on the ranch surrounded by people I trust to keep me safe, then I'll never be able to move into a place of my own off the ranch.

As she was trying to talk herself into moving into the house Charlotte was moving out of, there was a knock on her door before Becky, Jen, and Julie barged in carrying boxes, packing tape, and Sharpies.

"The packing fairies have arrived," Becky announced as she plopped down on the bed and started folding the first of the flattened boxes to prepare them for packing.

"I thought the plan was for us to all meet on the ranch to move Char's stuff first?" Cait looked at her friends quizzically, as she continued to empty her dresser into the suitcase she'd been packing with her clothes while waiting for Brody to wake up. "Why are you guys here before eight in the morning?"

"Oh, yeah, that was the plan," Jen agreed, nodding as she taped up the bottom of a box.

"But Char's been packing a few boxes a day for the last week, so all that's left to be done there is for the guys to do all the heavy lifting," Julie finished for her sister, as she took a prepared box and moved to Cait's bathroom.

"So, we decided to head over here to help you pack and send Ian and Brody to the ranch to deal with my bossy sister," Becky added with a grin, as she affixed a rod in a wardrobe box that was only a few inches shorter than her.

Before she could reply, Mikey stuck his head in the door. "I finally got Brody up and dressed. But I wanted to check and see if you have anything ready to move before we drive an empty vehicle to the ranch."

"Just these two suitcases," Cait admitted, closing the second one and zipping it up before handing it over to her brother and pointing at the first one she'd packed with all the necessities she'd need her first night in her new space. "And they need to be the first things I unpack this evening. So please put them where I can find them when I get there."

"Have you decided which house you're moving into?" Mikey arched an eyebrow at her as he picked up the other suitcase.

"No, not yet," Cait confessed sheepishly.

"Then do you want me to put them in your car? Or pick where I think you should live and put them there?"

As much as Cait wished she could let her brother make the decision for her, so she didn't have to fret over it, she knew she needed to face her fears and pick for herself. "Just put them in my car," Cait sighed.

"Take them to Mom and Dad's house," Becky corrected, as she carried the wardrobe box toward the closet. "No matter whether you decide to live with us, or in the house next door to us, you need to stay in the room you used in the spring for the next week or so while we repaint wherever you decide to stay. So, let's make sure you have enough stuff for a week, and then focus on packing Ian and Brody's stuff to move first. We can get the rest of your stuff next weekend, once you've had time to make the decision and redecorate your new living space."

"Perfect," Mikey agreed before he stepped out of the room without another word.

Cait stood there staring at her empty doorway, feeling like she'd just been played in some way, but she wasn't sure how. "Did you guys plan this to try to sway my decision?"

"Of course," Jen chirped, grinning as she packed the books and knick-knacks from the bookshelf in Cait's bedroom. "But we're not trying to sway you one way or the other."

"We're just trying to give you time to decide where you're most comfortable," Julie added, carrying the small box she'd filled with bathroom stuff back out to the bed to tape it closed and label it with a Sharpie.

"That's why we brought the wardrobe box for your clothes," Becky interjected with a grin as she stuck her head out of the closet, "so you can just open the side and use it like a closet until you're sure you've decided where you want to live, so you only have to unpack it once."

"Thank you," Cait choked out, struggling to keep from tearing up at the thoughtfulness of her friends. "I really appreciate how supportive you all are in helping me start to deal with my issues and take charge of my life again."

"Of course, that's what besties do for each other," Becky smiled before ducking back into the closet to continue packing that large wardrobe box.

"You'd do the same for any of us," the twins chimed in unison, as they continued prepping boxes and packing.

"You do realize that I don't need everything in my room for the first week, right?" Cait was confused about why the twins were packing things that weren't necessities after they'd just all agreed to only pack a week's worth of Cait's things before moving on to packing Mikey and Brody's stuff. "I already packed most of what I need for that short a time in my suitcases, other than maybe a few more outfits from the closet."

"Oh, yeah, we know," Jen nodded as she taped up the box of books she'd just packed. "It's just easier to pack everything quickly when we're all working in the same room, so we're not running back and forth to talk to one another."

"That's why we're labeling each box with whether it's move now or next week," Julie added, turning the bathroom box for Cait to see it was marked as *[Cait's bathroom stuff, move next week]*. "And I assumed you won't need the unopened products from under the sink in the next week, since you didn't pack them when you packed the toiletries you use daily, and we have plenty of extra tampons and toilet paper at our place that we can easily smuggle over to you at Aunt Hazel's if you need it."

"And now that I'm done with this box," Becky informed them as she pushed the wardrobe box out of the closet. "We can probably move on to packing up the rest of the house and preparing the furniture to be moved."

As they stepped out of Cait's room to move over to Brody's to start packing it next, they started discussing the things Cait might want to change in both the house Charlotte was moving out of and the master bedroom that had belonged to the Burlesons' grandparents, which none of them had felt comfortable living in after they passed away.

Realizing that her friends intended for her to stay in the bedroom that had belonged to their grandparents, if she moved in with them, pushed Cait over the edge to choosing Char's former home for her new living space. It was the only room in their home that they hadn't been able to bring themselves to change since losing their grandfather and moving in, so there was no way Cait could step in and change it now.

If I don't want anyone else to decide when it's time for me to move forward, I can't force them to push past their grief when they're not ready yet.

Cait just hoped she really was as strong as everyone kept trying to tell her she was, so she wouldn't regress in her mental healing during her time alone in her new home.

"Do you think anyone in your family would be upset if I paint over the exposed brick to lighten up the rooms in my new home?"

"No, not at all," Jen assured her with a smile.

"That house really is cave-like if Char doesn't turn on every light in the place," Julie added with a curl of her lips to show her distaste for the current color scheme.

"I suggested whitewashing it when Char moved in years ago," Becky added with a nod and a smile. "But Char thought it would be too much like Mom's style, so she wanted to keep the dark brick and woodwork."

"I was thinking more of a distressed off-white to allow a little of the brick to show through, and painting the cabinets to match whatever slipcovers I decide on for whatever mismatched furniture I end up with, once Mikey and Char decide how to mix and match their stuff."

Cait relaxed once the decision was made, allowing her mind to wander to all the possibilities for decorating her home to make her feel both comfortable and secure. *And if I can find some sunny yellow slipcovers, maybe the happy color will help keep me cheerful, instead of living fearful.*

Chapter Twelve

Josh couldn't believe he was back home to start his four weeks of terminal leave before he signed his final paperwork to end his time in the Navy. After nine years of not living on the ranch for more than a brief vacation, he was really looking forward to being able to come home for good. Unfortunately, even though he was on terminal leave, Josh wasn't permanently home just yet. He was taking this first week to be home for all the events surrounding his sister's wedding. Then he was planning on going back to Virginia to stay with Jake in Alexandria while continuing the search for his son, since none of his one-day excursions to the library had been successful. He'd have to spend a few days in Virginia Beach packing his things and moving out of his apartment, right before his final trip to the base to sign paperwork and do his exit interview, but he planned to spend the majority of his leave time looking for his son and the mother of his child.

Josh had finally told Jake about his plans on their trip back to Virginia after Independence Day. Jake had been shocked that Josh was leaving the Navy, knowing he'd dreamt of being a SEAL since he was a kid. But he wasn't surprised to hear that Josh planned to spend as much of his time off as possible in Alexandria, understanding Josh's need to step up for his child.

Jake had actually apologized for not being able to find the boy or his mother online. Apparently, his twin felt some of his pain from not knowing anything about his son. Because of that feeling, Jake had confessed to regretting getting his master's degree because of the time it added to his minimum service requirement, which was keeping him from getting out at the same time as Josh to devote all his resources to the search.

While Josh appreciated the sentiment, and their talk made him feel even closer to his brother than he already had, he didn't want Jake to give up his career aspirations for what he hoped would be a short search. He'd had to explain to Jake that needing the time off to find his son wasn't what prompted him to decide to leave the Navy at the end of his minimum service requirement. He'd actually made that decision back at Christmas, the day he met Cait, to be able to move home and pursue a relationship with her.

Josh was actually fairly happy with how things were going between him and Cait since he'd been home for leave at the end of June and beginning of July. They'd managed to go back to the easy friendship they'd developed earlier in the year and had maintained it through a continuous text conversation while he was back on base, even though the dialog wasn't as deep and meaningful as he wanted to get with her.

He missed being able to flirt with her the way he had before he found out he was a father. But he was hopeful that they could progress to a more romantic relationship in the near future.

Just as soon as I get things settled with my son's mother and can move back to the ranch permanently.

Because they'd kept things superficial when they texted, mostly sharing jokes and funny memes, or talking about humorous things that happened in the course of their days, Josh was surprised to see Cait sitting with his sisters and cousins when he walked into Tully's Roadhouse for Ian and Charlotte's joint bachelor and bachelorette party.

Damn! Maybe I shouldn't have backed off so much that she doesn't feel like she can tell me about her progress with going out in public, Josh thought as he stopped in his tracks, unable to take his eyes off Cait.

Or maybe you shoulda asked her how she was doing, instead of tryin' to make her laugh every time you texted her. Josh's inner voice sounded an awful lot like his dad.

Yeah, I'm gonna hafta get a whole lot better at takin' care of all her needs, instead of just tryin' to keep her spirits up by joshin' around. Having to back off on the flirting doesn't mean I can't be the best friend she confides in. Now I just hafta figure out how to step up for her and show her I can be serious when she needs me to without coming off like a possessive boyfriend.

"You're not being very subtle, Bro." Jake stepped in front of Josh, blocking his view of Cait, as he growled the words in a tone low enough that only Josh would hear him. "Ya need to keep moving toward the bar and quit starin' like a love-sick puppy, or everyone in the room is gonna know how you feel about Cait."

"Sorry. Just surprised to see her here." Josh shook off his momentary daze and followed Jake to the bar to order a beer.

Once they had their first round in hand, they made their way over to congratulate their sister before heading to the back room to hang out with the rest of the guys.

"Congrats, Char." Josh leaned down to give his sister a one-armed hug.

"You and Ian are perfect for one another," Jake added, hugging her from the other side.

"Thanks, guys." Charlotte slapped them each on the back before pushing them away. "But I can't have the shots required to be able to handle the two of you being all nice and lovey, so go hang out with the guys."

"We're goin'," Josh placated his sister by raising his hands in surrender as he stood back to his full height. When his gaze met Cait's, he couldn't stop himself from smiling at her.

"Hey, are we goin' with the dancy intros for the whole wedding party like at Anthony and Kay's wedding?" Jake questioned their sister. "Or more low-key with just ya'll being introduced when you enter the reception like at Bobby and Brooklyn's? I need to make sure I clear it with Rick before I dance with his wife, and everyone else probably needs to practice this week."

Damn! I didn't even think about getting to spend the week practicing a dance with Cait. Considering the only times I've seen her dance, she just swayed back and forth with Brody, I bet I'll have to teach her to two-step.

"Yeah, it'll just be me and Ian being introduced as we enter the reception," Char clarified, bursting Josh's bubble of hope about getting to hold Cait in his arms.

Fuck! But maybe I can salvage something from this failed opportunity.

Josh grinned at Cait. "I'll still teach ya how to two-step, if ya wanna learn before the wedding, Sunshine."

"That's okay," Cait smiled and shook her head at Josh. "The girls already had JJ teach me what I needed to know, so I can dance with more than just Brody at this wedding."

Josh just nodded and faked a smile, hoping it hid how his jaw had tightened as he ground his teeth together to keep from saying something he shouldn't if he ever wanted a shot with Cait. *My fucking cousin better have been a perfect fucking gentleman the whole fucking time. 'Cause I'm gonna kill the asshole if he touched her even the slightest bit inappropriately. Or had the fucking audacity to make a move on my girl.*

Josh had to turn and walk away before he lost his shit and yelled at his sisters and cousins for pushing JJ and Cait together while he was gone.

"Hey, chill, Bro," Jake admonished as he caught up with Josh, just as they reached the archway leading into the back room of the bar. "You can't kill our cousin. It'll ruin Char's wedding if Bobby has to arrest you for murder."

Josh cut his eyes at Jake, glaring at his brother as he tried to calm down.

"Give him that look when you stake your claim, and I'm sure it'll be enough to deter him from dancing with her again," Jake smirked. "But you might want to make that claim public knowledge, so the rest of our friends know not to piss you off by hitting on her, too. 'Cause I'm not sure some of them believed me when I told them you're serious about her."

"Damn, dude," Aiden Walker stopped Josh from getting too far into the room full of pool tables. "Who pissed in your Cheerios?"

"Make sure your brothers and cousins all know Cait's off limits," Josh growled, his jealousy at JJ for teaching her to two-step combining with his frustration at not being able to make his move on her yet and coming out as rage at anyone who might try to come between him and his girl.

"Dude," Aiden raised his hands in a placating gesture. "We all figured that out months ago. You kinda made it obvious when you snuck out of your own birthday party to go hang out with her."

"Don't worry, Cuz," Justin stepped in to try to calm the situation. "We didn't let the news of you spending the rest of the night in her bedroom get back to her brother."

"But we did spread the word to the rest of the guys from town, and the GWA guys who were in town for James and Randi's wedding while you weren't here, so it's pretty much public knowledge that she's taken," Aiden added. "So, you don't have to worry about any of us goin' after her."

"He's upset because he just found out JJ taught her to two-step in the time since we were home last," Jake informed two of the three guys they'd been closest to in school.

Josh, Jake, and Justin Burleson had been best friends with Aiden and Leo Walker, forming their own little clique from being in most of the same classes from kindergarten through twelfth grade. They still hung out with their siblings and cousins and their friends from other grades when they were around one another, but the guys they were with daily in school just felt like closer friends.

Once they hit high school, and were the most popular guys in their grade, they'd started hanging out with the most popular girls in their grade. Fiona Harrison, Cassidy Reilly, Kayla Scott, Kara Thompson, and Lexi Wilder were collectively known as the Fab Five of the graduating class of 2010. They mostly went on group dates, and as far as Josh knew, only Justin and Fiona ever considered themselves as boyfriend and girlfriend.

Oh, Josh had hooked up with a couple of the girls back in high school, but only after making sure none of his family or friends might someday be seriously interested in them. And only with the girls he knew were just looking for a good time and a few orgasms. He'd had a code from the first time he'd gotten a boner, consisting of two major points. Number one, to make sure anyone he was with knew it was a one-time thing because he wouldn't get serious until he met *The One*, and number two, to never poach someone else's girl. Now he just had to hope that his friends and family all still lived by that same code.

"Shit," Justin cursed, shaking his head. "I told him you wouldn't like that, even if he was only tryin' to be a friend."

"Yeah, well, I think I need to talk to JJ, instead of gettin' everyone else's opinions on whether he kept it friendly or not," Josh growled, unsure how to control the rage inside him, which was stirred up by his overwhelming jealousy at not being the man to hold Cait in his arms as she learned the most popular form of dance in the state of Texas.

His friends and family obviously knew not to get in his way as he stomped over to where JJ was hanging out with the two guys he'd been closest friends with in school, Dusty and Ridge Deere. Considering Dusty was Josh's brother Bobby's second-in-command at the police department and Ridge was a local firefighter, he knew they were capable of putting a stop to any fight that might break out between him and JJ. But since he didn't want to risk spending his time in jail when he could be hanging out with Cait, Josh hoped it wouldn't be necessary for their friends to intervene.

"What's goin' on with you teachin' Cait to two-step?" Josh glared at his cousin as he placed his full beer on the table between them, unconsciously squaring his shoulders and standing to his full height to emphasize the inch of height and thirty pounds of muscle he had over his older cousin.

"Just doin' what my sisters asked me to do, Cuz," JJ placated, holding up his hands in surrender. "When Ian and Char moved in together and Cait moved to the ranch, he asked the girls to help him push Cait a little outside her comfort zone to help her get over her fear of socializing in public places. So, we've all been gently topping her to help her feel prepared for facing places she's not familiar with."

Josh unconsciously balled his fists. He knew all about JJ's sexual proclivities and didn't like his cousin talking about topping Cait, even if he didn't mean it in a sexual manner.

"Chill, Cuz," JJ barked, not realizing his Dom voice wouldn't work on Josh. "Topping doesn't have to be sexual. It's more about making her feel safe enough to push her boundaries a little. Maybe manipulating situations a little to guide her toward making decisions that will lead to her achieving her dreams, but none of us have done anything inappropriate with your girl. In fact, I'm probably the only one who even thinks of the things we've all been doing to coax Cait out of her shell as topping. I'm sure everyone else thinks of it as being a supportive friend when she needs it."

"What exactly have *you* done?" Josh knew he was being unreasonable as he growled the question, but he couldn't stop himself. He needed to hear from JJ that he hadn't made a move on Cait.

"Cait was trying to use the excuse of not knowing the various dances the girls are all gonna be doin' tonight as an excuse to not come to the party," JJ explained, smoothing his tone to decrease the hostility between the cousins. "So, when they finally convinced her to let them teach her the different line dances, they asked me to teach her the partner dances because none of them know how to lead. I swear, my physical contact with her was limited to one hand holding hers and the other hand on her waist with her free hand on my shoulder. We followed the leave-room-for-Jesus rule that Pastor Harrison insisted on when we were all learning to dance as kids."

Josh had to smile at the memory of Pastor Harrison coming to the elementary school to observe when he found out his daughter was learning to square dance in gym class.

"Damn, I forgot about that rule," Aiden chuckled. "I'm surprised he didn't enforce it at Fiona and Rick's wedding."

"Considering how Rick is constantly touching Fiona whenever they're in the same room, I doubt even her dad could convince him to leave room for Jesus when they dance," Ridge chortled, nodding over to where Rick sat with his wife on his lap, where she'd just joined him in the back room of the bar.

"So, we good, Cuz?" JJ lifted his chin at Josh.

"Yeah," Josh sighed, letting go of his irrational anger as he released a deep breath. "But I still wanna know how else ya'll've been pushin' Cait." *And ya'll better not have manipulated her into doing anything she wasn't ready to do, even if it is good for her to get past her fear.*

"It hasn't been much," JJ shrugged. "I know the day we started moving the Campbells to the ranch, the girls insisted Cait stay at your mom and dad's place to have another week to decide where she wanted to live and redecorate the space she chose while the rooms were empty. They might have mentioned it being extra work to move our grandparent's stuff up to the attic before she could move in with them, but it wasn't more than a gentle nudge toward living on her own to feel more independent again."

"I think Becky might have put a little more pressure on her to get her to switch jobs," Justin added, lifting his right shoulder in a half-shrug. "But she made sure that Nico or one of the other guys is there whenever she has to work in the office at the theater, so she feels safe."

"I actually think it was Aunt Hazel pushing to spend more time with Brody that convinced her to work at least one day a week at the theater," JJ snickered. "But you'll need to get the particulars from Cait on that."

"And since it looks like the girls are through with their games," Dusty pointed out, nodding at the influx of women in the back room. "Ya might wanna go talk to her now, so she doesn't have the chance to ask another guy to dance with her."

"Oh, yeah, that's not happenin'." Josh didn't even realize he'd voiced the thought aloud as he turned and rushed back to the front room, totally forgetting all about the beer he hadn't even taken a drink of yet.

He found Cait on the dance floor with Becky, Jen, and Julie. She was a beat behind them as she tried to follow along as they did *The Git Up* with Blanco Brown on the jukebox.

Damn, she's cute, Josh thought, smiling as he watched her hips sway from side to side as she danced. *And sexy as fuck in boots and blue jeans. But she clearly needs a strong partner to help her find the rhythm when she dances.*

Josh jumped out in front of the girls and mirrored their moves, making sure he had the dance down before he lined up directly in front of Cait. "Follow my lead, Sunshine. It's easier to stay on beat when you mirror someone, instead of trying to follow the people beside you."

Cait gave him a skeptical look, but quickly got on beat when she started following him instead of looking back and forth between the women around her.

"When did you learn this line dance?" Becky yelled the question to be heard over the music. "It's brand new!"

"Just now," Josh replied to his sister as he spun around as directed by the song.

"You're nauseating!" Becky rolled her eyes at him. "We've been practicing for weeks to get this down to be able to do it tonight!"

"I can't help it that I'm both beautiful and a gifted dancer," Josh teased as the song ended. When the next song to come on was *Look What God Gave Her* by Thomas Rhett, Josh realized it described Cait perfectly. *And it's perfect for two-stepping,* Josh thought as he extended his hand to Cait, ignoring the over-exaggerated gagging act his sister was putting on beside them. "Care to show me your two-steppin' skills, Sunshine?"

"I guess I can let you show me how to get on beat with that dance, too," Cait acquiesced, placing her small hand in his much larger one. "Then maybe I won't step on anyone else's feet at the wedding next weekend."

"With me as your teacher, I guarantee you won't be steppin' on anyone else's feet," Josh promised as he spun her into his arms to start the dance, not voicing the rest of his thought. *'Cause you'll only be dancin' with me.*

Josh knew he was holding her closer than JJ had, but he couldn't resist putting his hand on the small of her back to guide her around the dance floor. She still only rested her free hand on his shoulder, but her hands weren't the only body parts she touched him with. They were so close that she rested her forehead on his chest to look down at their feet to make sure she was stepping in time with him. Josh couldn't help but smile at how adorable he found her actions as they danced.

Once she seemed to be sure she had the steps down, she lifted her head, looked up at Josh, and smiled shyly.

Josh hoped he kept his expression on the friendly side of neutral as he returned the smile, knowing he couldn't let her see his feelings for her yet. "My cousins told me you started your new job since I was home last. How're ya likin' the change?"

"It's good," Cait nodded, her smile widening. "Most of the time, I go down to either Kay or Brook's house to work with them. But one day a week, I ride to the office with Becky to work there."

"And you're doin' okay goin' more places like that?" While Josh was thrilled that she seemed to be doing so much better with being out in public, he hoped his family hadn't pushed her too hard or made her feel like she was forced to start doing things she wasn't ready for yet.

"Yeah," Cait nodded again, not missing a step as they continued dancing while talking. "It helps that I switched during the summer when Brody spends most of his time with Mikey. And that Kay's been home on maternity leave from the GWA, so I've had more I could do on the ranch. Though now that school is about to start and they're going back to work, we're going to have to rearrange the schedule for me to go to the office a little more, and for your mom to watch Brody on the days I'm not working with Brook or from home. And I'm sure it'll all change again in a few weeks when Brook has Maddie, and we both have to start working around her naps and feeding times. But at least, having gone through the newborn phase with Kay and Sam, I kind of have an idea of what to expect then."

"How does that work?" When Cait arched an eyebrow at him like she didn't understand his question, Josh elaborated. "Working with Kay and Brook to convert their books into screenplays. How do ya'll do it?"

"I start out by reading the book," Cait explained with a wide smile, obviously excited about her new job. "Which is totally the best perk of this job. I get paid to read books I would have read anyway. Then I sit down with the author, and we discuss the characters, their personalities, and the image they have in their head for anything I'm unclear about in the book. Then I take the dialogue from the book and put it in a screenplay format, taking out all the inner monologues and thoughts of the characters, or converting them to more dialogue if needed. And then I put in all the scene descriptors that the actors will need to portray on screen. After that, I have the author read over it and we work together to tweak it until everyone's happy with the final product."

Josh loved watching how passionate she was as she went into detail, telling him about the screenplays she'd completed in the six weeks since she started working full-time as a screenwriter. She caught him up on how much closer the entertainment division of Burleson Incorporated was to actually producing the films that would eventually air on the streaming service they were starting, and actually held his interest more than his sister had during the update she'd given during the last board meeting.

Yeah, that's probably because it's Cait telling me about it. I'd be more interested in watching paint dry if Cait was talkin' to me while watchin' it. The subject doesn't matter as long as she's the one talkin'.

As they continued two-stepping, they talked a little more about his plans for working with his dad while he was home on the ranch this week before the songs changed to another line dance. Josh hated losing that physical contact with her as they separated, but he loved seeing how much fun she was having with his sisters, cousins, and the other women in town.

While he wasn't sure he was able to keep his feelings for her off his face all night, he was at least successful in keeping himself from stepping over the boundary of friendship that he had to keep between them for now. He just wasn't sure how much longer he could maintain that extreme level of self-control to keep from kissing her perfect pink lips.

It's just until I find my son and get the legalities of being part of his life squared away. Then I hope she's prepared for me to focus a hundred-and-ten percent on winning her heart.

~~~

Sunday, September 1, 2019

As Cait walked into the wedding shower for her brother and Charlotte, she couldn't help but reflect back on how much she'd changed her life since the last wedding shower she attended two months ago. While she had started driving herself to and from the Burleson ranch and the house she lived in with her brother, she'd still felt like he needed to drive if she went anywhere else back when they attended Fiona and Rick's wedding shower after church. Now, she was able to drive herself to the church, though she still preferred having someone in the car with her when she went anywhere else.

Her driving habits weren't the only things that had changed in the last couple of months, either. She was now living alone in the house Charlotte formerly occupied, instead of having to live with her brother or someone else to help her feel safe. And she'd switched over to be a full-time screenwriter for the entertainment division of Burleson Incorporated, so she only had to keep her own house on the ranch clean.

She'd had a couple of nights when the nightmares returned right after the move. But she made it through them without calling anyone to come check her house for intruders in the middle of the night, so she considered it a win. She'd also talked to her new therapist about the dreams and implemented a few new strategies to combat them, which was probably why they didn't last long this time around.
~~~

The new therapist was also working with her on ways to deal with her anxiety about going out in public, which seemed to be helping. Having someone with her that knew about her issues to talk through her overwhelmed feelings as they happened seemed to be the most effective. But spending time each day helping care for the horses on the ranch, and thinking of them if she felt overwhelmed without a friend to talk to, was also working for her.

Maybe I should try imagining the feel of the horses' hair as I'm petting them next time I try to go to the grocery store or put gas in my car without someone going with me? If it works for driving to church by myself, maybe it'll work for those other things too?

Or should I take a little time with just the changes I've already made to feel more comfortable before I push myself to do more? Yeah, I want to be able to go back to living a normal life where I'm not afraid to go out in public on my own. But I don't want to risk a setback by trying to do too much too soon, either.

She didn't have much time to think about it as Hazel ushered her over to the table where she insisted the wedding party had to sit. Well, minus the kids, since she had most of them sitting a table over with her and Bob.

As she took her seat between Josh and Becky, Cait noticed an empty chair between Jake and Fiona, who would be walking back up the aisle together at the end of the ceremony. She looked around the table that was set up to seat ten to figure out who might be missing. She saw Charlotte beside Jake with Mikey on her other side. Mikey's best friend from San Diego, Trent Jones, was on his other side, with Becky between him and Cait. On Josh's other side, Fiona's husband, Rick, sat between Josh and Fiona.

I guess Mikey and Char didn't think about how it would throw off the seating by not pairing up the matron of honor with her husband and picking another bridesmaid to pair with Jake?

Not that Cait really cared if it seemed awkward to have an empty seat at the table to make up for the fact that they also had an extra person who wasn't part of the wedding party. She'd rather just enjoy the fact that she was paired with Josh for each of the festivities leading up to the nuptials.

After dancing with him the night before, she'd pretty much given up on trying to protect her heart by keeping her distance from him. In fact, she was kind of hoping that all the extra time they'd have to spend together this week would prompt him to bring them back out of the friend zone and start to flirt with her again.

Not that she'd be brave enough to instigate any flirting, but she'd certainly reciprocate it if he initiated it. *And I definitely won't try sending him a sexy selfie again, unless he actually asks for one.*

"I'm surprised Mom let you get away with having Jake walk Fiona back up the aisle at the wedding." Becky's words brought Cait back into the conversation going on around her.

"I think she's more focused on setting you up this time," Char smirked, pointing at Becky. "Since you keep rejecting the guys she's tried to fix you up with, I think she's hoping Trent might pique your interest with him being a fresh face in town and all."

"Oh yeah, she's definitely targeting me this week," Becky agreed, nodding her head. "But she's also still working with the rest of the Matchmaking Mommas to pair up our single cousins and her friends' kids. And I'm sure she pushed to have Josh and Cait paired up. So, I don't understand why she hasn't at least moved someone over here to sit by Jake to try to fix him up, too."

Cait wasn't sure how to respond to Becky's statement about Hazel pushing to pair her and Josh. She knew they were one of the couples the Matchmaking Mommas hoped would get together eventually. But she'd also talked to Hazel to make it clear that while she was interested in Josh, and would be agreeable to being set up with him in the future, she needed time to deal with her issues first, and Josh would probably have to retire from the Navy before anything could happen between them.

She also knew that both Becky and Char knew about her attraction to Josh, so she couldn't lie and say that she only ever wanted to be his friend the way Amy had before she finally gave in to her feelings for Justin. With no other ideas for what to say, Cait kept her mouth shut and hoped her friends kept the matchmaking conversation focused on Jake.

"Ma's only pairing me and Cait up 'cause she thinks her previous efforts are workin' on us," Josh interjected, surprising Cait as he bumped his shoulder against hers. "And I'm happy to let Ma think we might turn into more than friends, 'cause it keeps her from pushin' a whole bunch of different women on me every time I'm home. And

Cait's cool, so it's not hard to hang out with her like it is with some of the other women in town."

Cait was immensely grateful for every acting class she'd ever taken at that moment, needing those lessons to keep her expression neutral, so nobody at the table would see how Josh's words had hurt her.

"Josh!" Becky reached around Cait and slugged Josh in the shoulder. "Why would you say something like that?"

"What?" Josh put a hand up to block his sister's aggression. "Cait and I are friends. I don't see what's wrong with our friendship coming with the benefit of avoiding Ma's matchmaking."

"It's fine, Becky," Cait defended Josh, not letting her mind wander to the other *benefits* she wished their friendship *came* with. "He's right. We are friends. Besides, I don't think your mom is trying to fix us up. She knows about my issues and that I trust that Josh's SEAL training will kick in to keep me safe if a mass shooter shows up. And I'm happy to reciprocate his protection from bullets by protecting him from the Thirsty Threesome."

Cait hoped her lighthearted comment and slight smirk effectively covered the heartbreak she was feeling at realizing that Josh would only ever see her as a friend.

"I've definitely got the better end of that trade," Josh chuckled.

"Damn it," Jake cursed, pointing at Josh. "When did you become the smart twin? And why didn't you share this epiphany sooner, so I coulda talked a friend into hanging out with me while we're home, too?"

"You're still the smart twin," Josh assured his brother, grinning mischievously. "But after not seeing you every day for the last few years, I forgot that your brain is too full of computer geek stuff to have room for all the common-sense stuff. Sorry, Bro. I'll try to remember to help you out with that from now on."

"Do you need me to get Lexi or Kayla over here to be your shield, Jake?" Fiona joked.

"Or maybe Cassidy or Kara?" Charlotte added, teasing her brother.

"Or I could call Liam over here," Rick suggested. "Surely I can trust you not to take pictures with him here in the church to cause more of a marriage uproar on social media than I've already had to deal with for the last couple of weeks."

The conversation turned to the fallout in the GWA from the pictures several of the wrestlers were in after their last pay-per-view show in Las Vegas and Cait relaxed, glad to not feel like she was in the hot seat the way she had when they were talking about the matchmaking.

Although, from the way Rick just described the scene Allissa's mother caused with the wrestlers in Vegas, I have to wonder if she'll be an official member of the Matchmaking Mommas before the end of her stay in town. Cait hadn't met Windy Walters or her friend Kandi King yet, but Rick had pointed them out where they were sitting with the Hunters while he relayed the story. *Considering how close Dean and Allissa seem to have gotten since the last time they were in town, and now her mom is here to visit with his family, maybe she'll be here longer than the week Rick thinks she'll be, so she can be in on planning that Thanksgiving wedding Dean was talking about at Rick and Fiona's wedding?*

Cait took advantage of the changing flow of topics to distract herself from any thoughts about Josh and his lack of romantic feelings for her. When they sat back down after getting up to fix their lunch plates, and everyone at the table started talking about Mikey and Charlotte's plans for building a bigger house on the ranch for their growing family, Cait appreciated that her brother's best friend from San Diego was in attendance because Trent was the only other person there that didn't call him Ian.

When she thought back over the last decade since Trent had gotten close to their family, she realized that he'd always called her brother Mike or Campbell. *Oh wow! Why didn't I realize that he'd just gone to using our last name after Mikey dropped his first name after the shooting?*

Cait knew her brother went back and forth between calling his friend Trent or Jones, and only had him listed in his phone as Jones to help protect any cover he might use as a DEA agent. But she'd always called him by his first name, not wanting to associate him with the man her mother claimed was Cait's sperm donor because of his very common last name.

Not that Cait really believed her mother's convoluted stories about some sailor named Earnie Jones providing half of her genetic material. If her mom had claimed to have gotten pregnant by some random druggie, whose name she couldn't remember, Cait would have believed her. But there was no way on earth the Lorna Campbell Cait remembered from her childhood would have ever had an affair with an upstanding Naval officer.

Of course, Cait also didn't believe her brother's story about her mom dating a farmhand named Hector Gonzales before she was born either. She might not care enough about finding out her ethnicity breakdown to spit in a tube and send it off to have her DNA tested like her brother, but she was pretty sure her pasty white complexion was proof enough that she wasn't half-Hispanic.

When she was a teenager and curious enough to Google the two names, she'd quickly figured out that both her mother and brother were wrong. Cait had found an article about a man named Earnest Jones being promoted to Commander in the Navy that was dated about the same time she remembered her mom making the claim, and assumed she'd pulled the name from the paper. And the only Hector Gonzales she found with the spelling her brother insisted was correct was a fictional character from an old James Bond movie. So, she assumed her brother had confused the names of a farmhand their mother flirted with and a movie character he might have seen while watching television with their grandfather as a child.

After that failed attempt at finding her biological father to help her brother with some financial support for her, and the subsequent discussion with Mikey about how both of their biological fathers were probably deadbeats who were just as strung out as their mother, Cait had given up. She took babysitting jobs for people in their apartment building to help Mikey with their bills, until she was old enough to start waiting tables, and finally talked her brother into letting her go on a few casting calls for local commercials and modeling jobs.

She hadn't thought anything more about finding out about her ancestry until the Burlesons mentioned doing DNA tests back at Christmas. While she was happy that the Burlesons had been able to find their long-lost cousins and was a little interested in what Mikey had learned about their Campbell ancestors since sending in his sample and starting their family tree, Cait had no desire to send in her own sample. The only thing she might learn from that which she hadn't already learned from Mikey's research was which of her mother's druggie boyfriends wasn't coherent enough to use protection. And she wasn't about to risk one of those losers coming back into her life.

Why am I thinking about those losers now? Lorna and her junkie boyfriends have no place at Mikey's wedding shower.

Today is supposed to be about celebrating Mikey and Charlotte finding each other and falling in love. So that's what I need to focus on. Not any of my childhood baggage or my heartbreak at realizing Josh isn't my happily ever after.

I'm thrilled to pieces for Mikey and Char, so I need to get out of my own head and start acting like it.

Cait jumped back into the conversations around her as they finished lunch and got started on the games. She just hoped her smile didn't appear as fake as it felt every time she took her eyes off her brother and his bride-to-be.

~~~

Tuesday, September 3, 2019

As Josh rode back to the family stable on Leonardo after working all day on the ranch, he started wondering if this was what the Navy therapist had in mind when he suggested equine therapy to help him come to terms with the things he'd had to do as a SEAL. When his platoon deployed a couple of weeks before Josh's terminal leave started, Josh took advantage of his time on desk duty to talk with the therapist on base about how to transition to civilian life. He'd learned that his feelings about going to a dark place in his head while in mission mode were normal, and he was one of the lucky ones who was getting out without a bad case of PTSD. After a couple of times talking with the therapist, Josh already felt better about being able to transition to life on the ranch without having any more of those dark thoughts. But the therapist had suggested equine therapy if Josh needed a little more help settling in once he was able to finally move home.

But I think he meant I should meet with a therapist who specializes in equine therapy, not just spending time with my horse while separating spring calves from their mommas to wean them, and moving pregnant heifers to the pastures closest to the birthing barn to prepare for fall calving, like I did today.
~~~

Leah Mae Wright

Come to think of it, I wonder if there's a therapist in our area that might be able to use some of our older, family horses for a therapy program? I'm sure there are lots of people who could benefit from that form of therapy. Possibly other vets, or maybe the women and children living at the Ashbury House?

I'll have to ask Bobby if they've looked into that possibility for one of the services they're offering. If not, maybe I'll look into starting something, once I find my son and can finally move home.

Josh dismounted and led Leonardo to the bathing stall on the backside of the stable. He tethered the horse to the wall and started untacking him, carrying the leather saddle and equipment to the tack room, so it wouldn't get wet when he turned on the water.

As he stepped back out after putting the saddle in the tack room, Josh was greeted by the glorious sight of Cait walking into the stable. "Hey, Sunshine, whatcha doin'?"

"Oh, uh, hi," Cait sputtered, clasping a hand to her chest, obviously surprised to see him in the stable. "Just sneaking in a little equine therapy before dinner."

"Were you reading my mind?" Josh couldn't stop himself from chuckling at the irony of her mentioning equine therapy just a few minutes after he was thinking about it.

"No," Cait shook her head, her nose wrinkling in confusion.

"Then great minds really do think alike," Josh grinned, nodding toward the back exit of the stable to coax Cait to follow him back out to where he had Leonardo waiting to be taken care of in the bathing stall. "I was just thinking about how our older horses that we've retired from working the ranch every day might be beneficial in an equine therapy program."

"Seriously? That would be amazing," Cait gushed, her smile widening as they walked out to where Leonardo was waiting. "I'm not really doing equine therapy, but when I told my therapist about moving to the ranch, she mentioned how working with horses could be beneficial for my anxiety. So, I've been coming out here every evening to pet them and give them treats. And then when I feel overwhelmed while out in public, I can visualize those times to keep from having a panic attack."

"Has it helped?" Josh questioned as he grabbed the hose and turned on the water. After filling the troth for Leonardo to drink from, he started hosing down the horse to cool him off after working in the South Texas heat.

"Yeah, I think so," Cait replied, stepping back to keep from getting wet. "I still prefer having someone with me to talk to, just in case I can't stop the panic attack from starting. But I have been successful in driving myself to the church and the B and B without incident from using the technique. Now I need to start trying to go a few other places on my own to make sure it's really working."

As Josh used a squeegee glove to wipe the water off of Leonardo, he tried to think of ways he could help Cait with her anxiety in public places. But since her goal was to be able to go to more locations alone, he couldn't think of a single thing he could do to help her.

Finally, he gave up trying to think of ways to be supportive on his own and just asked her what the therapist recommended. "So, uh, has the therapist suggested anything your friends can do to support your efforts?"

"Yeah, in fact, your family has really been stepping up to help me with everything she's suggested. Mostly going with me to new places, and meeting me at the places I feel comfortable going by myself, to keep me from wanting to rush right back home." Cait stepped back up to help Josh dry Leonardo off after he turned off the water.

"What new places have you gone?" *And where can I take you while I'm home this week?*

"You already know about the Destiny Playhouse and Tully's Roadhouse," Cait smiled over Leonardo's back as they each wiped a side of the horse with a towel. "But I've also been to the bowling alley, shopping, and to a few places to eat here in town. I haven't been brave enough to go anywhere outside of Heart's Destiny with anyone but Mikey yet. And since I didn't want to risk having a panic attack when he and Char were trying to have family time with Brody, I haven't gone to any of the attractions in San Antonio that they visited over the summer."

"Would you feel safe going to some of those places with me?" Josh knew he was jumping the gun to start thinking of dates he could take her on in San Antonio, but he had so many ideas of fun things they could do together that he couldn't stop himself from hoping she'd trust him to protect her in the city. "After seeing how much more relaxed you were in the park yesterday at the Labor Day picnic and Maria's birthday party than you were on the Fourth of July, I'd love to take you to the Alamo. It's not as crowded as say, SeaWorld or Six Flags. And it's not too far from the Tower of the Americas, where we can see the whole city in the revolving restaurant at the top."

"Yeah, I would trust you to keep me safe," Cait smiled momentarily before her glow dimmed and her expression flattened. "But I'm not sure when we could go. I'm working with Kay and Brook for the next three days, trying to get the screenplay for **Heart's Desire** finalized before Kay flies out with the GWA on Monday. And then we'll both be busy on Saturday with all the last-minute details for Mikey and Char's wedding."

"We could go on Sunday after church," Josh suggested, untying Leonardo to walk him into his stall in the stable for brushing and feeding. *Fuck, I hope we can at least get one friendly outing in before I head back to Virginia to look for my son. But if not, then I'll just plan to take her when I'm home for the holidays, if I haven't found him and settled everything to be able to move home before then.*

"Sounds good," Cait smiled as they continued caring for the horse. "But I should probably skip the potluck after church. And maybe wait on the revolving restaurant until after I know if the anxiety is going to make me nauseous or not."

"Deal," Josh chuckled at the adorable face she made as she flushed lightly from being embarrassed about mentioning nausea. "And if you can't handle the Tower, I'm sure I can find someplace else we can eat at the RiverWalk."

And maybe I can keep myself from thinking of it as a date, Josh hoped.

With plans made, they finished taking care of Leonardo before going to their separate homes to clean up for dinner at his parents' house.

Chapter Thirteen

Cait couldn't believe how much prep work went into getting the women of the wedding party and the bride's family ready on the day of a wedding in Heart's Destiny. The way Lexi, Kayla, and Cassidy multi-tasked nails, hair, and makeup for all of them reminded Cait of being backstage at a runway show back when she was modeling, only without the rapid wardrobe changes.

Cait had been awoken by Mikey and Brody barging into her home after Hazel and the Glam Squad had kicked them out of the house they were currently living in while their new house was being built. At first, she'd momentarily forgotten about how everyone just walked into all the houses on the ranch, since she wasn't awake to hear their announcement of "knock, knock" as they entered her home. She had a small panic attack, thinking someone was breaking in, but she'd quickly calmed down, when she recognized her brother and nephew's voices, and remembered she'd moved to the ranch where it was safe to leave the door unlocked. Once she'd calmed down and admonished them for frightening her, she dressed for the day and left the guys there to get ready, while she joined the ladies for a day of girl talk while they were primped and pampered.

Once her nails, hair, and makeup were done, she popped back over to her house to grab her garment bag with her dress and shoes before riding with the other women of the wedding party to the church. She had to run interference to make sure her brother didn't see Charlotte as she walked through the church to get to the bride's room behind the baptismal. But she didn't mind that since she got to see Josh in his tuxedo pants and dress shirt before he finished getting dressed in the groom's room.

Leah Mae Wright

A girl can still dream, even if there's not much hope we'll ever be more than friends.

Once there, Cait put Josh out of her mind as the ladies all changed into their dresses, helping one another with the back fastenings they couldn't reach themselves. As Bob, Hazel, and Maria arrived and started talking to Char, Becky, and Fiona about the traditional good luck tokens every bride needed before walking down the aisle, Cait started wondering what her own wedding would look like, if she was ever able to get over Josh to fall in love with someone else.

I always thought I'd just have a spur of the moment courthouse wedding on a random day in the middle of the week, like Mikey and Mari did. But after seeing all the weddings here in Heart's Destiny this year, now I kind of hope to have a smaller version of the big festivities they have here. Maybe not as many people in the bridal party and none of the pre-parties that the bride's parents are supposed to host, but a church wedding and an actual wedding reception, instead of just grabbing a sheet cake from the grocery store on the way home from the courthouse.

Would it be weird to ask Mikey to walk me down the aisle? He is the closest thing to a dad I've ever had, so it seems appropriate to me. But I can't help but wonder if he'd be okay with it? Or if he'd rather stand up as my man of honor?

Will I still be able to be friends with the Burlesons to have Becky, Jen, and Julie as my bridesmaids, if I end up with someone other than Josh? Thinking his name made his image pop into Cait's head instantly. *Who am I kidding? I doubt I'll ever meet a man who affects me the way Josh does, so there's no point in even thinking about possibly getting married one day.*

Unless he suddenly changes his mind about whatever caused him to quit flirting with me and keep us firmly in the friend zone, I'm going to spend the rest of my life celibate, with no chance of ever walking down the aisle to my happily ever after. And even if he starts flirting again, I doubt he'll want more than a short-term fling.

No, it's better to quash any wedding fantasies now, before I start picturing him as the groom, waiting for me at the end of the aisle.

"Are ya'll tryin' to get started on the honeymoon before the wedding?" Becky teased her sister, pointing to the phone in Char's hands and bringing Cait back to the moment.

"Something like that," Charlotte admitted, typing another message before putting her phone in her purse.

"Oh, Char, you're such a beautiful bride," Hazel gushed as she hugged her daughter. "Now, I need to make sure I have a box of tissues before I take my seat." Hazel was wiping her eyes already as she made her way to the door.

"I've already put a box on the pew for you," Kathy Harrison assured Hazel as she opened the door for Hazel to leave before lining the rest of them up to walk down the hallway to the vestibule to prepare for entering the chapel for the wedding.

Once Kathy double-checked that everyone was in their seats and ready for the ceremony to start, she directed Maria to lead the processional.

"Don't be nervous, Sweetheart." Bob patted Char's hand reassuringly, as Maria stepped through the door to enter the chapel first. "Ian might not be much of a rancher, but he's a good man who'll do right by you and your babies."

Cait had a momentary pang of jealousy at how lucky the Burlesons were in having their parents in their lives. She quickly quashed the brief desire to have a similar relationship with her own parents. *Quit it, Caitir! No point in wishing for a fairy tale, when you know good and well a relationship with Lorna and whatever loser she screwed without a condom would just be a nightmare, not the dream come true you always wanted.*

"Thanks, Daddy." Charlotte leaned her head over to rest her cheek on her dad's bicep, as Cait stepped through the doors next.

She missed whatever else was said as her eyes locked on Josh already standing in place at the front of the chapel. Her thoughts about having a family of her own quickly morphed from her parents back to the happily ever after she no longer thought she could ever have.

Yeah, there's no way I'll ever get married if he's not the groom, Cait thought, as she appreciated the way Josh filled out that tailored navy-blue tuxedo. *I'm not sure if I like the way he looks now better than when he had the shirt unbuttoned at the neck and was putting in his cufflinks. But damn, that cowboy's F-I-N-E, fine, no matter what he's wearing.*

When she got to the end of the aisle, Cait turned and took her place exactly opposite Josh. But it took all her willpower to turn and face the back of the church to watch as Fiona and Becky walked down the aisle, instead of turning to look at Josh once more.

When the music changed to Richard Wagner's **Bridal Chorus** and the doors opened for Charlotte to walk down the aisle on her father's arm, Cait turned to watch her brother's reaction to seeing his bride in her wedding gown. Seeing the pure love for Charlotte in Mikey's eyes made Cait wish she had a couple of Hazel's tissues, as she teared up at seeing how happy her brother was on his second wedding day.

While she knew that Marisol would always have a special place in Mikey's heart, it was clear that Charlotte was the love of his life. Cait vowed right then to never settle for anything less than the love she saw between Mikey and Charlotte.

As Char and Bob stepped to the end of the aisle, Cait kept her eyes focused on Mikey and Charlotte, not wanting to chance looking at Josh and feeling heartbroken by not seeing that same type of love for her shining in his eyes that was clearly shining in both Mikey and Charlotte's eyes. She also didn't want to risk anyone recognizing her own love for Josh shining in her eyes.

"Dearly beloved, we're gathered here today to join Michael Ian Campbell and Charlotte Anne Burleson in holy matrimony," Pastor Harrison began. "Who gives this woman to be married to this man?"

"Her mother and I." Bob leaned down and kissed Charlotte's cheek before shaking Mikey's hand. He then placed Charlotte's hand in Mikey's before stepping back to take his seat in the front row of the church beside Hazel.

"I love you," Mikey mouthed to Charlotte as Pastor Harrison gave a speech about love and the sanctity of marriage.

Cait couldn't see Char's face, but based on the way Mikey's lips turned up in a smile, she assumed Charlotte had returned the mouthed sentiment. It was so poignant a moment that Cait sniffled as the tears started to escape from her eyes. Thankfully, her position at the front of the church was the closest to the first pew on the bride's side of the church, and Hazel was kind enough to discreetly pass her one of the tissues from the box she was holding.

Cait dabbed the tissue under her eyes, hoping not to disturb her makeup, as she watched Mikey and Char recite their vows. She was so worked up at realizing she'd probably never have a wedding of her own that Hazel ended up passing her another tissue before they each finally said, "I do."

Yeah, I'm going to need to rush straight to the ladies' room to fix my makeup before I can pose for pictures, Cait decided as Mikey, Charlotte, and Brody stepped over to the other side of the church to light a family unity candle. *Even if the waterproof mascara didn't run, I'm sure I wiped off all the concealer under my eyes.*

Thankfully, Josh turned to watch this part of the ceremony, so he's not looking at how messed up my face must be now. And hopefully, he won't notice if I don't look up at him when we walk to the back of the church together.

After the unity candle, Pastor Harrison spoke about the significance of the rings. "They are made of a precious metal to remind us that love is not cheap or common; but indeed, love is very costly and dear to us. The rings are also made in a circle and their design tells us that we must keep love continuous throughout our whole lives, even as the circle of the ring is continuous. As you wear these rings, whether you are together or apart for even just a moment, may these rings be a constant reminder of the promises you are making to one another this day. Let us pray. Father, bless these rings which Michael and Charlotte have chosen to be visible signs of the inward and spiritual bond which unites their hearts. As they give and receive these rings, may they testify to the world of the covenant made between them here."

Wow, I never realized the significance of wedding rings before now, Cait thought. *The justice of the peace certainly didn't describe them like that at Mikey's first wedding.*

She didn't have time to contemplate why she hadn't registered the pastor saying something similar at the other weddings she'd attended this year, as a collective "amen" echoed throughout the church along with the pastor. Pastor Harrison held out his hand for Mikey to take Char's ring as he spoke to him. "Michael, will you please take this ring and place it upon the third finger of Charlotte's left hand, and holding her hand in yours, please repeat this promise to her, saying after me: With this ring, I thee wed. I seal my promise, to be your faithful and loving husband, as God is my witness."

"With this ring, I thee wed. I seal my promise, to be your faithful and loving husband, as God is my witness." Mikey grinned as he slid the ring on Char's finger.

Pastor Harrison extended his hand with Mikey's ring to Char and directed, "Charlotte, will you please take this ring and place it upon the third finger of Michael's left hand, and holding his hand in yours, please repeat this promise to him, saying after me: With this ring, I thee wed. I seal my promise, to be your faithful and loving wife, as God is my witness."

"With this ring, I thee wed. I seal my promise, to be your faithful and loving wife, as God is my witness." Char pushed Mikey's ring on his finger.

"Charlotte and Michael, you have come here today before us and before God and have expressed your desire to become husband and wife," Pastor Harrison continued the ceremony. "You have shown your love and affection by joining hands, and have made promises of faith and devotion, each to the other, and have sealed these promises by the giving and the receiving of the rings. Therefore, by the power vested in me by the State of Texas, I now pronounce that you are husband and wife. Michael, you may kiss your wife."

"Gladly," Mikey grinned as he cradled Charlotte's face in both of his hands before pressing their lips together.

"Keep it clean, Campbell," Jake joked. "She might be your wife now, but she's still my sister, and I don't need to see more than a peck between ya'll."

Mikey shook his head as he broke the relatively chaste kiss. But he was smiling at Jake's joke, which caused Cait to smile with him.

"Sorry, Ian, you're stuck with my whole family now," Charlotte teased, giggling. "There are no do-overs to keep from getting my idiot brothers as brothers-in-law."

"I wouldn't have it any other way," Mikey chuckled before turning his head to grin at Jake. "But get it right, Jake. It's Burleson-Campbell now."

I still can't believe Mikey's changing his and Brody's last name to match Charlotte's, Cait thought as the preacher cleared his throat to get everyone to focus once more on the ceremony that wasn't quite finished.

"Ladies and gentlemen, it is my privilege to introduce to you for the first time, Mr. and Mrs. Burleson-Campbell," Pastor Harrison announced as the music for the recessional started.

Mikey took Charlotte's hand in his, kissing the back of it before they led the wedding party to the back of the church. Brody stepped up and presented his arm to Maria like a perfect gentleman. Cait couldn't help but smile as Maria placed her hand on the crook of his elbow before the kids followed Mikey and Char.

Once Becky & Trent and Fiona & Jake did the same, Cait stepped to the center of the aisle and placed her hand on Josh's arm in a similar fashion. She felt that ever-present rush of tingles traveling through her body from the point where she touched him straight to her core.

Great, now I need to go dry my panties in the bathroom, too. And I should probably do that before I fix my makeup.

~~~

Josh couldn't get the vision of Cait walking down the aisle out of his head, as he sat beside her at the reception after giving their speeches and sitting down to dinner. When she'd walked into the church earlier, he hadn't seen her in the bridesmaid's dress of various shades of blue that she was currently wearing. Though he couldn't help but think how amazing she looked in it. In his mind, he'd seen her in a white wedding dress, and he wasn't in the navy-blue tuxedo he was wearing for Charlotte and Ian's wedding, but his Navy dress blues as her groom. She'd taken his breath away and made it damn near impossible for him to pay attention to anything but her during his sister's wedding.

He'd wanted so badly to be the one wiping her tears when she quietly cried during the ceremony. But he knew it wasn't the right place or time for him to step up to comfort her.

After the ceremony, when he tried to offer her a shoulder to cry on, Cait had made sure he knew they were all happy tears right before she ran off to the ladies' room to touch up her makeup in case the tears left streaks. Josh hadn't seen any streaks in her makeup, and if anyone would have noticed them, it would be him because of how closely he constantly examined her, but he'd let her go with the rest of the ladies
~~~

to "freshen up" before the pictures. Only because he knew hovering over her the way he wanted to would make his feelings for her clear to everyone in attendance, and he couldn't do that just yet.

The guys might all know that he wanted more with her when he got out of the Navy, but most of them didn't know he was on terminal leave. And until he had some definitive news to share about his son, he didn't want his future plans to be common knowledge, on the off chance that something screwed them up when he finally found his child.

He just hoped he could keep up the I-only-want-to-be-friends act with Cait until he got everything squared away for them to be a couple. Josh didn't want to inadvertently hurt her by starting something, when he couldn't stay in town to see it through.

"So, how did ya'll manage to escape the Matchmaking Mommas' nefarious plans tonight?" From her seat between Cait and Trent, Becky glared across the table at Jake and their single cousins, who took up the other four seats at their table without being matched up with dates by their moms.

"I don't know about Jake and JJ, but we," Jen pointed back and forth between herself and Julie, "got lucky when Rick put the GWA guys in time-out."

"Because of the Vegas wedding chapel pictures on social media?" Cait looked over at the table where the wrestlers were sitting with Byron Avington and his wife, Blair, before turning to look at Jen and Julie.

"I thought they were all sitting with the Avingtons because of Allissa's stalker?" Josh arched an eyebrow at his cousins, curious about how things had changed since the night before, when Jen and Julie had been seated with Liam and Dion at the rehearsal dinner.

"I'm sure both of those things factored into Rick asking our cousins to babysit the wrestlers and Allissa's mom and her friend," Jake chuckled before stuffing his mouth with the last bite of his dinner.

"But Windy and Kandi thinking the matchmaking was working better than it was last night, and offering to host bachelor parties for Dion and Liam at the brothel where they work is probably a bigger factor," Julie giggled, shaking her head before taking a sip from her wine glass.

246

"So, we figured it was probably best if we all made it clear we're happily single," Jen added with a grin.

"Considering the offers I've gotten this week from Kandi, I don't think it matters if we're single or not," JJ sighed, shaking his head as he placed his napkin on his empty plate. "But since our Avington cousins are getting paid to be their bodyguards, I figured it's their job to deflect those advances tonight, while I happily hide away behind all ya'll."

"What's the matter, Cuz? Can't handle a little attention from a couple of cougars?" Josh couldn't resist teasing JJ, thinking it was funny that the big, bad Dom was being treated like a boy toy.

"No," JJ barked adamantly. "Which is why I'm looking into opportunities to purchase a couple of out-of-state oil companies, which I'll be presenting at the next board meeting. If Windy and Kandi stick around to plan Dean and Allissa's wedding, then I wanna be anywhere but here in town for the next couple of months."

More like he wants to buy the company Deanna works for, so he can go to Tulsa and try to win her over.

They all chuckled as the emcee asked the single ladies to step out on the dance floor for the bouquet toss. The girls all got up and congregated together between the reception tables and the center of the dance floor, where Charlotte and Ian were standing with their mother.

Yeah, I'd better keep an eye on this toss, so I can catch the garter if Ma convinces Char to toss the bouquet to Cait. Lucky for me, that means watching Cait the whole time she's out there.

Once Hazel stepped away from the newlyweds, Charlotte turned her back to the crowd of women on the dance floor and loudly announced, "Just because I'm married and a momma now, doesn't mean I have to join the Matchmaking Mommas. So, I'm going to make sure nobody can accuse me of targeting them by looking at my hubby, instead of where I'm tossing the bouquet."

Charlotte pushed up on her tiptoes and pecked her lips on Ian's. Then, without any kind of countdown, she took a step back from him and tossed the bouquet backwards over her head.

Fuck yeah! Josh thought when the blue and white flowers sailed through the air in a perfect arc and landed in Cait's arms. *Is it wrong to be jealous of a bunch of flowers because of the way she cradled 'em against her tits when she caught 'em?*

Josh didn't wait for the emcee to announce that it was the men's turn, jumping from his seat to be front and center when Ian tossed the garter.

"I suppose you want me to toss the garter the same way. Huh, Princess?" Ian arched an eyebrow at Charlotte, who nodded her head in agreement.

"Yeah, I've got a better idea." Ian grinned at her before turning and calling Brody over to help him. Brody ran over from the table where he was sitting, as Charlotte sat down in the chair that had been brought out on the dance floor. "Want to help me toss the garter?"

"Yeah!" Brody bounced with excitement, slipping on the dance floor in the shoes he wore with his tuxedo to match the men in the wedding party.

"Okay, yeah, you do have a better idea." Charlotte grinned, as Ian went down on one knee in front of her and lifted the hem of her wedding gown up to just above her knees, so he could see to remove the garter.

"Oh, I like the way Ian does this," Aiden Walker shouted from the group of guys gathering on the dance floor. "It's way better with a little leg showing."

"Hey, those are my sister's legs," Josh barked toward where the Walkers were congregated to his left on the dance floor. "And you'd better not be looking at them."

"Dude, it's not a big deal." Aiden held up his hands in surrender toward Josh. "All the girls show off more leg than that every summer in their short shorts."

"Doesn't matter if a girl is wearing short shorts that show off her legs or not," Jake interjected from beside Josh. "You don't get to look unless a lady asks you to, so avert your eyes."

"How about you hurry this up, hubby?" Charlotte suggested, "so we don't have a riot on our hands before you can toss the garter."

"As you wish, wifey." Ian winked at Charlotte as he removed the garter from just above her knee and lowered her dress back to the floor. He gave her a quick peck as he stood back up. Then turned and picked Brody up, handing him the garter.

"How am I supposed to throw it? And who am I throwing it to?"

Oh fuck! This might not be as easy as I thought, Josh realized, feeling unsure if his new brother-in-law would go along with the

Matchmaking Mommas' plans for whom to pair up with his sister. Or if Ian had someone else in mind whom he'd rather see with Cait than Josh.

"Shoot it like a rubber band," Ian suggested, not giving away who the recipient should be.

"No, you throw it like a baseball," Charlotte protested, jumping up out of the chair, and stopping Brody from looping it around one finger. "I can't believe you taught him to shoot people with rubber bands." Charlotte shook her head and glared at Ian. "That's going to get him in trouble in school next year."

"No, Mom, we only shoot rubber bands at Aunt Cait when she doesn't put them back in the bathroom," Brody informed her.

Josh had to chuckle at how her nephew had just outed Cait as being a slob when it came to putting away the rubber bands she'd worn in her hair all summer.

"That'll still get you on Santa's naughty list," Charlotte warned Brody. "You should pick them up and put them away for her instead."

"Okay," Brody shrugged, not seeming to care for the life lesson. "Who am I throwing the garter to?"

"Uncle Josh," Ian suggested, grinning at Charlotte.

Thank fuck! Josh was momentarily relieved to realize his brother-in-law had just shown the first sign of giving his blessing to Josh to pursue a relationship with Cait. *Yeah, Brody, throw it to Uncle Josh,* Josh agreed, grinning at his new brother-in-law as he stepped away from the guys, who would probably try to fight him for the garter as a way to rib him.

"Just close your eyes and throw it," Charlotte countered. "That way, it'll be a surprise to see who catches it."

Ian turned his back to the group of guys gathered to catch the garter, which put Brody facing out at them over his father's shoulder.

Josh grinned and waved at Brody as the boy partially opened his eyes to look around before he actually threw the garter toward the crowd. Unfortunately, Brody didn't throw to the area where Josh was standing, but to the other side of the dance floor, where he had no chance at all of being able to reach out and grab it.

Damn, I thought I had favorite uncle status with Brody. Why didn't he listen to his dad and throw the garter to me?

"Oh, aren't you a cutie," the photographer, Philippe, gushed as Josh turned to look with everyone else to figure out who caught the garter. "Come on up here for the pictures and bring your dad to be in it with you."

"I'm, uh, here to meet my dad." The little boy in navy-blue slacks and a light blue button-down, who looked to be about eight or nine years old, tentatively stepped forward, looking around like he wasn't sure where his parents were in the room.

Holy shit! He looks just like me!

Could he be my son? Is he Triple J?

Like, maybe he and his mom came to town to check me out before calling me?

"What's your name?" Ian knelt down, placing Brody on the floor beside him.

"His name's Josh," Brody answered for the kid. "We were playing before, while ya'll were taking pictures. You said to throw the garter to Josh, so I threw it to him."

My son's name is Josh? Did his mom know he was mine and name him after me?

No, it can't be. Surely, if she'd known who I am to name him after me, then she'd have told me when she was pregnant.

So, he's probably not my kid. I'm just so frustrated with looking and not finding him that I'm getting delusional.

"I said to throw it to Uncle Josh," Ian explained. "I didn't know you knew anyone else named Josh."

"Is your uncle's name Josh Burleson?" The kid's eyes widened as he looked at Brody expectantly.

Wait! He knows my name? Maybe it's not wishful thinking after all.

"Yeah," Brody nodded, turning to point at where Josh was momentarily frozen in place. "He's right over there."

"Oh my goodness! He looks just like our Josh when he was a little boy." Josh's mom squealed and covered her mouth with her hand as the little boy turned and walked up to Josh.

"I'm Joshua Jacob Jones."

Joshua Jacob Jones. Triple J! Holy shit! Holy! Fucking! Shit! This little boy really could be my son!

The child extended his hand to Josh to shake. "And I think you're my dad."

Holy fucking shit! Fuck! Fuck! Fuck! I need to get my shit together, so I don't look like a dolt the first time I meet my son.

"It's nice to meet you, Joshua," Josh choked out. He took Joshua's hand and shook it as he knelt down to eye level with the little boy. It was like looking into a mirror and seeing himself, only twenty years younger. "Is your mom here, so we can all go somewhere to talk and get to know one another?"

Joshua shook his head, clearly fighting to keep his emotions from showing on his face. "My mom's an angel now."

An angel? His mom's dead? Fuck! How the hell am I supposed to comfort him within the first few minutes of seeing him for the first time?

"I'm sorry to hear that," Josh whispered, unsure what else to say to ease the boy's pain at such a loss. He knew he needed to be supportive of his son at this moment, but Josh couldn't help the way he instinctually compartmentalized death as if he was going into mission mode. He knew he'd need to deal with all the emotions he felt deep inside, but it didn't seem like the right time or place at the moment. "I've been looking for her, and you, since I saw you and I matched on the Ancestry site. You are Triple J, right?"

Instead of responding verbally, the little boy just nodded, looking a little nervous, as most of the guys left the dance floor and the rest of Josh's family started to surround them.

Feeling overwhelmed by the situation and uncomfortable trying to talk to his son for the first time with such a large audience, Josh did the only thing he could think of — he looked to his dad for help. Thankfully, his parents took charge of the situation without him even having to ask for their assistance.

"Hey, Joshua, I'm your Pappaw. How 'bout we go to the parlor, where you can officially meet the rest of your family, while everyone else gets back to dancin'?" Bob extended his hand to Joshua, who reached out and shook it, instead of moving off the dance floor in the direction Bob was pointing.

"Okay," Joshua shrugged when they released one another's hands. "But what's a Pappaw?"

"It's what we call a grandpa in our family," Josh chuckled, placing a hand on his son's back and gently ushering him to go with them as the rest of his family joined them in walking out of the ballroom and into the nearest parlor, where they could close out the rest of the crowd attending the wedding.

"And I'm your Memmaw, or grandma," Josh's mom added as they walked. As soon as they were in the room with a little more privacy, or as much privacy as Josh could hope for with his large family, Hazel continued. "But I prefer hugs to handshakes, so is it okay if I hug you?"

Joshua nodded before walking into his grandmother's arms for the first time. As the little boy returned the exuberant hug, Josh felt a little jealous of his mom getting to hug his son before he did.

"Okay, let's get the introductions out of the way, so you can start getting to know all your aunts, uncles, and cousins," Hazel choked out, wiping the tears from under her eyes as she released the embrace. "Pappaw and I are your dad's parents, making us your grandparents. The little boy who threw you the garter is your cousin Brody. His parents are your Aunt Charlotte and Uncle Ian."

Hazel pointed to each person as she said their names, giving everyone the chance to wave at Joshua for him to put a name to each face. "I don't know if you met them earlier when you were playing with the other kids, but Tia, Maria, Antonio, and baby Sam are your other cousins. Their parents are your Uncle Anthony and Aunt Kay."

"Your Uncle Bobby and Aunt Brook are going to give you another cousin in about a month. And then you have your Uncle Jake and Aunt Becky, who aren't married and don't have kids yet, but we're hopeful they'll be giving you more cousins soon."

"Ma," Jake groaned, shaking his head. "Now's not really the time for that discussion."

"Your grandchild count has already gone from zero to seven in the last year," Aunt Susan playfully chastised Hazel. "So you really should let the rest of us catch up before you start complaining about not having more."

"You're getting a two-fer in a few months, so you're catchin' up just fine," Hazel grinned at Susan before turning back to Joshua. "That's your Great-Aunt Susan. She's married to your Great-Uncle Jon, who's Pappaw's brother. Their kids would be your second cousins, JJ, Jen, Julie, and Justin. Justin is engaged to Amy and they're going to have twins at the end of the year."

"We call them our aunts and uncles too, 'cause they're too old for us to call them cousins," Maria interjected.

"And technically, they're our first cousins once removed," Tia added for her sister. "Which is way too long to call someone when you're asking them to pass the mashed potatoes at dinner, so aunt and uncle works better. And we do the same with our Avington, Harper, and Whitman cousins, but they didn't come back here to meet you yet."

"No, we figured the Burlesons were overwhelming enough," Uncle Jon chuckled. "But you've got a whole lot more family out in the ballroom who are all eager to meet you, Joshua."

"Wow, your family is a lot bigger than Mom's," Joshua remarked with a slight sense of awe in his tone as he looked up at Josh. "And a lot friendlier."

"Yeah?" Josh sat down on the sofa closest to Joshua, so he was on the little boy's eye level before patting the seat beside him to invite the kid to sit and talk. "Can you tell me about them? 'Cause I don't know anything about your mom or her family. Shoot, I don't even know anything about you, other than you're listed as Triple J on Ancestry and share half my DNA. And I'd love for you to tell me everything I missed in your life so far."

"Um, before you guys get to know one another, we should probably find your mom or the adult who brought you here, Joshua, so they don't get worried," Brook suggested.

"I, uh, came by myself," Joshua stuttered as he sat on the other end of the sofa from where Josh was sitting, leaving the space of a cushion empty between them. "My mom got sick and went to heaven to be an angel watching over me."

"Where'd you come from?" Bobby knelt down where he was standing beside his wife, obviously trying to keep his size from being too intimidating as he talked to the child.

"I, uh, kinda snuck out of the boarding school in Roanoke that Grandmother and Grandfather put me in," Joshua confessed sheepishly to Bobby before turning to look at Josh and gushing the rest of his story. "They were mean and took away the phone Aunt Tawny gave me, so I couldn't call you when I got on the website to find my dad.

But they didn't know about the debit card she gave me when my grandparents took me away from her, so I used it for a bus ticket to come find you. Mom always told me you're a superhero in the Navy, so I figured you'd be able to convince the judge to let me live with you or Aunt Tawny, instead of my mean grandparents or at the school my grandparents put me in. And since your message on the website said you'd be moving back to Heart's Destiny when you get out of the Navy, I came here to find you. Then when I got off the bus, I walked around town until I found a park with some kids playing and asked for directions to find the Burleson Ranch. They told me the Burlesons were all at the bed and breakfast for a wedding and sent me here."

Holy shit! Josh thought, trying to figure out how a child so young could travel that far by themselves without anyone noticing.

Apparently, he wasn't the only one in his family having those thoughts, as there were several gasps at the same time his mother exclaimed, "Goodness gracious! How on earth were you able to travel so far by yourself without anyone noticing?"

"I used my debit card to buy dinner for a guy I met in the Roanoke bus station to get him to buy me the ticket and check me in as an unaccompanied minor," Joshua shrugged like it was no big deal. "Then when I got here, I waved to some people on the other side of the bus station to convince the driver they were there to pick me up. As soon as they waved back, he let me go and got back on the bus, so he didn't know I didn't really go with them."

"How old are you?" Josh had guessed eight or nine based on his size, but the kid was acting more like a teenager with the way he thought out his plan to come to Texas. "And where did you learn about traveling as an unaccompanied minor?"

"I just turned eight on June nineteenth," Joshua admitted proudly. "And Mom's favorite movie was *The Parent Trap*, so we watched it a lot before she got sick. But I also traveled to the school in Roanoke from my grandparents' house in Annapolis as an unaccompanied minor on a bus, so I knew how it worked in real life and not just the movies before I went to the bus station to come here."

Holy fuck! Josh was in awe of his son's resiliency and ability to navigate such a trek across the country, but he also vowed to do whatever he had to in order to keep Joshua from having to do something so dangerous again.

"Well, we're just glad you were able to get here safely," Hazel blubbered, sitting down beside Joshua, and squeezing him in another hug.

"Yes, we are," Josh agreed, smiling at his son to try to hide his worry about the things that could have happened to him on the trip.

"We are all so glad to meet you, Joshua," Charlotte added, looking around at the rest of the family before turning her smile back to Joshua. "And as much as I look forward to getting to know you, nephew, we should probably let you and your dad talk first, while we go back to the reception before our guests cut the cake without us."

After a chorus of "Good-to-meet-you's" and "Welcome-to-the-family's," most of the family left the room, leaving Josh alone with Joshua.

"So, you were born on June nineteenth, two-thousand-eleven?" Josh prompted, counting back nine months to realize he would have been conceived during Josh's first month in the Naval Academy. *He did say his grandparents lived in Annapolis, so that makes sense.*

"Yep," Joshua nodded. "In Alexandria, Virginia, where I lived with my mom and Aunt Tawny, after my grandparents kicked Mom out when she was pregnant with me. But Aunt Tawny's not really my aunt. She's my mom's best friend, but since they're like sisters, I've always called her my aunt."

Josh tried to remember back to picture Joshua's mother and had a vague memory of meeting a girl named Tawny, who hooked up with Jake while Josh hooked up with her friend. He couldn't remember the name of the girl he'd met that night, but he knew it started with J.

Jane? Janie? Fuck, how can I remember meeting Tawny because of her mentioning it was the same name as the chick from the Whitesnake videos, but I can't remember her friend's name, who I actually fucked and apparently have a kid with? Jamie? I know it's Jay-something.

"Your mom's name is Jay…" Josh trailed off, feeling like an ass for not remembering the name of the woman who gave birth to his son.

"Jaina," Joshua filled in for him. "Jaina Evangeline Jones."

Their talk was interrupted by a brief knock on the door.

"Come in," Josh called out, confused about why anyone would knock before entering a public space in the hotel. Byron and Blair Avington stepped in. "Hey, Uncle Byron and Aunt Blair."

Josh smiled when Byron arched an eyebrow at the unusual use of the uncle and aunt monikers. "I'm embracing Maria and Tia's way of thinking," Josh explained. "And calling anyone in my parents' generation aunt or uncle, instead of cousin once removed."

"Ah," Byron chuckled. "Makes sense."

"Joshua, Byron and his family are actually our cousins, who we just found this year through the same site where I found out about you," Josh explained. "The Burlesons have been looking for our second-great-grand-aunt, who was the Avington's first or second-great-grandma, since the end of World War I. So, finding them solved a hundred-year-old mystery in our family."

"Wow!" Joshua's eyes bugged out in surprise as he turned to look at Josh. "I'm glad it didn't take a hundred years for me to find you."

"Me too, buddy. Me too," Josh agreed, feeling a little less guilty about the eight years he missed of his child's life after realizing he could have missed out on finding him altogether.

"I just spoke to your dad as the family went back to the reception," Byron explained his appearance in the room after the Burlesons had mostly left. "And while I know you need to spend this time getting to know Joshua, I wanted to see if I could get some names from him to have my cyber team start the legwork on the legalities ya'll are gonna have to deal with in the next few weeks."

"Yeah, that's probably a good idea," Josh agreed, realizing that he was probably going to have to fight Jaina's parents for custody of his son.

"Whose names do you need to help my dad fix it to where I can live here?" Joshua looked at Byron, his expression obviously hopeful.

"Yours and your mom's to start," Byron clarified, pulling out his phone to type the names into a text message to his cyber team. "And anyone else you've lived with or that might have talked to a judge about you living with them since your mom passed away."

"I'm Joshua Jacob Jones and my mom's name is Jaina Evangeline Jones," Joshua started. "My mom wanted me to live with Aunt Tawny, or my dad, if we could find him on the internet after spitting in a tube and sending it to be tested. Aunt Tawny's last name is Ireland, like the country, but she's not my real aunt, just my mom's best friend. Mom's parents are Earnest and Evelyn Jones. And after they found out Mom was sick, they talked to a judge to take me away from Aunt

Tawny. But they didn't really want me to live with them. That's why they shipped me off to boarding school and told the headmaster not to let me even call Aunt Tawny."

"Thank you, Joshua," Byron smiled at the boy before turning his gaze to Josh. "I'll get my team to pull all the records they can, so you can file for custody. Considering he was able to travel here by himself after being dumped in boarding school by his grandparents, I'm sure we can get a judge to grant you temporary custody on the grounds that they can't keep him safe. But you can expect to have to go back to Virginia to go to court to make it permanent, once they can fit you on the docket."

"I'm not sure if Uncle Doug can sign off on the temporary custody thing or not, since we're related," Josh offered, wishing getting custody of his son could be as easy as having his uncle grant it as the local judge. "But Tyler Reilly is the attorney Anthony and Kay used to adopt Antonio, and that Char used to adopt Brody, so I'm sure he can handle whatever family law stuff we can do here in Texas by getting the case in front of a judge over in Hondo next week. And if he can't handle the part we'll have to do in Virginia, or Maryland, since that's where Joshua's grandparents live, then he can coordinate with an attorney there. So, send him everything you find."

"Is he here at the reception?" Byron tilted his head at Josh after typing the lawyer's name into his phone. "So I can give him a heads up on what I'll be sending him?"

"Yeah, I'm sure he is," Josh nodded. "If he's already left, then you can probably let his daughter Cassidy know what's going on to give him a call. She's one of Char's good friends, so I'm sure she's still here."

"Excellent," Byron smiled. "Then I'm going to go get all this started, and hopefully make it back to my table in time to get a piece of wedding cake."

Josh noticed how his son's eyes lit up at the mention of cake. *I guess he shares my sweet tooth as well as my looks.* "I think we'll join you in snagging a piece of cake or two," Josh grinned before turning to his son. "Did you eat dinner earlier, or should we run by the kitchen for a plate before we fill up on cake?"

"I ate a sandwich earlier when we stopped on the bus," Joshua informed him, standing up and appearing eager to go get some cake.

"That was probably at lunchtime, though, right?" Josh arched an eyebrow as he stood and started walking with his son out of the parlor.

"Yeah," Joshua admitted as his shoulders slumped, obviously realizing he needed to eat a real meal before he got dessert. "But it looked like everyone had assigned seats at the wedding, so I waited 'til they got up to dance and stuff before coming in there, 'cause I didn't have a seat."

"Well, I'm sure we can find you one. Shoot, my family will all probably fight over who gets to sit by you," Josh chuckled. "And I think it's only right that we celebrate finding each other by having dessert first tonight."

"Really?" Joshua's eyes lit up as they walked back into the ballroom.

"Yeah, really," Josh nodded, his smile matching his son's.

"Wow, Dad, you're even cooler than Mom said you were!" Joshua threw his arms around Josh, hugging his dad for the first time.

Fuck! I love hearing him call me Dad.

It wasn't an "I love you, Dad," like Josh hoped to one day hear from his son, but Josh was happy to be considered cooler than Joshua expected. And thrilled to hug his son for the first time.

~~~

"I'm Joshua Jacob Jones. And I think you're my dad."

The little boy's words as he looked up at Josh just kept running through Cait's head on a loop. From the first moment she heard those words, her world felt like it tilted on its side and the sounds around her became muffled to the point that she didn't even register the gasps of surprise or conversations going on around the room. She was so shocked by the revelation that she felt lightheaded and had to struggle to keep the world from fading to black. Cait was so dazed by the news that she completely missed the rest of what was said before Josh and his family ushered the little boy out of the room.

Holy shit! Josh might have a kid. A kid who looks just like him, according to Hazel, so it's a safe bet to think Joshua is actually Josh's son.
~~~

He must be flipping out at finding out about a child he didn't know about. Who am I kidding? The whole town is flipping out at this shocking news!

And where is the little boy's mom? Who is the little boy's mom? Is she someone Josh is going to get back together with, so they can provide their son a complete family?

I didn't see a woman here with Joshua. So maybe his mom has issues to cause the child to run away? If so, then he's gone to the perfect person to protect him by finding Josh.

But no matter why the little boy is here now, Josh must be freaking out at finding out he's a father. While I'm sure he'll be a great one, I'm sure he's worried that his SEAL training didn't prepare him for this kind of mission in life.

"Are you okay, Doll?" Philippe brought her out of her daze as he and his husband, Nico, checked on her after the Burlesons all left the room to talk privately with Josh's son.

"Yeah," Cait waved off their concern with the bouquet she still held in her hand. "I think I'm just as in shock as everyone else."

That was when she finally noticed the camera in Philippe's hand and realized they were coming to her for a decision about the pictures they were supposed to be taking right then, because she was the only person closely related to the newlyweds who was still in the room. "I think we're going to skip the bouquet and garter pictures for now, though. Maybe we can recreate them later."

"Yeah, I think the candids I took during the toss will have to do," Philippe agreed.

"But we still wanted to check on you because we know this has to be hitting you hard with your feelings for Josh and being left alone in a crowded public place," Nico added.

Who knew shock was a great cure for being afraid to be alone in a crowd? Cait thought, still in a bit of a daze.

Cait had gotten to know Nico from working with him on the days she went to the Destiny Playhouse to work with Becky. After her small panic attack on the first day she'd gone there for her new job, he'd made it a point to stick close whenever she was there to help her feel like there was someone bigger and stronger there to protect her.

Cait thought it was very sweet of him, even though she knew Becky or Ashlyn were more likely to actually defend them all if someone ever tried to attack the theater. While Nico was a very good actor, it was obvious that he was more of a lover than a fighter, no matter how tough he tried to act.

"I appreciate that," Cait smiled as she leaned over and gave Nico a one-armed hug. "But I'm really okay. I think we all need to focus on how we can be supportive friends to the Burlesons as they're figuring everything out."

"I think that's her way of telling us to get this party back on track, so when they come back, they'll know we're all celebrating adding another to their ranks along with the wedding," Nico informed his husband with a grin. "So, why don't we get the band going again…" Nico trailed off as most of the Burleson family returned to the reception.

"Or check with the bride and groom to see what they want us to do," Philippe suggested, nodding to where Mikey and Charlotte were walking toward the head table, while the rest of the Burlesons, minus Josh and Joshua, were headed back to their seats at the reception.

Cait went back to her seat as Nico and Philippe walked over to check with Charlotte and Mikey about the rest of the reception. She wasn't sure how she could help her friends, when she was in just as much shock as they were, but she wanted to make sure they all knew she was there for them.

Though I have no idea what to say. "How'd that go?" No. "Are you guys okay?" Maybe?

Luckily for her, she didn't have to say a word as Mikey and Char walked over to the table set up with the wedding cake, and the emcee handed over the microphone.

"Thank you all for being so patient with us while we took that little break," Charlotte announced over the sound system as Becky, Jen, Julie, Jake, and JJ rejoined her and Trent at the table. "But now we're going to get back to the party."

Char laid the microphone down before picking up the knife for her and Mikey to cut the cake. Cait watched in silence along with the other guests, as Mikey covered Charlotte's hand with his for them to slice into the beautiful multi-tier, blue and white cake. They were way more prim and proper feeding each other the cake than Cait imagined she'd be if she ever got married.

If I ever got to live out my dream of marrying Josh, we'd definitely be more playful and smash the cake into each other's faces. Though I guess that's even less likely to happen now. Between spending most of his time off on Navy missions and now having a child he'll want to spend all his free time with, he's not going to have time for any other relationships in his life, even if his son's mother isn't in the picture.

I'll still try to be there for him as a friend, though. I'm sure he's going to need someone to talk to about everything he's got on his plate now. And I want to help him deal with it all if I can, especially after the way he's tried to help me deal with my anxiety and agoraphobia issues. I just wish we could be there for each other as more than friends. Cait sighed, lost in her own thoughts, and not hearing Mikey's toast to his new bride and their ever-growing family before they opened up the dance floor and turned the party back over to the band.

But maybe it's a good thing we never crossed that line to see if we could have more than just this underlying attraction to one another. He's got so much going on right now that he doesn't need the added baggage I come with weighing him down. He needs to be able to focus on taking care of his son and forging that bond that all kids need with their parents, without getting distracted by whatever could have happened between us.

"You okay, Cait?" Becky reached over and placed her hand on Cait's forearm.

"Yeah, I'm fine," Cait smiled at her friend. "Just tired. It's been a long day. And really, I should be asking how you guys are doing after…" Her voice trailed off as she waved over at the dance floor where Joshua had surprised the whole town, unsure how to describe the incident.

Some screenwriter I am! Geez, I should be able to come up with something to say to my friends right now.

"We're good," Becky chuckled ruefully. "I think we're all still in shock. Well, those of us who didn't already know Josh had matched up with his child on Ancestry are still in shock. But it's a good kind of shock. If there is such a thing."

"Wait!" Jen squealed, reaching over her brother to slap Jake on the shoulder. "Joshua said something about Josh sending him a message about getting out of the Navy and moving home. Is he actually getting out soon?"

"And did you know anything about that before now?" Julie continued her twin's line of questioning. "Like you knew about Josh looking for his son for the last several months?"

"Yes, he's getting out of the Navy as soon as his minimum service requirement is up," Jake confirmed. "But he didn't want to mention it to anyone yet because of not being sure he'd be able to move home, until he found his son and worked out the details of being a part of his life. And since we hadn't found anything but a username and location where the account was created, he didn't want to deal with everyone calling and asking a whole bunch of questions he couldn't answer. So, he made those of us who knew promise not to mention anything to anyone else."

Josh is getting out of the Navy? When? And is he really moving home? Or will he move to wherever his son lives to be with his family?

"Who else knew?" Becky crossed her arms over her chest as she glared at her brother. "Let me guess. Char, because she was working on the family tree even after we all stopped trying to trace our DNA matches. Who else?"

"Yes, Char knew," Jake confirmed. "And I think Ian knew because he was at Char's house working on his family tree, when Josh called her the first day we looked at our results."

My brother knew? Mikey knew Josh had a son and didn't tell me? Even after he saw how close Josh and I got and how devastated I was when he ghosted me?

Holy shit! Is that why Josh ghosted me? He found out he had a son, and instead of letting me be a supportive friend to talk to about what he was feeling when he found out, he just cut things off because he couldn't deal with me at the same time? I guess even our friendship was more one-sided than I thought.

Cait completely missed the rest of the conversation as Jake informed his sister and cousins who else had been in the loop on Josh's life when they'd all been cut out.

Yeah, it's definitely a good thing that I never let him know I wanted more than friendship. At least, this way, I'm the only one of us who knows how brokenhearted I am over losing out on the dreams I had of happily ever after with him.

Well, the girls might figure out I have a broken heart because of knowing how I feel about him already, but they'll all be there to eat our weight in ice cream with me and won't say a word to Josh. Even though it hurts like hell to know he didn't care enough about me to share even a sliver of something meaningful about his life with me, I don't want him to know it hurts. He needs to be able to focus on taking care of Joshua, not be burdened with even an ounce of guilt for hurting my feelings.

"Hey, Cait, what do you say to heading out early and stopping for a couple gallons of rocky road and wine?" Becky leaned over and bumped her shoulder into Cait's just as the wedding cake was being served.

"Sure, but are we buying the ice cream by the gallon or the wine?" Cait agreed, grabbing her handbag, and standing up to leave with Becky.

"Both," Jen and Julie chimed in unison, standing to join them.

If nothing else, it'll be an interesting night, Cait thought as the ladies left the reception, only waving at the bride and groom on their way out.

Chapter Fourteen

Sunday, September 8, 2019

Josh had a lot on his mind as he prepared to show his son around the family ranch. On top of trying to figure out everything he had to do to get custody of Joshua and establishing a relationship with his son, he had to deal with the logistics of providing for Joshua's basic necessities, while also determining his son's emotional state and finding a way for them both to grieve the loss of Joshua's mother. And he wasn't completely sure his normal laugh-it-off attitude about the harsher side of life he'd had to deal with the last few years was the best way to handle everything his son had been through recently.

Since the kid had only come to town with what he could fit in a backpack for his bus trip to Texas, Josh had skipped church that morning to take Joshua to the twenty-four-hour superstore in Lytle. His mom hadn't thought it was necessary to miss the morning service for the errand, but Josh couldn't stand the thought of his son only having a couple of stuffy school uniforms and way too hot for South Texas flannel pajamas to wear. So, he'd decided to take Joshua shopping first thing in the morning after getting him settled into Bobby's old room the night before.

Oh, he knew the clothes and stuff they bought while the rest of his family was at church were just a drop in the bucket of all the things his parents would be spoiling Joshua with, once the stores in Heart's Destiny were open the next day. But he also knew how overwhelming it was for Joshua to have so many people coming up to their table to meet him, once they'd gone back to the reception the night before, so he felt it was best to not have a repeat performance at the Sunday morning service and potluck lunch after church.

Besides, the kid needs clothes he can get dirty in and boots he won't worry about ruining the first time he steps in a cow patty.

Josh had initially been upset to see Cait leaving the reception the night before with Becky, Jen, and Julie, just as he and Joshua walked back in. He'd actually looked forward to introducing Cait to Joshua and asking her for ideas about how to help his son through the grieving process. Since she'd been there for her nephew when Brody lost his mom, Josh assumed she'd be able to help him just as well as her brother could with helping Joshua the same way. Only he could ask Cait his questions now instead of having to wait until Ian and Charlotte got back from their honeymoon to ask Ian.

Besides that, he thought his personal grief over the loss of Jaina Jones was probably closer to what Cait felt for her first sister-in-law than the love he knew Ian had felt for his first wife. Considering he barely remembered the brown-haired girl he'd hooked up with one night almost nine years ago, Josh knew his sense of loss at finding out she'd died couldn't compare to the feelings of losing a loved one. He knew his sense of regret for her passing had more to do with how her loss affected his son than any feelings of friendship he might have developed for the woman had they gotten the opportunity to co-parent Joshua.

But shit, maybe it's a good thing I haven't been able to talk to Cait about any of this yet. With the way she's mentioned being friends with Mari, she might assume that I cared more about Jaina than I really did, if I tell her I'm feeling the same kind of grief for her loss that she feels from Mari's death.

And considering she was injured in the same shooting incident that ended Mari's life, I'm sure she's felt a lot more mental anguish from the loss of her sister-in-law than just the empathetic grief I'm feeling for Joshua's loss of his mother. Hell, I'm probably only feeling a third of what she felt back then, if that. So, I definitely shouldn't try to commiserate and bring back those painful emotions for her.

Thinking about Cait reminded him that he needed to cancel their plans for the afternoon. *Fuck, I hate to do it, 'cause I know how much she needs the help getting over her fear of public places,* Josh thought as he pulled his cell phone from his pocket and shot off a text. *But Joshua and I need this time alone to build our father-son bond that we've both missed out on the last eight years. Maybe she'll understand and we can try again in a week or two, after Joshua feels more comfortable with his place in our family.*

         Josh: Have to cancel the Alamo today. Raincheck for a week or two, once everything's settled with Joshua?

    Cait: NP. No rush on the raincheck. Enjoy your day with your son. :)

I'd enjoy it a hell of a lot more if you were here with us, Josh thought, just as Joshua barreled down the stairs with his cowboy boots clomping the whole way down from the third floor. *Now I understand why Ma always insisted we leave our boots in the mud room,* Josh chuckled to himself, as Joshua scuffed up the marble floor in the foyer as he came to an abrupt stop. *Guess I'll hafta have her teach me how to get those scuff marks up when she gets home from church.* "What do you wanna do first? Take the four-wheeler around to see the ranch? Or go meet the horses?"

"Horses!" Joshua bounced with excitement. "And cows. I wanna meet them too. And the barn cats Brody and Antonio told me about last night."

"I'm sure we'll run into a cat or two between here and the stable," Josh assured Joshua, grinning at his son's excitement.

"I always wanted a cat or a dog," his son informed him as his enthusiasm wavered and his expression turned more melancholy. "But Mom always said no because we lived in an apartment and didn't have a yard to go out and play with them."

"We have some dogs on the ranch too," Josh told his son as they stepped out of the house and started walking over to the family stables. "But they stay in the bunkhouse with the ranch hands to help herd the cattle when we're rotating pastures."

"Cool, then I wanna meet them, too." Joshua's smile returned, but it wasn't quite as bright as it was before he thought about his mother.

Damn it, Josh mentally berated himself. *I don't want to make him sad by asking about his life with his mom, but I don't know how else to get to know him. Hopefully, the horses and other animals will have the same calming effect on him that they've had on me this last week, so we can get through some of the harder conversations we're gonna hafta have today.*

Just as they got past the family houses and started walking through the paddocks, where they trained the horses and taught the kids to ride, to get to the family stable, one of the barn cats ran past them, causing Joshua to giggle with excitement once more as he ran to catch up with the kitten. "What's his name?"

"Actually, that's one of the new babies that just started venturing out of the barn," Josh grinned as Joshua picked up the kitten, who didn't look like he was sure he wanted to be held. "And I don't know if he has a name yet. But based on his coloring, I think his dad's name is Speckles."

"Speckles? That's a weird name for a cat." Joshua made a face as he cuddled the cat for a moment before putting him down to run around once more.

"Yeah, I think Brody wanted to call him Spot, but Maria told him that was a dog's name," Josh chuckled. "But since that one doesn't have a name yet, maybe you can come up with a better cat name for him than Speckles."

"I'll call him George," Joshua decided as they continued walking toward the family stable.

The horses weren't actually in the stable at the moment, having been moved out to one of the pastures for some free play time after breakfast and giving the hands time to be able to clean all the stalls. But Josh still wanted to show his son where the horses were kept when they weren't out and about on the ranch. The Burlesons actually liked to let the horses roam in the pastures as much as possible, when it wasn't too hot or wet for them to be comfortable outdoors.

"George sounds like a good cat name to me," Josh agreed with his son, wondering if talking about the names of the animals on the ranch would be a good way to transition to asking how Joshua ended up with both his and his brother's names.

"Whoa! Do you have air conditioning in the barn?" Joshua held his hand up to feel the breeze caused by the industrial-sized attic fans they used in the stables to keep the horses cool during hot weather. Or in this case, that the ranch hands ran while mucking out the stalls to keep themselves cool.

"Not exactly," Josh chuckled. "Just really big attic fans that circulate the outside air through the stables to keep everyone cool without having to try to keep the barn doors closed like we'd have to do with an air conditioner."

"And where are the horses?" Joshua looked in an empty stall before turning to look at Josh with a confused expression.

"They're out in the pasture getting in some play time while their stalls are being cleaned out, so they'll have clean beds for the night," Josh explained as he walked his son through the stable, stopping only long enough to grab the bucket of treats he'd prepared while Joshua was changing clothes earlier. "This stable is where our family horses live. But there's another stable over by the bunkhouse for the horses the ranch hands use to herd the cattle between pastures and to ride around checking the fences and doing wellness checks on the cows each day."

Once they walked out the other side of the family stable, Josh pointed to the bunkhouse and stable on the other side of the pasture where the family horses were currently hanging out. "That's where the ranch hands and cattle dogs live, and the stable over there is where the working horses sleep at night."

Not that Joshua seemed to care. He was too fascinated by the horses running around in the pasture to look past them to the buildings Josh was pointing out.

"Which one is your horse, Dad?" Joshua didn't take his eyes off the horses, as he ran up to the fence and climbed up on the bottom rail to get a better look.

Josh walked over and leaned against the fence beside his son and pointed to Leonardo. "See that brown and white horse with the blue harness?"

Joshua nodded, but didn't say a word.

"That's my horse, Leonardo."

"Like the Ninja Turtle?" Joshua turned his head to look at Josh for a moment before turning back to look at the horses.

"Yep," Josh nodded and smiled. "And the one with the red harness is Raphael, my brother Jake's horse."

"Are the one with the purple harness and the one with the orange harness Donatello and Michelangelo?" Joshua looked excited at figuring out the other horses' names.

"Yeah, Donatello is my brother Anthony's horse, and Michelangelo is my cousin Justin's." Josh pointed out each of the other horses in the pasture, telling his son the horses' names and the names of the family members who rode them the most often when they were kids. When he got to the two newest horses to be moved to the family stable, Lightning and Thunder, Josh had to admit to not knowing if any of the kids had claimed them yet or not.

Damn, guess we need to work on finding a few more horses for the kids, so they can each have one of their own.

"We're gonna hafta tell Pappaw to get on the ball with buying and training some more horses, so we can make sure all you kids have one of your own," Josh chuckled when Joshua asked what they did when everyone in the family wanted to ride at the same time since they had more people than horses. "This time last year, we didn't have any kids in the family. But then Anthony met Kay and adopted her daughters when they got married, so Pappaw started working on retiring a couple of the ranch horses."

"Thunder and Lightning?" Joshua questioned, appearing interested in hearing more about the two horses that had wandered over to the fence for some attention.

"Yep, Thunder and Lightning," Josh chuckled as Thunder nudged Joshua with his nose to ask for a treat. Josh grabbed a couple of carrots from the bucket, handing one to Joshua and showing him how to hold it out for the horses, as he continued telling him about how fast their family was growing. "Then Anthony and Kay surprised us by adopting Antonio in May, and Charlotte and Ian got together for her to adopt Brody, so Pappaw's been talking about buying a couple more horses this fall to try to keep up with how fast our family's growing. And now that you're here, too, he's three horses behind, and that's not counting the babies, who are gonna be ready to learn to ride as soon as they can walk. So, we might need to build a second family stable and let ya'll raise a few foals, since we don't really have any more ranch horses old enough to retire."

As Josh explained how they'd had to share family horses when he was a kid because of having more kids than horses ready to retire from ranch work dand having to wait until the foals they were raising were old enough to ride, he realized they were going to have a bigger problem with that in this generation of Burlesons than they had in his.

Leah Mae Wright

When the Burleson baby boom happened in the early 1990s, they went from zero to ten kids on the ranch over four-and-a-half years. But when Josh counted all the kids that had recently joined the family and that he knew were due to be born in the near future, he realized they were going from zero to ten kids in only about sixteen months this time around. And that was with only half of his generation procreating.

Yeah, I definitely need to get with Pop about picking up a few foals this fall. We might only have five kids old enough to ride as of now, but who knows how many we'll have in the next couple of years? Especially if Ma keeps pushing her matchmaking schemes and finds more single parents to marry the five single people left among my siblings and cousins.

While technically, he and Cait weren't a couple, Josh didn't consider himself to be part of that single group, knowing they would be a couple, eventually. In his mind, he hadn't been single since he gave Cait his heart back on December twenty-ninth of the previous year.

"So, if we get them as foals, do we get to name them? And how old do they have to be before we can ride them?"

"Yeah, you'll get to name your foal," Josh assured his son as they continued feeding the cleaned carrots from the bucket to the horses, who had all started wandering over to them once they realized there were treats to be had. "How do you think we ended up with a bunch of horses named after the **Teenage Mutant Ninja Turtles** and Disney princesses? And it depends on the horse and when their bones are strong enough to support a rider, which usually happens when they're somewhere between three and six years old."

"So, when we get the foals, can we name them after the **Avengers**?"

"Sure," Josh chuckled, realizing his brothers and cousins would probably rib him like crazy if his son named a horse the same thing he'd named his dick when they were kids.

Since he went with George for the kitten, maybe he'll stick with the character's name, instead of the superhero name. Not that it'll matter. The guys will still heckle me if Joshua names his horse Steve Rogers instead of Captain America. Hell, the teasing will be ten times worse if he picks Thor or Ironman like Bobby and JJ. But I won't really care as long as he doesn't pick Bruce like Jake.

"So, who's your favorite Avenger?" It might not be the most important thing he wanted to know about his son's life, but at least they'd found common ground for him to be able to get to know Joshua.

"Hawkeye," Joshua replied, giving the answer Josh least expected.

"Really?" Josh arched an eyebrow at his son, as they finished feeding the bucket of carrots to the horses. "Why do you like Hawkeye?"

"Because he's just a plain old guy from Earth," Joshua shrugged as they walked back to the stable to put the empty bucket away before going to get on a four-wheeler to ride around the ranch. "And he only needs a bow and arrows to fight the bad guys. He doesn't have to have super soldier serum or gamma radiation to be strong, or come from another planet to have superpowers, or build a special suit that nobody else can have. He's just a normal guy fighting evil in the world, like you. And Mom always said the real heroes in the world are the normal people like you, who protect others and fight for our freedom, even though they don't have superpowers."

Josh felt extremely humbled by the words of his eight-year-old son. Any guilt he felt for having to kill in the line of duty was wiped away at that moment, as Josh looked back at the missions he'd gone on during his time as a SEAL, and the raid on the cartel compound to rescue his sister, from the perspective Joshua had just shown him.

Could he have captured more and killed less? Possibly. Was it possible that not everyone he'd had to kill in the line of duty had been guilty of crimes bad enough to deserve the death penalty? Josh couldn't know for sure, no matter what reassurances his commanding officers had given him beforehand. But every single time he'd gone on a mission where he had killed someone, he did it as a normal guy fighting the evil of the world.

While it felt amazing to realize his son saw him as a hero, Josh didn't want to stroke his own ego by dwelling on that point in the conversation. Instead, he transitioned the discussion to find out more about Joshua's life with his mother. "So, your mom mentioned me before you did the DNA test for us to match up on Ancestry?"

Joshua nodded, as they walked to the barn where the four-wheelers were kept, but he didn't elaborate.

"I guess she remembered mine and Jake's names since she seems to have named you after us," Josh prompted, hoping to get his son to talk about the other things Jaina might have mentioned about him over the years. "What else did she tell you she remembered about me?"

And if she remembered my name, why the hell didn't she tell me she was pregnant back then? Josh knew he couldn't ask his son that question, but he was planning on asking Jaina's best friend Tawny, just as soon as Byron got her contact information for him.

"She said you met at a party right after you and your brother joined the Navy and that you just started training, so you couldn't leave to come live with us when I was born. She only knew your first names, so she named me after both of you because she didn't know your middle name to just name me after you. What is your middle name?"

"Bennett," Josh admitted as he opened up the barn where they stored the ATVs and started looking for a helmet to fit Joshua.

"I wish Mom woulda known your middle name. Then you could call me Ben, and nobody would be confused by there being two Joshes. Since she named me after your brother Jake, I can't even use my middle name to keep from confusing people. And there's already a JJ in the family, so I can't even use my initials."

"Maybe I can get everyone to start calling me Ben, so you can be Josh instead of Joshua," Josh suggested, unsure if his family could switch over after calling him Josh for the last twenty-eight years. "But it'll probably take a while to get everyone to switch over."

"I'm fine with Joshua," the boy shrugged as he took the helmet Josh handed him.

Yeah, I'm definitely gonna hafta come up with a nickname for him, Josh decided as they tabled the discussion while riding around the ranch on the loud four-wheeler. *Something that fits his personality and has nothing to do with his name. Hopefully, the perfect nickname will come to me while we're spending time together today and I'm getting to know more about him. As of now, I could call him Hawkeye after his favorite Avenger, but I don't wanna be lazy with picking his nickname by going with the first thing he's told me about himself.*

During the time they spent at the birthing barn and whenever they stopped to turn off the four-wheeler for Josh to explain the various stages of cattle growth based on whichever pasture full of cows they were looking at, they continued talking about Joshua's life in

Alexandria. Josh learned that Jaina had remembered Josh mentioning that he wanted to become a SEAL during their short time together. So, even though she didn't know his last name to find him, she'd told their son stories about the SEALs to explain why Josh wasn't able to be with them.

While Josh wasn't sure how she'd been so certain that he was Joshua's father after only spending a few hours together one long-ago September night, he was glad that she'd painted him in a positive light in their son's eyes. But he also felt bad for not remembering much about the night they'd conceived a child to be able to tell Joshua about the things Jaina might have mentioned that night to return the favor now that she was gone.

Maybe Jake remembers more than I do from the night we met Jaina and Tawny, so he can help me out with that. I guess we'd better head back to the house before he has to fly out this afternoon, so I can ask him.

His brother having to change his travel arrangements was another thing Josh felt guilty about. But after his brief talk with Tyler Reilly the night before, Josh felt it best to stay in Texas to start the custody proceedings, so the state of Virginia couldn't take Joshua back to his grandparents, or put him in a foster home until everything was settled. So, he couldn't leave to fly Jake home like they'd originally planned.

Technically, they couldn't accuse him of kidnapping his son, since Joshua ran away from the boarding school he was in and came to Texas on his own. But after the stories Joshua told him about his maternal grandparents, Josh was afraid they'd try, if he crossed state lines with Joshua without something in writing from a legal authority giving him permission.

At this point, all Josh could be accused of was harboring a minor without the consent of his legal guardian. But since he'd reported the whereabouts of the child to the local police chief, who just so happened to be Josh's older brother, he didn't think he would really be charged.

Bobby and Brook actually used their contacts through the Madeline Ashbury Foundation, which Brook started in honor of her late mother, to get permission from the Texas Department of Family and Children's Services for Joshua to stay on the ranch while jurisdiction was being established through the various court systems in Texas, Virginia, and

Maryland. Those conversations backed with documentation were probably what was most likely to keep Josh from any legal hot water. Regardless, Josh was just happy to have family and friends with the right connections to help him take care of his son.

And hopefully, all this legal stuff won't take too long, so I can ease Joshua's worries about his future living situation.

~ ~ ~

Cait felt terrible about leaving her brother's wedding reception early the night before. And her horrid feelings had nothing to do with the slight hangover she had from imbibing an entire bottle of wine once she and her friends got back to the ranch. She'd been so preoccupied with her inner turmoil over Josh and Joshua that she forgot she was supposed to be watching Brody while Mikey and Charlotte were on their honeymoon.

Granted, she'd known the original plan was for all the kids to go to Hazel and Bob's house for a sleepover with their grandparents after the wedding reception. Since Anthony, Kay, and their kids were flying out with the GWA on Monday morning with their leave for having baby Sam ending, they needed a night alone as a couple before fitting the six of them in hotel suites for the next couple of days. And, of course, with his cousins all sleeping over at Memmaw and Pappaw's house, Brody wanted to go with them. So, when Cait left the party the night before, she thought she had a free night and would see her nephew the next morning after the sleepover.

Unfortunately, she hadn't realized Joshua's arrival would put the kibosh on the kids' sleepover plans. She'd just assumed that since Josh was already staying at his parents' house, Joshua would join the other grandkids in the sleepover while also spending time with his dad. But when she'd walked over to find out who was riding with whom to church, Cait found out that Brody ended up going to spend the night with his cousins at Anthony and Kay's house. Apparently, there were legal issues with having Joshua stay on the ranch that had to be dealt with, and making sure none of them were arrested for harboring a runaway by taking care of Joshua kept Bob and Hazel from being able to leave the reception with all their grandkids.

Cait had apologized profusely for not being there to take all the kids back to her house for the night when she saw Anthony and Kay at church, hating that they'd missed out on a night of couple time. With four kids, she knew they couldn't have as much alone time as they probably wanted, especially since they hadn't even been married a year yet and were clearly still in the honeymoon phase of their relationship.

Cait had also been disappointed to not see Josh at church that morning, or really at any part of the day, since Josh had taken Joshua shopping while everyone else went to church, and then disappeared out onto the ranch before she and the rest of the Burleson family returned to the ranch in the mid-afternoon. Cait had spent some time with Brody and the horses, thinking Josh might eventually turn up near the stables, so she could ask how everything was going. But it wasn't until she'd gone back inside to fix dinner and sent Brody to the bath that she saw the two of them walking back toward Hazel and Bob's house.

Normally, she and Brody would have gone over to Hazel and Bob's for the traditional Sunday supper Hazel hosted every week for the whole family. But with everything going on that weekend, she'd opted to give the Burlesons their privacy to bond with their newfound family member. Considering how Josh had avoided bringing Joshua around anyone all day, she thought it was pretty obvious that he wanted that privacy for a little while as he got to know his son.

The Burlesons may have all tried to make her feel like part of the family since she moved to town, and especially since she moved onto the ranch, but Cait still felt like an outsider when it came to sensitive subjects like long-lost children showing up out of the blue. Her brother and nephew may have added Burleson to their names the day before, but she was still just a Campbell.

The last Campbell, Cait thought as she stepped out her back door to do a little stargazing after Brody went to bed. *At least, the last of the Campbells I want to be around and consider family.*

She'd been struggling to hold herself together and be there for her friends for the last twenty-four hours. Yeah, they'd all mostly talked about other subjects because of knowing how she felt about Josh, but he and his son had never been far from her mind all day. Now that she was alone, she finally felt free to give in to the pity party in her head and needed to find someplace to have a good cry without any witnesses or waking up her nephew. *If only I could go over to the stable, where nobody else could hear me, and still hear Brody if he wakes up. Maybe petting the horses could help me climb out of this hole of depression I seem to have fallen into today.*

She'd set up his old baby monitor in the spare bedroom for the nights that Brody stayed with her, so she could hear him if he had a bad dream in the middle of the night. But even though she had the monitor clipped on the waistband of her jeans, Cait wasn't sure it would reach all the way over to the stables on the other side of the paddocks. So, she stopped walking when she got to the fence that separated the paddocks from what she considered her backyard, leaning back against it to rest her head on a fence post and look up at the stars.

As she stared up at the cloudless sky and tried to pick out the few constellations she knew from the few stars that she could see with the diffuse light of the three-quarter moon making the dimmer stars almost disappear, Cait contemplated how alone she felt. Yes, she knew she still had a family with her brother and nephew. Technically, Charlotte was part of her family now, too. But for some reason, instead of feeling like Mikey and Char's wedding gave her a new sister-in-law, Cait felt like she'd lost her family.

Brody is literally asleep in my guest room, Cait mentally lamented. *So why do I feel so lonely and desperate to feel loved? I'm still going to see them every day. Well, not Mikey this week while he's on his honeymoon with Char. But that just means more time with Brody. So, why aren't his random hugs throughout the day and cuddles while reading his bedtime stories enough for me?*

Am I really so selfish that I can't be grateful for what I have in my life and have to feel so envious of my family and friends who are finding love and building families instead of being happy for them? Or am I just so pissed that some other woman is getting the family I want with Josh that I can't see past my anger to enjoy the other aspects of my life that are finally coming together?

Am I pushing away my friends because I'm being a bitch about not getting to join their family the way I want to? If so, then how the hell do I stop it? Because I don't like the angry bitch that seems to be taking up way too much space in my brain lately.

Cait didn't have the chance to ponder the answers to her mental questions, as Josh's deep voice boomed through the dark night and brought her back from the somber place she'd gone in her head. "That fence post doesn't look like a very comfortable pillow."

"No, but I was afraid if I brought a pillow and blanket outside to do a little stargazing, I'd fall asleep in the middle of the yard," Cait quipped, lifting her head from the top of the fence post to look in the direction she'd heard Josh's voice coming from. She was surprised to see him wearing an apparatus on his head that held what looked like binoculars over his eyes, as he got close enough she could make out his form in the moonlight.

"Yeah, I wouldn't suggest laying on the ground in the dark," Josh chuckled as he casually leaned against the fence beside Cait. "Especially not this time of year."

"Oh, why not?" Cait looked up at him curiously. "And what's with the binoculars?"

"It's the end of birthing season for snakes, and they're all trying to fatten up to survive their brumation period over the winter," Josh replied, pointing to the apparatus over his eyes. "And these aren't binoculars. They're night vision goggles, so I can watch for snakes without having to find a flashlight before going for a walk to clear my head."

"Of course," Cait giggled. "Because night vision goggles are so much easier to find than one of the flashlights hidden in junk drawers in every house on the ranch."

"These were in my room," Josh shrugged and smirked. "And the flashlights were either in the kitchen or garage. So yeah, they were much easier for me to find."

"And what are you going to do if you come across a snake on your walk?" He wasn't carrying a rifle like she'd gotten used to seeing the men on the ranch strapping to their horses when they went on a ride or out to work with the cattle to be able to take out predators before they could harm the herd or the horses. So, she wasn't sure he could do anything more than she would do if she saw a snake, which would be scream and run away from it.

"Depends on what type of snake it is," Josh shrugged. "If it's non-venomous, I'll leave it alone to go fill up on field mice. And if it's venomous, I'd shoot it, then try to find the nest in case it had babies nearby that I don't want to risk biting one of the kids or animals on the ranch."

"You're carrying a gun now?" *It must be concealed in a back or ankle holster like Mikey wears,* Cait thought as she did a visual scan of his body for weapons.

"Sunshine, I'm pretty much always carrying a gun," Josh confided, pulling a handgun from behind his back to show her before putting it away again. "Well, except on base when I'm not gearing up for a mission. But I have a concealed carry permit, so I'm always prepared to deal with coyotes, bobcats, or venomous snakes on the ranch, or snakes in human form in the case of a robbery or mass shooter situation when I'm out in public."

How did I not notice that the couple of times I've hugged him? Cait wondered, but she didn't have the guts to ask aloud, so she only nodded her approval. She knew he understood her gratitude for helping her feel safe, so it wasn't necessary to tell him yet again.

"If you really wanna be comfortable looking up at the stars, we need to head over to one of the barns with a hayloft," Josh suggested. "I can make sure there aren't any snakes lingering around, and then we can open the hatch we use to load and unload the small hay bales we store there to be able to lay down and look up at the stars."

"Yeah, I, uh, don't know that I can go that far and still hear Brody on the monitor in case he has a bad dream." Cait tapped the monitor on her waist as she explained to Josh why she hadn't even gone as far as the stables.

"Then we'll just go to the barn behind Memmaw and Pappaw's place," Josh countered her objection, nodding toward the house where Becky, Jen, and Julie lived before shaking his head. "Or what used to be Memmaw and Pappaw's place," he corrected. "We don't keep hay in the loft there anymore, since we quit keeping the cattle close to the houses to keep the girls from wanting to keep them as pets and started using the nearest fields for makin' hay. But I can go grab a couple of horse blankets to lay out up there and we'll still be close enough you can hear if Brody wakes up."

Cait wasn't sure it was wise on her part to go off somewhere so private with Josh, when she hadn't yet convinced herself that she was happy just being friends with him. She knew he wouldn't try anything inappropriate with her, but she didn't trust herself not to give in to the extreme urge she often had to kiss him if they were all alone with no chance of someone walking outside to see them.

"Oh, no, we don't need to go to all that trouble," Cait quavered, hating how nervous her voice sounded. "I've already found all the constellations I know, so I don't want to keep you from your walk any longer, especially when I was about to go back inside, anyway."

"Please," Josh implored, flipping his goggles up on top of his head and giving Cait a lost puppy dog look that she found hard to say no to. "I could really use a friend to talk to about everything I learned last night and today, but I don't wanna talk where my sister or one of my cousins could walk out and overhear."

Damn it! I can't really claim to be his friend if I'm not willing to offer him the same ear I gave the girls last night, when they were trying to process why he didn't confide in any of them as soon as he found out he had a kid.

"Okay," Cait conceded, praying she was mentally strong enough to put up a wall between them to protect her fragile heart as he confided in her. "But I don't think we need the horse blankets to lay on, unless you'd feel more comfortable talking if you're looking at the stars."

"Naw, I can see the stars anytime," Josh shook his head and grinned before flipping his goggles back down over his eyes and leading her around the houses to the barn.

They entered through a small side door, instead of opening up one of the big doors that they used to drive the tractors and large equipment through.

"Stay right here while I check to make sure there aren't any critters lurking around," Josh directed as soon as she followed him inside.

Cait stopped in her tracks, not able to see a thing in the barn as the door shut behind her, blocking out the moonlight that had previously allowed her to see Josh and where they were walking. She heard wood creaking from him shuffling around, but she couldn't tell where he was or what he was doing in the pitch-black darkness of the space.

"Why do I suddenly feel like I'm in a bad horror movie remake, waiting for a creep with a chainsaw to jump out and kill me?" Cait joked, wishing she'd grabbed a flashlight before leaving her house.

"Don't worry, Sunshine," Josh chuckled from somewhere above her. "There aren't any chainsaws in this barn. Just a couple of tractors with mowers and hay balers attached to them."

She heard more wood creaking before the sound of a stomp, which she assumed was Josh jumping down from the hayloft. A few moments later, she felt Josh approaching a second before he took her hand to lead her through the barn.

"I didn't even see any snakes, possums, or field mice hiding out in here," Josh informed her as he guided her around the heavy machinery to the ladder leading up to the hayloft. Once she was closer to that side of the barn, she saw a little bit of light coming from somewhere in the loft. "I already opened the hatch, so you should be able to see well enough to move around once you get to the top of the ladder. And I'll be right behind you as you climb up, so I can catch you if you slip in the dark on the way up."

Josh placed her hands on the ladder, which she assumed was his way of pushing her to start climbing. *Oh, I hope his night vision goggles don't magnify things like binoculars,* Cait thought when she realized Josh would be looking up, right at her butt, as they climbed the ladder. *I am not going to ask if they make my butt look big.*

Night vision goggles make everything look green, right? Not bigger? Cait thought as she climbed the ladder, feeling her cheeks flush at the thought of Josh's view at the moment. *Hopefully, the color distortion will keep him from being able to tell I'm blushing at the thought of him looking at my ass.*

As soon as she got to the top of the ladder, Cait scrambled into the loft, moving over near the opening in the wall that looked out on the grassy field that took up several acres in the far northeast corner of the Burleson Ranch. With the moon being about three-quarters full that night, it provided just enough light that they could clearly see each other when they were standing in her backyard. But with the moon's position in the sky being blocked by the roof of the barn, the stars became more visible as Cait looked out from the hatch.

"Wow, what a beautiful view," Cait mused aloud as she felt Josh walk up beside her.

"Yes, it is," Josh agreed, sounding as awestruck as she felt.

But when she turned to look at him, it was clear he was looking at her and not out at the stars, making Cait blush once more. Knowing she was probably projecting her attraction to Josh, wanting to see it returned the way she'd dreamed of, Cait quickly turned the subject back to his need to talk, as she sat down on the small patch of flooring that was faintly illuminated by the moonlight coming in the hatch. "So, what did you learn in the last twenty-four hours that you need to work through with a friend?"

"I, uh, should probably confess that unlike most everyone at the wedding reception, I didn't learn I'm a father last night," Josh admitted as he too sat down, dangling his feet out of the hatch as he leaned back on his hands. "I actually found out back in April, when I first looked at my DNA test results online. But all the site said about my son was a username, a last login date in March, and that we share fifty percent of our DNA."

"Okay," Cait nodded, having already figured that out from her talk with his sister and cousins the night before. The girls had claimed that was why Josh had ghosted her and suddenly stopped his previously flirtatious behavior when they talked, but Cait wasn't so sure they knew him as well as they thought, especially since he hadn't confided in them about his son or his plans for leaving the Navy.

"Anyway, I've been trying to find out about him ever since, and had decided to go stake out the library, where Jake found out his account had been created, as soon as my time in the Navy was up."

"And when is your time in the Navy up?" Cait wondered, remembering back to the night before when Jake mentioned Josh leaving the Navy as soon as his minimum service requirement was completed, but not actually saying when he would be finished.

"Technically, I'm on terminal leave now," Josh confided. "So, I only hafta go back to sign some paperwork and do a final debrief, or exit interview, or whatever they wanna call the final meeting with my CO on the thirtieth. I also hafta move the last of my stuff out of my apartment that week. And now I'm hoping I can get the courts in Virginia to schedule whatever custody hearings I need to do for then too, but I'm not sure how much luck I'll have with that."

"So, you're going to try to get custody of Joshua? Or just work something out with his mom to share custody?" Cait tried to maintain a neutral expression, not wanting to embarrass herself further by showing him that she hoped Josh didn't plan on trying to make things work for Josh, Joshua, and Joshua's mom to be a family.

She knew her feelings on the subject were selfish and petty. And a small part of her actually felt bad for wishing Josh would have a contentious relationship with his son's mother, so she might have a chance of a romantic relationship with him instead. But no matter how much she disliked herself for wishing the other woman wasn't in the picture, she couldn't prevent her stupid heart from wanting to be with Josh more.

"Yeah, um," Josh stuttered, stalling his reply as he looked up at the sky in silence for several long moments. Cait gave him the space he clearly needed to gather his thoughts, wishing she could comfort him in some way. "Joshua's mom died right after they sent in the DNA samples trying to find me. So, I'm apparently gonna hafta fight her parents for custody of Joshua."

Oh, God! I wanted her to be a bitch that Josh couldn't fall in love with, not dead! Cait was mentally freaking out, her guilt over the ill feelings she had for the woman multiplying exponentially. *And why the hell didn't the girls mention this last night? Or any of the Burlesons say anything today? So I wouldn't have stuck my foot in my mouth just now.*

Cait felt spastic with the way her mind was whirling at the moment. But she knew she wouldn't be the good friend Josh needed if she let out a little of her inner crazy right then, so she tamped down her own turmoil to offer him her condolences. "I'm sorry to hear that. Joshua must be devastated. If there's anything I can do to help you guys during your time of loss, please don't hesitate to ask."

"Thanks." Josh's lips turned up slightly in what Cait could only describe as a sad half-smile. "Since you took care of Brody after he lost his mom, I could really use your experience in helping a kid get through that. Maybe you can watch him for me while I go talk to the attorney tomorrow and get a better idea of how he's feeling than I got today?"

"Of course," Cait agreed. She wasn't sure how much she could really help Josh understand his son's emotions, but she could certainly help Joshua and Brody bond over having both lost their mothers and share her observations with Josh, the way she had with Mikey for the last couple of years since she'd been taking care of Brody. "He's welcome to hang out with me and Brody anytime you need to take care of stuff that he doesn't need to witness. But, um, is there something I should be looking for while he's hanging out with us?"

"I have no idea," Josh sighed. "I'm just thinking that maybe since he's used to living with his mom and her best friend, maybe he'll open up more with another woman than he has with me. Don't get me wrong, he's been extremely open with talking about his life today, but he's not really showing the emotions I'd expect him to be feeling after all he's been through."

"What do you mean?" Cait tilted her head, trying to get a better view of Josh's expression in the moonlight as she thought back to what she'd seen of Joshua from across the ballroom the night before and the yard earlier in the day. *He actually looked like a fairly happy kid.*

"I don't know. Maybe I'm wrong, and he cried it all out when his mom first died back in April. But he seems much more resilient than I think I'd be if I were in his shoes," Josh confided, taking off the headgear he was wearing to run a hand through his hair. After laying the night vision goggles on the floor of the hayloft between them, Josh continued. "He's obviously sad when he talks about her, but he's not breaking down, the way I would if I'd lost my mom. And I haven't even seen him tear up, much less cry, over losing his mom."

Cait worried that Joshua's lack of emotion over losing his mom was a sign that his mother had been more like Cait's than Josh's. *Hell, I'd break down if something happened to Hazel, and I'm just an employee, not an actual family member.*

But if I were to get a call that Lorna Campbell got out of prison and overdosed, I doubt I'd shed a tear. I'd be sad for her, but I don't think I'd mourn the way I have after losing Mari.

So, if Joshua's mom had some of the same issues mine did as a single mom, then I'm not really surprised that it's so hard to tell by looking at him that Joshua recently lost his mom.

Before Cait could come up with a way to respond to Josh's statement that wouldn't sound derogatory toward the deceased, Josh continued telling her about the conversations he'd had with Joshua since they met the night before.

"Joshua obviously doesn't know all the details surrounding his birth, but from what he's told me so far, I think Jaina's parents kicked her out when she got pregnant. Joshua and Jaina, that's his mom, lived with Jaina's best friend, and never had any contact with his maternal grandparents, until she got sick and called them to get some family medical records for her doctor. And apparently, they argued with her over the phone then, but didn't actually go see their daughter before she died."

"Geez, they sound like worse parents than mine," Cait blurted without thinking, covering her mouth with her hand, as soon as she realized she'd spoken the words instead of just thinking them.

"Wait." Josh turned his head to look at her with a slightly confused expression. "I thought you said you don't even know your dad?"

"I don't," Cait shrugged. "But when I was shot, my mom at least called me from jail to check on me, and actually sounded concerned about both me and Mikey. Although, it was strange because she called while Mikey was still in surgery, so I couldn't tell her how he was. Then Trent got to the hospital and confiscated our phones and started the process to fake Mikey's death and hide us from the cartel, so I didn't hear from her again after that. And I never did find out how she knew we'd been shot when it hadn't even made the news yet."

"Are you sure she was still in jail?" Josh arched an eyebrow as he questioned her.

"No, not really," Cait admitted, shaking her head. "I was thirteen when she went to prison and Mikey got custody of me, so I have no idea how long her sentence was, or even what all she was charged with. We went to see her a couple of times when I was a teenager, but didn't really stay in touch with her after the first year or so. And, when I was shot, I also hit my head, so I was concussed at the time. For all I know, I just dreamed that she called me while I was in the emergency room."

When Cait really thought about it, she was pretty sure the call she remembered had to be a dream, something her concussed brain had made up because of how much she'd longed to have a better relationship with her mother throughout her youth. "But even if it was a dream and she didn't know we'd been shot to call us, I know she wouldn't have argued with me if she had called. Lorna Campbell may be a druggie with terrible taste in men, but when she was clean and sober, she did care about her kids. She probably cared more about having us around to increase her welfare checks than because she loved us, but she wouldn't have argued with either of us if we were terminally ill. That's beyond fucked up."

"FUBAR," Josh chuckled as Cait tried to figure out what the acronym stood for. "Fucked up beyond all recognition," Josh clarified with a grin. "And I think that aptly describes Joshua's maternal grandparents. After Jaina died, they showed up to take custody of

Joshua from Jaina's best friend Tawny, and promptly sent him off to boarding school. Luckily, Tawny was able to sneak Joshua a phone and prepaid credit card during one of the visits she was allowed with him. I'm not sure if it was before they took custody, or as they were going through court, but she at least had the foresight to give him a means of escape. Not that the phone did him much good, since the school confiscated it to keep him from contacting Tawny. But he was able to sneak out of the school and use the credit card for his bus ticket here, after he went to the Ancestry site during one of his classes when he got to use a computer. Thank God, I sent that message on there, telling him all about my family and Heart's Destiny. Otherwise, he'd have never found me."

"When did you send this message?" Cait was curious about whether the timing of finding out about his son was why he'd ghosted her or not. While her friends had tried to convince her the night before that Josh probably needed to figure out the whole situation surrounding his son before he felt like he could have any kind of relationship with her, Cait still wasn't convinced they were right. She still thought she'd come on too strong with the attempt at a sexy selfie and turned him off.

"Back in April, after hitting the first dead end with Jake only being able to trace my son's profile to an anonymous email address." Josh turned once again to look at Cait, examining her intently before continuing. "Remember when I came home at the end of June and apologized for not texting you because of having a lot of stuff going on?"

Cait could only nod in recognition, nervous about what else Josh was about to tell her.

"Yeah, the news kinda hit me hard," Josh confessed, his expression full of regret. "And I felt like I couldn't stick with my plan to move us out of the friend zone, when I didn't know what kinda mess I was gonna hafta deal with when I found my son. So, I had to quit texting you to keep from flirting the way I wanted to. I didn't want to start something with you that I might not have been able to move home and finish."

Holy shit! Holy shit! Holy shit! Is he saying what I think he's saying?

"Hell, depending on what happens when my lawyer is able to talk to the right people in Virginia this week, I might still have to go back and stay there for a while. At least, while we're settling all the custody stuff. But I want you to know that when that's all taken care of and I'm able to move back home, I'm planning on asking you on a date."

No fucking way! The girls were right? Cait was stunned speechless, simply staring at Josh in shock at his declaration.

"I hope I didn't screw things up too bad by backing off so much. That's my biggest fear, ya know. Finding my son, only to lose my shot with you. I really hope you'll give me another chance, but I understand if I need to work for it."

"Of course, I'll give you another chance," Cait choked out, surprising even herself as she continued. "But we don't have to wait until everything's settled and for you to move back home to try being more than friends."

OMG! Did I really just say that out loud?

"Oh, we're gonna do more than try, Sunshine," Josh smirked as he moved his goggles out from between them to scoot closer to her. "I knew the first time I saw you that we're meant to be together. That's why I started the process to get out of the Navy as soon as I got back on base in January."

"You are not feeding me a line about love at first sight more than eight months after we met," Cait scoffed, lightly slapping her hand against Josh's upper arm as he leaned in close to her.

"Actually, I think I said something about feelin' lightning strike when you first sat down at the table for Christmas dinner," Josh smirked, wagging his eyebrows suggestively.

"But unless lightning strikes the instant you meet someone in our family, you don't have to worry about a trip down the aisle. It's either love at first sight or not at all for the Burlesons."

Cait remembered the exact words Josh had said, as well as how she'd been compelled to look up at him the instant he said them because of the strange feeling she got every time their eyes met. She also remembered wondering if he felt the same connection she did and that was why he'd looked at her so intently as he said those words.

"Yeah, Sunshine, that tingly feeling we both get every time we look in one another's eyes is exactly what I was talkin' about back then."

"But you didn't say you felt it when we first met," Cait objected, shaking her head to try to clear the Josh-induced lust fog she found herself in at the moment. "You were talking about how everyone in your family either falls in love at first sight or not at all. You didn't say anything about feeling that way about me."

"I might not have specifically mentioned that we fell for each other that day in front of both our families, but that's only because I had to figure out the plan for getting out of the Navy and moving home first. Besides, it was clear as day in your eyes that you understood my meaning, so I didn't think I had to clue anyone else in, when my siblings and cousins would have all made comments that might have scared you off."

Shit! He's got me there. Only I didn't really think he reciprocated my instant attraction back then. Cait opened her mouth as if she was going to contradict him, but she promptly closed it when she realized she couldn't chalk up those tingles they felt from day one to him joshin' around back at Christmas.

"Don't worry, Sunshine," Josh smirked. "I'm a patient man. I can wait as long as you need to hear you admit to falling for me the first time we saw each other. But since you said we don't hafta wait until everything's settled and I'm officially moved home to start dating, I think we should start off this new phase of our relationship by makin' out in the hayloft."

"Oh, no!" Cait put both palms on Josh's firm pecs as he leaned in as if to kiss her, pushing him back way easier than she expected, considering their size difference. "I don't make out on the first date."

"Oh, but Sunshine, this isn't our first date," Josh playfully argued, grinning at her like he thought he'd found a loophole. "We've had countless dinners together, gone to both the Independence Day and Labor Day celebrations in town, gone for target practice when it was just the two of us, and that's not counting the wedding stuff this last week, when you know Ma and all the other mommas in town considered us there as each other's dates. So, this is more like our twentieth date, at least."

"You're incorrigible," Cait teasingly chastised, grinning with excitement at the lustful look in Josh's eyes. In the low light, the amber starburst in his hazel eyes seemed to glow as he leaned in close enough that their breath mingled.

"Yeah, but you're still gonna let me kiss you," Josh grinned, wagging his eyebrows suggestively. "Aren't you, Sunshine?"

Oh-my-god, oh-my-god, oh-my-god! He's really going to kiss me? Cait was so overwhelmed with excitement that she couldn't form words at the moment, especially when Josh rested his forehead against hers.

"Say yes, Sunshine," Josh commanded, his voice so thick with lust that the sound alone felt like a sexual act.

"Yes, Sunshine," Cait echoed his words just before Josh pressed his lips to hers for the first time.

The kiss started off soft and sweet, the way she imagined a first kiss would be scripted in a romcom meant for a teenaged audience. But as their arms wound around one another, Josh deepened the kiss, taking her breath away as his tongue invaded her mouth. With one large hand on the center of her back and the other in her hair, Josh held her in place so he could ravish her.

Any doubts Cait still had about Josh reciprocating her attraction were blown away in an instant, as Josh claimed her with the most passionate kiss she'd ever experienced. Cait gave in to her womanly desires and returned the kiss with equal ardor, running her hands over Josh's muscular back as they pressed their upper bodies together.

The feel of finally being in Josh's arms and kissing him was more magnificent than she'd imagined. It felt like more than just a way to show their attraction to one another. Like they might feel more than lust. For the first time in her life, Cait actually felt like she might have found her place in the world.

Before she could contemplate whether Josh's love-at-first-sight theory was true for them or not, Cait heard a thud, followed immediately by another crash, over the baby monitor clipped to her jeans. They instantly broke apart as Cait jumped up, ready to rush back to the house where Brody was sleeping.

"It's okay, Aunt Cait," Brody's soft voice came over the monitor. "I just dropped my book and knocked over the lamp, tryin' to turn it off to go to sleep. But it didn't break, so you can stay in bed. I'm goin' to sleep now."

"Yeah, that sounds like somethin' ya might wanna check on," Josh chuckled as he stood, grabbing his goggles to be able to see for them to leave the barn. "So, I'd better walk you back to the house for the night."

"Yeah, I thought he was already asleep, or I never would have walked outside." Cait rolled her eyes at how her nephew pretended to be asleep, only to turn on a lamp and read when he thought nobody would notice. "And while he says he's turning off the lamp and actually going to sleep now, I'm sure if I wait ten minutes to go check on him, the lamp will be back on, and he'll be reading again."

"At least when he disobeys, it's to read, instead of doing something destructive or dangerous," Josh chuckled as he helped her back down the ladder and through the barn full of equipment.

"True," Cait conceded, chuckling with him as she imagined the shenanigans Josh probably pulled at Brody's age. "Thankfully, his dad is a literary nerd, so Brody's late-night antics mimic Mikey's when he was a kid. After hearing about frozen underwear and sneaking around to scare your sisters when they had slumber parties, I'm sure you'll have a lot more to worry about with raising Joshua, if he takes after you."

"Damn, I'm gonna hafta install a ton of video surveillance equipment and maybe some alarms on the bedroom doors to stay a step ahead of him," Josh joked as they walked back to her house. "Hell, with my siblings and cousins having kids now, we should probably put together a schedule to wire all our houses, so we can all watch when the cousins start pranking each other."

"Yeah, I have a feeling you wouldn't get to watch it live," Cait giggled as they got to her back door. "Because you'd be right there in the middle of whatever pranks the kids are pulling, helping them set it up, so your siblings and cousins would be the victims of the pranks, instead of their kids."

"Maybe," Josh shrugged, grabbing her hand, and stopping her from opening the door. "But I'd make sure you're in on 'em too, so you wouldn't end up doused with a bucket of water on the way out the door the next morning, or wake up to find your house covered in silly string."

"Why do I have a feeling that you've actually done those things before?" Cait grinned as she looked up at Josh.

"Sorry, Sunshine," Josh smirked as he wrapped her in his arms once more. "SEAL missions are classified, especially the ones we come up with ourselves to welcome the new guys to the teams."

Cait had to laugh at Josh's feigned serious expression.

"Now be a good girl and let me kiss you goodnight before you go get Brody to actually go to sleep," Josh instructed as he dipped his head to brush his lips over hers.

Unlike the kiss in the barn that came close to getting out of hand, this kiss was soft and sweet. The perfect way to end the day, with hope for what the future might hold for the two of them.

"Sweet dreams, Sunshine," Josh smiled as he released her from the tender embrace.

"Goodnight, Josh." Cait returned the satisfied smile before going inside to envision the happily ever after she and Josh might just get after all.

Chapter Fifteen

Josh felt amazing after finally getting to kiss Cait the night before. When he'd gone over to see if she was still up after putting Joshua to bed, he'd only planned to talk to her as a friend, thinking he had to get everything settled with custody of Joshua and figure out his future living arrangements before he could even give her a hint of how he wanted their relationship to move to the next level. But as they talked, he couldn't stop himself from confessing the real reason why he'd backed off on their flirtation earlier in the year. And after she told him they didn't have to wait until everything was settled to start dating, he was really glad he hadn't held back his feelings for her any longer.

Oh, he knew he still needed to take things slow to give her the space she needed to completely heal from the traumatic events of her past and feel as strong and capable as he knew she was before she'd be ready for everything he envisioned for their future. But in his opinion, taking things slow meant not moving in together immediately, and watching her closely for cues as to when she was ready for a more sexual relationship with him.

Fuck! After having to jerk off several times in the last eight hours 'cause of how sweet her lips tasted, I really hope she's ready for more than just kissin' a lot sooner than I expect it'll take for her to be ready for marriage and more kids. Yeah, my hand has been satisfying enough since meeting her back in December. But now that I know what her kiss tastes like, I really wanna know if her pussy tastes as sweet. And I'm absolutely dying to know how tight and wet she's gonna feel on my cock.

His dick instantly started swelling at the thought, which Josh had to quash before his son made it back downstairs from cleaning up after breakfast, so he wouldn't embarrass himself on the walk over to Cait's to formally introduce her to Joshua. *Think about baseball stats, or cows giving birth. Or even better, the look on Ma's face this morning when I told Joshua my plans for the day and called Cait my girlfriend.*

His mom had gone with Aunt Susan and Rosa to the grocery store before they had to start working on lunch and dinner for the ranch hands, but just her image in his mind was enough to deflate his cock. Hazel had been thrilled to hear Josh use the term "girlfriend" in reference to Cait, and she'd immediately started to ask all kinds of questions about how the relationship had evolved. Thankfully, Josh was able to deflect when Joshua started asking questions about Josh's plans while he was staying with Cait and Brody this morning.

"Okay, I'm ready," Joshua announced as he slid into the kitchen in his socks à la Tom Cruise in **Risky Business**. He had to chuckle as he remembered that his parents had compared his actions to the same movie when Josh did the same thing as a kid.

Damn, I can't get over how much he's just like me, Josh thought, grinning at his son and standing up from the table, so they could both put on their boots in the mud room. *I think I'd have known he was mine the instant I met him, even if I hadn't been forewarned by the DNA test that I had a son.*

"Let's go put our boots on then," Josh chuckled as he rinsed out his juice glass and put it in the dishwasher before following Joshua to the mudroom. "And when I get back from the lawyer's office, we'll get Brody to come hang out with us while we work with the horses and practice ropin' some more."

"What's Miss Cait gonna do while we're ridin' and ropin'?" Joshua looked up at him expectantly as they stepped out the back door to walk over to Cait's house.

"I'm not sure," Josh admitted. "I guess it depends on if she's able to get any work done this morning while hangin' out with you rowdy boys. If so, maybe she'll come play with the horses with us. And if not, then she'll probably enjoy some peace and quiet to work on her next screenplay."

"What's a screenplay?"

"Um, it's kinda like the script for a movie, but with all the information about what the set's supposed to look like and how the actors are supposed to move around the set during each scene." Over the past few months of being around his nieces and nephews while home on leave, Josh had seen that half the time his siblings spent parenting consisted of answering the most random questions the kids could come up with, several of which he'd had no idea how to answer without a little assistance from Google. But he hadn't realized just how many questions a kid could ask in a day until he spent ninety percent of the last thirty-six hours with his son. *Thank fuck, Joshua has been mostly focused on asking questions about ranching and stuff I actually know how to answer.*

"And Miss Cait writes them?"

"Yep," Josh nodded as they crossed the gravel drive separating the houses in this section of the ranch.

"If she writes for movies, doesn't she need to live in Hollywood?"

"No, because she works for the entertainment division of Burleson Incorporated," Josh explained. "Remember I told you about how we have several different divisions in our family business, not just the cattle and oil wells I showed you yesterday on the ranch?"

"Oh, yeah," Joshua nodded as they walked up Cait's driveway. "When are you gonna show me the rest of it?"

"I haven't even seen all of it," Josh chuckled. "But hopefully, I can show you the refinery, theater, and a couple of the gas stations here in town this week. And maybe the corporate headquarters in San Antonio, if we can convince the judge in Virginia to let you stay here with me until we have to go back there for court."

"That's why you're going to talk to the lawyer now, right? So I can stay with you instead of having to go back to Somerset?"

Josh had learned that Somerset Academy was the name of the boarding school Joshua's grandparents had sent him to in Roanoke. From the way Joshua described the place, it was exceptionally pompous and pretentious. And the absolute worst place Josh could imagine for a child to go to school. At least for a child who was anything like he was growing up — slightly hyperactive and not really interested in learning anything that required him to sit still for hours. He might not know everything about his son yet, but he was pretty sure he could say with a high degree of certainty that Joshua was very much like him in those respects.

"Yeah, that's the plan." Josh knocked on Cait's door. "But considering how slow the legal system can be, and the fact that your grandparents have already been given custody of you, I can't guarantee you won't have to go back there for a few weeks, until I can actually appear in court to fix the situation."

"Okay," Joshua sighed, his shoulders slumping with the despair he felt at the thought of going back to Somerset Academy. "But if I have to go back there, you're gonna come get me just as soon as you talk to the judge, right?"

"I will do absolutely everything I can to make it where you can live with me as soon as possible," Josh promised, just as Cait opened the door. She looked amazing standing there barefoot in jeans that were cut off at the knees, but had the lower legs reattached inside out to reach just below her calves, and a v-neck t-shirt that allowed only the slightest peak of her cleavage. Josh's boner was quickly making a reappearance, until his eyes traveled up to her face and he saw the panicked look in her turquoise eyes.

"Why did you knock instead of just walking in like everyone else does on the ranch?" Cait looked up at him with wide eyes and a hand clutched to her chest, like she was holding her heart because of being frightened. "I freaked out wondering who might have gotten on the ranch to come looking for me."

Oh shit! I didn't mean to frighten her. I was just trying to be respectful of her space. But I can't tell her it's because I only just walk in like that on family, when I wanna make her feel like she's already a part of my family.

"Sorry," Josh shrugged and smiled sheepishly, trying not to make a big deal out of the situation. "I guess I've spent too much time away from the ranch. And when I'm home, I generally only walk in like that at Mom and Dad's, which will always feel like home because it's where I grew up. I didn't mean to scare you by respecting your personal space."

"No, I'm sorry," Cait apologized for nothing. "I don't know why I freaked out. If I was still living in San Diego, I would fully expect everyone to knock or ring the doorbell. I guess in the two months I've lived here, I've just gotten used to everyone walking in and announcing 'knock, knock,' instead of actually knocking, way faster than I've adjusted to anything else."

"No worries," Josh grinned, hoping to settle her nerves a little before he left Joshua with her to go to his meeting.

Cait backed up and motioned for them to enter the house. "Please forgive my bad manners this morning. Come in and have a seat. Can I get you anything to drink?"

"We're good, Sunshine." Josh leaned over and kissed Cait's cheek as he walked past her into the living room, which was much lighter and brighter than it had been when his sister Charlotte lived in the house.

Instead of the bulky, formal living room set that had taken up all the space when Char lived there, Cait's furniture was minimal. She had a loveseat and several chairs arranged around a plush cream rug for more intimate conversations with guests. The only table in the room was the one under the television, which was hanging on the wall, and it wasn't really a table. Josh considered it more of a cabinet or bookcase with doors since he could see her books and DVDs on the shelves through the glass doors. The DVD player and a stereo sat atop the cabinet, along with a couple of knick-knacks.

Apparently, the furniture wasn't the only thing that changed when Cait moved into the house. She'd also painted over the brick walls and dark wood trim with an off-white color that allowed for some of the brick to show through, giving the walls a little bit of a distressed look. She'd also put up sheer curtains over the windows to allow in lots of light. The loveseat and chairs were all covered in mustard yellow slipcovers to match the color he assumed she'd painted on the kitchen cabinets based on the corner he could see through the door into the kitchen.

And she wondered why I call her Sunshine. The bright, sunny color scheme she chose totally matches her personality.

Once they were all in the living room, Josh formally introduced his son. "Joshua, this is my girlfriend, Cait, and our nephew, Brody, who is also your cousin since his dad married my sister Charlotte. Cait, Brody, this is my son, Joshua."

"We already met at the wedding," Brody announced, looking at Josh like he'd lost his mind.

"I met you, but I didn't meet your Aunt Cait," Joshua corrected the younger child as he stared at Cait with a strange expression.

"It's nice to meet you, Joshua." Cait extended her hand to Joshua, who looked at it for a long moment before finally taking it for a quick shake.

As soon as he released Cait's hand, Joshua turned to Josh and blurted, "Mom was right. You do have a type."

"What?" Josh chuckled uncomfortably, unsure what Joshua was talking about as he continued examining Cait.

"When Mom realized my grandparents were gonna take me away from Aunt Tawny, and they came up with the plan to do the spit tests to find you to help me, Aunt Tawny said she'd marry you to make the case stronger for me living with you and her," Joshua explained. "But Mom said that wouldn't work because Aunt Tawny isn't your type. Aunt Tawny said something about being everybody's type that didn't make sense. But Aunt Tawny has blonde hair, where Mom and Miss Cait both have brown hair. So, Mom was right. You like girls with brown hair, so Aunt Tawny isn't your type."

Josh wasn't going to point out that he'd never been that picky about the women he'd hooked up with in his younger years. His parents had raised him to not discriminate for any reason. And his cock had followed those early life lessons by happily banging a wide variety of women, regardless of race, size, or any other characteristic besides personality. Captain America didn't like mean girls. But before Josh met Cait, they were the only women his dick objected to fucking. Since meeting Cait, things had changed, though. And now she was the only woman that caused the Captain to stand at attention.

Josh floundered over what to say, unsure how to talk about attraction with an eight-year-old. *Yeah, I'm gonna hafta find Pop to ask his advice about how to talk to my son about girls as soon as I'm through in Mr. Reilly's office.*

Before Josh could come up with anything appropriate to say, Brody interjected, "It's not right to not like someone because of what color hair they have. I like Maria and Tia's yellow hair just as much as I like Bella's black hair and Aunt Cait's brown hair."

"You're right, Brody," Cait giggled. "We don't care what color a person's hair or skin is because those things aren't what matters."

"And I don't think I ever really had a type other than nice," Josh added. "I prefer to look at a person's attitude and personality when deciding if I wanna be friends with them. And as you boys will learn, growing up with the rest of your cousins, as Burlesons, you'll have a lot of friends of all different colors. But once you meet *The One*, the person you're meant to marry, it won't matter if they're purple with green hair and warts all over. To you, they'll be the most beautiful person you've ever seen. And instead of having a type of person you're into, you'll say your type is that person. So, now my type is Cait."

Cait held her arm out in front of her face like she was examining the color of her skin. After a second, she pulled some of her hair up in front of her eyes to inspect the strands. "I guess you got lucky, Josh. Either that or we need to get your eyes examined because I don't see any purple skin, green hair, or warts."

"No, but you're still the most beautiful person I've ever seen, Sunshine," Josh grinned, as the boys giggled at Cait's silly antics. He pulled her into a quick hug, kissing the top of her head as she returned the embrace. "Unfortunately, I can't stay and hang out with ya'll all morning, though."

"I know," Cait sighed as they released the hug. "It's too bad you're going to miss out on making cookies. I was hoping you could tell me what piece of farm equipment one of the cookie cutters I just got actually is, so I'd know how to decorate it."

"You bought farm equipment cookie cutters?" Josh chuckled.

"Oh yeah, Uncle Josh. They're so cool," Brody blurted excitedly. "There's a tractor and a barn and a cow and a horse and a pig and a couple of chickens..."

"Actually, I think one of those is a chicken, and the other is a rooster," Cait corrected with a grin as she mussed her nephew's hair.

"And a goat, and a sheep, and a bunny rabbit," Brody added enthusiastically. "But we can't figure out what the other one is 'cause Aunt Cait said you don't use a bulldozer on a farm."

"It's probably a combine," Josh chuckled, thinking that might be more common for cookie cutters than a hay baler. He was surprised when neither of the kids asked what a combine was, but Brody's excitement about decorating cookies with Joshua was too intense to be derailed by asking questions.

"We've got all kinds of icing colors to decorate them," Brody informed them as he took Joshua's hand and pulled him toward the kitchen. Josh and Cait followed the boys through the doorway into the newly painted, bright, sunny kitchen. "We're gonna have so much fun, Josh. And Aunt Cait said we get to eat any of the icing that gets on our hands while we're putting it on the cookies."

"You're gonna get the boys hopped up on a sugar high and then send them with me so you can work this afternoon, aren't you, Sunshine?" Josh shook his head and grinned at Cait, as they watched Brody and Joshua looking at the various cookie supplies in the pantry.

"I've got to make sure they have plenty of energy for roping fence posts and riding horses this afternoon," Cait shrugged and grinned back at him. "Besides, baking is a great activity to do while getting to know someone new."

Cait leaned in close to whisper so only Josh could hear her, "And cookies are excellent bribes for getting information from little boys."

"Thank you, Sunshine." Josh kissed Cait's temple, thankful for her planned efforts to help him figure out his son's emotional state. "You good, Joshua?"

"Yep," Joshua nodded, as he and Brody moved things Josh wasn't familiar with from the pantry to the kitchen island. "You can go tell the judge I wanna live here forever while I make you a horse cookie that looks like Leonardo."

"Yeah, I should probably go supervise that," Cait giggled, pushing up on her toes to kiss his cheek. "Good luck in your meeting."

"Yeah, I'll try to hurry, so maybe I can help with some of that decorating," Josh chuckled as Cait walked over to help the boys organize the things they were pulling from the pantry.

Seeing her with his son and their nephew, happy in her natural element working with the kids, Josh could see his future. Coming in from working on the ranch to see her playing with as many kids as she wanted them to have, sounded like the perfect way to spend the rest of his days.

Not that Josh could stand there all day and relish the joy of watching her bond with Joshua to start building their family the way he wanted. He had to force himself to walk out to his truck and drive over to Tyler Reilly's office at the corner of Brangus Street and Mustang Lane for their meeting.

Once there, he had to wait a few minutes while Mr. Reilly finished a phone call before he was shown to his office. "Good morning, Mr. Reilly," Josh extended his hand in greeting as he walked into the attorney's staid office.

"Good to see you, Josh. And please, call me Tyler," the lawyer directed, as the two men shook hands before sitting down on opposite sides of his large mahogany desk. "It was Mr. Reilly when you were a kid, hanging out with my daughter and the rest of ya'll's friends. But now that you're an adult, it just makes me feel old. Although, don't tell the Walker boys about that. They might technically be adults, but I still need them to fear me like they did as teenagers 'cause not a one of 'em is mature enough to date my daughter."

"Your secret's safe with me, Tyler," Josh chuckled, knowing he was going to have some fun with his friends, Aiden and Leo, whenever they were at a town function, and they first noticed Josh calling Cassidy's dad by his first name. "But the first time they hear me calling you Tyler at church, I'm gonna hafta tell them it's a privilege only granted to a select few people of our generation when we're mature enough to handle it, so I can rib them about not being grown-up enough yet."

"Oh, that's fine," Tyler smirked. "Just don't tell them it makes me feel old."

"Never," Josh shook his head solemnly before grinning. "So, what do we need to do to get this custody thing started?"

"I've actually already started on your case," Tyler informed Josh. "Because of the time difference, I came to the office early this morning, so I could contact the Department of Family and Children's Services in Virginia as soon as they opened. And surprise, surprise, they had not been notified that Joshua ran away from the boarding school his grandparents put him in. In fact, they didn't even realize that his grandparents had gone back to Annapolis and sent Joshua to a boarding school in Roanoke. They thought the three of them were happily settling into life in a house in Alexandria."

"Seriously? They didn't know he'd run away? Does the prison, I mean, school not report escapees?" Josh was shocked to hear that nobody had realized Joshua was missing when he'd left the boarding school on Thursday of the previous week. "And how could they not know that his grandparents live in Annapolis and not Alexandria? Didn't they have to do home visits like DFACS does here before deciding custody of an orphaned child?"

"Oh, yeah, they did the home visits," Tyler chuckled ruefully. "But they didn't ask to see a deed to the house, or even a rental agreement, to realize that the Joneses were staying in an Airbnb. From what I can gather, their attorney advised them to temporarily move to Virginia, so they didn't have to deal with the courts and DFACS in two different states, which might have delayed their claim for custody long enough for paternity to be established."

"So, they knew Jaina was trying to find me to keep them from getting custody," Josh assumed, feeling even more pissed at Earnest and Evelyn Jones than he already had based on what Joshua had told him since arriving in town. "So, they did whatever they had to in order to rush through the system before I could find out about Joshua and fight for him?"

"Yeah, pretty much," Tyler nodded. "But luckily for us, most people don't like being played. And the people I talked to this morning really don't like being played when a child suffers because of it. So, they are currently working on the paperwork to rescind the Jones's custody of Joshua. They're also conferencing with the Texas Department of Children and Family Services, since Joshua is here, instead of being in Virginia. And yes, I gave the caseworker in Virginia the contact information for the caseworker Brook called on Saturday for the emergency placement."

"I also talked to her this morning to find out the status of getting you listed as Joshua's official foster parent, instead of the Ashbury Foundation. And that should be done sometime today. It's just a matter of her boss signing off on the new site checks she did over the weekend and your information being entered into the computer."

"Really? I thought I was going to have to do all kinds of interviews and stuff to get approved." Josh had assumed the only reason the caseworker had allowed Joshua to stay with him at the ranch was because they were staying in his parents' house, and both Hazel and Bob were listed on the Madeline Ashbury Foundation paperwork as secondary supervisors for the group home they'd turned the south bunkhouse into back in the spring. So, he was really surprised to hear that he could officially be his son's foster parent so soon. "And he's gonna get to stay here with me until this all goes to court to determine the final custody arrangement?"

"Yes, for now," Tyler nodded and smiled, lifting a huge worry from Josh's shoulders. "They originally wanted to discuss the logistics of sending him back to Virginia to go into foster care. But when they found out how the Ashbury Foundation is privately funded and refuses to take the standard payment from the state for fostering the kids in their care, the state of Virginia decided it might be best to leave Joshua here for the time being. We just got lucky that best for their budget and best for Joshua coincide."

"Of course," Josh huffed. "I would never expect to be paid for taking care of my son."

"Yes, well, that's the thing. The courts won't accept the Ancestry DNA test to establish paternity, because there are no official records or witnesses to verify exactly who was tested. So, you do have to take Joshua for a blood test to establish paternity, which I've already scheduled for tomorrow morning at nine in Doc Hayes's office. And in addition to paying all his expenses while he's in your care, you have to cover all his travel expenses, as well as your own, when you go to Virginia to appear in court at the beginning of next month. That was the soonest we could get the case on the docket. Or rather added to the case already on the docket. And because you don't have his records to enroll him in school yet, and he wouldn't be able to attend while ya'll are traveling back and forth for court dates and such, you'll need to homeschool him until final custody is established for you to get all the proper paperwork to enroll him in the local school."

"Okay," Josh sighed, feeling slightly overwhelmed at everything he was hearing. "I guess I'll call Anthony this afternoon to find out what he and Kay do for homeschooling my nieces. Since Maria is not quite a year older than Joshua, I'm sure they can tell me where to get all the materials they used for her last year. And if there's anything that's confusing for me, I can get Charlotte and Ian to help me when they get back from their honeymoon."

"I'd definitely get on that as soon as possible," Tyler warned him. "While having everyone else on the ranch already in the foster system because of the Ashbury Foundation was extremely beneficial in rushing your foster parent status, DFACS is still going to have to do random home visits before you can be considered for full custody of Joshua. And they're going to want to see records of what you've been teaching him to verify you're meeting the homeschool requirements."

"Then I'll work on that first thing as soon as I leave here," Josh assured his attorney.

They talked for a few more minutes with Tyler giving Josh the contact information for the law firm in Alexandria, Virginia, that he was coordinating with to represent Josh in the courtroom, and Josh putting everything Tyler already had set up on the calendar in his phone to make sure he didn't miss anything that might impede his ability to get custody of his son.

Tyler also informed Josh that Tawny Ireland had also filed for custody of Joshua, claiming that the wishes in his mother's will should override the Jones's claim for custody. Apparently, her claim would also be heard when Josh went to court in October, but without having an official copy of the will, Tyler couldn't advise Josh on how to deal with that claim yet. So, instead, Tyler advised Josh not to contact Tawny at all, at least until they knew she wouldn't be a hindrance to his claim for custody.

For now, Josh decided to just focus on taking care of his son, jumping through all the hoops the caseworkers put before him, and spending time with Cait, both as a couple and as part of the family he hoped to build with her, Joshua, and any other children they might have in the future. He'd worry about working something out with Tawny Ireland later. And then only if Joshua wanted to keep in contact with his mom's best friend.

~~~

Cait mentally berated herself for how freaked out she'd gotten when she heard Josh knocking on her door that morning. Yeah, she'd freaked out like that whenever salespeople knocked on their door in San Diego since the shooting. But that was before the cartel had been dealt with, when she was afraid they'd found her to keep her from identifying the shooters. She'd also been nervous about the cartel when she lived in town in Heart's Destiny, leaving answering the door to her brother, just as she had in San Diego. But since moving to the ranch, where she now lived alone, she hadn't had anyone come over to visit her who hadn't just walked in the same way she'd been instructed to walk into each of the homes she'd cleaned while working in her first job with the Burlesons. And those visitors had all been members of the Burleson family, or her brother and nephew, which she supposed were also now part of the Burleson family. So, Josh knocking that morning had caught her off guard.
~~~

Thankfully, his easy affection and jovial personality had quickly set her at ease. Not that her heart rate had slowed down any once she saw him and realized there wasn't a threat at her door. Seeing him in his typical outfit of a t-shirt, jeans, and cowboy boots while on the ranch might have actually jacked it up higher than the fright of someone knocking on her door.

That cowboy is better at getting my heart rate up than any of the dance videos I've used for exercise over the last couple of years, Cait thought as Josh left for his meeting. *Hopefully, I won't get so excited that I end up having a heart attack the first time we make love. But maybe I should increase my cardio workouts to help prevent it.*

Not that Cait could think about any of that at the moment, when she had two little boys pulling way more baking ingredients from her pantry than were necessary for basic sugar cookies. "Alright, guys, let's put most of this stuff back and only get out the things we need for the cookies. After we wash our hands."

"But we need all the colors, Aunt Cait," Brody pouted when Cait started by putting the box of Wilton Icing Colors back in the pantry as the boys moved over to the sink to wash their hands.

"Eventually, yes," Cait agreed to placate her nephew as they finished putting everything back in the pantry while she took her turn at the sink to wash up. "When it's time to make the icing and decorate the cookies. But if they're on the counter now, they'll be in the way while we're making the cookies. So, let's just get the cookie ingredients out now. Once they're baked and cooling, then we'll get the icing ingredients out, including all the colors."

"What ingredients do we need to make the cookies?" Joshua looked at the pantry shelf, obviously not sure what to get and what to leave in place. He seemed wary of her and kept giving her strange looks that made her wonder if she had more in common with his mother than just the hair color he'd mentioned. Or if he was just afraid his dad having a girlfriend would cause an issue with his future living situation.

Oh, I hope his trepidation isn't because his mom had boyfriends like my mom had, who gave him the impression that people who date his parents might not love and accept him in their lives.

"From the pantry, we need all-purpose flour, baking powder, granulated sugar, salt, and vanilla extract. But you have to read the labels to make sure you don't get the self-rising flour, baking soda, or brown sugar confused with the ones we actually need."

Cait loved having baking days with Brody as he learned to read. Having a father who was an English teacher, Brody had learned to read way younger than most kids, but he tended to rush through books without noticing the subtle nuances of language. So, she'd started challenging him by making him look for specific ingredients whenever they baked together. It didn't matter that she now had three different types of flour in her pantry to make the reading challenge a little more difficult for him. Helping her nephew focus on comprehending what he was reading was way more important than a crowded pantry.

While Joshua was several years older than Brody, Cait thought the same activity would be beneficial in helping assess his reading ability for Josh to know if he might need help catching up with his peers when it came time to enroll him in school. Considering how bright and articulate he seemed while the boys worked together to pick out the proper ingredients, though, Cait had a feeling that Joshua might be more likely to be intellectually gifted than to need the extra help she had in school. Unlike Brody, who would have asked her several times to make sure he was picking out the correct flour, Joshua remembered the full list of things she'd mentioned needing and repeated them back to Brody to help him as they looked on the pantry shelf for each ingredient.

"Oh, Little Josh, before we get started, I need to know if you have any allergies, like to gluten or the dyes in food coloring," Cait inquired, hoping he wouldn't have an allergy to something she didn't know how to substitute in the cookies to make them safe for him to eat. She had rice flour to substitute if he had a gluten allergy and could look up the natural food coloring recipes online, which she'd had to use when she was in college and one of her friends had a sensitivity to FD&C dyes.

"I'm not little," Joshua made a face as he shook his head at her.

"I knew that wouldn't work as soon as it came out of my mouth," Cait confessed with a sigh, twisting up her mouth in a perplexed expression that she hoped would make him smile. "But Joshua sounds too old and stuffy for both you and your dad, so I need to figure out what to call you guys to keep everyone from being confused about which one of you we're talking to when we're hanging out with both of you. And while it worked when the GWA was in town to call Surfer Josh by his stage name, you and your dad don't have stage names for me to add to Josh to keep from being confused. So that's why I was trying to go with Big Josh and Little Josh."

"Dad has a call sign as a SEAL," Joshua suggested, tilting his head thoughtfully the same way she'd seen Josh when he was pondering a problem. "You could use that for him."

"Do you know his call sign?" *That really seems like something I should know about my boyfriend*, Cait thought, smiling at the memory of Josh introducing her to Joshua as his girlfriend. "Because I don't know it, or I'd start using it until we come up with a better nickname than Big Josh for him."

Joshua shook his head again, but he didn't elaborate on how he knew about call signs for SEALs without knowing the one Josh used with his team.

"Do I need to start calling him Uncle Big Josh?" Brody made a face almost as disgusted as Joshua's when Cait had called him Little Josh.

"No, that's way too long of a name," Cait scrunched up her face, mimicking the boys and making them giggle. "That would be like me calling you Brody Michael Burleson-Campbell all the time. That would sound like you're in trouble when I'm only calling you in for dinner. And we definitely don't want to go with long names all the time to make everyone think they're in trouble when they aren't. So, I'll just have to keep thinking of a shorter nickname for Joshua while we get started on the cookies. Now, I'm assuming the second head shake was because you don't know your dad's call sign, but was that first head shake because of the horrible nickname I tried? Or because you don't have any allergies for me to need to modify the recipe before we get started?"

"I don't have any allergies," Joshua smiled. "So, what else do we need to get out to make the cookies?"

"From the fridge, we need the unsalted butter and eggs," Cait replied, continuing to think of nickname ideas as the boys gathered the last two ingredients and she pulled out the mixer to start preparing the dough. Once they got started working together to measure the ingredients, Cait tried gently coaxing Joshua to tell her more about life with his mom before she passed away. "So, Joshua, have you ever made cookies before? Or done anything in the kitchen with your mom?"

"No, not really," Joshua shook his head as he watched the mixer do the job of creaming the butter and sugar together. "Mom and Aunt Tawny only cook in the microwave, so even on weekends when Mom was home during the day for us to do stuff together, I didn't help her in the kitchen."

Damn, it sounds like he grew up on TV dinners the same way Mikey and I did before I discovered cooking shows on TV when I was a teenager and insisted we both needed to learn how to cook.

"My mom only cooked in the microwave, too," Cait commiserated, nodding as she cracked the egg to add to the mixer. "But after Mikey and I lost her, I started watching cooking shows on TV to learn how to do more in the kitchen."

"Did your mom get sick and die, too? Like my mom?" Joshua looked up at her with wide eyes.

Damn it! I don't want to lie to the kid. But I don't want to have a heavy conversation with him about Lorna's drug use and prison time, either. Compromise, Caitir. Just tell him enough of the truth to show him you understand what he's going through without going into the gory details.

"She got sick and left when I was thirteen," Cait confided, thinking drug addiction was a type of sickness, so she wasn't really lying to the kid. "I haven't talked to her in so long that I don't know if she's still alive or not."

"My first mom died," Brody stated matter-of-factly as Cait measured out the vanilla extract and added it to the mixer. "But she didn't get sick. She was hurt by bad guys, so my dad arrested them and found me a new mom."

Cait wasn't sure if she should point out that Mikey had actually fallen in love with Charlotte and would have married her even if Brody hadn't wanted her to adopt him at the same time. At three months away from turning five, she wasn't sure Brody was old enough to understand the differences between a stepmom and an adoptive mom.

"Does your new mom look like your first mom?"

"No," Brody shook his head. "My first mom had black hair and brown skin like Antonio, Bella, and Mrs. Rosa. But Miss Char, my new mom, has peach skin and brown hair like Aunt Cait."

Cait wasn't sure what the boy's fascination was with comparing people's looks, but she knew it was probably best if she steered the conversation in a different direction before she found herself trying to explain the genetics of why Joshua looked like a clone of Josh, while Brody's bronze skin tone and umber hair color were a mix of his pale-skinned, blond-haired, Caucasian father and copper-skinned, ebony-haired, Hispanic mother, instead of him looking more like one parent than the other.

"Is Miss Char nice, like your first mom? Or more like Cinderella's evil stepmom?"

"I don't 'member my first mom, but Miss Char is really nice. She started teaching me about the horses and let me ride Westley with her way before she agreed to 'dopt me and be my mom."

Cait started to correct her nephew's pronunciation as she turned off the mixer, knowing he was dropping letters on some of his words because of rushing to get the words out in excitement. But quickly decided it was probably best to go ahead and change the subject to keep Joshua from casting her in the role of potential evil stepmom.

"JoJo, can you measure two-and-a-half cups of flour for me?" Cait pushed the measuring cups across the counter toward Joshua before getting out a second bowl to mix the dry ingredients. "And put it in this bowl?"

"The cup is the same one we used for the butter, right?" Joshua looked around the room, trying to find the measuring cup they'd previously used, which was in the sink, without acknowledging the nickname she'd just come up with for him using the first two letters of his first and last names.

"Yes, but you can also use the half cup and fill it up five times, since the full cup is in the sink to be washed," Cait informed him, realizing he was probably a little too young to have learned about fractions in school already, as she pointed out the correct measuring cup. "Brody, why don't you help JoJo by counting how many times he fills the half cup with flour?"

Brody nodded and counted as Joshua scooped the flour into the measuring cup, scraping the flour off even at the top the way she'd shown them to do with the butter. Cait picked up the measuring spoons and added the correct amount of baking powder and salt to the same bowl before handing Brody a whisk to blend the dry ingredients.

Cait turned the mixer back on and slowly added the dry ingredients while the boys watched as the dough came together.

"So, JoJo, what kind of things did you like doing with your mom?" Cait continued, trying to get Joshua to open up a little as soon as they could carry on a conversation without the sound of the mixer drowning them out.

"When it was warm outside, we'd go to the park and play. And when it was too cold or snowy, we'd go to the library and read or get on the computers," Joshua informed her as they prepared the counter for rolling out the dough. "And we watched movies a lot, whenever I didn't have to go to bed early to get up for school."

"It sounds like you used to have a lot of fun with your mom," Cait smiled, hoping his earlier childhood really had been happier than she'd expected to hear from him.

"Yeah," Joshua sighed. "I miss her a lot, but I know she's watching over me from Heaven. Her cardinal followed me all the way here, so I know she's always with me."

"Her cardinal?" Brody looked confused.

Cait wasn't quite sure what Joshua was talking about either, but she just listened as she turned the dough out on the floured countertop and started rolling it out.

"Yeah, it's a red bird that angels send down from Heaven to show the people they love they're still with them, even though their spirit doesn't live in their human body anymore," Joshua explained. "I promised Mom that anytime I wanted to cry from missing her, I'd look out the window to find the cardinal she sent me. And I've seen it every day since my mom died."

Cait wasn't about to burst the kid's bubble by pointing out that he'd probably seen several different cardinals between Texas and Virginia. From what little he'd said, Joshua seemed to have had a decent life with a loving mother before she got sick. And it sounded like she'd prepared him fairly well for dealing with the emotional aftermath of her premature passing. So, Cait wasn't about to say anything that might undo even the slightest aspect of her excellent job of parenting.

With a better idea of what to tell Josh about the reason his son didn't appear as lost in grief over his mother as they'd expected, Cait decided to get them refocused on the cookies and happier topics. "Alright, boys, pick your cookie cutters and start laying them out as close together as possible, so we can decide the best way to cut the cookies to not have to roll the dough a bunch of times."

As the morning went on, Cait enjoyed talking to the boys about their favorite things, especially the animals on the ranch, and getting to know Josh's son. While the cookies were baking, Cait cleaned up the kitchen and the boys played a game in the living room. When the cookies were on the cooling racks, they took some time to go for a walk around the ranch to make some mental notes about what colors things were to be able to decorate the cookies accordingly.

While Cait didn't feel comfortable venturing too far from the house when she didn't know exactly when Josh would be back, she did walk the kids around behind all the houses to see the different pieces of equipment being used to cut and prepare the grass for being baled as hay. Unfortunately, the only things she could identify were the tractors and the mower attachment being used to cut the field between the gate and the backyards of the three houses on the opposite side of the gravel drive from where she lived. So, when the boys started asking questions she couldn't answer, Cait decided it was time to go back to the house and start making the frosting for the cookies. She promised to ask Josh to repeat the walk with them when he got home, assuming he'd be better equipped to explain the process of harvesting grass for hay.

Throughout the entire time they were hanging out, Joshua never commented on her calling him JoJo, even when Brody picked up on the nickname and started using it, too. It wasn't until they were halfway through decorating the cookies and Josh arrived that the subject came up in conversation.

"Knock, knock," Josh announced as he walked in the door instead of scaring her by knocking again.

"Dad! You made it back in time to help decorate cookies!"

"I did," Josh beamed at his son as he sauntered across the room to join them around the kitchen island. "And I've got good news!"

"Oh, I like good news," Cait grinned at him as Josh reached for a cookie. "But wash your hands before you touch the food."

"Yes, ma'am," Josh saluted Cait playfully before turning to the kitchen sink and washing his hands.

"What's the good news?" Joshua inquired as soon as Josh turned back to face them.

"Guess who doesn't have to go back to Virginia this week," Josh directed, smiling brightly.

"Me?" Joshua looked up at Josh hopefully.

"JoJo!" Brody guessed at the same time.

"JoJo?" Josh arched an eyebrow at Brody before turning to look at Cait for an explanation.

"That's the nickname we've been trying out for Joshua today, so nobody gets confused with two Joshes on the ranch," Cait quickly summarized.

"It's way better than Little Josh," Joshua rolled his eyes. "And since we can't go with JJ like Mom called me because you already have a JJ in the family, I guess Cait thought using the first two letters of my first and last names would work instead of just the first letters."

"Yeah, I think I like JoJo better than Little Josh, too," Josh chuckled, giving his son a fist bump. "It reminds me of an anime series I used to watch, ***JoJo's Bizarre Adventure***. JoJo was the hero who used martial arts to defeat the bad guys."

"Cool! Can we watch it together?" Joshua's eyes lit up as he turned to his dad.

"Maybe when you're a teenager," Josh chuckled before picking out a horse-shaped cookie to decorate with them. "It's a cartoon that's really not meant for little kids."

"Okay," Joshua shrugged before going back to his task of decorating a barn-shaped cookie. "As long as you're sure JoJo is the good guy, I'm okay with being nicknamed after a character I'm too young to see."

"Yeah, JoJo is definitely the good guy," Josh grinned and pulled the whole bowl of chocolate icing they'd made for brown over in front of him. Josh lifted the spoon from the bowl and looked at it for a moment before turning to Cait. "You got a butter knife I can put this on with?"

"You're supposed to put it in a bag and squeeze it on," Brody instructed Josh as he demonstrated with the green icing he was putting on a tractor. "Like this."

Cait put the last spot of brown on the cow cookie she was working on before handing the decorator bag of chocolate icing across the island to Josh. "Here, I'm done with the brown on this cow. But while you're decorating your horse, you need to tell us your good news."

"Thanks, Sunshine," Josh grinned as he took the icing from her hand, turning to watch how both Joshua and Brody were decorating their cookies before trying to position his large hands properly to squeeze the icing from the bag onto the cookie in front of him. "The boys already figured it out. JoJo doesn't have to go back to Virginia, like I was afraid they were gonna tell us when Tyler called the caseworker in Alexandria."

"I get to live here forever with you and Cait and Brody?" Joshua's eyes widened in excitement at the thought.

Cait's heart warmed at being included in his statement of people he wanted to stay with forever. Not that she really thought she'd completely won him over in just a few short hours of getting to know him.

"Not forever yet," Josh warned. "But you don't have to go back until our court date on October first. And if everything goes according to plan in court that week, then it'll be forever."

Joshua dropped the decorator bag of red icing that he was using on his barn cookie, and jumped from his stool to hug Josh. "Awesome! I knew you could fix it where I don't have to go back to Somerset!"

Josh also dropped his icing bag as he caught his extremely excited son and squeezed him to his chest.

"That's not just good news," Cait smiled, enjoying the family bonding moment, even though she wasn't truly a part of it. "That's great news! We should do something special to celebrate."

"How 'bout I take ya'll to the Burger Barn for lunch?" Josh grinned at her as JoJo released him from the hug and moved back to his seat.

"We already ate lunch," Cait confessed, wishing she'd waited until after Josh got home to make sandwiches for her and the boys. "Since you haven't eaten yet, would you like me to make you a sandwich? That's what I made for us after our reconnaissance mission to determine the colors of farm equipment. Which reminds me, we really need you to tell us what all those pieces of equipment are called and explain what everything but the mower does."

"Thanks, Sunshine," Josh grinned. "But I can wait 'til after we're finished decorating cookies to eat. And when we're all done and hopped up on sugar, I'll actually teach ya'll how to use some of that equipment, instead of just telling ya about 'em."

"Cait had as many questions about how the grass gets turned into hay as I did about the different fields you used for all the cows yesterday," JoJo chuckled as he went back to decorating his barn cookie.

"That's because she's a city girl," Josh whispered as if he was sharing a secret with his son while winking at Cait.

"Well, we can't all be farm boys like you," Cait teased, grinning at him.

"No, Sunshine," Josh shook his head, feigning a disappointed look. "This isn't **The Princess Bride**. I'm a cowboy, not a farm boy. In fact, I'm so much of a cowboy that the guys in my unit call me Cowboy when we're on ops."

"Cowboy is your call sign?" *Yeah, I'm not going to tell him that I called him Cowboy Hottie in my head, when I first saw him and didn't know his name. Or that I call him Cowboy half the time when I'm fantasizing and using my vibrator in bed at night.*

"Yeah," Josh nodded, examining her closely. Maybe a little too closely considering where her thoughts had just gone. "How do you know about call signs?"

"I, uh, read about them in one of the books I'm converting into a screenplay," Cait fibbed, wishing she could turn off her tendency to blush right about then. She didn't consider it a real lie, since she had read about call signs in several of the military romance novels she'd read recently, one of which she was actually working on making into a screenplay. It didn't really matter that she'd read a few of those books long before she started working as a screenwriter.

"And Mom told me that SEALs have call signs, so I told Cait she could call you by yours to keep from having two Joshes in the family," JoJo added.

"But we didn't know it, so she came up with JoJo," Brody continued.

"I guess now you can call Dad Cowboy and me JoJo, and the wrestler you guys know can stay Josh without confusing anyone." Joshua put his decorated barn on the plate with the finished cookies and picked out a combine to decorate next.

"Yeah, I doubt you'll get the rest of the family to change over to callin' me Cowboy," Josh chuckled and smirked. "But I'll answer to it if that's what you wanna call me, Sunshine."

Based on the way Josh waggled his eyebrows suggestively at her while the boys were focused on their cookies, Cait had a feeling Josh had somehow read her earlier thoughts and already knew when she'd used the moniker in her mind. Since she couldn't exactly respond the way she wanted with little ears listening, Cait looked down at the bunny cookie she was decorating with white icing and hoped her blush wasn't too noticeable.

If this is what raising a family with him will be like, we're going to have to work hard not to gross out our kids with our flirty innuendo in the future.

That is, if things really do work out between us the way he seems to think they will. Cait was still slightly afraid to get her hopes up for living out her happily ever after with Josh. As much as she wanted it to happen, life had knocked her down too many times for her to not have a sliver of doubt. *But I really hope that Cowboy is right about us being meant for one another.*

Chapter Sixteen

Josh was looking forward to spending some time with Cait and JoJo to start bonding them all together as the family unit he hoped they'd soon become. Oh, they'd done lots of things together over the last few days, but none of it had just been the three of them. With Cait babysitting Brody until Ian and Charlotte returned from their honeymoon that morning, they hadn't gotten any time together without his newest nephew in tow. Even though Josh loved Brody and enjoyed having him hang out with them, he knew the only way he'd be able to make things work with Cait was to spend time with just her and JoJo, so they could all connect and build a loving foundation for the nuclear family he wanted them to be in the future.

We're no different than Char or Anthony and the families they've built recently through adoption, Josh thought as he drove them to San Antonio for the visit to the Alamo that he'd promised Cait before JoJo came into their lives. *Well, other than the fact that neither one of us has known JoJo his whole life to already have a bond with him. But just like Anthony had to spend time with Kay and her daughters before they could become a family, and they all had to spend time with Antonio before they could adopt him, Cait and I both need to spend time with JoJo, as well as each other. And just like Char had to spend time with Ian and Brody while Cait wasn't around to establish her role in their immediate family, Cait needs to spend time with JoJo and me while Brody isn't around, so she and I can eventually form a parental unit to raise JoJo and any other kids we'll have someday.*

Unfortunately, Josh wasn't sure Cait was looking at this outing in the same way he was at the moment. While JoJo sat in the back seat with headphones on to watch the Texas history lessons Josh had found for him as he set up his homeschool curriculum with the help of his youngest brother on Wednesday, Cait was practically bouncing out of the passenger seat from being so nervous about the outing. Josh was afraid Cait's anxiety over going out in public kept her from understanding that he had more than one goal for their trip to San Antonio for the day.

Apparently, her trepidation about going with Ian, Char, and Brody when they went to the various tourist attractions in San Antonio was less about interfering with their family bonding time than she'd originally led him to believe. He'd figured some of that out when he'd first suggested they do this outing earlier in the week, and she'd expressed her concern about not being able to protect the kids if she had a panic attack in the middle of a crowded public space. She'd been so scared that when he thought it would be both boys they'd have with them, Josh had agreed to push off the outing until Ian and Char were home from their honeymoon.

When he found out that Char insisted they come back early from the beach to take Brody to a rodeo in Seguin before they had to go back to work on Monday, he thought it was perfect timing for him to take Cait and JoJo to the Alamo. He was confident in his ability to protect both Cait and JoJo should they find themselves in a dangerous situation. As many times as he'd had to protect multiple women and children, who were innocent bystanders, while his team went after high-value targets during his time in the Navy, Josh hadn't even been worried about failing to protect them, even if they'd planned to bring all their nieces and nephews with them. But Cait didn't appear to be as confident in her ability to get through the experience without having a panic attack.

As he watched Cait fidgeting nervously in her seat through his peripheral vision while driving to San Antonio, Josh wished he'd had some time alone with her this week to address all her concerns before pushing her precariously close to the limit of what she could handle to make sure she was fully prepared and didn't feel like he'd shoved past her boundaries.

Fuck! I probably should have thought about the fact that when she was shot and Ian's first wife died, he was only able to protect Brody from catching a bullet. And now she probably thinks that if something similar happens, I'm gonna do the same thing he did that day and cover JoJo's body with mine while leaving her to fend for herself.

And granted, that probably would have been my first instinct before becoming a SEAL. Though I probably would have tried to cover both her and JoJo if we'd been in that situation before my training. But now I know I'd find the nearest cover for both of them and then take out the tangos.

Would it help her feel less stressed about today if I tell her that my military training prepared me better than Ian's police training for situations like that? Or would it be better if I give her something else to focus on to take her mind off of what we're doing until we get there?

I know once we're there, I'm gonna hafta stick close to her to make her feel safe. That's why, before we met her to leave the ranch, I talked to JoJo about holding her hand today if I have to step away from them for any reason, and made sure he's comfortable going to the bathroom by himself, so I can stand guard outside the restrooms whenever they have to go.

Between his teenage years working on the ranch, when he was afraid of getting poison ivy on his dick if he pissed outside, and his training for the SEALs, Josh had pretty much trained himself to only need the restroom once or twice a day. It probably wasn't all that great for his kidneys to only urinate first thing in the morning and right before going to bed at night, but controlling his bladder that much was certainly useful on long ops when the SEALs didn't want to leave any evidence of their presence in hostile territory. And now he assumed it would be a valuable skill he'd be glad to have, so he didn't have to leave Cait's side whenever they went somewhere in public where she struggled to feel safe.

But should I tell her how I've planned to stick close to keep her safe? Or will making her think about the precautions I'm taking ramp up her anxiety before we even get there?

Damn it! I really shoulda talked to a therapist about the best way to help Cait get over her fear, instead of following JJ's advice to subtly top her into pushing her boundaries.

"Hey, it's gonna be okay, Sunshine," Josh assured her, finally deciding it was best to tackle the problem head-on as he reached over to take her hand to stop her from picking at a loose thread on her jeans.

"I promise, I'll be able to keep you both safe, even if some lunatic shows up with a gun today."

"Are you sure?" Cait turned to look at JoJo in the back seat before settling her gaze on him for reassurance.

"Positive," Josh promised, lifting her hand to his lips for a gentle kiss. "It's kinda my job to protect innocent bystanders in hostile situations. And I don't mean to sound cocky or brag too much, but I'm damn good at my job."

"I thought your job was baling hay and taking care of cows now," Cait quipped, grinning lightly, even though Josh could still see the tension around her eyes. "I'm not sure how knowing when it's time for a calf to be born is going to be all that beneficial anyplace but on the ranch."

"That's gonna be my new job," Josh countered, smiling at how they both tried to deal with the bad shit in life through humor. "Next month, after everything's settled in Virginia. But until those discharge papers are officially signed and filed, I'm still a SEAL. Hell, even after I've been out of the Navy for fifty years, I'll still be a SEAL at heart, and my job will always be defending the people I love from harm of any kind. So, no matter when or where we go, I will keep you and everyone else in our family safe."

"You're right," Cait sighed. "I'm just nervous because I've avoided being out in a major city for so long. I mean, you saw how long it took for me to feel comfortable going to an outdoor event in Heart's Destiny, and how I had to be surrounded by practically everyone I know to feel safe among the other fifteen-hundred people who live there. So, going to San Antonio, where there's like a thousand times that many people, kind of feels like I'm going back out in San Diego."

"Yeah, but you were able to go out there to get on the plane to move here," Josh pointed out, hoping to make her feel a little less nervous about their outing by comparing it to an event she'd already completed with no negative repercussions. "The only difference is that you're going with me and JoJo, instead of with Ian and Brody."

"Oh, no," Cait chuckled self-deprecatingly. "We had a police escort from our house to the small airport where we got on a private plane arranged by Trent, Mikey's former DEA partner, to fly out here. And we didn't fly into San Antonio, but to a small airport between San

Antonio and Heart's Destiny, so I didn't have to freak out about being in a densely populated area once we left San Diego."

Well, shit, I guess it is a little different, Josh realized as he tried to think of a way to put Cait's mind at ease with a little joshin' around. "So, just how many DEA agents does it take to do the same job as one Navy SEAL?"

"What?" Cait looked adorable with her confused expression.

"You said you had a police escort and that the plane was arranged by a DEA agent, so I'm assuming the officers escorting you were also DEA agents," Josh clarified. "So how many DEA agents did you need covering your six to feel safe enough to leave the house in San Diego?"

"Four," Cait smirked. "Five if you count Mikey, but he'd been out of the agency for two years by then."

"And what about the pilot? And the rest of the staff on the plane?" Josh arched an eyebrow at Cait as he grinned.

"It was a small plane, so it was just the one pilot." Cait shook her head at him. "Mikey knew him from his time in the DEA, but I'm not sure if he was an agent or not."

"I'm gonna guess he probably was," Josh teased. "So, it took six DEA agents to do the job I'm doin' solo today."

"I thought you said you didn't want to sound cocky earlier," Cait giggled, rolling her eyes at him. "And since we're not flying anywhere today, the pilot doesn't count, so it's only five."

"Oh, but Sunshine, did I not tell you my plans for an aerial tour of the area after lunch?" Josh grinned even wider than before at the thought of taking Cait and JoJo up in his Cessna for the afternoon. He hadn't really thought about taking them up until right then, but now that he had, he thought it was a great idea. Not only would it be a better way of showing Cait the San Antonio area than looking out the window of the revolving restaurant at the Tower of the Americas, so she wouldn't have to be around a bunch of people at the time, but it would also be a good idea for finding out if JoJo got airsick before flying back to Virginia in a couple of weeks.

"You do not have plans for an aerial tour of the area," Cait scoffed, not realizing he could add a quick flight to their agenda at the drop of a hat.

"Did I forget to tell you about my plane?"

"Quit teasing, Josh!" Cait reached over and lightly slapped his thigh. "You do not have a plane! If you did, you'd have suggested flying before now."

"No, seriously, I have a plane," Josh chuckled, catching JoJo's eyes in the rearview mirror, and seeing that he'd finished his videos about the Alamo.

"You have a plane?" JoJo tilted his head at Josh curiously as he removed his headphones. "When do we get to see it?"

"I was just telling Cait my plans for taking ya'll on an aerial tour this afternoon after the Alamo and lunch," Josh explained, catching his son up on this portion of his and Cait's conversation. "I thought you might want to check out the Skyhawk and make sure you don't get airsick before we fly it to Virginia in a couple of weeks."

"You're gonna fly us to Virginia when we have to go?" JoJo's eyes got wide, and Josh wasn't sure if it was in excitement or from a fear of flying.

"That's the plan," Josh grinned at his son through the rearview mirror and hoped his love of flying would carry over to his son. If not, their travel plans for Josh to sign his discharge papers and go to court for custody of Joshua would have to change pretty quick. "Unless you have a problem with riding in a small plane and need me to come up with different travel arrangements."

"No!" JoJo shouted, rapidly shaking his head to make his point. "I've always wanted to fly, but Mom always drove when we went somewhere."

"When did you learn to fly a plane?" Cait inquired, smiling as she looked him over like she didn't recognize him for a moment. "I knew SEALs were trained to jump out of planes, but I didn't think your training included how to fly them."

"No, I went to flight school on weekends when I was in the Naval Academy," Josh clarified. "Jake and I both did during our sophomore year. That was when Anthony joined the Navy and all he could talk about was how he was gonna learn to be a pilot. We couldn't let our little brother show us up by learning to fly before we did. Then, when I got my first big check from being on the Burleson board, I bought the same kind of plane we learned to fly in, to be able to fly myself home on leave instead of having to deal with commercial flights."

"Is flying yourself faster than taking commercial flights?" Cait questioned, tilting her head in thought. "Or just less stressful because of not having to cram in like sardines with a bunch of other people?"

"Oh, it's definitely not faster," Josh chuckled. "In fact, since my plane is so small, it takes me about three times as long to fly somewhere than the airline flights or even Anthony in his little jet. And I wouldn't even say space is a benefit, since it's only a four-seater and is a snug fit for larger people. But I can fly on my own schedule and not have to worry about being bumped to a later flight if an airline overbooks. And I can fly into the littlest airports, so there aren't any issues with crowded airports, long TSA lines, or restrictions on the size of any liquids I wanna pack in my carry-on."

Talking about the plane and flying distracted them completely for the rest of the drive, calming Cait's nerves until they got to the Alamo. Josh wasn't sure what else he could do to ease her anxiety, as she started fidgeting once more as soon as he parked the truck.

"It'll be okay, Sunshine," Josh assured her as he helped her down from the truck and took her hand for the short walk from the parking garage near the RiverWalk to the Alamo Plaza.

"I'm gonna help Dad keep you safe," JoJo added, stepping around them to take Cait's other hand. "So, you don't have to be scared of getting hurt again, 'cause we won't let any bad guys come close enough to hurt you."

Cait looked shocked at Joshua stepping up to help defend her. "Oh, um," Cait sputtered, obviously at a loss for words.

Shit! I should have warned her that I'd talked to JoJo about her anxiety this morning. She seemed so open about it with the rest of our family, so I thought it was common enough knowledge that it was no big deal. But maybe I was wrong?

"Hey, Sunshine, look at me," Josh commanded, hoping JJ was right about her needing him to take charge and guide her through getting past her anxiety. When her eyes popped up to his instantly, he was reassured that he was following the best course of action for her by the trust he read in them. "I only told him that you've been hurt before when some bad guys showed up while you were at a public park, so now you get a little scared whenever you go someplace with a lot of strangers around. So, now he knows to stay close to us and to help you hide, while I take care of any bad guys who might show up while we're out in public."

"Oh," Cait nodded as his words sunk into her consciousness. "Thank you." Cait turned to look down at JoJo and added, "Both of you. Thank you for being my brave protectors."

Josh had been given service medals for some of the missions he'd gone on as a SEAL, but none of those military honors made him feel as proud as Cait's genuine appreciation. And all he really felt like he'd done was stand by her side to support her as she fought through her fears.

Josh didn't want to continue dwelling on the psychological obstacle Cait was overcoming, knowing that would only set her back in her progress. So, he opted to continue trying to distract her with stories about his ancestors who'd been at the battle of the Alamo from the research his sister had done on their family tree.

He'd been surprised to learn that not only had they had two great-uncles on his mother's side of the family that defended the Alamo, but the Burlesons had also had a great-uncle through their great-grandmother Sylvia Davis's branch of the family tree, and another through their second-great-grandmother Sarah King's branch of the family tree. He couldn't remember how many greats went in front of each of those uncles, but he was proud to be able to point them out when they looked over the list of Defenders carved into the Alamo Cenotaph.

"Hey, there's a Campbell listed here, too," JoJo pointed out. "That's your last name, Cait. Did you have ancestors who fought for Texas' independence, too?"

"I don't know," Cait shrugged. "You'd have to ask Mikey if he found a Robert Campbell on our family tree, who could have been here back then."

"You still haven't looked at any of the information he found?" Josh inquired, knowing she wouldn't send in her DNA to be tested, but still unaware of why she refused to search for her biological relatives. "Or sent in your DNA to verify his findings?"

"No," Cait sighed. "But after coming here, I'll definitely ask my brother about our Campbell ancestors."

"Why haven't you sent in your spit to be tested?" JoJo questioned Cait. "It's not really gross to spit in the tube. And you might find a whole family that you've been missing out on, like I did."

"Some of us aren't as lucky as you, JoJo," Cait quipped, touching her finger to the tip of Joshua's nose as she smiled at him. "To find out you have a wonderful dad who came from a great family. Sometimes fathers turn out to be bad guys. And since my mom didn't know my dad well enough to know if he's a good guy or not, like your mom knew your dad, I don't want to take the chance of him being as bad or worse than the stories my mom and Mikey told me about the guys they think could be my father."

Fuck! From what little she told me about her mom, I should have realized she was afraid her bio-dad would be just as messed up. No wonder she doesn't want to submit a DNA sample that could lead to finding out just how fucked up his life was when he abandoned their family.

"They don't know who your dad is?" JoJo looked up at Cait like questioning paternity was a foreign concept for him.

Damn! Did we get lucky that his mother sheltered him from the reality of life? Or is figuring out how to explain one-night stands and sleeping around to my eight-year-old son my punishment for being a man-whore most of my adult life?

"No, they don't know for sure." Cait shook her head. "My mom dated a couple of different men before I was born, so she wasn't sure which one of them could be my dad. And DNA tests back then weren't nearly as accurate as they are now, so even if she had one done, I'm not sure the results were right. Since I never saw the results of the test she claimed she had done, I don't know if I can believe her story about my dad being a Navy officer or not. I did see the money he paid her to keep me away from him, though, so I'm sure whoever she thought was my dad wasn't a nice person. And Mikey was only seven when I was born, so the person he remembers our mom dating around that time might not have been dating her at the right time to help make me. But even if Mikey's right about the farmer he remembers being my dad, the man left town when he found out I was on the way because he didn't want to be my dad. So, I don't really want to do a DNA test to find out which one of the guys who didn't want a daughter is actually my biological father."

"But what if it's not either one of those guys? What if he's really nice like my dad, and would have loved you if he'd known about you like my dad does me?"

As much as Josh loved hearing his son recognize that he already loved him and would have been there from day one had he known Jaina got pregnant the night they hooked up, he hated that JoJo was putting Cait on the spot. Especially since it appeared she was a lot less ready to deal with the issue of her paternity than she was to tackle her anxiety in public places. So, once again, he decided distraction was his best option for the moment. "Hey, ya'll, we should probably get moving on the rest of the tour if we wanna get through it all before lunch."

His distraction technique seemed to work well as the subject was dropped, and they went back to talking about the Alamo and its role in Texas' history, while they crossed the street to check out the church and long barracks. Cait seemed to relax more and more the longer they walked around. More so whenever they were inside one of the buildings than when they were walking around the various courtyards and the gardens. But Josh still felt like the experience seemed to be an overall positive one for her mental health.

That is, until they started toward the exit of the Alamo Plaza, and a car on one of the nearby downtown streets backfired. Cait jumped at the sound, breaking their connection where he had his hand on her low back as they'd walked side by side trailing Joshua. She tackled JoJo, covering his body with hers.

Josh was surprised by how quickly she reacted to the sound, barely having registered what had set her off before she dove to cover JoJo. He looked around to double-check that his initial assessment of the noise was correct, as he knelt down beside them and rubbed a hand over Cait's back. Once he was assured by the reactions of the other people around them that it was indeed just a car backfiring, Josh relayed the info to Cait in as soothing a manner as he could, cooing the words softly close to her ear. "It was just a car backfiring, Sunshine. You're safe. JoJo's safe. We can get up and go straight from here to the truck, so you don't have to stress anymore today."

"It was just a car?" Cait slowly lifted her head until their eyes met, hers still wide with fear. "Not a gun?"

"Yeah, Sunshine, it was just a car," Josh reassured her, helping her up to a seated position, so JoJo could also get up.

"Sorry, I, uh, I guess I overreacted," Cait stuttered out an apology, blushing with embarrassment at being the only person around them who seemed to think it was a gunshot she'd heard. "I didn't hurt you when I tackled you, did I?"

"No," JoJo reassured her, shaking his head. "But the middle of the sidewalk isn't really a good place to hide."

"No, I guess it isn't," Cait laughed as JoJo jumped up and reached out a hand to help her up. Josh extended his hand as well, so she could grasp each of them to pull herself up from the ground. "Next time I think I hear a gun go off, I'll make sure we look for a better place to hide."

"Naw, you did exactly right, Cait," Josh informed her as he ushered them out of the middle of the plaza and toward the parking garage. "You got JoJo down where it was safer than standing had it been real gunfire, so I could assess the situation and find a place you could crawl to for cover if you needed it. Though maybe I should make ya'll wear helmets whenever we go out like this, so neither one of you end up with a concussion from hitting your head on the ground."

"Naw, that's okay, Dad," JoJo disagreed, continuing to hold Cait's hand as they walked. "I lifted my head like Tia showed us the wrestlers do when they take a bump, so I didn't hit my head."

"I guess that wrestling training ya'll did for P.E. yesterday was beneficial after all," Josh chuckled as he walked along on Cait's other side with his hand on the small of her back. "Now it's time to find out if you worked up the appetite of a wrestler with your extra practice just now."

"Um, would you mind if we skipped the Tower of the Americas and just grabbed some fast food instead?" Cait looked up at him nervously, obviously still a little on edge as they walked through downtown San Antonio.

"Yeah, we can do that, Sunshine," Josh agreed, smiling as he slid his hand up her back and put his arm around her shoulders to walk the rest of the way to the truck. "The view from my plane will be better than the one from the restaurant, anyway."

"Thank you." Cait showed her appreciation by wrapping her arm around his waist and giving him a little squeeze.

Josh leaned over and kissed her temple before whispering, "And after the drive-thru, we'll go straight to the hanger," *where I've fantasized about fucking you,* "so you won't have to worry about any more crowded places today."

I'll just have to try to keep from getting a hard-on in front of my son while remembering the fantasies I've had of pounding you against the side of the plane.

~~~

Monday, September 16, 2019

Cait felt like all her dreams were on the cusp of either coming true, or crashing down around her, as she sat with Josh and JoJo in the game room on the third floor of Hazel and Bob's house playing a Lego superheroes video game. Technically, she was watching Josh and JoJo play the game after she'd proven Brody's opinion of her lack of video game-playing ability correct. But even though she wasn't the one holding the controller, she was enjoying the time with the father and son she was rapidly starting to consider *her guys*. Due to her lingering doubt and fear that something would tear them apart, that was as close as she was willing to come to calling them *her family* just yet.

Even though they'd spent most of their time together over the last week, and Josh had made it clear to his family and friends that they were officially a couple, Cait knew they still had some hurdles to get over before they could do more than casually dating. While the largest of those hurdles was the upcoming court hearing for Josh to try to get full custody of JoJo, there were also a lot of personal issues for all three of them to tackle, so they could each be mentally ready to be a family. And she wasn't sure any of them were going to be easy to overcome. In fact, she thought it might be their individual issues that would ultimately derail them from being the family she wanted.

While the outings Josh and JoJo had taken her on the past couple of days were helping Cait tremendously in dealing with the remnants of her agoraphobia, Cait feared that she wasn't doing as much to help JoJo and Josh with their issues. With the way JoJo pointed out a similarity between her and his mom at least once a day, she worried
~~~

she might actually be setting him back in his grieving process, instead of helping him move forward.

To be totally honest, if only with herself, she felt a bit weird whenever JoJo made a comparison between her mannerisms and those of his mother. Little things, like telling her she made the same silly face his mom had while they were at the Sea Life Aquarium the day before, felt like he was trying to cast her as his mom's stand-in, instead of seeing her as an individual. At the time, she'd blown it off as it being common for everyone to puff out their cheeks when looking at puffer fish. But the more she thought about how he'd compared her looks to his mom since the first day they officially met, the more she worried that it could be a major red flag for them as a blended family.

Would Cait love to be able to marry Josh and adopt JoJo? Absolutely. But even though she dreamed of one day legally being his mom, she didn't want to be a carbon copy of his biological mother any more than she wanted to replace the woman in his heart. She wanted him to see her as an extra parental figure who loved him and for them to forge their own relationship, different but not better or worse than the one he'd had with his mother. And she wasn't sure how to do that when JoJo kept commenting on how she smiled like his mom, or hugged like his mom, or whatever else he found to compare between them.

She was at just as much of a loss as to how to help Josh with the dark shadows she sometimes saw in his eyes. He hadn't shared whatever was bothering him besides the worry about the upcoming court hearing, but she could tell there was something.

Not that they'd really had any alone time to talk, or do any of the other things a couple needed to do to build intimacy between them. Their outings, and time hanging out with JoJo after dinner the way they were currently, were the closest they'd gotten to alone time. And those still came with the possibility of more than one member of their families walking in on them at any moment.

"Hey, Josh," Bob walked into the room, carrying an envelope that he handed to Josh, and emphasizing Cait's internal point on why she hadn't gotten any alone time with Josh in the last week. "I was just goin' through the mail before bed and thought you might want yours immediately."

"Thanks, Pop." Josh paused the game and put down the controller to take the envelope, turning it over to open it before Cait could see the name of the sender.

Cait sat back and watched Josh's face, not wanting to snoop by reading the letter over his shoulder. When she saw his smile widen, her curiosity got the better of her, causing her to ask about the letter without thinking it might be something he didn't want to talk about in front of his dad or son. "What is it?"

"It's a copy of what the lab sent to the court and DFACS in Virginia," Josh grinned, looking up at his dad then over at Cait before settling his gaze on JoJo. "That officially tells them I'm your dad."

"Like we didn't already know that," Bob scoffed with the slightest grin.

"Yeah, but the courts wouldn't take our word for it," Josh chuckled. "So, we had to do this test to prove it legally. And now they have to acknowledge my rights as JoJo's father, so I just have to show my fitness as a parent to get primary custody when we go to court in a couple of weeks."

"Primary custody? I thought you were going for full custody?" Bob looked as surprised as Cait felt at hearing the change in his goal coming from Josh's mouth.

"I'm petitioning for full custody," Josh clarified. "But with Joshua's grandparents trying to do the same, and Jaina's best friend petitioning for partial custody per Jaina's will, it's possible the judge could rule for a shared custody situation. Tyler seems to think that with everything else they've been fighting over for the last few months, and JoJo being shipped off to boarding school when his grandparents got full custody, it's most likely I'll get primary custody with everyone else getting visitation rights. But we'll just have to wait and see how it all settles out after all our cases are heard."

"Is that why Tyler was calling to find out your specific titles and salaries with Burleson Incorporated? To show that you're gainfully employed after leaving the SEALs, so the court knows you can provide for him better than everyone else fighting for custody of him?" Bob nodded as if he was answering his own questions in his head.

"Yeah, probably," Josh nodded. "What did you tell him? I know you're putting me in as a VP like Becky and our cousins. But did you finally decide between the beef and agriculture divisions for my official title?"

"No," Bob sighed, shaking his head. "And after talking to your brothers about what they want to do when they retire from their other jobs and can take over some of the other areas, I'm thinking we might just have to combine beef and ag into one division since you're gonna be stuck doin' both."

"Really?" Josh looked surprised. "I know Jake wants to head up the IT and cyber technology aspect of the company, but I thought Bobby or Anthony would be interested in doing something on the ranching side of things."

"Yeah, me too," Bob agreed with a chuckle. "But Bobby wants to head up security, and Anthony thinks we're gonna need a fleet of company jets to go check on all the non-local sites we've added to the company in the last few years."

"And managing them is his way of planning to get in the cockpit regularly," Josh chuckled.

"Exactly," Bob laughed along with his son. "So, I told Tyler to hold off on listing your official title until after the board meeting at the end of the month, so we can have all the details worked out. But we can discuss all that tomorrow. I need to hit the rack to get up early enough to get through the extra feeding of the bred heifers and cows before we start overplanting the winter grazing pastures."

"Can I help you feed the cows in the morning, Pappaw?" JoJo jumped up from his chair, excited about the possibility of working on the ranch the next morning.

"Sure ya can," Bob agreed, grinning at his grandson. "But you'd better get to bed too, 'cause cows get hungry a lot earlier than people."

"I thought they ate the grass in the pastures where they live." Cait was confused about what they had to feed the cows that they weren't already getting as grass-fed beef out in the fields on the ranch. "Can't they eat whenever they want?"

"They can, to some extent," Josh chuckled. "But just like humans, cows need more calories and nutrients when they're pregnant, especially in the late stages when the calves are bulking up for birth. And this is also the time of year when the nutrients in the forage in the pasture starts to decline. So, we give them a supplemental feeding each day, in addition to the grass they can eat anytime in the pasture, to make sure they get everything they need."

Cait was impressed by how Josh and his father kept everything running so smoothly on the ranch when they had to organize multiple breeding and birthing seasons, sort two-thousand cows and bulls into specific pastures based on where each was in the life cycle, figure out the proper nutritional plan for each animal that lived on the ranch, including at least fifty horses, cats, and dogs, in addition to the cattle, and managed everything that went into planting the various types of grass the cattle and horses ate and harvesting the fields the animals didn't graze in for hay production. There was no way she could handle the office portion of their jobs, much less do all that, and then find the time to complete the physical tasks they did regularly on the ranch.

Oh, she knew most of Bob's time on the ranch was spent supervising the ranch hands as they did the more strenuous tasks. But she'd seen how sweaty and hot Josh got working alongside the ranch hands, wanting to earn their respect before stepping into the managerial part of the job when Bob was ready to turn over the reins.

"Yeah, I don't know how you guys manage everything you do on the ranch," Cait marveled in awe. "I'm going to have to stick to screenwriting and leave the complicated stuff to you cowboys."

After a brief chuckle, they said their "goodnights" as Bob left the room. JoJo rushed to the bathroom between the game room and his bedroom, brushing his teeth and changing for bed before coming back to give them both a goodnight hug and finally going to bed.

"Finally, some alone time with my girl," Josh practically moaned the words as he slid his arm around her shoulders.

"Oh, no, Cowboy," Cait hissed, pushing on his chest when Josh reached around with his other arm and turned her to face him. "Don't even think of trying anything when JoJo is still wide awake and close enough to hear us."

"But, Sunshine, kissin' is a quiet activity that he can't overhear," Josh argued, wagging his eyebrows suggestively. "But if you want to do more than that, we can either go across the hall to my bedroom. Or I can walk you over to your house where we can be all alone, so we can get as loud as you want."

Even though Cait wanted to make love with Josh almost as much as she wanted her next breath, she knew she needed some reassurances that they could get past the other obstacles she feared might end their relationship before she could go that far with him. She was ninety-nine-point-nine percent sure sleeping with Josh would ruin her for all other men. And she wasn't sure her heart could handle knowing what making love with him felt like if she couldn't be with him in the future.

Like you aren't already so deep in love with him that you'll never be able to be with anyone else, her inner voice chided, trying to keep her from putting on the brakes as Josh lowered his head to kiss her. *Even if things end up not working out, it's better to enjoy the time you have with him than to never know the wonderous pleasure of making love with him.*

"I promise, I'm just planning on kissing you tonight, Sunshine," Josh assured her as their breath mingled from how close their mouths were right then. "And we'll go at your pace for doin' anything more."

Cait could only nod in response, bumping her forehead against his in her haste to agree to kissing on the sofa in the game room like teenagers. *I'll talk to him about my other concerns later. Or tomorrow.*

Not giving him a chance to ask for her verbal agreement, Cait slid her hands up from his chest to cup his jaw as she pressed her lips to his. Not that Josh let her control the kiss for long. Cait relished the passionate way he took over, as he pulled her close in a loving embrace and claimed her with his mouth.

The dominating feel of his tongue demanding entry as he parted her lips and deepened the kiss caused her core to gush and her nipples to harden against his firm pecs. *I wonder if he can feel how hard they are through our clothes?*

Cait returned his ardent affection, tangling her tongue with his as she moved her hands from the stubbly five o'clock shadow of his jaw around to weave her fingers through the soft, short strands of hair on the back of his head. She knew he'd kept it as long as the Navy allowed to be able to blend in and not look like he was in the military while doing reconnaissance before some of his missions. Now that she was getting to run her fingers through his hair, she wondered if he would let it grow out a little longer once his career as a SEAL was officially over.

Maybe he'll decide to keep it a little longer once he realizes how much I love playing with it when we make out, Cait hoped, loving the way he'd moved one of his hands from her back up to play with her hair as well. *I hope he enjoys having his hair played with as much as I do.*

As the drugging reaction of Josh's kisses took effect, Cait lost the ability to think. She forgot all about where they were or who might walk in on them, only able to feel the overwhelming need to be closer to Josh. If it were possible, she would have fused their bodies together so tightly that they could never be split apart.

Josh somehow used his other hand to shift their positions on the sofa, covering her body with his while never breaking their kiss. She wasn't sure what kind of magic he used to move them from sitting side by side with only their torsos turned toward each other to laying face to face with him between her spread thighs. But with his hard length grinding against her soaking wet core, Cait was really glad Josh possessed the powers of a sexually wicked wizard.

As their hands roamed, Cait knew she should say something about getting rid of their clothes, but her lust-addled brain couldn't form the complete thought, much less the words to verbalize it. Josh stopped playing with her hair to stroke down her body and under her, clamping a hand on her ass and pulling her up into his groin, where she registered that he had a very hard, very large member. She had a flicker of thought about not being able to take such an enormous cock. But it flittered away as he rocked his hips to press his shaft against her clit.

Josh's other hand moved to her breast, kneading gently, and sending a jolt of electricity straight to her pussy that quickly convinced her that he knew exactly how to use what he was packing. So what if it felt like he was three times the size of her vibrator? As wet and soft as her sex felt at that moment, she was confident her body could accommodate the man she loved, even if his dick felt like it was almost as big as her forearm.

Cait moaned into Josh's mouth, unable to contain the pleasure she felt from his denim-covered cock rubbing against her clit. Josh released her lips, giving her a chance to breathe as he kissed down her neck. The juxtaposition of his soft lips and tongue with the light scratchiness of his stubble felt amazing, making her wonder how decadent it would feel on other parts of her body.

Cait pulled her hands from Josh's back, needing to get her clothes off and out of his way. Josh caught her wrists with his hands, pinning her arms over her head as he arched his back to look down into her eyes.

"No, Sunshine," he groaned, closing his eyes momentarily before pecking her lips once more and pushing up off of her completely. "Just kissin' tonight, remember? Which we should probably stop now before we take things further than we should in the kids' game room at my parents' house."

It took a moment for the fog to clear before Cait registered the meaning of Josh's words. Slowly, her surroundings started to come back into focus around them, and Cait blushed with mortification at the realization of just how far she'd been willing to go with Josh, when JoJo could have walked in on them at any moment.

"Yeah, I think it's time I head home." Cait motioned over her shoulder with her thumb, not realizing that she was actually pointing toward the pasture between the Burlesons' houses and the main gate of the ranch, instead of in the opposite direction toward where she lived.

"I'll walk you home, Sunshine," Josh chuckled, standing, and offering her a hand to get up from the sofa.

"Thanks," Cait replied as she stood and fought not to wobble on her knees, which were still weak from the swoony feelings Josh induced in her with his kisses.

Holy shit! If I'm this loopy from just making out with him, then I'm going to need to be in bed for the night when we finally get the chance to make love.

Chapter Seventeen

After almost coming in his pants from dry-humping Cait the night before, Josh was eager to finish up his duties on the ranch to see if he could sneak in another hot make-out session with her. As JoJo sat on the fence watching the first-calf heifers after Josh and Bob filled the troughs with their supplemental feed that morning, Josh had taken a moment to talk with his dad to ask his advice on how to get some alone time with his girlfriend, now that he had a son to take care of twenty-four-seven. Bob had reminded him about all the times he and his siblings had spent with Memmaw Judy, when they were JoJo's age, while their mom joined their dad in "working" on the ranch. Apparently, all the times they'd thought their mom was going to help mend fences and herd the cattle from pasture to pasture were falsehoods portrayed to the kids to keep them from interrupting intimate moments between their parents. Armed with the advice to make sure Carlos, the ranch manager, knew which barn to keep the hands out of while JoJo and Brody were occupied with Hazel and Bob, Josh set off to extend his lunchtime with Cait in the hayloft he was claiming as their special spot on the ranch.

Josh's dad had already taken JoJo to the house for lunch with him and Memmaw Hazel, while Josh finished disking the pastures to prepare them for overseeding that afternoon. Bob mentioned stopping to get Brody to join them for lunch and bringing him back out with JoJo to ride on the tractors while they overseeded the pastures with a mix of rye and clover for the cattle's winter grazing. So, if luck was on Josh's side, he'd find Cait alone at her house before she got focused on writing her latest screenplay.

Leah Mae Wright

"Knock, knock," Josh announced as he stepped through her back door to find Cait at her kitchen sink, washing up from lunch. She was wearing her typical wardrobe of jeans and a t-shirt, which Josh found just as sexy as the dresses he'd seen her in at various weddings and other events over the last few months. Especially when he looked down to see her bare feet. Taking off her shoes as soon as she stepped into her house was a habit she'd only started since moving into the house on the ranch as far as he knew.

Unable to resist, he walked over and wrapped her in his arms from behind, kissing her cheek when she only tilted her head to look at him instead of turning around. Josh inhaled deeply, loving how she always smelled like fresh flowers and baked goods. "Did Brody go with Pop and JoJo?"

"Yes, I think he's planning to have a second lunch before the big adventure of riding on a tractor this afternoon," Cait giggled as Josh bent to nuzzle her neck.

"If he wanted an adventure, he shoulda come with us at five this morning to see Pop being chased by a couple dozen hungry heifers," Josh chuckled.

"Why were they chasing him?" Cait turned the water off before twisting around to look up at him as she looped her arms around his neck.

"I guess we were too slow in getting the feeding troughs set up," Josh shrugged as he laced his fingers together at Cait's low back. "And they weren't happy that we moved them into the pasture empty, so they tried to follow him out the gate to get to the feed."

"Now I'm going to be worried about you being trampled by hungry cows every morning," Cait sighed, shaking her head at him.

"Don't worry, Sunshine," Josh chuckled, bending down to give her a peck of a kiss. "Our cattle aren't like the running of the bulls in Spain. They tend to trod along at a nice leisurely pace, and gently nudge us with their noses to get us to put the food out faster. Hell, they're so tame, we set JoJo up hand-feeding them through the side fence to keep them from getting out when we had to have the gate open to move the troughs into the pasture."

"Yeah, maybe I should come with you one morning to see that for myself," Cait suggested, biting her lip nervously.

"You're welcome anytime, Sunshine," Josh smiled, knowing that Cait's fear was most easily quelled by showing her more than telling her that something was safe. "But while we have a little while when the boys are otherwise occupied, I'd rather we sneak off to the hayloft for a little private time with no chance of interruptions."

"Are you suggesting we blow off work to fool around?" Cait's eyes lit with mischief as she grinned up at him.

"I am." Josh wagged his eyebrows suggestively. "But I'm only delaying going back to work and hoping I can get a taste of you for lunch."

"I don't think I'm a very nutritious lunch," Cait quipped as she leaned a little closer to him. "But I'm more than willing to feed you lunch and let you have me for dessert."

"Deal, but I want dessert first," Josh declared, gripping her waist to lift Cait up and drape her over his shoulder to carry her out of her house toward the barn with the empty hayloft, where he'd laid out a couple of blankets after their last rendezvous there.

"Josh!" Cait squealed, bracing herself with her hands on his back. "Let me at least put some shoes on first!"

"No need, Sunshine," Josh argued as he crossed the lawn between the houses to get to the barn. "You'll just have to take 'em right back off when we get to the barn 'cause they'll be in the way of takin' your jeans off."

"But I don't want to get a splinter in the bottom of my foot climbing the ladder up to the hayloft," Cait protested, playfully slapping his ass as he reached the door to the barn. "And I'm not taking my jeans off in the barn."

"So I'll carry you up the ladder," Josh decided, swatting her ass right back. "And I'm totally cool with spanking games, Sunshine, but I prefer to administer the spanking with you naked and draped over my lap."

Josh wasn't as into the whole BDSM scene as his cousin and a couple of his Navy buddies, but he knew enough from hanging around with the lifestylers in his circle of friends to safely play once in a while if that was what Cait wanted.

"You planning on roping me like a calf to get me over your lap, Cowboy?" Cait wiggled on his shoulder, as Josh weaved through the tractors and other equipment in the barn to get to the ladder going up to the hayloft.

"Only if you wanna be tied up, Sunshine," Josh assured her as he tightened his hold around her thighs before climbing the ladder.

"Oh, Josh!" Cait shrieked, tightly gripping his waist, as if she was afraid of falling, and completely dropping the whole bondage subject.

Damn, I suppose it is kinda scary to be carried up a ladder while hanging upside down. Josh grimaced as he reached the top and strode over to the blanket he'd laid out by the hatch before setting her down. "Sorry, Sunshine. On the way down, we'll go piggyback, so the ladder won't be so disconcerting."

"I can't believe you carried me up here." Cait gaped up at him with wide, surprised eyes.

Josh hoped it was a positive form of surprise, like maybe she was a little impressed with his show of strength, and not because she felt like he was being high-handed with her. "Of course, Sunshine. I'm always gonna do what I can to take care of you. I even put down a blanket for us to lay on, so there's no chance of gettin' splinters anywhere while we're foolin' around."

"I suppose making out on a horse blanket is your idea of being romantic?" Cait arched an eyebrow at him, like she was questioning his sanity, but she couldn't contain the slight upturn of her lips that gave away her mirth.

"I got it fresh from the laundry in the bunkhouse, so I know it's clean," Josh grinned.

"It still smells like hay and horses," Cait argued, putting a hand on her hip as she tried to act indignant.

"We're in a hayloft. In a barn. On a ranch, Sunshine," Josh laughed. "The whole place smells like hay and horses. Just be glad the wind's blowin' the smell of the cow manure in the opposite direction of the houses."

"Yeah, I'm surprised I don't really smell the cows all that often living here." Cait dropped the playful banter to let her curiosity show as she sat down on the blanket. "Is that because of the way you rotate them in the various pastures?"

Josh joined her on the blanket, scooting over close enough to pull her into his arms, so they could cuddle with her back to his front as he explained. "Not really. That's more to make sure the cattle get the right nutrients from the grasses they eat in the pastures, and that the pastures have time to recover from being trampled and depleted by the herd. The smell traveling away from the houses has more to do with the direction of the wind. While most of the year, the wind is coming from the south, it's not moving due north, but more to the northwest, which is why we put all the processing plants in the northwest corner of the ranch. Between December and February, when the wind is coming from the north, the smell from those plants can get pretty bad out on the pastures and oil fields on the southwest side of the ranch. But luckily, we seem to be in the sweet spot on the ranch where we don't often get those smells because the wind is usually more east to west like now, or southeast to northwest most of the rest of the year, so we typically only get the smell of the trees on the Hunters' property and the hay when we cut the fields around the houses, instead of the smell of the animals and stinky stuff on the west side of our ranch."

"It's fascinating how you know all this stuff," Cait whispered softly as she twisted in his arms to look up at him. "But I believe you said something about eating me for dessert before lunch. So, I think we should table this discussion for later and get on with the hanky-panky now."

"I like the way you think, Sunshine," Josh chuckled before bending his head down to claim her mouth with a soul-searing kiss.

Kissing Cait was like nothing Josh had ever experienced before. He hadn't ever had a problem with kissing the women he'd hooked up with in the past, but he'd never felt the extreme urgency to kiss anyone the way he did with Cait, either. Kissing was one of those things that was cool if the woman was into it, but he was also fine if he never kissed a woman he was with for a one-night stand.

Because of his take-it-or-leave-it attitude toward kissing, he'd always thought his brothers made too much of a big deal about kissing being too intimate when they complained about hookups not understanding their no-kissing rules. But now that he'd gotten a taste of Cait's lips, Josh finally understood where they were coming from when they'd set those rules.

With Cait, kissing was an intimate act, not the lackadaisical precursor to fucking he'd previously thought it was. Whenever he kissed Cait, Josh felt like they were connecting more than just their lips and tongues. It was more of a physical manifestation of the joining of their hearts and souls.

He'd overheard his sisters, cousins, and female friends talking about the love scenes in romance novels, where the couples bond so deeply during sex that they couldn't tell where one of them ended and the other began. And for the first time in his life, Josh actually understood the concept.

Fuck! If I feel this connected to her from just kissing, how fucking amazing is it gonna feel when we finally make love? How the hell am I gonna force myself to stop making love to her, so I can take care of everything else going on in our lives?

They let their hands wander as Josh rolled them to a more horizontal position on the floor of the hayloft, with him hovering over her as he continued to devour her sweet mouth. As Cait ran her hands under the back of his t-shirt, Josh lifted hers from the front and palmed her lace-covered tits.

As much as he wanted to strip her naked and make love to her then and there, Josh understood her trepidation in believing that they were completely safe from prying eyes walking in on them in the middle of the day. So, he settled for only moving her clothing out of the way enough that he could touch her without exposing her completely.

He also had other plans for making their first time together special, and he didn't want to forgo them for a quicky in the barn. Quickies were fine for random hookups and one-night stands, but not for his first time with the woman he wanted to spend the rest of his life with. Cait might not believe just how special she was to him just yet, but Josh intended to show her in the way he made love to her. Yeah, he'd always been more into hard and fast fucking, but Cait made him want more. He wanted to take his time and memorize every inch of her body, as he mapped out all the places and ways she liked to be touched and kissed.

"Oh, Josh." Cait broke their smooch to moan his name before teasing her lips over his neck.

"Fuck, Cait," Josh reciprocated, licking his way down her neck until he ran into the barrier of her heather-gray t-shirt. "I need to touch you and kiss you everywhere, but I want you to stop me before I go too far."

"I don't think you can go too far, Josh," Cait hypothesized breathlessly as Josh scooted down to bury his face in her cleavage.

"I'm glad to hear you're ready for us to move past kissin', Sunshine," Josh breathed against the alabaster skin that peeked out of the top of her dove gray bra. "But I can't go as far as we both want in our current surroundings. You're too special to me for our first time together to be a quick fuck in the hayloft, though I do see a lot of those in our future."

Josh lifted his gaze to meet her eyes, grinning as he rested his chin in the valley between her breasts. "I wanna make it perfect the first time we make love, Sunshine. In a bed by candlelight with soft romantic music playing in the background, so you can be comfortable while I spend all night worshiping your body the way you deserve."

"That sounds wonderful, Josh," Cait cooed, lifting her head as she gripped his biceps. "But I'm not sure it's realistic for us, unless you're planning to wait ten years for JoJo to go off to college first."

"Oh, no, Sunshine," Josh balked, shaking his head, and jiggling her tits with his chin. "We may have to wait a couple weeks for the custody situation to be settled, so he can have sleepovers with his cousins and the friends he'll make when we enroll him in school here, but that's as long as I'm willing to wait to be inside you."

If Josh had it his way, he'd be sneaking over to Cait's house every night after JoJo went to bed. But since JoJo had woken up in the middle of the night and come looking for Josh several times since they'd officially met ten days before, Josh didn't want to scare his son by not being easily accessible when his abandonment issues reared their ugly heads. He could possibly squeeze in an hour or two right after JoJo went to sleep, when he could hang out with Cait like he had the second night JoJo had spent on the ranch. But a couple of hours wouldn't give him the time to make love to Cait the way he wanted for their first time.

"But having to wait a little while to make love doesn't mean we can't do other things now," Josh teased as he shifted his weight onto one arm, freeing up his right hand, so he could unclasp the front closure on Cait's bra. "Like finding out how many different ways I can make you come without using my cock."

And I'm definitely gonna start spending the hour or two after JoJo goes to bed each night on a little foreplay to build up the anticipation for our first time together.

Cait's eyes lit with excitement, as Josh lowered his head once more and trailed his tongue over her newly exposed flesh. He licked his way to her turgid, dusky rose-colored nipple before lightly sucking it into his mouth. He laved the tip with his tongue while cupping her other breast and stimulating the other nipple with soft passes of his thumb.

Cait moaned in pleasure, arching her back to push more of her luscious mound into his mouth. She slid her hands up from his arms to muss his hair as she held his head in place.

Josh loved how responsive she was, but he needed to know if she was equally sensitive on both sides. So, he released the tit he was cupping to put his arm down on her other side, shifting his weight once more as he trailed his mouth to her other nipple. He repeated his ministrations after switching sides, both tactile and oral, eliciting more erotic sounds from Cait's soft lips.

Cait's response seemed just as intense as before. Only this time, instead of lifting her chest to press her tits to his face, she wiggled her hips to rub her pussy against his upper abs that were now between her legs.

Fuck yeah, Sunshine! Rub that little clit on me until you come.

Josh would have vocalized the command, but he had his mouth full with her perfect C-cups and had no desire to stop nibbling her nipples to speak at the moment. He did try to help her out by pressing down with his torso, applying enough extra pressure to send her over the edge.

Fuck, if only I was a little higher up her body, so she could rub my cock with her cunt like that.

"Oh, Josh, Josh, Josh," Cait chanted his name repeatedly as her whole body convulsed with her release.

Josh looked up with only his eyes, just in time to see her O-face, continuing to suckle her breasts as he witnessed her rapturous expression. His cock was as hard as steel and eager to blow his load at any second. But Josh wasn't about to come from humping the floor of the hayloft. Besides, he didn't think he'd enjoy his own release as much as he enjoyed watching Cait climax from him sucking her tits and applying just a little pressure to her clit. At least, not as long as his cock wasn't deep inside Cait when he came along with her.

Josh popped his mouth off her boob long enough to growl, "Fuck, I need to know how wet you are, Sunshine."

"So wet," Cait panted breathlessly as she released her death grip on his hair and slid her hands down between them to unfasten her jeans. "Need you to touch me to feel how wet."

"As you wish, Sunshine," Josh agreed, releasing his hold on her tit to slide his hand down into the front of her pants. He rolled to the side of her, giving himself a little more room to move his arm between them, even though his dick protested the loss of anything to rut against.

More lace, he thought as he slipped his hand under her panties and went back to ravishing her tatas with his mouth. *I bet the panties match this sexy-as-fuck bra. If only we had the time for me to look...*

Josh's thoughts trailed off in his head as he moved his hand under her panties to feel the soft patch of neatly trimmed hair over her pussy. As he separated her folds with first one finger and then two, Josh found the flood of her juices and wished he could lap them up with his tongue.

"Fuck, you're drenched, Sunshine," Josh growled against her tit. "I wish we were somewhere more private, so I could lick you clean."

"Oh, Josh," Cait moaned, gripping his head once more as he breached her tight entrance for the first time.

She was so tight he could only slide one finger inside her at first. He massaged her inner walls, relaxing her enough that he could insert a second digit as he continued to lavish her breasts with his oral affection. "So, fucking, tight. You're gonna choke my cock. How long has it been, Cait?"

Surely she's not still a virgin? But damn, she feels tighter than I remember the girls I was with back in high school feelin'.

"Too long," Cait panted out, bucking her hips in time with the thrusts of his fingers. "A few years."

A few years? Fuck, does it start to grow back together after that long? Josh wondered as he worked her open enough to take a third finger.

"Unless you count my vibrator, but it's not that much bigger than one of your fingers." Cait turned her head to look at the hand he had resting by her shoulder. "Yeah, the part that goes inside is only about as big as one and a half of your fingers."

"But it's big enough to get you off?" Josh didn't know much about sex toys, but he couldn't imagine a vibrator that small being very effective. *Does it even reach her G-spot? I mean, if it's as long as my fingers, it might. But if it's not as big around as a cock, or flexible like my fingers, it's gotta be awkward to try to get it in the right spot for it to work to get her off.*

"No, but I think that part is only there to hold the clit stimulator in place," Cait informed him breathlessly as he searched for the internal spot he wasn't sure she'd successfully stimulated on her own. "That's what actually does the trick. I don't usually come from penetration."

Fuck, no wonder it's been a few years for her, if the guys she was with were too inept to find her G-spot. Josh resisted the urge to push his palm down on her clit, wanting to show her that he didn't have to rely on the easy way of making her climax. He quickly proved he wasn't as inept as her former partners, stroking the pad of his middle finger over the rough spot on the front wall of her pussy.

"Oh, Josh," Cait cried out as she writhed in pleasure. "Holy, wow! Yes, right there. Oh-my-god! Yes, Josh, yes!"

Josh smiled around the nipple in his mouth as he took her up and over the edge once more. Her pussy clamped down on his fingers as she spasmed with each wave of her release. Josh varied the amount of pressure he applied to her G-spot, drawing out her orgasm for as long as possible, relishing being the only man to make her come in such a way. *Damn, it's gonna feel fucking amazing when she comes on my cock like that.*

He gentled his strokes, allowing her to come down from the high gradually before pulling his fingers from her snug sheath. He licked between her glorious tits one last time before pushing up to a seated position once more and lifting his cream-coated fingers to his mouth. He savored her salty-sweet taste as he licked them clean, while Cait stared up at him in a post-orgasmic daze.

"Hmmm, tastiest lunch ever," Josh declared, just as his phone signaled an incoming text. Knowing it was probably his pop letting him know that he was taking the boys back to the pasture to start overseeding, Josh quickly started helping Cait put her clothing back to rights. "Too bad I don't have time for seconds."

"But I didn't get a chance to have my dessert," Cait playfully pouted as she reached over and cupped his crotch while licking her lips suggestively.

"Fuck," Josh groaned, removing her delicate hand from his dick, and standing up before she tempted him to ignore his responsibilities for the afternoon. "We'll have to save that for later, Sunshine."

Josh hated having to cut their time together short, especially since he was going to be driving a tractor all afternoon with an epic case of blue balls. But seeing her look of disappointment at not being able to reciprocate right then was going to haunt him even more.

~~~

Cait floated through the rest of her afternoon on an orgasm high like nothing she'd ever felt before. But at the same time, she also felt guilty for letting things go that far between her and Josh, without voicing her concerns about the issues that might derail them from the happily ever after she hoped they'd one day have together. So instead of basking in the afterglow the way she wanted, she spent her writing time vacillating between doing what she wanted to do with Josh that night after JoJo went to bed, and what she knew she needed to do the next time she got a moment alone with Josh.

She felt terrible for spending the whole time they had alone at lunch with Josh focused on her pleasure, and not leaving any time for her to satisfy him. While she wasn't confident enough in her hand job or blow job skills to think she could give him two orgasms in as short a time period as he'd given her two, she felt like she owed him at least one before he gave her more. But she wasn't sure if she should try to reciprocate the O's before or after talking to him about the issues she feared might become major problems for them in the future.

Needless to say, by the time Josh walked her home after they spent the evening playing board games with their families and JoJo went up to bed, Cait was still torn about how to spend the hour or so she hoped to have alone with him. If she could convince Josh to stay for a little while, maybe they'd have time to both talk and take him to O-town. But knowing how dedicated he was to being easily accessible when
~~~

JoJo woke up in the middle of the night, she wasn't sure they'd have time for both.

Wanting to support Josh in being a good father, and understanding how much JoJo needed him right across the hall to be reassured that his dad hadn't deserted him when he awoke from a nightmare, Cait didn't want to push Josh to stay at her place for very long. *JoJo's needs have to come first*, she decided as they stepped onto her porch. *So, I'll just ask him to stay long enough to discuss JoJo for now.*

"Can you come in and talk for a few minutes? I know you have to get back before JoJo wakes up and comes looking for you, so I promise not to keep you very long." *Geez, can you sound any more nervous, Caitir?*

"Actually, if he sticks to his pattern of not waking up before midnight, I can stay for a couple of hours," Josh informed her as he opened the door for her. As soon as they stepped into the house, he spun her into his arms and leaned them against the door to close it, wagging his eyebrows suggestively. "And maybe we can have another round or two of dessert to bookend our talk."

Josh dipped his head to kiss her before she could respond, stunning her into submission. Unlike the soft pecks they'd shared while others were around, this kiss was daring and bold. Josh's hand magically moved from her waist up to cup her face, holding her gently in place for his oral exploration.

Cait lifted her arms under his, running her hands over the sculpted muscles of his upper back. She loved the feel of his hard body against her soft one. While it probably wasn't politically correct, or the popular opinion among her feminist friends, Cait delighted in the way their size difference made her feel dainty and petite. At five-foot-eight, those weren't things she'd felt often in her life.

While Josh was naturally thin like the rest of his family, it was clear his physical training as a SEAL provided the defined beefiness the other Burlesons lacked. Not that he was bulky, like a bodybuilder, or some of the GWA wrestlers she knew. In Cait's opinion, Josh was the epitome of the perfect, athletic body type. She just hoped that leaving the Navy wouldn't mean cutting out so many of his current workout habits that he lost the muscular definition that kept him from having the same tall and lanky look of the rest of the men in the Burleson family.

Cait knew it was shallow of her to find him more attractive for his fitness model physique, so she told herself she was more attracted to his personality. It wasn't really a lie, since she did find the funny, jokester side of him immensely attractive. And if anyone asked, she'd blame that small part of her that was drawn to his strength on her lizard brain and point out that it was hard to fight thousands of years of evolution that caused women to be attracted to the men who appeared most capable of protecting them.

Her lizard brain was definitely doing the thinking right then, causing her to forget everything but Josh and the connection they shared at the moment. Their tongues tangled as she returned his ardent kiss lick for lick, wanting him to feel as claimed by her as she did by him.

When they finally broke their lips apart enough to breathe, Cait didn't give Josh the chance to kiss down her neck, or try to remove her clothes the way he had earlier in the day. Instead, she dropped to her knees and reached for the button of his jeans, eager to give him the orgasm he'd missed out on at lunchtime.

"Oh, no, Sunshine," Josh protested, gripping her under her armpits and lifting her back to her feet. "I might be able to stay for a couple of hours, but we don't have time for everything I'm gonna wanna do if Captain America comes out to play."

"Captain America?" Cait laughed, unable to contain the humor she found in the name he'd given his cock when he was a kid. "Kay, Brook, and Amy all said you guys had all named your dicks when you were kids, but none of them knew what you'd named yours."

"Hey, don't laugh at Captain America," Josh commanded, but his slight smile kept him from appearing serious enough for her to obey him. "I was nine at the time and wanted to go along with my older brother and cousin to be cool, instead of lame like Jake, Justin, and Anthony. And the *Avengers* were as cool as we could think of back then."

"Okay, the girls filled me in on the other guys' names for theirs, and I agree that The Anaconda and Mr. Happy are both lame. But none of them knew what Jake picked. Is it really as bad as Justin and Anthony's ideas?"

"He named it Bruce," Josh snorted. "Because he couldn't decide between Bruce Wayne and Bruce Banner."

"I guess he was at least still sticking with the superhero theme?" Cait giggled, trying to picture Josh when he was a little older than JoJo hanging out with his brothers and cousins, as they picked out the names for their most prized appendages.

"Yeah, I tried to talk him into going with the Hulk," Josh shrugged before picking her up and carrying her over to the loveseat. "But he was afraid he'd never get a girlfriend if the girls heard the name and thought his dick was green."

"Do boys really think about girlfriends and sex at nine years old?" Cait looped her arms around his neck and her legs around his waist, so Josh had to sit down with her on his lap.

"Oh, we didn't think about doin' more than kissin' a pretty girl back then, and had no idea what we'd wanna do with our dicks a few years later," Josh chuckled as he pressed his large hand on the small of her back, moving her close enough that she could feel the appendage in question standing at attention between them. "But we knew any body part turning green was probably a sign of infection of some type and not attractive to anyone."

"True," Cait agreed, smiling at him, and thinking it was probably time to actually talk about the more serious matters she had to discuss with him. "But while we're on the subject of what little boys know and think about girlfriends, we should probably talk about what JoJo thinks about us as a couple."

"What do you mean?" Josh's brow furrowed as he contemplated her segue from his childhood antics to his son's thoughts and feelings now.

"I'm a little worried about him," Cait confessed, hoping this discussion wouldn't prevent them from enjoying more carnal pleasures later that night. "Specifically, how he compares me to his mom all the time. It's so soon after her passing, and it kind of feels like he's trying to cast me in her role in his life to keep from missing her or something. I mean, I adore him and could see being a motherly figure for him in the future. But that needs to be based on him and I getting to know one another for who we are as individuals, not me being her replacement. I don't want him to think we're interchangeable because we have some physical characteristics in common."

"You don't think he sees you for you?" Josh tilted his head in contemplation.

"Not all the time," Cait confessed, unable to maintain eye contact for fear of her irrational jealousy of Jaina showing. "I'm not an expert on grief or anything like that to be able to say for sure what's going on. But sometimes it feels like he's trying to see me as a clone of her. I get the whole kids-wanting-their-parents-to-be-together thing, but I'm afraid that his grief over losing his mom might be coming out in an unhealthy way. Kind of like he's making up so many similarities between us to pretend I'm her, so he doesn't have to grieve her loss and gets to have his parents together. And that has to be just as unhealthy for him as trying to forget her completely and pretend someone else is his mom."

Josh closed his eyes, dropping his head back on the loveseat as his hands fell away from her hips, where he'd been holding her. Cait wasn't sure what to do, wanting to wrap herself around him to comfort him, but feeling like he was pulling away from her and wouldn't be receptive to the gesture. Finally, she moved off his lap to give him the space he seemed to need to contemplate her words.

Maybe I should go fix us something to drink to give him a little more time, she wondered as she sat stiffly on the edge of the loveseat, leaving a foot of space between her and Josh. *But I don't want to leave his side when he's obviously worried and in need of a friend to lean on right now.*

"I think maybe I need to get him in to see a child psychologist or something," Josh breathed out, finally breaking the silence between them. "Because I have no idea how to talk to him about any of this. Hell, maybe I should be seeing a therapist to deal with my feelings about all this, too, so I don't screw him up more."

Is that why he's looked so haunted lately? Cait didn't think they'd have time to handle more than one issue in the short amount of time they had to talk right then. But if the issue she'd seen Josh trying to tackle on his own was his worry about being a good father, then she reasoned that she could help him with it easily enough that they might be able to circle back to the issues she worried about with JoJo.

"Oh, Josh," Cait sighed, unable to stop herself from scooting closer and wrapping her arms around him once more, giving him the comfort he so desperately needed. "You aren't going to screw him up. It's obvious to anyone who sees you with him that you love him too much to ever do anything that's not in his best interest. You're already a great dad. And you're only going to keep getting better at being a father as you get to know your son."

"Yeah? You think?" Josh scoffed, shaking his head as he pulled her sideways onto his lap once more. He buried his face in her hair as he cuddled her close. "I can't tell him anything I remember about his mom, 'cause I only vaguely remember the night I met her. Hell, I only remember part of that night because her best friend introduced herself by saying her name was Tawny, like the chick in the old Whitesnake videos. If the girl Jake hooked up with that night hadn't made the rock band reference, then I doubt I'd have remembered anything from one random night that far back. And I'm pissed that she didn't come tell me she was pregnant back when I woulda still remembered her name and hooking up with her."

"She didn't even know your last name, Josh," Cait defended Jaina, which felt really weird for her as she sat in his arms, trying to comfort him. But as someone who was just removed enough to see both sides of the situation, she felt like she had to point out the difficulties Jaina would have had in tracking him down back before online DNA databases were easily accessible. "So, it would have been pretty difficult for her to find you again to tell you back then."

"She knew I was in the Naval Academy with my twin," Josh huffed, lifting his head to look her in the eyes. "And she remembered both of our first names well enough to give them both to JoJo. And I can guarantee that we were the only twins in the Naval Academy named Josh and Jake at the time, so it wouldn't have been all that difficult to find me if she'd actually tried. Don't get me wrong, I'm glad she remembered enough about me to tell JoJo about me being in school and planning to be a SEAL and all. But actually letting me be a part of his life woulda been a hell of a lot better than whatever made-up stories she told him about SEALs over the years."

Cait couldn't argue, understanding his anger at having lost so much time with his son. While she didn't think it would have been as easy to find him back then as he thought, she didn't know for sure. Besides, it seemed like a moot point so many years later, especially since Jaina wasn't able to explain her thought process at the time. So, she just nodded along and let him rant to get it all out.

"And now I feel like an ass for being mad as fuck at a dead woman," Josh vented as she felt his hands fisting at the small of her back. "So, I can't talk to JoJo about his mom without risking my anger showing and fucking with his feelings for her. That would be just as bad for his mental health as pretending you're her, or trying to make him forget her and replace her with you. But I have no fucking clue how to get past my anger, or help him deal with his grief in a healthy way, so we can be the family I want us to be."

"I don't either," Cait commiserated with an encouraging smile, unsure if she was included in the family he wanted in the future or not. "But I think you're on the right track with thinking about therapy. I know it's helped me quite a bit."

"Maybe JoJo and I should see your therapist," Josh speculated, leaning his forehead against hers. "Then maybe we could do some joint sessions, so all three of us can help each other deal with our issues."

Cait examined his unique hazel eyes, looking closely at the gold bands of color that resembled rays of sunlight shining from his pupils out into the greener outer portion of his irises. She couldn't be certain, but she thought she could see his desire for them to have a sunny future as a family in them.

"She does offer family therapy sessions. In fact, when I saw her last month, she suggested Mikey sit in on my session this month to help me with the changes happening recently in our family dynamics. When we do that tomorrow afternoon, I'll ask her if she works with kids, if you're serious about us all seeing the same doctor."

"Yeah, I think family therapy sounds perfect," Josh smiled. "Especially since I hope we'll be a blended family one of these days. And I don't think that can happen until we're all three ready for it."

A blended family? Yeah, I like that idea.

"Well, my appointment tomorrow is at four." Cait ran her fingers through Josh's hair, unable to resist caressing him now that she knew he wanted them to be a family the same way she did. "So why don't you come over a few minutes before five to use the last few minutes of my session to ask your questions, and see about setting up sessions for you and JoJo, and us as a family? Even if she doesn't end up being the right therapist for you guys, maybe she can refer you to someone who specializes in helping kids through their grief."

"I will most definitely do that, Sunshine," Josh smiled before pressing his lips to hers once more. He kept the kiss chaste in comparison to the one when they first got to her house, only brushing their lips together briefly before lifting his once more. "But now I need to make you come a couple more times before we have to go to our separate beds for the night."

"Oh, no, Cowboy," Cait protested, wiggling on his lap until she was straddling him and able to rub her core on his impressive erection. She slid her hands down from his head to trail over his pecs on the way to the waistband of his jeans. "I owe you at least one before I get to come again."

"Sorry, Sunshine," Josh grinned, shaking his head, and gripping her wrists to stop her from getting her hands on the part of his body she most wanted to touch. "But I was serious earlier about us not having time for everything I'd wanna do if my cock leaves the confines of my jeans. And I'm not about to come in my pants like an untried teenager, so you're just gonna hafta give up any ideas you have about keeping things even between us. You're always gonna come first and way more often than I do."

"But that's not fair," Cait whined, wanting to give him as much pleasure as he gave her.

"Oh yeah it is," Josh chuckled, carefully moving her hands behind her back, and holding them there. "Why do you think God made women capable of coming multiple times in a row, while we guys have to have recovery time between orgasms?"

"To make up for the pain of childbirth?" Cait guessed, half-heartedly shrugging.

"Well, maybe that too," Josh chuckled, grinning at her. "But since I get just as much pleasure from watching you come as coming myself, I think it's His way of keeping it fair without us having to keep count."

"Whatever." Cait rolled her eyes at the line of bullshit he was spewing. "If you really believe that, then you're the only man I've ever met who thinks that way."

"I'm sure you know more than a few who share my opinion," Josh claimed, shaking his head. "You just don't know it because you haven't dated them. Hell, for my sister's sake, I hope your brother agrees with me and isn't a selfish douche, like it sounds like the guys were that you've been with before now."

"I do not want to even think about my brother and your sister right now," Cait cringed, curling her lips in revulsion as she shuddered at the image that popped into her head.

"Agreed," Josh nodded, his expression turning more serious. "Though we should probably talk a little about our sexual histories, so we're prepared for when I'm able to schedule a whole night to ourselves."

"Oh, um, okay," Cait stammered, unsure what he wanted to know about her sexual history, and fairly hesitant to hear about his. "What do you want to know?"

"I, uh, don't need specific numbers or anything like that," Josh stammered, breaking their eye contact by dropping his gaze as if he was embarrassed about what he was about to admit. "Hell, I can't even give you a specific number, 'cause it's never been anything more than scratching an itch before now. And it's only been my hand since right before coming home on leave at Christmas last year. After I met you, I pretty much blocked out all memory of anyone else, which really made it difficult to try to come up with a list of everyone I've been with for Jake to try to find my son's mother online."

Cait wasn't exactly thrilled at hearing there'd been so many women before her that he couldn't even guess a number, but she was ecstatic at finding out he'd quit hooking up when he met her. "Well, I can tell you it's only been three for me," Cait sighed, feeling slightly pathetic for having such a low number. "All college boyfriends. I told you it's been a few years, but what I meant was that the last one was about a year before I was shot, and there've been none in the over two-and-a-half years since. Though I was tested when I was in the hospital, so I know I'm clean."

"I'm clean, tested regularly by the Navy, and have never had sex without a condom, which was why JoJo was such a shock when I first found out about him." Josh ran a hand through his hair as he stroked the other one up and down her side. "Since condoms don't seem to be as reliable as I thought, we should probably consider other birth control options until we're ready to add to our family."

"You really see us having a future as a family, don't you?" Cait tilted her head as she ran her hands back up to his shoulders.

"Sunshine, if it was up to me, we'd already be married, or at least planning our wedding," Josh smiled sincerely. "But I know you need time to feel comfortable living on your own, and JoJo needs time to grieve the loss of his mother, before ya'll will be ready for us to deal with the legalities of making us a family. So, I'm willing to wait and take it one step at a time for now. But yeah, I'm plannin' on marryin' you just as soon as we get all our ducks in a row."

"And what do you think about having more kids?" Cait bit her lip nervously as she awaited Josh's answer. After having unpleasant side effects when she tried going on the pill while she was in college, she didn't really want to risk more health issues by going back on hormonal birth control, even if there were other options besides the one she'd tried before. But if Josh wasn't ready to risk another condom failure resulting in a child, she wasn't sure what other option they might have other than not having full, penetrative sex.

"I'll have as many as you want, Sunshine," Josh grinned before his expression turned more pensive. "I just don't wanna rush our timeline by makin' a baby before you're ready."

Cait could see the wariness in his green and gold eyes, and wished she knew how to wipe it away. Unfortunately, she feared the revelation she was about to make would only heighten it. "I can't go on birth control," she anxiously confessed. "I tried it in college, and it jacked up my blood pressure and made my periods go wonky. So, if condoms aren't effective enough for you, we'll have to wait…"

"Fuck, no," Josh interjected, cutting off her statement and surprising Cait with his vehemence to the point she flinched back from him. "I'm sorry. I didn't mean that the way it sounded."

Josh wrapped his arms around Cait, not letting her leave his lap as he clarified. "I'll wait as long as you wanna wait, Cait. I meant that 'fuck, no,' as 'fuck, no, you won't get on birth control if it causes you any kind of bad side effects,' not 'fuck, no, we won't wait.' But how long we wait is absolutely up to you. I only said that about condoms not being as effective as I thought 'cause I wanted you to know the risk of pregnancy before you made that decision. Like I said earlier, I'm ready to marry you and start trying for more kids now. Hell, I woulda started tryin' the day we met, but I knew I had to get outta the Navy first."

"So, you're okay with me deciding to take the risk with just using condoms, and leaving it up to fate when we're ready to take the next step in building our family?" Cait wound her arms back around Josh's neck as she leaned in to press their foreheads together once more.

"Absolutely," Josh smiled, mischief flashing in his hazel eyes as he sealed their decision with a scorching hot kiss.

Cait scooted back over his erection as she returned the ardent kiss. Josh gripped her hips, holding her in place as he bucked up to grind his impressive bulge against her sensitive core. They didn't bother coming up for air as they dry-humped on the loveseat like teenagers until Cait came a couple of times.

Unfortunately, they talked too long for them to have time for any clothing to be removed, or them to go any farther, before Josh had to go back over to his room at his parents' house. Not that being in separate beds stopped them from sexting while Cait used her vibrator a few minutes later.

Josh: Send me a pic of you in bed.

Cait: What are you going to do with it?

Josh: Jerk off while thinking about fucking you.

Cait: {Sexy Selfie in blue silk nightie} Okay, but you need to send me a pic to look at while using my vibrator.

Josh: {Shirtless Selfie in bed} Fuck I wish it was me inside you instead of your vibrator.

If only Josh wasn't so dead set on having all night before we can make love for real.

353

Chapter Eighteen

Cait felt exceptionally frustrated after almost a week of what felt like one-sided foreplay with Josh. *So what if I've had more orgasms in the last week than I've had in the rest of my life? I still don't think it's fair that he hasn't let me give him one. And no, talking to him on the phone while he jerks off doesn't count, no matter how freaking hot it is when we come at the same time like that. I want to actually see his dick. And touch it. And taste it. Fuck! I want his dick inside me and not just his fingers!*

Cait was tempted to talk to their therapist about how soon it would be appropriate to seduce Josh into getting naked with her. But since she didn't have a one-on-one session scheduled with her until the middle of October, she didn't know if she could wait that long without going insane. And there was no way she could bring up the subject during one of the sessions she had scheduled with Josh and JoJo present.

Josh had actually been able to set up sessions for him and JoJo the previous week, both one-on-one and for the two of them together. Apparently, they'd gone so well that the therapist felt they'd benefit from the three of them being included in all their sessions starting this week. Cait thought it seemed kind of fast to completely move away from one-on-one sessions, especially for JoJo so soon after losing his mom. But she trusted her psychologist, so she followed the plan laid out by the mental health professional to be there to support Josh and JoJo, even though it meant going into San Antonio with them for an in-person appointment, instead of a telehealth session like she was accustomed to doing.

Considering how the majority of Cait's last session had been spent reviewing how well she did going with Josh and JoJo on their outings to the Alamo and aquarium in San Antonio, she had to wonder if Dr. Edwards was trying to push her to leave the ranch more often by setting their joint appointments in her office. After how much better she'd done on the trips to the San Antonio Zoo and The DoSeum on the weekend since she'd talked to Dr. Edwards, Cait was actually looking forward to updating her psychologist on her rapid progress thanks to Josh and JoJo's help.

Cait also hoped the doctor would be able to instruct her on how she could best help Josh and JoJo when they went to their first joint session the next day, as well as at the subsequent sessions they had scheduled each week for the next month. She wasn't sure how they planned to handle the session they'd scheduled for the first week in October, when Josh and JoJo would be in Virginia, and she'd be stuck on the ranch worrying about them. But maybe they could teleconference from three different locations.

Thinking about Josh and JoJo leaving Heart's Destiny on Sunday brought down Cait's mood, even as she sat down with them surrounding her to watch the new live-action version of *Aladdin*.

Forget the therapy session. That will be easy to deal with. But how am I going to get through a week or more without them here?

The last two weeks of spending time with "her guys" daily totally spoiled Cait. She knew she'd miss them terribly while they were in Virginia, dealing with the legalities of Josh claiming custody of his son. She also felt guilty for letting her fear prevent her from being there to support Josh and JoJo when they went to court.

"Why aren't you laughing, Cait?" JoJo looked up at her from where he'd squeezed onto the loveseat in her living room on the opposite side of her from Josh. "Do we need to wait until the sun goes down to watch the movie, so you can see it without the glare from the windows?"

"Maybe?" Cait looked over to Josh for his opinion on how hard it was to see the television, not having paid attention earlier to realize just how hard it was to see when they had at least another half hour before sundown.

"I suppose we can push back bedtime by a few minutes," Josh shrugged before picking up the remote and pausing the movie. "But you've gotta tell us why you suddenly look so sad, Sunshine, so we can fix it to make you smile again."

"It's nothing," Cait smiled as she shook her head.

"I think we're gonna hafta tickle it outta her, Dad." JoJo grinned at Josh before attacking Cait's ribs with his fingers.

"Maybe I'll tickle it outta you," Cait retorted, laughing as she retaliated with the tickle torture.

Josh momentarily got in on the action, using one hand on Cait and the other on JoJo. But somehow he managed to stay in a seated position while Cait and JoJo wrestled around on the other end of the loveseat.

Maybe I should have insisted on taking the sofa from Mikey's furniture, instead of the loveseat, Cait thought when she somehow ended up on her back with her head on Josh's lap, her legs hanging off the end, and JoJo hanging upside down across her midsection.

But I figured they'd need the bigger sofa for roughhousing in their game room, since Brody doesn't really watch TV here and this is plenty big enough for me to curl up on to watch TV or read when I'm home alone. I guess, now that Josh and JoJo are hanging out more here, I should probably look into buying a sofa to finish filling up the space and give us a little more room for getting comfortable on movie nights.

Cait wasn't sure if Josh moved the throw pillow she kept on the loveseat over his crotch to cover getting hard from how close her head was to his cock, or if it was his attempt at trying to make her more comfortable laying there by providing some cushion between her head and his hard thigh. But either way, it was obvious she probably shouldn't stay in this position while JoJo was right there with them, or she might forget there was a child present. She was just too tempted to move the pillow and turn her head to tease him.

"Okay, okay! I give up!" Cait laughed as Josh continued tickling her with one hand while JoJo wiggled around and knocked the breath out of her.

JoJo put his hands on the floor and kicked his feet off the back of the loveseat to flip down onto the rug. Cait was having such a good time that she didn't even care that she'd have to wash the slipcover to get his footprints off of it.

It's my own fault for not reminding him to take his shoes off like Josh and I did when we came in earlier. Maybe one of these days I won't be distracted by thinking that even Josh's bare feet are sexy, so I can be more attentive to JoJo.

Oh, who am I kidding? I'm always going to be distracted when Josh starts taking off clothing, even his boots and socks.

"If you give up, you gotta tell us why you were sad," JoJo insisted, holding his hands out and making a clawing gesture with his fingers. "Or we're gonna go back to tickling you."

"I was just thinking about how much I'm going to miss you guys when you're in Virginia next week," Cait admitted as she sat up.

"You should go with us," JoJo suggested as he grinned and sat down beside her once more. "Then we won't have to miss each other."

Damn it! I can't let my fear keep me from being there for this precious little boy.

"JoJo," Josh growled his son's nickname in a tone that made it clear it was a warning to not push the issue. "I already told you we have to wait for Cait to decide when she's ready for a long trip like that with us."

"But she only got scared the first time we went to San Antonio," JoJo pouted. "And you said the bad guys who hurt her before are all in jail, so she doesn't have to be scared of them anymore. So why can't she come to Virginia with us?"

Geez, he's right. And even if they weren't in jail or dead, they'd be in San Diego or San Antonio. Not a couple thousand miles away in one of the suburbs of our nation's capital. How the hell can an eight-year-old realize that when my twenty-six-year-old subconscious can't seem to comprehend it?

"She has a job, too," Josh pointed out. "She can't just take off work for however long we end up having to stay there while going through court."

"But she can write anywhere," JoJo argued, standing back up to glare at his dad. "So, she can still work while I'm doing my school work like we've been doing here."

"She also has to watch Brody while Uncle Mikey and Aunt Char are at work," Josh ratiocinated, finally switching over to using the name Cait called her brother.

With all these arguments for why I need to stay here, maybe Josh doesn't want me to go with them. Or is he just trying to give me an out in case I can't handle the trip?

"But Memmaw can watch Brody," JoJo huffed, stomping his foot. "Memmaw can't come to Virginia 'cause she's gotta stay here to cook for the cowboys. And I don't like the nannies she interviewed today, so I don't want one of them to go with us. I like Cait. And I know she won't let Grandfather take me while you're on the base for your meetings. Those nannies won't be able to stop him, just like Aunt Tawny couldn't stop him."

Cait felt like she was sitting front and center at a tennis match with the way her head kept turning back and forth as Josh and JoJo debated. She just thought she felt guilty earlier for letting her fear hold her back from volunteering to go with them. Hearing JoJo practically beg for her to go tore her heart to shreds, especially since his desire to have her there seemed rooted in a fear of his grandparents and he was trusting her to keep him safe.

I am not going to let my fear keep me from being the best stepmom this kid could ever hope for, Cait decided as Josh assured his son that his grandfather wouldn't get the chance to take him.

"Josh, other than my anxiety, is there a reason you don't want me to go to Virginia with you?" Cait interrupted, unable to handle seeing JoJo so worked up a moment longer.

"No, I'd much rather have you with us than some nanny I don't know." Josh reached over and took her hand to comfort her. "But I would never ask you to go so far outside your comfort zone, when I know I can't stay by your side the whole time."

"But when you have to go to base, we can stay in your apartment, right? And if JoJo isn't able to be in the courtroom, then we can stay in our hotel while you're in court, right?" Cait knew she could handle being left alone with JoJo while Josh took care of his business as long as they stayed indoors in a private space where she didn't have to interact with strangers, even in a large city she'd never visited before. She was less confident about having to leave their hotel room to get lunch while Josh was in court, but she already loved JoJo enough to brave it for him. *If the anxiety is too overwhelming for me to take him to the restaurant in the hotel, then I'll just order room service. I can handle one of the staff delivering food. Hopefully.*

"I was planning on staying with Jake in Alexandria for our court dates," Josh nodded. "But yeah, ya'll can stay in either his apartment or mine whenever I can't be with you."

"Even better," Cait smiled, feeling a little more confident in her ability to handle the trip without having an anxiety attack. "Then I can cook for us there and won't have to order room service if you're gone over lunchtime. So, it'll be just like being here on the ranch or going sightseeing with you in San Antonio. And I can handle that."

"Are you sure?" Josh examined her with a skeptical expression.

"Yes, I'm sure. But we can check with Dr. Edwards tomorrow if you need more reassurance," Cait nodded, smiling at him before being tackle-hugged by JoJo.

Cait wrapped the excited little boy in her arms, as he squealed a chorus of "Thank you! Thank you! Thank you!" right in her ear.

"If you're sure, I'll tell Ma to stop interviewing nannies then," Josh nodded, smiling at Cait around JoJo's head in between them. "But now, we need to hurry up and get this movie started or we won't be able to watch it all tonight."

JoJo released Cait from his vise-grip hug, wiggling around to lay across both Josh and Cait's laps as Cait snuggled into Josh's side to watch the movie.

Oh, I really hope I can pull this off, Cait sighed as Josh wrapped his arm around her shoulders, kissed the top of her head, and restarted the movie. *Going to a suburb of Washington D.C. for an undetermined amount of time is a way bigger step toward taking back my life than the baby steps I've taken here in Texas. But it's one I absolutely have to take to be the woman my guys need me to be, so we can be a family.*

As they snuggled on Cait's short sofa watching the movie, Josh could only focus on the sense of peace and contentment he felt with having family time with Cait and JoJo. While he knew there were no legalities binding them together yet, in his heart, they were already a family in all the ways that mattered. He also knew that Cait was still too skeptical to believe they loved each other from the first moment they met, so he continued to hold back those three special words that were always on the tip of his tongue, waiting until she said them first. Though it was really hard to do when she showed her love for both him and JoJo the way she had that evening.

Josh didn't want to pressure her to go to Virginia, even though he desperately wanted her by his side when he went to court to fight for his son. No matter how much he wanted her with them on the trip, he knew she had to go at her pace when it came to healing from her past trauma enough to venture away from her safe spaces. So, he'd tried to be the supportive boyfriend by keeping her informed about when he and JoJo had to be out of town, without mentioning his wishes for her to come with them.

Fuck! I hope her decision tonight isn't because JoJo guilted her into coming with us. But damn, I'm fuckin' awestruck at how brave she's being in facing her fears to be there for him. Whether she knows it or not, just being willing to try to step up for him like that shows how much she already loves him.

Now I just have to figure out how to get her to recognize the unconditional love she feels is reciprocated, so we can all start sharing the words.

"I don't think you have to worry about JoJo staying up past bedtime," Cait whispered, reaching over to wipe a drop of drool off JoJo's face before it hit the pillow he was using on Josh's lap. She wiped the drool off her thumb onto her jeans before turning to look up at Josh.

"No," Josh chuckled, stopping the movie before turning off the television. "I'm not sure his bedtime was really nine o'clock when he was with his mom. Not with as hard a time he has staying awake past eight, especially on days when we breeze through his schoolwork and get to spend extra time with the horses."

"Learning to ride is just as exhausting for us humans as it is for the horses. Besides, eight o'clock here is nine o'clock in Virginia, so his internal clock is probably set to the Eastern Time Zone," Cait giggled. She dropped her gaze to JoJo once more as her expression turned from humorous to hopeful. "You know I have a guest bedroom you can put him in, so you don't have to carry him all the way across the ranch and up three flights of stairs to his bedroom. And you're both welcome to stay the night, so he won't be scared waking up in a strange room."

Josh wasn't sure exactly what Cait was suggesting. *Is that an invitation for me to spend the night in her bed? Or to share the guest room with JoJo?*

"What exactly are you suggesting, Sunshine?" Josh kept his voice low, not wanting to wake his son in the middle of what could turn out to be an adults-only conversation.

"A trial run for how we're going to work out the sleeping arrangements on the trip to Virginia?" Cait quirked an eyebrow curiously as her lips turned up in a mischievous smile.

"I'm a firm believer in being consistent as a parent," Josh informed her as he twisted his upper body slightly, so he could brush Cait's hair behind her ear and see her true feelings on her expressive face. "So that means," *parents*, "adults in separate bedrooms from kids with the kids knowing it's okay to come wake us up if they have a nightmare. You understand that'll mean you and me sharing a bed with the possibility of JoJo coming to get me to help him go back to sleep if he has a nightmare? Are you ready for what that's gonna mean for us as a couple?"

"Extremely ready," Cait assured him, leaning her face into his hand.

They wouldn't have all night to be naked the way he wanted for their first time, but Josh wasn't strong enough to resist the temptation to make love to Cait for however long it would take to schedule a whole night alone with her. The way she looked up at him with desire shining brightly in her aquamarine eyes destroyed the last bit of his resolve to wait.

"Then give me a few minutes to make sure he's settled," Josh grinned, leaning down to lightly brush his lips over hers. "And I'll meet you in your room, Sunshine."

Josh scooped JoJo up in his arms and stood, carrying his son to the smaller of the two bedrooms in the house, assuming Cait had set it up as the guestroom. He removed JoJo's shoes, socks, and jeans, leaving him to sleep in his white t-shirt and Captain America Underoos before tucking him into bed.

"Did we finish the movie?" JoJo mumbled without even opening his eyes.

"No, but we can watch the rest tomorrow night," Josh assured his son before bending over and kissing his forehead. "Or maybe in the morning, since we're staying at Cait's tonight."

JoJo opened his eyes then, looking around briefly. Josh pointed out the door to the guest bathroom that was accessible from both the bedroom and the hallway as he gave his son a lay of the land. "That door goes to the bathroom without having to go through the hall. And I'll be across the hall in the other bedroom with Cait if you need me."

"Okay, goodnight, Dad." JoJo lifted his shoulders from the bed and opened his arms, signaling Josh to lean in for a hug. "I love you."

"I love you, too, Son." Josh returned the goodnight hug, brushing his lips over the soft, light brown hair on top of JoJo's head. "Now get some sleep and I'll see you in the morning."

JoJo's eyes were closed before they even released the hug for him to lay back down. Noticing how JoJo's breathing had already evened out before he could stand from the side of the bed, Josh wasn't sure his son had woken up enough to remember their brief interaction the next morning. As he walked to the door, he hoped that having spent some time in Cait's house over the last couple of weeks would make it clear where he was, if JoJo woke up and didn't remember Josh telling him where they were sleeping.

Josh noticed the monitor on the bedside table and the nightlight that stayed on in the room as he turned off the light and shut the door behind him. *Damn, I guess her having that room set up for Brody will make it easier for us to know when to make sure we have clothes back on, if JoJo has another nightmare tonight.* Josh smiled at the thought as he walked across the hall into Cait's bedroom.

Unlike the blues and greens in her guest bedroom, Cait's bedroom was done up in a brighter sunny yellow than the mustard yellow in the living room and kitchen, even though the walls were painted the same creamy white as the rest of the house. Since she'd already turned the light on in the room, he could tell where the black fuzzy throw pillow that was out on the loveseat she used for a sofa was usually kept in the house. Its twin was stacked on top of her bed pillows in crisp white pillowcases with a couple of fuzzy yellow throw pillows that matched the canary yellow bedspread.

I guess the black pillows are supposed to help the black wrought-iron canopy frame and black metal bedside lamps blend with the yellow and white bedding, without it being so much yellow and black that it looks like a bumblebee bedroom?

Josh didn't understand home décor, choosing his furniture and linens based on comfort and functionality rather than style. His color palette leaned more toward blacks and grays, which didn't show dirt if he didn't have time to clean before being spun up for an op. But as he looked around the room while waiting for Cait to finish whatever she was doing in the ensuite bathroom, Josh decided he could definitely get used to living in a home done up with Cait's sense of style and pops of color. All that yellow made it obvious it was a woman's room, but he could see all the black and gray stuff he had in his apartment in Virginia blending in well with her sunny yellows sometime in the future.

"I, um, put out toothbrushes for you guys," Cait sputtered as she walked out of her bathroom still dressed in the capri-length jeans and light gray t-shirt she'd been wearing earlier. "I didn't know if JoJo was awake enough to use it before bed or not, so I just left one for him in the package beside the sink in the guest bathroom. I don't know if he'll want to use it in the morning before going back to his room where he could use his own. And the one for you, I put beside the sink in this bathroom."

Cait was so cute as she pointed over her shoulder with her thumb that Josh couldn't help but smile. "Then I'd better go use it, so I'm minty fresh for kissing you all over."

Cait faintly flushed from embarrassment as he stepped by her on his way to brush his teeth, briefly pausing to tenderly kiss her temple and take a deep inhale of her lightly floral scent as he passed her. *Fucking adorable.*

As he stepped into her bathroom, Josh realized Cait's flowery aroma that he loved smelling every time he was near her had to come from the lavender bath products he saw around the bathtub and on the pearl white granite countertop surrounding the dual sinks and making up the vanity between them. Josh took a moment to bask in her scent as he opened the blue toothbrush she'd left beside the sink for him, tossed the package in the sunny yellow wastebasket at the end of the counter, and loaded up the toothbrush with her minty toothpaste.

He quickly went through a limited version of his normal nightly routine, washing the important parts with her girly soap after brushing his teeth, since he didn't need to shower to jerk off as he'd done almost every night since meeting Cait. He pulled his wallet from his back pocket and double-checked that the condoms he had in there weren't expired, since the last time he'd swapped them out was before Christmas. Once he was assured they weren't too old to use, he stuffed them in his front pocket instead of putting them back in his wallet, knowing he'd want to have easier access once they got started.

When he walked back into the bedroom, he found the lights off with a couple of candles flickering on the dresser and Cait already in bed with the blankets pulled up to her neck. Josh pulled his phone out of his pocket and activated the flashlight app to be able to see to get to the bedside table, where he turned on one of the lamps. "Oh, no, Sunshine, I need to be able to see your beautiful face the first time I make love to you."

Josh turned off the flashlight app and pulled up Pandora, selecting the country love songs station for mood music before placing it on the bedside table. He took the condoms from his pocket and dropped them on the table beside his phone.

Cait turned and switched on the lamp on the other side of the bed, giving him a glimpse of her naked back. "Sorry, I knew you said something about candles, so I thought that meant lights off."

Damn, I was lookin' forward to undressing her slowly and taking my time getting her worked up with my mouth on every inch of her as I exposed her sexy body.

"Yeah, the more I thought about the scene I pictured in my head and described to you the other day, the more I realized that the number of candles we'd need so I could see you would be a fire hazard," Josh chuckled as he reached behind his head with one hand to strip off his t-shirt before he crawled into the bed.

He intentionally left his jeans on, knowing he needed that barrier to keep him from jumping straight to the main event when he wanted to make her come with his fingers and mouth first. He pulled the blanket and sheet down when he got to the middle of the bed and could finally reach Cait, exposing the alabaster skin over her collarbone, down to her perky tits with coral-pink nipples that were already almost as hard as his dick.

"I didn't realize being able to see each other was so important," Cait grinned as she ran her hands up his arms to rest her palms on his shoulders as he moved over her, trailing the hand he wasn't braced on from her cheek, down her neck, and across her chest until he could finally cup her ample breast. "But that's probably because my past experience has all been with college boys fumbling in the dark. And nobody wanted to see that."

"I don't want to think about anyone from the past right now," Josh growled, squeezing the creamy mound in his hand as he tried to clamp down the irrational anger that made him want to go find her past boyfriends and kill them for having the audacity to touch her. "As far as I'm concerned, we've never been with anyone else before now."

"So, we're pretending JoJo came from the stork?" Cait teased, her lips turning up as she fought not to giggle.

"No pretending, Sunshine," Josh grinned, loving how they could laugh together even in otherwise serious, intimate moments. "Since I don't remember anyone before you, he had to have come from the stork."

Cait lost her fight not to giggle, barking out a laugh as Josh chuckled with her. *Damn, I love seein' her smile.*

He couldn't resist a second longer, needing to kiss her more than he needed his next breath. He pressed their lips together as he gently pinched her nipple between his thumb and pointer finger. Cait wound her arms around his neck, as he deepened the kiss, relishing the taste of mint and sweet Cait on his tongue for several long moments.

As much as Josh loved spending hours kissing Cait, he didn't stick to his usual modus operandi of just making out with her for the entire time he had alone with her after JoJo went to bed. He broke the kiss fairly quickly to lick his way down her body, taking only a few minutes to focus on her glorious rack before pushing the blankets further out of his way and trailing his tongue down the gentle curve of her belly.

No matter how badly he wanted the blankets completely out of his way, Josh didn't keep pushing them down the bed as he moved down to get between Cait's legs. He knew they might have to quickly cover up if they heard JoJo stirring on the monitor he saw sitting on the bedside table closest to Cait's head. So, he just pushed them down low enough that he could move Cait's legs out from under them, eagerly anticipating her wrapping those long, sexy legs around his neck while he ate her pussy.

Cait apparently understood his unspoken request to free her lower legs from the confines of the bedding, kicking the leg free that he hadn't started trying to move yet as Josh trailed his tongue down from her belly button over her mons pubis. The tangy sweet scent of her arousal mixed with her faint lavender lotion filled his nostrils as he ran the tip of his tongue through the neatly trimmed small triangle of chestnut hair at the top of her vulva and over her labia to find the pearl of her clit, already swollen and poking out between her lower lips to get his attention.

Fuck! No wonder she comes so fast from dry-humping. She doesn't have a hood to keep her clit covered when she's not aroused, so I bet just her panties rubbing over it can get her off if she gets even the slightest bit turned on for it to pop up past her outer labia.

Finally getting the chance to closely examine Cait's pussy made Josh's dick as hard as stone, knowing he'd have the imprint of his zipper on his cock from waiting to remove his jeans until he could plunge inside her sweet cunt. For now, Captain America had to be satisfied with the tight confines of the rough denim instead of her silky soft sheath.

"Oh, Josh," Cait moaned when he hit his target with the tip of his tongue, causing him to smile before he wrapped his lips around her little nub and sucked. "Oh, that feels so much better than I expected."

Holy shit! Does that mean nobody's ever sucked her clit before? Did her previous boyfriends not go down on her at all? Or did they just not know what they were doing? As curious as he was, Josh wasn't about to ruin the moment to stop and ask. *Fuck, not that I'm an expert since I haven't done this since high school. But I at least remember enough from sex ed to know how to make her come apart with my mouth.*

"Tastes amazing too," Josh murmured as he lapped up her sweet cream while relishing the feel of her feet digging into his upper back.

She was already dripping wet before he even teased through her folds with his fingers. But as he inserted a digit and swirled the tip of his tongue around her clit, she gushed even more. He fucked her with his finger for a little while, coating it in her arousal before slipping it out and sliding it back between her cheeks to rim her puckered hole.

He had no intention of any rectal insertions, but he had to get his hand out of the way so he could lick through her slit and fuck her with his tongue. Josh used the thumb from his other hand to stimulate her pink pearl at the same time, wanting to overwhelm her with pleasure.

Josh didn't even realize he was humping her bed as she writhed beneath him and dug her nails into his scalp, mumbling incoherently until her inner walls clamped down on his tongue.

"Oh, Josh," Cait cried out breathily as she came, pumping her mound into his face and squirting into his mouth.

Holy fuck! That's a first, Josh thought as he gentled his strokes to bring her down from the peak gradually. He'd seen porn where women squirted when they came, but he'd never experienced it in person before. *I mean, shit, I've always made sure the women I was with were good and wet, but I thought they faked the squirting I saw in videos online. But damn, now I've gotta see if I can get her to do that again.*

He swapped his hand and mouth between her clit and her slit, inserting two fingers while she was relaxed enough to take them easily. He licked her clit, swirling his tongue until she pulled his hair to lift his mouth from her mound.

"No, not your fingers, Josh," Cait panted breathlessly. "I need your cock inside me now, please."

"Not yet, Sunshine," Josh regretfully denied her plea as he smiled up at her. "You're too tight still. I have to get you opened up for me first."

She made the cutest pouty face, but she released her death grip on his hair to let him have his way. "I'll try to hurry, Sunshine," Josh chuckled as he scissored his fingers inside her to open her up enough to get a third finger in her tight channel. He dipped his head back down, alternating between licking and sucking her clitoris as he stroked her G-spot.

He used his thumb and pinky to hold her outer lips apart, so he could enjoy the view of his other three fingers stroking in and out of her slick opening. "So, fucking, hot," he groaned against her needy nub as she bucked her hips and pushed his face down to direct him where she wanted him.

"So, close," she panted, rocking her pelvis in an erratic rhythm that backed up her breathless words. "Need more."

"I'll give you exactly what you need, Sunshine," Josh growled, diving in to devour her pussy like a starving man. He licked, sucked, and stroked until her creamy cunt started to spasm around his fingers, drinking down her release when she squirted in his mouth once more.

"Oh, Josh, Josh, Josh," Cait chanted his name repeatedly, clamping her thighs around his head as her whole body convulsed in pleasure.

Josh wasn't sure which would kill him first, suffocating or drowning. But either way, it was a glorious way to go. *Fuck! If this was how I was being waterboarded, I don't think I'd classify it as being tortured. Maybe in my exit interview, I should suggest this as a way for future SEALs to train for if they're ever captured by the enemy. But they'll have to find their own squirters, 'cause Cait's all mine.*

Josh had to chuckle at the strange place his mind went to keep from coming in his jeans, when Cait finally went limp and released him from the vise-like grip she had on his head.

"What's so funny?" Cait barely lifted her head from the pillow to smile at him. She was sexy as hell, sprawled across the bed and eyeing him hungrily.

"Just thinking that I like the way you waterboard me much better than the way they did it as part of my SEAL training," Josh admitted, grinning as he stood and walked around the bed to get a condom from the bedside table, unable to take his eyes off the gorgeous curves she had on display for him. The instant he unhooked the button and lowered the zipper of his jeans, his cock sprang out, finally filling to its full size and eagerly pointing in Cait's direction.

"Oh, wow, you're…wow." Cait stared at his cock with wide eyes, biting her lower lip nervously as Josh shoved his jeans down and stepped out of them. "Bigger than I expected from what I could see and, um, feel in your jeans."

"Yeah, well, denim doesn't exactly stretch to allow more than a semi," Josh chuckled as he tore open the gold and black foil package, removed the condom, and tossed the wrapper back on the bedside table. He'd throw it away later when he disposed of the used rubber.

"Are you sure you, um, stretched me out enough to handle all that?" Cait looked a little worried as she gazed up at him from the bed.

"Don't worry, Sunshine," Josh assured her as he lowered his knees to the side of the bed and walked on them back over between her legs. "You were made to take me, so I'll fit just fine. But we'll still go nice and slow to make sure it's amazing for both of us."

Josh lifted her legs, propping her ankles on his shoulders to hold her open for him. He used his left thumb to rub her clit, spreading her juices around even as more oozed from her pretty, dusky-pink pussy.

Josh gripped his dick in his right hand and slid the tip up and down along her slit while stroking his hand up and down his shaft to lube up with her arousal. Once his head was coated in her cream, Josh slowly pushed inside her. He stopped with just the head inside her, allowing her to get used to his girth before working his full length into her tight channel.

"Oh," Cait moaned, gripping the bedding in her fists as she wiggled her hips as if she was trying to get him to move faster.

Josh could only smile, unable to form words as he reveled in the feel of sinking his cock into Cait for the first time. Going so fucking slow was torturous, way more difficult for him to handle than the feeling of drowning during her last orgasm. He had to fight to stay in control. To not shove balls-deep from how eager he was to be completely connected to her.

The feel of her tight heat surrounding him was other-worldly, even with the barrier of the latex between them. He didn't want it there, wanted nothing separating them from being completely lost in one another. *Fuck, I hope she doesn't wanna wait too long before we start actively trying to make a baby. I can't wait to feel her wet cunt choking my cock with nothing between us.*

"Fuck, you feel amazing, Caitir," Josh groaned as he finally bottomed out inside her. Just as slowly as he'd pushed into her, he pulled back out, leaving only his head inside her before reversing direction once more. "Even better than I imagined in all my fantasies."

"Yes. So full. So good." Cait's eyes locked on his as she slid her feet off his shoulders and wrapped her luscious long legs around his waist. She released her grip on the bedding to grip his forearms, using her legs to help propel him forward, so he had no choice but to cover her body with his. "Need to touch you, Josh."

"Then touch me, Sunshine," Josh growled before claiming her lips in a passionate kiss. He braced his weight on his left arm while using his right to fondle her breasts as he matched the movements of his tongue and cock stroking inside the woman he loved. Thankfully, she didn't seem averse to tasting herself on his tongue, licking into his mouth in perfect time with each sweep of his tongue through hers.

Cait ran her hands up and down his back, delicately scoring her nails over his skin as she bucked and writhed beneath him. Gradually, her movements became more frantic, urging him to move faster as her inner walls fluttered with the first waves of her next climax.

"Fuck, yes, Cait," Josh rumbled, nipping her lips as he swiveled his hips to make sure he stroked her G-spot with his dick. "Come on my cock. I wanna feel you soak me from coming so hard."

"Oh. Yes. Josh." Cait paused between each word to take a breath, marking him with her nails on his back as her pussy squeezed down forcefully on his cock.

Josh maintained his slow and steady rhythm as she rode the waves of her release, chanting his name repeatedly as she came. Hearing his name on her lips as she shattered around him was his undoing. He couldn't hold back a second longer, urgently needing to thrust harder and faster into her slick sheath.

When the final wave passed and she collapsed onto the bed in a satiated state, Josh took advantage of the way her body relaxed into an almost limp form, unwrapping her arms to push back into a more upright position. He unwound her legs from around his waist to prop her ankles on his shoulders once more, gripping her hips to hold her in place as he started to pound into her pliant pussy.

He was fascinated with how her tits bounced as he plowed into her, watching the rosy peaks that he hadn't spent nearly enough time worshiping with his mouth.

"Oh, yes, Josh, more, please," Cait panted, rocking her hips in time with his thrusts. "Harder. Fuck me, Josh."

Josh couldn't believe his ears, surprised to hear his sweet Cait begging to be fucked. He didn't know how she was able to form the words when all he could get out were grunts as he rutted into her like a wild animal, completely lost in the oblivion of pleasure.

When she gripped his arms once more, trying to pull him forward, Josh turned the tables on her, taking control. He leaned forward the way she wanted, but he gripped her wrists, moving them to one hand as he pinned her hands above her head. The new position practically folded her in half with her ankles still braced on his shoulders. But the way she moaned, "Ride me, Cowboy," made it clear that Cait enjoyed his show of dominance.

"Fuck, yeah, Sunshine," Josh growled, grinning at the woman who was his perfect match in all ways and loving her apropos use of his call sign.

Josh used his free hand to position her tits between her shins, loving the feel of the turgid tips brushing against his chest as he claimed her mouth with his and continued fucking her. He felt a familiar tingle spread from his spine down to his balls, causing them to tighten up with his impending release. Josh knew he couldn't hold off much longer, desperately aching to spill inside her.

So, he broke their carnal kiss to command her to, "Come now, Caitir. Come with me." He barely waited until he felt her vaginal muscles ripple around his cock before he let loose with jet after jet of his cum into the condom. He felt his eyes roll back in his head from the intensity of his release, fearing he might pass out and collapse on top of her.

Cait's breathy moan of, "Oh, Josh, I love you," brought him back from the brink.

Josh snapped his eyes open, locking his hazel orbs on her blue-green eyes as he finally uttered the words he'd been holding back for far too long. "I love you, too, Caitir. So, fucking, much."

Josh released her hands and moved her legs back around his waist, so he wasn't bending her in half as he sealed their vows of love with an earth-shattering kiss. He wanted to roll them across the bed and bask in the pleasure of slowly shrinking inside her, but he didn't want to risk the condom leaking and creating another wet spot that they'd have to try to dodge in their sleep. So, he cut the kiss short and gripped his dick to hold the condom in place as he slowly pulled from the hot clutch of her cunt.

He jumped up and ran to the bathroom to dispose of the condom, barely remembering to pick up the empty wrapper from the bedside table on the opposite side of the bed on his way. He wiped off as much of his excess cum as he could with a few squares of toilet paper, which he flushed before rinsing the rest off in the sink. He then searched the cabinets for a washcloth and hand towel, drying his junk with the towel before running the washcloth under a warm stream of water and taking both to the bedroom to clean Cait up.

Wiping her girl cum up after sex wasn't something he'd ever thought of doing for a partner in the past. But with as much as Cait had squirted each of the four times she came, he assumed it was something that would become a habit for him with her. One he would thoroughly enjoy.

"What are you doing?" Cait looked at him skeptically as he wiped her up with the wet washcloth.

"Just taking care of you, Sunshine," Josh grinned, leaning down to brush his lips over hers before drying her off with the hand towel.

"I know you said you wanted to pretend this was both of our first times," Cait giggled, waving her hand around in a circle in the direction of his hand on her inner thigh. "But this is actually a first for me. But then again, so were the O's with a partner."

"We've had a few firsts tonight, Sunshine," Josh admitted as he tossed the washcloth in the laundry hamper in the corner of her bedroom. "Wanna roll and see if we can get some of the wet spot up with this towel?"

"Yeah, I don't think that towel is big enough," Cait chuckled as she rolled to the center of the bed and revealed the small pond they'd made on her side of the bed.

Josh just shrugged and spread the towel over the spot as best he could before walking around to the other side of the bed and laying down. "Well, maybe it'll get some of it up, so we don't have to change the sheets before going to sleep. And we can look for a waterproof mattress pad tomorrow, so we're better prepared for next time."

"I already have a waterproof mattress pad on the bed," Cait informed him as he moved the extra pillows out of his way to lay his head on just the bed pillow.

Josh couldn't help but look at her in surprise at the revelation. *Does she gush like that when using her vibrator?*

"Brody had issues with wetting the bed while being potty trained," Cait shrugged. "And since he developed a habit of crawling in bed with me after changing his underwear, it was necessary right after I moved in with them. While he outgrew that phase, I found the mattress pad saved my mattress when I spilled soda in bed a couple of times, too. So, I continued to use it to protect the bed on the nights I stay up late reading in bed and want a snack or something to drink while I'm reading."

"Makes sense," Josh grinned as he reached for the blanket and top sheet.

Once he pulled the covers up over them, Cait rolled to his side and cuddled against him with her head resting on his shoulder. "So, what other firsts did I not realize we had tonight?"

"My first time making love instead of just fucking," Josh admitted as he wrapped his arm around Cait and held her close. "My first time having sex on the ranch."

"Seriously?" Cait twisted her head to look up into his eyes. "You didn't sneak a bunch of girls up into the hayloft when you were a teenager?"

"No," Josh chuckled, shaking his head. "There were always too many people around to risk getting caught. I might have snuck in a kiss or two when we did haunted hayrides for Halloween when I was a teenager, but you're the only girl I've ever even really made out with here."

"Wow, that makes me feel special," Cait smiled before laying her head back down and twirling a finger through the light smattering of hair on his chest.

"You *are* special, Cait." Josh lifted his head from the pillow to brush his lips across the top of hers. "I wasn't just repeating your words in the throes of passion earlier. I love you. I've loved you from the first moment I saw you. And I will never stop loving you."

"I love you, too," Cait started, kissing his chest. "So much that it's hard to believe we might be lucky enough for everything to work out for us."

Before Josh could reply to try to ease Cait's too-good-to-be-true feelings, they heard a blood-curdling scream through the monitor on the bedside table. "Fuck," Josh cursed under his breath as he jumped up from the bed and grabbed his jeans from the floor. He didn't bother with his t-shirt, rushing out of the bedroom to his son as he was zipping up and buttoning his pants.

Josh flipped on the light as soon as he opened the guest bedroom door, finding JoJo sitting up in bed with wide eyes, looking around frantically. He strode quickly across the room and sat down on the side of the bed, pulling his son into his arms, and stroking his hand up and down the boy's back to soothe him. "Hey, JoJo, it's okay. I'm here."

JoJo's arms clamped around Josh as he cried into his father's chest. "I, I," JoJo sniffled as he sobbed. "Didn't know where you were."

"We're at Cait's," Josh informed his son once more. "You fell asleep during the movie, so Cait suggested we sleep over and finish it up in the morning before going to see Dr. Edwards. I'm sorry I didn't realize how good you are at sleeping with your eyes open to know you didn't hear me tell you that earlier."

"Wow, that's a true hidden talent," Cait giggled from the doorway, apparently having thrown on her PJ's before following him to check on JoJo. "Think you can teach me how to do that, so I can nap through the next time Mikey practices one of his school lectures on poetry?"

JoJo just shook his head into Josh's chest, though Josh wasn't sure Cait could see his response. He looked over his shoulder at her and arched an eyebrow. "Not a fan of poetry, Sunshine?"

"Some poetry is okay," Cait shrugged. "But the last time Mikey had me and Brody sit and act as his students, it was a lesson on Edgar Allan Poe. And I'm not really a fan of his work. So, I would have loved to be able to sleep with my eyes open like JoJo to keep from hearing it while still giving Mikey an audience to practice with."

"I don't know how to teach you, though." JoJo finally pulled out of his father's arms to look over at Cait. "But I can be his audience next time, so you don't have to. Dad will too, won't you Dad?"

"Sure," Josh chuckled, surprised at how Cait didn't even have to come into the room to get JoJo's mind off his nightmares a thousand times faster than he'd been able to accomplish it the last couple of weeks.

"Oh, well, if you guys are going to be his audience, then I want to be there too." Cait grinned mischievously. "Mikey says he only needs to have an audience to practice his lectures like a speech, but I think he needs to prepare for dealing with the naughty kids who pass notes and act out in class. And I think you guys will be a lot better at helping me with that than Brody has in the past. You know, since you're both experts at joshin' around."

"We are both named Josh, so it's kinda in our blood to be experts at joshin' around," Josh teased as JoJo nodded in agreement. "But it's a little late for much of that right now, so we should probably all go back to bed and sleep for a few more hours."

"Can we go home to sleep?" JoJo looked up at Josh tentatively before turning to look at Cait. "We don't have pajamas here, and we need to put on our pajamas to sleep."

Josh realized then that JoJo was holding the blanket at his waist, obviously uncomfortable with the possibility of Cait seeing his underwear. *Damn it. I should have thought about him being old enough to know that private parts need to be covered up around girls.* "Yeah, we can go home to sleep."

"I'll, uh, just go to the kitchen to give you guys some privacy to get dressed." Cait pointed over her shoulder with her thumb before turning and walking away. "Goodnight, guys. See you in the morning."

Fuck! I hate not being able to spend the whole night with her, especially right after our first time making love. But surely, she understands I have to do what's best for JoJo right now.

"Where are my jeans?"

"Over on the dresser," Josh automatically answered, standing and planning to go get his t-shirt and phone from Cait's room. "And your shoes and socks are on the floor right beside it. I'm gonna go get my shirt and stuff while you get dressed."

"Okay, Dad."

Josh walked out of the room, closing the door behind him to give his son the privacy to get out of bed and get dressed. He went to Cait's room for his shirt and phone, stuffing the other two condoms from the bedside table in his pants pocket as soon as he got the music app turned off and his phone in the back pocket not already holding his wallet. He put his shirt on as he walked down the hall to find Cait in the kitchen, where he'd left his boots and socks beside the back door.

"I'm sorry, Sunshine," Josh apologized for his sudden departure as he pulled her into his arms for an agonizingly brief moment.

Cait wrapped her arms around his waist, returning the embrace. "Nothing to be sorry for, Josh. JoJo's needs are our top priority right now. And I completely understand that he's not ready for sleepovers just yet."

Leah Mae Wright

"You are an amazing woman, Caitir Skye," *Burleson. Fuck, I can't wait to give her my last name. But I've gotta get JoJo's last name changed to Burleson before I can start workin' on changin' Cait's.*

Hopefully, it won't take too much longer before my son's ready for both of those changes.

Chapter Nineteen

Cait was nervous as she walked into Dr. Edwards' office with Josh and JoJo. Not because of being in a public place in San Antonio, but because she was afraid they might have screwed up by trying to have a sleepover the night before, when JoJo wasn't ready for another change in his home life while custody and his primary residence were still up in the air. *It's no wonder he woke up and screamed last night. After all the other changes in his life, I'm sure it's scary as hell to wake up in an unfamiliar place. We should have stuck to the routine of Josh carrying him to the bedroom he's used to sleeping in, so the trauma of waking up in a strange room wouldn't have happened. Now it'll probably take him twice as long before he's comfortable having a sleepover with his cousins or friends, not just at my place.*

It didn't take long after Josh got them checked in for Dr. Ariel Edwards to call them back to her office. Her office was bigger than Cait expected, having only ever seen the area behind Ariel's desk during their telehealth appointments. In addition to the desk with two chairs in front of it, there was a separate section with a sofa and a couple more chairs in a seating area around a coffee table, and a corner off to the side of the sofa with a Lego table, several toys, and small children's chairs for Ariel's youngest patients.

Cait was tempted to ask which of them was supposed to lay on the couch, but decided it probably wasn't the best time to joke around.

"It's so good to see you in person, Cait," Dr. Edwards greeted her with a smile, as she and Josh took a seat on the sofa, while JoJo beelined to the Lego table.

"I told you these guys are working miracles with getting me out and about," Cait smiled back at the psychologist.

"Yes, you said something last week about the Alamo and flying," Ariel nodded.

"Cait's gonna fly with us again this weekend when we go to Virginia," JoJo announced, grinning up at them for a moment before going back to whatever he was building with the Legos.

"Oh, really?" Dr. Edwards' eyes widened as she looked at Cait, obviously surprised at Cait planning to go on the trip.

"Yes, Josh needs someone to stay with JoJo while he takes care of some things on base, and if JoJo isn't allowed in the courtroom during the custody hearing," Cait explained as Josh squeezed her hand supportively. "And I figured staying at his or his brother's apartment won't be too much different than staying at home on the ranch. Plus, it'll probably be easier for me to go out in public in a state where I don't have bad memories, or haven't heard about the cartel that hurt my family being in the area."

"And you're sure you're prepared for such a major undertaking?" Dr. Edwards maintained a placid expression, not showing any signs of being confident Cait could handle the trip, but also not showing any doubts.

Cait looked back and forth between Josh and JoJo, reassuring herself that she could do it for the two of them. While she knew most people would say that it was healthier to find her own well of inner strength as she healed from her mental scars, she knew herself well enough to know that her true strength came from the people she loved. She'd never been intrinsically motivated, always able to accomplish more when she was doing things for the people she loved than if she was doing them for herself. Just as Mikey and Brody motivated her to leave the comfort zone of their house in San Diego to move to Texas, now Josh and JoJo were motivating her to leave her new comfort zone to be by their sides. "Yes."

"And we're going up this weekend to give her some time to feel comfortable before I have to report to base on Monday," Josh filled the doctor in on the backup plan he'd set up that morning. "Plus, my youngest brother and his family are joining us in Alexandria on Monday evening. So, if it's too much for Cait, Anthony can fly her back home, while Kay stays with the kids while I'm in court."

Cait felt terrible that morning when Josh first told her about the arrangements he'd made with his family to be there as her backup, thinking she was ruining their time off from the GWA by trying to take such a major step to get past her fears. But then Josh had filled her in on the other members of his family, who planned to take off work to be in Virginia to support him in court, so she knew their plans weren't being altered just for her. Becky, Jen, Julie, JJ, Bob, and Hazel were also planning to be there. And of course, Jake, who lived in Alexandria.

Cait had been surprised to hear that Bob and Hazel were going to Virginia, considering Hazel had been looking for a nanny to go instead of her watching JoJo. But apparently, they had to go to the hearing in case they were needed to represent the Madeline Ashbury Foundation, since it was technically their house that JoJo was currently residing in, thanks to the DFACS social worker in Texas, who approved his living arrangements on the night of the wedding when JoJo first arrived in Heart's Destiny.

Bobby and Brooklyn would have gone to represent the Ashbury Foundation for their part in helping Josh get temporary custody of JoJo, but with Brooklyn's due date looming, they weren't leaving Heart's Destiny to even go into San Antonio, much less attempting to fly to Virginia. Justin and Amy would have also planned to be there to support Josh, but Amy's doctor insisted she couldn't fly after the thirty-week mark in her pregnancy because of the risk of early delivery with her carrying twins. Jon and Susan would have planned to go as well, but with Bob and Hazel going, they had to stay to cover their responsibilities to Burleson Incorporated and the ranch.

The only other members of the Burleson family not going to support Josh and JoJo were Mikey, Charlotte, and Brody. But after taking off work for their honeymoon, Mikey and Charlotte couldn't take another week off from the middle school so soon. Apparently, it had been difficult to get a substitute for both English teachers at the school during their honeymoon, so the principal had informed them that they could only be off work on the same days if they gave her ample time to find subs. So, in addition to covering the cooking that Hazel normally did for the ranch hands, Susan and Rosa would be watching Brody while Mikey and Char were at work.

"Well, then it sounds like you're taking the right precautions," Dr. Edwards smiled at Cait and Josh, her eyes dropping momentarily to their joined hands. "But please make sure you have my number with

you, so you can call me if you need to talk while you're gone." She
then turned to look over at JoJo. "And what do you think about Cait
going with you, JoJo?"

"It's way better than Memmaw hiring a nanny to come with us,"
JoJo stated without looking up from the tower of Legos he was
building. "She's one of my extra moms like my mom told me about,
so she needs to be there to talk to the judge, too."

Extra moms? Having not heard him use the term before, Cait
wondered what JoJo was talking about, but she didn't get the chance to
ask because Dr. Edwards did it for them.

"What did your mom tell you about *extra moms*?"

"That once she went to Heaven, Aunt Tawny and my dad's wife or
girlfriend would be my extra moms," JoJo explained matter-of-factly.
"That she would always be my mom, but once she couldn't be here to
take care of me anymore, they'd love me like she does, and do the
stuff a mom normally does."

"And what are you supposed to call your extra moms?"

JoJo tilted his head at Dr. Edwards then, obviously confused by her
question.

"Are you supposed to call them Mom?"

"No, silly," JoJo laughed as he shook his head and went back to
building the tower of Legos. "I'm supposed to call them by their
names. Mom's the only person I'm supposed to call Mom. They
didn't carry me in their belly when I was a baby, so they aren't really
my mom. Just extra people who love me like a mom."

"What's the difference between your *extra moms* and when you and
Brody were talking about his *new mom*?" Cait couldn't stop herself
from blurting the question, still confused about the different things
JoJo had said over the past couple of weeks. Specifically wondering
about the evil stepmom comments from the first day she met him.

"Brody's still little," JoJo shrugged, not looking up from the Legos.
"I didn't want to confuse him by telling him that Aunt Char's his extra
mom, not his new mom. You can't replace your mom and dad, but
you can have extras of both."

*Okay, so maybe all the comparisons between me and Jaina aren't
his way of trying to cast me in her role. And hopefully, he doesn't see
me as an evil stepmom, since he seems happy to call me his "extra
mom" along with Jaina's friend Tawny.*

"Do you have an extra dad we need to see while we're in Virginia?" Josh's grip on her hand tightened as he asked the question, making Cait wonder if he was worried about yet another person who might fight him for custody of JoJo. Or if he was jealous of the men who might have had a role in Jaina and JoJo's life over the last few years.

"No," JoJo smiled as he looked up at his dad. "Just you, Dad."

"Your mom never had a boyfriend to be your extra dad?" Cait was grateful for Dr. Edwards voicing the question she wanted answered, but didn't feel was appropriate for her to be the one to ask.

"She had a couple of boyfriends," JoJo sighed, focusing back on the tower he was building, like he was ashamed to look any of them in the eyes as he continued. "But none of them liked me enough to wanna be my extra dad."

"Then they were dumb," Cait blurted, unable to stand seeing JoJo hurt by the rejection he'd felt at the hands of Jaina's former fuck buddies. And that's all she assumed they were, since anyone who truly wanted a relationship with Jaina would have had to love JoJo. "You're the most loveable kid I've ever met, so if they didn't love you from the first moment they met you like I did, then they weren't worthy of being your extra dads."

JoJo looked up at Cait and smiled. "That's what Mom said, too. That none of the men she dated after Dad were worthy of being my extra dad."

"You've pointed out a lot of similarities between your mom and Cait." Dr. Edwards took over the conversation with JoJo once more, finally asking about the issue Cait had been most concerned about. "How do those things make you feel?"

"I don't know," JoJo shrugged, looking down at the block in his hand.

"Do they make you miss your mom more? Or do they help you remember the good times with her, so you can smile instead of being sad?"

Cait hadn't even thought of the possibility of those similarities helping JoJo with his grief the way Dr. Edwards just mentioned.

"They make me smile." JoJo backed up his statement by looking up at them with a bright grin. "And they prove Mom was right when she said that Dad has a type of girl he likes."

"I guess I did and just didn't know it until I met Cait," Josh chuckled, running his free hand through his hair as he conceded the point that he and JoJo had been lightheartedly arguing about since the first day Josh had introduced JoJo to Cait. "But I didn't know Jaina long enough to really see the similarities."

The similarities between me and Jaina? Or the qualities in me that he could have fallen for in Jaina if he'd spent more than an evening with her nine years ago?

As they finished out the session, Cait really started to feel more comfortable with how JoJo saw her having a place in his life. He had a much better understanding of the love shared by kids and their non-biological parental figures than she had at his age. And she was certain that they could have a strong, loving stepmom-stepson relationship in the future.

Unfortunately, she started to wonder if Josh's feelings for her were as true and strong as her love for him. *Would we be together at all if Jaina was still alive? Or would he have seen her again and picked her over me? Maybe he just thinks he's in love with me because I'm so similar to the mother of his child?*

Not that she could voice her concerns in the current therapy session with JoJo present. She wasn't even sure she could ask him about them when they were alone. At least, not before the trip to Virginia.

There's no way I'm going to take a chance on causing a fight that might make him change his mind about me going with them. Whether Josh really loves me or not, I love him and JoJo enough to be there to support them when they need me. Even if it'll lead to more pain from my broken heart if, or more likely when, Josh realizes he's not really in love with me.

But when we get back from Virginia, we're going to have to schedule some sessions with Dr. Edwards that are just for me and Josh. No matter how much I love him and want us to be a family, I don't want to be with him if he's just settling for second best because he can't be with Jaina.

~~~
~~~

The last few days felt strained, and even flying all day to take Cait and JoJo to Virginia wasn't enough to settle Josh's nerves. Surprisingly, he wasn't worried about the upcoming court appearance. But more so that the trip was pushing Cait too far outside her comfort zone and causing her strange behavior for the past few days. *Fuck! I hope Anthony doesn't have to fly her back to Texas as soon as we get to Alexandria on Monday.*

He'd thought their group therapy session on Tuesday had settled the last of her concerns about JoJo slotting her in as a substitute for his mom and would make things easier for them moving forward as a family. And when he looked back at the interactions between Cait and JoJo since then, it was obvious that it had in some ways.

But when he and Cait were able to sneak in some couple time, Josh felt a sense of desperation in every kiss and touch from Cait that he hadn't felt before. Oh, he still felt the urgent need to fuck her every chance he got and had taken advantage of his parents watching the boys, so they could sneak off to the hayloft as often as he could get away with it. But there was something different about Cait's kisses and her eagerness for them to make love each time now that he couldn't quite figure out.

Fuck! It was like she thought every time we've been together since Tuesday was gonna be the last time between us or something. And the only reason I can think of that might be making her think that is this trip.

I don't know if she's afraid she's gonna have a panic attack, or if she's afraid the judge will insist I move to Virginia to be able to see JoJo. But it's obviously something about this trip that has her spooked. Hell, maybe she's afraid she'll have a panic attack in front of the judge and cost me custody of JoJo? I don't know, but whatever it is, I need to get her to talk to me about it tonight, so I can put her mind at ease.

Whatever was bothering Cait, Josh knew it wasn't something she'd want to discuss in front of JoJo. Otherwise, she would have brought it up in their family therapy sessions earlier in the week. So, he planned to wait until JoJo was asleep in his guest room to bring it up.

Hell, maybe I should switch half our family sessions to couple's sessions when we get back to Texas.

Josh wasn't allowing himself to think about possibly having to move to Virginia for more than a week or two while going through the Alexandria Juvenile and Domestic Relations District Court to get custody of his son. With everything his Avington cousins had sent him about the Joneses and Tawny Ireland, he was ninety-nine percent sure he'd be awarded primary custody of JoJo. They might have to take trips once or twice a month for JoJo to visit with his maternal grandparents and honorary aunt, but he didn't really think the judge would order them to live in Virginia full-time to share custody with any of them.

So, when he scheduled therapy sessions for him and JoJo, he only asked to skip the one week when he knew he'd be in Virginia. And he hadn't changed that request when Dr. Edwards agreed that it would be most beneficial for Cait to join them in the sessions. But now that he knew what the group sessions would be like, he realized that he and Cait might benefit from having a few sessions without little ears listening in on their more adult conversations.

Thank fuck, SEAL team two is deployed right now, Josh thought as he parked his 2018 gunmetal gray Chevrolet Equinox in his assigned parking space at his apartment in Virginia Beach. *If they were here to see me now, they'd be merciless with pickin' on me about going to couple's counseling so soon after getting together with Cait.*

"Wow, I thought we were going to the beach," Cait giggled, looking around at the trees surrounding the nondescript brown buildings of the apartment complex as they got out of the SUV. "Not going to the middle of the woods."

"We're actually not too far from several beaches," Josh informed her as he got their suitcases out of the back of the vehicle. "Chesapeake Bay is a little closer than the Atlantic, but we can go check out both tomorrow, since I've already packed up everything but what we'll need while we're here."

"Yeah, I'm still confused by why you packed up most of your kitchen stuff, when you knew you'd have to stay here for another day or two." Cait rolled her eyes at him as she passed him before carrying their fast-food bags for dinner up the stairs, where he directed her and JoJo to his apartment.

"It's not like back home, where there are other people around to cook," Josh shrugged, hating not being able to look at her heart-shaped ass any longer as he stepped around her and unlocked the door. "So, I usually eat out and only have a few dishes here, not a fully stocked kitchen like you. And I figured it was easier to go ahead and pack everything but my bedding and electronics, so I don't have to do much on Monday after signing my discharge papers to be able to ship all my stuff home."

"Are you shipping your car home, too?" JoJo looked at him in confusion as he walked past Josh into the apartment.

"Yeah, buddy," Josh nodded at his son, who walked over to the small table in the section of the space designated as a dining room and sat down the drink holder he was carrying. "It won't exactly fit on the plane, so I picked a shipping company located at the airport where I normally keep the plane to send everything back to the ranch without having to get a rental car here."

Josh turned to Cait and addressed the obvious question in her eyes before she could even open her mouth to ask. "And yes, Sunshine, I already have a rental car lined up for when we fly to Alexandria on Monday."

"Dad's smart. He plans for everything." JoJo beamed as he looked around the small, combined spaces of the living room, dining room, and kitchen. "Which of those doors goes to my room?"

"The one straight ahead." Josh pointed at the three-foot-by-three-foot space he didn't consider big enough to call a hallway. "The door on the left is my room and the door on the right is the bathroom. Sorry, there's only one bathroom that we've all gotta share, but I'm not used to having anyone but Jake come stay with me here."

"It'll be fine, I'm sure." Cait smiled as she placed the food bags on the table beside their drinks and looked at the two boxes of kitchen stuff he had stacked in the corner. "We don't have a timetable for tomorrow, and JoJo and I can wait until after you leave to go to base on Monday to shower and stuff."

Josh just smiled at how Cait was already planning for them to work around the limitations of his small living quarters. He carried their suitcases to the bedrooms, dropping JoJo's in the guest room and his and Cait's in his bedroom. He only paused long enough in his bedroom to hang the garment bags with their dress clothes for court in the closet. He didn't think JoJo would mess with the gun safe he kept in his spare bedroom, but just in case the boy got curious, he took the time to double-check that the weapons inside were all unloaded before he relocked the safe.

Maybe when I talked to him about the sleeping arrangements here, I should have reminded him about our earlier talks about weapon safety and not touching the ones in my room on the ranch to make sure he knows that goes for all weapons and not just back at home.

After their failed attempt at a sleepover at Cait's earlier in the week, Josh had spent some time talking to JoJo about the sleeping arrangements while they were in Virginia. Primarily, he wanted to make sure his son didn't have a repeat of the fear he'd experienced waking up in a strange room. But he also wanted to prepare JoJo for seeing him and Cait in bed together, in case he walked in on them after a nightmare.

Fuck! I hope he continues on the trend he's been on for the past couple of nights and doesn't have any more of those episodes while we're here. But considering how frequent they were during his first couple of weeks in Texas and the stress of going to court this week, I'm pretty sure they're gonna come back with a vengeance while we're here.

Guess we'll just have to make sure we're quick with any naked time and put some PJ's on before actually going to sleep.

Since his table only had chairs for two, they ended up sitting on the sofa and streaming a Disney movie while they ate dinner. At eight-thirty, Josh instructed JoJo to go brush his teeth and get ready for bed. Again, he was trying to keep JoJo from waking up in an unfamiliar environment by having him go to bed while he was still wide awake, instead of letting him fall asleep during the movie and carrying him to bed. Their new routine seemed to work better for preventing the little boy's nightmares back on the ranch, so he hoped it would work in Virginia, too.

"Do I get to read to Cait tonight, too?" JoJo grinned as he came out of the bedroom in his *Avengers* pajamas a few minutes later.

Having JoJo read to him was another thing they'd added to their bedtime routine the last few days. Josh had originally planned to read to JoJo, but he quickly learned his son felt he was too old for bedtime stories. Since JoJo was advanced enough to read chapter books, Josh found that they had just enough time between brushing his teeth at eight-thirty and bedtime at nine for one or two chapters a night.

"I would love for you to read to me," Cait beamed, standing from the sofa to follow JoJo and Josh back to the bedroom.

"Do we need to start over, so you know what's going on? Or just read the next chapter?" JoJo looked to Cait to answer his question as he climbed into bed and picked up the book they'd just started a couple of days earlier.

"I haven't read that one before, but I hate to ask you to read the chapters you've already read again. Can you just tell me about what I missed before you go on with reading where you left off?" Cait sat down on one side of JoJo while Josh sat on his son's other side.

"It's about a boy like me who hasn't met his dad yet. But his dad's a spy and sends him secret messages to keep from blowing his cover," JoJo started, giving a thorough overview of the first few chapters of the book before reading the next one to them. Because of the detailed description JoJo gave, they only had time for one chapter that night before his bedtime rolled around. But since the boy was yawning, he didn't balk at calling it a night when Josh informed him it was time for lights out.

After goodnight hugs, Josh and Cait went back to his living room, with Josh thinking it was the perfect time to talk while waiting for JoJo to go to sleep before moving to the bedroom for the night. Unfortunately, Cait seemed to think it was time to pick up the cups that still sat on the coffee table after dinner.

"Hey, come sit down, Sunshine," Josh commanded, reaching out to grab her hand and pull her down onto the couch beside him. "Our empty cups are fine for now."

"Don't we need to wait until JoJo's asleep before we start doing, um, other things he shouldn't overhear?" Cait's eyes widened as she tilted her head in the direction of the bedroom doors, making it obvious what she thought he intended for them to do on the sofa.

"Yeah, but we can put another movie on, so he can't hear us talking," Josh suggested, grabbing the remote and switching the streaming service over to a Marvel movie, knowing the musical accompaniment and sound effects during the action scenes would drown out their voices, even if he turned the volume down to keep from disturbing the downstairs neighbors. "And I think we need to talk before we go to bed and do those *other things*."

Josh grinned and wagged his eyebrows to emphasize his last two words, making Cait giggle a little as she relaxed on the sofa beside him.

"And what exactly do you think we need to talk about, Cowboy?" Cait purred in the sultry tone usually reserved for when they were wearing fewer clothes.

Josh's cock instantly responded to the sexy way she used his call sign. *Not now, Cap. You've gotta wait 'til after we find out what's goin' on in her head lately.*

When Josh's inner thoughts didn't deflate his dick, he switched to thinking about his SEAL team to try to get it under control.

Thank fuck, I'm not going on any more missions as a SEAL. It'd be damn inconvenient to get a hard-on from thinking about the way Cait calls me Cowboy every time one of the guys used my call sign on a mission. Hell, if any of them actually come for a visit once they get home from this deployment, I'll hafta tell them they can't use it anymore 'cause it's reserved for my girl from now on.

"I just wanna make sure everything's okay with you." Josh held her hand between both of his, so he could feel her pulse at her wrist under his fingertips as a way to judge her response to their talk. "You've seemed on edge the past few days, so I need to know what's goin' on to be able to fix whatever's botherin' you."

"It's nothing." Cait shook her head, unable to make eye contact with him as the pulsing in her wrist with each heartbeat sped up.

"It's something," Josh contradicted her, knowing she was hiding something from him. "So, don't lie and tell me it's nothing. Just tell me what's wrong, so we can fix it together."

"It's stupid," Cait sighed, pulling her hand from his and flopping back on the opposite end of the couch from Josh.

Josh didn't let her retreat dissuade him, turning to face her, and pulling her feet up into his lap, so he could rub her feet while they continued talking. "I highly doubt you've been all worked up about something stupid, Sunshine. So, just tell me what it is."

"I'm just having a hard time believing that what we feel for each other is real," Cait finally confessed, still not looking him in the eyes. "And when you said something in our therapy session the other day about not realizing you have a type until you met me, it made me wonder if you actually fell for Jaina years ago, and just thought it was love at first sight with me because of all the similarities JoJo keeps pointing out between us."

Fuck! I've really gotta start thinking before I speak, so she doesn't get any more dumb ideas like that again. Starting with not telling her that she's been worked up for a stupid reason. Her feelings are valid, even if I don't think there's a legit reason for them.

"So, it made me wonder if we'd even be together if Jaina was still alive," Cait continued, her voice low and mournful, as Josh kneaded the balls of her feet with his thumbs. "And that made me wonder if what we think we feel will really last or if we'll break up when someone else who's more like her comes along and catches your eye. Someone without all my baggage, who doesn't have to talk herself down from a panic attack every time you want to go someplace new in public."

"Oh, Sunshine," Josh sighed, pulling her feet around his waist to slide her up on his lap. He released her feet to take her hands and pulled her up into a seated position, so he could hold her in his arms. "How many times do I have to tell you that I've only felt that lightning strike of true love with you before you believe me?"

Cait shrugged as she slipped her arms around him and leaned into his embrace.

Josh pressed his forehead to hers, wanting to kiss her, but knowing they needed to finish this talk first. "As I told you before, I barely remember meeting Jaina. I didn't feel a fraction of what I feel for you when I hooked up with her. Yeah, I'll always be grateful to her for giving me a son. But even if she was still alive and your identical twin, I'd never choose her over you."

"Oh, please, like you could tell the difference between me and my hypothetical identical twin," Cait scoffed, rolling her eyes.

"I'm sure I could," Josh assured her, pecking her lips with his. "If you don't believe me, ask Justin. He'll tell you all about how he only gets that tingly feeling we get when our soulmate enters our space with Amy, and not her identical twin. Hell, next time they're in town, Randi and Allissa will probably tell you the same thing about the Hunters. And they're so close to identical that when we were kids, I could only tell them apart based on which one of them spoke while other people were around."

"That's how I tell them apart now," Cait giggled. "Well, unless Randi or Allissa are around. Then it's easy based on which woman they can't take their eyes off of."

"True," Josh chuckled. "But you get my point, right? There aren't enough similarities between you and anyone else for me to confuse my feelings between you. I'm in love with you. Only you. And won't ever fall in love with anyone else but you, Caitir Skye Campbell. And the only things I ever wanna change about you are your marital status and last name."

"Josh," Cait gasped, looking surprised at his declaration.

"I know you're not ready to marry me," Josh acknowledged, giving her another peck of a kiss. "Yet. But I'm patient enough to wait to change your name to Caitir Skye Burleson." Josh paused to let his words sink in before adding. "At least, I think I can wait until we get JoJo's last name changed to Burleson and get him moved to the ranch for good first. But as soon as that's all done, I'm probly gonna start trying to talk you into marryin' me sooner rather than later."

<p style="text-align:center">~~~</p>

Holy shit! Holy shit! Holy shit! Cait mentally flipped out, unable to respond to Josh's declaration that he wanted to marry her. It took all her willpower not to agree on the spot, letting go of all her doubts about their love for one another. But as much as she wanted to skip straight to happily ever after with Josh, she knew they needed to take their time and do a few more family therapy sessions with JoJo to make sure he was totally on board with them getting married and living together as a family.

"Yeah, well, you're going to have to do a lot better than that with your proposal, if you ever expect me to say yes," Cait declared, placing her hands on Josh's shoulders, pushing back from him slightly, and grinning mischievously. "And it'll probably take quite a few sexual favors between now and then to convince me."

"Oh really?" Josh grinned and arched an eyebrow as he pulled her in close enough to feel the rod in his jeans pressed against her core.

390

Geez, I still can't believe how much bigger he gets when he's not confined by his jeans. Or how well all of him fits inside me.

"Really," Cait confirmed, wiggling in his lap to tease him a little more.

"Then I should probly get started on those now," Josh drawled, his colloquial pronunciation of "probably" coming out as he reached over and clicked off the television.

Cait had to admit, even if only to herself, that she found his Texas twang far more arousing than any of the foreign accents she'd thought sounded sexy before meeting Josh. Even the way he dropped the g on a lot of words, and mispronounced a few others, sounded hot coming from his lips.

After he tossed the remote on the coffee table, Josh gripped her hips, lifting her with him as he stood. Cait instinctually wrapped her arms and legs around him to keep from falling, even though she knew Josh would never drop her, as he carried her into his bedroom. With her wrapped around him like a monkey clinging to a tree, he couldn't exactly throw her on the bed, so they both flopped down, with him landing on top of her. As she opened her mouth to remind him to shut the bedroom door, Josh cut off her words with a claiming kiss.

As she always did when Josh got his lips on her, Cait melted against him, reveling in the possessive way he kissed her while also seeming gentle and romantic. When he traced his tongue over the seam of her lips, she opened her mouth, eagerly allowing him entry.

Cait forgot for a moment that the bedroom door was standing wide open, returning Josh's kiss with equal ardor as she ran her hands over the muscular planes of his back. Luckily, hearing a door shut in the apartment below them was enough to bring her out of her Josh-induced lust fog long enough to remember the need for that barrier between them and little ears.

"Josh, we have to shut the bedroom door," Cait breathed out the words as she turned her head and pushed on his shoulders to break the kiss. "What if JoJo gets up to go to the bathroom one more time before going to sleep?"

"I'm sure he's asleep by now," Josh groaned, pecking her lips once more before pushing up off of her. "But I'll shut the door, just to be safe."

Josh walked backwards to the door, not taking his eyes off of her as he found the door, shut it, and locked it. The way he ate her up with his eyes made her feel more attractive than she'd ever felt before in her life, even when she was modeling and had flirty photographers trying to pull sexy looks from her.

Cait crab-walked to the center of the bed, glad they'd removed their shoes before sitting down to eat, as Josh stalked back over toward her with a predatory gleam in his hazel eyes.

"Now I get to do what I missed out on Monday night." Josh pulled his phone from his pocket and fiddled with it momentarily before placing it on a charger on his bedside table. Cait wasn't sure what he'd done on his phone to generate the soft, country music playing from the Bluetooth speakers on his bedside tables, but she was glad for the added buffer of the music to cover the sounds she knew they would soon be making.

"What did you miss out on Monday night?" Cait tried to think of what he might have done later if he'd stayed after JoJo woke up, assuming he meant cuddling after they made love and not helping her change the sheets.

"Kissing every inch of you as I slowly undress you," Josh crooned as he slid onto his belly beside her on the bed, stopping when his head reached her waist. He gradually pushed her t-shirt up, trailing his lips over every part of her abdomen that he exposed before moving the shirt a little further.

"Oh, Josh, I don't know if I have the patience for this," Cait moaned, loving the feel of the butterfly kisses he continued to deliver as she ran her hands up and down his powerful arms.

"I think you can handle it, Sunshine." Josh's warm breath tickled over her belly button. "And if not, then I'll just tie you to the headboard, so you have to wait for me to finish exploring every," *kiss*, "delicate," *kiss*, "sexy," *kiss*, "inch of you."

Josh continued trailing his lips over her body as he took his time undressing her. Cait moaned in pleasure, eagerly trying to lift Josh's t-shirt as soon as he moved far enough up her body that she could reach the hem. Not that he let her slide it up very far before he pulled her arms from around him and placed them up over her head.

"Hold onto the headboard, Sunshine," Josh commanded as he deftly unfastened her bra.

Cait did as he directed, arching her back as he lightly grazed her breasts with the edge of his teeth. She was so focused on the way he worshiped her breasts that she didn't realize he slid the straps of her bra down to her wrists, and somehow twisted them and her t-shirt to bind her wrists, before fastening the bra around the slats in the headboard to hold her in place.

Cait wiggled her hands, assessing how thoroughly he'd bound her. *Wow, that's actually pretty comfortable,* she thought, realizing he'd only twisted her clothes around her wrists tight enough to make her feel confined, but loose enough that she could easily escape if she turned her head to look at what she was doing. *But I probably should have expected that from Gentleman Josh. He's always going to make sure I'm comfortable, even when we're being kinky.*

"No fair, Cowboy," Cait whined half-heartedly as Josh leisurely sucked one nipple before trailing his tongue through the valley between her breasts to repeat the erotic torture on the other nipple. "I didn't think you could tie me up without the rope you left on the ranch."

"I'm more resourceful than that." Josh grinned around her breast as he gently nibbled her nipple. He released the soft bite to suck her whole areola into his mouth, pulling off with a pop before wagging his eyebrows and continuing. "Besides, your t-shirt is much softer and provides enough padding to keep from leaving abrasions like the rope on the ranch would. But if you wanna try a little rope play, maybe we can get some made from silk or somethin' that won't mar your soft skin."

"Yes, please," Cait moaned, writhing beneath him as Josh moved to repeat the nibble and suck routine on her other breast. "But don't I need a safe word for stuff like this?"

"For now, your safe word is stop," Josh instructed, kissing his way up her neck. "Or no, or don't, or any other word you might use to object to what I'm doing."

"Yeah, those won't work," Cait snorted as Josh stopped her from laughing with a kiss.

"They'll work just fine, Sunshine," Josh disagreed when he finally broke the kiss to move his mouth back over her neck and shoulders, nipping, licking, and sucking places on her body she never knew were erogenous zones.

"But what if I'm really into what you're doing," Cait argued in a breathy tone. "And begging you to continue comes out as, 'Please. Don't. Stop. Josh.'?" She deliberately paused between each breathlessly moaned-out word to make her point clear.

"Fuck," Josh groaned, rocking his hips between her thighs in a crude imitation of making love while their jeans and her panties still separated them. "Then I guess you'd better hurry up and pick a safe word, Sunshine."

Cait was too caught up in the wonderful sensations Josh was creating in her body with his mouth and hands running all over her upper body to be able to think of a creative safe word right then. "How 'bout we stick to the stoplight system?"

"Like green means go, yellow means slow down and prepare to stop, and red means stop immediately?" Josh didn't stop teasing her with his tongue as he slid down the bed and started playing with the button on her jeans.

"Yes," Cait breathed out her agreement as she wiggled her hips to try to get him to remove her jeans faster. "And right now, I'm greener than the grass before you cut it to make hay."

"Guess it's a good thing we cut it before the yellow seed heads sprout," Josh chuckled, finally unbuttoning her jeans. He slowly lowered the zipper, trailing the tip of his tongue down her lower abdomen about an inch behind where he was unzipping, until he got to the top of her light blue lace panties. "'Cause I don't think you want me to go any slower."

"No, don't slow down," Cait pleaded. "Bright, emerald, green." Cait almost added, "like the outer part of your irises," but she feared any mention of his eyes would lead to him pointing out that the gold starburst around his pupils was in the yellow color spectrum. "And that kind of green means go, go, go," she whisper-shouted, trying not to be so loud that she woke JoJo.

"Considering you're so soaked that you made a wet spot on your jeans, maybe I should slow down just long enough to prepare the bed before I finish undressing you," Josh smirked as he stood and walked out of the room. When he returned, he was carrying a gray bath towel, which he dropped on the bed beside Cait after shutting and relocking the bedroom door.

"Is that to keep me from having to wash the sheets daily while we're here?" Cait arched an eyebrow as Josh walked on his knees back into place on the bed.

"Somethin' like that," Josh chuckled and finally pulled her jeans and panties down in one fell swoop. As soon as she was naked, Josh opened up the towel, so it was only folded in half before lifting Cait's legs and sliding it under her hips, protecting the bedding from the base of her spine down to her knees. "But since you're already dripping for me, I guess I'll save learning your lower body for tomorrow night, Sunshine."

"Yes, tomorrow," Cait panted as Josh stood up and reached over his head with one hand to remove his royal blue t-shirt in that sexy way that she'd only read about in romance novels before meeting Josh.

Before his t-shirt could even hit the floor where he dropped it, Josh shoved his jeans down, freeing his gloriously long, thick dick. Cait had never thought male genitalia was particularly appealing in the past. Of course, the college boys she'd been with before weren't packing nearly as much heat as Josh.

His cock was beautiful, standing tall and erect with a slight curve toward his stomach that apparently allowed him to easily find her G-spot whenever they were facing one another while making love. He also manscaped, keeping the whole area neatly trimmed, so she wasn't deterred from wanting to taste him by long, unruly hair she didn't want to risk swallowing. Or inhaling.

"Maybe it's a good thing you tied me to the bed." Cait licked her lips to keep from drooling at the thought of sucking his miraculous member. "But one of these days, you're going to have to let me suck your cock before you get me so worked up that I can't wait to have you inside me."

"I don't think either one of us has the patience for that, Sunshine." Josh palmed his cock with one hand while opening the bedside table with the other. He quickly pulled out an unopened box of condoms, looking down as if he was reading it while removing the outer plastic from the box. After tossing the clear cellophane into the wastebasket beside the bed, he opened the box to pull out a single condom.

"Need to read the directions first, Cowboy?" Cait teased, grinning at him.

"No, Sunshine," Josh chuckled as he opened the gold foil wrapper and rolled the Magnum down his length. "Just making sure they aren't expired, since I bought them last year."

Cait knew Josh had told her he hadn't been with anyone else since the first time he met her back in December. But a small part of her hadn't really believed it until just then. Not that she had time to reflect on that as Josh crawled over her on the bed. He did a one-armed plank as he used his other hand to slide his tip through her folds.

"Wrap your legs around me, Sunshine," Josh commanded right before dipping his head and covering her mouth with his.

Cait followed his instructions as their tongues tangled in a passionate imitation of what she wanted him to do with his dick. She hooked her feet together at the top of his rock-hard butt, wishing her hands were free to grab two handfuls of his ass and pull him into her center.

They continued kissing as Josh worked his cock inside her one agonizing millimeter at a time. Cait desperately tried pulling him in faster with her legs, but Josh used his superior strength to maintain control of their coupling. He laughed into her mouth when she groaned her frustration at his tedious pace.

Cait turned her head to break their kiss, planning to beg him to move faster.

"Maybe I should call you Bunny, instead of Sunshine," Josh chuckled before she could even take a breath before speaking. "'Cause you're as impatient as a hare tonight."

"If you do, then I'm going to start calling you Turtle instead of Cowboy," Cait quipped, loving how they could laugh and joke with one another, even in the middle of making love. "Though if you don't hurry up and fuck me, I might just change it no matter what you call me."

"Guess I'd better find a happy medium then, huh, Sunny Bunny?" Josh grinned as he finally thrust all the way home.

Cait couldn't help but giggle in response. The laughter didn't last long, though, as Josh set a steady pace, stroking in and out and swiveling his hips at just the right point in each thrust to swipe the head of his cock over her G-spot. She rocked her hips to match his rhythm, feeling her orgasm building to epic proportions deep in her core.

"Oh Josh," she cried out softly as the first waves of her release washed over her. She dug her nails into her own palms, wishing her hands were free, so she could cling to Josh instead. "Yes, Josh, yes."

"That's it, Cait," Josh growled in a low tone against her ear as he lightly pinched her nipple with the hand not supporting his weight. "Come on my cock. I love how tight you squeeze me when you come."

Josh maintained his steady rhythm, extending her climax until one orgasm rolled into the next. Cait felt like she was floating away to another realm as her whole body convulsed in pleasure, flooding the towel under them as she rode wave after wave of orgasmic bliss.

"Oh, Josh. I. Love. You." Cait panted out each word in sync with the spasms wracking her body.

"I love you, Caitir," Josh growled as he thrust in all the way to the hilt, shuddering with his release.

Josh rolled them to their sides as the convulsions started to fade, maintaining their connection while they recovered. He reached up and deftly untied her wrists while kissing her passionately, as they floated back down from that state of nirvana that only Josh had ever taken her to.

Cait wrapped her arms around Josh, touching him the way she'd missed while being tied to the bed as she returned his amorous kiss.

Josh groaned as he released her lips and pulled back, reaching down to hold on to the condom as his only slightly deflated cock slipped from her body. "Damn, Sunshine, I hate havin' to pull out of you to deal with the condom."

Cait couldn't help but giggle at the forlorn look on Josh's face as he rolled off the bed to remove the condom. He tied it off and stepped back into his jeans, which he left unfastened as he quickly crossed the room and snuck across the short hallway to the bathroom, quietly pulling the bedroom door shut on his way out. Cait used the towel she was still laying on top of to wipe up the excess moisture between her legs, not realizing that Josh would return a few minutes later with a wet washcloth and a hand towel to clean her up.

"I, uh, already used that towel to clean up," Cait informed him as she sat up and twisted to dangle her legs off the side of the bed, preparing to get dressed for bed in case JoJo walked in on them as Josh expected.

"Well, then, I'll just make sure you didn't miss a spot," Josh grinned, wagging his eyebrows as he bent down and gently pushed her knees apart to wipe the washcloth over her sex. When he was finished making sure she was completely cleaned up and dried off, Josh brushed his lips over hers once more. "Now we need to hurry and get ready for bed before JoJo wakes up."

Cait appreciated his minty fresh breath, where he apparently brushed his teeth while he was in the bathroom dealing with the condom and cleaning himself up. *We probably should have both done that before we started kissing earlier. But I guess not minding that we both had burger breath while making love just proves how much we love each other.*

Cait couldn't contain her smile as she quickly put on her sleep shorts and matching tank top while watching Josh swap his jeans for a pair of sleep pants. As she walked across the hall to the bathroom to brush her teeth and wash her face before bed, Josh followed her to put the towels they'd dirtied in the hamper in the bathroom, along with their dirty clothes.

As soon as they were both done with everything they needed to do before bed, Josh turned off the music before wrapping her in his arms to sleep. "Goodnight, Sunshine."

"Goodnight, Josh." Cait snuggled in close, resting her head right over his heart to let the steady beat lull her to sleep.

Oh, yes, I could definitely get used to cuddling every night, Cait thought as she drifted off to dreamland, where Josh holding her while they slept peacefully was a nightly occurrence.

Unfortunately, they were awakened less than an hour later by JoJo knocking on the bedroom door. "Dad? Cait? Are you both still here?"

"Yeah, JoJo, we're here," Josh replied, sitting up to turn on the bedside lamp, just as JoJo peeked his head through the door.

"Can I have another hug, just to be sure I'm not dreaming you?" JoJo tentatively stepped into the room, wiping his eyes with the sides of his balled-up hands.

"Of course, Son." Josh opened his arms just in time for JoJo to launch himself onto the bed and into his father's arms.

They embraced for several long moments before JoJo pulled back and turned to look at Cait. "You too?"

"Absolutely," Cait agreed, sitting up and opening her arms to JoJo. He squeezed her tight, as she rubbed her hands up and down his back, hoping to soothe his fear of abandonment. She felt extremely honored to be included in the small group of people JoJo trusted to never desert him.

After another round of "goodnights" from each of them, JoJo went back to his bed. Josh turned the lamp back off, and they settled back into bed to sleep snuggled together for the rest of the night.

Before she drifted off to sleep the second time, Cait realized she felt more at home than she ever had before. Not because of the building she was in or the city she was in, but because she was in Josh's arms.

Chapter Twenty

Cait was proud of herself for how well she was doing on this trip with Josh and JoJo as she walked into the courtroom to support them during the first, and what she hoped would be the last, court appearance to grant Josh custody of JoJo. Oh, she knew the attorneys warned them that they could spend the rest of the week in court with three different parties petitioning for custody of JoJo. But even if it took them a couple of weeks of daily court appearances, she hoped this would be the only time they had to fly to Virginia before Josh gained custody of his son.

She'd been pleasantly surprised when they met with Josh's Virginia attorney the day before and had been instructed to bring JoJo to the hearing, so the judge could talk to him about where and with whom he wanted to live. While she was sure she'd have been fine alone with JoJo at Jake's apartment or the hotel where they ended up staying, she really felt like her place was by Josh's side to support him and JoJo during the court proceedings.

Considering the way things had gone the past couple of weeks with them spending all their free time together, and especially with the talk they'd had Saturday night, Cait was really starting to believe that she might get her happily ever after with Josh and JoJo, after all. She wasn't just babysitting him when JoJo spent his days with her and Brody while Josh worked on the ranch or met with his attorney. She'd also stepped up to help with his homeschool lessons, and spent quality time with just JoJo whenever Brody's parents had other plans for him, and Josh was otherwise occupied. She'd also spent every weekend going to the various attractions in South Texas with the man and little boy she wanted to officially claim as hers.

While she wasn't sure JoJo would ever be ready for her to adopt him the way Charlotte had adopted Brody when she married Mikey, Cait already felt like she'd stepped into the stepmom role because of everything she was already doing to help Josh in parenting JoJo. And she really didn't mind if JoJo only wanted to call her his "extra mom" for the rest of their lives. She was just honored to be allowed to have that role in his life.

The last month of having Josh and JoJo at home in Heart's Destiny had totally spoiled Cait. She felt like her days of feeling lonely while living alone among the Burlesons' extended family were over. At least, they could be, if the court hearing for custody of JoJo ended up the way she hoped, with Josh being granted full, permanent custody.

Would it be easier on JoJo if we live together before getting married? Maybe give him time to get used to the idea first? If so, how long should I wait before asking them to move into the house with me, so it'll finally feel like home for all of us? Cait wondered as she sat in the courtroom with Josh, JoJo, and several of the Burlesons, waiting for the judge to come into the room and their case to be called. *After the last couple of nights with him seeing us sharing a bed, surely, it won't be as big a deal for JoJo to convert the guestroom to his room and for us to make our home together? Will it?*

Or will he always have bad memories of that room after our disastrous sleepover attempt last week? Maybe I should ask Josh if he has plans to build a house on the ranch like the rest of his siblings and cousins are doing. If that's the case, maybe it'll be better if we wait to move in together after it's built? I can wait that long to feel at home every night when we go to bed, if it'll make things easier on JoJo.

Regardless of where we end up living, it should probably be a family discussion to make the transition as smooth for JoJo as we can. Would it be too soon for that discussion as soon as we get back to the ranch from this trip? Or should I wait until after the holidays to give them time to adjust after the legalities of their relationship are settled to bring up the possibility of sharing a home and truly living as a family?

She didn't get the chance to ponder her questions for long as an older couple stopped at the end of the bench, where she was sitting with JoJo between her and Josh at the end of one of the two benches of Burlesons there to support them. Josh was seated at the end of the bench, which she assumed was his way of positioning himself to protect them from anyone walking up the center aisle.

"I assume you're the ne'er-do-well who got my daughter pregnant and deserted her," the gentleman bleated, snarling down at Josh.

"Ne'er-do-well?" Josh chuckled. "That's somethin' I've never been called before."

I bet that's something nobody in the Burleson family has ever been called before, Cait thought, hearing a few of the Burlesons behind her chuckling as she looked over the couple that looked eerily familiar. Maybe not the platinum blonde, obviously botoxed woman, but she'd definitely seen that man before. He had medium brown hair with streaks of silver at the temples that gave away his age, otherwise, he would have looked closer to forty than the fifties or sixties she guessed they had to be in order to be JoJo's grandparents.

I guess Jaina's parents are a lot more concerned with keeping up the appearance of being wealthy than the Burlesons or any of the other families in Heart's Destiny. Oh, wow, I just realized that JoJo's grandparents could be the Joneses everyone talks about trying to keep up with.

Her opinion was validated when she turned her head and observed the Burlesons on the bench behind her as they took notice of the couple representing the other side of JoJo's family tree. They were all dressed professionally in clothing that was probably just as costly and high-end as the older couple standing in the aisle. But none of the Burlesons had that high-and-mighty air about them, still appearing approachable and down to earth, even in their Sunday best.

"But if you mean I'm the lucky man who recently found out I'm JoJo's dad, then yeah, that's me," Josh smirked, not pointing out that his suit was just as high quality and expensive as the clothing the older couple was wearing, even though it was from Benny's Formalwear in Heart's Destiny, instead of being part of a line by a high-fashion designer.

Cait loved how down-to-earth Josh and the rest of the Burlesons were, but she worried not flaunting their wealth might be detrimental to his case for custody, if the old-money attitude of this couple was what he was up against.

"Our grandson's name is Joshua, not JoJo," the woman scoffed, looking down her haughty nose at them.

"Yeah, so's mine," Josh retorted, turning to look at Cait and JoJo. "That's why my girlfriend came up with a nickname JoJo likes, so we'd quit getting confused whenever someone hollers 'Josh' across the paddocks or cow pastures."

When Josh mentioned his girlfriend, the older couple turned their gazes toward Cait for the first time. The man's face turned beet-red as he stared at Cait with pure hatred shining in his blue-green eyes. Eyes that looked an awful lot like her own. *Oh, God, no! He can't be Earnie Jones!*

"You," he hissed, pointing at Cait like he was accusing her of the most heinous crime imaginable. "Did your druggie, whore mother send you here to try to get more of my money through my grandson, since she couldn't get any more after I got her DNA tests thrown out and replaced with the one from my lab? If so, then you're as stupid as she is and you're both going to be sorely disappointed."

Holy shit! Was Mom not lying about who my father is? And did he just admit to falsifying the DNA results the way she claimed back then?

"What did you just say?" Josh stood, towering over the older man as he blocked Cait's view of the man she just realized was the same man her mother claimed was her biological father. "I don't care if you're JoJo's grandpa or not. You need to apologize to Cait right now."

Holy shit! What are the odds that JoJo's grandpa would be the same man my mom claimed was my father? I mean, I knew JoJo's last name is Jones, but it's such a common last name that I never thought it was possible that they could be related. Hell, Trent's last name is Jones, too, but he's not related to Earnie. At least, not as far as I know. So, why would I think JoJo might be?

Oh, crap on a cracker! If Earnie falsified those results to get out of having to pay child support, then that means Jaina was my half-sister. No wonder JoJo keeps seeing similarities between us!

"I'm not apologizing to that trollop," the man she now knew was Earnie Jones scowled. "And if that's the kind of trash you associate with, then winning custody of Joshua just became an easy victory for us."

With that, the Joneses turned and walked to the other side of the courtroom to take their seats as the Burlesons whispered among themselves. Cait felt several of their hands reaching out to pat her shoulders reassuringly, but she couldn't acknowledge their support at the moment.

Cait sat frozen in place, unsure what to do or say in response to the strange turn of events. *I guess I should have asked JoJo's grandparents' names before I decided to come on this trip.*

"Hey, are you okay, Sunshine?" Josh sat back down and reached behind JoJo to rub his hand over Cait's shoulder, trying to comfort her.

"Yeah, uh, maybe?" Cait mumbled, unsure how she should feel at the moment. Then Earnie's parting words started to sink into her brain and Cait got worried about her presence hurting Josh's chance of getting custody of JoJo. "Do I need to leave, so he can't use my family history to keep you from getting custody?"

"I'm not sure I understand what he knows about your family history," Josh sighed, running his free hand through his hair.

"I don't want you to go, Cait," JoJo implored her with fear-laced words, reaching over to take her hand and squeeze it. "But I don't want to live with them or go back to Somerset either."

"Yeah, that's not gonna happen," Josh vowed, taking JoJo's free hand in his right hand while also lightly squeezing his left hand on Cait's shoulder. "You're both staying with me. I just need to know what that pompous windbag was talking about, so I can have Uncle Byron look into it before I present my side of the case. Hopefully, if I text him before the judge enters the courtroom, then he'll be able to get back to me before the other parties are through presenting theirs."

"I don't really know the details," Cait choked out. "When I was ten or eleven, my mom claimed that Earnie Jones was my father, and I had to go have blood drawn for her to be able to prove it to get child support. She never showed me the test results, just told me that they went to her attorney to be used in court. And for a few months, she actually seemed to have some money coming in that Mikey and I thought was child support. Then it stopped and she complained about the Navy falsifying a test for him to get out of having to provide for me. After that, she never said anything more about him or who else my father might be."

"Fuck," Josh cursed under his breath, but just loud enough for her and JoJo to hear.

"That's a dollar for the swear jar, Dad," JoJo informed him, lightening the moment enough that both Cait and Josh chuckled, along with several of the Burlesons around them.

"I'll give you five as soon as we get out of here today," Josh told JoJo as he pulled out his phone and started texting. "'Cause I'm sure I'm gonna wanna say it at least four more times during the course of this hearing, even if I hafta bite it back when the judge comes in."

"Yeah, I might need a pencil and piece of paper to keep track of how much you owe me," JoJo quipped with a grin. "But I'll give you a discount for every time I think those bad words when Grandfather is talking to the judge."

"Don't say that out loud in court," Cait whispered, leaning in close so only Josh and JoJo could hear her. "The judge might not consider letting you get away with cussing in your head as good parenting."

"But it's supposed to be okay if I confess my sins and ask forgiveness." JoJo tilted his head and looked perplexed. He then leaned forward to turn and look at Bob and Hazel, who were seated on the other side of Cait. "Isn't that right, Memmaw?"

"Yes, it is," Hazel agreed with a smile, obviously having heard more of the conversation than Cait realized.

JoJo looked back up at Cait and then over at his dad. "Would he think it was better for me to be a bad kid by not telling you when I do something wrong? I think teaching a kid to admit their sins is good parenting, even if you don't punish me for little things like thinking bad words."

Cait had to admit that JoJo made a good point, but she wasn't sure how a judge might perceive it. Worrying about the perceptions of the judge brought her right back to worrying about how her presence at Josh and JoJo's side might impact their case.

"Give it up, Sunshine," Josh grinned as he finished texting and put his phone back in the pocket of his suitcoat, obviously reading her mind since she hadn't voiced her concerns aloud. "You can't beat Burleson logic. Even if we're wrong, we're stubborn enough to argue until everyone else gives up and agrees with us."

"I'll have to remember that next time I have an actor or producer try to argue with me," Becky chuckled from behind them.

She wasn't sure if Josh was referring to the argument about her leaving the courtroom or the discussion about parenting she'd inadvertently started with JoJo, but she didn't get a chance to debate either topic as the bailiff ordered them all to rise for the judge to enter the courtroom. After all the pomp and circumstance of introducing Judge Levi English concluded and everyone was seated once again, the case for custody of Joshua Jacob Jones was called with the representative from the state of Virginia, the three petitioning parties, and all of their attorneys being instructed to step forward and take seats at the two tables at the front of the courtroom.

Since they were already having to squeeze so many people around the two small tables, Cait suggested she and JoJo stay in their seats in the audience. With so many of the Burlesons there with them, she was pretty sure she'd be safe enough, if she stayed where she was while Josh and his attorney stepped to the front of the courtroom for the proceedings.

"Nope," Josh objected, keeping his voice low as he reached for their hands and pulled both her and JoJo with him toward the front of the room. "The only person who really needs to be up there to give his opinion to the judge is JoJo, and he needs both of us to support him right now. Besides, the best way for me to make sure I can protect you both is to keep you both close."

Cait didn't fight him, unable to argue against sitting with him at the front of the courtroom, when she really would feel safer being closer to Josh than in the gallery seating with the rest of the Burlesons several rows back. *I just hope my presence at his side doesn't bite him in the ass.*

~~~

Josh was so livid at the audacity of Earnest Jones that he didn't realize he'd chosen to sit at the same table as Tawny Ireland and her attorney, instead of sitting with the representatives from the state of Virginia, the way he'd planned when he was informed that the four parties would have to share two tables during the hearing. He wouldn't have cared about sitting in a specific spot, if it hadn't been made clear to him by the attorneys he'd hired that whoever sat next to the DFACS representative would appear to have their department's endorsement for custody of JoJo. And by delaying his walk to the well of the
~~~

courtroom to convince Cait and JoJo to come with him, he'd unwittingly given that advantage to the Joneses.

Fuck! I wish we could have settled all this back home, where all this pretentiousness doesn't matter. I hate havin' to act all hoity-toity like the Joneses to convince the judge I'm worthy of being JoJo's primary caregiver.

"Since we find ourselves in the highly unusual situation of having multiple parties contesting the previous custody arrangements temporarily ordered by this court, instead of being able to meet today to make those arrangements permanent, I feel it best to allow each party to present their full case for why they deserve custody before asking for the state's recommendation." Judge English looked over everyone at the two tables in the well of the courtroom from his bench before turning to look directly at the Joneses. "You'll present your cases in the order the claims for custody were filed with the court, beginning with the Joneses."

As the Joneses' attorney gave his opening statement, Josh placed his phone in his lap and did a quick search of the family tree that Charlotte had put together for the name "Levi English" to satisfy his curiosity about why the judge's name sounded so familiar. Sure enough, he found Captain Levi English, who had married Matilda Jane Burleson in 1839. Matilda's cousin was the fourth-great-grandfather that Josh's generation of Burlesons was embarrassed to have in their family tree.

Yeah, I probably shouldn't mention how I might be distantly related to the ancestor the judge was probably named after.

Josh switched over to his texts to watch for when he heard back from Byron as Evelyn Jones was called to the stand as the first witness. She wove a tale about how devastated she was at the loss of her only child, telling the court that she felt like she and her husband were the only people who knew Jaina well enough to be able to raise her son the way she would have wanted.

It took all of Josh's willpower not to object to the lies she was spewing. Fortunately for him, his phone vibrated in his lap with reply texts from Byron Avington, so he had something else to focus on instead.

Byron: Sorry my guys missed it the first time, but we didn't think to look for records of Earnest Jones on the west coast.

Byron: Feb-June 2003, Lorna Campbell v Earnest Jones, Paternity & Child Support case, San Diego County, CA court. I just emailed the files to your attorney in VA. And I'll send what I can find on the DNA tests & labs by lunchtime.

Byron: But from what I can tell so far, it looks like he might have used his Navy contacts to influence the 2nd lab & possibly the judge to get the case to go his way.

Byron: If Cait's willing, I know a lab in the DC area that can compare her & Joshua's DNA with next-day results, so you can prove his misconduct in the 2003 case to give you a stronger case now.

Josh discreetly passed his phone under the table to Cait, who looked down and read the messages before nodding her agreement. When she passed his phone back, Josh replied to let Byron know Cait agreed. He then scrolled back to his messages to Byron, outlining what he'd learned that morning about Earnest Jones possibly being Cait's biological father before passing it to his attorney, Gabriel Adams, so he could prepare for presenting the evidence against Earnest Jones.

Mr. Adams scrolled through the messages before turning to look at Josh with wide eyes. His eyes darted to Cait next, which Josh assumed was to verify Cait's agreement to be tested to see if she shared any DNA with JoJo. He then whispered, "We'll discuss this at lunch," as he handed Josh's phone back to him.

Josh tuned back into the proceedings as Tawny's attorney stood to cross-examine Evelyn Jones. "Mrs. Jones, you weave a very compelling tale. But I must ask, how many times did you speak to your daughter Jaina in the last eight years of her life?"

"I don't remember a specific number, but it was not as often as I would have liked," Evelyn stated snootily.

"Really?" The young female attorney representing Tawny narrowed her eyes and creased her brow in disbelief. "You can't remember that you only spoke with your daughter once since you and your husband kicked her out of your home when she told you she was pregnant with Joshua?"

"No, it was more than that," Evelyn argued, appearing slightly ruffled by the attorney's accusation at the same time her attorney, who looked even older than the Joneses, objected to the question, claiming Tawny's attorney was badgering the witness.

"Ms. Ireland is prepared to present phone records for the accounts she and Jaina Jones shared for the last nine years to prove that the only time Jaina spoke to her parents since they kicked her out was in February of this year, when she called them to ask for her family medical history to give to her doctor." The attorney pulled a two-inch thick file from her briefcase and held it up for everyone in the courtroom to see. "So, I'm merely asking her to clarify that she can't remember the one phone call in February that we can prove. If I were badgering her, I'd ask if she has dementia or Alzheimer's that prevents her from recalling the conversation where she insulted her daughter and refused to provide the family health history that might have helped Jaina's doctor pinpoint her illness before it was so far progressed that she couldn't be saved."

Holy shit! I knew from the records Byron found that Jaina only went to the doctor a couple of months before she died, but I didn't realize that her parents didn't give her any family medical history to try to help her doctor figure out what was killing her! How the fuck can they live with themselves after not trying to help their daughter?

"Objection overruled," Judge English boomed, glaring at Tawny's attorney. "But I will caution you, Ms. Baker, not to embellish your commentary any further with things you cannot prove with verifiable evidence. And restate your question more succinctly, so Mrs. Jones can understand it and answer accordingly."

"Yes, your honor." Ms. Baker appeared suitably chastised before turning back to look at Mrs. Jones on the witness stand. "Mrs. Jones, do you recall any other conversations you had with your daughter Jaina between June nineteenth, two-thousand-eleven, when Joshua was born, and February first, two-thousand-nineteen, when she called you from the hospital at Dr. Johansen's request?"

Leah Mae Wright

"No, I do not recall any specific conversations between those dates," Evelyn bit out in a clipped tone.

Because there weren't any conversations to remember. Josh sighed. *This woman has to have some mega-sized balls to try wording her answers to make it sound like there might have been conversations that would paint their relationship with Jaina in a better light, without blatantly lying on the stand to catch a perjury charge.*

As Ms. Baker went on to ask questions about how many times the Joneses saw Joshua before Jaina died, Josh had to calm JoJo down. "But she's lying, Dad," JoJo hissed a little louder than a whisper, drawing the judge's attention. "I never met them until the day they showed up to take me away from Aunt Tawny. And the judge needs to know she's lying."

"Don't worry, Son," Josh whispered as he and Cait both put an arm around JoJo to comfort him. "We'll tell the judge the truth when it's our turn to testify."

"Remember, we're supposed to keep our lips zipped in the courtroom unless we're on the witness stand," Cait added in a hushed tone, miming zipping her lips to get JoJo to do the same.

Josh repeated the movement as he smiled at the only two people in the room he cared about.

"Is there a problem we need to address?" Judge English looked pointedly at Josh and JoJo.

Josh shook his head, causing the judge to arch an eyebrow at him. Josh didn't want to just speak again and undermine the playful way Cait helped him get JoJo to stop talking, so he mimed unzipping his lips before he answered the judge. "No, your honor. Just reminding JoJo that we're supposed to keep our lips zipped in the courtroom unless we're on the witness stand or you ask one of us a specific question. And reassuring him that he'll get his turn to talk to you later in the proceedings."

"Very well," the judge nodded, not quite hiding his slight smile as Josh rezipped his lips.

They somehow remained quiet the rest of the day as the Joneses presented the remainder of their case, though Josh wasn't sure how he managed to bite his tongue. Actually, it wasn't really hard for him to keep from pointing out their lies as they tried to present themselves as upstanding citizens and pointed out all the reasons Tawny Ireland wasn't fit to gain custody of JoJo. He didn't even have a problem with wanting to argue with them when they cited his job as a Navy SEAL as too unpredictable and dangerous for him to be capable of providing a stable home for his son.

Those were things he could easily laugh off, knowing whatever private investigator they'd hired for their opposition research wasn't thorough enough to have the most up-to-date information. So, Josh knew his attorney could make sure all the mistruths were cleared up when they finally got to present his side of the case and he recalled them to the witness stand. He even understood Gabe Adams' reasoning for deferring his chance to cross-examine them, knowing he needed to review the new information from Byron that evening and get the results of the DNA test they did at lunch to devise the right strategy for his questions.

But when they got back from lunch, after going to the lab Byron referred them to, so they could have their blood drawn for comparison, and Earnest started spewing lies about Cait, Josh had to sit on his hands to keep from jumping up to wrap them around the son of a bitch's throat. The only thing that stopped him was knowing he'd go to jail for murder, and wouldn't get to marry Cait and raise JoJo and all the kids he wanted to have with Cait. But in his head, he called Earnest Jones every derogatory name he could think of, racking up at least a fifty-dollar debt to JoJo's swear jar.

Fuck! I'm not looking forward to sitting through another day of bullshit like that tomorrow. Hopefully, Tawny's lawyer won't take so fucking long to present her case, so maybe we can get to our turn before Thursday.

Well, if we get the DNA results back tomorrow like Byron thinks we will, anyway. Hell, maybe it'll be better if Ms. Baker gets as long-winded as Mr. Stephenson was today. Then we'll have plenty of time for the results to come in before we present our case.

~~~

Cait felt shell-shocked at the way Earnie Jones attacked her from the witness stand earlier in the day. He'd actually tried to claim that Cait was just like her mother, addicted to drugs and making her living as a
~~~

prostitute with the hopes of getting knocked up and conning some poor schmuck into supporting a kid that wasn't his. The only good thing that came out of his convoluted testimony about how he suspected Cait was working with Lorna to get revenge on him for defeating their scam in court more than fifteen years ago was how she knew he'd look like a fool when Josh's attorney finally got to present the true facts about her life.

Hell, I don't even know where Lorna is, if she's even still alive. So, there's no way I could be in cahoots with her on some elaborate long con the way he thinks.

After her talk with Josh when she realized her memory of talking to her mom after being shot was only something she'd dreamed up in her concussed state, Cait had asked her brother for more details on when and why they'd lost touch with their mother just a few years after she'd gone to jail. Mikey had filled her in on how Lorna's sentence had only been three years and that when she was released, she vanished instead of trying to take custody of her then-sixteen-year-old daughter from her son, who'd finished college and become a cop during the time she was incarcerated.

Learning their mother had abandoned both her and Mikey gave Cait a little more understanding about JoJo's feelings after losing his mom. Not that the situations were the same in any way, but whether they were separated by death or because of a neglectful parent who walked away, they both felt abandoned. Mostly, though, the news just eased the undeserved guilt she'd felt from thinking she and Mikey had been the ones to cut all communication with their mom.

And obviously, whoever Earnie had look into Josh before the hearing did a terrible job. If they'd looked past Josh's time as a SEAL, they'd have found the rest of his family and everyone else living on the ranch, including me. So, seeing me today wouldn't have caught him by surprise the way it did. But I guess that's a good thing, since being surprised I was there is why he talked out his ass on the stand. And no matter how the DNA test turns out, Earnie making stuff up on the stand can't be good for his case.

She couldn't believe Earnie Jones's hatred for Lorna Campbell was so vehement that he carried it over to Lorna's offspring. For that matter, she couldn't believe how easy it was for her to decide to go take a blood test at lunch to try to prove the jackass was her biological father. When Josh had shown her the texts from Byron Avington that basically corroborated her hunch after Earnie's rant before the hearing, though, she didn't need a second to think about it before she agreed.

She'd only refused to do the DNA test with her brother on the Ancestry site because she didn't think anything good could come from finding out who inseminated her mother. But if her DNA could prove Earnie's prior misdeeds in a child support case and strengthen Josh's chances of getting custody of JoJo, then she'd gladly give a whole lot more than one vial of blood. Her love for Josh and JoJo was stronger than any fears she had, regardless of whether those fears were being out in public or finding out about her sperm donor.

Not that she was a hundred percent certain that the test would turn out the way they anticipated. Yeah, Earnest Jones obviously knew Cait's mom back in the day. But that could be because Lorna had seen him in the paper and thought she'd be able to con an easy payday out of him, not necessarily because he really was the man she'd been with to conceive Cait. And yeah, his eyes looked an awful lot like hers. But a lot of people had eyes that straddled the border between blue and green. That didn't necessarily mean they were related.

Oh, I hope I'm right about Earnie sinking his own ship today, so the results of this blood test won't really matter for Josh's case for custody, Cait thought as she brushed her teeth to get ready for bed now that they were back at the hotel for the night. *Then Josh will get custody of JoJo, no matter whether Earnie is my sperm donor or not.*

The plan to stay at Jake's apartment had changed quickly when a dozen Burlesons, not counting Josh, JoJo, and Cait, showed up on his doorstep the night before. Like Josh, Jake only had a two-bedroom apartment, so there was simply not enough room for everyone to be able to stay there all week. Even with two bathrooms and a washer and dryer in his apartment to make things a little easier than they'd been at Josh's apartment, they'd have been miserable trying to cram more than a dozen people in the small space. Instead, they managed to procure an entire floor of suites at one of the local hotels, thanks to Julie having negotiated a deal for Burleson Incorporated to buy out a chain of hotels back in the summer.

Now that they were all back at the hotel for the night, Cait was taking a little time alone in the bathroom attached to the bedroom she was sharing with Josh, knowing he and JoJo still had access to the other restroom in the suite if they needed it, while she was getting ready for bed and thinking about the day's events.

With Lorna's track record, it's more likely she was trying to con Earnest into paying her off than actually telling the truth about him being my father. I guess, at least, Mr. Adams deferred cross-examining the Joneses today, so we'll know what the test says before he brings it up in court. If he even brings it up, she mentally corrected, knowing the results might not be beneficial the way Josh believed.

As much as I hate the thought of being related to Earnie, and how weird it will be if we find out Jaina was my half-sister, since Josh has slept with both of us, it would be a lot worse for Josh in court if his attorney had mentioned the possibility today, and then we find out tomorrow that Lorna was lying. Hell, that might actually have been as bad for Josh as the Joneses' testimony was for them today.

"Hey, you okay in there, Sunshine?" Josh knocked on the bathroom door.

"Yeah, I'll be out in a second," Cait replied, washing her face one more time to get rid of the streaks from the tears she'd unconsciously shed while trying to wrap her mind around all the possible ramifications of the DNA test she and JoJo had taken that afternoon. *At least I have Josh to talk this all through with before we go face another day in court tomorrow.*

Josh was already in bed, waiting for her when she finally came out of the ensuite bathroom. She put her dirty clothes in the laundry bag Josh had started and placed on the chair in the bedroom of the suite. Then she put her phone on the charger before sliding under the covers beside him.

"You sure you're okay, Sunshine?" Josh rolled onto his side, facing her as he rested his head on his hand. "Today was a lot for you to handle, in more ways than one, and I wanna make sure it wasn't too much for you."

"Yeah, I'm okay," Cait sighed as she rolled onto her side to face him while they talked, grateful that he knew her so well that he'd given her the space she needed all night. He'd stayed close and kept a hand on her while they ate with his family, but he didn't push her to talk. Not when it was the whole group at dinner, or when it was just the three of them once they got to their suite. He'd even been patient with her when she was still stuck in her head after JoJo went to bed, not upping the affectionate touching and chaste kisses between them from the normal levels they'd been all day with others around to their typical level of heat when they were alone. "Just worried about how my family history with Earnie is going to affect the judge's ruling."

"I'm sure you're my ace in the hole in this case," Josh smiled, reaching out to brush her hair behind her ear. "And that blood test is gonna prove his history of undermining the judicial system to be the final nail in the coffin we're gonna bury his case in. Between that and proving he lied on the witness stand today, there's no way the judge will give the Joneses more than supervised visitation with JoJo."

"But what if that blood test shows no familial relationship between me and JoJo? You heard what Mikey said about Lorna the other day. If running off to find her next high was more important than seeing her kids when she got out of jail, then can we really hope she wasn't so high when I was conceived that she might actually remember who she slept with back then?" Cait sniffled, reaching up to wipe her involuntary tears before she continued. "I can guarantee you she was wasted most of the time when I was a kid, so I really think her naming Earnie Jones as my father was only because she saw his picture in the paper and thought he'd be an easy mark. And if Lorna was lying, like she was pretty much every time she opened her mouth back then, we have no way of proving his version of past events isn't accurate. Yeah, we have my employment records and such to show he was lying about me now, but without proof about the past, he's going to sound at least somewhat credible."

"No, Sunshine," Josh disagreed, shaking his head as he slid his hand down from her face to her hand to squeeze it reassuringly. "Proving he's lying about you will make him seem less credible about past events. And even if Lorna was lying about him being your bio-dad, you can't be held responsible for whatever she did when you were a kid. Since she hasn't been a part of your life in the last decade, her actions, past or present, won't have any bearing on this case. And Gabe's gonna point that out when he finally gets to present our side of the case. So, you don't have to worry about that DNA test, no matter what it shows."

"If it's not going to matter to the case one way or the other, then maybe we shouldn't have taken it," Cait mused aloud, wishing she'd taken a day to think things through before going to have her blood drawn.

"I'm sorry. I shouldn't've put you on the spot to do it." Josh flopped over onto his back, released his hold on her hand, and stared up at the ceiling. "I was just so blindsided by the craziness of the situation and desperate to make sure we have all the facts as soon as possible to be able to lay it out for the case that I didn't think about you not wanting to know if he's your father or not."

"No, don't apologize." Cait reached over and ran her hand along his slightly scruffy jaw. She kind of wished he didn't have to shave for court the next morning, so he could let the light beard grow out long enough to soften up, instead of being so scratchy after only a little more than twelve hours of growth. "You're fighting for your son, so of course, you want every possible piece of evidence you can use in court."

"But I shouldn't have asked you to take a test that's going to be bad news for you, no matter what the results show, just in case it goes against the odds and gives me one more piece of damning evidence against Earnie's character." Josh rolled back onto his side, reaching over to cup her face in a soothing gesture. "Just know that no matter what the test results show tomorrow, it won't change how I feel about you in any way."

"Really?" Cait scoffed, afraid she wouldn't be the only one who thought it was beyond weird for her to be in a relationship with Josh, if he had a child with her half-sister. "And you don't think people will look at us like we're freaks for being together if it turns out Jaina was my half-sister?"

"No, Sunshine," Josh chuckled wryly. "Nobody's gonna bat an eye at us being together."

Cait arched a disbelieving eyebrow at Josh.

"I mean, yeah, it's a crazy coincidence. But it's not any more freaky than my sister marrying your brother, especially since you weren't raised with Jaina to have any kind of a sisterly bond."

"Wait, does that mean if you and I were to get married, I'd basically be marrying my brother-in-law?"

"No," Josh chuckled again before leaning in to peck her lips. "I'm Mikey's brother-in-law and you're Char's sister-in-law, but you and I aren't related in any legal sense. So, *when* we get married, it'll just make me Mikey's brother-in-law twice over, and you Char's sister-in-law twice over. But our only legal relationship will be husband and wife."

Cait couldn't help but smile at the way Josh put special emphasis on the word "when" and didn't say "if we get married" the way she had. "You seem awfully confident about me accepting your proposal, Cowboy."

"I am, Sunshine," Josh grinned, rolling her onto her back as he hovered over her. "But just to make sure you're amenable when I put together my proposal plan, I should probly get started on some of those sexual favors you suggested I bribe you with."

"Oh, you're bribing me now, huh?" Cait giggled and rolled her eyes.

"Yeah, since you want me for my dick and not my money, that's probably not the right word to describe how I'm persuading you."

Before Cait could come up with a witty reply, Josh covered her mouth with his, shutting down her brain with his panty-melting kiss. Cait wrapped her arms around his neck, returning his passion lick for lick.

When they finally came up for air, Josh smirked and suggested, "Since we're cuttin' it so close tonight on when JoJo might wake up, I was thinkin' we might try to be stealthy tonight."

"Stealthy? How?" Cait was curious about what Josh was proposing.

"Well, since we're already in our PJ's, I was thinkin' we might just move them out of the way and do a little sporkin' under the covers, so it's not obvious what we're doin' if he wakes up while we're still in the middle of makin' love." Josh rolled back off of her before taking her hand to urge her to roll with her back to him. He ground his erection into the crevice between her butt cheeks as a demonstration of his plan while sliding his hand down the front of her sleep shorts. "Though this would be a lot easier if you slept in nightgowns with no panties."

Noted. Guess I'll be going lingerie shopping with the girls when we get back to Texas. I wonder if any nightgowns in the back room of Destiny Dresses will be demure enough if JoJo sees me wearing them, but will give Josh the easy access he seems to want?

417

Leah Mae Wright

"And how are we going to keep from soaking the sheets and our pajamas with this plan?" Cait wiggled her hips to give him a little friction on his cock, as he slid his fingers between her folds.

"We can put a rolled-up towel between your thighs while I fuck you from behind," Josh contended, his voice low and gravelly with desire. "And maybe put another one under us."

Cait wasn't sure how effective that would be if they didn't move their pants and shorts far enough out of the way, but she was willing to try it. *And we'll be under the covers, so JoJo won't see any wet spots even if he comes in before we can completely get our clothes back in place*, she thought as she got up to grab a couple of towels from the bathroom while Josh got a condom from his bag and sheathed himself before getting back in bed.

It took a little longer for her to put one towel down, lay back down on top of it, shove her shorts and panties down past her knees, and roll the second towel up to put it between her thighs than it took Josh to push his pajama pants down, don the love glove, and hop back in bed. But in the grand scheme of things, it didn't take them long at all to prepare for stealth sex.

Josh pulled her hair up into a makeshift ponytail and pushed it toward the top of the pillow, getting it out of his way, so he could kiss her neck while reaching around to finger-fuck her to make sure she was opened up and ready for his dick.

"I'm not sure I like these positions where I can't touch you," Cait playfully pouted, trying to reach back with her hand to grab his ass. She would have grabbed for his cock to reciprocate the hand job, but with him humping between her cheeks, there wasn't exactly room for her hand between their lower bodies.

"Sorry, Sunshine," Josh drawled in her ear. "You'll just have to wait 'til our shower in the morning for that. Just like I'll have to wait 'til then to suck on your gorgeous tits and eat your sweet pussy."

Ah, the other benefit of our current accommodations that I'm going to miss when we're back on the ranch and living in separate houses.

They hadn't been able to shower together while they were at his apartment in Virginia Beach. But since the hotel suite had two bathrooms, they were able to shower together either before JoJo woke up or while he was getting ready for the day in the other bathroom. They still had to be quiet because the bathrooms seemed to back up to one another in the suite. But at least, they were able to get in a morning quickie that morning and planned to have repeats all week while they were scheduled for court.

Cait had thoroughly enjoyed giving Josh a hand job while soaping him up that morning. Especially since he'd forgotten to bring a condom to the shower, so he had to let her drop to her knees and finish him off in her mouth after rinsing off the soap. She was still way behind in the oral favors, but she no longer worried about her lack of experience equating to sub-par BJ skills.

"Hmmm, will I still get to suck your cock if you remember the condom in the morning?" Cait mused aloud as she rocked her hips to rub her clit on the palm of his hand while he continued to finger-fuck her.

"I do believe it was you surprising me in the shower this morning, Sunshine. So, I wasn't the one who forgot the condom. But I'll be sure to set my alarm for an hour earlier than we have to wake up JoJo, so you have plenty of time to do whatever you want to me the rest of the week." Cait could feel the vibration traveling down her spine from Josh's deep growl as he pulled his fingers out of her.

"Hmmm, good idea." Cait shuddered with the erotic sensations tingling through her body from knowing they were about to make love.

Josh adjusted his position, moving his lower body far enough back that he could slide his dick between her thighs. He rubbed the head through her dripping wet folds, coating the outside of the condom in her juices before he repositioned to slip inside her.

"Finally," Cait groaned, arching her back to try to work him in deeper.

"Quit complainin'," Josh chuckled, his warm breath blowing over her neck as he finally filled her completely. "You know it's way better because I take my time and make sure you're completely ready to take all of me before I start uppin' the intensity."

"Yeah, I know," Cait agreed as Josh reversed direction and slowly pulled out, only leaving the head inside her. "I just wish I could handle all of you from the very first thrust and didn't need such a long adjustment period every time."

"I don't," Josh disagreed, nipping the sensitive spot where her neck met her torso. "I love how tight you are. If you were able to take all of me from the first stroke, it wouldn't feel nearly as wonderful as it does. For both of us."

"True," Cait giggled, not wanting to remember the lackluster experiences of her past right then. "But I wouldn't mind if you want to try straddling that line between pleasure and pain once in a while."

"Are you sayin' you don't like what I'm doin', Ms. Campbell?" Josh growled as he ramped up the pace of his lovemaking.

"Oh, no, I love what you're doing, Mr. Burleson," Cait purred, rocking her hips in time with his thrusts. "Just letting you know that I'm open to whatever you want to try and trust you to test our limits."

"Fuck," Josh groaned in her ear as he thrust a little harder and reached around to circle her clit with his fingertip. "Then you'd better come on my cock, Caitir. 'Cause I need you nice and lubed up before I let loose, so I don't push too far over to the pain side of that line."

Cait wasn't sure if it was the extra pressure on her clit or Josh ordering her to come that took her over the edge, but her orgasm hit her out of the blue. When she squirted into his hand, Josh grabbed the rolled-up towel between her knees and shoved it closer to the apex of her thighs.

"Oh, yes, Josh," Cait chanted breathlessly, repeating his name with each wave of her release. "Josh, Josh, Josh…"

"Fuck, yes, Cait," Josh growled low in his throat as he frantically pounded into her. "Keep coming. Milk my cock."

With Josh hitting that perfect balance where pain morphed into intense pleasure every time his dick hit her cervix, Cait couldn't tell where one climax stopped and the next one began. It could have been one hour-long orgasm or a hundred shorter ones, but she couldn't tell the difference. All she knew was that Josh took her to the zenith of bliss once more, keeping her there until he joined her.

"Caitir," Josh grunted her name almost incoherently as he shoved in as deep as he could go one last time, holding himself there as his whole body convulsed with his release.

"I love you, Josh." Cait was so blissed out that she drifted off to sleep before Josh could recover enough to return the sentiment. Though when she awoke later in the night to find the towels had been moved and her shorts and panties pulled up, she had to wonder if his softly whispered "I love you, Caitir," while cleaning her up was a little bit of reality coming through in her dreams.

Chapter Twenty-One

Josh couldn't concentrate on the proceedings in court because he was too distracted by catching glimpses of Cait in her sleek, black, pinstriped skirt and blazer. He knew she was wearing a silky camisole top under the blazer that barely covered the sexy black strapless bra that matched the little black thong she was wearing under the skirt. So, every time he caught a whiff of her lavender lotion or saw a flash of silk in the V-neckline of her blazer, Josh remembered back to her coming out of the bathroom after doing her hair and makeup, wearing only that bra and panties, and the sexy fuck-me pumps she still wore on her feet. As she'd passed by him to get to the closet, she'd run a hand over his dick, which was hard as steel and determined to get out of his slacks, and whispered her regret that they didn't have time for her to get on her knees and suck him off again.

Remembering her sultry words instantly took him back to how she'd done just that in the shower the day before and how he'd had to stop her in the middle of the act that morning, so he could actually make use of the condom he'd taken into the shower with them. *Fuck! I hafta stop thinking about Cait's amazing oral skills,* Josh mentally moaned, adjusting in his seat and hoping nobody noticed how his body responded to the memories. *Getting a hard-on in court can't be good for my case.*

As Ms. Baker called Tawny to the stand, Josh tried to focus on the testimony she was about to give, knowing he had to look away from Cait in order to deflate his dick. But when he saw the minuscule skirt and low-cut top Tawny was wearing, he couldn't help but compare the two women.

Leah Mae Wright

Fuck, she looks like she's dressed for the role of slutty secretary in a bad porno, Josh thought, turning to watch the judge instead of Tawny, so he didn't accidentally see what color her underwear was when she sat down on the witness stand. *Cait's way hotter in her classy, professional pencil skirt and the jacket that actually conceals her nipples.*

Luckily for Josh, looking at the judge while thinking about how hot his girlfriend looked negated his cock's normal response to such thoughts. So, Josh was able to focus once more on the hearing.

Once Tawny was sworn in, her attorney started by asking why she'd petitioned for custody of JoJo.

"Because I love JJ like he's mine. Jaina was my best friend. We were as close as sisters, so when her parents flipped out about her being knocked up, she came to live with me. I've been her partner in taking care of him since before he was born. I mean, I was in the room when he was born, so I'm as close to him as any parent can be without actually giving birth."

Really? Then why haven't you even tried to say "hello" to him during our time in the courtroom so far?

"And I know Jaina wanted me to continue raising him after she was gone," Tawny sniffled, grabbing a tissue from the box on the edge of the witness stand and dabbing it under her eyes like she was crying. Josh didn't believe there were any real tears, otherwise, her caked-on dark eye makeup would have run down to be caught on the tissue. "She didn't just tell me that, either. She also wrote it out in her will."

The attorney presented a hand-written piece of paper to the judge, entering it as their first piece of evidence. "Do you know why Jaina's wishes, as stipulated in her last will and testament, weren't honored during the preliminary hearing when the Joneses were given temporary custody of Joshua?"

"Yeah, because the court didn't even get to see it, since I didn't know they were petitioning for custody until the day they showed up to take him away from me." Tawny glared at the Joneses. "And when I tried to show it to the social worker they brought with them from DFACS, she said it wasn't legal because it wasn't notarized. But I didn't know it needed to be notarized, and neither did Jaina, or else we woulda done that when she wrote it out back in March. Which is why you had me bring in all Jaina's diaries and anything else I could find

422

with samples of her handwriting, so you could have that expert confirm she was the one who wrote it for us to be able to use it now."

The attorney presented a letter from a handwriting expert that supposedly validated Jaina's will and discussed the need for the expert to actually testify with the judge and the other attorneys before continuing to question Tawny. After reading the copy of the handwritten will that Tawny's attorney had provided to each of the other parties to the case, Josh's attorney had no objections to it being admitted as evidence. So, Gabe Adams left it up to the Joneses' attorney, Mr. Stephenson, to bluster out his objections.

From what Josh had seen, Jaina had worded it to where Tawny was to get custody of Joshua, only if his biological father either couldn't be found or was unfit to raise a child. Since Josh was clearly more than fit to raise his child, he and his attorney believed the will would actually work in their favor, only giving Tawny rights to visit JoJo as his honorary aunt, but making it clear that Jaina wanted Josh to raise their son.

"While you can't read the will for the court to hear Jaina's exact words until the handwriting expert testifies, can you please tell us about the conversations you had with Jaina leading up to her deciding to write out a will?"

"I was actually in the room with Jaina and Dr. Johansen the first time she was admitted to the hospital, and heard the conversation with her parents when Dr. Johansen asked her to call them for a more complete family medical history. It was obvious after that phone call that Jaina didn't want Earnest or Evelyn anywhere near JJ. Then over the next couple of months, as Jaina's health got worse and worse, with Dr. Johansen trying every test and treatment she could think of, Jaina realized that whatever it was might be deadly. She started talking about wishing she'd found JJ's dad before then, and ordered an online DNA test to try to locate him."

JoJo reached over and squeezed Josh's hand at the mention of the DNA test. Josh smiled down at his son, returning the three squeezes that his family had all started using as a silent way of saying "I love you" since Anthony and Kay met a year ago and introduced the silent show of love to the rest of them.

"She was hopeful that the man she remembered would either be on there, or have a close enough family member on there, that she could link to him to find JJ's dad. But she knew it was a long shot, so she told me she wanted me to raise JJ. She told me she wanted me to marry her baby daddy so we could raise JJ together. That's what she really wanted. For me and Josh to raise JJ together, preferably as a couple, but if he was already married or whatever, then as co-parents."

JoJo shook his head, his grip on Josh's hand tightening. Josh looked down at his son to see the disappointed look on his face and knew it was because he thought Tawny was lying, the same way his grandparents had the day before. *Fuck! He's gonna contradict her when he gets on the stand, telling the judge the same thing he told me and Cait about Jaina saying Tawny's not my type.*

"But then she died before we even got the results of the test. And the Joneses took him away from me before I could even log into the site to try to find his dad. So, I was too busy gathering all our evidence to try to get him back and didn't get the chance to check the site before Josh and JJ did to find each other."

Really? She didn't have a couple of minutes to look between the end of April and the beginning of September? How hard was it to find the will Jaina had just written and a couple of diaries to prove it's her handwriting?

Josh felt his phone buzz in his pocket and pulled it out to see a text from his brother.

Jake: Not true. I went back to look at when the Ancestry site was accessed & found a login in May that had to be her.

Yeah, I know. I remember getting pissed that my son's mother had apparently logged in and didn't reply to my messages back when you told me that the first time. That's why I questioned JoJo about when he was able to access the site. And found out he couldn't get on there until the day after Labor Day, when his new computer class started at Somerset. So, I know it had to be her that got on back in May when the Joneses first took him. But I still can't figure out why the fuck she didn't reply to my messages to get me to help her get him out of there before he had to endure the summer term?

Josh: You think she read my message & didn't want to fight me for custody too?

Jake: Most likely.

Unfortunately, Josh knew they couldn't use the knowledge they gained from Jake's hacking in court, so he didn't bother informing his attorney that Tawny was lying on the stand, again. *Would it even be worth it to subpoena the login records? Or is her case already flimsy enough, with only a handwritten will that she misrepresented in her testimony and no blood ties to JoJo, that the judge will likely only give her limited visitation?*

Hell, JoJo loves her, so I don't wanna be the bad guy who points out she perjured herself to push her out of his life. Obviously, I don't trust her enough to have too much of an influence on him as he grows up, but I can tolerate visits to make my son happy.

Josh just sat back and listened as Tawny continued testifying, presenting the phone records her attorney had mentioned the day before, as well as Jaina's diary as evidence that the Joneses hadn't been a part of their daughter or grandson's lives since the day they kicked Jaina out of their home because she was pregnant. He trusted his attorney to emphasize her testimony against the Joneses while not presenting her in a poor light in front of JoJo.

Once she was done on the stand, Ms. Baker called the handwriting expert to the stand, as well as Jaina's doctor, Tawny's boss, and a couple of her friends as character witnesses. While she had a few more people testify than the Joneses had the day before, they weren't nearly as long-winded. So, Tawny's attorney was able to wrap up their side of the case just in time for them to break for lunch.

Guess we'll be having lunch with Gabe to figure out how he wants to handle recalling Earnest without proof of his prior misconduct.

~~~

Cait was ready for a reprieve from the Tawny Ireland show by the time they broke for lunch. Oh, Tawny hadn't stayed on the witness stand all morning, but even once she'd stepped down, her witnesses had all
~~~

sung her praises as if she was Mother Teresa, instead of a bartender at a local dive bar. While she was pretty sure Tawny had delivered a couple of blows to the Joneses' case for custody in the form of the diary entries and telephone records, she didn't think the other woman had much of a chance of even getting visitation with JoJo because she hadn't painted herself in the best light as a parental figure.

Not that there's anything wrong with honest work as a bartender. But come on, she had to know it wouldn't look great in a custody hearing, especially compared to the decorated Navy officers she was facing off against. So, I'm surprised her attorney didn't advise her to find a job the court would see as more respectable, like in an office or something, to make her look like a more suitable guardian.

But I guess she doesn't have to appear as the perfect parental figure, since she's only going for joint custody of JoJo with Josh. Lord knows, Josh has the perfect parent thing well covered.

"Ms. Campbell, I believe this is for you." As they walked out of the courtroom, Josh's attorney interrupted her thoughts to hand her an envelope that had just been couriered over from his office.

"Thank you." Cait's hand shook as she took the envelope that she knew contained the test results because of the lab name listed as the sender.

"Why don't we go somewhere more private to open that?" Josh suggested, rubbing his hand on her back reassuringly. "Either in the car, or maybe in the private room we have reserved for lunch?"

"Of course," Gabe Adams agreed. "Remember, regardless of what they say, I only need to know the results if you want me to present them in court. Our case is solid either way, so I don't actually have to present those results, even if there's a DNA connection that reveals Mr. Jones's prior misdeeds. So why don't the two of you take a moment to discuss the findings before you get to the restaurant? That way you don't have to discuss them in front of anyone who doesn't need to know the details."

"Thank you," Cait nodded, relieved to hear the attorney's opinion that the results weren't required for Josh to have a solid case for getting custody of JoJo.

"Do you want JoJo to ride with us to the restaurant, so ya'll can talk without little ears overhearing?" Hazel smiled at Cait as she ran her hand over JoJo's hair.

"If you wouldn't mind," Josh answered for them, not giving Cait a moment to think over a reply.

"But I wanna know if Cait's mom's sister," JoJo pouted, as they got to the parking lot for everyone to disperse into their fleet of rental vehicles.

Cait was torn between wanting a few moments alone with Josh to deal with the emotional aspect of opening the envelope, and wanting JoJo with her when she found out if she was his biological half-aunt or not.

"We'll tell you first thing when we get to the restaurant," Josh assured his son.

"No, I've got a better idea," Cait interjected, opening the car door to sit down, so she was at eye level with JoJo. "How about we open it now together, and then you ride with Memmaw and Pappaw to the restaurant while your dad and I talk about the legal stuff?"

"Yes!" JoJo stepped in close to Cait, obviously wanting to see the paper as soon as she removed it from the envelope.

"Here, you do the honors, JoJo." Cait handed the envelope to the little boy, wanting him to feel important to her whether or not they were biologically related.

JoJo tore into the envelope with a zeal only a kid could show at such a time. He pulled out the paper and handed it to Cait, so they could both read it at the same time. There was a bunch of information at the top of the letter such as their file number and notations that Cait was Individual A, JoJo was Individual B, and Josh was Individual C. But it was the body of the letter she was most interested in reading.

> Individual A shares 890 cM on 36 segments, equating to 13% shared DNA with Individual B. Therefore, we can say with 99% certainty that Individuals A and B are most likely related through one of the following relationships: first cousins, great-grandparent and great-grandchild, grandaunt/granduncle and grandniece/grandnephew, or half-aunt/uncle and half-niece/nephew.

> Individual A shares no DNA with Individual C.
> Therefore, Individuals A and C are not considered
> biologically related.
>
> Individual B shares 3456 cM on 29 segments,
> equating to 50% shared DNA with Individual C.
> Therefore, we can say with 100% certainty that
> Individuals B and C share a parent-and-child
> relationship.

"We're half-aunt and half-nephew," Cait mumbled, feeling more than a little shock at realizing that her mother was correct in naming Earnest Jones as her biological father. *Sperm donor,* Cait mentally corrected herself, not wanting to honor Earnie with a title that should be reserved for loving parents.

"Can I just call you Aunt Cait? 'Cause Half Aunt Cait is too long." JoJo grinned up at her, reminding her of the crazy conversation about long nicknames the first day they met.

"Yeah, I don't think halves or wholes matter," Cait agreed, smiling at the little boy she couldn't believe shared a small portion of her DNA. "So, you can just call me Aunt Cait if you want. Or you can just keep calling me Cait if it's easier, since that's what you're used to calling me."

"Yeah, I'll probly do that," JoJo agreed, turning to look at his dad and grinning before turning back to Cait. "But when you marry Dad, will it be okay if I call you Momma Cait sometimes, like Brody calls Aunt Char Momma Char sometimes?"

"Absolutely," Cait sobbed, unable to resist pulling him in for a hug as her tears started to flow. She wanted to tell him that he didn't have to wait for all the legalities to be settled to start calling her that, but she was so overwhelmed by JoJo's easy love and acceptance that she couldn't form words at the moment.

"I'm sorry," JoJo apologized, returning her hug, and rubbing his hand up and down her back the same way Josh did when he was trying to comfort a loved one. "I didn't mean to make you sad."

"I'm not sad," Cait corrected his misperception, smiling through her tears as she pulled back from the embrace just enough that he could see her face. "These are happy tears 'cause I love you so much, and feel honored that you want me to be your extra mom and share a similar term of endearment with your mom."

JoJo gave her a skeptical look. "But I don't wanna make you cry."

"Get used to it, Son," Josh chuckled, squatting down to wrap an arm around each of them. "I don't like it when she cries either, but girls are weird like that. So, we've just gotta make sure we only make 'em cry when they're happy."

"I hate to break up such a poignant family moment, but we need to hurry up if we wanna have time to eat before we hafta be back in court," Hazel interrupted to pull JoJo out of their group hug.

They snuck in one more quick squeeze before JoJo went off with his grandparents, while Josh walked around to the driver's side of the car and prepared to drive them to the restaurant.

"So, now that you don't have to put on a brave face for JoJo, how do you really feel about those test results?" Josh didn't even get the car turned on before he checked on Cait's emotional state.

"I feel like I got the best of two evils for a spcrm donor," Cait chuckled ruefully as she buckled her seatbelt, thinking Earnest Jones wasn't much of a step up from the drugged-out guys she remembered her mom dating and previously feared could have provided half her DNA. "And the only reasons I consider it good news are because I'm related to JoJo, and you can use it to prove what a pompous, lying jackass Earnie is to strengthen your custody case."

"You know we don't have to use these results if you don't want your paternity to be public record," Josh offered after buckling his seatbelt, starting the car, and pulling out of the parking lot.

"No, I want you to use these results," Cait admitted. "Being honest about my paternity doesn't negate all the other ways that Lorna was a horrible mother. But being able to show the world that Earnie is just as terrible a parent will help me feel like I got a little vindication of my feelings toward both of them. And if it's the final piece of evidence you need to get custody of JoJo, even better."

"Are you sure? You know he's gonna try spewing more of that bullshit about you if Gabe brings up your paternity when he calls him up for cross-examination. We don't have to risk putting you through more of that, if we don't mention these test results." Josh kept darting his eyes back and forth between Cait and the road, trying to check on her without impeding his ability to safely drive them over to the restaurant where they were meeting everyone for lunch.

"I'm sure," Cait declared, her voice sounding stronger than she felt. But the fact that she only felt a little woozy from the revelations and wasn't having palpitations or other panic attack symptoms that made her feel like she was having a heart attack just proved how much her anxiety was reduced with Josh by her side. "Yeah, that was hard to sit through yesterday, but the judge will shut him down if he tries to say stuff not pertaining to the questions he's asked."

At least, I hope Judge English will do the same thing he did yesterday when Tawny's attorney was cross-examining Earnie, and he tried to go off on a tangent about Tawny's character, instead of answering the questions Ms. Baker posed.

"But maybe we should suggest to Gabe that he have Earnie declared a hostile witness before he starts the cross," Cait giggled, feeling so much lighter than she had sitting in court worrying about the test results that morning. "Or is that reserved for criminal cases on television?"

"Oh, I'm sure witnesses can be declared hostile in civil cases, too," Josh chuckled as he pulled into the parking lot of the restaurant. "But I think it's only the attorney who actually called them as a witness who can ask for them to be declared hostile. It's kinda expected they'll be hostile when being cross-examined."

When they got to the restaurant, they clarified with Gabe Adams that Josh was correct. Only Earnest Jones's attorney could ask for Earnie to be declared a hostile witness.

"Well, either way," Cait shrugged as she took her seat at the table between Josh and JoJo. "I hope there's a team of paramedics close by when you call him out for tampering with evidence in my paternity case."

"Oh?" Josh's attorney arched a curious eyebrow from across the table. "Why do you think we're going to need paramedics?"

"Because Earnie's liable to have a heart attack or a stroke if his blood pressure gets up so high that he turns as beet red as he did yesterday when he was ranting about me. And while I'm disgusted to think he had any part in making me, and won't ever think of him as anything more than a sperm donor, I don't hate him so much that I wish him dead." Cait shuddered as she thought of the men she had hated that much. Her biological father might be a conceited asshole, but he wasn't half as bad as the cartel members who'd killed Mari and attempted to kill Cait, Mikey, and Brody.

She turned to look at Byron Avington, who'd joined them at the hotel the night before in case he needed to testify in regards to what his team had found while investigating the other parties in the case. "Unless you found links to the cartel or some other heinously criminal acts he's committed that are much worse than being a lying deadbeat?"

"No, it seems his crimes are all of the white-collar variety," Byron boomed, mirth clear in his tone. "Though after having my team dig a little deeper yesterday, it became evident that he's never been faithful to his wife, and has bribed more than one DNA lab over the years, when the women wouldn't take a payoff and walk away."

"Are you saying I have more siblings I don't know about?" Cait blanched, suddenly worried about how her potential unknown siblings might have been raised if their mothers were as bad or worse than hers had been.

Crap, maybe I should send in a DNA sample to that Ancestry site, so they might have a chance at finding me. Even if we're related through that scumbag, it's not their fault he's their sperm donor any more than it's mine.

"Possibly," Byron shrugged. "We found three other cases where he used the same lab that he used with your case, but there weren't prior lab results that were thrown out and supposedly proven false by his lab results in those cases, so I can't say for sure."

"Can you get me contact information for those individuals? Or their mothers, if they're still under eighteen?" *It might be too late for him to have to pay back child support for me, but if any of my siblings are underage, it might not be too late for them to hit him where it'll hurt the most — in his wallet.*

"I can put you in contact with their mothers," Byron informed her, a cautious expression on his face. "But after having dealt with Earnest Jones, I don't know that they'll want to speak to you."

"Oh, they'll want to speak to me," Cait grinned, hoping her thirst for vengeance wasn't showing too prominently in her expression.

"What are you thinkin', Sunshine?" Josh smirked, his eyes glinting as if he'd read her mind.

Leah Mae Wright

"That I might just have to make my DNA and family tree widely available, so those innocent kids can have the proof they need for their mothers to go after Earnie for back child support. While I was lucky to have Mikey raise me to be able to provide for myself, and don't want or need Earnie's money, his other kids might not be so lucky. So, they deserve to have a fighting chance against him in court. And to take him for every dime he's worth."

"Your girl's got a vindictive streak, Cuz," JJ quipped from the end of the table. "I like it. Maybe you should bring her to the office next week to help me figure out how to deal with some of our more unscrupulous competitors."

"No," Josh growled in response to his cousin, his comical version of an evil eye making Cait laugh. He didn't get to say anything more as the server interrupted their conversation to take their order.

Once the server left the room, their conversation turned to how Gabe planned to present Josh's case. Since Anthony's family had to report back to the GWA on Friday, they specifically had to make sure Gabe planned for them to give their testimony as Josh's character witnesses on Thursday. They all rushed through eating lunch to make it back to the courthouse on time.

When they were back in their seats in front of the judge, Gabe Adams presented his opening arguments, laying out how Josh and Jaina met and lost touch, as well as how Josh found out he had a son back in the spring and how he'd searched for his son all summer. He culminated his statement with how JoJo had dramatically entered the lives of the Burlesons after escaping the boarding school where the Joneses had sequestered him, without regard to JoJo's best interest or his mother's wishes for how he was raised after her passing.

"Before I call Josh and Joshua to the stand to present my case for why it's in the boy's best interest to live with his father, I'd like to recall Earnest Jones to the stand for the cross-examination I deferred yesterday."

The judge agreed and reminded Earnie that he was still under oath as he took the stand.

"Mr. Jones, yesterday during your testimony, you referenced Mr. Burleson's girlfriend, Caitir Campbell. Please tell us how you know Miss Campbell."

"Several years ago, her mother tried to claim that I fathered her," Earnie snarled, pointing at Cait. "I don't know how she came across my name to try to con me out of child support. But thankfully, DNA evidence cleared me and proved her to be nothing more than a lying con artist."

"You're referring to the DNA test administered by Gen One DNA Labs and submitted to the San Diego County Court in June of two-thousand-and-three?" Mr. Adams flipped through a folder of papers on the table in front of him.

"Yes," Earnie confirmed with a smug expression.

"And what about the DNA test originally presented to the court in February of that same year that showed you were Caitir's biological father?" Gabe held up a piece of paper, implying it was the test he was questioning Earnie about.

"That test was thrown out because I didn't submit a sample of my DNA to be tested. Obviously, Lorna used the girl's actual father's toothbrush and put my name on it when she took it to the lab." Earnie glared at Cait. "That's why I don't trust the DNA test they claim to have that shows that Joshua is Mr. Burleson's son. I'm sure Caitir and her mother taught him how to fake a DNA test."

"Yes, you mentioned that yesterday." Gabe placed the piece of paper back in the folder, closing it before he pulled another folder from his briefcase. "I believe you specifically stated that you only trust DNA tests that have been witnessed by court officials, which is why I had my client go for additional testing yesterday with a court official witnessing the blood draws. So, now we have the original Ancestry data showing Josh and Joshua are father and son, as well as two blood tests, one done in Texas through Dr. Eric Hayes's office and submitted to the Departments of Family and Children's Services both in the state of Texas and the state of Virginia, and one done here yesterday, witnessed by Judge English's court clerk."

Gabe turned to the judge as he continued, "Your honor, at this time I'd like to present Burleson exhibit nineteen, the report from yesterday's blood test comparing Josh Burleson and Joshua Jones."

"Did you forget exhibits one through eighteen, Mr. Adams?" Levi English arched an eyebrow at the attorney.

"No, your honor. But I already have those designated for other items that I intend to present with our witnesses, and I just received these results over lunch along with some other documents that will be exhibits twenty through twenty-five."

Since neither the Joneses nor Tawny had presented even a dozen exhibits for their cases, Cait was surprised to hear Josh's attorney say they had so many pieces of evidence to present.

The judge nodded once before accepting the exhibit, which Gabe pulled from the folder he'd just gotten out of his briefcase and passed to him through the bailiff. He then looked it over before offering it to Earnie to review.

Earnie gave the document a cursory glance, not even taking it from the judge to actually read it before turning back to face Gabe Adams. "Yes, well, just because Mr. Burleson got lucky with my daughter one night when she was in college, that doesn't prove he's fit to be a parent," Earnie bellowed. "My wife and I share just as much DNA with Joshua, and have been in a committed relationship for over thirty years, so we're much better suited to raise him."

"Oh, yes, combined, you and Evelyn do share fifty percent of Joshua's DNA," Gabe smirked. "And I thank you for submitting that DNA test for the court. Though you probably should have studied a little more about DNA before you tried to claim that the twenty-five percent of Joshua's DNA you each share makes you as closely related to him as Mr. Burleson. Especially since you're claiming you're more fit to raise a child because you've been in a committed relationship with your wife for over thirty years."

"I beg your pardon," Earnie glowered at the attorney.

Gabe ignored Earnie's interruption, pulling a copy of the letter Cait had received from the lab before lunch from the folder he still held in his hand. *I guess, since he already had a copy of his own, he just meant I didn't have to be embarrassed by telling him about the results earlier when he said I didn't have to tell him if we didn't want to use them in court. I probably should have realized that he'd get a copy too, since I did sign off on having them sent to his office yesterday.*

Gabe turned back to Earnie to continue his questioning, blocking Cait's view of the paper in his hand. "Did you pay off someone at Gen One DNA Labs to falsify the DNA report you submitted to this court, Mr. Jones?"

"No, absolutely not!" Earnie yelled, turning as beet red as Cait had expected.

"So, you only paid them off to falsify the reports when you were being sued for child support of your illegitimate children? And was that only in the case of Caitir Campbell? Or do you have other children you refuse to take responsibility for by having Gen One DNA Labs falsify DNA results that you submitted to the courts to keep from being charged with perjury every time you lied on the stand about cheating on your wife and impregnating your various mistresses?"

Holy shit! Gabe's not pulling any punches with Earnie the way he did this morning with Tawny.

"I haven't paid off anyone," Earnie raged, his face decidedly looking a lot more like a tomato than it had even just a moment before. "And I haven't cheated on my wife. Don't listen to this ignorant man's lies, Evelyn."

"Your honor, I'd like to present Burleson exhibit twenty, the lab report from yesterday's blood test comparing Caitir Skye Campbell's DNA to that of Joshua Jacob Jones and Joshua Bennett Burleson." Gabe handed the paper over to the bailiff for review by Judge English.

"You can't do that," Earnie objected from the witness stand, turning his irate glare at his own attorney. "Caitir Campbell isn't even a party to this case, so there's no reason for that test to be submitted. Tell them, Stephenson!"

Cait had to grin at the shell-shocked look on Mr. Stephenson's face as he floundered for words.

"I'll be glad to point out the relevance, your honor," Gabe added confidently.

"Very well," the judge nodded as he took the piece of paper from the bailiff and looked it over. "I'll accept Burleson exhibit twenty. Please continue, Mr. Adams."

"Thank you, your honor." Gabe Adams turned to face the witness stand. "Before I outline the findings in Burleson exhibit twenty, would you care to revise your statements about not paying off Gen One DNA Labs to falsify the DNA results in the case regarding Caitir Campbell's paternity and claiming to have never cheated on your wife of over thirty years? Or perhaps you have another child you'd like to claim?"

"No," Earnie barked defiantly. "Jaina was my only child. And there's nothing in that test that can prove your outrageous claims otherwise."

435

Leah Mae Wright

"Science doesn't lie, Mr. Jones, unlike you. And the scientific test done yesterday comparing your grandson, Joshua Jones, and Caitir Campbell's DNA shows a very clear familial relationship. They have thirteen percent shared DNA. There was also a third person whose DNA was compared with the two of them, with whom Caitir shares no DNA. Josh Burleson, the father from whom Joshua inherited fifty percent of his DNA. So, therefore, Caitir has to be related to Joshua through Joshua's maternal line. Through your daughter, Jaina."

"That doesn't prove a thing," Earnie bellowed, pulling a handkerchief from his pocket, and wiping his brow. "One of my wife's cousins could be Caitir's father to give them that familial relationship."

"Not with thirteen percent shared DNA. That much shared DNA means they have a ninety-nine percent chance of being categorized in one of four familial relationships. And their ages make it highly unlikely they share a great-grandparent and great-grandchild relationship, a grandaunt and grandnephew relationship, or are first cousins. Therefore, they can only be half-aunt and half-nephew, with one of Joshua's grandparents also being Caitir's parent. As it has been established that Joshua and Caitir have to be related through Joshua's maternal line, that means either you or your wife have to be Caitir's parent."

Gabe then turned back to the judge and picked up another folder from his briefcase. "Your honor, at this time I'd like to present Burleson exhibit twenty-one, the San Diego County Court record in the case of Campbell v. Jones regarding the paternity of Caitir Skye Campbell."

"I'll allow Burleson exhibit twenty-one," Judge English nodded to the bailiff to take the folder from Josh's attorney, speaking before Earnie Jones could make a sound to object. "Please summarize the relevance, Mr. Adams."

"The relevance is simple, your honor," Gabe smiled. "It's a legal record including Caitir Campbell's birth certificate listing Lorna Campbell as her mother, making it impossible for Evelyn Jones to be the DNA link between Caitir and Joshua Jones. The rest of the documentation in that file provides the names of the lab tech and court officials that are currently being investigated for taking bribes from Earnest Jones to hide the fact that he is Caitir Campbell's father."

"Sperm donor," Cait automatically corrected, hating hearing the word "father" being used to describe Earnie Jones. *He's not good enough to be called a father. Not just for me, but for Jaina and however many other siblings we have out in the world, too.*

"What was that, Miss Campbell?" The judge gave her a pointed look.

"Sorry, your honor," Cait blurted, unable to stop herself from elaborating, even though it really wasn't the right time for her to speak her mind. "I have an extreme aversion to deadbeats being labeled as 'dads' or 'fathers' in general. And apparently, when I'm the child being referenced in relation to the deadbeat, my aversion morphs into a full-blown allergy that makes me sneeze out the correct term for the loser who isn't man enough to be my father. So, from now on, if you don't mind, anytime Earnie donating half my DNA is being discussed, please refer to him as my *sperm donor* because he hasn't done a single thing to earn any other title. For that matter, when you're discussing my relation to Lorna Campbell, you can refer to her as my *egg donor*. My brother Mikey is the only person who ever acted like my parent."

"I thought we were supposed to zip our lips in court," JoJo giggled, reaching over, and squeezing her hand as Josh rubbed his hand up and down her back.

Crap! Now I'm being a bad example as his extra mom. Cait closed her eyes as she mimed zipping her lips. *At least I didn't use any bad words to owe money to his swear jar.*

Now I just have to hope the judge understands that I'm completely off-kilter today from finding out those DNA results and won't hold my outburst against Josh. Or worse, decide to go with Tawny's interpretation of Jaina's wishes by giving her and Josh joint custody, since I've proven to be a worse mother figure than she has.

"My apologies, Cait. I will definitely use the proper terminology for your DNA donors in the future." Cait didn't miss the mirth in Gabe Adams' tone.

Since she didn't open her eyes until Josh's attorney went back to questioning Earnest Jones, she did miss the slight smile on Judge Levi English's face from her rambling, however.

~~~
~~~

While Cait seemed flustered by having to wait to testify until the next day, Josh was glad the judge had called an early recess to give everyone a cooling down period after Earnest Jones's time on the witness stand that afternoon. He enjoyed having the extra free time to do a little sightseeing with his family, even though he wished Cait could have relaxed and enjoyed it a little more than she did. Oh, she put on a fake smile and tried not to let her unease show for the rest of the evening. But Josh could see she was on edge. Now as they went through their normal bedtime routine with JoJo, Josh had to work through everything in his mind to figure out how to best soothe Cait, so they could both get a good night's sleep before going back to the courthouse the next day.

While the revelation about her paternity had to be what had Cait worked up, Josh thought it was actually the other items Gabe had presented as Burleson exhibits twenty-two through twenty-five that would actually sink the Joneses' case for custody of JoJo.

I still can't believe Byron's team was able to dig up that Airbnb lease paperwork to show that they didn't intend to stay in Alexandria with JoJo any longer than they had to for DFACS to sign off on a home visit. Between that and the records from Somerset Academy, showing that JoJo transferred in there immediately after that Airbnb lease ended, with him having to be picked up at the bus station by a Somerset employee, I'd say it's pretty obvious that the Joneses don't really want custody of JoJo. They just don't think it'll look good to their high-society cronies if they let their grandson live in a loving home with someone they see as beneath them.

Josh hated the fact that Cait was going to have to get on the witness stand the next day and tell her whole life story because Earnest Jones was cruel enough to bring it all up in court. *Fuck, if I could testify for her to keep her from having to suffer through being cross-examined by Earnie's attorney, I would.*

Unfortunately, this was another battle that Josh couldn't fight for her. So, just like with her agoraphobic tendencies and anxiety, he had to stay relegated to the supportive boyfriend role, letting her tackle the challenging situations on her own while being by her side to make her feel safe in doing so.

For a protective man like Josh, it was a lot harder to hold back when she was facing off against a human foe than when she was working through the mental hurdles impeding her from living her life to the fullest. With the mental hurdles, all he had to do was take her in his arms to shut them down. And if that wasn't enough, he could kiss her until she couldn't think about anything but the two of them.

But with people like Earnest Jones, Josh had to fight his first instinct, which was to shut him up by punching him in the mouth. *The bastard can't talk trash about Cait if his jaw's wired shut.*

Oh, hey, maybe I'm not as fucked up from my time in the Navy as I thought. Wanting to punch him is a whole lot better than wanting to shoot the son of a bitch right between the eyes.

"What's that strange look for?" Cait questioned as JoJo closed the book he'd been reading to them.

"I'll tell ya later," Josh grinned, wagging his eyebrows suggestively at Cait as she placed the book on the end table beside the sofa bed JoJo was using in the hotel. He then turned to his son for their goodnight hugs. "I love you, JoJo. Sleep well."

"I love you, too, Dad," JoJo muttered through a yawn as the two embraced.

Josh brushed his lips over his son's head before he released him from the hug to let Cait have her turn.

"Goodnight, JoJo." Cait kissed the sleepy little boy's cheek as the two of them hugged. "I love you."

"I love you, too." JoJo smooched Cait's cheek as the two pulled back from their embrace.

Josh made sure the room was secure before following Cait to the bedroom in the suite, where she was already stripping off the sweater she'd put on when they changed to go sightseeing after court. *Thank fuck! She left on the sexy underwear.*

Josh stepped up behind Cait, wrapping his arms around her and cupping her satin-covered breasts in his hands. "Finally," he groaned, trailing his lips over her shoulder, lightly kissing the small exit wound she had from when she was shot before working his way up her neck to whisper in her ear. "I've been fighting a hard-on all day from thinking about what you were wearing under your clothes."

"You have not," Cait scoffed, covering his right hand with hers while holding her sweater in her left.

"I have," Josh confirmed, nibbling her earlobe as he lightly pinched her taut nubs through the fabric of her bra. "How do you think I managed to keep from losing my temper in court this afternoon?" He didn't give her a chance to formulate an answer. "Instead of looking at that fuckwad on the stand, I glanced over at you and pretended I had x-ray vision to see through your prim and proper business woman outfit to this sexy bra. Then I imagined taking it off of you before fuckin' you in the shower, so I was really glad I was wearing a suit with a long enough jacket to keep anyone from noticing how hard I got thinking about fucking you tonight."

Cait released his hand and spun around in his arms, tossing her sweater toward the bed, so she could place both her palms on his pecs as she grinned up at him. "You do realize that fantasizing about sex while in court makes you a pervert, right?"

"Yeah, but I'm your pervert, so it's okay, 'cause all my fantasies are about sex with you, Sunshine." Josh didn't give her a chance to reply, dipping his head to cover her mouth with his at the same time he slid his hands down to grip the globes of her ass.

Cait wrapped her arms around his neck as their tongues tangled and her legs around his waist when he lifted her up to carry her to the bathroom for that sensual shower he'd been dreaming about all day. As soon as they were in the ensuite, Josh placed her back on her feet and moved his hands around to the button on her jeans, eager to get her undressed.

"Wait." Cait stilled his hands, breaking their kiss to take a step back. "You didn't tell me what that weird look was a few minutes ago. And I know it wasn't your typical horny look, so don't even try lying about it to get to naughty naked time faster."

Josh had to think for a second to remember what had been running through his mind as JoJo read *Charlie and the Chocolate Factory* earlier. "Oh, I was just thinking that my time as a SEAL hasn't skewed my people skills to the dark side as much as I'd feared," Josh finally explained, stripping off his Henley before stepping closer to Cait once more.

"Why were you thinking about that?" Cait's eyes narrowed as she looked at him with a confused expression.

"I was thinking about how hard it was to keep from following my first instinct while Earnie was on the stand today," Josh admitted, knowing he'd have to explain everything before she'd let him distract her with sex to help her quit stressing about testifying the next day. "And I realized that my first instinct was to punch him in the mouth, so he'd have to have his jaw wired shut and couldn't spew his lies anymore. It was refreshing to know that I'm not programmed to shoot first and ask questions later, since that's what I had to do so often on ops."

"You don't consider punching him in the mouth as being skewed to the dark side?" Cait chortled, rolling her eyes at him.

"Naw, a single punch is barely light gray when compared to some of the things I could think of doing instead." Josh chuckled to keep the mood light, not wanting to mention how his first thought a couple of months before would have been to shoot the asshole. Besides the fact that she didn't need the reminder of being shot in her head, Josh never wanted to give her a reason to think he was capable of being a cold-blooded killer, like the wastes of humanity she'd had to face in the cartel. "Now, is there anything else we need to discuss before you let me get you dirty and then clean you up in the shower?"

Cait bit her bottom lip, clearly still worried about something to the point that she couldn't relax yet.

"Spit it out, Sunshine," Josh commanded, running his hands down her arms from her shoulders to her elbows. "Tell me what you're worried about, so I can allay your fears before giving you something much more pleasurable to focus on."

"You don't think finding out I was born from that genetic cesspool will cause the judge to not want me to be around JoJo, do you?" Cait's lip trembled and her eyes filled with unshed tears as she choked out the question.

"No, I don't," Josh assured her, pulling her close as he slid his arms around her back. "Environment has obviously had a greater impact on you than genetics. So, the only thing those DNA results prove about your character is how strong you are to have overcome the piss-poor genetic influence of your DNA donors."

"But what if he thinks Tawny will be a better parental figure for JoJo and awards her joint custody?" Cait whimpered, wrapping her arms around his waist as she buried her face in his chest. Her warm tears lightly tickled as they ran down Josh's torso.

"Then we'll work out a schedule where he spends some of his time with her and some of his time with us," Josh surmised, petting her hair the way he knew calmed her. It wasn't the outcome he wanted from the hearing, but he'd live with it as long as he wasn't cut out of his son's life. "But even if that happens, nothing's gonna change between you and me. And after we present our case tomorrow, the judge is gonna know we're the best parents for JoJo."

Josh held Cait for a few more minutes, waiting for her sobbing to subside before changing the subject to getting naked once again. "Now that we know there's nothing else for us to worry about, can we please get naked and do something about the serious case of blue balls I've been suffering with all day?"

"Can you really classify it as blue balls when you just got some this morning?" Cait giggled, pulling back from him to look down at where his dick was clamoring to escape his jeans.

"That was more than twelve hours ago, Sunshine," Josh playfully pouted as he reached out and unfastened her bra. "So, yeah, I can."

Josh deftly freed her perfect peaks from the scrap of satin, not caring where the bra landed as he bent to get his mouth on her turgid brownish-pink tips. He cupped her pillow-soft flesh in his hands, sucking on one nipple while gently pinching the other between his thumb and forefinger.

"Oh, Josh," Cait moaned, no longer bothering to banter as he alternated the tactile treatment and oral affection between her bountiful breasts.

Instead of running her fingers through his hair as he expected, Cait slid her hands around his waist until she reached the button of his Levi's. She quickly unfastened them, shoving them off his hips and freeing his engorged cock. As soon as the jeans were out of her way, she stopped fussing with them, leaving the waistband around his thighs as she grabbed his dick with both hands.

"As much as I love what you're doing, Cowboy," Cait purred as she jacked his shaft with one hand while spreading his precum over the head with the other. "I should probably take the edge off your blue ball situation first, so we can go longer in the shower."

"Oh, fuck, Cait," Josh groaned as she dropped to her knees, taking away the toys he was enjoying playing with a moment before. Not that he would complain too much, since she quickly closed her lips over the head of his cock and sucked. Hard.

He couldn't take his eyes off the glorious sight of a topless Cait on her knees with his dick in her mouth. The way she used her hand to stroke the part of him that wouldn't fit in her mouth as she alternated between sucking and licking him felt wonderous. The amazing sensations of Cait blowing him were only amplified by watching her use her free hand to play with her tits at the same time.

"Fuck, yeah, Sunshine. That's so hot," Josh growled, unable to stop himself from running his fingers through her hair and gripping it at the back of her head.

The gesture was more to push the long chestnut tresses back, so they wouldn't obscure his view, than to control her head movement. But Josh still used his hold on her hair to keep her from deep-throating him and causing him to come too soon, like a virgin getting his first blow job.

"Get those jeans off and play with your pussy while you suck my cock," Josh commanded, wanting to make sure she was getting as much pleasure from the experience as he was.

He might not have ever had a serious girlfriend before, but he knew the secret to maintaining a meaningful relationship was to always make sure she got off first. And twice as many times as he did during every encounter. With his prior hookups, he'd still tried to make sure he abided by that first rule. But Cait was the only woman who'd ever inspired him to follow through with the second.

Cait followed his commands up to a point. She only wiggled her jeans and panties down to her knees, not being able to move them any further one-handed while still sucking and stroking his cock. Watching her fingers delve between her folds as she flicked her bean, Josh didn't really care that neither one of them had managed to lose the jeans.

Between her tits bouncing with every bob of her head up and down his length and her pussy dripping from how aroused she was, Josh relished the visual aspect of their foreplay almost as much as the sweet heat of her mouth on his dick. He praised her profusely while keeping his voice low so it wouldn't carry throughout the suite. He was especially prolific with his words when her lips and hand clamped down on his dick as she made herself come. "Fuck, yeah, Sunshine.

Just like that. Feels so good. That's it. Come from suckin' my cock. Fuck, Cait, you're so fuckin' perfect."

Josh enjoyed several more minutes of her exceptional oral skills before he finally pulled her from his dick to keep from coming until he was buried balls-deep in her tight cunt. "Have to have you now," he growled as he hauled her to her feet.

They shucked their jeans in a hurry, with Josh only being a moment slower because of having to grab his wallet from the pocket to grab a condom. "While I'm puttin' this on, turn on the water, so it'll drown out the noises we're about to make."

"Yeah, we probably should have done that earlier," Cait giggled as she opened the shower door and fiddled with the knobs to turn on the water.

"I don't think either one of us were thinking with the right head earlier," Josh chuckled as he ripped open the foil packet and sheathed his dick.

"Um, in case you haven't noticed," Cait giggled, shaking her head at him as she moved her hand under the stream of water to test the temperature. "I only have one head."

"Yeah, well, if I can think with my dick, you can think with your clit," Josh teasingly argued as he gripped Cait's hips and lifted her up to carry her into the shower. "Hope the temp's good enough, 'cause I can't wait any longer for your tight pussy."

Cait wrapped her arms and legs around him just as he impaled her on his cock while stepping under the tepid spray coming from the shower head. "Oh, Josh." Her mouth formed a perfect O, and Josh could've sworn he saw her eyes roll back in her head momentarily.

"Oh, shit, Cait." Josh pulled most of the way out, unsure if the way she squeaked out his name was good or bad. "I didn't hurt you, did I?"

"No, just surprised me," Cait assured him, smiling as she rocked her hips to let him know she was ready for more. "In a really, *really* good way."

"Are you sure? I know you said you like it when I lose control a little and get more intense. But I usually do that toward the end, not right at the beginning. And I don't ever want to do anything to hurt you, Sunshine. I love you too much to enjoy anything that causes you pain."

"I'm sure, Josh," Cait smiled before pressing her lips to his. "And I love you, too."

Josh slowly started to press back into her slick cunt as he tried to deepen the kiss. Cait, however, had other ideas, nipping his tongue lightly when he tried to sensually make love to her.

"Now quit teasing me, Cowboy," Cait insisted, squeezing his waist with her legs to try to push him in deeper. "And fuck me already."

"Yes, ma'am," Josh chuckled, pressing her back against the shower wall to show her just how her Cowboy liked to ride. Hard and fast. With multiple orgasms for both of them before rinsing off in an unfortunately cold shower.

Chapter Twenty-Two

After multiple rounds of shower sex, both the night before and that morning, and a really outstanding sporking in the middle of the night after JoJo went back to his bed, Cait was much less apprehensive sitting in court than she'd been the afternoon before, even knowing she was going to have to testify. She'd been exceptionally worked up when Levi English adjourned the proceedings early the day before, thinking the judge was wrong about everyone needing a cool-down period after Earnie's testimony. She was afraid waiting overnight before countering his lies about her life would only amp up her unease, not cool her anger in any way. But once again, Josh had proven to be better for her anxiety than any of the medications that her doctors in San Diego had tried to help her with her anxiety right after being shot.

I guess instead of meds or a service animal for my PTSD and anxiety, I just need to make love with Josh. I wonder if Dr. Edwards can write me a prescription or some kind of medical letter. Maybe something like they do for service animals, only stating that I need to be allowed to go off for private time with Josh whenever I feel overwhelmed and close to having a panic attack? Maybe we should have called her and asked about that before court, so I'd have it to use if I need a timeout during my time on the stand today.

Cait couldn't help but smile at thinking about having that conversation with Josh and their therapist, knowing she probably wouldn't be the only one blushing through it. *Aw hell, I'm blushing now just from thinking about it. Talk about inappropriate timing. Though I guess it's better than remembering the way Josh held me up against the shower wall and fucked me multiple times both last night and this morning. While those events are much more pleasant to think about than what's going to happen here today, it's really not appropriate to fantasize about sex while sitting next to JoJo and Josh in court.*

Not that Josh was sitting with them for long. Since he'd finished cross-examining Earnest Jones the day before, Gabe Adams started presenting his case for Josh to get custody of JoJo by calling Josh to the stand first. As Josh was being sworn in, Cait shut off her earlier mental rambling to focus on listening to his testimony.

"Josh, please tell the court how and when you met Jaina Jones," Gabe started with a much more laid-back demeanor than he'd had while cross-examining the other witnesses in the case.

"It was September of twenty-ten, just after the start of my first semester in the Naval Academy," Josh stated, turning to speak directly to the judge. "My twin brother Jake heard about a party near one of the other colleges in Annapolis, from someone he was talking to online, and he convinced me to go with him. I think it was actually some upperclassmen at the other school who thought they were gonna embarrass a couple of freshmen Navy nerds, since everyone there was at least two or three years older than us. But it kinda backfired since we didn't look like the scrawny computer geeks they were expecting. I mean, Jake's a computer geek, but working on the ranch throughout our teens kept him from looking like a stereotypical skinny geek."

Josh turned to look at his brother in the audience and grinned mischievously. "As we mingled, we asked around for the person who actually invited him. But we never found them to see what kinda prank they might've had planned. But not knowin' anyone hasn't ever stopped me from makin' friends, so we met Jaina and Tawny and ended up spendin' the whole evening hangin' out and havin' fun with them."

"Jaina and Tawny weren't in on the prank?" Gabe turned to look at Tawny where she was seated at the other end of their table in the well of the courtroom.

"No," Josh chuckled and shook his head. "They were cool. They didn't care that we were three years younger than them and didn't go to their school. So, like typical college kids, we ended up pairing off to talk and stuff."

"And stuff?" Gabe chuckled as he tried to get Josh to elaborate. "You're going to have to be a little more specific than that."

"Aw, come on man, my mom's in the courtroom," Josh blushed, making Cait and several others in the courtroom giggle. "And so's my son and a couple of my nieces and nephews. None of them need to hear the details about how JoJo was conceived."

"JoJo? You mean your son, Joshua Jones?"

"Yeah, with our family all living so close on the ranch, it was confusing with two Joshes, and we couldn't call him JJ 'cause that's what we all call my cousin, Jon Junior," Josh confirmed. "So, my girlfriend, Cait, came up with the nickname JoJo."

"So, your son was conceived that night? You didn't have an ongoing relationship with Jaina?"

"Yes, JoJo was conceived that night. No, I didn't have an ongoing relationship with Jaina. I didn't see her again after that night. Though I really wish I would have." Josh sighed, his shoulders sinking with regret as the jovial side of his personality receded and his more serious side showed through in his body language.

His regret is because of the time he missed with JoJo, not because he wanted a relationship with Jaina, Cait had to remind herself, not wanting to spiral back to a fear that Josh had already settled in her.

"Why is that?"

Josh looked at his attorney with his Duh face. It was an expression Cait had seen several times on both Josh and JoJo whenever someone asked them a question they thought was dumb.

"Because I missed eight years of my son's life." Josh blew out a harsh breath through his nose, obviously still trying to come to terms with his feelings about Jaina not telling him about their son when she was pregnant. "I wasn't there when he was born. I wasn't there when he said his first word, or took his first steps, or for his first day of school. I missed so many milestones in his life because she didn't reach out to tell me she was pregnant."

"And now that I finally found out about him, she's not here to explain why she kept him from me all these years. That's the hardest part of all this — the not knowing why she didn't try to find me and tell me. I've loved my son since the moment I saw his username as my DNA match back in April, and it breaks my heart that I lost out on loving him for the eight years before then. I feel blessed beyond measure at finally having him in my life, and I'm having a blast getting to know JoJo now, but I feel like she stole eight years from us when we coulda bonded even more than we have in the last month. Everything coulda been so much different for all of us, if she'd only told me as soon as she found out she was pregnant."

"How so? It's my understanding that students enrolled in the Naval Academy aren't allowed to get married or have children. So, you would have had to sign away your parental rights if she had told you, correct?" Cait was surprised to hear that information as part of Gabe's question.

"No, I woulda left the Naval Academy to be there for my child," Josh declared adamantly. "Not that Jaina knew that much about me to know that back then. But after talking with a therapist the last couple of weeks, I figured out that's probably part of why she didn't tell me. That night when we talked, I told her my plans to become a SEAL, so she probably thought telling me wouldn't have changed anything because of those rules. But I know it would have. I'd have taken care of her and the baby from day one. If she didn't want to move to Texas, I'd have gotten a job and found a different college wherever she wanted to live. And who knows, if she'd moved back to the ranch with me, she might not have been exposed to whatever caused the tumor that killed her. But we won't ever know for sure, since she didn't give me the chance to step up."

"You said the Naval Academy rules about cadets not being allowed to be parents was *part* of the reason why you believe she didn't inform you," Gabe pointed out. "What other reasons do you think she might have had for not telling you?"

"Everybody keeps trying to tell me that it was probably because she didn't have a way to find me and didn't know my last name, but I don't believe that." Josh leaned forward, looking around the judge's bench to glare at the Joneses. "We were all on Facebook by then, and she knew enough about me and Jake to find me on there if nothing else. But after everything I've learned in the last month about Jaina's parents, I think they're the main reason she didn't contact me. I'm sure it was hard for her to trust a nineteen-year-old guy to be capable of loving and taking care of his child, after growing up with parents who don't seem to know how to love anything but their bank account and public image."

Cait heard hushed whispers coming from the Joneses, but she couldn't make out what they were saying to their attorney. *Probably*

449

trying to get him to object instead of just waiting to try to negate Josh's statement in cross-examination.

"Take us back to how you found out about your son, and how you were ultimately reunited with him," Gabe directed Josh.

"My family all decided to do one of those online DNA tests to trace our family history," Josh grinned, relaxing back in the chair on the witness stand. "My great-great-great-grandparents died in the nineteen-twenties not knowing what happened to their daughter, my great-great-grandaunt, at the end of World War I because she didn't come back to the ranch after serving as a nurse. So, we figured if enough of us did the DNA test, we could find her descendants to give them their rightful inheritance and solve a hundred-year-old family mystery. So, most everyone sent off their saliva samples in January and found our Avington cousins in February."

"Your honor, at this time I'd like to submit Burleson exhibit one, printouts of Josh Burleson's Ancestry profile, DNA match list, match comparison with the Triple J profile, and the messages Josh sent to the Triple J profile on the website." Josh's attorney handed over a stack of papers.

"I'll accept Burleson exhibit one," Judge English agreed.

Gabe then turned back to Josh and continued questioning him. "But you didn't send in your DNA at that time?"

"No, I was on base in Virginia Beach when most of them sent in their samples, and halfway around the world on an op when they all got together to pour over DNA match lists and made the connection with our fourth cousins." Josh looked down like he was embarrassed to admit to his location when that connection was made.

Because he wasn't a part of solving the mystery? Or because he mentioned an op that is supposed to remain classified?

"When did you send in your DNA? And why did you do the test at all if the mystery had already been solved?"

"Jake and I both sent ours in while we were home on leave at the end of March. I honestly didn't think we'd find anything different than the rest of the family," Josh shrugged, his lips lifting at the corners in the slightest smile. "But Jake and I had joked at Christmas about figuring out which one of us was switched at birth, since we're twins but so different from one another. So, since the tests were there waiting for us, we kinda had to follow through."

Josh turned to look at the judge once more before adding, "My family will tell you I'm the jokester of the family, but they're all just as bad, only sneakier about it. So, we had to be proactive about sending in our samples to keep them from pranking us by having a friend send in their DNA with our names on the samples to try to make us think we really were switched at birth."

After the pranks he pulled on Becky, I wouldn't be surprised if Becky had tried sending in her sample multiple times to try to make them believe their genetic sex didn't match their genital organs.

"And when did you look at the results for the first time?"

"April twenty-eighth, right after I got the email telling me that they were ready. Like I said, I didn't expect to see anything other than what my siblings had told me they saw on their profiles. But then I saw an extra person besides my mom and dad in the Parent-Child section of the match lists with fifty percent shared DNA. When I looked at the Immediate Family section and saw Jake with forty-nine percent shared DNA, I momentarily thought the Triple J profile could be a triplet that was stolen at birth. But deep down, I knew the truth. I was just upset because I didn't know how to find him. Then I called my sister Charlotte, who'd been doing most of the research on our family tree, and she looked at her match list to see that she didn't share enough DNA with Triple J for him to be another sibling, so I knew my gut reaction was correct. He had to be my child."

"What did you do once you realized that you had a child?"

"I fu…freaked out and called Jake to help me try to find him," Josh chuckled, using his boyish charm to cover his almost use of an expletive. "The profile only listed Triple J with a blue icon for a boy and that he, or I assumed his mom, had last logged into the site in March. It wasn't enough for me to find him on social media, but Jake's computer skills are much more advanced than mine, so I thought he might be able to find him online somehow."

"Was Jake able to find Joshua?"

"No," Josh sighed and shook his head. "There wasn't enough information for him to track either. At least, not without a warrant for the user data from the website. And without the legal name to go along with the username, I couldn't file a case for custody to have a reason for the court to grant a warrant for the site to give me the legal name associated with the profile. So, I sent a message on the Ancestry site to the Triple J profile, and spent the next four months eagerly awaiting a response."

"Did you do anything else to try to find your son?"

"Yeah, I bugged Jake constantly for ideas on how else we could search for my son and his mom. That led to him suggesting I try to remember every hookup I've ever had, so we could scour social media to find my child's mother. And since I pretty much forgot every other woman I've ever met the instant I first saw my girlfriend Cait back in December, that was a virtually impossible task."

Cait grinned, feeling herself blush when Josh smiled and winked at her.

"How did you end up finding Joshua?" Gabe continued the questioning, getting Josh back on track.

"I didn't," Josh chuckled. "He found me. After being shipped off to boarding school by the Joneses, he finally managed to log onto the website and saw the messages I'd sent. Well, he saw the first message before his teacher caught him on the site, made him log out, and watched him too closely for him to read the rest or reply to me. But since the school had confiscated his cell phone, he couldn't call me, even though he did see the message where I gave him my phone number. So, he snuck out of the school and got on a bus to my hometown, which I'd mentioned in that first message on the website."

"Objection, hearsay," Mr. Stephenson interjected. "Mr. Burleson cannot testify to what happened with Joshua prior to his arrival in Texas."

"Sustained," the judge ruled.

Damn it! He's not supposed to rule in favor of what the Joneses' attorney wants.

JoJo squeezed Cait's hand, drawing her attention away from what the judge and attorneys were saying for a moment.

"I can tell the judge when it's my turn to talk, though, right?" JoJo whispered, looking up at Cait imploringly.

"Yes," Cait whispered back, nodding her head before turning back to face the front of the courtroom.

"Tell us about the first time you saw your son," Gabe smiled at Josh.

"It was surreal," Josh replied, his voice tinged with awe. "I was trying to get in a good position to catch the garter at my sister's wedding, 'cause Cait had just caught the bouquet and I didn't want anyone else trying to pair up with my girl for the pictures. But my brother-in-law had his son toss the garter, and it didn't quite go the way I thought it would. Apparently, when Mikey told Brody to throw it to 'Uncle Josh,' he just heard 'Josh,' so he threw it to the boy he met that night named Josh."

Josh paused to chuckle and grin at JoJo. "The instant I saw him, I thought I must be hallucinating or something. Like I thought, my mind must be playing tricks on me because of being frustrated with not finding my son, so maybe I was imagining him there. It was like looking at myself when I was his age, so I didn't think he could possibly be real. Then he said he was there looking for his dad and said my name. And all I could think was, 'If I'm dreaming, I hope nobody wakes me up'."

"We ended up going to a private room off the ballroom where the reception was being held, so he could meet the family and tell us how he managed to get to Heart's Destiny, Texas, on his own. And then we had even more to celebrate when we went back to the reception."

"I believe you did a lot more than celebrate when you went back to the reception." Gabe arched an eyebrow at Josh. "Please tell us about the legal steps you started taking that night."

"I admit, I was so excited about finally getting to meet my son that I immediately went for the cake and celebrating," Josh chuckled and gave a half-shrug. "But luckily, I have a fabulous family who helped me through the legal issues I didn't even know I needed to navigate. My Uncle Doug is our city court judge, and my oldest brother, Bobby, is the Heart's Destiny police chief. And they both knew there could be legal ramifications for harboring a runaway. Bobby's wife, Brooklyn, founded the Madeline Ashbury Foundation and turned an extra bunkhouse on the ranch into the second location of the Ashbury houses she's opening up around the country. So, Brook called her contact person in the Texas Department of Family and Children's Services to get everything set up for JoJo to be placed in the care of the Ashbury Foundation over the weekend, until the DFACS office in Virginia opened on Monday morning for them to coordinate everything, since JoJo is technically a resident of Virginia."

"That Monday morning is when Tyler Reilly contacted my office about representing you, correct?"

"Yes, sir," Josh nodded in agreement with Gabe Adams' statement.

"Please inform the court how you know Mr. Reilly and why you hired him to act as your liaison with our office," Gabe instructed Josh, as he pulled out another piece of paper and a folder full of papers from his briefcase.

"We live in a small town, so I guess there's a lot of ways you could say I know him," Josh half-shrugged. "His daughter is one of my friends from high school, but he's also friends with my parents, so I guess the most appropriate is to say he's a family friend. But he's also a family law attorney, and I actually hired him to represent me, thinking this might be able to be handled in Texas, since that's my permanent residence and where JoJo was at the time. And he did handle everything he could from there, scheduling the home visits and background checks needed to list me as JoJo's temporary guardian, instead of the Ashbury Foundation, as well as scheduling the appointment for the first blood test to prove I'm JoJo's dad. But since custody cases have to be tried in the child's state of residence, which for JoJo is Virginia, he couldn't represent me here, which is why he coordinated with your office to represent me this week."

"Your honor, at this time, I'd like to submit Burleson exhibits two and three, the blood test results from Dr. Eric Hayes's office in Heart's Destiny, Texas, and the Texas Department of Family and Children's Services records showing their opinions on Josh Burleson's fitness as a parent."

After the judge accepted the exhibits, Gabe continued questioning Josh. "Do you know the contents of the two exhibits I just submitted?"

"I know the blood test confirmed what I already knew about being JoJo's dad," Josh grinned. "But I haven't seen the DFACS records to know what's in them. I'd be willing to guess they recommend giving me custody of my son, though, since they convinced their counterparts in Virginia to allow me to have temporary custody of JoJo while we're waiting to find out the judge's ruling in this hearing."

"Objection, speculation," Mr. Stephenson barked.

"Unfortunately, I have to sustain that objection," Judge English sighed, leaning over the side of the bench to hand Josh the folder Gabe had just submitted as Burleson exhibit three. "Please reword the question, Mr. Adams, so Mr. Burleson can answer with specific statements from the records."

"Yes, your honor," Gabe nodded at the judge before turning back to Josh. "Josh, please read the final line on the last page of the case summary."

Josh flipped through the papers in the folder until he found the page in question and began reading. "It is our recommendation that full and permanent custody of the minor child, Joshua Jacob Jones, be granted to his biological father, Joshua Bennett Burleson." After reading the line, Josh looked up and grinned.

Cait couldn't help but grin back, even though she knew Josh was actually smiling at his son, who was seated beside her, mirroring his father's dazzling smile. She'd always seen the resemblance between them, but when they smiled at the same time, it almost seemed like they could be identical twins, if they hadn't been born twenty years apart.

"In his testimony on Tuesday, Mr. Jones claimed that you aren't suitable to raise Joshua because of your limited income and unpredictable job as a Navy SEAL," Gabe moved on to the next point he wanted Josh to make on the stand. "In order to clear up any misconceptions his testimony might have given the court, please explain your income and job status."

"As a former Navy officer, I was really surprised to hear Mr. Jones classify my income as limited," Josh chuckled. "But then again, it's been a few years since he was a lieutenant, so maybe he's not familiar with the current pay rate for an O-3. Since earning that rank in the Navy, I've been making about a hundred-thousand dollars a year as a Navy SEAL, which is a little more than half of what he made as a rear admiral lower half and approximately the same amount he gets in retirement every year now. Maybe that's why he thinks it's a limited income. It has to be hard learning to cut back after having his income cut like that."

"Do you have other forms of income besides your Navy pay?" Gabe cut Josh off before he could veer too far off on a tangent of only slightly veiled insults to the Joneses and their financial status.

"Yes," Josh sighed, his expression suddenly melancholy. "Three years ago, when my Pappaw Jerry passed away, my siblings, cousins, and I inherited his share of our family business and were named to the board of directors. That provides a salary of two-hundred-and-fifty-thousand dollars a year, plus dividends on my portion of the company. Originally, my portion was five percent, but after finding our Avington cousins in February, the shares were recalculated, so now I only own like three-and-a-half percent. Pappaw Jerry's will also stipulated that each of his grandchildren are to inherit a trust fund, either on our thirtieth birthday or when we get married. Last time I checked, my trust fund was in the nine-hundred-million range, but with interest and such, I expect it to be right at a billion when I turn thirty to inherit it. If I don't get married to inherit it before then."

Holy shit! Cait's jaw dropped, as did several others around the room. *I knew the Burlesons were wealthy, but I didn't know they're that freaking loaded! And Josh is sitting there all calm, cool, and collected, talking about a billion dollars as if it's pocket change.*

Cait was so flustered by the realization that she missed hearing what Mr. Adams submitted for Burleson exhibit four, but assumed it had something to do with showing Josh's inheritance from his grandpa.

No wonder he wasn't intimidated by the Joneses and how rich they act. Evelyn might have boasted on the stand the other day about coming from a high-society family and wanting her grandson to grow up in the lap of luxury instead of on a "dirty ranch," but it sounds like the Burlesons are worth a hell of a lot more than the Joneses. Especially if each of his siblings and cousins are right there with him at billionaire status from their trust funds.

Holy shit! If he's serious about us getting married one day, he'd better have a prenup drawn up. No way in hell do I want anyone thinking I'm interested in him for his money. While my sperm and egg donors both seem to care more about money than people, Mikey raised me to be more self-sufficient than that. I'd be perfectly happy if we had to live on my income as a screenwriter. And now that I know just how freaking rich Josh is, I need to make sure he knows that, too.

Her mental spiral caused her to miss what was said about how Burleson Incorporated was structured and JoJo's future inheritance. She barely registered hearing Josh mention that no matter who got custody of JoJo, they needed to make arrangements for him to spend time with his cousins, whom he would one day work with on the Burleson Incorporated board of directors, and devote time for him to learn all about the company, so he wouldn't be overwhelmed with everything when he inherited his portion of the business.

She started to tune back into the proceedings when Mr. Adams submitted Burleson exhibits five and six, getting Josh back on track to discussing his current income and job, instead of the trust funds he didn't have access to currently.

After the judge accepted the exhibits, Gabe continued questioning Josh. "Please explain the significance of DD Form 214, hereby known as Burleson exhibit five."

"That's my certificate of release from the Navy," Josh explained with an affable smile. "I was actually on terminal leave from the end of August through the month of September, and just finished up my official time in the Navy on Monday."

"Since you will no longer be earning a salary as a Navy SEAL, does that mean your annual income has now decreased?"

"No," Josh chuckled. "While the United States Navy will no longer be giving me a paycheck, I accepted a higher paying job last Friday, so my overall income will be going up by about a hundred-and-fifty-thousand dollars a year."

"Tell us about the new job, specifically the details outlined in the human resources file hereby known as Burleson exhibit six."

"I'm now the vice president of agriculture and beef for Burleson Incorporated," Josh elaborated with a smile. "That file includes my offer letter, which outlines my salary and benefits, as well as my new duties and responsibilities in the position. In addition to the beef operation on the original Burleson Ranch where the majority of my family resides, I'll be overseeing all beef and crop operations on all the farms and ranches owned by the company throughout the nation."

"Would you consider this new job safer and less unpredictable than your last job as a SEAL?"

"Safer? Possibly," Josh smirked. "I'll probably get a lot more paper cuts in this job as opposed to when I was in the Navy. But even when I have to carry a weapon in case of snakes in the field when I'm checking on crops or predators trying to harm the cattle, the coyotes and rattlers won't be shooting back like the terrorists I faced as a SEAL."

Is he really joking around on the stand about being shot at? Yes! Yes, he is. Because he's a crazy cowboy, who thinks his mother named him Josh so he could spend his entire life joshin' around about everything. I bet even as a SEAL, he told the terrorists a bad joke or two before he killed them.

And I wouldn't want the big lug any other way. Cait finally smiled, choosing to embrace Josh's philosophy of laughing his way through life. *I guess, even the scariest things aren't as frightening when we're laughing as we face them.*

His expression turned contemplative as he thought for a moment before smiling once again and continuing his answer. "As for being less unpredictable, I'd have to say no. I'll use the skills I learned while getting my degree in operations research in a different manner in this new job than I did as a SEAL, so I can try to predict crop yields and steer growth instead of terrorist movements. But natural disasters and unexpected storms can still wreak havoc on our operations."

"I believe Mr. Jones was referring to the unpredictable loss of life on SEAL ops," Gabe chuckled. "Not unpredictable corporate profits."

"Well, I guess if you don't consider plants as living things, then yeah, the loss of life in my new job is a lot more predictable than it is for the SEALs," Josh smirked. "There's a lot more loss of life in the beef industry, but we have full control over how many head of cattle go to the slaughterhouse each year. While SEALs are the elite force of the U.S. military, even we can't train the terrorists to line up and walk into the slaughterhouse."

Cait giggled at the unexpected image that popped into her head at Josh's statement. *If only we could train the worst criminals in the world to willingly walk to their deaths like cattle, maybe we'd have fewer issues with violent criminals like the cartels and wouldn't have overcrowded prisons anymore.*

Apparently, Earnie didn't think Josh was as funny as Cait did. "You think this is a joke?" Earnie shouted, pointing at Josh on the witness stand. "I was talking about how you can't be a good father when you were off risking your life all the time. But maybe I should have mentioned how someone who jokes about death is obviously too deranged to be a proper parent."

"No, I don't think death is a joke," Josh barked back, glaring at Earnie with disgust and anger blazing in his eyes. "Especially the death of a fellow SEAL. But my point in injecting humor into my answers to these questions isn't to make light of death. It's to point out how asinine your opinion is when you claim SEALs aren't fit to be parents. The SEALs I've worked with are some of the finest men I've ever met. But you wouldn't understand the way we're willing to risk our lives to save innocent people we don't even know, since you're so incapable of caring about anyone but yourself that you wouldn't even give your own daughter your family medical history to try to save her life."

Josh closed his eyes for a moment, composing himself before he turned back to his attorney. "As for whether or not I'm more or less likely to die unexpectedly in this job than when I was an active-duty SEAL, I have no way of knowing for sure. Only God knows when my time on this earth will end. I don't believe I'm as likely to get shot again while working on the ranch or one of our other corporate locations as I was when I was an active-duty SEAL. But with mass shootings on the rise in recent years, I can't say the same about going to the park or the mall, or any number of other public places. Especially public places like this courthouse, where I'm not allowed to carry a weapon to be able to defend my family if some punk decides to come try to take out the judge who sent him to prison, or whatever other stupid reason criminals come up with for shooting a bunch of innocent bystanders. At least as a SEAL, I had enough Kevlar to protect my vital organs and plenty of firepower to take out the bastard who shot me, so being shot wasn't that big a deal."

Cait sucked in a breath at Josh's unexpected reveal of information she didn't think he wanted his mother to know. Considering the gasps she heard behind her, she assumed Josh would be having a few uncomfortable conversations with his family members after court, with Hazel being the first in line to reprimand him for not telling his family when he'd been shot. Her sympathy for Josh having to answer to his mom overrode any fear she might have had from Josh talking about mass shootings and him not being armed to protect them.

On the witness stand, Josh seemed to come to the same conclusion Cait had, saying a quick, "Sorry, Ma," before closing his eyes for a moment to calm down once more. After regaining his composure, he continued.

"I don't know how many people die each year from car accidents, heart attacks, cancer, etc. But I know it's a lot. That's why I do what I imagine most of the people in this room do to eat healthy, exercise, and pay attention while driving, trying to decrease my risk factors for those things, so JoJo doesn't have to worry about losing another parent."

Josh gave his son a sympathetic smile before turning back to speak directly to the judge. "I can also tell you we only had twenty-seven Navy SEALs die last year. *Twenty-seven.* Less than thirty SEALs died while there were over thirty-thousand people killed in terrorist attacks during the same twelve-month timeframe. There were also three-hundred-and-forty mass shootings in the United States last year that weren't classified as terrorist acts, resulting in almost four-hundred deaths and over thirteen-hundred non-fatal injuries. So, overall, I'd say it's safer to be a SEAL than to be a civilian. And more importantly, after rescuing more innocent bystanders than we've lost in my time as a SEAL, I'd say my training and experience in the Navy will keep my family safe if we're ever in a dangerous situation, even if I'm caught unarmed like now."

Josh paused to take a breath and smile at Cait and JoJo. "And since my dad taught me that one of the most important things a parent should do for their kids is protect them, I think being a SEAL shows I'm more than qualified to parent my son."

Josh turned his head and lifted his chin toward the Joneses' table. "Way more qualified than the Joneses, who turned their backs on their daughter and then shipped JoJo off to boarding school, instead of being there for him as he was grieving the loss of his mother."

"Speaking of your time as a SEAL," Gabe interjected, transitioning quickly to get Josh focused on something other than being aggressively argumentative with the Joneses. He pulled another stack of papers from his briefcase. "In preparing for this case, I contacted your commanding officer to obtain a little more information than the very-redacted file the Navy provided. While he gave me the same spiel you did about not being able to discuss classified missions, he did provide me with a few names of people I should reach out to for character references."

Gabe redirected his comments from Josh to the judge. "Your honor, at this time, I'd like to submit Burleson exhibits seven through eighteen, each a separate letter written by one of the people whom Josh Burleson has impacted during his time as a SEAL."

Seven through eighteen? That's like twelve different letters. The Joneses and Tawny only had half that many character references — combined.

After the judge accepted the exhibits, he scanned over them before handing them to Josh, presumably for him to be able to read certain passages from them.

Cait was impressed by the names of the high-ranking politicians and foreign dignitaries that took the time to write personalized letters detailing not only Josh's bravery on missions, but also how personable he was when they met him. Josh refused to read any sections of the letters that gave details about classified operations, but since one of them was from Senator Kurt Lexington, she assumed Becky had guessed correctly that he'd been involved in rescuing his daughter when the boat she was on was seized by pirates off the coast of Kala earlier in the year.

While she was exceptionally proud of him for all he'd done as a SEAL, she was also relieved that he wouldn't be going on such dangerous missions in the future.

The letter that made her most proud, however, was the one written by the former President of the United States, who had just left the Oval Office two years ago. Not because it was signed by the President, or even because it talked about Josh earning a Presidential Medal of Honor during his first year as a SEAL, although those were both impressive features of the letter. Cait was most impressed by how the President had described the interaction between Josh and the first family.

At that time, the President's youngest daughter had just turned sixteen, and Josh compared notes with her about the drastically different ways they learned to drive. Apparently, Josh had made learning to drive a tractor seem like so much more fun than she was having while learning to drive from the Secret Service that she tried to convince her dad to let Josh take over her lessons. The President had ended the letter by asking if Josh's invitation to the first family to visit the ranch was still open, now that they'd both changed jobs and could actually get some time off at the same time to make it happen.

"Of course," Josh chuckled when he read that section of the letter, grinning from ear to ear as he looked back up at his lawyer. "You'll have to give me whatever number you called to get this reference letter, so I can give Barry a call to set that up."

Only Josh would call a former President of the United States by a nickname. Cait grinned, knowing Hazel would invite the presidential family to stay at her house, instead of at the bed and breakfast in town.

"I'm sure that can be arranged," Gabe chuckled before moving on with his questioning. "Speaking of your family ranch, please tell the court your plans for living there with your son in the future."

"For the last month, we've been staying in my childhood home with my parents," Josh smiled at his parents in the audience before turning his gaze to the judge. "While there are several houses on the ranch that have been passed down since the mid-eighteen hundreds, currently, they're all occupied by my siblings, cousins, and my girlfriend, Cait. So, Mom and Dad's place was the best fit for me and JoJo while we're stuck in limbo with how this hearing is gonna go. I didn't want to get started on building something there until I know we won't have to move here to share custody of JoJo."

Josh turned to look at Cait and JoJo, grinning widely as he announced his plans for their future if he got sole custody of JoJo. "But ideally, JoJo will get to come home with the rest of us Burlesons when this is settled. Then we can move in with Cait while I convince her to marry me. Since the house she lives in is the smallest on the ranch, it won't be big enough for our family for long. But until I get a new metal barn built for the tractors, mowers, and balers and renovate the wood barn my great-grandparents built to make it into our home, the two bedrooms should be sufficient."

He wants to convert the barn we use when we sneak off to fool around in the hayloft into our home? That's so cool! And way more meaningful than the new construction Mikey and Char are talking about for their house. Cait couldn't help but smile at the sentimental man she loved as he winked at her once more from the stand. *Hope you can renovate fast, Cowboy, because hearing you talk about romantic plans like that is giving me ideas about making babies to fill all that space.*

~~~
~~~

Josh felt like he'd run through the entire gamut of emotions when he finally got through testifying and was able to get off the witness stand. Gabe had ended his questioning by asking about his relationship with Cait, setting up for her to be next on the witness stand. Talking about falling in love had brought his mood back up after discussing the other topics that highlighted his grief and anger. Unfortunately, he couldn't finish his testimony on that happy note, however, since he'd still had to sit through being cross-examined by the other attorneys representing the other parties in the case.

Ms. Baker questioning him about his willingness to allow Tawny to be a part of JoJo's life wasn't too bad. He'd been able to maintain a neutral façade as he stated clearly that he would gladly welcome Tawny if she wanted to come visit JoJo in Heart's Destiny, and would be happy to set aside time for them to visit whenever he brought his family to Alexandria to see Jake.

Mr. Stephenson's cross-examination was a different story altogether. After fighting to control his temper while the Joneses' lawyer badgered him with asinine questions, Josh wished Cait didn't have to take the stand at all.

He was half-tempted to tell Gabe not to call her to the stand. But he knew that was just his lizard brain being an alpha asshole in the way he wanted to try to protect her, even though she wanted the chance to stand up for herself. Since he knew she'd protest if he tried pulling that move, he quickly realized there was nothing he could do to keep her from being called up next. So, he paused beside her as he walked to his seat, pecking her lips as his show of support for what she was about to endure.

Cait smiled up at him as he lifted his lips from hers. Josh returned the sweet smile before stepping around her and JoJo to take his seat beside his attorney. Gabe then called Cait to the stand.

She didn't look even the slightest bit nervous as she confidently walked forward and was sworn in to testify. Josh was amazed by how far she'd come from the scared woman he'd first met in December. He wished he could take some of the credit for helping her heal from the ordeal she'd been through and grow into the exquisite, poised woman on the stand. But he knew he'd only been there to support her as she showed off her inner strength.

Leah Mae Wright

"Miss Campbell, please tell the court how you met Mr. Burleson," Gabe instructed, instead of asking a specific question.

"Josh pretty much told you our story already," Cait shrugged, smiling slightly. "But we met at a holiday party his family hosted last year between Christmas and New Year's, right after I moved to Heart's Destiny with my brother and nephew. I met all of the Burlesons that day, along with several other people, who all gave us a warm welcome to town."

"When did you and Josh start dating?"

"Officially? The eighth of last month," Cait replied with a grin in Josh's direction. "But just like most of the couples in Heart's Destiny, we fell for each other the first moment our eyes met on December twenty-ninth of last year. And we spent time together as friends pretty much daily whenever Josh was home on leave. So, it feels more like we've been a couple for nine months instead of one."

Josh knew he'd been committed to her from day one, even back before they'd said a word to one another. But it was still nice for him to hear that she'd felt the same.

"So, you officially became a couple the day after Joshua arrived in Heart's Destiny?"

"Yes," Cait nodded her agreement with Gabe's question.

"We've already heard about Josh wanting to make sure everything worked out with him getting out of the Navy and getting custody of his son to move home before asking you out. But it's the twenty-first century and no longer uncommon for women to make the first move. So, since you fell for Josh back in December, why did it take you eight months before taking that next step with Josh?"

"It might not be uncommon here, or even back in San Diego, where I grew up," Cait grinned cheekily. "But even though Heart's Destiny is more progressive than some of the surrounding small towns, it still has an old-fashioned vibe that makes it feel like we live on the set of a classic TV sitcom. Besides, even when I lived in San Diego, I wasn't the type to make the first move. And on top of it not feeling right for me to be the aggressor in our relationship, I felt like I needed to work through some of the issues I developed after…"

Cait's voice trailed off as she started one of the breathing exercises he'd seen her do whenever she talked about the shooting in the past. *Fuck! I didn't even think about her having to dredge all that up.*

Before Josh could get Gabe's attention to have him call for a break so he could console Cait, she locked her eyes on him and finished her sentence. "After I was shot in a drive-by at my nephew's second birthday party at Cesar Chavez Park."

Fuck! I didn't realize the park they were in was that close to Coronado. If it'd been two years earlier, I coulda been hanging out there with the guys between BUD/S and parachute training. Hell, if that's the park they went to most of the time, it's a wonder we didn't meet when I was there.

Gabe was clearly caught off guard by the revelation of information they hadn't previously disclosed to him, so Cait continued speaking, filling the silence that followed a few gasps from around the courtroom.

"On December third, two-thousand-sixteen, the Rodriguez Cartel targeted the park, trying to eliminate the undercover DEA agent who'd infiltrated their ranks. My brother, Michael, was that agent. Two people died, including my sister-in-law, Marisol, and thirteen people were wounded, including both myself and Mikey. Since Mikey's cover was blown, when we were released from the hospital, the DEA moved us to a safe house in the suburbs. But on top of my physical injuries, I suffered from PTSD and anxiety that developed into agoraphobia."

"When my brother told me about wanting to move to Texas for a new job in December, I thought the change of scenery would help me most in trying to get over the agoraphobia. And for the first week or so, it did. I was not only able to go to a couple of holiday parties full of strangers, but I also got a job outside my brother's home, and I even drove myself to the hardware store alone."

Cait paused to take a deep breath, not taking her eyes off of Josh. He hoped his smile conveyed how proud he was of her for being able to talk about all this in front of a courtroom full of strangers. *You got this, Sunshine. Keep goin'. Show 'em all how strong you are, and what a wonderful lesson in perseverance you're gonna be for our kids.*

Cait nodded as if she'd heard his unspoken words. "But then I found out that Mikey hadn't wanted to move to Texas for the new experience of teaching middle school, or to get away from the cartel specter hanging over us. Instead, he was there at the request of his former DEA partner to track down the head of the cartel, who'd escaped the DEA's raids in the two years since the shooting. And I regressed big time. I could only leave the house when Mikey drove me, and even then I only felt safe enough to get out of the car when he took me to the local church, the Burleson Ranch, or the bed and breakfast, where we'd stayed that first week in town. I was only able to keep my job because it was on the Burleson Ranch and the Burlesons made me feel as safe with them as I felt with Mikey."

"How did you manage to get to the point where you're able to be here in court?" Judge English interrupted Cait when it was obvious Gabe wasn't going to stop her to ask any questions.

Cait looked up at the judge but nodded her head in Josh's direction. "Josh and his family helped Mikey bring down the last of the Rodriguez Cartel. They also rallied around me, supporting me in my efforts to push past the fear and be more outgoing, like I was before the shooting. You've already got a dozen character references for Josh from people who are a lot more important in this world than I'll ever be, but I can tell you from first-hand experience that those twelve letters are just the tip of the iceberg of how many you'd be inundated with if everyone who's benefited from knowing anyone in the Burleson family sent them to you."

She turned to point out the Burlesons seated in the gallery of the courtroom. "Becky, Jen, and Julie stepped up to be my best friends even before anyone knew about romantic feelings between me and Josh, or between Mikey and Charlotte. And Char feels like my sister now that she and Mikey are married and she's adopted my nephew, Brody. Hazel has treated me like a member of the family since the first time I sat down to talk to her during my interview. Since my egg donor never acted very motherly, it took me a little time to get used to having Hazel mother me. But now I think of her as one of my extra moms. The same goes for Josh's Aunt Susan, who couldn't be here today because she's on baby watch back at the ranch. But I guarantee the rest of the Burlesons would have been here to support Josh and JoJo this week, if Brooklyn and Amy weren't so far along in their pregnancies that they're not allowed to fly, and Mikey and Char had been able to get substitute teachers for their middle school classes."

Josh had to chuckle at Cait mentioning why part of his family couldn't be in Virginia for the hearing.

"They're a very close-knit family with a lot of love to share, even for those of us who aren't biologically related. I don't think there's a better family anywhere on the planet, so the Burleson Ranch is absolutely the best place for JoJo to grow up."

"Objection. The witness is rambling about subjects not pertaining to the question," Mr. Stephenson interjected.

"Before you rule on the objection, your honor, I'd like to point out that Miss Campbell was originally on my witness list as a character witness for Mr. Burleson," Gabe pointed out. "So, we can save the court a little time by allowing Miss Campbell's testimony to stand, instead of making her repeat it all after I go through my original list of questions for her."

"Objection overruled," Judge English agreed. "But please get back to your list of questions, Mr. Adams, so we can move the hearing along a little faster."

"Thank you, your honor," Gabe nodded at the judge before turning back to Cait to continue his questioning. "Since we're able to skip the character reference questions, please state for the court why you believed you'd only be testifying as a character witness on Monday when you accompanied Mr. Burleson to my office, and how that changed on Tuesday."

"Honestly, on Monday when we first met with you, I didn't think I'd even be testifying as a character witness." Cait chuckled ruefully. "I only came to Virginia to be able to take care of JoJo if he wasn't allowed in the courtroom during these proceedings. It wasn't until you informed us that JoJo would need to be here that I offered to be a character witness. But I also didn't know Mr. Jones's first name, until I figured it out when he verbally accosted us on Tuesday morning before court."

"Why did you not know Mr. Jones's first name? And how did you figure it out?"

"Josh always referred to JoJo's maternal grandparents as the Joneses, never by their first names. And when we met with you on Monday afternoon, that was also how you referred to them." Cait shrugged and cocked her lips up on one side. "I don't know if you realize it, but Jones is one of the most common last names in America. So, it didn't dawn on me that Mr. Jones in Virginia could possibly be the Earnie Jones who'd been stationed in San Diego, and I'd been told might be my sperm donor."

Josh stifled a chuckle at Cait's look of disbelief, knowing she was calling on her acting background to ham it up a little.

"Then Tuesday, while we were sitting there minding our own business, the peaceful silence was broken by that pretentious old couple stopping at the end of the row where we were sitting to call Josh a *ne'er-do-well* and accuse him of deserting Jaina while she was pregnant." Cait pointed at the Joneses when she referred to them as "that pretentious old couple," making Josh chuckle.

"As if he was the one who knew she was pregnant and deserted her instead of them." Cait rolled her eyes. "Then when Josh corrected their misconception by saying he was the lucky man who just found out he was JoJo's dad, she objected to the nickname. It was when Josh explained why I came up with the nickname that they noticed me sitting there on the other side of JoJo. And that's when the ranting really started. I figured out he had to be Earnie when he mentioned Lorna and turned so red from anger that I thought he was going to have a heart attack or stroke before he quit spitting out his vile accusations toward me, which is why I warned you to have paramedics on hand before you asked him about that DNA test yesterday."

"So, you didn't recognize him when you first saw him?"

"No, and I honestly don't know how he recognized me, since I was ten and in school when they went to court during that paternity case." Cait shook her head. "Until Tuesday, I'd never been in the same room with him. At least that I know of. I suppose I could have been when I was a baby or toddler and don't remember it. And the only picture I've seen of him was one I found online, when I was thirteen or fourteen, from a newspaper article that ran in two-thousand-and-two. I don't exactly remember the details from a picture I only saw once over a decade ago."

"Were the 'vile accusations' he spat at you on Tuesday before this hearing the same as the claims he made on the stand later that day?"

"Yes, if you're referring to his claims that I'm a prostitute and in cahoots with Lorna to try to steal his money." Cait rolled her eyes. "You'd think, if he kept up with me enough to be able to recognize me so easily, he'd know my work history, and that I haven't been in contact with Lorna in over a decade, either."

"Why were you not in contact with your, um, Lorna Campbell?" Gabe smiled apologetically as he corrected his question to keep from referring to Lorna as Cait's mother.

"Because when I was thirteen, she was arrested for drug possession and my brother, Mikey, was awarded custody of me," Cait stated matter-of-factly, her face completely devoid of emotion. "We were able to talk to her a couple of times while she was in prison, but when she got out three years later, she disappeared. Not that Mikey would have willingly given her custody of me again, but it would have been nice if she'd cared enough to at least try to come and visit us. Though I suppose I can understand how uncomfortable it would be for an ex-con to visit the home of a cop, even though she gave birth to the cop."

"Can you please give us a brief overview of your work history, starting with the present and working your way back to when you first started working?"

"Currently, I work in the entertainment division of Burleson Incorporated as a screenwriter. My boss is Becky Burleson." Cait pointed to Becky in the gallery of the courtroom. "Prior to that, I worked as a housekeeper on the Burleson Ranch, reporting to Hazel Burleson." Cait smiled as she pointed to Josh's mom next. "And since she's here in the courtroom, Jen Burleson is the vice president of the human resources department, so she can probably pull up my HR file on her laptop for you if you need to submit it as evidence of my employment history since January."

"I don't think that will be necessary at this time," Gabe grinned at Cait. "Please continue with your employment history prior to your move to Heart's Destiny, Texas."

"From December of twenty-sixteen to July of this year, I was the live-in nanny for my nephew. But it wasn't an official, paid job. Just family taking care of family while we were all healing, both physically and emotionally. I still watch Brody when I'm home and Mikey and Char are working, but now the rest of the Burlesons pitch in, so it's not a full-time thing anymore."

"Prior to that, I worked with the Armsburger Agency in San Diego as a model and actress while I was in high school and then college at San Diego State University." Cait paused to breathe for a moment before continuing. "I started working with them in twenty-ten, when I turned eighteen. Prior to that, I did the typical teenage thing with babysitting and fast-food jobs."

"So, there's no truth to the claims Mr. Jones made about you having a criminal record for prostitution?"

"My brother had just finished the police academy and started working as a cop full time when he got custody of me." Cait rolled her eyes. "During my teen years, he worked his way up through the ranks at the SDPD and was recruited to the DEA. With my brother in the role of doting dad, I couldn't have gotten away with misbehaving if I'd tried. But if you don't believe me, run my name and social security number through N.C.I.C. and you'll see my record is spotless."

"And what do you know about the paternity case from two-thousand-three and the DNA tests run on you and Mr. Jones?"

"Mostly, just what you pointed out from the records you found and the test we had run this week." Cait sighed. "Like I said before, I was ten when Lorna filed that case. I vaguely remember going to the doctor after school one day to have blood drawn and her having some extra money for a couple of months that she claimed was child support because of it. But I wasn't in the courtroom and had no knowledge prior to this week of what might have happened then for the money to suddenly stop coming in. Whenever Lorna would start ranting about stuff like that, Mikey would take me to the library, the park, or the beach to avoid her."

Cait's expression turned wistful, as if she was thinking back on her childhood. "Pretty much all of my happy childhood memories are of times spent with Mikey at the library, park, or beach. At least, until we were able to move out of Lorna's apartment and get a nicer place on our own. Considering where my DNA comes from, I got lucky with having Mikey there to prove that a nurturing environment overrides genetics in human development."

"Thank you, Caitir." Gabe sat down, finished with his portion of the questioning.

Josh was shocked when neither of the other attorneys had any questions for Cait. While he hadn't expected Tawny's lawyer to have any, he'd been fully expecting the Joneses' representative to try to tear her apart on the stand.

I guess they aren't brave enough to give her the chance to fight back so publicly.

Once Cait took her seat, Gabe started calling up Josh's family members to testify on his behalf. One by one they took the stand to tell the court what they'd witnessed between Josh and JoJo in the last month. With the other lawyers not choosing to cross-examine any of them, their testimonies flew by. Then it was time for Gabe to call their final witness, JoJo.

Josh was impressed by how his son carried himself as he took the stand and was sworn in to testify. He acted mature beyond his years as he calmly asked for everyone to please call him JoJo instead of Joshua, so it would be clear in the records that he was speaking and not his dad.

"My apologies," Gabe grinned at JoJo. "I've been referring to you as Joshua and your dad as Josh, because that's how Mr. Reilly differentiated between the two of you when he first spoke to me about this case."

"Yeah, well, I'm only eight, so give a kid a break." JoJo gave an epic eye roll as he flung his arms out to the sides, flipping his wrists to flash his palms toward the ceiling. "Between you and the Joneses calling me Joshua and Aunt Tawny calling me JJ, I'm confused about if ya'll are talkin' about me, my dad, or Uncle JJ. All I know is that ya'll don't know how to be consistent the way Mom taught me adults are supposed to be."

Josh stifled a chuckle at how his son's personality couldn't remain hidden past his initial statement.

"What did your mom teach you about adults being consistent?" Gabe voiced a question that Josh didn't believe was actually on the list of questions he had planned for JoJo.

"That adults are supposed to do stuff the same way and not change things up all the time, especially when they're talking about rules, so kids don't get confused and get in trouble for stuff that wasn't against the rules before." JoJo smiled.

"That's an excellent point," Gabe chuckled. "And I will try to be consistent from now on, JoJo. Can you please tell the court why you specifically asked to testify today?"

"Because I need to tell the judge about the lies that were told on the witness stand yesterday and the day before," JoJo replied, his lips turning down. "And 'cause I'm the one who has to live where the judge decides, so I need to tell him where I want to live before he sends me someplace I don't wanna go."

"Who lied on the witness stand during this hearing? And what did they lie about?"

"Mr. and Mrs. Jones, and Aunt Tawny." JoJo pointed to each of them as he said their names.

"Let's start with your grandparents," Gabe directed JoJo. "What did they lie about on the witness stand?"

"I'm gonna call them Mr. and Mrs. Jones and not grandfather and grandmother like they told me to call them," JoJo informed everyone in the courtroom. "They lied when they said they talked to Mom all the time and came to see us a lot. I didn't meet them until they showed up with that lady," JoJo pointed to a woman at the table with the attorney representing the state of Virginia, "and made me go with them instead of staying with Aunt Tawny after Mom died. They also lied when they said they took care of me like any loving grandparent would. Loving grandparents would have treated me like Memmaw and Pappaw have since I met them. But instead of being nice and doing fun things with me like Memmaw and Pappaw, the Joneses ignored me and sent me to my room most of the time I stayed with them. And they yelled at me every time I did something I didn't know was against their rules, except when the lady came by to see where we were living. And they lied to her about us living there permanently. As soon as she said she had all she needed and wouldn't have to come visit anymore, they took me to their real house in Maryland for a night before sending me on a bus to Somerset Academy."

JoJo shook his head as he glared at the Joneses. "And there were even more rules at Somerset that I didn't know about before getting in trouble for not following them, like not being allowed to have a phone to call Aunt Tawny or get on a computer to find my dad. It was more like goin' to jail than goin' to school."

"Is that why you ran away from Somerset Academy?"

"I ran away from Somerset 'cause I wasn't supposed to be there. Mom told me I'd either live with Aunt Tawny or my dad if we could find him online after sending in my spit. And since Aunt Tawny hadn't come to get me out of jail after being stuck there for months, I took the first chance I had to look on the computer to see if the Ancestry site found my dad. I only got to read his first message before my teacher caught me and made me write lines for playing online after I finished my assignment instead of asking for another one, so I couldn't message him back. And since they'd taken my phone back in May, I couldn't call him once I was in my bunk for the night either. So, I figured if the bus could get me from Annapolis, Maryland, to Roanoke, Virginia, then it could get me to Heart's Destiny, Texas, too. And it did." JoJo gave the judge a beaming smile, obviously proud of himself for navigating the country the way he had.

Little stinker, Josh thought, diligently trying to flatten out his own smile, so the judge wouldn't think he condoned JoJo's actions when he ran away from Somerset.

"Before we get into the details about your trip to Texas," Gabe refocused JoJo. "Let's go back to the original question about the lies on the witness stand. What did Tawny lie about yesterday?"

"She lied when she said Mom wanted her to marry my dad and for them to raise me together," JoJo explained. "When they were talking about doing the spit test to find my dad, Aunt Tawny said she'd marry him since Mom couldn't. But Mom told her that she's not my dad's type, so he wouldn't wanna marry her. And she was right, 'cause he wants to marry Cait."

JoJo paused to smile at Josh and Cait. "I still don't understand what Aunt Tawny meant when she said she's everyone's type. But I'm glad she's not my dad's type, 'cause I want him to marry Cait, too. I know Mom said Aunt Tawny's supposed to be one of my extra moms now that she's gone, but she doesn't really do much mom stuff with me. Cait's done mom stuff with me every day since I met her."

"What do you mean when you talk about 'extra moms' and 'mom stuff'?"

"My extra moms are the women who love me, take care of me, and do stuff with me like my mom did before she died, but they can't be my mom because I didn't come out of their belly," JoJo explained, causing even the judge to grin at his response. "Mom said Aunt Tawny and my dad's girlfriend, or wife, would be my extra moms after she was gone. Only when Dad and Cait get married, she'll be my stepmom, which is the legal term for an extra mom."

"And mom stuff is like baking and decorating cookies together, helping me with my homework, playing games or watching movies with me, teaching me stuff, and just hanging out with me even when my mom or dad isn't able to do stuff with us." JoJo smiled as he detailed all the fun things he considered *mom stuff*, but his lips flattened out as he continued listing the not-so-fun things moms did. "Moms also have to discipline kids when they do something bad and make us do stuff we don't wanna do like cleaning up after playing."

"Tawny didn't do that stuff with you before the Joneses made you move out of her apartment?"

"Not really." JoJo shook his head. "She was there when Mom did some of those things, but she wasn't as interested in talking to me when Mom wasn't there with us. And when Mom was in the hospital and after she died, I spent more time with Mrs. Juanita next door than I did with Aunt Tawny 'cause Aunt Tawny was always working."

"And Cait has done mom stuff with you every day since you met her?"

"Yeah," JoJo nodded, flashing a beaming smile. "Cait does her work in her house or down at Aunt Brook's or Aunt Kay's house most of the time, so even when she's working, I can hang out with her and my aunts, uncles, and cousins. And Dad when he's not having to go talk to his lawyer or do gross stuff with the cows. I like feeding the cows and riding on the tractor when we're cutting hay, but I don't wanna ride along with Dad when he's gotta drive the machine to pick up their poop."

JoJo pinched his nose closed and made a gagging face that made most of the people in the courtroom chuckle.

"I really like staying with Cait when he does that stuff. We made cookies and decorated them the first day I met her. Dad helped too, when he got back from talking to his lawyer. She also helps me with my school work, and is the best at acting out scenes from history so I can actually remember the lessons. She plays video games with me, even though she's terrible at Mario Kart. And when we went to the Alamo, she tackled me to protect me from getting shot when a car backfired, and she thought it was a gun going off."

Josh could feel Cait cringing beside him as JoJo relayed the story. *Damn, I wish she could see that as the act of bravery it was, especially for someone with her background.*

"Dad had told me before we went that Cait was scared of being in crowded places outside like that, so if something happened, I was supposed to help him make her feel safe by holding her hand and staying where he told us to hide while he handled any bad guys. But instead of freaking out and being scared, she made sure I was safe while Dad assessed the situation to protect all of us."

Josh slid over into the seat JoJo wasn't currently using, so he could wrap his arm around Cait. "You did great that day, Sunshine," he whispered in her ear before brushing his lips over the side of her head.

Cait lightly nodded her agreement as she leaned into him.

"Cait also puts me in time-out when I say a bad word and makes sure I eat my vegetables before I can have dessert. She's so good at being an extra mom that she even put Dad in time-out when he tried to eat dessert before dinner."

There were several chuckles throughout the courtroom then, including Josh, Cait, and even Judge English. When the judge arched an eyebrow at Josh, he could only shrug. *Yeah, I'm the bad influence who wants to have dessert before dinner all the time. And yeah, I sat on the sofa in time-out with JoJo when Cait caught us trying to sneak a piece of chocolate cream pie thirty minutes before dinner was ready.*

Gabe redirected the questioning once the laughter in the courtroom died down. Only instead of going back to the topic of JoJo running away and traveling by himself to find his dad, he went straight to his final question for JoJo. "Alright, JoJo, let's wrap this up by getting to the main reason why you're on the witness stand. How do you want the judge to rule on this hearing?"

JoJo turned to look up at the judge before he spoke. "I want you to say I don't have to go back to Somerset or stay with the Joneses ever again. I want to live on the ranch with my dad, extra mom Cait, Memmaw, Pappaw, and all my aunts, uncles, and cousins. I want Aunt Tawny to come visit sometimes, and for us to come visit her sometimes. And I want to change my name to JoJo Joshua Jay Burleson, so everybody has to call me JoJo, but I'm still named after my dad and have part of my mom's name, too."

JoJo turned to look out into the gallery before continuing. "Uncle Jake, Mom only named me after you because she didn't know Dad's middle name, but I want you to have your name back, so you can have a son and name him after you. And if we change my middle name to Jay instead of Jacob, then I'll have part of Mom's name and still have part of your name, too, in case you only give me girl cousins and don't have a son to name after you."

Leah Mae Wright

Damn, I have a sweet kid! Josh knew he wasn't the only one in his family that was touched by how JoJo wanted to include his mom in his name while also not making Jake feel like he wasn't honored to have been partially named after him. *Now I just have to hope the judge sees that being raised as a Burleson is what's best for my amazing little boy.*

And that can only happen if I maintain control and don't lose my shit if either of these other two attorneys gets stupid with cross-examining him.

Damn, maybe I shoulda worn a mouthguard to court today.

476

Chapter Twenty-Three

Cait was caught in that hazy state between sleeping and waking, unsure if she was only dreaming about making love with Josh, or if he was actually following through on one of his teasing comments about being her oral alarm clock. Regardless if it was real or just in her head, she couldn't stop her hips from rocking in response to the feel of Josh's tongue licking through her folds and swirling around her clit.

"If I'm dreaming, don't wake me up yet," she moaned, running her fingers through Josh's hair as she writhed beneath his oral onslaught.

"You're not dreaming, Sunshine," Josh chuckled, his hot breath blowing over her sex before he dove back down to devour her once more. He licked and sucked, bringing her to the brink of orgasm before backing off, repeating the process ad nauseam and not letting her go over. "I told you this is what would happen if you slept in only my shirt."

"Okay, you've converted me, Cowboy," Cait conceded breathlessly, acknowledging he was right about the benefits of not wearing panties or sleep shorts to bed. "I'll only wear your shirts to bed from now on, if you'll wake me up like this every morning. But you've got to quit teasing me and let me come."

Josh didn't reply with words. Instead, he doubled his efforts with eating her out, sending her skyrocketing in seconds. Cait's whole body quivered as she rode the waves of her first orgasm of the day. "Oh, Josh, yes."

She was still amazed by how much stronger the little warmup O's Josh gave her were compared to the O's she'd previously achieved on her own, even when she'd used a toy for assistance. And she knew that he was just getting started with sating their lusts enough that they could make it through the day without sneaking off for a quickie, since they weren't home on the ranch where that would be possible.

Before she fully recovered, Josh scooped her up in his arms and carried her to the ensuite bathroom. Cait's knees were still weak from the climax, causing her to wobble slightly when he sat her on her feet.

Josh somehow managed to steady her, even as he stripped off his sleep pants, and the button-down shirt of his that she was wearing, so fast that she didn't have time to get her bearings. Cait had only just registered that she was naked as she watched him pinch the tip of the condom he was rolling down his thick length.

"What's the rush, Cowboy?" Cait grinned as Josh lifted her once more. She wrapped her arms and legs around him as he stepped into the shower, skewering her on his cock without even bothering to turn on the water to cover the sounds of their morning mating.

"Need you too much to wait, Sunshine," Josh groaned before covering her mouth with his. His tongue plunged between her lips, moving perfectly in sync with each powerful thrust of his dick.

Cait loved the momentary bite of pain as he stretched her out with that first full thrust, almost as much as the slight sting every time the head of his cock bottomed out against her cervix. Josh was such a gentleman, who never wanted to hurt her in any way, that she'd had to explain to him how barely crossing that pain threshold quickly morphed into the most exquisite pleasure she'd ever experienced, so he wouldn't feel guilty and stop giving her that edge of roughness she craved.

Oh, she loved it just as much when he was gentle and sweet and sensually made love to her. But sometimes a girl just needed a good, hard fuck. Besides, there wasn't always time for slow and sensual lovemaking, when they were having to sneak in sexual bonding between family time and their other responsibilities.

With the risk of JoJo waking up and interrupting them at any moment, Cait knew it was one of those times when she could only hang on for the ride. She let go of any hang-ups she'd previously had about giving as much as she received, and let Josh take care of getting them both off.

As Josh hammered into her relentlessly, Cait's normally cluttered mind cleared. She couldn't think about testifying in court, or DNA results, or even the large crowd of people they had to navigate their way through to get from the hotel to the courtroom later. All she could do was feel. And the only thing she could feel was the gloriousness of joining as one with Josh.

Cait didn't notice the juxtaposition of the cool tile against her back and Josh's hot body pressed into her front. He could have been fucking her against a block of ice or the heated wall of a sauna and she wouldn't have known the difference. She could only feel the parts of their bodies making contact with one another.

The roughness of his fingers digging into the globes of her ass as he held her in place for his plundering. The firm pressure of his pillow-soft lips against hers. The slide of his tongue over and around hers. The teasing tickle of his chest hair against her sensitive nipples. The firmness of his muscular body against her soft curves and under her exploring palms. And most intensely, the slick glide of his long, thick dick spearing into her tight pussy, stretching her inner walls to their limits.

Josh was the perfect size to hit her cervix with the head of his cock while stimulating her G-spot with the shaft and grinding his pubic bone against her clit. If she could form a coherent thought at the moment, she'd realize his dick was the epitome of what her girlfriends called a magic peen — the perfect penis capable of giving the best orgasms imaginable — because it truly was magic the way he made her come.

As the ripples of release started in her core and spread throughout her body, Cait cried out his name. Josh swallowed down her inarticulate moans, continuing to kiss her as he fucked her through what seemed like a never-ending orgasm. After what felt like a hundred waves crashed over her, she finally felt him push deep inside her, filling her to the hilt as he convulsed in simultaneous climax with her.

Though her body felt so limp she could barely cling to him, Cait took over the kiss, not wanting him to risk waking JoJo by calling out her name. She didn't allow him to release the lip lock until the aftershocks started to settle down.

"Fuck, that was amazing, Cait," Josh groaned into her ear, resting his forehead on the shower wall behind her.

"It was," Cait agreed, trailing the tip of her tongue down his neck and back up to nibble his earlobe. "I really like it when you go all caveman to wake me up, Cowboy. I might just need you to replace my alarm clock like that every morning."

"That can easily be arranged, Sunshine," Josh crooned, finally seeming to have recovered enough to not need the wall to hold them up any longer. He pushed off the wall and lifted his head to grin at her as she lowered her legs to try to stand. "But only after you agree that it's time for me and JoJo to move in with you."

"But I thought it was one of your special talents as a SEAL to be able to sneak in and out of the house without being caught," Cait teased, feeling a lot closer to being ready for them to live together than she'd let on to Josh. "No need for you to move in when you can sneak over anytime you want."

"I can sneak in and out of terrorist camps and pirate ships, Sunshine," Josh chuckled, finally releasing her now that she was stable on her feet. "But terrorists and pirates don't have the bat-like hearing of my mother and JoJo. Even highly trained SEALs can't be quiet enough to sneak past either one of them."

"Oh, please," Cait scoffed as Josh turned on the shower. "JoJo can't hear that well, or we would have woken him up multiple times this week."

"Okay, maybe I could sneak past JoJo, since his super hearing seems to turn off when he's asleep," Josh conceded with a grin as he picked up her shampoo and poured some into his hand to start washing her hair. "But I swear, Ma's hearing is so good that when we were teenagers, she could tell which one of us was tryin' to sneak out of the house and called us by name without even opening her bedroom door to see who it was. And it didn't matter if we tried using the front stairs, so the noise wasn't as close to her room, or if we carried our shoes, hoping walking around in only our socks would muffle the sound of our footsteps. She always heard us."

"I think that's just a trait parents develop when raising their kids, or even kids that aren't theirs," Cait giggled as Josh gave her a scalp massage with her morning shampoo. "Mikey could always hear me when I got up for a glass of water in the middle of the night, too. But then again, I probably wasn't trying to be as quiet as you were, since I wasn't trying to sneak out. I've even started being a lighter sleeper since I started helping take care of Brody the last few years."

Cait didn't mention that her brother had developed the ability to hear any movement in the house long before either one of them were teenagers and he became her legal guardian. He hadn't trusted any of Lorna's boyfriends not to do something stupid from the moment they moved to San Diego and away from the safety of their grandparents' farm.

"Maybe you're right," Josh shrugged before moving her over under the spray of water to rinse her hair. "I feel like I'm always on alert now that I have JoJo. Whereas before, I only listened intently in the middle of the night while on an op."

"Of course I am," Cait popped off sarcastically as she grabbed Josh's alpine-scented bodywash and started soaping him up before he could move on to conditioning her hair.

Their easy banter continued as they lovingly bathed one another, getting ready to start their day.

A couple of hours later, they'd all finished getting dressed and had breakfast together with the members of Josh's family, who remained in Alexandria. They then led the caravan heading to the courthouse for what Cait hoped would be their final day in court. This time as they walked in, Cait's wish for it to be their last day appearing before the judge was all about wanting the case settled for Josh and JoJo. And had absolutely nothing to do with her nerves.

By the fourth day of court, Cait was a lot more relaxed about being in the public space than she'd been on the first day. She'd like to say her lack of anxiety was because of being confident that Josh's case was the strongest and she was certain he'd be getting full custody of JoJo. But unfortunately, she was pretty sure it was the repetitive exposure to the courtroom that made it feel less intimidating to the part of her psyche that still struggled with agoraphobia.

I guess the therapists were right about exposure therapy helping ease my anxiety in certain situations. I just needed Josh with me instead of the therapist, so I could actually feel safe enough to try it.

And starting every day with an orgasm high from sharing my shower with Josh probably helps a lot, too. It's hard to be nervous and worried when I'm still feeling blissed out a few hours later.

Cait didn't have enough time to mentally relive their early a.m. amorous adventures, thanks to the judge arriving a couple of minutes early to restart the hearing. Finally, it was time for the state of Virginia to present its recommendations to the court.

Cait expected the state's portion of the case to take up the entire morning session, if not all day, the way Josh's and the Joneses' cases had earlier in the week. But instead of calling multiple witnesses to present their findings after reviewing the evidence presented by each of the other parties, or at least explaining why they'd so easily given the Joneses temporary custody of JoJo a few months earlier, the attorney read a statement that had been prepared in advance by the social worker, not even calling her to the stand to present it herself.

Not that Cait or any of the Burlesons were standing up to object to the Department of Family and Children's Services not putting forth a witness they could cross-examine, since the prepared statement was a recommendation for Josh to get full, permanent custody of JoJo.

Once the attorney was finished speaking, the judge called for each of the other parties to present their closing arguments before he ordered a recess until one o'clock that afternoon, when he would present his final ruling.

"I guess we have a little time for some sightseeing before lunch," Josh grinned, his confidence in his case evident on his expressive face. "Think we have time to check out the Lincoln Memorial for JoJo's history lesson this week?"

"Um, maybe?" Cait looked at her Fitbit to see the time, wishing she knew more about the traffic times in the area to know if they'd be able to get to the memorial, tour it, have lunch, and get back to the courthouse in the three hours they had free. "How far is the memorial from here?"

"It's only about fifteen minutes from here," Gabe informed them. "Just head west on King and turn right on the George Washington…"

"Um, excuse me," Tawny interrupted before Gabe could finish giving them directions. "I have a lot of JJ, ur, JoJo and Jaina's stuff at my apartment. Since my attorney just told me that the judge is probably going to award you full custody, I was wondering if we could schedule a time for you to come pick up anything JoJo wants."

Wow! I'm surprised she's conceding already instead of waiting to be sure of the judge's ruling. I mean, yeah, I'm pretty sure Josh is going to win the case, but I doubt I'd admit defeat so easily if I were her, Cait thought as their small group turned to look at Tawny. *Did she lose her confidence by dressing more demurely today?*

Stop it, she mentally berated herself. *I'm not the mean girl who looks down on someone else for how they dress. Wanting to bitch and moan about her being more confident when she was dressed in one of the sexier outfits she wore earlier in the week is just my own insecurity trying to rear its ugly head. And I'm not going to let that hideous bitch take up any more space in my psyche.*

"Yeah," Josh nodded, looking decidedly uncertain about when they should make these plans. "Um, if that's how the judge rules, then we'll need to plan that and when you might wanna visit with JoJo. But I'd rather wait until after his ruling to make any of those plans."

"Oh, okay," Tawny nodded. "I guess we'll talk this afternoon, then." She reached over and ruffled JoJo's hair, smiling at him as she directed her final comment to him. "Have fun sightseeing, squirt."

Cait wanted to be the bigger woman and invite Tawny to come with them, so JoJo could spend some time with her while they were in town. But even though Josh was talking about them moving forward as a family and JoJo made it clear he considered her his extra mom, Cait didn't feel like it was her place to extend that invitation. So, she just stood there mutely, as Tawny walked away and Gabe continued giving Josh directions to the Lincoln Memorial.

Hopefully, I'll feel more secure with my place in their family after the hearing is over and we're all back home in Texas.

After a far too brief sightseeing excursion, Josh was back in the courtroom with his stomach in knots as he waited for the judge to enter the room and render his decision on JoJo's custody. *Fuck! Now I understand what Anthony was talkin' about feelin' while Kay was in labor. Waiting to find out if the judge will legally make me a father shouldn't be as nerve-wracking as worrying about something going wrong during labor and delivery. But fuck, it sure as hell feels like it right now.*

Leah Mae Wright

Maybe I shoulda swapped seats with JoJo, so I could hold both his and Cait's hands to help me calm down.

Since JoJo was between them, Josh put his left arm across the back of JoJo's chair to rest his hand on Cait's shoulder and reached across his body with his right arm to hold JoJo's right hand in his. He didn't care if it made him less manly to admit he needed to touch the two of them to help keep him grounded during this stressful time. In his opinion, even the most alpha badass needed the loving support of his family once in a while. And it didn't make him less of an alpha badass to need their constant presence in his life.

Thankfully, he didn't have to wait long before the judge reentered the courtroom. Once everyone had stood and sat back down, Levi English didn't waste any time before he started delivering his ruling.

"This case has been quite outside the norm for what I usually see in my courtroom. Typically, when I see multiple parties petitioning for custody of a child, it's in the middle of a contentious divorce case. So, when I first reviewed the multiple petitions for custody in this case, I assumed it would be a nice change of pace with three parties loving JoJo so much that they just needed some help in planning an equitable split of his time between them. Unfortunately, what they say about assumptions is most definitely true in this case."

Josh pinched his lips together, trying not to laugh at the judge referring to the asses several people had made of themselves during the hearing. *Fuck! I hope I'm not one of the asses.*

"Thankfully, most of the actions of the petitioners, though sometimes quite antagonistic, weren't completely awful. The behavior of one party to this case made it abundantly clear which of the petitioners is best suited to raise JoJo in a loving home, where he can heal from the loss of his beloved mother and thrive from this point forward."

Please be me. Please let JoJo stay with me. Josh's mental chant drowned out all the case particulars the judge had to list out before he could officially state his ruling. Josh closed his eyes momentarily to turn his wish into a quick prayer. *Please, Lord, let the judge say I get full custody of JoJo.*

"Therefore, it is hereby ordered that Joshua Bennett Burleson is the legal father of the minor child previously known as Joshua Jacob Jones. It is further ordered that the legal name of the minor child previously known as Joshua Jacob Jones shall hereby be changed to Joshua Jay Burleson. It is further ordered that Joshua Bennett Burleson is granted sole legal custody of the minor child hereby known as Joshua Jay Burleson, with all the rights and obligations pertaining thereto."

"It is further ordered that the child's birth certificate shall be amended to reflect the new name and state that Joshua Bennett Burleson is the father of Joshua Jay Burleson."

Josh blinked back the tears in his eyes as he hugged his son, neither of them paying attention to the rest of the legal jargon coming from the judge's mouth. As JoJo returned Josh's embrace, Cait leaned over behind JoJo and wrapped her arms around both of them. Josh pulled one hand out from between JoJo's back and Cait's front to include her in the group hug.

When Judge English finished his legal spiel, he waited for Josh and his family to separate, and for Josh to pass his handkerchief to Cait to wipe her happy tears off her cheeks before addressing him more casually. "Mr. Burleson, it is completely up to you as to whether the other parties to this case are ever allowed to visit with JoJo. But after witnessing their complete lack of open affection for him during these proceedings, I suggest you allow only supervised visits, should you allow them at all."

"Yes, sir," Josh agreed, not letting go of JoJo or Cait's hands as he somehow ended up seated between them after their group hug.

The judge then turned to look directly at Earnest Jones. "Mr. Jones, I find your behavior toward your children and grandson exceptionally appalling. I will be forwarding the transcript of these proceedings to the district attorney to determine if you should be charged with perjury for your statements in this case. I will also be advising him to speak with his counterparts in the various states where there have been paternity cases brought against you, as well as the federal prosecutor to determine if you can be charged with fraud, bribery, or conspiracy for your actions in those cases that were brought to light in this courtroom. I suggest you find a criminal defense attorney as soon as possible. You might also want to find a new family law attorney, as I will be speaking with the bar association regarding Mr. Stephenson's criminal conduct in those cases as well."

Finally, the judge turned to look at Cait. "Miss Campbell, unfortunately, the statute of limitations has passed for you to appeal the decision in your paternity case in California. However, if you wish to file a defamation suit against Mr. Jones in the state of Virginia, you have one year to file it."

With that, the judge adjourned the court. Josh quickly found himself surrounded by family members, ready to celebrate their victory. In all the commotion, he barely remembered to have someone get Tawny's phone number, so he could call her over the weekend to schedule a time to pick up the rest of JoJo's things.

"Can we celebrate by doing more sightseeing this weekend before going home?" JoJo's big hazel eyes beamed up at Josh.

"Absolutely!" Josh agreed, ruffling JoJo's hair. "There's a lot of really cool stuff to see close to where you were born, so I say we try to see as much of it as possible while we're here."

After the complete lack of fear he'd seen in Cait this week whenever they were out and about, Josh was excited about taking a few extra days of family time. *And maybe the extra nights of sharing a bed will convince Cait that we can't live apart any longer.*

~~~

Saturday, October 12, 2019

Cait was glad to be home after spending some extra time in Virginia after the hearing was over. After not getting home until late the night before, she hadn't had the chance to restock her pantry and fridge, so she ventured over to Hazel's to partake in the big family breakfast Josh's mom cooked every morning. With it being a Saturday, and the first day Josh and JoJo were back on the ranch, everyone was there to hear about the week they'd had in Virginia, since everyone else had gone home the previous weekend.

Josh and JoJo took turns relaying the events as they'd unfolded. Josh seemed to be more focused on the various monuments and memorials they'd visited over the last week. But JoJo was most excited about getting to meet his favorite wrestlers and go to his
~~~

cousins' version of school backstage with the wrestlers' kids, when the GWA was also in Virginia while they were there.

As they were out sightseeing the previous Saturday, Josh had gotten a call from Byron Avington, asking him and Jake to scope out the airports and hotels in Richmond and Virginia Beach a day ahead of the GWA crew arriving there for their shows. Apparently, they believed Allissa's stalker was traveling on their schedule, only twelve to twenty-four hours ahead of them. So, they had tasked a couple of bodyguard teams from Avington Security to look for anyone suspicious.

Cait wasn't sure what had happened that put them short a team for a couple of days, but she understood when Josh wanted to team up with his brother to help fill the gap. After getting to know Allissa, Cait was more than happy to change their plans, so Josh could help keep the GWA women's division champion safe.

While Josh was off searching for the stalker until the Avingtons could coordinate another security team to meet up with the GWA tour, Cait and JoJo hung out with the GWA crew, either in the hotel or backstage at the arenas. Cait had been a little nervous at first to leave the hotel without Josh. But with Anthony, Kay, and their kids there with the GWA, plus Randi and James, Dean and Allissa, and Rick and Fiona, whom she'd gotten to know fairly well when they were in Heart's Destiny for weddings the last few months, she didn't feel nearly as worried.

She'd even made a few more friends with the rest of the GWA women welcoming her with open arms, while JoJo played with the other kids backstage. They'd even caught her up on all the latest gossip, clearing up the confusion of the tabloid speculation about who got married in Vegas.

I just hope Jen won't be upset with me for being friendly with Rylie this week, after she learns that Liam married her when they were in Vegas. I know Jen claims she's not really into Liam, but considering they always sat together at weddings and stuff whenever the GWA was in town, I can't help but wonder if she was only saying that to keep Susan and Hazel from thinking their matchmaking plans had worked.

I mean, Julie says the same thing about Dion whenever her mom or aunt are around. Of course, she also talks about how he's her soulmate whenever it's just us girls. But Jen doesn't really talk about her sex life as openly as Julie and Becky do when I'm around. So, who knows if she's really into him or not?

Either way, I think I'll wait for Kay to break the news to the Matchmaking Mommas that Liam is off the market.

Not that she would admit it to anyone, but hearing the gossip and thinking about the love lives of her friends had helped get her mind off of how much danger Josh was in while trying to help catch a stalker. Though to listen to him talk about it when he got to the arena to watch the show with her and JoJo, he'd been in less danger than she was hanging out backstage near Allissa. Since Allissa was always surrounded by multiple armed bodyguards, Cait wasn't so sure she believed him.

Then, after that stressful couple of days, they ended up going to Roanoke to pick up JoJo's school records and the belongings he hadn't been able to fit in his backpack when he ran away. Once they had that all sorted, they went back to Alexandria to get the stuff from Tawny's apartment that Jaina wanted to go to her son, and picked up JoJo's amended birth certificate that now listed his new name and Josh as his father.

"Oh!" Brooklyn cried out, interrupting the story JoJo was telling about being body-slammed by his favorite wrestler, Tank, while playing in the wrestling ring with his cousins. She clamped one hand on Bobby's arm while holding her protruding belly with the other. "I think it's time to call Dr. Magnum."

From the wide-eyed expression on Brook's face and the way she was puffing out her breath like Cait remembered Mari doing while in labor with Brody, it appeared to be getting close to time for baby Maddie to make her entrance into the world.

"Relax, Brie-Baby, I have her on speed dial," Bobby smiled as he used his free hand to pull his phone from his pocket.

"Are you sure it's not just more Braxton Hicks?" Hazel inquired from her seat across the table. "I know you've been having those for a while."

"No," Brook panted out, a truly pained expression on her face. "This. Is. Definitely. Labor."

"Yes, Dr. Magnum, this is Bobby Burleson. I think it's time for you to meet us at the birthing center."

While her husband talked to the obstetrician, Brooklyn's expression softened, and her breathing leveled out as the contraction seemed to pass. "And I'm gonna need to change clothes before we go 'cause my water just broke."

"Oh shit!" Bobby looked down at his wife's lap as the color drained from his face.

With that announcement, the room became a hive of activity. Everyone started rushing around to get the breakfast mess cleaned up, along with the puddle in and under Brooklyn's chair, while the expectant parents prepared to leave for the birthing center. Since she'd previously worked as a housekeeper for the Burlesons, Cait went to the mud room to get the towels and cleaning supplies she needed to clean up the amniotic fluid on the chair and floor, leaving dealing with the dishes and corralling the kids to her girlfriends and the male Burlesons who didn't look like they were about to get sick or pass out.

As she returned to the dining room, she heard Char ask for the location of their baby go bag and if it contained the change of clothes Brooklyn needed. Once Brook confirmed she had multiple changes of clothing for her and the baby in her go bag in the car, Charlotte directed Mikey to go get it from their car, while she and Bobby helped Brooklyn to the closest restroom.

Hazel quickly called Mary down at the Ashbury House, knowing Brooklyn would want the woman she considered her mother figure to be there with her when the baby was born. Then she joined Char and Bobby in helping Brooklyn into the bathroom off the foyer.

Since it was the weekend, the ladies who lived at the Ashbury House and worked as housekeepers on the ranch were off work. So, Cait assumed they'd be able to take care of their kids without needing someone to cover for Mary in her role as the house supervisor.

Cait quickly sopped up as much of the mess as she could, grateful the marble floors were sealed, so there wouldn't be any lasting damage. Unfortunately, the same couldn't be said for the cloth-covered seat of the chair.

I guess that fabric protector spray is only good for small spills. Not the massive gush that seat just got doused with suddenly.

Cait did her best to clean up the mess, but she was afraid that after a direct hit with what appeared to be at least a gallon of amniotic fluid, the chair would need to be reupholstered at the very least. If not replaced completely.

Once Brooklyn had changed her dress, everyone started to file out of the house, following Bobby and Brooklyn to the birthing center. Cait found herself being swept up with the crowd, barely having time to wash her hands after throwing the dirty towels in the washing machine before Josh insisted she get in the truck with him and JoJo to be present at the birth of his niece.

The scene at the birthing center was just as chaotic as it had been on the ranch, with all of the Burlesons, their significant others, and all the kids filling up the waiting room at the Heart's Destiny Clinic. They were all stuck waiting downstairs while Bobby and Brooklyn were ushered upstairs to the birthing suites.

"How many Burlesons does it take to birth a baby?" Josh quipped, grinning as he looked around the packed waiting room.

"Just one, Jokester Josh," Becky replied, rolling her eyes at her brother.

"Technically, just one." Josh held up a finger to his sister before motioning to the room full of people. "But ya know we're all gonna show up in case the kid has to be pulled out like a stuck calf."

"I'm pretty sure Bobby's not gonna pull Maddie out like a calf," Becky argued, not seeming to understand that Josh was joking. "If the baby's too big to easily fit through the birth canal, the doctor will do a C-section. Right, Kay?"

"Yes," Kay agreed, grinning. "Though I think they went with the C-section for me because I had the girls that way previously. For a first-time mom, they might try pulling the baby like a calf to keep the recovery time from being as painful as it is with a C-section, especially with all the Burlesons being so experienced in pulling calves."

"Oh, Kay, please tell me you're joking." Amy gripped Justin's hand tight, her normally glowing golden-brown complexion taking on a fearful pallidity.

"Don't worry, Sweetheart," Justin reassured his pregnant fiancée by rubbing her back with one hand while resting the other on her rounded belly. "I only watched while the rest of the guys pulled the calves, so I'll be leaving the birth of our babies up to you and the doctor. I'm pretty sure I'm only gonna be good for holding your hand and feeding you ice chips during labor."

"And I can testify that Dr. Magnum is excellent with pain management during labor." Kay held up her right hand like she was being sworn in for court. "I have no idea what the pain is like after vaginal delivery, but if you have a C-section, you'll be numb for hours afterward. Then you'll be on painkillers for a few days and will need a pillow to hold over your stomach every time you move for a couple of weeks, but it's all worth it when you hold your babies."

"Yeah, I've already decided I don't care how this baby comes out," Charlotte interjected, looking a little paler than normal. "I want all the drugs as soon as the contractions start. After Brook about broke my hand in the bathroom earlier, I'm seriously thinking I need to ask Dr. Magnum about setting me up with an I-V as soon as I start having Braxton Hicks."

"Ya'll need to stop talking about the painful part of having babies," Susan chuckled, shaking her head. "Before you scare everyone else in the room into not giving us any more grandbabies."

Cait looked around the room at the stricken expressions on Julie, Jen, and Becky's faces and had to laugh. While she wasn't especially looking forward to the pain of labor and delivery, she was certainly closer to wanting to have a baby than her dearest friends.

I wonder how soon Josh is going to want to give JoJo some siblings? Is that something he's going to want to do as soon as I agree to moving in together, so our kids will be close in age to their cousins? Or will he give me a few months of living together to get used to the idea before pushing for marriage and babies?

Oh, hell, who am I kidding? As soon as I get over my issues with not being independent and agree to him and JoJo moving in, I'm probably going to be the one pushing for marriage and babies. I'm not going to be able to handle my jealous feelings every time I have to hand one of the Burleson babies back to its momma for long before I'll need to have a baby of my own.

Seeing Josh hold his newborn niece a few hours later only solidified Cait's thoughts on having babies with him in the near future.

Chapter Twenty-Four

Cait felt like a completely different woman after the last few weeks. The trip to Virginia was a huge turning point for her, giving her the confidence to act more like her old self than she ever dreamed possible. She hadn't agreed to let Josh and JoJo move in with her yet, but only because she felt like she needed to live on her own for at least six months to prove to herself that she could do it without reverting to the fearful agoraphobic she'd been since the shooting.

She'd settled into a routine, adding the responsibility of picking JoJo up from school to her weekday schedule. Since Hazel insisted on taking over watching Brody more than the one day a week Cait had previously gone to the Destiny Playhouse to work, Cait now worked half-days there five days a week while Hazel watched Brody in the morning. Cait then took over babysitting duties when she got back to the ranch with JoJo in the afternoon, so Hazel could have a break before Josh, Mikey, and Charlotte were finished with work.

She still came home each day for lunch with Josh, which often included fooling around more than eating anything nutritious. No matter how many times he claimed cum was pure protein, Cait still insisted they, at least, eat a sandwich and some fruit as Josh went back to work and she went to get JoJo from school.

They had to be a little more creative with their noontime hideaways since he'd started the barn renovations. The new metal barn Josh had erected at the other end of the pasture from the barn where they'd first become a couple didn't have a hayloft, so they couldn't sneak in there for privacy while the crew from Walker Construction worked on the barn that was being converted into their future home.

She still couldn't believe that Josh had talked the Walkers into hiring a whole new crew to be able to start on their renovations while finishing up Justin and Amy's house down by Anthony and Bobby's houses and starting the bigger house Charlotte and Mikey were building between their future barn home and the ranch manager's house. *I wonder if he's planning to move in there without me if the renovations are done before my six months of living alone are up in January?*

Cait made a mental note to ask him about that when she saw him that afternoon, needing to get back to work on the first draft of the screenplay she wanted to finish that morning before she could go joshin' around with her guys. While Josh and JoJo both called any kind of joking they did "joshin' around," Cait used the term to mean any time she spent with her two Joshes, regardless of whether they planned a game or movie night on the ranch or took her out to have new experiences off the ranch.

As Cait was typing the final scene in the screenplay for the first Taryn Quinn book that Becky had secured the rights to make into a movie, her phone buzzed on her dining room table beside her laptop.

Josh: Emergency family meeting at Mom & Dad's.

What the fuck? Cait was confused by the strange message, not having received anything like that from Josh before. The closest she'd ever seen to that kind of message was when Hazel called all the women on the ranch together back when Charlotte was kidnapped. *Oh, gawd, I hope everyone's safe.*

Cait: On my way.

Cait barely took the time to reply, rushing to slip her shoes on to run across the road. The only reason she did was because she knew Josh would worry about her if she didn't. Of course, she was freaking out about who might be hurt because of his cryptic message. But she also knew he wouldn't give her really bad news over text, so she rushed out the door to get to him as soon as possible, knowing he'd ease her fear as soon as she saw him.

Cait wasn't the only one rushing to the house she considered the main hub of the Burleson Ranch. Becky, Jen, and Julie were running out of the house next door to her at the same time JJ came out of his house on the other side of her. Justin was helping Amy into one of their cars, obviously not wanting her to try to run from the opposite end of the cluster of homes while trying to keep from going into preterm labor with their twins.

Cait didn't see her brother, sister-in-law, or nephew, but assumed they came in the back door since they were staying in the house on the other side of Hazel and Bob until their new home was built. Sure enough, as soon as she stepped in the front door alongside her friends, she heard Brody asking why he needed to go up to the game room with JoJo, instead of staying for the family meeting.

"Because it's an adult meeting," JoJo explained, trying to usher Brody up the front stairs. "And if we stay down here, they'll have to report to Santa Claus that we've been eavesdropping, and we'll get coal in our stockings instead of presents at Christmas."

Even worried about why they were all meeting so suddenly, Cait had to smile at JoJo teaching his cousin about behaving for Santa. She'd tried that the last couple of years with Brody, but he hadn't seemed to comprehend the concept of Santa Claus until they moved to Heart's Destiny.

Once the kids were out of earshot and Bobby and Brooklyn had arrived with baby Maddie, Bob and Hazel sat them all down in the dining room to talk. Cait sat between Josh and her brother, holding Josh's hand, but glad to have Mikey close, since it appeared they were about to hear some bad news. She was surprised when it was the usually reserved, quiet Bob who spoke first.

"I just got off the phone with Anthony. There's been an incident at the GWA fan expo."

There were a few gasps from around the room, but nobody else spoke as they waited to hear the status of the Burlesons in attendance at the GWA's *Halloween Horror* weekend in New Orleans.

"Anthony, Kay, and their kids are all safe. So are David, Mandi, Rick, and Patty Hunter. And Allissa's mom, Windy, and her friend, Kandi. And most everyone else, including all the kids with the GWA." Bob paused momentarily to take a breath. "Unfortunately, Allissa was alone in the locker room when her stalker made a move to try to kidnap her. It appears that Dean, Liam, and Dion went in to try and help the security team. And at least one of them was caught in the crossfire between the stalker and the security team."

"Oh, God!" Julie cried out, covering her mouth and jumping up to run out of the room.

Cait wanted to follow her friend to support her as she dealt with the possible loss of her soulmate. Unfortunately, hearing about a shooting in the GWA locker room made her too lightheaded to be able to run after her like Jen and Becky.

Holy shit! We were just in the locker room area with the GWA less than three weeks ago! If the stalker had struck in Richmond or Virginia Beach, I could have lost Josh or JoJo!

Cait didn't hear what Bob was saying about waiting on an update from Anthony, once he found out what hospital the ambulance had gone to, or heard more from the authorities in New Orleans. All she could hear was the beating of her heart as if the blood rushing through her body was pounding on her eardrums.

"Hey, look at me, Sunshine," Josh commanded, releasing her hand to cup her face in both of his large hands. He turned her head, so she was forced to look him in the eyes. "It's okay. You're safe. It wasn't the same locker room we were in. Just breathe for me, Sunshine. Nice and deep. In through the nose, out through the mouth."

Focusing on the love shining in Josh's green and gold eyes, as she followed his directions to breathe, kept her world from fading to black.

Why the hell have I been so worried about being independent and showing I'm strong enough to live on my own, when I could have been living with them for the past couple of weeks? Because I'm an idiot, that's why.

Not anymore. I'm not going to waste another day of the time I could have them with me. Not after how close it feels like we just came to me losing them.

Just as soon as we find out the fate of our friends, I'm going to pull Josh aside and ask him to move in today.

"I'm okay," she assured him, once she no longer felt like she was about to pass out. "But I have to go check on Julie."

"You should wait a few more minutes before trying to stand up, Caitir," Mikey insisted, rubbing a hand up and down her back.

"Mikey's right, Sunshine," Josh agreed, grinning. "At least stop with the fainting goat impersonation first."

Josh joking around brought her out of the last of her foggy state. Cait grabbed his wrists and playfully pushed his hands away from her face. "Seriously? I'm freaking out about how you could have been caught in the crossfire, if this had happened in Virginia a couple of weeks ago, and you're comparing me to fainting goats?"

"It brought the color back to your face," Josh shrugged, smirking, before giving her a peck of a kiss. "Now I know it's safe for you to try standing up so we can go check on Julie."

Josh took her hand and helped her up from the chair, continuing to hold her hand as they walked to the hallway off the foyer where the Burleson women were all gathered, trying to talk Julie out of the bathroom.

"Come on, Sis," Jen pleaded, leaning against the bathroom door with one hand on the doorknob and the other hand resting against the wood up by her face. "At least unlock the door, so I can hold your hair back while you puke."

Oh, no. Cait covered her mouth as she heard retching sounds coming from the restroom. Julie had mentioned her period being late back on the eighteenth, when Cait's started while they were all out bowling. Combining that with Julie being nauseous made Cait wonder if her friend was the next of the Burlesons to get pregnant this year. *I can't even imagine how frightened she must be right now. Worrying about the man she loves is bad enough, but I'm sure that fear is multiplied by a million if she's pregnant with his baby. And maybe by a billion if she found out and hasn't had the chance to see him in person to tell him that he's going to be a daddy before now.*

Cait pulled Josh with her as she joined Jen, Becky, and Char in huddling around the door. Susan and Hazel were hovering nearby, but they'd obviously realized that the younger generation was more likely to get through to Julie at the moment.

"What can I do?" Cait inquired as the other women opened up their tight circle to allow her and Josh in, just as the water turned on in the restroom.

"I can take the door off the hinges to get in if you need me to," Josh offered, motioning for them to move away from the door as he lowered his shoulder as if he was about to bust his way into the bathroom.

"No," Hazel objected. "Do not bust that door down, Joshua Bennett Burleson."

"Alright, how 'bout I pick the lock instead?" Josh grinned at his mother.

Before anyone could reply to Josh, the door opened, revealing Julie standing there with a devastated look on her face. "He doesn't wanna talk to me," she sobbed. "He said he can't deal with a ring rat that he can't remember, trying to con him out of his money by taking advantage of his injury to claim we're in a relationship. And that I shouldn't bother trying to call him again because he's blocking my number."

Holy shit! What a prick! She's here worried sick about him possibly dying while trying to be a hero, and the douchebag has the audacity to brush her off like that?

The women all surrounded Julie, offering their support through hugs and crying along with her. Cait wasn't sure how long they stood there commiserating with Julie, but she was grateful for Josh's stoic silence as he stood sentinel at her back, as if watching over all of them.

Hearing about how callously Dion had disregarded Julie, Cait especially appreciated how Josh was more like the cinnamon roll alphas she loved reading about and not an alphahole like Dion was turning out to be. Unlike her friends, she avoided the alphahole and dark romance books like the plague. Life was too short to spend her leisure time reading about annoying characters. Not to mention how those dark romance novels could trigger her after being shot.

Finally, someone's stomach growled loudly, breaking the silence that had descended on the huddle of women as the crying had subsided.

"Sorry," Charlotte winced as she rubbed a hand over her small baby bump. "Being called to a family meeting interrupted my lunch prep and Judy is getting impatient."

"How about ya'll go back to the dining room to wait for an update while I go throw together a late lunch?" Hazel suggested, smiling sympathetically at Julie and the rest of the women who'd barely stepped back from her.

"Thanks, Aunt Hazel," Julie sniffled, wiping her tears with one hand while holding her phone up with the other. "But I got all the updates I need from my online news feed and my brief conversation with whoever it was that answered Dion's phone. So, I think I'm gonna go soak in a nice hot bath and get lost in a good book."

Cait wasn't sure she'd be up for reading if she was in Julie's situation. Before she could ask if her friend was planning to pick a book outside their favorite genre of romance, Julie shrugged and explained what she planned to read.

"I know we're supposed to review the newest *Crescent Cove* book on Monday night, but do you think we can switch it up to a paranormal or fantasy romance instead? I know everyone else is into the hot baby daddies right now, but I'm kinda sick of human men at the moment. So, I'm only gonna read about aliens and vampires and faeries for a little while."

"Absolutely," the women around her chorused.

"I have a whole list of recommendations in the fantasy and paranormal romance category," Becky added with a smile. "Let's head home so I can pull it up on my tablet for you."

Cait went with the girls, needing to get the list of book recommendations to try to read at least one before the next book club meeting on Monday, even though paranormal romance wasn't her top choice for reading material. *I'll just hang out with them until Julie goes up for her bath and then come back to talk to Josh about moving in.*

~~~

While Cait went with the girls to help get Julie's mind off of whatever had gone down between her and Dion, Josh ran upstairs to check on JoJo. As curious as he was about how what he'd previously thought was only a friendship between his cousin and the wrestler, brought about by their forced proximity when the Matchmaking Mommas seated them together at every wedding and holiday celebration in town, seemed to have turned into more, he had a feeling Julie wouldn't speak openly about the relationship between her and Dion with anyone but her closest confidants. Since she obviously needed to talk, he
~~~

stepped back and hoped Cait would share a few more details with him later in the afternoon.

Once he'd instructed JoJo and Brody to wash up and head down to the kitchen for lunch, he stopped in the restroom to wash up himself. Then he went back into the dining room with the rest of the men in his family. While Julie had alluded to getting more of an update on her phone than they'd gotten from Anthony, Josh didn't want to rely on whatever stories he could find online, knowing the websites wouldn't be nearly as accurate as the information they'd get from the family members they had on the scene.

And it didn't sound like whoever answered Dion's phone really gave her much info, either. Fuck, did Dion even answer his phone? Julie seemed to think it was him when she first came out of the bathroom, but then later, she referred to the person she spoke to as "whoever answered his phone" like it was someone other than him. Does she think it was actually someone else who answered it? Or does she think his injuries may have caused him to act like a different person than he normally is?

If he didn't answer his own phone, I wonder if the "he" she referred to when she was upset about him calling her a ring rat and implying she was a gold digger was Dion or the jackass who answered his phone?

If it wasn't Dion she spoke to, maybe the jackass on the phone didn't know about whatever was goin' on with them any more than I did before today. Considering those don't sound like things the Dion that I got to know this last year would say, I have to wonder if he's gonna be just as pissed at the jackass as Julie is when he realizes what just happened on his phone.

But then again, if he has a head injury, he could have a personality change that caused him to act like a jackass, when he's normally one of the nicest, easy-going guys I've ever met.

"Did I miss any updates?" Josh inquired, not wanting to think about his knowledge of head injuries from his time as a SEAL, as he settled into a chair at the table with his dad, Uncle Jon, JJ, Justin, Amy, Bobby, Brooklyn, Charlotte, and Mikey.

"We haven't heard back from Anthony, but I just got off the phone with Byron," Uncle Jon informed him. "Dean, Allissa, and Liam are all physically fine, with the exception of maybe a few extra bruises.

Dion was grazed by a bullet and hit his head as he tackled Allissa out of the line of fire. Because he was knocked out from hitting his head, he was transported to the hospital via ambulance. His brother is back in the ER with him and everyone else is waiting for him to come out to the waiting room to give them an update, since the hospital won't release any information to anyone but family."

Fuck! He does have a head injury. So, there's no telling if it was him that Julie spoke with or someone else in the emergency room with him.

Uncle Jon went on to inform them that the only casualty was the stalker, so the only people the Avington Security teams had to protect the GWA wrestlers from now were the paparazzi. But Josh didn't pay much attention to his uncle's exact words as he was thinking about Dion's injuries and how they might have affected his response when Julie called him.

Yeah, taking a bullet while tackling Allissa out of the line of fire sounds a lot more like the Dion that I know than the asshole who disrespected Julie over the phone. But then again, if he was knocked out by hitting his head, he might have some memory loss that prevented him from remembering whatever happened between him and Julie when she called.

But, hell, if he was still unconscious or off having scans or whatever, it might not have been him who actually answered his phone. Since nobody from the GWA has been allowed back to the ER to see him, it could have been anybody answering his phone. I doubt it was his doctor, but maybe an irritated nurse or orderly getting frustrated by his phone blowing up could have picked it up to turn it off and accidentally answered it. Or if his brother was there by then, maybe he answered her call?

Then again, if it was his brother covering his calls while he was unavailable, surely, he woulda known about them being friends, even if Dion didn't confide in him about any other details of their relationship. Wouldn't he?

Or maybe not. I don't remember hearing about Dion having a brother before now, so maybe they aren't close enough to share any kind of information about their relationships with women.

Josh didn't have the chance to contemplate it any further as they were all called to the kitchen to grab a few barbeque sandwiches and chips for lunch. It wasn't long after Josh returned to the dining room with a full plate before Cait returned to the house to join in on lunch.

"What did Jules decide we're supposed to read before Monday night?" Char asked as soon as Cait took her seat to eat.

Josh sat back and observed the ladies' discussion as he scarfed down his lunch.

"The first book in Lexi Blake's *Thieves* series," Cait informed her with a grin as she placed her napkin in her lap. "Since that's a series most of the girls have already read, it'll just be those of us who don't normally read paranormal and fantasy that have to squeeze it in over the next couple of days."

Damn, if she's gotta read this book in the next couple of days, maybe I can get her to read me the good parts after JoJo goes to bed. Might make for an interesting twist on the phone sex we've been having every night since we got back from Virginia.

As Josh tried to switch his mental train of thought to something less arousing while eating with his family, Cait picked up the barbecue sandwich to take a bite and he had to force himself not to watch. Seeing her lips wrap around the sandwich was too close to how they looked wrapped around his cock, and he couldn't have that visual in his head without having his dick turn as hard as stone. *Not now, Cap. Boners are only for when I'm alone with her.*

"Oh, good." Brook nodded her agreement after wiping her mouth with her napkin. "I've already read that whole series, so I'm actually prepared for a book club meeting more than five minutes before we get together."

"Me, too," Amy smiled and took a sip from her glass before continuing. "It's been a while since I read the first one, though, so maybe I'll listen to the audio version over the next couple of days during the relaxation time Justin keeps insisting I take."

"You need to rest now to save your energy for when the boys are born, Sweetheart," Justin insisted, leaning over to wrap his arm around Amy's shoulders and kiss his fiancée's temple.

"They're not due for another six weeks." Amy rolled her eyes at Justin, even as she leaned into his embrace. "I'm not a battery. I can't store up my energy for that long."

As the conversation around the table turned to the possibility of twins coming as much as a month early, and if they were planning a C-section or waiting for the boys to try to come naturally, Josh leaned over to whisper to Cait, "What are the chances we can sneak out of here while everyone else is occupied?"

He'd had plans to take her and JoJo out for lunch and then fly them down to Corpus Christi to meet his maternal grandparents. He thought they'd get a hotel for the night and then spend the next day on Mustang Island before flying home. But with the whole family worried about their friend, who might be more than a friend to his cousin Julie, Josh decided to scrap his plans and stick close to home to keep up with the latest updates.

While everyone was trying to be optimistic about Dion's injuries not being too severe, Josh had seen too many head injuries completely derail the careers of his fellow sailors to think Dion wouldn't be facing a hard battle to heal after the incident earlier in the day. He was more of an acquaintance to Josh than a true friend, but Julie was part of his family. And it was obvious that Julie's feelings for Dion were deeper than friendship, so she needed the support of everyone in the family to deal with the fallout.

"Depends on how far away you want to go?" Cait whispered back, her eyes wandering over the other occupants of the room. "We can probably sneak out of this room, and maybe out of the house, but I don't think we should leave the ranch…"

"No, I know we need to stick close now," Josh interrupted, not letting her finish her thought. "I just want a little privacy, ya know?"

"Oh, yeah, I know," Cait grinned, her turquoise eyes lighting up as she pecked his cheek before picking up her dishes to take them to the kitchen.

No, I don't think you do, Sunshine. Josh smiled as he picked up his place setting and followed her. Her demeanor made it clear she thought he wanted to sneak off to fool around. But while he wouldn't mind stealing a few kisses, he really wanted to talk about how the news of a shooting involving people they knew was affecting her.

Once they rinsed their dishes and put them in the dishwasher, Josh pulled Cait up the back stairs to his bedroom.

"Josh, what are you thinking?" Cait's voice was higher pitched than normal, betraying her frantic thoughts before she could voice the words. "We can't do anything here with everyone just downstairs."

"I'm thinking we can sit and talk for a couple of minutes before anyone comes looking for us," Josh assured her as he pulled her down to sit beside him on the side of his bed. "And I need to know how you're feeling after hearing about a shooting involving people we know."

"I'm okay," Cait insisted, rubbing her thumb over their joined hands as if trying to soothe him with her touch. "I freaked out at first, thinking I could have lost you or JoJo if this had happened a couple of weeks ago. But I know it's an isolated incident and not likely to happen again, if we go to another GWA show. So, I'm really okay. Worried about Dion and Julie, but otherwise, it actually clarified a couple of things for me."

"Oh, how so?" Josh wasn't sure how the day's events could have possibly had a positive impact on Cait's thought process.

"I don't want us to be like them," Cait shrugged. "They've been seeing each other in secret since the week of Anthony and Kay's wedding when they first met, but even though Julie claimed he was her soulmate just last week, they're over now because of not being open about their feelings for one another. Yeah, our friends and families know we're dating, so I know none of them would tell one of us off if the other was injured and couldn't answer the phone. But if something were to happen to you, I wouldn't be allowed in the ER with you. Or vice versa. And I don't want that for us. I want it to be so obvious to the world that we're together that an injury like this couldn't keep us apart."

"I can guarantee you that won't be an issue with us, Sunshine," Josh reassured her, pulling her onto his lap so he could wrap his arms around her. Cait ran her hands over his pecs before wrapping her arms around his neck. "But if it'll make you feel better, I'll call Tyler's office on Monday and have him draw up whatever paperwork needs to be done, so we're each other's emergency contacts and can't be kept out of one another's hospital rooms."

While he knew that would be unnecessary once they got married, Josh also knew Cait wasn't quite ready for that step just yet. She wanted to live on her own for six months before she even agreed to let him and JoJo move in with her, so he was trying to be patient and give her the space to see how strong he already knew she was before he proposed.

If it were up to him, he would have already proposed, and they would be planning their wedding for the one-year anniversary of the day they met. Yeah, he knew Justin and Amy were already planning their wedding for that same weekend, but he didn't see why they couldn't have two family weddings on back-to-back days the last weekend of the year.

Since she'd nixed his cohabitation plans, though, Josh was now planning to propose on the twenty-ninth of December. *Hell, if I start finding out what she wants for the wedding now, maybe I can set it all up in advance, so I can propose that morning and talk her into marrying me that night?*

Fuck! That probably won't work 'cause of not having any time for the other parties leading up to the wedding. Not that I want a bachelor party or wedding shower, but Cait might not want to miss out on all that stuff.

Fine, whatever, I'll just start asking about the stuff she wants for our wedding to plan it for some time in January, after her six months of independent living are up.

"Is that necessary if we're living together?" Cait's question brought him out of his mental rambling. "Or do we only get those rights after getting married?"

"I'm not sure," Josh shrugged. "But since we're not living together yet, I'll call Tyler to find out."

"Yeah, about that…" Cait ducked her head sheepishly, biting her lip momentarily before continuing. "Everything that happened today made me realize that I don't want to wait until I've lived on my own for six months before you and JoJo move in. I don't want to waste another good night of sleep, when I could be sleeping peacefully in your arms."

"You sure, Sunshine?" Josh was eager to move forward with their lives as a blended family, but he didn't want to take advantage of the tragic situation with the GWA to push Cait for more than she was ready for between them. "I know how much it means to you to live on your own for a few months, and I'm willing to wait as long as you need us to."

"I'm sure, Cowboy," Cait smiled at him, twirling her fingers in the back of his hair. "While we're here in your room, let's start packing your stuff and move you and JoJo over this evening."

"Fuck, yeah," Josh whooped before sealing their plans with a passionate kiss. Unfortunately, they were in his childhood bedroom with over a dozen family members just downstairs, so he couldn't take things further than a kiss at the moment. And he wasn't about to listen to his insistent dick that was clamoring to be let out of the confines of his jeans.

"I didn't mean for you to pack your tongue in my mouth," Cait giggled when they finally came up for air.

"No?" Josh arched an eyebrow as he slid his hands from her back to her sides, preparing to tickle her to keep her giggling. "Guess that means I can't pack my cock in your pussy, either, huh?"

"Not 'til we get you moved, and JoJo goes to bed tonight," Cait smirked.

"Deal," Josh agreed as he tickled her ribs, causing her to burst out laughing.

"What's so funny in here?" JoJo hollered as he threw the door open.

"Help me, JoJo," Cait squealed as she attempted to retaliate. "Your dad's trying to kill me in a tickle war. I need your help to make it a fair fight."

JoJo jumped on the bed to attack Josh with claw hands from behind. Josh twisted around to get one hand on JoJo's ribs while keeping the other on Cait's, tickling them both at the same time while they double-teamed him.

"I'll help you, Uncle Josh," Brody chimed in, having followed JoJo into the room. He climbed on the bed and went straight for Cait's armpits. "I know where Aunt Cait's really ticklish."

"Stop! Stop! Stop!" Cait hollered, no longer trying to tickle Josh because she was too busy trying to push his and Brody's hands off of her. "I give up!"

Josh released her to tickle JoJo with both hands. Brody followed his lead, also switching to tickling JoJo.

"Hey, no fair," JoJo protested through his laughter. "Cait surrendered for our team, so ya'll gotta stop tickling me, too!"

"Nope," Josh disagreed. "It's every man for himself in tickle wars, so you've gotta give up, too."

"I give up," Brody jumped back, obviously realizing if JoJo surrendered first, then he'd be Josh's next target to tickle.

JoJo wasn't about to give up so easily, however. He wiggled and squirmed, trying diligently to tickle Josh as much as Josh was tickling him.

"If you guys want to move tonight, one of you needs to surrender," Cait grinned, standing beside the bed to watch the roughhousing without being caught in the fray.

"Move?" JoJo stopped tickling Josh to twist around where he could see Cait, his eyes lighting up with excitement. "We're gonna move over to your house tonight?"

"If you want to," Cait nodded and smiled.

"Yes! Yes! Yes!" JoJo shouted, jumping off the bed to throw his arms around Cait.

Josh sat up on the side of the bed, smiling widely as he watched his son embrace his future wife. "I'm counting your retreat as you conceding that I'm the king of tickle wars," Josh joked. "And since I'm now the ruler of the family, I hereby decree that ya'll need to help us pack, so we can move enough of our stuff that we can sleep in our new beds tonight."

"I'm helping JoJo!" Brody announced, grabbing his older cousin's hand, and pulling him toward the door.

Once the kids left the room, Josh stood and pecked Cait's lips. "Guess that means you're helping me, Sunshine."

"Nope," Cait disagreed, popping the P as she chirped the word. "I'm going to go clean all my junk out of my former guest room, so JoJo can make the space his."

If Josh wasn't already hopelessly in love with Cait, he would have fallen for her right then. As it was, seeing her thinking of his son's needs first only deepened the feelings he had for her. "I love you, Sunshine."

"I love you, too," Cait beamed at him as she walked toward the door. "Now hurry up and pack 'cause I need you to help me carry a few boxes of stuff up to the attic, so JoJo has a clean slate to decorate."

"Yes, ma'am," Josh grinned and playfully saluted her as she sauntered toward the bedroom door.

As soon as she left his room, Josh quickly grabbed a couple of duffle bags from his closet and started packing his clothes. *Damn, I'm gonna enjoy our first official night cohabitating.*

Several hours later, they finally had most everything moved, and JoJo's room set up the way he wanted it, just in time for him to read one chapter of his current book before bed. Josh was hopeful that the pattern of JoJo sleeping through the night that they'd experienced the last three weeks wouldn't be broken by the move. But he also knew that any kind of change could trigger him to have another nightmare, so he wouldn't be surprised if JoJo came looking for him again, like he had before the judge granted him full custody.

Hopefully, this is another change like the custody hearing that makes him feel more secure in our family situation, so it won't trigger any more bad dreams.

Josh still couldn't believe how JoJo's nightmares had miraculously stopped the night Judge English awarded him full custody. When he'd brought it up in therapy, Dr. Edwards had pointed out that it was probably because he finally felt like he knew his place in the family and didn't have to fear being sent away anymore. So, Josh now hoped that moving in with Cait, and eventually into the home they were designing out of the barn where he'd first kissed Cait, would cement his security in the family even more.

As Josh and Cait left JoJo's room, which was now decked out in the cowboy theme he'd picked while shopping with Memmaw Hazel during his first week on the ranch, Josh scooped Cait up into his arms, bridal style.

"What are you doing?" Cait whisper-shouted, wrapping her arms around his neck as he strode across the hall into their bedroom.

"Carrying you over the threshold, Sunshine." Josh wagged his eyebrows suggestively as he kicked the door shut behind them.

"I think that's only for the wedding night, Cowboy," Cait giggled.

"Well, then, I guess I'm just practicin' for the weddin' night," Josh drawled as he carried her over to the bed. "But I kinda like carryin' you around, so I might just make it a nightly habit."

"It won't be special if you do it every night," Cait argued.

"But every night I spend with you is special, Sunshine," Josh confided, smiling as he gently placed her on their bed. "So, I've gotta do stuff that's normally reserved for special nights to show you how special you are to me."

"You're special to me, too, Josh," Cait cooed, reaching up to run her fingers over his stubble covered jaw as he crawled onto the bed beside her. He settled on his side, facing her with his head resting on his hand. Cait turned to mirror his position, running her free hand down his arm to rest on top of his between them.

"Speaking of things that are normally reserved for special times in our lives," Josh started, turning his hand over to clasp hers. "Maybe you should tell me now what kind of flowers you want for our wedding, so I can start making sure you always have some for the dining table." *And maybe describe what else you want for our wedding while you're telling me the flowers you want, so I can start getting things ordered.*

"Is that why your mom always has white lilies on the side table in their dining room?" Cait smiled, rubbing her thumb over his, as they laid there talking and holding hands.

"Yeah, Pop has a standing order with Flora's," Josh shrugged sheepishly, confessing where he got the idea. "He's brought her a bouquet similar to her wedding bouquet every week for as long as I can remember. So, I thought I might carry on the family tradition."

"Yellow gerbera daisies," Cait smiled.

"You thinking you'll have your bridesmaids in yellow like Amy's doing?" Josh wondered if their color schemes would match well enough that they would only have to decorate the church once if he could convince Cait to marry him the day after Justin and Amy's wedding.

"No, I'm thinking the flowers and decorations would be yellow, but I'd want the bridal party to wear navy blue, so the yellow bouquets and boutonnieres would really pop." Cait gave him a curious look, like she was getting suspicious of why he was asking what she wanted for their wedding. "But to be honest, I never really imagined a big, fancy wedding with all the parties beforehand like everyone seems to have here."

"No?" Josh was surprised to hear that she hadn't picked all this stuff out as a teenager like his sisters did. "What did you think your wedding would be like?"

"I always thought my wedding day would be more of a spur of the moment decision, where I'd pick a dress from my closet without worrying that it wasn't white," Cait confessed with a shrug. "No bachelor or bachelorette party, wedding shower, or rehearsal dinner, or anything else that my future in-laws would expect my parents to host."

Yeah, I bet her lack of loving parents was a huge factor in her not wanting all that in the past. Hopefully, now she feels like my family fills in any holes she has in her heart from a lack of family. Lord knows, Ma already loves her like a daughter. Hell, Pop probably does, too. He's just not as demonstrative as Ma, so she might not know it yet.

"I mean, I didn't even go to church until I moved here, so I just assumed if I ever got married it would be a courthouse wedding like Mikey had with Mari. A couple of witnesses, but no official bridal party. And a sheet cake from the grocery store, instead of a huge wedding reception."

"Yeah, Ma's not gonna let us get away with that," Josh chuckled. "But maybe if you let her help you pick a wedding dress and agree to get married at the church instead of the courthouse, we can cut out all the extra parties, bridesmaids, and groomsmen to make it a little simpler if that's what you want. Hell, I can even make picking our wedding attire simpler by letting you pick between the two navy blue tuxes I already own from being in my brother and sister's weddings this year and my dress blues from the Navy."

"Oh, that is simple," Cait giggled. "Your dress blues. There's no way I'm going to marry you when you're wearing a tux you've already worn in a wedding."

"Deal," Josh grinned before leaning over to brush his lips over hers. *Guess it's a good thing none of my Navy buddies have gotten married, so I've only worn my dress uniforms to official Navy functions.*

"But as of now, it's a moot point," Cait faltered, her smile fading, as they pulled back from the brief kiss. "Since you haven't asked me yet, there's no wedding to plan for."

"Don't you worry, Sunshine," Josh grinned, knowing he'd have plenty of help from the Matchmaking Mommas to plan the perfect proposal. "The proposal's coming. I've just been waiting until you got over your need to live alone before I started finalizing my plan for how I wanna ask you."

And I've gotta make sure our reno is far enough along that it's safe for me to take you up to our loft, so I can ask you in the same place where I first kissed you.

"And now that we've moved in together, I can promise it's not too soon for you to go dress shopping with Ma," Josh grinned, ready to be done talking so he could make love to his future bride. "Especially if you want me to make our wedding seem like the spur-of-the-moment thing you dreamed about by asking you to marry me on the same day I want us to have the wedding."

"You wouldn't," Cait gasped, closely examining his expression. "Oh, geez, you would!"

"It's the perfect way to get us out of havin' to do all those parties before the wedding," Josh smirked. "So, yeah, I would, especially now that I know you don't really wanna do all that stuff either."

"Fine, I'll agree to go dress shopping with your mom this week," Cait conceded, rolling her eyes in exasperation. "But you've got to promise that you won't ask me to marry you on my birthday, or one of the other birthdays or holidays coming up in the next couple of months. Pick a random weekday. Or maybe a Sunday, so everyone will already be at the church."

"Well, didn't I just get lucky," Josh teased, grinning widely. "The day I think will be perfect for us to get married just so happens to fall on a Sunday this year."

"And it can't be tomorrow," Cait added, her eyes widening as she obviously freaked out at the thought of him rushing her that fast. "I need at least a week to find a dress. And you're probably going to need at least that long to order my bouquet and coordinate the reception that you know your mom won't let us skip."

"It won't be tomorrow," Josh chuckled, a list of things he'd need to do starting to form in his head. "But it will be before New Year's."

"And you have to make sure Mikey and JoJo have navy tuxes in time to be in the wedding. I want Mikey to walk me down the aisle and JoJo to stand up with us as we become a family. And since you're not going to ask me until the day of, you're in charge of setting everything up."

"Navy tuxes with yellow gerbera daisy boutonnieres," Josh confirmed, leaning over to peck her lips once more.

Yeah, I'm definitely gonna hafta get some help from Ma and her matchmaking posse. And maybe Uncle Doug. Surely, as our local judge, he can help me get the marriage license on a Sunday. Or maybe the week before without Cait with me when I go to the courthouse.

"Now get naked woman," Josh jokingly commanded, releasing her hand to reach around and swat her jean covered ass. "I'm ready to christen our bedroom."

As Cait's eyes and mouth widened in shock from the single slap to her ass, Josh jumped up from the bed, so she couldn't retaliate. He quickly reached over his head to clasp his t-shirt in one hand to pull it off.

Just as Cait stood to join him in stripping off their clothes, the classic country station that had been playing through his phone since they started unpacking earlier switched songs to **Save A Horse, Ride A Cowboy** by Big & Rich, causing both of them to burst out laughing.

"I suppose you want me to do as the song says, too," Cait giggled as she removed her top revealing her lace covered C-cups. "Huh, Cowboy?"

"Abso-fucking-lutely," Josh agreed with a grin as he shoved his jeans off and jumped back into the bed. He laid back, propped his head on a pillow, and stroked his cock as he watched Cait finish removing her clothing. "But maybe I should set the song on repeat, so I can enjoy the strip show you're givin' me and you can still ride me while it's playin'."

"Yeah, I don't think that's necessary," Cait scoffed, not bothering to dance for him as she lost her lacy bra and thong panties.

She crawled back into the bed on her hands and knees, giving Josh a great view of her tits hanging down as she moved over him. He released his dick to reach up and cup her tatas as she straddled his hips and settled her creamy cunt over his cock, rubbing her dripping wet slit along the underside of his shaft. The hard nub of her clit ran over the most sensitive part of his shaft just below the head and made his dick twitch involuntarily.

"Fuck, yeah, Sunshine," Josh growled, lightly pinching her rosy pink nipples. "Rub your wet pussy all over me. Make yourself come, so you loosen up enough to take my big dick."

Josh had the best view imaginable, loving looking between her tits to see his cock sliding through her folds. The sight was such a turn on that he had almost as much precum dripping from the head onto his abs as she had cream lubing his cock.

"I want you to come once like this and then come sit on my face, so you can come on my tongue before you really start riding me." Even though they'd been having sex almost daily for the last month, only skipping the three days she was on her period, Josh knew she couldn't just slide right on due to his size.

She needed to come at least once to keep from wincing when he first entered her because her pussy was still so tight. And little orgasms from dry-humping or him using his fingers alone didn't count. He had to use his fingers and tongue to really get her loosened up from a couple of orgasms before he could go balls-deep on the first thrust. Luckily for them both, he loved eating her pussy almost as much as he loved fucking her.

"Oh, no, Cowboy," Cait shook her head, pushing off of him to lean over to the bedside table to get out a condom. "I'm not waiting that long to feel you inside me."

"But we need to make sure you're ready, Sunshine," Josh protested as she opened the condom packet and moved back to straddle his thighs to give her access for putting it on.

"I'm ready, Josh," she argued as she rolled the condom down his length. "And as much as I love how gentle you are and always want me to come at least once first to keep from hurting me, sometimes I want that little bite of pain to make sure I still feel you inside me the next day. And since I'm the one on top tonight, I insist you give me my rough and rowdy Cowboy, instead of my sweet, gentle Josh."

Cait pushed up on her knees, moved forward, and held his dick by the base to line it up with her opening. She circled the tip through her folds, coating him in her natural lube as he ran his palms up her thighs to her hips.

"Fuck," Josh groaned as she released her grip on his cock and dropped down suddenly, taking him balls-deep without him even thrusting.

He wanted to lift his pelvis as she rose up and grip her hips to control her frantic movements to keep from causing her too much pain, afraid she'd go too rough too fast, and they'd end up having to take a couple days off before making love again. But even though it went against all his tender instincts, Josh let Cait take the reins and ride him the way she wanted.

Instead of gripping her hips and slowing her bouncing up and down on his cock, Josh slid his hands up to cup her tits. He crunched up to get his mouth on her mounds, nibbling and sucking her nipples as Cait controlled their copulation.

He kept his eyes open, watching her expressive oval face to make sure her voracious riding style didn't cause her too much discomfort. Based on her rapturous smile, Josh was certain she was enjoying the fervid fucking as much as he was at the moment. *Guess I'd better get used to letting my primal beast out to play with her a little more often.*

Josh wasn't sure if it had been Cait's relative inexperience causing her to feel so much tighter on his cock than his previous hookups, or his deep, abiding love for her that had reined in his previously aggressive sexual nature. But seeing her hedonistic enjoyment of more forceful carnal activities eased his trepidation about letting her see that side of him more often.

He enjoyed the show she put on for him, fighting to stave off his own climax each time her tight cunt clamped down on his cock, as she took herself over the edge. "Fuck, I love feelin' you come on my cock, Sunshine."

"Come with me, Cowboy," Cait begged, her frantic, bouncing movements slowing down as she tried to catch her breath after her fourth climax.

"How 'bout I take my turn ridin'," Josh offered, sliding his hands around her back to pull her down until her breasts pressed against his chest, so he could roll her onto her back without leaving the tight confines of her pussy. "And let you rest a bit?"

"But I was having fun riding your big pogo stick," Cait playfully pouted, causing Josh to chuckle.

"You can ride my big pogo stick again later, Sunshine. But for now, reach up and push against the headboard, so we don't bump our heads as I'm pounding into your pussy," Josh grinned as he leaned down to kiss her.

"Yes, Sir," she grinned as she lifted her arms and placed her palms flat against the headboard to do as he'd instructed.

As their tongues tangled, Josh slid his hands down her sides to pull her legs up, hooking her knees over his elbows before placing his hands on the bed beside her shoulders. The new position gave him greater access, so he could shove his cock in even deeper than before.

Josh took a few gentle strokes, making sure she could handle taking him so deep from this angle. When her moans of pleasure made it obvious that she loved the deeper thrusts, he let loose, rutting into her like a wild animal until they cried out each other's names as they reached the ultimate peak as one. Josh came so hard, his vision faded to black and he was afraid the condom couldn't hold all the jets of cum shooting out of his dick.

"Fuck, I love you, Caitir," he growled, unable to move from her depths as the aftershocks washed over him.

"I love you, Josh," Cait panted out breathlessly, moving her hands off the headboard to run her palms over his biceps and shoulders.

When her inner walls stopped quivering and Josh's dick stopped twitching, he pushed up to his knees, releasing her legs as he secured the base of the condom before pulling out. While he went to the ensuite bathroom to dispose of the condom, Cait removed the comforter from the bed. Thankfully, it was thick enough she hadn't squirted all the way through to the sheets.

"Sorry, Sunshine," Josh apologized as he walked back into the bedroom. "Next time, I promise I'll remember to put down a towel first."

"Yeah, we might need to buy some more towels," she grinned as she walked over to the closet to get down another blanket. "Otherwise, I might end up spending more time washing our bedding than actually sleeping on it."

"Teach me how, Sunshine," Josh offered as he helped her spread the blanket over the bed. "And I'll gladly help clean up our sexy messes."

"Deal," Cait grinned as she grabbed one of his shirts to sleep in.

Fuck, yeah, Josh thought as he put on his sleep pants before they both went to brush their teeth for bed. *I'm definitely gonna enjoy all the benefits of our new living arrangements.*

~~~
~~~

After the past two nights of sharing her space with Josh and JoJo, Cait really wished she could stay home with them to enjoy more of their first week living together as a family. But she'd already committed to going to the book club meeting with her girlfriends, so she couldn't stay home for a movie night with her guys. Besides, she had the rest of her life to stay home with Josh and JoJo. Now she needed to go support Julie after her breakup. She was also curious what Julie found out at the doctor's appointment she had that day, and the book club meeting was her first opportunity to see her friend to talk to her.

I wonder if she'll share her news with all of us? Or if I'll have to try to get a moment alone with her to find out if my suspicions about her being pregnant are true or not?

Cait didn't have to wait long to find out. As soon as she got there, she noticed Julie declining the wine that was usually her staple drink of choice during book club meetings.

"Yeah, I'm gonna have to stick to lemonade and water tonight," Julie sighed, looking longingly at the wine bottles most of their friends were choosing for the evening.

"Are you sick?" Kara reached over and felt Julie's forehead with the back of her hand, like she was trying to estimate her temperature.

"Not with anything contagious," Julie assured them, pushing Kara's hand away. "But I confirmed with Dr. Magnum today that Dirtbag Dion knocked me up, so I can't have alcohol. And since my appointment was this afternoon, instead of this morning, I'd already exceeded the amount of caffeine I'm allowed to have in a day, so I can't even have a glass of tea now."

"Whoa! Why are you calling Dion a dirtbag all of a sudden?" Lexi looked at Julie in shock. "And when did you start sleeping with him without giving us the deets on his magic peen?"

"We've been hooking up since we met last November," Julie admitted to the women in the room who hadn't previously known about her relationship. "And I started calling him a dirtbag when I called him a couple of days ago and he accused me of being a ring rat, who was after him for his money."

Leah Mae Wright

"Seriously?" Kayla's jaw dropped in shock. "And here I thought he was some kind of hero for jumping in to save Allissa over the weekend."

While none of the online articles Cait had seen mentioned which of his female coworkers he'd been instrumental in rescuing, everyone in Heart's Destiny knew about Allissa's stalker issues after the town was asked to be on the lookout for any strangers in town when she was there for Rick and Fiona's wedding over the summer. So, it wasn't surprising to Cait that Kayla had figured out it was Allissa's stalker that had opened fire in the locker room over the weekend from the vague news stories on the incident.

"Yeah, well, as glad as I am that he helped keep Allissa safe, he showed his true dirtbag colors when I called to check on him," Julie informed them. "And I'm pretty sure it was just because I'd told him about the doctor's appointment last week when I told him my period was a week late. It's way too convenient that he suddenly started being an ass and blocked my number, so I couldn't get through to tell him the test results today."

"What a jackass," Cassidy scoffed as several of the other women chimed in their agreement.

"Ya'll haven't even heard the best part of it," Julie chuckled wryly. "Because my period in September was only one day of light spotting, Dr. Magnum did an early ultrasound to estimate my due date. And she saw two babies."

"Twins?" Several of the women shouted in unison.

"Yep, I'm not only a twin, I'm a carrier of twins," Julie nodded before swigging a big gulp of her lemonade. She then reached into her purse and pulled out a stack of ultrasound pictures to pass around for all of them to see. "When she started labeling them on the ultrasound pictures, I tried to convince her to label them as Thing One and Thing Two, in honor of Halloween coming up this week, but she didn't think that was funny."

"We can get out the markers and glitter pens to change that if you want," Becky offered, as everyone cooed over the fuzzy black and white images.

"So, how far along are you?" Cait wondered, unsure what the numbers on the edge of the scans indicated.

"As of tomorrow, I'll officially be ten weeks along, which I don't understand 'cause they were only conceived eight weeks ago. It makes no sense that they count the two weeks between the first day of my last period and the date of conception as part of the pregnancy, but whatever. At least, it means I'm already a quarter of the way through. And since they're due on May twenty-sixth and twins usually come early, Jen and I might get to share our birthday with my babies."

"That would be cool." Cait had to point out the bright side, unable to handle any more negativity surrounding the news of Julie's pregnancy. She considered all children a gift, and wanted to celebrate them, even if their sperm donor was an asshole. "I'd love to share my birthday with my babies."

"When's your birthday, Cait?" Sierra inquired, arching a curious eyebrow in Cait's direction.

"November nineteenth," Cait replied with a smile.

"Oh, that's only three weeks away," Lexi grinned. "Perfect for a pre-Thanksgiving party."

"Yeah, but there's no chance she'll share a birthday with her baby this year." Kayla looked her up and down as if looking for a baby bump. "And probably not next year, either. With the way the rest of the Burlesons have recently been pumping out babies as soon as they hook up, there's no way she can hold off 'til February before joining the Burleson Baby Boom, now that she's with Josh."

"The Burleson Baby Boom?" Becky spluttered as she choked on the drink of wine she'd just taken.

"Yeah, haven't you noticed?" Kayla nodded at Becky. "For the last year, every time a Burleson hooks up with someone, they end up pregnant before they even make it down the aisle, which is miraculous considering how fast your moms can put together a wedding."

"It's not just us, though," Jen objected, shaking her head at Kayla. "There are other babies being born in town besides the babies in our family."

"Yeah, but those are all born to couples who've been together for years," Cassidy pointed out, agreeing with Kayla. "Of the couples our ages who've just recently met and hooked up, it's only the Burlesons making babies almost immediately."

No, that can't be right. Can it?

Leah Mae Wright

"They're right," Lexi agreed, holding up a hand to count them off on her fingers. "Anthony met Kay, and less than two months later, her pregnancy was announced at their wedding rehearsal. But even though James and Randi got together during that same time frame, they haven't started having kids yet. Then Bobby and Brook got together and less than three months later, her pregnancy was announced at Bobby's birthday party."

"But even though there've been a few couples who've gotten together in the GWA during the same time frame of when Amy and Justin, and Char and Ian have gotten together and announced they're expecting, none of the GWA couples have announced a pregnancy," Kayla added with a half-shrug. "Well, except for Julie, but she's a Burleson, so Dion's GWA anti-baby mojo wasn't strong enough to counteract the super-fertility that runs in ya'll's family."

"Super-fertility?" Jen rolled her eyes at Kayla.

"She's got a point," Amy admitted, rubbing her hand over her round belly. "Justin knocked me up less than a week after we started having sex."

"I can beat that," Brook giggled. "Bobby hit a bullseye my very first time."

Holy shit! Maybe I should look into a more reliable form of contraception than condoms, at least, until Josh follows through with his proposal plans.

"Now I don't feel so bad about only knowing Ian for six months when we got pregnant," Charlotte chuckled.

"I guess the women in our family aren't as fertile as the men," Julie giggled. "Since it took Dion almost ten months to get the job done."

"Which brings me back to my point about Cait and Josh," Kayla smirked. "You know Josh is just as virile as his brothers and cousin, so I fully expect Cait to be preggo by the end of the year."

He did say he wanted us to get married before then. And he was okay with taking our chances with just condoms when we talked about birth control before, even knowing he'd conceived JoJo while wearing a condom. So, maybe it won't be a big deal if we go along with the trend and make a baby in the next couple of months.

"Yeah, I think I'm gonna avoid hooking up in this town," Ashlyn, Amy's twin sister, chimed in. "I'll stick to my vibrator or go to San Antonio for a hookup from now on."

"Don't worry, Ashlyn," Lexi assured her with a wide grin. "You're safe from the baby bug as long as you don't hook up with a Burleson. So, Jen and Becky are the only ones here who have to forgo man-made orgasms until they're ready for babies."

As the conversation about when the other women in the room wanted to have babies continued around her, Cait contemplated her thoughts on when she wanted to have a baby with Josh.

It would be nice to have our kids close in age to their cousins, so they always have a friend around. I didn't mind the seven-year age difference between me and Mikey, but it would have been nice to have some other kids closer to my age around when I was younger. And JoJo is already eight years older than any siblings Josh and I can give him, and would be nine years older even if I got pregnant this week.

But do we really want to actively start trying for a baby the first week we're living together? No, that's too soon. We should at least get married before we start trying to have a baby.

I guess we'll just keep leaving it up to fate and trust that his swimmers will get past the condom if we're meant to have babies sooner than we decide to actively try.

And in the meantime, we can have a lot of fun practicing making those babies.

Chapter Twenty-Five

Cait couldn't believe how much life had changed since her last birthday. Not only had she moved from San Diego, but she'd also mostly dealt with her agoraphobia, started dating and then living with Josh, and even gotten to speak with a couple of her younger half-siblings that she'd only learned about a month and a half before. She'd even had an actual birthday party for the first time in years. She hadn't really had them as a kid, only celebrating birthdays and holidays once Mikey became her legal guardian. During her high school and college years, the parties had gradually grown from having a few girlfriends come for a sleepover to keggers in her apartment. But after the drive-by, she'd been back to only getting a present or two from Mikey and a grocery store cake. This year, however, the Burlesons had thrown her a bash, showering her with more presents than she really needed.

At the party, Josh had gifted her with an upgraded laptop, one he'd had his twin custom build for her with all the bells and whistles. And the specialty security measures he felt she needed to keep her screenplays confidential. But once they got home from the party and were about to crawl into bed, he surprised her with another box for her birthday.

"The present you got me is already too much," Cait protested when she saw the large box sitting on their bed when she came out of the bathroom after brushing her teeth. "You know, all I really want is time with you, not all this expensive stuff, right?"

"Yeah, Sunshine, I know," Josh assured her with a peck of a kiss. "But it's because I know you don't care about my money or the material things in life that I trust you with full access to all of it and want to shower you with gifts that show you how much I love you. Now open this last present for your birthday, so you can show me what my sisters meant when they said it would be a present for both of us."

"Oh gawd, Josh, please tell me they didn't send you to Ashlyn's website to buy sex toys for my birthday." Cait felt herself blush as she thought about the things both Becky and Charlotte had recommended when they discussed the newest line with Ashlyn at the last book club meeting. *I really didn't need to know that Charlotte was the one who suggested the pierced dildo they added to the It's My Pleasure line back in the spring, or why she thought they needed to offer more options for different types of piercings on their newest products.*

"No, but damn, maybe I'll ask Justin if Amy has one of her sister's cards laying around, so I can check out that website for Christmas ideas," Josh grinned, wagging his eyebrows suggestively.

"Please don't," Cait cringed. "I really don't want to try the pierced dildo Charlotte mentioned at book club. Nor do I want to know if my brother is her inspiration for recommending pierced dildos to Ashlyn in the first place."

"Yeah, I don't want to know that either," Josh shuddered. "So, when I get a link, we'll avoid that section of the site."

Cait didn't mention that she could give him a link to Ashlyn's website for her It's My Pleasure side business, preferring to change the subject. "If this isn't sex toys, it must be lingerie if your sisters think it'll be a gift for both of us."

"Nope," Josh grinned, sitting down on the bed, and pushing the box over toward Cait. "Not lingerie."

As Cait went to pick it up, she realized it was way too heavy to be lingerie. Or even sex toys. She quickly tore off the paper and opened the box to find it full of paperback books.

"It's a signed set of the series they assured me was your favorite," Josh beamed. "Based on the covers, I'm guessing they think it's a series I'll enjoy reading, too."

As Cait pulled the books out of the box, she realized it was a full set of all fifteen books in Lexi Blake's original ***Masters and Mercenaries*** series, which was one of her favorite series of books, even though her girlfriends all compared her brother to one of the main characters. "Well, there are a couple of former Navy SEALs as main characters," Cait giggled, grinning over at Josh. "But you'll probably point out every possible inaccuracy in the spy stuff. So, I think they meant they could be a gift for both of us if we act out some of the sex scenes."

"Oh, yeah, we can definitely do that," Josh eagerly agreed, his eyes lighting with excitement as he picked up *Love and Let Die* and started flipping through it.

"Not that book," Cait warned him, reaching over to take it from his hands. "That's Ian and Charlotte's book, the one I told you about being glad I'd already finished before the girls started comparing my brother to the main character."

"Oh, yeah, we definitely don't wanna act out scenes that will make us think of my sister and your brother having sex." Josh shuddered once more before spreading the books out to examine the covers before pointing out *The Men with the Golden Cuffs* and *On Her Master's Secret Service*. "What about these two?"

"Please tell me you at least read the titles and didn't just pick these two because of the sexy women on the covers."

"I picked that one," he pointed at *The Men with the Golden Cuffs*, "because the laptop she's holding made me think of you when you're working, only naked, the way I'd love to watch you work sometime." He moved his hand to point at *On Her Master's Secret Service*. "And I picked that one 'cause the way her hands are tied together reminded me of tying you to the bed, so I thought it might have a scene where I could tie you up again."

"Oh, they all have scenes where you could tie me up again," Cait grinned as she moved to sit on Josh's lap. "They also all mention the use of butt plugs, especially *The Men with the Golden Cuffs* because Serena, Adam, and Jake end up in a permanent ménage, so the guys have to train her to take them at the same time."

"Holy shit," Josh hissed, looking down at the books spread out on the bed momentarily before looking back at Cait. "Would you be interested in trying some of that stuff, Sunshine? The anal, not the two-guys stuff. I can't stand the thought of anyone else touching you, so sharing you would be a hard limit for me."

She was surprised that he didn't seem to catch her mention of a character with the same name as his twin. *Huh, I wonder why the girls haven't compared Jake Burleson to Jake Dean the way they compared my brother to Ian Taggart? Maybe because the only thing Jake has in common with the book character is the name?*

"I've never really thought of trying any of the stuff in those books before I met you," Cait admitted honestly, even as she blushed at what she was about to suggest. "But I trust you enough that I'm willing to try anything you're interested in doing. And I have a couple of toys and lube in the bottom drawer of my bedside table if you want to try the double penetration thing without having to invite anyone else into our bedroom."

"You have a butt plug?" Josh's eyes widened in shock.

"No, but I have a couple of vibrators that can go in the front if you want to try going in the back." Cait wished she'd put on more makeup that morning to cover up how red her face must be during this conversation. "But since I haven't had anything in that hole before, it'll probably take a lot of lube and way more work with your fingers than the light teasing on the outside you've done there before to open me up enough that you'll fit."

"Oh, yeah, Sunshine," Josh nodded, gripping the globes of her ass in his large hands. "That's definitely a job I'm willing to take my time with to make sure we don't hurt you. Do any of these books go into enough detail to work as a training manual for an anal newbie, so I know what to do to make it feel better for you?"

"I don't remember any specific scenes off the top of my head," Cait half shrugged. "But we can read the series together if you want to look for specific instructions before we try any back door action."

"I suppose we can read a few chapters a night while we're waiting on JoJo to fall asleep, so he doesn't hear us when we're more likely to get loud while tryin' what we learn," Josh grinned.

They quickly returned most of the books to the box for Cait to find a place for them on their bedroom bookshelf later. Then they changed into their normal night clothes, just in case JoJo had a relapse of his nightmares. Finally, they settled into bed with **The Dom Who Loved Me** to start reading the first book in the series.

"How about you read the chapters that are from the male perspective and I'll read the ones from Grace's perspective?" Cait suggested, knowing she'd feel self-conscious enough reading the sex scenes from the woman's perspective and would really prefer hearing Josh read the whole book. *I wonder if he'll do the different voices like Ryan West does in the audiobook version?*

"Okay," Josh smirked, flipping to the first page to see who needed to read first.

"Yeah, you've got the first chapter, Cowboy," Cait grinned, snuggling into his side, so they could both see the book to be able to swap who was reading without having to pass the book back and forth. Truth be told, she could have pulled it up on her Kindle to follow along as he read without them having to share the book, but she wanted to cuddle so she could touch him while he read. "Luckily, the Taggarts are from Texas, so your twang will be perfect for reading their parts."

Josh began reading, not bothering to change his accent for the different characters the way Cait had hoped he would. *Oh well, at least that means I don't have to try to act out the male dialogue during Grace's parts later in the book either.*

"When you said these books talk about anal sex, I didn't think you meant the guy would be talking about it with his brother in the first chapter," Josh scoffed after he finished reading the first chapter. "And when you said I'd point out the inaccuracies, I didn't realize you meant I'd point out that brothers don't talk about our kinks with one another like this."

"Maybe brothers don't in your family," Cait giggled. "But your sisters do."

"I don't wanna know," Josh insisted, moving the book over in front of Cait's face for her to read the portion of chapter two that was from Grace's point of view.

Cait read her part, then poked Josh in the ribs when it was time for him to read the section from one of the bad guys' point of view. After that section, he had two more sections from Sean's point of view before she took over again.

"Seriously?" Josh shook his head as she motioned for him to take over again. "You only have to read two small sections in the first three chapters? I thought this was women's literature, meaning it should be from the woman's point of view most of the time."

"Sorry, Cowboy, but women prefer getting into men's minds, so we can try to figure out what you're thinking," Cait explained with a smile. "And it turns us on more when the audiobook is narrated by a sexy man's voice, so my favorite authors write at least half their books from the male perspective and either hire a male narrator or switch back and forth between male and female narrators to match the correct tone of voice to their audiobooks."

"Maybe I should read all your books to you from now on," Josh pouted, shaking his head. "That way, I don't have to worry about you getting turned on by another man's voice."

"Yeah, you might want to look into some voice acting lessons then, Cowboy," Cait laughed. "So you can change your tone and accent for each character to make it clear who's speaking without me having to read along."

"You haven't been changing your tone and accent for the different characters in the parts you've read," Josh pointed out.

"Only because you didn't," Cait informed him. *And because it's been so long since I've practiced different accents and tones that I'm afraid they'll come out croaky.*

"Whatever." Josh imitated her exaggerated eye roll before starting to read his next section of the book. This time he read a little slower, so he could concentrate on changing his tone and accent for each character's speaking parts.

Cait was impressed with his range for a voice actor, since she didn't think it was something he'd previously studied. When it was her turn to read again, she tried to keep up with the tones and inflections he'd assigned to each character, but she didn't have the range to hit the deep Dom voice of the male lead the way Josh did. They continued reading until they got through the first sex scene, which unfortunately didn't include anal. But since it did include a swimming pool, they couldn't act it out.

"Yeah, I can't wait any longer," Josh insisted, reaching over to his bedside table and rummaging around to find something to use as a bookmark. "We'll just wing it with the anal play tonight and go back to act out that scene after I figure out where we can install a pool that nobody else on the ranch will be able to see into."

Cait had to laugh when she realized Josh was so impatient to try playing with her back hole that he'd torn the lid off the box of condoms in his drawer to mark their place in the book without damaging it.

"Get out the toys and lube you mentioned earlier, Sunshine," he insisted as he jumped from the bed to lock their bedroom door. He shoved his sleep pants down as he stalked back to the bed.

Cait hated to turn her back to him to roll to the edge of the bed to reach into her bedside table. As curious as she was about how it would feel to have him in her anus, she didn't want to take her eyes off his glorious dick. It stood proudly at attention, jutting from the V of his thighs and reaching almost to his navel.

What the hell was I thinking? That monster isn't going to fit in my ass without a lot of training with plugs first.

"Maybe we should read a little more and check out the butt plug section of Ashlyn's website before we try this tonight," Cait muttered as Josh crawled back onto the bed.

"Don't worry, Sunshine," Josh crooned as he trailed his fingertips up her legs, causing her to quiver in anticipation as he pushed her nightgown up to expose her sex. "I know I'm just gonna get to play with my fingers in your ass tonight and maybe see if I can get you opened up enough to take the head of my cock. And we'll take our time and do all the research on what plugs to use to get you ready for me to fuck your ass."

The intensity in Josh's eyes made her want to try it all right then, but she didn't have the chance to state her wishes. Josh took her hands and pulled her up to a seated position, stripping her nightgown over her head and tossing it to the floor.

"Now, unless you want me to start with a spanking like in that book, I suggest you do as I instructed and get out the toys and lube, Sunshine," Josh commanded, his voice deep and gravelly from his aroused state.

"Yes, Sir," Cait choked out breathlessly as she twisted over onto her hands and knees and moved to the edge of the bed, so she could reach down and pull out the bottom drawer.

As she grabbed the bottle of lube and the two vibrators she owned, Josh ran his hands over her butt cheeks, spreading them apart to expose her anus. He circled her rosette with the tip of his thumb, heightening her arousal in a way she hadn't noticed the other times he'd lightly touched her there during their intimate moments. *Who knew having him rub my butthole would make my pussy even wetter than it was from cuddling with him while reading a sexy book?*

"Why do you have lube if you don't have any anal toys?"

"Because I need it for my other toys when I'm playing with them by myself," Cait confessed, glad she had her back to him so he couldn't see how embarrassed she was by that admission.

"So, all this cream is for me?" Josh ran his fingers over the lips of her sex, spreading her moisture up to her puckered back hole.

"Yes, Sir," Cait cooed, pushing back against the digit he pressed against her virgin entrance.

"No, Sunshine," Josh lightly slapped her ass with the hand not playing with her anus. "Call me Josh or Cowboy. I need to know you're with me and not imagining one of the Doms from those books."

"Yes, Josh." Cait reached back to hand him the lube, not sure her natural lubricant would be enough.

"Hand me your favorite toy, Sunshine," Josh instructed, taking the lube from her hand, but not using it yet. "Turn it on first," he corrected when she tried to hand him the G-spot vibe that curved to a clit sucker on one end.

Once she pushed the two buttons to turn on both the vibration and suction, Cait passed the toy back to Josh. He took a second to reposition on the bed before he inserted the vibe in her pussy, spreading her labia to make sure the suction head was right over her clit.

"Fuck, that's hot," Josh groaned, apparently enjoying being able to see her toy-filled pussy while also rimming her anus with his fingertip. He positioned his free hand so he could press on the vibe just right to move it in short strokes inside her.

Cait couldn't believe she was letting him play this way, always thinking of anal as forbidden territory before Josh. When he lifted his finger from her asshole, opened the lube, and drizzled it on her rosette, Cait shivered with excitement, feeling exhilarated by doing something so naughty and unexpected with her all-American good guy.

As he pressed his finger into her ass, Cait felt her body responding with the first little ripples of her impending orgasm. The pressure she felt as he worked his finger in and out was way more pleasurable than she'd expected. There was no discomfort whatsoever, as he massaged her inner muscles to open her up to take a second digit.

"Oh, Josh," Cait moaned repeatedly, feeling her core contract as her first orgasm struck her.

"Such a naughty girl, coming from having your ass finger-fucked," Josh playfully chided, though she could clearly hear the mirth in his voice.

As the waves of pleasure receded, Josh continued to work the vibe in her pussy while fingering her anus, not giving her any reprieve to catch her breath. She felt fuller than she had before her climax, making her wonder if he'd inserted a third finger in her rectum while she was preoccupied in the floaty feelings of her release.

Josh continued working her over while whispering his dirty fantasies about fucking her ass, taking her up and over the edge so many times that her upper body collapsed into the bed at some point without her even realizing it. Somehow, she stayed up on her knees with her hips tilted to give Josh easy access to both of her holes.

"Fuck, Sunshine, I hafta know what it feels like to be inside you here," Josh growled as he removed his fingers from her asshole.

She felt so empty, even with the vibe still in her pussy, while Josh moved out from behind her to retrieve a condom from his bedside table. He tore open the wrapper, but placed it on her low back instead of putting it on. He then removed the vibe from her pussy and drizzled on more lube before rubbing the head of his bare cock through the combined liquids dripping from her sex.

"Relax, Sunshine," Josh instructed as he separated her butt cheeks and lined his cock up with her puckered back hole. "I'm just gonna put the head in to know what it feels like. Then I'll put on the condom to fuck your tight little cunt. Now, flatten your back and push against me so I can get inside your perfect ass."

Cait pushed up on her elbows to follow his directions, pushing back as he split her open with the big, blunt head of his dick. "Oh, fuck, Cowboy. That feels a lot bigger than your fingers."

Cait wouldn't call it painful, per se, but it was definitely more discomfort than his fingers were moments before.

"I'm not goin' any farther, Sunshine," Josh assured her, holding still with just the head of his cock in her ass. "I want to stay here for a while to let you adjust to it, but you're so fuckin' tight that I'm about to blow without even moving."

"Then get that condom on and fuck me, Cowboy," Cait suggested, wiggling her hips now that she was accustomed to the fullness in her anus and needed him to move to take her over the edge once more.

Josh pulled out, smacking her ass with one hand while grabbing the condom with the other. "Remember, I'm in charge in the bedroom, Sunshine."

"Yes, Josh," Cait agreed as Josh sheathed himself.

Once the condom was in place, he ran the head of his cock through her folds once more, coating the condom in her cream, so it was easier for him to slide home in one deep thrust.

"Oh, yes, Josh," Cait moaned, bucking her hips to get him to move. "Please, fuck me, Cowboy."

"Oh, fuck, yeah," Josh groaned, taking control of her movements by gripping her hips and setting a furious pace with his powerful thrusts.

Cait was certain he would leave fingerprint bruises on her hips with how tightly he was clasping onto her, but she could only smile at the thought of him marking her in such a way. It seemed only fair that he left a few love marks, since she'd scratched up his back several times in the last couple of months. The animalistic way he took her sent her to the heights of nirvana within seconds, causing her to cry out his name once more.

Josh hadn't been kidding about how close he was, pushing in deep and holding the tip of his dick against her cervix as they came simultaneously. "Oh, fuck, Caitir."

Their mutual orgasms were so intense they both collapsed to the bed, with Josh rolling them to their sides, so he didn't crush her under his weight. They laid there spooning for several long moments as the aftershocks washed over them. Until Cait broke their silence by giggling when she realized her toy was still vibrating on the bed beside them. She couldn't stop laughing long enough to tell him why, so she hoped he'd figure it out when he saw her reach over and pick it up to turn it off.

"I think I like our new nightly routine of reading together and trying out some of the things from those books," Josh chuckled as they floated back down to earth.

"Me too," Cait smiled as Josh pulled out of her and got up to dispose of the condom. "Though I think we're going to have to work up to anal a little slower. And maybe save it for special occasions, so I'm not bedridden all the time."

"We can definitely do that, Sunshine," Josh agreed as he walked back into the bedroom from the bathroom, carrying a wet washcloth and a towel to go through his usual ritual of cleaning her up after sex. "And I promise not to ever use anything bigger than my cock, so you'll still be able to walk the next day."

"Deal," Cait giggled, getting up to grab her nightgown, so Josh could pick up the towel they'd put down to protect the bed earlier.

Once the cleanup was completed, they redressed for bed, unlocked the bedroom door, and snuggled in with a chorus of "I love you" and "goodnight."

~~~

Sunday, November 24, 2019

As he sat through yet another wedding shower after church, Josh was seriously glad Cait shared his opinion that they weren't necessary. They already ate lunch at the church almost every Sunday, so it seemed to him that the only thing that changed was putting a spotlight on the couple getting married. He supposed that was fine for the GWA couples who were accustomed to being in the spotlight for their jobs, but for his shy, quiet Cait, it would be a panic-inducing nightmare. And that was something Josh wanted to avoid at all costs. Besides, since everyone he knew suggested charity donations in lieu of gifts for all their wedding events, he didn't see the point in a party that was traditionally held to fill the newlyweds' home with presents.

But he considered Dean Hunter a friend, so he was there with his family to celebrate his impending marriage. When they'd originally sat down, he'd picked the table where Mikey and Char were sitting with Brody, knowing it would be where Cait and JoJo would be most comfortable. But when Anthony and Kay were called up to sit with the wedding party, where they had two rectangular tables pushed together to seat the bride and groom with everyone participating in the wedding, his mom went into Memmaw mode and insisted all her grandkids and their friends needed to go with her and Pappaw to the children's church classroom they had set up to keep the kids occupied during the party.
~~~

Apparently, she'd recruited Uncle Jon, Aunt Susan, Bobby, and Brooklyn to help her out with the various activities she had planned, so the rest of his siblings and cousins who were in attendance joined them at their table to avoid being set up with potential dates. Since the wrestlers that the Matchmaking Mommas usually paired them up with were all at the head table as part of the bridal party, Josh didn't think they had much to worry about. Especially since several of those wrestlers had apparently married each other in Vegas.

Then again, what do I know? Josh thought when he noticed how Dion was staring at Julie from across the room. *Dion didn't get married and he's obviously still interested in Julie. Now I wish I'd have gotten the chance to talk to him last night before he left Tully's, so I could find out why he hasn't contacted her before now.*

Cait had filled Josh in on the events he'd missed the night before while back shooting pool with the guys, when Dion showed up at the joint bachelor and bachelorette party, only to be immediately rebuffed by Julie and leave. But from the sounds of it, Julie hadn't let him say much to explain why he'd suddenly had a change of heart regarding their relationship.

Josh still believed his injuries had caused the miscommunication between them. But Julie had pretty much told everyone that she didn't want to talk about him when she'd announced her pregnancy to the family, so he had to respect his cousin's wishes. He was curious, but not curious enough to risk raising Julie's blood pressure while she was pregnant with twins. As was evidenced by how uncomfortable Amy was in the last few months of her pregnancy, just carrying twins was stressful enough.

Damn, Amy looks even more uncomfortable than normal today, Josh noticed as he started to tune back into the conversation going on around him after looking around the room. *I hope when Cait and I start having babies, she doesn't have as hard a time carrying our babies as Amy's had with her and Justin's twins. Hopefully, Tia's right and me being a twin won't make it more likely that we'll have twins, so she'll have an easier pregnancy like Kay and Brook had with just one baby at a time.*

"The next eight days can't go by fast enough," Amy mentioned as she moved in her seat to place a hand on her low back.

"I can't believe Dr. Magnum agreed to let you go that close to your due date before scheduling you to be induced," Char commented, rubbing a hand over her baby bump. "I thought they usually recommended delivering at thirty-eight weeks for twins, even if there aren't any complications."

"She originally planned for thirty-eight weeks," Amy replied, grimacing as she shifted in her seat. "But that's this week, and with it being Thanksgiving week, she was afraid of being short staffed and keeping us from spending the holiday with the family if we have any complications."

"Having a small staff that all want to be at home with their families for the holidays is the only drawback we've found to having the birthing center in town," Justin added, rubbing Amy's back that was obviously bothering her from carrying their twins. "But Dr. Magnum still has privileges at the hospital in San Antonio, so we have a backup plan to call her and meet her there if the boys decide to make their appearance on Turkey Day."

"Is that where everyone had to go to have babies before the birthing center opened?" Cait questioned, looking around the table at the Burlesons.

"Yeah, we were all born in the hospital in San Antonio," Josh replied, grinning at her.

"Not all of us," Charlotte chuckled, pointing with her thumb over her shoulder toward the head table where Anthony was sitting with the rest of the bridal party. "Anthony was technically born on the backseat of Memmaw Judy's car somewhere between here and the hospital."

"Seriously?" Amy's eyes went wide at the prospect of delivering in a moving vehicle.

"Yeah, seriously," Char confirmed. "I was only three at the time, so I don't really remember it. But Mom told me about it the other day when we were discussing my birth plan."

"Hopefully, ya'll won't have to go with your backup plan," JJ pointed back and forth between Justin and Amy. "'Cause I have a feeling I'll be the one driving ya'll to the hospital, and I am not cleaning that up off my upholstery."

Josh hadn't thought about the logistics of having babies before, but now that his family was pointing out the possibilities of backseat births on the way to the hospital in San Antonio, he realized the need to plan for holidays when deciding it was time for him and Cait to have more kids.

Is it weird to plot out dates on the calendar to decide when to try making a baby, so we can pick a birth month without any holidays?

As they ate lunch, Josh tried to picture the calendar in his head to figure out when it would be best to have a baby, also accounting for when he had the least amount of work to do on the ranch so there was no chance that he'd miss the birth.

January through June, we have our breeding seasons. October through March, we have our birthing seasons. That leaves July, August, and September when we're cutting hay and weaning calves and mostly just preparing for the busier months. But if we want to avoid holiday weeks at the beginning of July and September, then we need to plan for August babies. And since women and cows are pregnant for about the same amount of time, we need to get pregnant in November to have an August baby.

Shit! That means we'd have to get pregnant this week if we want a baby next year. And there's no way Cait's ready to start trying already. I'm pretty sure she's gonna wanna be married for a few months before she'll be ready to start thinkin' about addin' to our family. But I suppose I can ask her this afternoon when we get home to see if she's ready to plan it instead of just leaving it up to fate.

As they finished eating, people started getting up and mingling to prepare for the games, bringing Josh back to the moment just as Dion walked up to their table.

"Hey, um, Jewel, can we talk?" For such a large man, who usually came off as intimidating in the wrestling ring, Dion looked exceptionally humbled as he approached Julie.

"No," Julie huffed, shaking her head at him. "And I told you last night not to call me that anymore. My name is Julia, and that's what I expect you to call me from now on."

Oh, fuck, this is awkward. She's really pissed if she's insisting he call her Julia instead of Julie, like everyone else. Cait squeezed Josh's hand, obviously as uncomfortable witnessing this reunion as he was, even though she'd already been front row for the first time Julie saw Dion after he broke things off with her.

"I'm sorry, Julia," Dion pleaded. "I know in the middle of the wedding shower isn't really the right time for us to talk. But can I at least get your phone number so we can talk later this week?"

"You already have my phone number," Julie scoffed, shaking her head at him. "If you don't have it in your contacts anymore, try looking in your blocked number list."

"Yeah, about that, my brother…" Dion's words drifted off as he turned to the man who'd walked up to the table with him. "Damn, I should probably introduce ya'll to my brother. This is Darius, but we call him Dare." Dion then turned back to look around the table at the Burlesons, soon-to-be Burlesons, and Burleson-Campbells seated there. "I'm sorry, I've been told I've met ya'll before, but after my injury, I don't remember it. So, please forgive me for only being able to introduce you as the Burlesons."

When nobody else made a move to introduce themselves to Darius, Josh stepped in, hoping to cut some of the tension surrounding them at the moment. "Hi Dare, I'm Josh, and this is my girlfriend, Cait."

"Nice to meet you," Dare waved at them across the table.

Before Josh could go around and finish introducing the rest of the family, Amy cried out in pain and reached over to grab onto Justin. The rest of the introductions were forgotten, as everyone realized that the next set of Burleson twins didn't want to wait until the day the doctor had them scheduled to be born.

Thankfully, Dr. Magnum was just a few tables over and came quickly to check on her patient. Josh didn't understand half of what was being said as the doctor started questioning Amy about what she was feeling and if she had any kind of leakage that day.

"I think that was my first real contraction," Amy informed the doctor as soon as it had passed so that she could speak again.

"But you've been having back pain since last night, Sweetheart," Justin added. "Could that be the back labor I read about?"

"It could be," the doctor confirmed. "But your water hasn't broken yet?"

Amy shook her head. "No, I don't think so." She bit her lip and looked at Justin before looking back at the doctor. "Unless it can leak out slowly, like only when I laugh or during a contraction?"

"It can, yes," the doctor nodded.

"Then I probably should have called you last night, 'cause I've been wearing pads to catch what I thought was bladder leakage from having two babies sitting on it since we got home from the bachelorette and bachelor party."

"Let's get you over to the birthing center, so I can do a full exam," the doctor suggested, causing the Burlesons to all scramble to get their kids and the expectant grandparents to head to the birthing center for Jerry and Jonah's birthday.

"Guess I won't have any excuses for forgetting our anniversary, huh, Baby?" Anthony quipped as the family followed Justin and Amy out of the church.

"Not with the way our family is about birthday parties for all the kiddos," Kay grinned.

"Oh, damn, today is ya'll's first anniversary, isn't it?" Josh mused aloud, finally realizing the date. "Happy anniversary!"

"Thank you," Anthony and Kay said in unison.

"Hopefully, sharing their birthday with your anniversary won't give my nephews any ideas about being born in the car on the way to the hospital like you were," JJ teased, slapping Anthony on the back as he passed them on the way to his vehicle.

As Josh unlocked his Equinox and opened the passenger doors for Cait and JoJo, he turned to the woman he planned to marry in a little over a month and whispered so JoJo couldn't hear. "What do you think about trying to make a baby this week, so we're guaranteed an August baby?"

"Why do you want an August baby?" Cait looked at him like he had two heads.

"I figured August is the best time for us to have a baby, so there aren't any holidays the birthing center might need to close for. And that's when I'm the least busy on the ranch, so I won't be stuck in the middle of something and miss the birth," Josh shrugged. "But if we want an August baby, we've gotta make it this week. If we wait until next month, then we might have to risk a backseat birth on the way to the hospital on Labor Day."

"So, you want me to go through the worst part of pregnancy during the heat of summer when I'll be absolutely miserable because it works best for your schedule on the ranch?" Cait rolled her eyes at him as she got in the vehicle.

Leah Mae Wright

"Well, no, not when you put it that way," Josh sighed, realizing the heat stress of summer on heavily pregnant cows was part of the reason why they scheduled calving season for the late fall and early spring. *Damn! What was I thinking? Obviously, I don't want her to suffer through being pregnant in the heat of summer any more than I want to put our cattle through it.* He closed her door and walked around the vehicle to get in the driver's seat.

"How about we just keep leaving it up to fate?" Cait arched an eyebrow at him as he buckled his seatbelt and started the car. Josh looked in the rearview mirror to see that JoJo had put on his headphones and was watching something on his tablet, so he couldn't hear their conversation. "If we're meant to have an August baby, then it'll happen whether we try to make it happen or not. But if it doesn't happen by then, we can start trying in August for a May baby, so I'm not as big as a house in the middle of summer."

"Yeah, I guess May will work," Josh conceded as he drove them to the birthing center. "It's still in the middle of breeding season, but the bulls are doing most of the work then. And we can call the vet out for pregnancy checks, even if I can't personally be there."

"I'm glad that fits into your schedule," Cait giggled, smiling as if her thoughts had turned to all the ways they could practice making their babies. "I'll make sure to mark the calendar, so we remember when to start riding bareback."

Oh, hell, yeah! Josh was looking forward to August now, eager for his first time having sex without a condom.

Chapter Twenty-Six

BUZZ! BUZZ! BUZZ!

"Ugh!" Cait groaned as she woke up to Josh's early morning alarm. As much as she loved waking up in his arms, she really wished he didn't start his days so freaking early in the mornings. "Please tell me that you're going to let the ranch hands handle the early morning feedings for the next couple of weeks, while JoJo is on winter break from school, so we can sleep in over the holidays."

"Sorry, Sunshine." Josh leaned over and brushed his lips over her forehead before rolling to get out of bed. "The hands already handle most of the early morning chores, so I've gotta go check for any cows that might've gone into labor overnight. And with the way we double up our calving seasons, that's a daily job from the middle of September to the middle of April."

"Who did this job while you were in the Navy?" Cait grumbled, rubbing her eyes as she sat up in bed and watched Josh get dressed. With him going straight out to check the cattle, Josh opted to shower off the smell of whatever dirty jobs he ended up doing in the mornings after he got back to the house around lunchtime. Cait understood his need to shower later in the day, but she really missed the early morning showers they'd taken together when they were in Virginia. "And can't they continue doing it, so you can focus on the bigger picture, Mr. VP?"

"Pop or Carlos have always handled it before," Josh informed her as he buttoned up the blue Wrangler cowboy-cut shirt he layered over the long-sleeved t-shirt he'd already put on to keep from having to wear a jacket on forty-five-degree mornings during the winter. "And they'll both probably still be out there with me every morning until they finally retire. Hell, Pop will probably be out there every morning even after he retires. But if we have a backwards calf, it could take two of us to pull it. And it's not unheard of to have more than one cow in labor and needing assistance at the same time, so we still might have to pull some of the hands into the calving barn to help us out."

Josh had explained all that to her back in the spring when he first showed her the calving barn. But after hearing the description of his job during the hearing for JoJo's custody, she'd thought Josh wouldn't be spending so much time actually working with the cattle on the ranch each morning. During his testimony, it had sounded like he'd be checking in with the various ranch managers and doing more paperwork than actual physical labor.

After living with him for a couple of months though, she now knew he spent his mornings actually working the ranch and his afternoons making phone calls to the other locations and doing all that paperwork. Since his official job change, he only spent all day out with the cattle when he had a cow whose labor wasn't progressing and he had to assist in the birth. Thankfully, that hadn't happened all that often, so they were still able to have their midday rendezvous. *Guess we just combined our morning shower sex and midday quickies, since our schedules prevent us from having both.*

As Josh finished getting dressed, swapping his pajama pants for blue jeans, Cait got up and went to take care of her morning restroom needs. After emptying her bladder, she stared at the wet tissue. *Still nothing? Not even a little spotting?*

She dropped the tissue in the toilet as she stood, flushing the toilet before going to wash her hands and brush her teeth. *I'm officially a week late.*

Holy shit! I'm a week late! Is that late enough that an over-the-counter test will be accurate? Or should I just not worry about testing until the appointment I set with Dr. Magnum for after the holidays?

Cait had been concerned after she'd not started during the three days when she was supposed to have her period, so on Monday morning she'd called to get the earliest appointment with the OB-GYN all her girlfriends used. Unfortunately, due to the holidays, the only obstetrician in town was booked solid until January third.

And when should I tell Josh that I think I might be pregnant? After the doctor confirms it? Or after taking a home test to find out? Or should I just tell him now, so he can be with me for the appointment?

"You alright, Sunshine?" Josh gave her a curious look as he removed his toothbrush from the holder between the sinks.

"Yeah, why?" Cait looked up at him as she rinsed the soap off her hands under the running water in the sink she tended to use most often, while Josh turned on the water in the other one to wet his toothbrush.

"You've been washing your hands for like five minutes, and I don't think you even noticed when I walked into the bathroom," Josh informed her as he applied toothpaste to his toothbrush before starting to scrub his teeth.

Yeah, I should probably just tell him now, so he doesn't think I'm spaced out because of having second thoughts about marrying him.

She'd figured out his plan for them to get married on the one-year anniversary of the day they met, after he hadn't popped the question in November. The bouquets of yellow gerbera daisies he had delivered weekly since he told her about his parents' flower tradition showed he had a sensitive side that he covered with humor when dealing with most people. So, when the calendar flipped over to December and she saw that the twenty-ninth was a Sunday this year, she knew her sentimental man would pick the date they met to be their wedding day as well.

Wow! I guess we really are following the pattern of the Burleson Baby Boom to get knocked up before walking down the aisle. And we didn't even have to try like he suggested last month.

"Oh?" Cait shook her head as she dried her hands and grabbed her toothbrush. "Sorry, I was just lost in thought."

Josh spit the foamy toothpaste from his mouth before inquiring, "What's got you thinkin' so hard, Sunshine?"

"I'm, uh," Cait stammered, wishing she'd moved faster to put the toothpaste on her bristles, so she could think of how to tell him while she cleaned her teeth. Instead, she blurted, "I'm a week late," before shoving her toothbrush in her mouth.

Josh rinsed his mouth and spit once more before questioning her further as he rinsed off his toothbrush. "A week late for what?"

Cait took her time, making sure she brushed each tooth twice before she finally spit out the foam, rinsed her mouth, spit several times, and held her toothbrush under the faucet. Without anything left to block her from talking, she finally admitted, "My period's a week late." She watched the excess toothpaste flowing down the drain, instead of looking up at Josh to see his reaction. "And I can't get in to see Dr. Magnum until the third, so now I'm torn as to whether I should go get a home pregnancy test now, or wait until then for her to do a test, so I don't prove Kayla's prediction right."

When Josh didn't say anything, Cait continued rambling, unable to handle the silence. "And let me tell you, it's extremely disconcerting to have the girl you hooked up with on Prom night know enough about your virility to announce to our book club that I was going to be knocked up by New Year's, and then, two months later, be a week late getting my period. Like, how does she know your sperm is made up of a bunch of SEALs capable of getting past a condom to infiltrate my womb?"

Josh barked out a laugh as he pulled her into his arms. "I'm gonna hafta message the guys later to warn them that SEALs have SEAL sperm capable of defeating birth control to Infil into an unsuspecting uterus," he quipped, brushing his lips over the top of her head. "Might make a couple of 'em think twice before goin' home with a frog hog in the future."

Cait shook her head at his lame humor, even as she wrapped her arms around his waist and smiled into his chest.

"And I'm guessing that Kayla was basing her prediction on the way everyone else in our family seems to be procreating as soon as they meet their soulmates," Josh assured her, kissing the top of her head. "I guarantee, she doesn't have any first-hand knowledge of my virility. 'Cause for me, sex is only good enough to be memorable with you. Hell, even if she does remember something happening on Prom night that I forgot, it's probably only because of how much I fumbled around as a clueless high school kid."

"Whatever." Cait rolled her eyes at him, not wanting to mention how Kayla had coughed his name when the girls were discussing men with "magic peens" at one of the book club meetings she'd gone to over the summer, months after she'd let slip about Prom night.

"As for taking a test now or waiting until your appointment, I vote we go a couple of towns over to buy a home test today while JoJo is in school. That way we'll know before all the parties coming up, so we know if you need to skip the bachelorette party shots and champagne toasts at the weddings next weekend. But we won't tip off any of the gossipy Gertrudes in town to the possibility before we want them to know."

Weddings? As in plural? Cait stifled a giggle. *You're not very stealthy at keeping your proposal date a secret, Cowboy.* Cait hid her smile against his chest, not wanting to ruin his plans by saying what she was thinking.

"You'll go with me to get a test?" Once she contained her grin, Cait pulled back to look up into his heated, hazel eyes. "Don't you need to stay here and help with the calves?"

"I just need to go make sure we've got enough hands in the birthing barn to cover however many cows we have in labor," Josh assured her with a smile. "Then I'm gonna come back here to go with you to take JoJo to school and drive us over to Lytle or Atascosa to find a pharmacy where nobody will recognize us. And I'm gonna be right here in the bathroom with you when we look to see the results. I wanna be there for every single step of building our family with you, Sunshine."

"Yeah, I think you can wait in the other room while I pee on the stick." Cait cringed at the thought of him being there during that step. "I know we don't ever want to keep secrets from one another, but I don't think we actually have to witness certain bodily functions to know we both do them."

"From hearing my family talk about what can happen during the human birth process and having witnessed a few hundred calves being born, I'm pretty sure seeing you pee on a pregnancy test is nothing compared to what I'm gonna see when you give birth to our babies," Josh chuckled.

"Yeah, well, thankfully, I won't be able to see all of that while in labor." Cait gagged as she remembered the pictures she'd seen in the pregnancy books Mari had laying all over the place when she was pregnant with Brody.

"I could videotape it for you if you want," Josh joked, grinning mischievously.

"Don't you dare!" Cait pulled out of his embrace to lightly slap his rippled abs. "And you'll wait in the bedroom while I pee on the stick. But you can be the first one to look at the results if you want."

"Deal," Josh agreed with a smile before leaning down to peck her lips. "Give me a few minutes to check that the calving is fully covered, and I'll be back to get in the shower with you."

A few hours later, after Josh had verified the momma cows were being watched over by enough men to help them birth their calves, they'd snuck in a shower quickie, and gone through the morning routine to get JoJo off to school, they drove a couple of towns over to buy the test they needed. Looking at the shelves of tests, Cait felt overwhelmed by the number of choices available.

"Which one of these is the most accurate?" Josh looked as lost as she felt as they looked over the large selection. "And how come some of them come as one test in a large box, while others come as thirty tests in a small box?"

"I have no idea." Cait shook her head as she picked up a box with only one test in it to read the packaging. "I've never had to do one of these before."

While she was reading the packaging, Josh pulled out his phone. "Yeah, I'm just gonna Google it to figure out what we need to get."

"I thought you'd have a better idea of how this works with having to pregnancy test the cows," Cait joked.

"Yeah, trust me, Sunshine," Josh chuckled. "You'd much rather have me watch you pee than go through what the cows have to when we confirm their pregnancies."

"I thought you just did blood tests on the cows?" Cait assumed that would be how the doctor would test her on the third, so she didn't think it would be a big deal for Josh to come to the appointment with her and watch the blood draw.

"That's just something Pop has recently started using to try to test a month after breeding," Josh informed her with a grin. "But a month after that, we still have the vet come out and verify the results with rectal palpation. That requires a rubber glove that reaches all the way up to his armpit..."

"Don't!" Cait held a hand up to stop him from describing the process of rectal palpation in the middle of CVS.

"Don't worry, Sunshine," Josh grinned as he dipped his head to whisper close to her ear. "I've already shown you the only way I'll ever palpate your rectum. Though if you didn't limit that to special occasions, maybe we wouldn't be standing here confused about which pregnancy test to buy right now."

Cait rolled her eyes as she side stepped away from him to put the first package back on the shelf and pick up another. "Pervert," she coughed to cover the little laugh she let slip, hoping nobody else in the store heard her.

"No more than you, Sunshine," Josh smirked as he looked back down at his phone.

"Whatever." Cait rolled her eyes at him once more. "Now quit joshin' around and help me figure out which of these I need to get."

"Okay, so the strips, you pee in a cup and then dip them in," Josh explained what he was reading on his phone. "But they seem to be for people who are trying to conceive and need to retest often while trying. That's why they come thirty to a box."

"Yeah, I already figured out I don't need those," Cait scoffed, waving a hand at the shelf where the bulk tests were located. "That's why I'm looking at the ones on the shelf below those, that are more what I'm used to seeing in commercials and reading about in romance novels. I just don't know if I need the one that shows two lines, the one that shows a plus sign, or the one that actually says, 'pregnant' or 'not pregnant' in the test window."

"From what I've found online, they're all ninety-nine percent accurate, so maybe grab one or two of each kind?" Josh shrugged, pocketing his phone. "And we can grab a pack of Solo cups so you can dip them all instead of tryin' to pee on all of them."

"We don't need that many tests," Cait protested, thinking one would easily be enough to verify what she already suspected.

"Think of them as a second and third opinion in case one of them is a faulty test," Josh advised as he grabbed a package containing each of the types of tests Cait had pointed out that she was considering. "Only this way, you only have to pee in a cup once, instead of having to come back to the store for a different test and going again."

"Okay," Cait sighed, knowing that if she won the argument and only bought one test, it would end up being faulty and he'd gloat about how she should have listened to him.

Josh held the three boxes in one hand and placed his other hand on the small of her back to usher her through the store to the aisle by the food where the disposable cups were located.

"We've got plenty of cups at home, Josh," Cait pointed out, thinking he was being a little nuts by picking up a whole package of disposables when they only needed one.

"Yeah, but we're not gonna wanna drink outta your pee cup." Josh made a disgusted face.

"Well, obviously, I'd wash it after we're done with the tests," Cait argued.

"I'd still always wonder which one it was," Josh shuddered as he led her to the front of the store to checkout. "So, we're gonna save my sanity instead of the environment today. If we put them under the bathroom sink and only use them when we're testing for our kids, then we won't even do that much environmental damage."

Once again, Cait rolled her eyes at him. "Considering you insist on driving one of your big trucks instead of my little car anytime we go somewhere together, I don't think your plastic cup usage is the worst thing you do for the environment each day."

"Yeah, well, I do what I can while still supporting the family business," Josh shrugged as he put everything on the counter for the cashier to ring them up.

Eighty dollars and an hour later, they were back at home with Josh opening the various test boxes while Cait went to pee in one of the plastic cups he'd insisted on buying. As soon as she flushed, Josh stepped into the bathroom with the three opened boxes in his hands.

"These are all two packs, so we're ready to test for our next baby, too," Josh grinned as he placed the boxes on the counter beside where she'd placed the cup to wash her hands.

Cait thought he was acting a little over the top with how he meticulously laid out strips of toilet paper on the counter between the dual sinks to have places to put each of the test sticks after they were dipped. But she just smiled and let her goofy guy have fun playing mad scientist, as he set up their tests like they were experiments being done in the Burleson Incorporated lab.

Thankfully, JoJo is in school while we're doing this, Cait thought, as Josh swirled each stick in her cup of urine before placing them on their paper-covered resting places on the counter and setting separate alarms on his phone for each one. *If he'd been home, Josh would have had him in here playing Igor to his Dr. Frankenstein.*

Once they were all processing, Josh washed his hands and put the extra supplies in the cabinet under the sinks. Cait started to take the cup of excess urine over to the toilet to pour it out, but Josh stopped her.

"Wait, Sunshine. We've gotta make sure we don't have three duds first."

"I highly doubt all three of them will malfunction, Josh," Cait pointed out, disposing of the urine before rinsing out the cup and tossing it in the wastebasket. "But if they do, it'd probably be because I didn't use my first morning urine, so I'd want to wait to retest with the others in the morning, anyway."

"Oh, yeah, good point," Josh agreed, as Cait washed her hands again. "Now what can we do for the next few minutes while we're waiting for all the alarms to go off?"

Josh didn't give her a chance to respond, pulling her into his arms and covering her mouth with his. Cait wrapped her arms around him, as they made out like teenagers while waiting to find out if they were going to be parents in about eight months.

As much as she loved standing there kissing Josh, she pulled away as soon as the first alarm went off, unable to wait to see what the first test said.

"Oh, no, Sunshine." Josh held her tight with one arm while reaching over and swiping off his alarm with the other. "I wanna wait until I know they're all ready before we look."

The alarm blared a second time before he even finished his sentence. And when he swiped to turn it off, it only stopped ringing out for a second or two before it went off the third time.

"Now we can look," he chuckled as he finally got the shrill sounds to stop.

They turned as one, moving to where Cait was standing in front of Josh, as they looked down at the three tests. Two pink lines, a plus sign, and the word "pregnant" made it clear that they were expecting.

As Josh placed his hands on her still flat stomach, Cait's eyes welled with tears. "We're having a baby." Her voice was tinged with awe as she covered Josh's hands with hers.

"We are," Josh reiterated reverently, kissing her temple before reverting to his typical jovial nature. "Guess this means I need to hurry with the wedding plans, so you'll still fit in your wedding dress, and Mikey won't come after me with a shotgun."

Cait had to laugh at the way Josh made reference to the way everyone was picking on her brother about having a shotgun wedding back in September. "I don't want to tell anyone before the wedding," Cait informed him. "Unlike Julie, I didn't wait until I'm almost through the first trimester and starting to get a baby bump to take a test, so we should be able to keep it a secret for another month or two. Then after we're out of the first trimester, when there's less likelihood of miscarriage, we can tell everyone."

"Whatever you want, Sunshine," Josh agreed, hugging her close and kissing her cheek before resting his chin on her shoulder as they continued to stare at the three positive pregnancy tests. "Luckily for you, I'm way better at keeping secrets than my siblings or their spouses, so you won't have to worry about an unexpected early announcement from me."

Yeah, I'm a lot more worried about the possibility of having twins...

"How far along do you think we are?" Josh rubbed his hands over her still flat stomach, derailing her thoughts.

"Barely over a month," Cait sighed, realizing that she probably got pregnant right after Josh suggested trying that week for an August baby. "If that. I would have been ovulating the week of Thanksgiving. Please tell me you didn't tamper with our condoms that week to make sure we have an August baby like you suggested."

"No, Sunshine." Josh turned her in his arms to look into her eyes. "I might joke around a lot, but I'd never do something like that. I swear I've followed your plan to let fate decide when we have more kids. Though I wouldn't be surprised if we get to Heaven one day and find out that Memmaw and Pappaw heard us talking about when we wanted to start adding to our family and talked God into stepping in to make it happen when I said I wanted our next child."

"More like JoJo might have overheard us through his earphones and convinced your mother to pray for it," Cait giggled, knowing that would be something Hazel would love taking the credit for, just like she took credit for them falling in love because she and Susan had a plan to seat the Campbells with their kids.

"Possibly," Josh chuckled. "But when we finally announce our impending parenthood, don't mention that theory around Ma. She'll claim the credit whether it happened that way or not."

~~~

Sunday, December 29, 2019

Josh was both excited and a nervous wreck now that his wedding day had finally arrived. He wasn't nervous about asking Cait to marry him. He was positive she'd say yes. But he was nervous about whether or not she'd like the arrangements he'd made for their special day.

Fuck! I hope I didn't screw up by sneaking out of bed this morning to try to recreate the first time I saw her for the proposal. Maybe I shoulda stuck with my plan to propose in the area of the hayloft we're making into our bedroom?

He'd left a note with directions to wear the same emerald green dress she'd worn the first day they'd seen each other and meet him at his parents' house for breakfast before church. He'd even put on the same blue jeans and Henley he'd worn back then, not caring that his mom had complained about him not planning to wear a suit like the rest of the men in his family would be wearing for church.

There were a couple of things different about his proposal plans than when they'd met a year before. Besides being breakfast instead of lunch, there were a half dozen more children present, most of them babies who might interrupt the proposal by crying for a bottle or diaper change.

It was also only going to be the Burlesons (or soon to be Burlesons) and Burleson-Campbells present, instead of having the whole extended family, as well as the Hunters and all their guests from the bed and breakfast for a party. They'd been able to have Christmas dinner on Christmas Day this year instead of having to postpone it like last year, since Kay's family from Oklahoma came down to spend the holiday week and attend Justin and Amy's wedding, so they'd already had their big celebration earlier in the week.
~~~

With Mikey and Char now being married, Josh had also changed things up by tasking JoJo with accompanying Cait to the house, instead of her brother and nephew, as they had the year before. But he'd made sure JoJo knew to walk her over to Pappaw and Uncle Bob the same way the Hunters had first introduced the Campbells the previous year. Now, Josh waited impatiently as he stood talking to his siblings and cousins, eagerly anticipating the moment when their eyes would meet across the room as they had twelve months before.

"Dude, how'd you ever survive being a SEAL if you're this jumpy following a plan you've set up?" JJ grinned at him.

"SEAL ops are a lot different than proposal plans," Josh replied, shaking his head at the cousin who had no idea what his life had been like in the Navy.

"Yeah, you coulda died on those ops," JJ chided. "While the worst that can happen here is that she gets so choked up, she can't say anything and has to nod her acceptance."

"No, the worst would be if she says no," Josh disagreed, though he really didn't believe she'd turn him down, especially now that they knew they were expecting.

"She's not gonna say no," Jake reassured him. "Hell, you probably coulda asked her anytime in the last year and she'd have said yes, even back on that first day."

"No, we both needed this year to deal with some issues and build our friendship first," Josh corrected his brother's inaccurate assumption. "And I don't really think she's gonna turn me down. I'm just excited because the day is finally here."

"I still can't believe you planned a surprise wedding for her for tonight," Jen mused aloud.

"I can't decide if that's the most romantic thing ever or just him being the biggest caveman on the planet," Becky quipped as the girls giggled.

"Because it's Josh and Cait, I'm voting romantic," Julie chimed in. "But if Dion tried to pull this shit on me, I'd say it was because he's a Neanderthal."

"She knows I'm planning it," Josh informed his family. "The day we moved in together, we talked about what she always pictured for her wedding and she said she thought it would be spur of the moment, decide to do it, and hit up the courthouse the same day. So, I told her

I'd plan everything and propose on the day of the wedding to make it seem spur of the moment like she wanted, and all she had to do was go dress shopping with Ma to be ready for when I surprised her with the proposal."

"I wondered why we all had to give her our opinions on wedding dresses on Halloween and then she didn't end up dressing up as a vampire bride for the holiday," Julie remarked, informing him of how many others she'd asked for advice while dress shopping with his mom, when she refused to let him see the dress.

"I told you she was preparing early because she expected Josh to pop the question and Aunt Hazel to plan the wedding in a month." Jen pointed at her twin.

"I bet Mom has the dress stored somewhere here in the house waiting for her," Becky added with a grin.

Josh didn't get a chance to confirm his sister's suspicions, as the door opened and Cait walked in holding JoJo's hand. He couldn't think about the conversation he'd had with his mom about making sure Cait's dress was purchased in plenty of time because he was speechless as he felt that bolt of lightning once again when he saw her.

Just like it had happened the previous year, he couldn't take his eyes off of Cait, as she and JoJo walked through the room to greet his father and uncle first. As soon as they stopped walking, she turned and smiled directly at him.

Unlike the previous year, Josh didn't stay glued to his spot. He strode across the room with a wide smile on his face, dropping to one knee as soon as he reached the woman of his dreams. He joined their left hands as he reached into his pocket and pulled out the three-carat sunburst diamond ring he'd picked because the large center stone surrounded by fifteen smaller stones matched her sunny personality.

"Oh, Josh," Cait gasped, covering her mouth with her right hand, pulling JoJo's hand up with her since they were still holding hands.

Josh placed the ring at the tip of her left ring finger as he stared up into her expressive blue-green eyes. "A year ago today, I saw you walk in this room just like this, and instantly fell head over heels in love with you. As we've gotten to know each other, I've only fallen deeper in love with you each day. You've been my Sunshine since day one, and I will love you for all eternity. Caitir Skye Campbell, will you marry me tonight?"

"Oh, yes, Josh," she gushed, dropping her right hand so he could see her smile beaming at him, as he slid the ring onto her finger. "Oh, wow, it's a perfect fit. How'd you know my ring size?"

"I tied a string around your finger while you were asleep," Josh shrugged as he stood, pulling her into his arms to kiss his fiancée.

Since he wouldn't even get to call her that for twelve hours before he changed her title to wife, he wanted to, at least, get a few engagement kisses in during their super short engagement period, knowing there was no chance he'd get to make love to her while she was his fiancée. Between the wedding breakfast his mother insisted on hosting in place of the wedding shower, and the women of the family insisting on having their day of beauty to get dolled up between church services like they had at all the other family weddings, Josh was certain he'd only be allowed a few chaste kisses before they went off for their wedding night alone.

"I'm surprised I didn't wake up," she informed him after he released the way-too-short lip lock.

"There are certain times of the night when you're more soundly asleep than others," he smirked, referring to those times when he wore her out with orgasms. "And because I know you well enough to know those times, you didn't move a muscle as I tied a knot in the string and slipped it off your finger to take to the jeweler's."

"Uh-huh," she grinned as their family surrounded them to offer their congratulations. "I think you used some kind of sneaky SEAL trick to make sure I slept through it."

Only if fucking you into an orgasm coma is a sneaky SEAL trick, Sunshine, Josh thought, not wanting to share his thoughts in front of his parents.

Once everyone had taken a turn hugging Cait and welcoming her to the family, his mom insisted they get started with breakfast, so they wouldn't be late with the other things they had planned for the day.

As they sat down in the same seats that she and Jake had occupied the year before at their late Christmas dinner, Josh filled Cait in on the plans for the day. "Since Ma is counting this breakfast as our wedding shower, right after church, you can go with her and the other women in the family for whatever beauty treatments they have planned before the wedding, which is replacing the evening service at church tonight."

"And you've got everything set up, so it's actually legal? We won't have to do it all over again after going to get a marriage license next week?" Cait questioned him between bites of breakfast.

"Yes, it's all legal," Josh grinned. "I've already set up everything with Uncle Doug, so you just have to sign the paperwork at church this morning for the marriage license, which I actually applied for last week."

"Is that why I couldn't find my wallet on Monday?" Cait arched a quizzical brow at him.

"Yeah, I had to show your driver's license and social security card to get the marriage license," Josh confessed. "Even with Uncle Doug promising to witness your signature on the paperwork, so you didn't have to apply in person, the clerk still had to physically see those things to verify I'd accurately filled out the license application."

"You know I would have gone with you to get the license anytime in the last two months, right?" Cait rolled her eyes at him. "I mean, I did know it was coming, so it wouldn't have ruined the surprise if you'd have asked me to go with you for that errand."

"Yeah, but I figured if I asked you to go get the license, then you'd figure out when I was planning everything," Josh shrugged.

"Oh, my sentimental Cowboy," Cait cooed, reaching over to place her hand on his jaw to pull him down for a quick peck of a kiss. "I figured it out when you hadn't asked me in the first month after we talked about it, and I looked at the calendar and saw the anniversary of the day we met was a Sunday this year. I just didn't tell you I knew because I love your sappy, sentimental side and agreed that today is the perfect day for us to get married."

"Sounds like you're gonna have a harder time surprising your girl than you thought, Bro," Jake chuckled from across the table.

"Maybe with some things," Josh smirked, knowing she'd never guess his plans for their wedding night. "But I've still got a few tricks up my sleeve to keep her on her toes."

"I'm looking forward to figuring out all your secrets, Cowboy," Cait teased back.

"No secrets, Sunshine." Josh shook his head before leaning over to peck her lips once more. "Just surprises for special occasions."

Like the toys I stashed at the cabin the other day, so you can have double penetration for our wedding night.

Leah Mae Wright

After overcoming every obstacle that had come their way in the last year, Josh was looking forward to the adventure of life as Cait's husband. He was fully prepared to fight any battles they had coming at them in the future, knowing they would tackle them as a team. And have a lot of fun joshin' around along the way.

~~~

Cait felt like she was floating on cloud nine as she danced with Josh at their wedding reception later that night. If anyone had suggested she'd be married and expecting a baby within a year, back when she'd first met Josh and the rest of the Burlesons the previous year, she'd have thought they were insane. But here she was, living out the dream life she'd thought she'd only ever get to fantasize about back when she was mired in the depths of her agoraphobia. Oh, she was still hyper-vigilant whenever she went off the ranch on her own and preferred having Josh go with her when she had to leave the relative safety of the Heart's Destiny city limits. But she wasn't being held back by her PTSD or fears any longer. She had goals for her life that she knew she'd achieve thanks to having a loving support system to bolster her strength whenever she felt lacking.

Mikey and Brody had provided the first rungs on her ladder out of despair by giving her a reason to go on after the shooting and moving her to a place where she felt safer than she had in San Diego. But after the move, the Burlesons had quickly provided the rest of the rungs on her ladder to help her climb to the heights she wanted to reach in life. And Josh had proven more than capable of catching her if she slipped and carrying her up over the obstacles in life if she needed him to keep her from faltering.

JoJo had also surprised her as they were eating breakfast that morning, asking if they could include something in the wedding, making her his legal mom since they'd asked him to stand up with them. They'd had to take a few minutes after church to talk to Pastor Harrison about adding vows as parents to their ceremony and set an appointment with Tyler Reilly for the next day to draw up the adoption papers, but they were able to get it done. So, now she wasn't just Mrs. Joshua Burleson, she was also JoJo Burleson's Mom, even if they still
~~~

had to wait for all the paperwork to go through the court system to make it legal.

"So, my beautiful bride, who did Ma convince you we need to target with the bouquet and garter toss?" Josh smirked, referring to the way Hazel had cornered Cait earlier in the day to discuss her admittance into the Matchmaking Mommas Club.

"She surprised me with her suggestions, actually," Cait admitted as Josh twirled her around the dance floor. "I thought, for sure, she'd push to pair off Becky or Jake next, so she could get all her kids married off. But she actually suggested JJ and Deanna."

"Yeah, that's not surprising," Josh smiled knowingly. "They've been pushing to get those two together since Anthony and Kay got married. And I think they're hoping something will happen between the two of them when he goes to Tulsa next month for the takeover of OK Oil."

"Wait." Cait looked up at her husband in shock. "That's the company Deanna works for, right? She's like the executive assistant to the CEO or something, right?" Josh nodded and smiled. "Does she know Burleson is buying them out?"

"I don't think so," Josh shook his head before turning to look over at where Deanna was sitting with Kay, Anthony, and their kids. "From what JJ has presented on his buyout efforts in our board meetings, I think he's been negotiating with their board of directors or individual stockholders and not the CEO. And considering the bad blood between JJ and Beau Irvine, I'm pretty sure JJ insisted on being the one to fire him when we buy out the last stockholder. So, I'm pretty sure he's had each of the stockholders he's been in negotiations with for the last few months sign non-disclosure agreements to keep Beau from figuring it out."

"Oh, she's going to be furious when he shows up and fires her boss out of the blue without giving her any kind of heads up beforehand." Cait didn't know Deanna very well, only talking to her briefly when she'd come down to visit with Kay and her family a couple of times in the last year. But while she had seen some sparks between Deanna and JJ, she'd clearly heard Deanna say that nothing could happen between them because she wasn't the marriage and family type and had to break off the fling they'd had years ago because she didn't want to break his heart. *But with the way she's looking at him, I'm not sure*

Leah Mae Wright

I believe her about not wanting a family with him now. "I don't know that the magic of the bouquet and garter toss will work on them after that."

"Maybe not. But it's worked for several other couples in the last year or so, even when the toss went awry and my son caught the garter instead of me." Josh grinned and winked at her as he referred to when she'd caught the bouquet and JoJo caught the garter at Mikey and Charlotte's wedding. "Only time will tell if things will work out for the couples who caught them at the last couple of weddings. But I'm sure JJ needs all the luck he can get in winning over Deanna, so I'm not opposed to tossing the garter to him tonight."

"Well, then by all means, let's toss the bouquet and garter to Deanna and JJ," Cait chuckled, hoping they really could pass along a little of the happiness of being a couple to Josh's cousin and Kay's friend. "And then we've got to hurry through cutting the cake, so you can surprise me with our honeymoon destination."

They weren't taking a long honeymoon, only going away for a couple of days and coming home on New Year's Day, so Cait didn't think they were going very far. But she was eager to find out where they'd be spending their wedding night.

"I suppose I could go ahead and tell you where we're goin' tonight," Josh grinned, leaning down to whisper in her ear, so none of the guests dancing near them could hear his honeymoon plans. "I'm taking you to the secret lair Jake and I rebuilt as teenagers to sneak off for some peace and quiet where the rest of the family couldn't find us."

"You have a secret lair?" Cait giggled, thinking he had to be joking around.

"Yeah, only a handful of people know about it," Josh confided with a smile. "Just me and Jake, and Leo and Aiden Walker 'cause we had to get them to help us with the septic system. And Mikey, 'cause Jake let him use it as his tactical operations center when he was searching for Rojo. And maybe a few girls that Jake hooked up with back in high school, but he made them wear blindfolds so they couldn't find it again if he took them there. But you'll be the only girl I've ever taken there."

"Am I going to have to be blindfolded to go there for our honeymoon?" Cait arched an eyebrow, curious about why he was still being so secretive about his teenage hideout.

"No, Sunshine, seeing how to get to my secret lair is one of the privileges of marriage," Josh assured her teasingly, wagging his eyebrows. "But we might try that blindfold in the bedroom later if you want."

"Oh, we can definitely try it later in the bedroom, Cowboy," Cait giggled, looking forward to a long, exciting marriage with the man of her dreams. "And maybe that silk rope I gave you for Christmas?"

"I love you and your sexy ideas, Mrs. Burleson."

"I love you, too, Mr. Burleson."

Epilogue

Josh couldn't believe how drastically life had changed for the Burlesons in less than a year and a half. When he'd first heard that his little brother, Anthony, had met his soulmate and wanted him to come home for Thanksgiving to be at his wedding, Josh could never have dreamed that the Love Bug would spread through his family and friends like wildfire. And he certainly didn't imagine he'd be one of the family members to find his true love, get married, and have kids so soon after the first of them fell.

As he looked around the room at the Heart's Destiny Birthing Center to see his family, where they'd gathered to welcome their newest member, he was awed by the amount of love and happiness in the room, even with several members of the family unable to be there because of their job responsibilities. Anthony, Kay, and their four kids were off flying around the country with the GWA. Josh's twin brother, Jake, was still in Washington D.C. with another year and a half on his minimum service requirement with the Navy. And their cousin JJ was still in Tulsa, dealing with transitioning the holdings of the former OK Oil into the Burleson Energy division of Burleson Incorporated. But the rest of the Burlesons and Burleson-Campbells were there to welcome Judy Carol Burleson-Campbell to the family.

And in just a few more months, we'll all do this again to welcome mine and Cait's child to the family, Josh realized as he sat there with Cait on his lap while the family all discussed how Char was doing after delivering Judy that morning. *I wonder if we should tell them we're expecting while we have most of the family here?*

"I can't wait 'til it's my turn in that bed," Julie sighed, rubbing her rounded belly.

"How far along are you now?" Amy inquired as she rocked one of her twin sons, while Justin held the other.

"Twenty-five weeks," Julie smiled. "Finally in that sweet spot between the morning-sickness phase and the too-big-to-tie-my-shoes phase."

As the ladies in the room discussed the various stages of pregnancy, Josh brushed Cait's hair off her shoulder so he could whisper in her ear. "You think we should tell them our news?"

Cait nodded her agreement before bending down to pick up her purse, where he knew she'd stashed the ultrasound pictures they'd gotten that afternoon.

"So, um," Josh interrupted the conversation going on around them. "While we've got most everyone here, we wanted to let ya'll know that we're adding another Burleson baby to the family in August."

"Oh my goodness! Really?" Hazel beamed as she bounced baby Judy in her arms.

"Yes, really," Cait giggled as she pulled the ultrasound pictures from her purse to pass them around the room.

"Michael Ian Burleson-Campbell, don't you dare laugh!" Charlotte shouted from her hospital bed, pointing at her husband as she gave him a dirty look.

"Sorry, Princess, I can't help it," Mikey chuckled as he stood up and walked over to hug his sister, Cait. "Congratulations, Caitir. I can't wait to meet my next nephew or niece."

Cait quickly returned the brief embrace. "Thanks, Mikey."

Once they released the hug, Mikey shook Josh's hand to congratulate him on his impending fatherhood. "Your little one will be the lucky number thirteen to help me win a bet with Charlotte."

"What?" Josh was confused by the way his sister and brother-in-law reacted to the news.

"You may have won the bet, but this just proves I was justified in naming Judy after Memmaw," Char huffed as Mikey walked back over to her bed and brushed his lips over her forehead.

"Ya'll are gonna hafta explain this one to the rest of us," Bobby pointed to Char and Mikey.

"Does this have something to do with the dreams you had about Memmaw last year?" Becky asked Charlotte.

"Yes," Char confirmed, nodding at Becky. "And while trying to distract me during labor, Ian bet me that Josh and Cait would be the ones to have the thirteenth of the great-grandbabies Memmaw told me she'd have by Christmas this year."

"Wait a minute, I'm lost," Josh interjected, not understanding if Memmaw actually had a conversation with Charlotte or if Char had just dreamed it. "What dreams? And when did you talk to Memmaw about us all having kids? Hell, we were all still kids when she passed away."

"I didn't actually talk to her about it when we were kids," Charlotte explained. "But last year I had a bunch of dreams where she sat on the side of my bed and talked to me about the future of our family. She told me I'd met my soulmate and was going to give birth to a daughter within the next year. And then within a couple of months, I found out I was pregnant, so I decided if she was right about the baby being a girl, I was going to name her Judy after Memmaw."

"It was Char's way of getting back at Memmaw for proving her wrong about prophetic dreams," Becky elaborated.

"Anyway, she also told me that she'd have thirteen great-grandbabies by Christmas this year, and three dozen great-grandbabies by the time we're all finished falling in love and having babies," Charlotte went on. "At the time, I thought there was no way we'd get to thirteen kids added to the family in less than two years, 'cause Anthony and Bobby were the only two of us who'd gotten married, with Anthony adopting Tia and Maria, and then both Kay and Brook announcing they were having babies. I didn't think there was any way we'd go from four to thirteen without everyone else getting married by the end of the year."

Charlotte held up both hands, but only put up four fingers as she started counting off the rest of the kids being added to the family. "But then Anthony and Kay adopted Antonio, bringing the total up to five." She extended her thumb on the first hand. "And then I found out I was pregnant right before Justin and Amy announced they were having twins, so the total jumped to eight." She extended three fingers on the other hand. "A couple weeks later, Brody asked me to adopt him, making it nine. Then we found out about JoJo, ten." Char held up both hands with all her digits extended before reaching over for Mikey's hand to use his fingers to add the next three. "Then Julie made her Halloween announcement of twins, bringing the total up to twelve." Mikey extended two fingers on the hand Char had pulled over by hers. "And now ya'll just announced number thirteen." Mikey extended another finger. "So, now I have to wonder if Memmaw really had to have visited me in my dreams to tell me the exact number of great-grandkids she'd have by Christmas."

"I just hope I get a few more from the twenty-three that are yet to come than I did from the first thirteen, so I can have as many grandkids as Hazel," Aunt Susan giggled. "And hopefully, things will work out with JJ and Deanna, so they can give us the first of the next batch at the beginning of next year."

"Thank you, Cowboy," Cait grinned, turning to peck his lips with hers as the rest of the family continued talking about the possibilities of who would be next to add to the family.

Josh arched an eyebrow at her when she pulled back from the brief smooch, curious about what she was thanking him for.

"For sharing your big, crazy family with me," Cait laughed, clearly reading his mind.

"You're welcome, Sunshine," Josh chuckled. "And thank you for helping me expand our big, crazy family."

I wonder how many of those three-dozen great-grandkids, Memmaw and Pappaw are plannin' on watching over from Heaven, Cait and I will get to raise?

Next in Heart's Destiny

<u>*Dion's Dream Girl*</u>
Heart's Destiny Book 7

Dion Davis didn't remember the most important events of his life after helping to rescue one of his fellow wrestlers from a deranged stalker. Truth be told, he didn't remember meeting Allissa, much less helping to rescue her. But he did remember his good friend, Dean Hunter, who just so happened to be Allissa's fiancé, so he couldn't say no when they asked him to be in their wedding.

From what he'd been told after waking up in the hospital with amnesia, he spent a lot of time in Dean's hometown over the last year. So, he hoped his trip to Heart's Destiny for their wedding would bring back a few of the memories he lost. Especially if those memories revealed the identity of the woman he dreamed about nightly since he woke up in the hospital after the altercation with Allissa's stalker. *Jewel. My Dream Girl. My Jewel. She has to be real. Making love to her in all those different hotel rooms has to be my memories trying to come back to me, not just dreams, like the, uh,…guy in the white lab coat thinks they are.*

After almost a year of sneaking around to see Dion without letting on to her matchmaking mother that she'd met *The One*, Julie Burleson was almost ready to announce to the world that they were in love, and possibly starting a family. Then, two days before she was scheduled to see her doctor to verify her suspicion that she was pregnant, Dion was injured while helping to rescue one of their friends from a stalker. After frantically trying to call him in between bouts of nausea at hearing the news, Julie finally got through, only to be told not to call him again because he was blocking her number.

Devastated by the sudden rejection of the man she thought was her soulmate, Julie struggled with her emotions as she tried to move on with her life. Hurt and angry, she didn't want anything to do with him when he returned to Heart's Destiny for Dean and Allissa's wedding, no matter how much her heart and her libido contradicted the thoughts in her head.

But Dion was nothing if not determined. Determined to heal, not only his injuries, but also his relationship with his Jewel. Could this former professional wrestler win the biggest battle of his life — the emotional wrestling match for Jewel's heart? He might not ever be able to step into the squared circle as a pro grappler again, but he planned to spend the rest of his life fighting for his family. Dion knew the most important victory of his life would be winning the heart of his dream girl.

DISCLAIMER: This small-town, second chance, multicultural, surprise pregnancy, amnesia romance contains scenes depicting the physical and mental symptoms experienced after a traumatic brain injury, profanity, and graphic sex scenes. It is intended for adult readers (18+) who are not easily offended.

Next in the GWA

Mistakenly Married?
Galactic Wrestling Association Book 3

What happens when the Galactic Wrestling Association celebrates a little too hard after a successful show in Las Vegas? Too much drinking that leads to a night several of the wrestlers have completely forgotten. Especially when one of their meddling, matchmaking mommas instigates an excursion to take pictures at a local wedding chapel.

The photographic evidence on social media of thirteen inebriated performers stopping at a wedding chapel caused quite an uproar, making them wonder if some of their angles needed to be rebooked. But with all of them waking up in their own rooms at the hotel the next morning, with only vague memories of what had happened, they all believed they'd stayed outside the chapel, as the pictures indicated.

Until a few weeks later, when Rylie Long checked her mail while the GWA was in her hometown for a show, and learned that what happens in Vegas doesn't always stay there. Finding out she'd actually married Liam Connery that night in Vegas was a shock. She hadn't wanted to let on to anyone in the company that she had a little crush on the older wrestler. Now she had to figure out if she wanted to take advantage of their situation to see if her little crush could turn into more.

When Rylie took her marriage license to the arena to inform her boss, several of her coworkers suddenly scrambled to check their mail to find out their marital statuses as well. Apparently, Rylie and Liam weren't the only GWA wrestlers who got mistakenly married.

Teagan Shields and Josh Parker also got married while drunk that night, as did Aiken Pearson and Brent Crockett. Now they all had to figure out how they wanted to handle the legalities of their situation, while the GWA bookers reworked their angles to try to control the celebrity gossip. Would any of them stay married? Or would they get divorced? Or have their marriages annulled? And how did the fact that none of them had their legal residences listed in the same state as their spouses, or the state where they got married, factor into their options?

Taking the time to meet with attorneys and determine the requirements for each of their situations was difficult with them traveling with the GWA. Especially when their coworkers conspired to keep them together by pairing the three couples in the bridal party for Dean and Allissa's wedding, so they couldn't go home for their Thanksgiving break.

DISCLAIMER: This multicultural, age gap, forced proximity, friends-to-lovers, drunk Vegas marriage, sports romance contains profanity, graphic sex scenes, and references to infertility issues. It is intended for adult readers (18+) who are not easily offended.

Books by Leah Mae Wright

Heart's Destiny Series

A Brief History of the Founding Families of the Fictional Small Town of Heart's Destiny, Texas – Free on Book Funnel

Courting Kay – Anthony Burleson and Kay Lee

Courting Kay Bonus Scenes

Wrestling with Randi – James Hunter and Randi Lee

Bobby's Bride – Bobby Burleson and Brooklyn Barns

Adoring Amy – Justin Burleson and Amy Lawton

Charlotte's Wedding – Ian Campbell and Charlotte Burleson

Joshin' Around – Josh Burleson and Cait Campbell

Dion's Dream Girl – Dion Davis and Julie Burleson

Destined for Deanna – JJ Burleson and Deanna Wolfe (Coming Soon)

Lights, Camera, Ashlyn – Darius Davis, Ashlyn Lawton, and Cade Starling (Coming Soon)

Galactic Wrestling Association Series

<u>Glossary of Professional Wrestling Terms</u> – Free on Book Funnel
<u>Fighting for Fiona</u> – Rick Robertson and Fiona Harrison
<u>Dean's Darlin'</u> – Dean Hunter and Allissa Walters
<u>Mistakenly Married?</u> – Liam Connery and Rylie Long, Brent Crockett and Aiken Pearson, & Josh Parker and Teagan Shields
<u>Winning Rylie</u> – Liam Connery and Rylie Long
<u>Blade's Botched Bump</u> – Brandon "Blade" Braddock and Caitlyn Sullivan (Coming Soon)

About The Author

Leah Mae Wright lives in Florida with her husband and fur babies.
Her head has been filled with romantic stories for as long as she can
remember, beginning with fairy tales as a small child growing up in
Oklahoma and carrying through to countless ideas of her own
throughout the years, as she has moved around to live in several
different states. Now that her children are grown and life has slowed
down, she's letting them out of her head, so they can join the libraries
of her fellow fans of romance. Leah's literary world is a wonderful
place that has no Covid, no real politicians, and a few unreal towns.
Her favorite part about her characters living in her literary world is
knowing that they are guaranteed a happily ever after.

You can keep up to date with Leah's future book plans at:
www.leahmaewright.com –Be sure to sign up for the Newsletter to
receive emails about new releases, sales, and freebies.
www.facebook.com/LeahWrightAuthor
www.amazon.com/author/leah_wright
https://www.instagram.com/leahmaewrightauthor/
https://www.pinterest.com/LeahMaeWrightAuthor/

Provide your feedback to the author at:
Leah's Literary World Facebook Group
LeahWrightAuthor@gmail.com
Leah@LeahMaeWright.com

You can also review Leah's books on Amazon, Goodreads, Bookbub, and Fictiondb.